An A

Three Investigators
Mysteries

*All the mysteries solved by the Three Investigators
are available in Armada*

The Three Investigators Mysteries

The Green Ghost

TheVanishing Treasure

Skeleton Island

Text by Robert Arthur

Armada
An Imprint of HarperCollins*Publishers*

This Armada Three-in-One was
first published in the UK in 1993

Armada is an imprint of
HarperCollins Children's Books,
part of HarperCollins Publishers Ltd,
77–85 Fulham Palace Road,
Hammersmith, London W6 8JB

Printed and bound in Great Britain by
HarperCollins Book Manufacturing, Glasgow

Contents

THE GREEN GHOST

The Green Ghost was first published
in the USA by Random House Inc in 1965
First published as a single volume
in the UK by Armada in 1970

Copyright © 1965 Random House Inc

Warning to the Reader!

I DO NOT WANT to alarm anyone, but I feel it is my duty to warn you that in the pages ahead you will meet, as the title of this book suggests, a green ghost. In addition to the ghost you will encounter some strange pearls, and a little dog who plays no part in the story because he does nothing at all. Or does he play a part? Sometimes doing nothing is as important as doing something. It will be worth thinking about.

I could tell you of many other strange episodes, exciting adventures and suspenseful situations that you will be encountering, but I feel sure you would rather read about these for yourself. So I will content myself by introducing, as I promised them I would, The Three Investigators.

This is the fourth time I have introduced them, and I admit that in the earlier cases I had grave doubts. However, I have now grown rather fond of Jupiter Jones, Bob Andrews and Pete Crenshaw. I think you will find them good companions for an evening of mystery, adventure and suspense.

The three boys have formed the firm of The Three Investigators and use their spare time to solve any mysteries that come their way. They live in Rocky Beach, California, a town on the shore of the Pacific Ocean some miles from Hollywood. Bob and Pete live with their parents and Jupiter Jones lives with his uncle, Titus Jones, and aunt, Mathilda Jones, who own and operate The Jones Salvage Yard, a rather fabulous junk yard where one can find almost anything.

In this junk yard is a 30-foot mobile home trailer, that had been damaged in an accident, and which Titus Jones was never able to sell. He allowed Jupiter and his friends to use it, and they have rebuilt it as a modern Headquarters for an investigation firm. It has a small laboratory, a darkroom, and an office with desk, typewriter, telephone, tape recorder, and many books of reference. All equipment was rebuilt by Jupiter and the others from junk that came into the salvage yard.

Jupiter has had Hans and Konrad, the big, blond Bavarian brothers who are the yard helpers, arrange stacks of junk all round the trailer so that it is invisible to the outside world. The adults have forgotten about it. Only The Three Investigators know of its existence, and they keep the secret by using hidden entrances into Headquarters.

The entrance they use most often is Tunnel Two, a length of corrugated iron pipe which runs from their outdoor workshop partly underground, beneath some junk and under Headquarters. After crawling through it, they emerge into Headquarters through a trap-door. There are other entrances, but we will discuss them when we come to them.

The boys have the use of a gold-plated Rolls-Royce automobile, complete with chauffeur, when they need to travel long distances. The use of this automobile, for thirty days, was won in a contest by Jupiter Jones.

For ordinary purposes of local travel, they use their bicycles, or sometimes get Hans or Konrad to drive them in one of the salvage yard trucks.

Jupiter Jones is stocky, muscular, and a bit roly-poly. Some people of an unfriendly nature call him fat. He has a round face which often looks stupid. This is misleading. Behind it is a very sharp intelligence. Jupiter has an excellent mind, and he is rather proud of it. He has many good features, but undue modesty is not one of them.

Pete Crenshaw, tall, brown haired, muscular, is capable of many athletic feats. He is Jupiter's right-hand man at trailing suspects and other dangerous activities.

Bob Andrews is slighter of build, has lighter hair, and is more studious. Though he has great nerve, he is chiefly in charge of records and research for the firm. He has a part-time job at the local library, and this enables him to hunt up much information that is helpful in the firm's investigations.

I have told you all this, so that the following narrative need not be interrupted to repeat information which some of you may have previously acquired, if you have read about the firm's earlier cases.

In any event, onward! The green ghost is about to scream!

ALFRED HITCHCOCK

1

The Green Ghost Screams

THE SCREAM took Bob Andrews and Pete Crenshaw by surprise.

Standing in a driveway overgrown with weeds, they were studying an old, empty house, as big as a hotel, one end torn down where the demolition men had begun on it. Moonlight made everything misty and unreal.

Bob, with a portable tape recorder slung round his neck, was talking into it, describing the scene. He interrupted himself to turn to Pete and say:

"A lot of people think that house is haunted, Pete. It's too bad we didn't think of it when Alfred Hitchcock was looking for a haunted house for one of his pictures." He was referring to the time they had become acquainted with the famous movie director when they had solved the mysterious secret of Terror Castle.

"I bet Mr. Hitchcock would have liked this place, all right," Pete agreed. "But I don't. In fact, every minute I'm getting more nervous. What do you say we get away from here?"

That was when the scream came from the house.

"EEEeeeee-*aahhhhhh!*" It was a high-pitched sound, almost more animal than human. The hair stood up on both boys' necks.

13

"Did you hear that?" Pete gulped. "Now we *are* getting out of here!"

"Wait!" Bob said, standing his ground despite an impulse to run. As Pete hesitated he said, "I'll turn up the tape recorder in case we hear anything else. That's what Jupiter would do."

He was referring to Jupiter Jones, their partner in the firm of The Three Investigators, who was not with them.

"Well——" Pete began. But Bob had already turned up the volume control and pointed the microphone at the empty, mouldering old house among the trees.

"Aaaaaaahhhhh—ahheeeee—*eeeeee!*" The scream came again and died out slowly, in a most unsettling manner.

"Now let's go!" Pete said. "We've heard enough!"

Bob was in full agreement. They spun round and started to run down the old driveway to where their bikes were parked.

Pete was fleet as a deer, and Bob ran faster than he had run for many years. After a fall down a rocky slope, he had broken his leg in several places and for a long time he had had to wear a brace. However, the leg had healed well, and after a long period of exercises, Bob was told, just the previous week, that he could discard the brace.

Now, without it, he felt so light he could almost fly. But fast as they ran, neither he nor Pete got very far.

Strong arms suddenly and unexpectedly stopped them.

14

"Ah-ulp!" Pete grunted in surprise as he ran head-long into someone. Bob, too, was brought up short by plunging into a man who grabbed him and held him.

They had run full tilt into a group of men who had come up the driveway behind them as they stood listening to the eerie screams.

"Whoa, boy!" the man who had grabbed Pete exclaimed good-naturedly. "You nearly knocked me down!"

"What was that sound?" asked the man who had stopped Bob from falling after the boy had run blindly into him. "We saw you boys standing and listening."

"We don't know what it was," Pete spoke up. "But it sounded like the ghost to us!"

"Ghost, nonsense! . . . It could be someone in trouble! . . . Maybe it was just a tramp. . . ."

The five or six men in the group into which the boys had plunged all began to speak at once, ignoring Pete and Bob now. The two boys could not see their faces clearly. But they all seemed well-dressed and spoke like typical dwellers in the pleasant neighbour-hood that surrounded the overgrown grounds and the empty house, known as the Green Estate.

"I think we should go inside!" One man with an unusually deep voice spoke loudly. Bob couldn't make out his features, except to see that he had a mous-tache. "We came over here to look at the old building before it got torn down. We heard somebody scream. Somebody may be inside, hurt."

"I say we should call the police," said a man in a checked sports jacket, a little nervously. "It's their duty to investigate such things."

"Someone may be hurt," the deep-voiced man said. "Let's see if we can help. If we wait for the police he might die."

"I agree," spoke up a man wearing thick glasses. "I think we should go inside, and look round."

"You can go inside, I'll go for the police," said the man in the checked coat. As he turned away, a man who led a small dog on a leash spoke up.

"It may be just an owl or a cat that's got inside," he said. "If you call the police for that, you'll look pretty foolish."

The man in the checked coat hesitated.

"Well——" he began. At that point a large man, the biggest in the group, took the lead.

"Come on," he said. "There's half a dozen of us and we have several torches. I say we look inside first, and then call the police if it's necessary. You two boys—you can go on home, you're not needed here."

He strode up to the flagstone path that led towards the house, and after a moment's hesitation, the others followed him. The man who was leading the small dog picked it up and carried it, and the man in the checked coat, somewhat reluctantly, brought up the rear of the group.

"Come on," Pete said to Bob. "Like he said, they don't need us. Let's go home."

"And not find out what made that noise!" Bob yelped. "Think what Jupe would say. We'd never hear the end of it. We're supposed to be investigators. Anyway, there's nothing to be scared about now, there's so many of us."

He hurried up the path after the men, and Pete

followed him. Outside the big front door, the men were milling around uncertainly. Then the big man in the lead tried the door. It opened, showing a black cavern of hallway inside.

"Use your torches," he said. "I want to find out what it was we heard."

Flashing his torch, he led the way inside. The others crowded close at his heels, and three more torches cut bright paths into the darkness. As the men entered, Pete and Bob quietly slipped inside behind them.

They found themselves in a big reception hall. The men who had torches shone the beams around, and they could all see that the walls were covered with what once had been cream-coloured silk tapestries, with Oriental scenes on them.

An impressive flight of stairs curved down into the hall. One of the men shone his light on it.

"That must be where old Mathias Green fell down and broke his neck fifty years ago," he said. "Smell the air! This place has been shut up for the whole fifty years."

"The house is supposed to be haunted," someone else said. "And I'm willing to believe it. I only hope we don't see the ghost."

"We're not getting very far with our search," said the big man. "Let's start by searching the ground floor."

Staying in a group, the men began to go through the big rooms on the ground floor. They were empty of furniture and dust lay everywhere. One wing of the building, which was obviously in the process of being demolished, had no back wall.

The men found nothing and only their hushed whispers echoed around as they walked hesitantly through the rooms. Then they tried the other wing of the mansion, finally entering what must once have been a big parlour. There was an impressive fireplace at one end and tall windows at the other. The men gathered in front of the fireplace, uneasily.

"We're not doing any good," one man said in a low voice. "We should call the police——"

"Sssh!" another voice cut him off. Everyone froze into silence. "I thought I heard something," the second man said in a low whisper. "It may be just an animal. Let's turn off all the lights and see if anything moves."

All the lights winked out. Darkness engulfed the room, except for some very faint moonlight coming through the dirty windows.

Then someone said in a gasping tone, "Look! Over by the door!"

They all turned. And they all saw it.

A greenish figure was standing by the door through which they had entered. It seemed to glow slightly, as if with an inner light, and to waver a bit as though it were insubstantial mist. But as Bob stared at it, unconsciously holding his breath, it seemed to him to be the figure of a man in long, flowing green robes.

"The ghost!" a rather weak voice gulped. "Old Mathias Green!"

"All lights on!" the big man said sharply. "Shine them that way!"

But before the lights went on, the greenish misty figure seemed to glide along the wall and dart out through the open door. It vanished as three torches beamed light towards it.

"I wish I was somewhere else," Pete whispered into Bob's ear. "Beginning about an hour ago."

"It may have been a flash from a car headlight," a man said firmly. "Just coming in a window. Come on, let's have a look in the hall."

They all trooped noisily out into the hall and flashed their lights around again. There was nothing to be seen. Then someone suggested that they turn the lights out once more. They waited in silence and darkness again; the small dog one man carried in his arms whimpered slightly.

This time Pete spotted the figure. The others were looking around them, but he happened to glance up the stairs and there, on the landing, was the greenish figure.

"There it is!" he shouted. "On the stairs."

They all turned. They all saw the figure move from the landing and glide up towards the second floor.

"Come on!" shouted the big man. "It's someone pulling a gag on us. Follow him and catch him!"

He led the way pell-mell up the stairs. But when they got to the second floor, they found nothing.

"I have an idea." It was Bob who spoke. He was asking himself what Jupiter Jones would have done if he had been there, and he thought he knew.

"If anybody came upstairs ahead of us," he said, as the men turned to him and someone shone a light on his face so that he had to squint, "they'd leave

"Look! Over by the door!"

tracks on the dusty floor. If they left tracks, we can follow them."

"The boy's right," the man with the dog exclaimed. "You fellows, shine your lights here on the floor of the hall, where none of us has walked yet."

Three torches glowed on the floor. There was dust, all right, plenty of it, but nothing had disturbed it.

"Nobody's been up here!" The speaker sounded baffled. "So what did we see go up these stairs?"

Nobody answered that, although everyone knew what everyone else was thinking.

"Let's turn out the lights and see if we see it again," a voice suggested.

"Let's get out of here," someone else said, but there was a chorus of agreement with the first speaker. After all, there were eight or nine of them—counting Pete and Bob—and nobody wanted to admit to being scared.

In the darkness at the head of the stairs, they waited.

Pete and Bob were staring down the hall when someone whispered sharply.

"To the left!" he said. "Half-way down the hall."

They spun round. A green glow, so faint it could hardly be seen, stood beside a doorway. The figure grew clearer. It was definitely a human-shaped figure in green flowing robes like a Mandarin's.

"Let's not scare it," somebody said in a low voice. "See what it does."

They all waited silently.

The ghostly figure began to move. It glided down the hall close to the wall, to the very end. Then it turned the corner, or seemed to, and vanished.

"Follow it, slowly this time," someone murmured. "It's not trying to get away."

Bob spoke up again. "See if there are any footprints now, before we go down the hall," he suggested.

Two torches winked on and played up and down the hallway.

"No footprints!" The deep-voiced speaker sounded a bit hollow. "Not a trace of a print in the dust. Whatever it is, it's floating on air."

"We've come this far, we have to go on," someone else said firmly. "I'll lead the way."

The speaker, the big man, strode out boldly down the hall. The others followed. They came to a cross corridor, where the green figure had turned, and stopped. Someone shone a light down the other hallway. Two open doors showed in its beam. Beyond the doors the hallway ended in a blank wall.

They shut off the lights and waited. In a moment the green, ghostly figure glided out of one of the open doors and, hugging the wall, went down the hall, stopped at the blank wall and then, very slowly, faded out.

As if, Bob said later, it had oozed right through the wall.

But there were no footprints in the dust.

Nor, when the police came later after the men had called them, could Chief Reynolds or any of his men find a thing. There was no trace of a human being in the house, no one hurt, no animal. Nothing.

Being a policeman, Chief Reynolds did not like to believe that eight reliable witnesses had seen a ghost, or heard a ghost scream. But he had no choice.

Later that night a watchman reported that he had seen a greenish, ghostly figure lurking near the rear entrance of a big warehouse. It had faded away when he approached. Still later, a woman phoned to the police in a panic, saying a moaning noise had awakened her and she had seen a greenish figure standing out on her patio. It had vanished when she turned the light on. Two truckers at an all-night restaurant said they saw a ghostly figure beside their truck.

Finally, Chief Reynolds had a call from two radio patrol car officers who said they had seen a figure in Rocky Beach's Green Hills Cemetery. Reynolds hurried down there and stepped inside the big iron gate of the cemetery. Standing against a tall white monument was a green, ghostly figure that, as he approached it, sank into the ground and was gone.

The chief flashed his light on the monument.

It was the monument to the unfortunate Mathias Green, who had fallen down his stairs and broken his neck fifty years before in the great, old mansion.

2

Summons for Bob and Pete

"Aaahhhhhhhh—*eeeeeeee!*" The ghostly scream sounded again. But this time it did not bother Bob and Pete. It was coming from the tape recorder.

The Three Investigators were in their concealed, mobile-home Headquarters in The Jones Salvage Yard, and Jupiter Jones was listening intently to the tape that Bob had recorded the previous evening.

"There's no more screams, Jupe," Bob said. "The rest is just conversation when those men met us, before I remembered the machine was running. I shut it off when we went into the house."

Jupiter, however, listened to everything. The voices of the men who had spoken the previous night were quite clear, for Bob had had the recording volume all the way up. When the tape ended, he shut it off, pinching his lower lip, a sign that his mental machinery was spinning.

"That sounded to me like a human scream," he said. "It sounded like somebody screaming as he fell down a flight of stairs, and at the end dying out because he didn't have strength enough to scream any more."

"That's just what it does sound like!" Bob exclaimed. "And that's what happened in that house fifty years ago. Old Mathias Green, the owner, fell down the stairs and broke his neck. He probably screamed as he fell!"

"Now wait a minute, wait a minute!" Pete objected. "Why should we hear him screaming fifty years later?"

"Perhaps," Jupiter said solemnly, "the scream was a supernatural echo of a scream first uttered fifty years ago."

"Don't say things like that!" Pete objected. "I don't

like to hear them. How could we hear a fifty-year-old echo?"

"I don't know," Jupiter answered. "Bob, you are in charge of records and research for the firm. Please give me a detailed account of what happened and what you have learned of the history of the Green Mansion."

Bob drew in a deep breath.

"Well," he began, "Pete and I rode over last night to look at the place when we heard they were starting to tear it down. I thought I could do a good story on it and have it ready for the first issue of the school paper in the autumn. I took along the tape recorder so I could talk my impressions into it, to use later for the writing.

"We'd been there about five minutes, and the old house was looking mighty spooky, when the moon came up. Then came the scream. The first one. I turned up the volume of the recorder in case there was another scream because I knew it would be important for you to hear it."

"Very good," Jupiter said. "You are thinking like a detective. I've already heard on the tape what the men said. Proceed with your entry into the house."

Bob described in detail how they had searched the house, how they had seen the ghostly green figure first downstairs, then on the landing, then upstairs, and then how it had finally glided down the hall and melted through a solid wall.

"And no footprints," Pete said. "Bob thought of that, and he made sure the men with torches examined the floor carefully."

"Excellent work," Jupiter said. "How many men saw this green apparition with you?"

"Six," Pete told him.

"Seven," Bob contradicted him.

They looked at each other. Pete spoke first.

"Six," he said. "I'm positive. The big man who led us, the fellow with the deep voice, the man with the little dog, the man who wore glasses, and two others I didn't notice much."

"Maybe you're right," Bob admitted, unsure of himself. "I counted them inside, when they were all moving around. Once I got six and twice I got seven."

"It probably doesn't matter," Jupiter said, forgetting for a moment his own rule that in any mystery the smallest fact might be very important. "Now give me the background of the old house."

"Well," Bob said, "we left the house and the men broke up into groups. One group said they'd call the police. This morning the papers were full of the story. I stopped at the library on the way over here, but they don't have any information about the Green mansion because it was built so long ago—before Rocky Beach was even a town or had a library.

"But according to the story in the papers, it was built way back, sixty or seventy years ago, by old Mathias Green. He was a skipper in the China trade, and supposed to be a very tough man. Not too much is known about him, but it seems he got into some kind of trouble when he was in China and had to leave in a hurry. He came back here with a beautiful Chinese princess for a bride. One story says he quarrelled with his only relative, a sister-in-law up in San Francisco, and came down here to live.

"Another story says he feared the vengeance of some Chinese nobles, maybe the family of his wife, and he built his big house down here to hide. This region was pretty wild back then, you know.

"Anyway, he lived in style in the Green mansion with a whole bunch of Oriental servants. He liked to put on green robes like a Manchu noble. He used to have his supplies brought up to him by team and wagon from down in Los Angeles, once a week, and one day the driver of the wagon found the house empty. Except for Mathias Green. He lay at the bottom of the stairs with his neck broken.

"When the police finally got there, they decided that he had been drinking and had fallen down and killed himself and that the whole bunch of servants had fled in the night, afraid they'd be blamed. Even the Chinese wife was gone.

"They could never find anybody to tell them anything. In those days most Chinese in this country were very secretive and afraid of the law, so all the servants either went back to China or went up to San Francisco and lost themselves in Chinatown, there.

"Anyway, the whole thing stayed a mystery. His widowed sister-in-law in San Francisco inherited his estate and used the money he left her to buy a vineyard up in Verdant Valley, near San Francisco. She refused either to live in the house or to sell it. Even after she died, it was just left to rot. Finally, though, this year a Miss Lydia Green, the sister-in-law's daughter, sold the property to a developer who is

27

going to tear down the house and build some modern houses on the grounds.

"That's why the house is being torn down. And—well, that's about all I can tell you."

"Very well summed up, Records," Jupiter complimented Bob. "Now let us examine the newspaper accounts."

He spread out several newspapers on the desk of the tiny Headquarters office. There was a Los Angeles paper, a San Francisco paper and the local paper. The local paper had the biggest headlines about the strange events of the night before, but the big city papers gave it plenty of space, too, with dramatic headlines such as:

SCREAMING GHOST LEAVES WRECKED HOME TO BRING TERROR TO ROCKY BEACH

GREEN GHOST AT LARGE IN ROCKY BEACH AS HOME IS TORN DOWN

GREEN GHOST LEAVES WRECKED HOME TO SEEK NEW LODGINGS

The stories that followed were written in a humorous vein, but they gave the facts as Bob had just stated them. Missing was the fact that Police Chief Reynolds and two of his men had actually seen the green figure in the cemetery. The chief preferred to keep that to himself. He didn't want to be made a laughing stock.

"The paper says," Jupiter remarked, referring to the *Rocky Beach News*, "that the ghost was seen outside a big warehouse, then later in a woman's patio, and finally among some big trucks outside a truckmen's diner. It almost looks as if the ghost was looking for some place else to stay, now that his home is being torn down."

"Yeah," Pete said with a note of sarcasm. "Maybe he was hitch-hiking away from Rocky Beach."

"Perhaps." Jupiter chose to take the remark seriously. "Although ghosts are not commonly supposed to need mundane means of transportation."

"Long words," Pete groaned. He put his head down on his arms as if floored by Jupiter's language. "Long words Jones! You know I don't know what mundane means."

"It means ordinary or everyday," Jupiter told him. "The whole thing seems very mysterious. Until further facts emerge——"

He was interrupted by his aunt's voice. Miss Mathilda Jones was a large woman, and her voice was a powerful one. It was she who really ran The Jones Salvage Yard, the family business.

"Bob Andrews!" the boys heard her calling. "Come out from behind all that junk and show yourself. Your father is here and wants you. Pete, too."

3

The Hidden Room

IN A MOMENT all three boys were scrambling through
the long section of corrugated pipe which formed
Tunnel Two, the secret entrance they used most.
They had put some old carpets on the bottom, so that
the corrugations didn't bruise their knees, and they
could slither out through the exit as fast as eels. In a
moment they were threading their way through the
stacks of junk which Jupiter had had Hans and
Konrad, the yard helpers, arrange to hide their workshop and Headquarters. They emerged in the open
space around the neat shack which served as the office
for the salvage yard.

There Mathilda Jones waited, talking with Bob's
father, a tall man with twinkling eyes and a brown
moustache.

"There you are, son!" he said. "Come along, we
have to hurry. Chief Reynolds wants to talk to you.
You, too, Pete."

Pete gulped. Chief Reynolds wanted to talk to him?
He thought he knew what about—the events of the
previous night.

Jupiter's round features looked eager. "May I go,
too, Mr. Andrews?" he asked. "After all, we're a
team. All three of us."

"I guess one more boy won't matter." Mr. Andrews

smiled. "But come along. Chief Reynolds is outside in a police car and we're going to ride with him."

Just outside the gate a black sedan was waiting. Police Chief Reynolds, a bulky man with balding hair, was at the wheel. His mouth and chin were set grimly.

"Good work, Bill," he said to Bob's father. "Now let's get there fast. And listen—you're a local man—we're neighbours. I'm counting on you to help me handle the outside press if this thing—well, if this crazy business turns into something even crazier."

"You can count on me, Chief," Mr. Andrews said. "While we drive over to the Green mansion, why don't you let my son tell you what he and his friend observed last night."

"Yeah, shoot, boy," Chief Reynolds said, starting the car down the road at breakneck speed. "I've heard it from a couple of the men who were there, but let's hear how you saw it."

Bob swiftly told him what he and Pete had observed the previous evening. Chief Reynolds chewed his lips as he listened.

"Yes, that sounds just like what the others told me," he said gloomily. "Even with so many witnesses I'd say it was impossible, only——"

He stopped. Bob's father, who was a very good reporter, looked at him sharply.

"Something tells me, Sam," he said, "that you saw that green ghost yourself. That's why you aren't speaking up louder to say that it is impossible."

"Yes." The chief let out a gusty sigh. "I saw it, too. At the cemetery. Standing by the marble shaft erected to old Mathias Green. And, confound it, as I watched

31

it, that green figure just sank down into the ground where the grave is and vanished!"

Pete, Bob and Jupiter were sitting on the edge of the seat, listening with great excitement. Bob's father looked quizzically at the chief of police.

"Can I quote you on that, Sam?" he asked.

"No, you know darned well you can't!" Chief Reynolds exploded. "That's off the record. You boys! I forgot you were here! Don't go repeating what I've said, you hear?"

"We won't sir," Jupiter assured him.

"Altogether," Chief Reynolds continued, "that green figure was seen by—let me see now. Two truckers at the diner. The woman who telephoned in. The night watchman at the warehouse. Myself and two of my men. The two boys——"

"That makes nine, Sam," Mr. Andrews put in.

"Nine, plus the six men who wandered over to look at the old place," Chief Reynolds said. "Fifteen altogether. Fifteen witnesses to a ghostly figure!"

"Were there six or seven men at the Green mansion, Chief?" Jupiter asked eagerly, "Pete and Bob can't agree."

"I'm not sure," the Chief grumbled. "Four men reported what happened. Three of them said there were six, and one said there were seven. I didn't talk to the others—couldn't locate them. Guess they didn't want publicity. But either way, there were fifteen or sixteen witnesses and that's too many to imagine something. I sure wish I could play it down as a gag or something, but after seeing it myself—watching it just disappear into a grave—well, I can't!"

Now the car turned up the weed-grown driveway of the old Green mansion. By daylight it looked very impressive, even though one wing was partly torn down. Two policemen stood guard at the door, and a man in a brown suit seemed to be waiting impatiently with them.

"Wonder who that is?" Chief Reynolds muttered as they got out. "Probably another reporter."

"Chief Reynolds!" The man in the brown suit, an intelligent looking man who spoke rapidly in a pleasant voice came towards them. "Are you the chief? I've been waiting for you. Why won't these men let me go into my client's house?"

"Your client's house?" The chief stared at him. "Who are you?"

"I'm Harold Carlson," the man said. "Actually it is Miss Lydia Green's house. I'm her lawyer and also a distant cousin of hers. I represent her interests. As soon as I read this morning's paper about the events of last night, I flew straight down here from San Francisco, rented a car and drove out here. I want to investigate. The whole thing sounds like fantastic nonsense to me."

"Fantastic, yes," Chief Reynolds said, "but I don't think it's nonsense. Well, I'm mighty glad you're here, Mr. Carlson. We'd probably have had to send for you otherwise. I posted my men to keep out curiosity seekers and that's why they wouldn't let you in. But we'll all go in now and look around. I have here two boys who saw everything last night, and they'll point out exactly where the—er, strange manifestations took place."

33

He introduced Mr. Andrews, Bob, Pete and Jupiter. Then Chief Reynolds led the way into the house, leaving his two men outside, on guard. Inside, in the big, dimly lit rooms, there was still a sense of the spookiness of the night before. Bob and Pete pointed out to the chief exactly where they had all been, and where the greenish figure had first appeared.

Then Pete led them upstairs.

"It just glided up these stairs and along the hall," he said. "Before we followed it, the men examined the floor for footprints. That was Bob's idea. But there wasn't a mark in the dust.

"Good work, son," Mr. Andrews said, and clapped Bob on the shoulder.

"Then the ghost went down that hall"—Pete pointed—"and stopped against the wall at the end. After that it just melted through the wall and vanished."

"Mmm." Chief Reynolds scowled as they all stood staring at the blank wall. Harold Carlson, the lawyer, was shaking his head helplessly.

"I don't understand it," he said. "I just don't understand it. Of course, there have always been stories about this house being haunted, but I never believed in them. Now—I don't know. I just don't know."

"Mr. Carlson," Chief Reynolds asked, "have you any idea what's behind that wall?"

The other man blinked. "Why—no. What could be behind it?"

"That's what we're here to find out," the chief said. "And why I'm glad you're here.

"This morning, one of the men engaged to demolish

34

the house was working on a ladder, ripping some of the siding off the outside. Apparently this hallway is over the section downstairs that has been partly taken down, and this upper portion came next. Anyway, he saw something. So he stopped work and called me."

"Saw something?" Mr. Carlson frowned. "Good heavens, what?"

"He couldn't be sure," Chief Reynolds said bluntly. "But he thinks there's a secret room behind that blank wall. And now that you're here, we're going to open it up and see what's inside."

Harold Carlson rubbed his forehead and looked at Mr. Andrews, who was busy making notes.

"A secret room?" he said, in utter bewilderment. "There's no mention of a secret room in any of the family stories about this house."

Pete and Bob and Jupiter were almost hopping with suppressed excitement as the two policemen came up the stairs, one carrying an axe and the other a crowbar.

"All right, men, get an opening in that wall." Chief Reynolds said. To Mr. Carlson he added, "I'm sure that's what you want, isn't it?"

"Of course, Chief," the man from San Francisco told him. "After all, the house is coming down anyway."

The two policemen attacked the wall with vigour. Soon they had a hole in it. It was plain that beyond it lay a sizeable space, now quite dark. When the hole was big enough for a man to get through, Chief Reynolds approached it and flashed a beam of light inside.

"Good grief!" he said, and climbed through the opening into the secret room. Hastily Mr. Carlson and Bob's father followed him, and the boys could hear their exclamations of excitement and consternation from within.

Quietly Jupiter slipped through the hole, too, and after him Pete and Bob. They were in a small room, about six by eight. A little daylight came through a crack in the outside wall that the demolishers must have pulled loose.

It was no wonder the men were excited.

There was nothing in the room but a coffin.

It rested on two trestles, objects of polished wood similar to sawhorses. The coffin was magnificently carved and polished on the outside, but it was the inside that was receiving the men's attention.

The three boys crept up beside them and peered in also. All three gasped.

There was a skeleton in the coffin. They could not see it very well because it was partly draped in what once had been magnificent robes. But it was sure enough a skeleton.

For a moment no one said anything. Then Harold Carlson spoke.

"Look!" he said. "This silver plate on the coffin. It says, 'Beloved wife of Mathias Green. Rest close by and undisturbed.' "

"Old Mathias Green's Chinese wife!" Chief Reynolds said huskily.

"And everyone always thought she had run away when he died," Bob's father added, in a hushed tone.

"Yes," agreed Harold Carlson. "But look at this!

This is something I'm going to have to take charge of Chief, for the family."

He reached into the coffin. What he did the boy couldn't see because the bodies of the men blocked their view. But a moment later Mr. Carlson held up a long string of round objects which were a curious dull grey colour in the beam of the chief's torch.

"These must be the famous Ghost Pearls that Great-uncle Mathias is reported to have stolen from a Chinese noble. They were the reason he had to flee China and go into hiding. They're immensely valuable. We thought they were gone forever—that when Great-uncle Mathias broke his neck, his Chinese wife cleared out with the pearls and went back to the Orient.

"Instead, they've been here ever since."

"And so has she," Bob's father commented.

4

An Unexpected Phone Call

IN HEADQUARTERS, the next day, Pete was busy clipping stories and pictures from the newspapers, while Bob pasted them in a large scrapbook. Mr. Andrews hadn't been able to do much about cutting down on the publicity Rocky Beach received in connection with the story of the Green mansion and the green ghost.

Probably the story of the ghost would not have held the public's interest very long. But when it was followed by the discovery of a secret room and the skeleton of Mathias Green's wife wearing a rope of famous pearls round her neck—some of the headlines seemed bigger than the front pages they were on.

Now the reporters were digging back into the past and recounting the events of Mathias Green's history. Their articles told that he had been a reckless captain in the China trade, and had sailed into the teeth of any storm he met, daring the elements to daunt him.

They revealed that he had been a personal friend and adviser of several Manchu nobles, and that he had received gifts of jewels from them. But the Ghost Pearls hadn't been given to him. He had stolen them and then hastily left China with his bride, never to return. The rest of his life had been spent in seclusion in the Green mansion.

"Imagine all this happening right here in Rocky Beach!" Bob paused to exclaim. "You know what Dad and Chief Reynolds have figured out?"

He was interrupted by the scrape of metal. That was the iron grating over the outside entrance to Tunnel Two being moved aside. Then, presently, there was a muffled scrambling noise—that was Jupe crawling through the long corrugated pipe that formed Tunnel Two. Next came the code rap on the trap-door, which now opened upwards to allow Jupiter to crawl in looking sweaty and hot.

"Whew!" he said. "It's hot." Then he added, "I've been thinking."

"Better be careful, Jupe," Pete said. "Don't overdo

it. By the sweat you're in, your brain bearings must have been overloaded. We wouldn't want them to burn out and leave you just an ordinary guy like the rest of us."

Bob chuckled. Pete was actually very proud of his friend's mental ability, but he still couldn't help cutting Jupe down to size once in a while. It didn't hurt any because Jupiter Jones was not by nature an especially modest boy.

Jupe gave Pete a sour look.

"I have been deducing." He lowered himself into the swivel chair behind the partly-burned desk with which their Headquarters office was furnished. "I have been figuring out what happened there in the Green mansion many years ago."

"You don't have to, Jupe," Bob said. "My dad told me what he and Chief Reynolds have figured out."

"What I have decided," Jupe said, seeming not to hear Bob, "is that first——"

"Dad and Chief Reynolds agree that Mrs. Green probably died of some illness," Bob went right on. He was seldom in possession of inside information like this, and he didn't intend to be cheated out of telling it.

"Then her husband, the old sea captain, put her in that wonderful coffin but he couldn't bear to be really parted from her. So he put her in that little room at the end of the corridor and closed up the window. Then he plastered and papered over the door so no outsider would guess there was a secret room.

"That way she stayed with him, you might say.

39

How long this lasted there's no way of guessing, but then one night Mathias Green stumbled coming down the stairs.

"When the servants saw he was dead, they panicked. They slipped away in the night. They either went up to Chinatown in San Francisco and lost themselves there with their relatives, or they went back to China. Some of them may have been in this country illegally. In any case, Chinese people in those days were very clannish and gave no information to white men if they could help it, so their running away was perfectly natural.

"The only relative was Mr. Green's sister-in-law, who inherited everything. She used the money to buy a big vineyard up near San Francisco—Verdant Valley Vineyard. She never came down here at all. Neither did Miss Lydia Green, her daughter, who now owns Verdant Valley and is the owner of the Green mansion since her mother died.

"For some unknown reason they just let the old house sit there all this time. Until this year when Miss Green finally agreed to sell it to developers."

"And when they started to tear it down, old Mathias Green's ghost got annoyed," Pete put in. "That's why he screamed, and was seen going into the hidden room. He was paying a last visit to his wife. After that he—well, apparently he just left."

Jupiter looked slightly annoyed. This was just about what he had figured out himself. However, he contented himself by assuming an air of superiority.

"You seem pretty sure it was a ghost," he remarked. "And also that it was Mathias Green's ghost."

40

"We saw it. You didn't," Pete retorted. "If that wasn't a ghost, I've never seen one!"

Of course, he never had seen one—at least not previously. But he ignored that fact.

"If it wasn't a ghost, what was it?" Bob asked. "If you can think of any other possibility, Chief Reynolds would probably give you a reward."

Jupiter blinked. "What do you mean?"

"Yes," chimed in Pete, also looking interested. "What about the chief?"

"Well, we all heard him say yesterday he saw the ghost," Bob told them. "And Dad tells me the chief is pretty upset because officially he can't admit there is any such thing as a ghost. And so he can't order his men to try to catch it for him. But he still can't forget he saw it, and so maybe there *are* ghosts. He would certainly be grateful to anybody who could either prove it was a real ghost, or if it wasn't, exactly what it was we all saw."

"Mmm." Jupiter was beginning to look pleased. "I believe we should take on this case of the green ghost just as a favour to Police Chief Reynolds. Besides, I have a feeling there is a lot more to this mystery than any of us guess."

"Now wait a minute!" Pete yelled. "He hasn't asked us to take on any case for him. And I draw the line at investigating green ghosts!"

Bob, however, was as interested as Jupiter.

"Our motto is, 'We Investigate Anything'," he reminded Pete. "I'd like to know for myself if we really saw a ghost or not. But how would we start trying to catch one?"

"We will review the case from the beginning," Jupiter said. "First, was the ghost seen again last night?"

"Not according to the papers," Bob said. "And Dad said he heard from Chief Reynolds that no new reports have come in."

"Did your father interview the men who saw the phantom figure the other night?" Jupiter asked Bob.

"He went round with Chief Reynolds," Bob answered. "They could only find four of them. The big man, the man with the little dog, and two neighbours. They all said the same thing—exactly what I've put in my notes."

"What about the other two?—— Or three?"

"They couldn't locate them. Dad said they probably didn't want publicity, didn't want to be kidded by their friends about seeing a ghost. Though I'm sure there were three others, not two."

"How did these men come to visit the old Green mansion anyway?" Jupe asked.

"They all said a couple of men came along from up the road and suggested they all go and see the mansion by moonlight before it was torn down. They made it seem like a good idea. So the men went. As they came up the driveway, they heard the scream, and you know the rest."

"Has the demolition of the mansion stopped?" Jupiter asked.

"For the time being, anyway," Bob said. "The chief has had the house searched for more secret rooms, but there aren't any. Still, he's having it guarded against sightseers and Dad said there was some talk that the whole deal for tearing it down and building a new development might fall through now, because of the bad publicity."

Jupiter thought hard for several minutes.

"Well," he said finally, "we might as well play over the tape you recorded, Bob. It's just about all we have in the way of clues."

Bob switched on the tape recorder. Once again the eerie scream rang in their ears. Then they heard the conversation of the men who had joined them that night. Listening, Jupiter frowned.

"Something about that tape stirs an idea in my mind," he said, "but I can't quite get it. I heard a dog bark a little. What kind of dog was it?"

"What difference does it make what kind of dog it was?" Pete exploded.

"Anything may be important, Pete," Jupiter said loftily.

"It was a little wire-haired fox terrier," Bob told him. "Do you have any ideas yet, Jupe?"

Jupiter was forced to admit he didn't. They played the tape again and again. Something about it bothered Jupe, but he couldn't figure what it was. Finally they put the recorder away and began to study the newspaper clippings, one by one.

"It certainly looks to me as if the green ghost has moved out of town," Pete said finally, with satisfaction. "They were tearing his house down so he left!"

Jupe was trying to think of an answer to that when the phone rang. He picked it up.

"Hello?" he said. They could all hear the conversa-

43

tion through the loudspeaker attachment he had rigged up on the telephone.

"This is long distance," a woman's voice said. "I have a call for Robert Andrews."

The boys stared at each other. It was the first long distance call any of them had ever had.

"For you, Bob," Jupiter handed Bob the receiver.

"Hello," Bob said. "This is Bob Andrews." His voice squeaked slightly from excitement.

"Hello, Bob." It was another woman's voice that spoke. This one was obviously quite an old woman, though her voice was strong. "This is Miss Lydia Green, calling from Verdant Valley."

Lydia Green! The niece of old Mathias Green whose ghost—if it was a ghost—Bob and Pete had seen!

"Yes, Miss Green," he said.

"I want to ask a favour of you," Miss Green said over the phone. "Could you and your friend, Peter Crenshaw, come to Verdant Valley?"

"Come to Verdant Valley?" Bob asked in bewilderment.

"I very much want to talk to you," Miss Green said. "You saw my uncle's—well, his ghost two nights ago and I want all the details from an eyewitness. What he looked like, what he did, everything. You see——" and for a moment her voice faltered—"you see, the ghost has come to Verdant Valley. Last night I—I saw him in my room."

The Ghost Appears Again

BOB LOOKED at Jupiter. Jupe was nodding his head, to say yes.

"Why sure, Miss Green," Bob said into the phone. "I guess Pete and I could come. That is if it's all right with our families."

"Oh, I'm so glad!" Miss Green seemed to sigh with relief. "Naturally I called your families first and your mothers said they were sure it would be all right. Verdant Valley is a very peaceful place, and I have a great-nephew here, Charles Chang Green, who will be company for you. He has spent most of his life in China."

The rest of Miss Green's call was about arrangements. Bob and Pete were to catch the 6 p.m. jet flight to San Francisco, and she would have them met at the airport and driven to Verdant Valley. Then she thanked them again, and hung up.

"Gleeps!" Bob said. "She wants to know all about the ghost from an eyewitness so we get a nice trip out of it!" The realisation struck him. "But she didn't invite you, Jupe!"

If Jupe was disappointed, he was working hard to conceal it.

"That's because I didn't see the ghost," he said. "You two did. Anyway, I couldn't go because to-

45

morrow Uncle Titus and Aunt Mathilda are driving down to San Diego in the big truck to buy a lot of Navy surplus material, and I have to stay to take care of the business."

"Just the same, we're a team," Pete objected. "I hate to be going somewhere without you, Jupe. Especially," he added, "if there's going to be a ghost around!"

Jupiter pinched his lip.

"Perhaps this is a fortunate circumstance," he said. "If the ghost has been seen up in Verdant Valley, you two can carry out an investigation there for Chief Reynolds. Meanwhile, I'll follow up all the leads I can think of here. The value of having a team of investigators is that we can follow up two or even three different lines of investigation at the same time."

They left it at that. After all, what Jupe said made sense. Presently Bob and Pete rode home to get ready. Their mothers had packed suitcases for them, and the boys made sure to add a torch, and to be certain each of them carried his special piece of chalk—green for Bob, blue for Pete—for leaving the sign of The Three Investigators, when necessary.

Mrs. Andrews drove them to Los Angeles's busy, modern International Airport, and Jupiter came along.

"Phone me any developments," he told Bob. "We have some money saved up to pay for calls. If the ghost is really up there, I'll think of some way to get there to join you."

Mrs. Andrews's final words to Bob were, "Now be sure to watch your manners, Robert. And if you can

46

tell Miss Green anything that will help her, I'll be very glad, though I have to admit this whole business is very puzzling. Even your father says he thinks there is a lot more to it than meets the eye.

"But Miss Green has a fine reputation, and her Verdant Valley Vineyard is known to be well-run. It's a winery, too, because they make wine out of the grapes. I think they call it the Three-V Winery. They have horses, Miss Green said, so you two and the great-nephew she mentioned can go riding together. You should have a nice time."

A few moments later they were on the plane, and the great jet was in the air, arrowing northwards. The trip only took an hour, which hardly gave them time to get used to it, especially since part of the time was taken up by a dinner served in plastic trays.

After eating they resumed watching the clouds flow by underneath them until they swooped in for a landing at the San Francisco airport.

They were met by a boy almost as tall as Pete, but with broader shoulders, who stepped forward to greet them. He was a good-looking youth, who seemed very American except for the slight Oriental appearance of his eyes.

He introduced himself as Charles Green, better known as Chang, told them he was one-quarter Chinese and had lived most of his life in Hong Kong. Then he helped them get their bags from the luggage section. When they had their suitcases, Chang Green led them across a busy street to a huge parking lot.

Here a small, bus-type station wagon was waiting, a young Mexican-looking man at the wheel.

"Pedro, these are our guests, Pete Crenshaw and Bob Andrews. We'll go straight back to Verdant Valley. They ate on the plane so we don't have to stop."

"Si, Señor Chang," Pedro said. He grabbed the boys' bags, stowed them in the back and took his place behind the wheel. The three boys took their places directly behind him, where they could sit side by side. Pedro put the wagon into gear and they were off.

During the ride, Pete and Bob tried to talk and ask questions and look around them, all at the same time. Somewhat to their disappointment, they did not go into the city of San Francisco itself, but skirted its edges and then were rolling through hilly but more or less open country.

"We are going to Verdant Valley, where my honourable aunt operates the 3-V Winery," Chang Green said. "Actually, my aunt says that I am the rightful owner of the vineyard and winery, but I could not dream of taking them away from her."

At this statement, Pete and Bob looked at him with new interest. They waited for him to explain, and he did, as they sped along.

It turned out that Chang was actually the great-grandson of old Mathias Green. Mathias Green had taken as his second wife the Chinese princess whose skeleton the boys had helped to find. His first wife had travelled with him on all his voyages, and she had died of a fever during one voyage to the Orient, leaving him with a small son, Elija, to bring up.

Unable to care for the boy, Mathias had placed

him in an American mission school in Hong Kong to be reared and educated. Then, a short time later, Mathias had got himself into trouble with the authorities for illegally taking the Ghost Pearl necklace, had married a beautiful young Chinese princess, and had hurriedly sailed back for America, leaving his son still in Hong Kong.

Elija Green, whose father never sent for him, had grown up to become an American medical missionary in China and had married a Chinese wife. When they both died of yellow fever, their son Thomas in turn had been brought up in the American mission school. Thomas, Chang's father, had known nothing of his American relatives, for his father had refused ever to speak of Mathias Green. He, too, had spent his entire life in China as a doctor. He had married an English missionary's daughter, and they had been very happy until a flood in the Yellow River had overturned their boat, and they had drowned.

Chang paused as he said this, and Pete and Bob could see him swallow hard.

"Those were troubled times in China," he said. "I was just a baby and I was rescued from the flood by a Chinese family with whom I lived for several years. Then they heard my life was in danger because I was an American, and they slipped into Hong Kong with me to safety.

"I did not know my real name then, so for some years I grew up in a missionary school, just as my father and grandfather had done. Then one of my teachers, when I told him my mother's and father's first names, which I remembered, looked up the old records and told me that my real name was Green. He got in touch with Aunt Lydia in this country, and she sent for me.

"I have been living with her ever since. She has been very kind to me and I want very much to help her, because she is upset now. Uncle Harold is also trying to help her, but he is deeply troubled, too. Now come these stories of my great-grandfather's ghost appearing, and everything is much worse. I cannot explain it all now, for there is much I do not understand, but you will see for yourselves."

Bob started to ask a question. But he couldn't remember what it was. It had been an exciting day, and an exciting trip, and now the motion of the little bus was a soothing one. His eyes closed, and he fell asleep.

He woke up with a start when they stopped. The sun, he noticed, had set behind a high ridge. Facing them was a large, old house, built of stone and timber, behind which the mountain ridge rose abruptly. Apparently they were in a long, narrow valley. He could not see too much because the valley was already in deep twilight, but he could make out what looked like miles of cultivated ground where small bushes grew, undoubtedly grape vines.

"Wake up!" Pete said. "We're here."

Bob stifled a yawn as he came fully awake. He clambered out. Chang led them up a long flight of wooden steps to the porch of the old house.

"This is Verdant House," Chang told him. "Verdant, as I'm sure you know, means green. My aunt chose that name for the vineyard and the house because our name is Green. Now you will meet her. I know she is anxious to see you."

They entered a big hall panelled in redwood, and a tall, dignified, rather frail-looking woman came out of a room to greet them.

"Good evening, boys," she said. "I'm so glad you are here. Did you have a good trip?"

They assured her they had, and she led them into a dining-room.

"I know you're probably hungry," she said. "Even though you may have eaten earlier. Boys are always hungry. So I'm going to leave you to eat something and get acquainted with Chang. We'll talk to-morrow. To-day has been a very busy and troublesome day and I am rather tired. I'm going to bed early."

She beat on a small bronze Chinese gong, and an elderly Chinese woman came into the room.

"You may serve supper now, Li," Miss Green said. "Chang will probably be ready to eat another meal, too."

"All boys all time starve," said the shrivelled little Chinese woman. "I feed um good."

She bustled out. As she did so, a man entered the room. Bob and Pete recognised him as Harold Carlson, whom they had seen in Rocky Beach the day before, when the skeleton in the secret room had been discovered. He looked worried.

"Hello, boys," he said in his light, pleasant voice. "Never dreamed when we met yesterday under such strange circumstances we'd be meeting again here. But—" He paused and shook his head. "Frankly," he sighed, "*I* don't know what to make of it. Neither does anyone else."

"Good night, boys," Miss Green said. "I'm going up to bed. Harold, will you assist me?"

"Certainly, Aunt Lydia." The man took Miss Green's elbow lightly and walked with her out of the room and up the stairs. Chang switched on the lights.

"It gets dark suddenly here in the valley," he said. "It's practically night outside now. Well, let us eat and I'll try to tell you some more about us. Perhaps you'd like to ask questions?"

"No time talk, talk, talk!" exclaimed the Chinese woman, Li, as she pushed a serving trolley into the room. "Now time for boys to eat. Eat to make big men. Come sit down."

She put a platter of cold roast beef, plates of bread and pickles and potato salad and other cold dishes on the table. Bob suddenly realised that he was starving. That meal on the plane seemed a long time ago, and awfully small, too.

He and the others started towards the table.

But their meal was to be postponed.

Just as they started to sit down, they heard a piercing scream from upstairs. It was followed by an ominous silence.

"That was Aunt Lydia!" Chang cried, jumping up. "Something's wrong!"

He ran for the stairs. Bob and Pete automatically followed him, and so did Li and several other servants who appeared from nowhere.

Chang led the way up the stairs and down a hall. At the end of the hall a door was open, the light on, and

Anxiously he massaged her wrist.

they could see Harold Carlson bending over Miss Green, who lay stretched out on a bed. He was massaging her wrists and speaking to her urgently.

"Aunt Lydia!" he said. "Aunt Lydia, can you hear me?" He saw the others. "Li!" he said. "Bring missy's smelling salts!"

The old Chinese woman scurried into a bathroom and came back with a small bottle. While the others crowded at the door, she held the open bottle under Miss Green's nose. After a moment Miss Green shuddered slightly and opened her eyes.

"I've been foolish, haven't I?" she said. "I fainted? Yes, I screamed and fainted. It's the first time in my life I ever fainted."

"But what happened, Aunt Lydia?" Chang asked anxiously. "Why did you scream?"

"I saw the ghost again," Miss Green said, trying to keep her voice steady. "After I said good night to Harold I entered my room. Just before I turned on the light, I looked towards that alcove."

She pointed to a small alcove near the windows.

"And the ghost was standing there, as clear as day. It looked at me with terrible, burning eyes. It wore green robes, just as Uncle Mathias used to, and I'm sure it was he, although the face was just a misty blur, except for the burning eyes."

Her voice dropped to a whisper. "He is angry at me. I know he is. You see, many years ago my mother promised him that after his death the mansion in Rocky Beach would be closed and never opened again. She made a solemn vow that neither the house nor the ground it was built on would be sold or disturbed in any way. And I have broken that promise. I agreed to sell the house, and now the body of Uncle Mathias's bride has been disturbed and he—he is angry at me!"

6

Startling Developments

SUPPER, when Pete and Bob and Chang finally got to it, was gobbled in bites between bursts of excited talk.

Miss Green had been put to bed with a soothing drink by Li, who seemed to be a combined cook and housekeeper. When the servants had been sent about their business with stern orders to say nothing of what had happened—orders bound to be disobeyed—the boys went back to the dining-room.

Mr. Carlson joined them, looking very upset.

"Did you see the ghost, sir?" Pete asked.

Harold Carlson shook his head.

"I just saw Aunt Lydia to her room," he said. "It was dark and she went in alone. I was just turning away when she screamed. Her door was partly open and as I turned, I saw the light go on. Apparently she had had her finger on the light switch, and when she saw the—well, whatever she saw, she unconsciously finished turning on the light. Naturally, with the light on, there was nothing to see or at least I couldn't see anything.

"She had her hand to her mouth, horrified. Then, as I rushed in, she slumped in a faint and I was there just in time to catch her. I put her on her bed and was rubbing her wrists to revive her when you arrived."

Worriedly, he rubbed his forehead.

"The servants are bound to talk," he said. "It's impossible to shut them up. By morning the story that the ghost has been seen will be all over Verdant Valley."

"Are you worried because maybe the newspapers will learn about it and print the story," Bob asked.

"The newspapers have already done as much harm as they can do," the man replied. "I'm worried about the effect on our workers. I believe Aunt Lydia told you over the phone that she saw the ghost in her room last night?"

Bob and Pete nodded.

"Well, two of the maids saw it, too, or they say they saw it—outside, on the patio, where they were sitting and chattering. They were frightened half out of their wits. I thought I had persuaded them that they had imagined it, but I guess I didn't because this morning there were rumours all over the valley about the ghost having moved here from Rocky Beach. All our workers were buzzing with gossip about it."

"You think that the ghost will frighten the workers, is that it, Uncle Harold?" Chang asked.

"Yes!" the man burst out. "That ghost will ruin us! Ruin us completely!"

Then, as if he regretted the outburst, his voice became calmer.

"But that's not the concern of our guests. Perhaps

you boys would like to see the pearls that I recovered yesterday when you were present?"

Bob and Pete agreed they would. They had only had a glimpse of them there in the secret room in the Green mansion.

Mr. Carlson led the way out of the dining-room and down a hall into a small office, equipped with a big roll-top desk, a number of filing cabinets, a telephone, and a large, old-fashioned safe in the corner.

He knelt and spun the dial of the safe. In a moment, he rejoined them carrying a small cardboard box, which he placed on the desk and opened. Then he lifted out the necklace inside and placed it on the green blotter of the desk, where it showed up clearly.

Bob and Pete leaned over, and Chang joined them. The pearls were large, but all of them were irregular in shape and had a strange, dull grey colour. They were not at all like the lustrous round pink-white pearls in the small string which Bob's mother owned.

"That's a funny colour for pearls," Pete said.

"It's why they are called Ghost Pearls," Mr. Carlson told them. "I believe all such pearls came from one tiny bay in the Indian Ocean, and are no longer found. In the Orient rich nobles value them highly, but I don't know why because their shape is not perfect and their colour is very unattractive. Just the same, their value is high. I'm sure these could be sold for a hundred thousand dollars or more."

"In that case, Uncle Harold," Chang began, "Aunt Lydia could pay off the debts she owes and save the vineyard and the winery!" And he added, "Surely the pearls now belong to her!"

57

"There's a complication." Mr. Carlson shook his head. "Obviously Mathias Green gave these pearls to his Chinese wife. So they were hers, not his. By the law of inheritance, if you can follow me, they would belong to *her* nearest relative."

"But her family disowned her," Chang said, puzzled. "They said she was no longer a daughter. Besides, since the revolution and war in China, her family has vanished."

"I know." Mr. Carlson mopped his brow. "Just the same, I have had a letter from a Chinese lawyer in San Francisco who claims he has a client who is a descendant of the bride's sister. He warns me to keep the pearls safe because his client claims them. The whole matter will have to be tried in court and it may take years before we know to whom the pearls belong."

Chang's brow furrowed. He seemed about to say something when outside in the hall they heard hurrying footsteps. A strong knock sounded on the door.

"Come in!" Harold Carlson said, as they all turned.

The door opened and a burly, middle-aged man with swarthy features and piercing eyes came in. He was breathless as he spoke, ignoring the boys.

"Mr. Carlson, sir, the ghost has been seen down by the Number One pressing house. Three Mexican grape pickers saw it, and they have panicked. You'd better come."

"Oh, this is terrible! I'll be right with you, Jensen," Mr. Carlson groaned. Hurriedly he put the necklace back in the safe and swung the door shut. Then, with the three boys at their heels, he and the other man hurried out of the house to a waiting jeep. They all managed to climb in, Bob sitting on Pete's lap, and the little vehicle took off with a roar, spinning round and dashing through the darkness down the alley.

Bob and Pete were too busy holding on as the jeep bumped along the dirt road to see much, even if it hadn't been night. But the ride only lasted five minutes. Then they came to a skidding stop outside a low building that the headlights showed to be made of concrete and concrete bricks. It looked new.

They all got out. The smell of grapes, and of freshly pressed grape juice, was heavy in the air.

"Mr. Jensen is the foreman of the planting and picking operation," Chang whispered to the boys. "He oversees the labour force for that part of the operation."

Mr. Jensen shut off the headlights, just as a young man, somewhat raggedly dressed, came forward from the darkness around the building.

"Well, Henry?" Mr. Jensen barked at him. "Seen anything since I left?"

The young man shook his head.

"No, sir, Mr. Jensen," he said. "Not anything, sir."

"Where are those three pickers?" Jensen asked. The young man was now close enough for them to see him spread his hands.

"Who knows?" he said. "They fled as soon as you left. They ran, and"—he chuckled—"I have never seen them run before. Probably they are in a café in Verdant," he pointed towards the little cluster of lights at the other end of the valley, "telling everyone that they saw the ghost."

"That's just what I didn't want," Mr. Jensen said grimly. "You should have stopped them."

"I tried to speak sense to them," the young man said. "They would not listen. Fear had turned their minds."

"The fat's in the fire all right," Harold Carlson said dejectedly. "What were those men doing down here after dark anyway?"

"I told them to meet me here, sir," Jensen reported. "They are the ones who have been mainly responsible for spreading stories about the ghost, and I wanted a chance to tell them to keep their mouths shut or be fired. But I was delayed getting here and while they waited for me, they imagined they saw something."

"I'm sure that's just what it was—imagination. They've been talking so much about ghosts that they thought they saw one."

"Whether it was imagination or not, the harm is done," Mr. Carlson said. "Maybe you can go into the village and calm them down, though that's probably hopeless."

"Yes, sir. Shall I drive you all back to the house first?"

"Yes and——" Harold Carlson clapped his hand against his forehead with an exclamation. "Good heavens!" he cried. "Chang! Did I lock the safe after I put the pearls back?"

"I don't know, sir," Chang replied. "Your back hid the safe. I couldn't see."

"I could," Pete spoke up. He was trying hard to search his memory for what he had actually seen back in the office. "You put the pearls inside—and you slammed the door shut and turned the handle——"

"Yes, yes," Harold Carlson broke in. "But did I turn the dial?"

Pete thought hard. He couldn't be sure. And yet—

"No, Mr. Carlson," he said finally. "I don't think you did."

"I don't think I did either," Harold Carlson groaned. "I went away and left the safe unlocked with the Ghost Pearls in it. Jensen, quick, get me back to the house. Then you can come back and pick up the boys."

"Right. Here, Chang, take my torch." Jensen pressed a powerful torch into Chang Green's hand, then the two men leaped into the jeep and roared off.

"Golly!" Bob broke the silence that followed. "First up at the house. Now down here. But why is everybody so worried about the people talking, Chang?"

"It is because the grape-picking season has commenced," Chang said. "Now the grapes are ripening, they must be picked and brought to the presses to have the juice extracted. Every day more grapes ripen, and if they are not picked, soon they are too ripe for good wine, or else they rot.

"It takes many men to pick the grapes, but it is not a year-round job, so we have many workers who come here just for the picking season, then go elsewhere. Some are Mexicans, some are Americans, some are of Oriental ancestry, but they are all poor, hard-working people who are very superstitious.

"The pickers have been uneasy since the stories of the green ghost at Rocky Beach first appeared in the papers. Now, if the ghost is here in Verdant Valley,

61

many of the pickers will flee in superstitious fear. They will quit their jobs, and we will not be able to get other pickers. The grapes will rot on the vines, we will not be able to press the juice, and the crop will be a failure. The 3-V Winery will lose much money—and I am sure my aunt is worried because a great deal of money is owed and every penny counts."

"Gosh, that's tough," Pete said in awkward sympathy. "All because they started to tear down your great-grandfather's house and his ghost started roaming."

"No!" Chang said stubbornly. "I do not believe it is my great-grandfather's honourable spirit. He would not wish to do harm to those of his own family. It is some other evil spirit seeking to work mischief."

He spoke with such conviction that Bob wanted to believe him. But he had been at the Green mansion and he had seen that misty figure in the flowing Mandarin robes, and he was afraid Chang was wrong.

The three boys were silent a moment longer, trying to decide what to do next. It was Bob who spoke first.

"If the ghost was seen here," he said, "then we ought to look round and see if we can see it again."

"Well——" Pete's voice sounded reluctant— "I guess that makes sense. But I sure wish Jupe were here."

"The ghost has harmed no one," Chang said. "It has only shown itself. We need not fear it. And if it is the honourable spirit of my ancestor, it cannot intend harm. I agree, Bob. Let us look round the pressing house and see if the ghost still lingers there."

He led the boys in a slow circle round the building.

He seemed to know his way well, and did not turn on the torch because, as he said, light would make it impossible to see the green ghost.

They strained their eyes, watching, but saw nothing except the darker shadow of the building. As they walked, Chang explained the work of a pressing house. "Here is where the ripe grapes are put into big tanks. Large rotary paddles crush the grapes and press out the juice, which flows to a gathering tank. From the gathering tank it is pumped into vats in the ageing cellars. These are really caves cut into the nearby mountain, where the temperature and humidity remain constant all year round."

Bob was only half listening. He was straining to catch a glimpse of anything that might look like a glowing figure, but they circled the building completely without seeing anything.

"Perhaps we should go inside," Chang finally suggested. "I will show you the machinery and the tanks. It is all very new. It was just built last year when Uncle Harold bought much new machinery, and a great deal of money is owed. That is why my honourable aunt worries so. She is afraid she cannot repay the money."

But at that moment headlights came into sight and a moment later the jeep pulled up beside them.

"Hop in, boys," Jensen said. "I'll take you back to the house. First, though, I have to do an errand in the village. I have to try to find those three pickers who claim they saw the ghost, make them keep their mouths shut, and try to undo the damage they've already done."

63

"Thank you, Mr. Jensen," Chang said. "But we can walk. It's only a little over a mile. Here's your torch. The moon is up now so we can see the road easily."

"Anything you say," the burly man agreed. "I only hope those three haven't panicked all our pickers, or there won't be a dozen showing up to-morrow."

The jeep roared off down the valley towards a small cluster of lights which must have been the village the man had referred to. Pete turned to Bob.

"You don't mind walking, do you, Bob?" he asked.

"My leg feels fine," Bob told him. He explained to Chang, "When I was a little kid I rolled down a hill and broke my leg in umpteen places. From that time I wore a brace, until last week when Dr. Alvarez took it off. He said I was okay now and that exercise would do my leg good."

"We will not hurry," Chang said, and they started strolling down the dusty road in the moonlight, smelling the ripe grapes all around them. Chang was silent for some moments.

"Excuse me," he said at last. "I have just been thinking of the way in which this ghost business will be a disaster for the Verdant Valley. All our pickers will desert, as I said. The crop will rot. We will lose a great deal of money. Aunt Lydia will not be able to pay off the notes she signed, and Verdant Valley will be taken away from her.

"That is why I was silent. I was worrying for her sake. I know how much the vineyard and the winery mean to her. After all, first her mother, and then Aunt Lydia, spent their lives in building up the business. To lose it now will crush her. There is one hope.

If we can clear up the title to the Ghost Pearls, and prove they do not belong to someone else, she can sell them for a great deal of money and pay off the debts."

"I sure hope you can," Pete said. "But what do you really think, Chang? Is it your great-grandfather's ghost we've been seeing, or what?"

"I do not know," the other boy answered slowly. "I cannot believe my grandfather's spirit would mean harm, even though he was a rough man in life. In China I learned not to disbelieve in spirits, either good ones or evil ones. I think this is an evil spirit at work, and not my great-grandfather at all. Yes, it is an evil spirit!"

By now they had reached the house. A few lights were on, but everything seemed very quiet. They climbed the stairs, entered, and went in. Chang seemed surprised to find the big living-room empty.

"The servants have all gone to bed," he said, "but I was sure Uncle Harold would be here. He said he wanted to ask you some questions. Perhaps he is in his office."

He led them down the hall to the office. The door was shut. Chang knocked. The only answer they got was a muffled groan and a bumping noise.

Alarmed, Chang thrust the door open. All three boys stared at the sight of Harold Carlson lying on the floor, his wrists and ankles tightly tied and brought together behind his back. A brown paper bag covered his head.

"Uncle Harold!" Chang cried.

He rushed in, Bob and Pete at his heels, and

65

snatched off the paper bag. Harold Carlson's eyes bulged up at them, and he tried to utter words through a thick gag that filled his mouth.

"Don't try to talk, we'll cut you free!" Chang said swiftly.

He whipped out a pocket knife and cut loose the gag which was made from a bandana. Then, as Harold Carlson gasped for breath, he freed the man's legs and wrists. Mr. Carlson sat up, rubbing his wrists.

"What happened?" Pete asked.

"When I returned to the house and entered the office, someone was hiding behind the door. Whoever it was grabbed me from behind, held me while a second man gagged and tied me. Then they threw me on the floor and tied my ankles and wrists together and put a paper bag over my head. I heard the safe door clang open—the safe!"

In sudden anxiety he turned and rushed to the big iron safe. They could all see it was open an inch or two. Mr. Carlson jerked the door wide open and reached in. His hands came out empty.

He stared at them, his lips working, his face grey.

"The Ghost Pearls!" he said huskily. "They've been stolen!"

7

Jupiter makes Deductions

BACK IN ROCKY BEACH, sitting alone in the living-room of the cottage where he lived with his Uncle

Titus and Aunt Mathilda, Jupiter Jones had been pinching his lip and thinking hard for an hour. Now he abruptly straightened up and screamed as loudly as he could. Then, pink-faced from the effort, he sat back and waited.

A moment later there was the sound of footsteps outside. The front door burst open and Konrad, the big, blond yard helper, thrust his head in. Hans, his brother, was in San Diego with the Joneses. Konrad's eyes bulged as he gaped at Jupiter.

"Who was that yelling just now, Jupe?" he asked excitedly.

"That was me," Jupiter said. "So you heard me?"

"Sure bet I heard you!" Konrad said emphatically. "Your window open, my window open, I heard you okay. Sound like you sat on a big tack or stubbed your toe or something."

Jupiter looked at the window behind him. It was wide open. His round face registered vexation.

"What you yell for, Jupe?" Konrad asked. "I don't see anything wrong."

"There isn't anything wrong except I forgot the window was open," Jupiter told him.

"Then why you yell?" Konrad persisted.

"I was practising screaming," Jupiter told him.

"You sure you hokay, Jupe?" Konrad asked. "Not sick or something?"

"I'm fine," Jupe told him. You can go back to your cottage now, I won't scream any more to-night."

"That's good," Konrad said. "You sure scared me."

He closed the door and returned to the small cottage

67

he shared with his brother Hans, about fifty yards behind the Joneses' home.

Jupiter sat where he was, his brain buzzing. An idea was trying to break through in his mind—an idea about the green ghost, but it wouldn't come. Presently he sighed and gave up. It was time for bed anyway.

As he stood up to go upstairs, he wondered what Bob and Pete were doing up in Verdant Valley.

As if in answer to his thoughts, the telephone rang. It was a reverse charge call from Bob. Jupe accepted the call eagerly.

"What's happened, Bob?" he asked. "Did you see the green ghost?"

"No, but Miss Green saw it," Bob said excitedly. "And then you'll never guess what happened. The——"

"You are excited," Jupiter told him. "Please tell me everything that happened, slowly and in sequence. Don't skip any details."

This was not easy for Bob to do, because he wanted to get right to the fact that the Ghost Pearls had been stolen. However, Jupiter had been training him to get all facts in order, and not to skip anything because small details could turn out to be very important. So now he began with their meeting with Chang Green, and told Jupiter everything he could remember, just as it had happened.

Finally, to his great relief, he got to the theft of the pearls, and told about that.

"Hmmm," Jupiter said, as Bob paused for breath.

"That is an unexpected development. What's happening now? Is an investigation being made?"

"Mr. Carlson sent for the local sheriff, Sheriff Bixby," Bob told him. "Sheriff Bixby is pretty old and doesn't seem to know what to do. The house here isn't in any town so there isn't any police force to call on. Just the sheriff and a deputy who keeps saying, 'I'll be danged.'

"The sheriff has a theory, though. He thinks that with all the publicity in the papers about the pearls, some criminals from the city came down here to steal them. When they saw Mr. Carlson rush out, they slipped in through a window from the side porch. They got the pearls and were searching for anything else that might be valuable when Mr. Carlson returned unexpectedly. They grabbed him as he came in, gagged him and put a paper bag over his head, so he couldn't see a thing. All Mr. Carlson can tell us is that one of them was rather short, but very powerful. The sheriff says they're probably halfway back to the city by now. He's going to phone to the police in San Francisco, but he doesn't think it will do much good."

Jupiter pinched his lip. The sheriff's theory certainly sounded reasonable. With all the publicity the Ghost Pearls had had, it would probably have been surprising if some city thieves hadn't taken the opportunity to try to steal them. It was just bad luck that Mr. Carlson, in his excitement, had left the safe unlocked to make things easier for them.

And yet Jupiter couldn't help wondering if there might not be some connection between the green ghost and the theft of the jewels. He couldn't imagine what it could be, but he wondered.

"You and Pete keep your eyes open, Bob," he said at last. "I certainly wish I was there," he added, wistfully, "but I have to stay here because Uncle Titus and Aunt Mathilda will be away for at least another day. Phone me if anything else happens."

With that he hung up. He was tempted to stay up and think about what Bob had told him, but sleepiness overcame him and he went up to bed. He slept heavily with many dreams, in one of which he kept hearing a voice he almost recognised but didn't.

The following morning, he could not remember what he had been dreaming about.

Jupiter hoped it would be a quiet day at The Jones Salvage Yard, so that he could think about all Bob had told him the previous evening.

However, as things usually happen, it was a very busy day at the salvage yard. Jupiter had to run the whole place, with Konrad's help, and he didn't have a minute to be alone and think. But at about five o'clock, business slackened off. Jupiter made a swift decision. An idea had come to him—an important idea.

"Konrad," he said to the big yard helper, "you take charge. Close up at six o'clock. I have some investigating to do."

"Hokay, Jupe," the man said good-naturedly. "I do my best."

Jupiter hopped on his bike and sped across town to the wooded area near a small stream which was the site of the Green mansion. As he rode up the drive way, he saw a police car parked in front of it. A uniformed policeman leaned out the window of the car as Jupiter rode up. It was one of the men who had been at the house the previous morning.

"Just keep right on riding, sonny," the policeman said, a bit wearily. "I've been shooing sightseers and souvenir hunters away all day."

Jupiter got off his bike and reached into his pocket.

"A lot of people have been out here?" he asked.

"Ever since the ghost was seen," the policeman said.

"We've had to guard this place to keep souvenir hunters from tearing it down. Now run along. I'm tired of shooing people off."

"I'm not here for souvenirs," Jupiter said. "Didn't you see me come here yesterday with Chief Reynolds when the secret room was discovered?"

The officer took a better look at him.

"Well, yes, now you mention it," he said. "You did come with the chief."

Jupiter took out a card and handed it to the officer. It was one of the firm's business cards. It said:

THE THREE INVESTIGATORS

"We Investigate Anything"

?   ?   ?

First Investigator – JUPITER JONES
Second Investigator – PETER CRENSHAW
Records and Research – BOB ANDREWS

The officer started to grin, then stopped. After all, Jupiter had come in the chief's car the previous day.

"You investigate things, huh?" he asked. "You investigating something for the chief?"

"I'm making an investigation that I'm sure will interest him if my idea works out," Jupiter said.

He told the officer what he wanted to do, and the man nodded.

"That sounds all right," he said. "Go ahead in."

Jupiter trudged up the flagstone path to the house, studying it. It was solidly built, and the wing that was partly torn down showed that the walls were thick.

He went inside. He did not waste time looking round for more secret rooms or anything like that, because Chief Reynolds had said a thorough search of the house had been made. Instead, he went upstairs to the upper hall. There he stood on the top step, faced downstairs—and screamed.

He waited a minute, then went downstairs and in the lower hall screamed again. After that he went outdoors and walked down to the waiting policeman.

"Well?" he asked. "Could you hear me?"

"I heard a couple of yells," the officer told him. "One very faint one and one a little louder. The door was shut."

"The door was shut the night the ghost appeared," Jupiter said. He looked round. There was a big clump of ornamental bushes at the corner of the house. "Listen this time," he requested, and headed for the clump.

He stationed himself behind it, then leaned out a

72

bit and gave another loud yell. When he walked back to the police car, the officer nodded.

"I heard that all right," he said, "loud and clear. Say, what are you trying to prove, anyway?"

"I'm trying to deduce where the ghost was when it screamed," Jupiter said. "According to my observations it must have been outside the house. If it was inside, it would have had to have a very powerful pair of lungs."

"I don't know whether ghosts have lungs or not," the policeman chuckled, but Jupiter didn't smile.

"That's exactly the point," he said, and the man scratched his head. Jupiter started towards his bike, but the officer called after him.

"Say," he called, "what are the question marks on your card for?"

Jupiter suppressed a chuckle. Those question marks always attracted attention.

"The question mark," he said, in a very adult manner, "is our symbol, our trade-mark. It stands for mysteries unsolved, enigmas unanswered, conundrums requiring an answer."

He got on his bike, leaving the officer still scratching his head, and rode away. He rode only a few blocks, however. By then he was away from the extensive grounds of the old Green mansion, and in a neatly built, modern suburb.

He had with him a clipping from the local newspaper, giving the names and addresses of the four men who had reported to the police after seeing the ghost and hearing the scream.

He picked the address farthest away from the old

mansion, and got there just as a car turned into the driveway and a man got out. It was one of the four men, a Mr. Charles Davis, and he answered Jupiter's questions readily.

He and a neighbour from across the street had been sitting in his patio, smoking and discussing baseball, when two men had walked by and called out to them. He hadn't recognised the men, but assumed they lived nearby in the development. They had suggested a walk up to look at the old Green mansion by moonlight before it was torn down, and one of them, a man with a deep voice, had been so persuasive that the two had joined them. He himself had taken two torches from his garage and given one to his friend.

Then the four of them had walked towards the Green mansion. On the way they had seen two more residents of the development and the man with the deep voice had talked them into joining the group. He'd made it seem rather a lark, to be visiting a supposedly haunted house before it was torn down, and had laughingly suggested they might see the ghost.

"He actually said you might see the ghost?" Jupiter asked, and Mr. Davis nodded.

"Something like that," he said. "And as it turned out, we did. The whole thing was mighty peculiar, if you ask me."

"You didn't know the first two men?" Jupiter inquired.

"I thought I might have seen one of them," Mr. Davis told him. "The other was a stranger to me, but I judged he lived in the development some place. We have lots of neighbours we don't know here. Most of us have only been here a year or so."

"How many of you were there when you reached the house?" Jupiter asked.

"Six," Mr. Davis told him. "Although somebody else said there were seven, I know there were only six of us when we started up the driveway. Of course, somebody could have followed us out of curiosity. After we heard the scream and then started to look inside, nobody thought much about counting. And it was mighty dark. After we left, we split up. My friend and I and our two neighbours decided we'd better notify the police. I don't know what happened to the others. I guess they just didn't want any publicity."

At that moment a small wire-haired terrier came dashing across the yard and leaped around Mr. Davis's legs, yapping a happy welcome.

"Down, boy, down!" the man laughed, and patted the dog, which subsided on to the lawn, where he stretched out, panting, and watched his master.

Jupiter remembered, from Bob's account, that one of the men at the Green mansion had had a dog. He ventured a question.

"Sure," Mr. Davis told him. "I had Domino here with me. I always take him for an evening walk, so I took him along."

Jupiter stared at the dog. The dog met his eye. Its mouth open, panting, the dog seemed to be laughing at him as if it knew something Jupiter didn't. Jupiter scowled. Again an idea was trying to come to him, and couldn't quite make it.

He ventured a few more questions, but Mr. Davis

75

could tell him nothing new, so Jupiter thanked him and remounted his bicycle.

He rode home, slowly now, thinking furiously. When he got back to the salvage yard, the big main gates were shut. The sun was setting—he had spent longer in his quest for information than he had realised.

Jupiter found Konrad comfortably smoking a pipe in his little cottage.

"Hi-yup, Jupe," Konrad said as Jupiter entered. "You look like you're thinking so hard you're pretty close to busting."

"Konrad," Jupiter said, hardly noticing the remark, "last night you heard me yell."

"Sure did," Konrad agreed. "Sounded like stuck pig, Jupe, hope you don't mind if I say it."

"I was trying to sound as hurt as I could," Jupiter told him. "But you wouldn't have heard me if my window and your window hadn't been open, would you?"

"Don't think so. What you getting at?"

Jupiter's face turned pink with sudden excitement. The scream that everyone had heard—and the dog! The dog that had seemed to be able to tell him something. Suddenly he remembered that in a Sherlock Holmes story there had been a dog that had told Sherlock Holmes a lot too! By not doing a thing!

He turned and hurried back to the cottage where he lived. All of a sudden ideas were tumbling in his mind and taking form.

The policeman at the Green mansion hadn't been able to hear him yell, when he was inside with the door shut. But outside—yes, he'd heard him clearly! That was very significant!

Once inside the house, Jupiter got out the tape recorder and prepared to play the scream again, and along with it the bits of conversation Bob had recorded. He played it all through once, then sat very still for several minutes. He recalled exactly what Bob had told him the previous night. It all fitted! It had to fit!

The scream—the fact that no one was sure whether six or seven men had been in the house—even the dog! Now he knew what the dog could have told him if it could speak. There were a lot of other things he still didn't know, but he knew that much, he felt sure.

It was dark in the room, but he didn't bother to turn on the light as he grabbed up the telephone and put through a person-to-person call to Bob Andrews in Verdant Valley. After a long delay, it was Miss Green herself who answered the phone.

"Is that Bob's friend, Jupiter Jones?" she asked, and her voice seemed to tremble.

"Yes, Miss Green," Jupiter answered. "I wanted to talk to Bob. I believe I have some ideas and——"

But her voice stopped him.

"Bob isn't here," she said, sounding very distracted. "Neither is his friend Pete. My great-nephew Chang is missing, too. All three of them have just—just disappeared!"

8

Runaway !

THE MORNING AFTER his telephone call to Jupiter—the same morning Jupiter was so busy at the salvage yard—Bob, together with Pete and Chang, was exploring Verdant Valley on horseback. None of the three boys had any notion of the dangerous and exciting events that were ahead of them that day.

They weren't planning anything more exciting at the moment than a look at the caves which the 3-V Winery used as ageing cellars in which to store the wine made from the grapes grown in Verdant Valley. These caves, as Chang explained, were really old mines, most of them dug into the high ridge to the west of the valley long before.

Mostly, the boys' plan was to stay away from the house for the day. They couldn't very well investigate the theft of the Ghost Pearls, because if Sheriff Bixby was correct, and city thieves had taken them, both thieves and pearls were probably back in San Francisco by now.

But the big house was swarming with reporters, brought there by the news of the appearance of the ghost and the theft of the pearls. Miss Lydia Green, looking very haggard and worn, had asked Pete and Bob not to give the reporters the chance to guess that they were the boys who had first seen the ghostly manifestation at the empty house in Rocky Beach. She was afraid this would just make the reporters write bigger and more sensational stories, speculating about the ghost and why the boys had come. As she said, the stories were going to do enough damage anyway.

So Bob, Pete and Chang had eaten breakfast in the kitchen and had quietly slipped away to the stables, where they had saddled three horses. Chang did most of the work, for Bob and Pete had only limited experience with horses while visiting dude ranches.

Now, with torches clipped to their belts for use later in exploring the wine caves—or mines—they rode slowly through the cultivated fields, between the bushy grape vines, where purple grapes were ripening fast in the hot sun.

Chang was visibly gloomy.

"There should be at least a hundred pickers in the fields now," he told them. "And several trucks carrying the picked grapes to the pressing houses. But look. You can hardly see a dozen people picking. And only one truck. The others have all left for fear of the ghost. If this keeps up, Aunt Lydia and the vineyard will be ruined. She'll never be able to pay off the notes, and they will be due very soon."

Bob and Pete couldn't think of anything to say to cheer him up, but Pete tried.

"Our partner, Jupiter Jones, is working on the mystery of the ghost right this minute, back in Rocky Beach," he said. "Jupe is pretty brainy. If he can solve the mystery and quieten down the ghost some-how, maybe the pickers will come back."

"Only if it happens very soon," Chang said. "Other-wise the pickers will go elsewhere. This morning old Li told me that I am the one causing such ill-fortune to Verdant Valley. She said I brought bad luck with me when I came from Hong Kong a year and a half ago and that I should go back."

"That's silly," Bob said promptly. "How could you bring bad luck?"

Chang shook his head. "I do not know. But it is true that since I have been here, there have been many misfortunes. Batches of wine have spoiled, casks have leaked, machinery has broken down time and time again. Nothing has gone right."

"I don't see how anybody can blame you for that!" Pete declared.

"Perhaps it is true, though," Chang said. "Perhaps if I were to go back to Hong Kong, the ghost would go with me and fortune would smile again on Verdant Valley. If I could be sure that was the case, I would go to-morrow. Not for anything would I bring trouble and misfortune to my honoured great-aunt!"

Chang seemed so gloomy, Bob decided it was time to change the subject.

"You call Miss Green your aunt, and Mr. Carlson your uncle," he said. "I haven't been able to figure out the actual relationship. Old Mathias Green was your grandfather——"

"My great-grandfather," Chang said. "Miss Green is really my great-aunt, but I call her aunt by courtesy. Uncle Harold is a distant cousin of hers. I don't know the exact relationship, but I call him uncle, also by courtesy. We three are the only living members of this branch of the family."

Pete looked ahead, down the long, narrow valley, walled on both sides by steep mountain ridges. As far as he could see, grape vines grew.

"So this place is really all yours, Chang?" he asked with interest. "I mean, as the only direct descendant of old Mathias."

"Oh, no, no," the other boy said. "It belongs to Aunt Lydia. Her mother started it and Aunt Lydia worked all her life to build it up.

"She wants to deed it to me, but I will not permit it. So she is leaving it to me in her will. I have decided that then I will give half of it to Uncle Harold. After all, he has worked hard as Aunt Lydia's business manager to make the vineyard and the winery prosper. Only——" he looked gloomy again "——if the vineyard and the winery are lost because there is no money to pay off the loans, none of us will have anything."

A jeep came down the dirt road towards them. They pulled to a stop to let it pass. Chang was riding Ebony, a big black colt full of life and spirit, which he had to hold in tightly. Pete was riding Nellie, a young mare who was a bit nervous, and he, too, had to keep her under tight control. Bob was on an older mare, called Rockinghorse, because of her easy motion and placid disposition.

The jeep stopped. Mr. Jensen leaned out.

"Hi, Chang," he said. "I suppose you see how few pickers we have this morning?"

The boy nodded.

"Those varmints last night did their work well," Jensen continued. "Every time they told about the ghost they claimed to see, they made it bigger and uglier, until at last it was breathing smoke and flames. They scared the daylights out of the other pickers. I've sent out word for help, but I'm afraid we won't get it."

He shook his head.

"I'm on the way up to report to Miss Green," he said. "It doesn't look good."

The jeep roared off. The boys started their horses walking again and with an effort Chang threw off his gloomy mood.

"What can't be helped, can't be helped," he said. "There's nothing we can do, so let's try to enjoy ourselves."

They rode the length of the valley, stopping now and then, while Chang showed them the other pressing houses. Some time after noon they began to get hot and hungry. They had sandwiches and canteens with them, and feed for the horses in their saddle bags.

"I know where we can be cool and comfortable," Chang told them. He led them past an old grape-pressing house, now only used at rush periods, and on a few hundred yards until they were in the shadow of the western ridge of the valley wall. Around an outcropping of rock they found a small, shaded space where they dismounted, tied up their horses and gave them the grain they had brought.

Then Chang led them round the other side of the rocky outcropping and they found themselves outside a heavy door set into the rock wall of the ridge.

"This is one of the entrances to the ageing caves, or mines, I told you about," Chang said. He pulled the door open with an effort. Beyond it was a shaft of darkness that ran straight into the ridge. "We'll explore this after we eat."

He reached for a switch inside the door and clicked it, but nothing happened.

"Darn," he said. "I forgot. The dynamos aren't on. We have to make our own electricity here, and the dynamos for different sections are only turned on when there's work being done inside. Oh well, we can use our torches."

He unbuckled his own light and shone it forward. Pete and Bob saw a long corridor, rock walled, with timbers overhead supporting the roof. On each side of the corridor was a long row of large casks, bigger than water barrels, lying on their sides. Down the middle of the corridor ran two narrow rails, and a small flatcar stood a few feet away.

"The casks can be put on that flatcar and rolled down here to the entrance," Chang explained. "If we want to ship a whole cask, we just load it on to a truck that backs up to the entrance. That way the heavy casks are pretty easy to handle.

"Well, suppose we sit here inside the door and eat, and take it easy for a while."

Pete and Bob were delighted to flop down beside him with their backs against the stone, and start their lunch. It was cool inside, though the heat of the afternoon was only a few feet away.

As they ate, they could look out at the valley. The

old pressing house was in their line of vision, but no one, looking in their direction, could see them inside the cave.

They finished eating and talked for awhile, enjoying the coolness. Chang was telling them about his life in Hong Kong, where he had always been surrounded by people in contrast to the quiet life in Verdant Valley, when the boys saw several old cars pull up outside the pressing house a few hundred yards away.

Half a dozen men, all of them big and powerful looking, got out and stood in a little group. They seemed to be waiting for something.

Chang broke off what he was saying, and frowned.

"I wonder why they aren't busy picking," he asked aloud. "To-day we need every hand available."

A moment later, Mr. Jensen's jeep drove up and they saw the burly man get out. He went inside the old pressing house. The men followed him and the door shut.

"I suppose Mr. Jensen is going to work on the machinery," Chang murmured. "Since the pressing house isn't being used to-day. Well, it's his business. I don't like him very well, but I have to admit he knows how to handle the workers, even though he does get rather rough with them at times."

He leaned on an elbow and turned to Bob and Pete.

"Want to explore the ageing tunnels now?" he asked.

They agreed and unsnapped the torches from their belts. Pete stood up and as he did so, slipped. His hand shot out to steady himself. The torch seemed to zip from between his fingers and fell on the rock with a tinkle of broken glass. When he picked it up, the lens and bulb were both broken.

"Darn!" Pete said, disgusted with himself. "Now I haven't got a light."

"We could get by with just two," Chang said, "but——"

He was gazing at the jeep parked outside the pressing house.

"I have it," he said. "Borrow Mr. Jensen's. The one he loaned me last night. He carries it in the toolbox with the other gear during the day. We'll get it back to him long before dark. I'll ride over and get it."

But Pete insisted that as he had broken his torch, it was up to him to do the chore of getting the replacement. Chang wrote out a note, to leave in the toolbox, telling Mr. Jensen that they had borrowed the torch and would return it later.

"When he's busy he hates to be interrupted," he said. "Besides, the torch actually belongs to Aunt Lydia, so he won't mind our using it for a while."

Pete got on his horse and started trotting across the field towards the pressing house. In a couple of minutes he reined up beside the parked jeep. His horse, having rested, was feeling frisky, and he had to hold the reins tightly to keep it from bolting away.

With one hand, he flipped open the toolbox of the jeep and saw inside a jumble of tools. The torch was not in sight. Then he saw it, tucked well down into a corner. He pulled it out and slipped it inside his belt. It was an old fashioned torch, with a large, black fibre barrel, and had no ring that he could use to hang it to his belt clip.

He dropped the note Chang had given him into the toolbox and left the box open so Mr. Jensen would be sure to see it. Then, with some difficulty, he remounted and started trotting back to where Pete and Chang waited.

He had covered a hundred yards when he heard a voice shouting behind him. Pete looked back. Mr. Jensen was standing beside his jeep, shouting at him. Pete held up the torch, then pointed to the jeep, to indicate that the note explained everything, and kept on trotting.

A moment later the man leaped into the jeep and raced the sturdy vehicle across the field, between the grape-vines, after Pete. The other men who had been in the building with him crowded outside to watch.

Obviously, he wanted Pete to stop. Wondering at the man's excitement, Pete reined in his horse, which danced a little.

"Steady, girl, steady!" he said soothingly.

But the horse, eyeing the approaching jeep, still sidestepped nervously.

The jeep roared up and stopped. Mr. Jensen practically catapulted out of it and ran towards Pete.

"You young thief!" he roared. "I'll tan your hide! I'll teach you to——"

The rest of what he had to say was lost.

As he came closer, the nervous horse under Pete gave a great leap. Then, before Pete could get himself set, it bolted.

At a dead run it started tearing down the vineyard,

angling towards the mountain slope, and Pete could do nothing to stop it.

Knees pressed tightly against the horse and unashamedly clutching the pommel of the Western type saddle, Pete hung on for dear life.

9

A Desperate Flight

THE MARE thundered along between the rows of grapevines, heading straight for the rocky ridge of the western wall of the valley. Pete, unable to do anything but hang on, saw that there was a trail slanting up the slope, narrow but not too steep.

The frightened horse automatically selected the trail and continued galloping upwards. Pete hoped the slope would slow her down, and it did, but only enough to let him get set better so that he was in less danger of tumbling out of the saddle.

He risked turning his head to look back. Mr. Jensen had jumped back into his jeep and was chasing him. The little car, driven pell-mell across the fields, pulled up to a stop where the narrow trail up the slope began. Jensen leaped out and shook his fist after Pete.

Then Pete saw Bob and Chang. As soon as his mare bolted they must have run to their horses, mounted, and set out after him. They swerved round Mr. Jensen and the jeep and came up the trail behind

A hurried glance showed Chang and Bob fast pursuing him.

Pete. Chang, on his big black stallion, Ebony, was in the lead, urging the animal on and gaining on Pete.

Bob, on the slower Rockingchair, was behind and losing ground.

A sudden swerve by Nellie as she went round a rocky outcropping nearly unseated Pete. He grabbed the pommel tightly and held on again. Coming to a short level stretch, the nervous mare picked up speed.

Then Pete heard pounding hooves behind him. Chang pulled up daringly beside him on the narrow trail, reached out and grabbed Nellie's reins just behind the bit.

Chang slowed Ebony, meanwhile holding tight to Nellie's reins and forcing the mare to slow. Almost as if she had made up her mind to stop running anyway, Nellie stopped. Ebony stopped beside her and both horses, their flanks wet with sweat, heaved deeply for breath.

"Golly, Chang, thanks," Pete said with fervour. "This horse acted as if she wanted to run right over the mountain."

Chang was staring at him with a peculiar look.

"What is it, Chang? Did I do something wrong?"

"I was just thinking," Chang said. "Why did Jensen make your horse bolt?"

"He wasn't trying to," Pete answered. "He was yelling at me. Calling me a thief. He was pretty angry."

"When I passed him," Chang said, "his face was twisted like the mask of an evil spirit. He was in a mindless fury. In his pocket he carries a revolver—to kill rattlesnakes that are found among the rocks—

and he half drew it as if he was going to shoot at you."

"It beats me," Pete said, scratching his head. "Why should he get so upset because I borrowed a worthless old torch like this one?"

He pulled the old, fibre-cased torch from his belt and held it up. Chang stared at it.

"That's not Jensen's torch!" he exclaimed. "I mean it isn't the one he usually carries in the jeep, the one he loaned me last night."

"Well, it was in the toolbox," Pete told him. "It was the only one, so I took it because you said it was okay."

"Looks as if I was wrong," Chang muttered. "Pete, may I please see the torch?"

"Why, sure." Pete passed it over and Chang held it in his hand, weighing it.

"It is very light," he said. "It does not feel as if it has any batteries in it."

"Then it's useless," Pete said in disgust. "Why should Mr. Jensen get so riled up over a worthless torch?"

"Perhaps——" Chang began. At that moment Bob caught up with them. He was breathless, more from excitement than anything else. His old mare had decided she didn't want to run uphill and had slowed to a walk.

"Here you are!" he said in relief. Then he noticed their expressions. "What is it?" he asked. "Something wrong?"

"We are going to see what made Jensen so angry," Chang told him in a quiet voice. He unscrewed the base of the torch. Then he reached in and pulled out a wad of tissue paper. As Pete and Bob watched, he carefully unfolded the tissue paper. Something was coiled up inside. He uncoiled it and held it up in the sunlight. It swayed in his hand.

"The Ghost Pearls!" Pete shouted.

"Mr. Jensen stole them!" Bob yelled.

Chang's lips were set tightly.

"Yes, apparently Jensen stole them, or, more likely, had two of the men who work for him steal them," he said. "He had them hidden in this old torch, in his toolbox, all along. What better place of concealment? A torch is just the right size to hold them, and it doesn't look suspicious, especially if it is in among some old tools. He could just drive right out of the valley with the pearls, and never have to risk taking them from some other hiding place."

"It was a good hiding place, all right," Bob agreed. "He couldn't figure that we'd need a torch."

"No. He couldn't see us, and no one else was around. He had no reason to think anyone would come along while he was in the pressing house," Chang said. "I wonder what he was doing in there with those men? Plotting something, perhaps. Indeed, I begin to wonder many things. One of them is whether Jensen does not know more than he has told us about the accidents, the wine spoilage, and other incidents in recent months."

"Say," Pete interjected, "hadn't we better get back to the house with these pearls, tell Mr. Carlson and your aunt, and get the sheriff after Jensen?"

"It may not be that simple," Chang said slowly.

"Jensen is a dangerous man, and can be very brutal and reckless. He will not let us reveal his guilt without trying to stop us."

"What can he do?" Bob asked anxiously.

"I think we'd better have a look first," Chang told him and slipped off Ebony. "Bob, you stay here and hold the horses. Pete, you and I will go down the trail until we can see back down into the valley."

The two boys gave Bob their reins. Then together they eased down the trail towards the rocky projection that hid the valley.

Crouched low, they peered round the rocks. Now they could see the valley below. Two men stood at the foot of the trail by the slope, as if on guard. Bob and Chang could see the jeep bouncing swiftly towards the tiny village at the end of the valley. Then they saw the two cars that had been parked by the old pressing house swaying and bumping over the cultivated ground. These were manoeuvred up to the trail. One drove several yards up the trail, effectively blocking it to a horse, and the other was parked across the trail behind it as an additional barrier.

Chang drew his breath.

"Jensen is going for horses!" he said. "He's had his men block the trail so we can't ride down and gallop past them. If we do ride back down, we'll have to dismount to get past those cars, and they can grab us."

"You mean he has us trapped?" Pete aked.

"He thinks he has. We can't go back. If we go forward, across the ridge and down the other side, we come out into Hashknife Canyon. It's a very rugged box canyon. That is, at one end there is no way out. At the other end there is a trail, which becomes a rough road that eventually joins up with the main road to San Francisco."

"If we take that trail, Jensen will easily follow us. Also, he will send men in cars to block the other end of the trail. He plans to capture us and take the pearls back."

"He can't get away with it!" Pete exclaimed. "Even if he does get the pearls, we'll tell someone."

"I'm sure he's thought of that." Chang's quiet tone made a shiver go down Pete's spine. "And he will see to it that we can't tell anyone—ever. Remember, all those men are his accomplices. No one else knows what happened."

Pete understood. He swallowed hard.

"Come on!" Chang said abruptly, pulling Pete back. He was grinning now, his black eyes shining with excitement.

"I have an idea!" he exclaimed. "Jensen will need time to get to the village, get horses, and get back here. He thinks he has us bottled up. But we'll fool him. We have to hurry though."

They ran back to their horses, where Bob was waiting impatiently, and remounted.

"Well?" Bob asked. "What's happening?"

"Jensen has cut us off," Pete said. "He wants the pearls back and he doesn't care what he does to get them. Apparently all those men we saw are working with him."

"But I have a plan to make him look foolish!" Chang said jubilantly. "We have to ride over the ridge—this trail leads to a pass—and down into the canyon beyond. I'll lead the way."

He urged Ebony up the trail and the big stallion set a fast pace. Chang made all the speed possible without exhausting the horses. Bob came second, with Pete behind him. Bob's slower mare, obviously disliking all this activity, was kept moving by the nervous mare at her heels.

In half an hour they reached the top of the pass, and could see down into the canyon beyond. It looked rugged and narrow and desolate.

Chang paused only for a moment, then started Ebony on the down trail. The going was easier on this side, and in half an hour they reined their panting horses in on the rocky floor of the canyon.

"The trail out of Hashknife Canyon goes that way." Chang pointed. "It becomes a road that, as I said, joins the main road in a few miles. Jensen will expect us to head that way. So we're heading in just the opposite direction."

He turned Ebony, and the horse started picking its way along through the rocks, between the narrow cliff walls.

"Now we have to look for two yellow rocks, about twenty feet above the floor of the canyon," Chang called to them. "One rock is just above the other."

They rode on for ten minutes, then Pete, who had very keen eyesight, spotted the rocks.

"There they are!" he pointed. Chang nodded. At a point directly below the two yellow rocks he dismounted.

"We get off here," he said. Pete and Bob dismounted. Unexpectedly, Chang slapped all three horses on the rump. Ebony, startled, bolted away down the canyon and the others followed.

"From here we go on foot," Chang explained. "And on our knees and stomachs, too. There's a small pool of water at the closed end of the canyon. The horses will smell it and head for it to drink. When Jensen realises we've given him the slip and comes back to hunt in this canyon, he'll find them, but that'll be hours away."

He looked up. "There used to be a trail here," he said. "Rock slides took most of it away—luckily for us. But we can climb it. We have to get on the top of that first yellow rock."

He started up, finding rocky toe-holds. Bob followed him. Pete was behind Bob and gave him a helping hand when necessary. In a couple of minutes they stood on top of the yellow rock. Bob and Pete were startled to see an opening in the cliff. The second yellow rock overhung it, like a roof, and hid it from sight from below.

"A cave," Chang said. "Many years ago a miner found a rich lode inside, so he started tunnelling, using the cave as the mouth of his mine. This is where we're going. Quickly before Jensen or his men have a chance to spot us."

He ducked into the cave. Bob and Pete followed him into the darkness without the slightest idea of where they were going or what would come next.

10

Captured!

CHANG LED THEM to the rear of the cave, which seemed quite large once they were inside. Then Chang's light showed them the mouth of the tunnel—an old mine gallery, really, dug many years before. Old timbers were still in place, bracing the roof, though some rocks had fallen to the floor.

"I'll tell you my plan," Chang said. "There's a whole network of mine galleries under this ridge. When I first came to this country, the old mines fascinated me. There was an old fellow named Dan Duncan, a little shrivelled old man who'd spent his whole life scratching tiny bits of gold out of the old mines."

"He knew them like you know the streets of your home town. He's sick in hospital now, but before he got sick, he showed me through these old mines. And if you know exactly how to go, there's a way from this cave all the way through to the wine cellars on the other side of the ridge."

"Golly!" Pete exclaimed. "You mean we're going back through the mines while Jensen and his men are looking for us outside?"

"That's it," Chang agreed. "Many of the workers must be in league with Jensen. But this way we'll come out only a mile from the house and be there with our story before anyone can stop us. There are two pretty tricky spots where only a boy or a very small man can squeeze through, but they were passable last time I tried it six months ago."

Bob gulped slightly. They seemed a long way underground, and the darkness was awfully black. He put his hand in his pocket, and his fingers touched his piece of green chalk.

"Shouldn't we mark our trail?" he asked. "Then if we did get lost, we could find our way back."

"We won't get lost," Chang said. "And if Jensen found the marks he could follow us without any trouble."

He seemed very confident of himself, but Bob knew that you can get lost when you least expect it. So did Pete.

"Listen," Pete said. "Our secret mark is a question mark. Suppose we mark our trail with question marks, but put up arrows, too, leading in different directions. Then only we know for sure which marks indicate the real trail. Anyone who came after us would lose a lot of time following the fake marks."

Chang approved of this.

"Anyway," he said, "Jensen doesn't know about this mine or the fact that it connects with the wine cellars. But you're right, we could get lost ourselves. However, we won't mark the entrance. That would be a giveaway. We'll start the marking once we're inside the gallery."

With that they started into the old mine diggings. The way was narrow, and at times the roof was low. Occasionally they came across intersecting or branching galleries, where miners years before had followed a wandering vein of ore in the rock. Bob marked the proper route with question marks. He also drew bold arrows pointing down the wrong galleries. The trail he left would have confused anyone who didn't know the secret.

But presently they came to a spot where the gallery ahead had partly caved in. Rocks and dirt on the floor almost closed the passage. Chang called a halt.

"We have to crawl now," he said. "I'll go first."

He pulled something from his waist and handed it to Pete.

"Here's the old torch with the pearls," he said. "You take care of them, Pete. They'll be in my way if I have to dig."

"Sure, Chang," Pete agreed. He thrust the old torch with its precious contents inside his belt and buckled the belt tight so the torch couldn't slip. "I certainly wish I had a real light, though."

"That's a problem." Chang considered a moment. "We only have two lights. Look, Bob, suppose you let Pete have your light? I'll go first, with my light. You follow me. Pete will follow you. That way we'll all have light, because the light behind you will shine ahead and show you your way, too."

The idea didn't appeal to Bob much. Down there in the pitch blackness the torch was something nice and solid and bright to hang on to.

However, Chang's idea was sensible, so he passed his torch to Pete. As it happened, being rid of the torch helped him crawl better, and this was fortunate because the leg which recently had the brace on it was beginning to feel quite tired.

The caved-in section was only a hundred yards long, but it seemed as if they would never get through it. Ahead of Bob, Chang at times lay flat on his stomach and pulled himself along. Then Bob followed. Behind him, Pete, his light shining up to assist Bob, repeated the process. Like inch-worms they moved ahead. Several times Chang paused to dig a wider opening or to push small rocks to one side.

Once Bob brushed against the roof and a small rock fell on his back and wedged him there so that he could not move in either direction. He had to fight a feeling of panic while Pete crawled up behind him and, lying on his legs, reached up and wiggled the rock loose.

"Thanks, Pete," Bob gasped. Then he wriggled on. Behind him, Pete, who was bigger, stopped to scoop out a little dirt so he could get through without having the same thing happen to him.

Bob was panting for breath when they finally crawled out into a place where they could sprawl out full length with their backs against the rock wall.

Overhead, the lights showed the old timbers, used to brace the roof, bulging downward under the weight above them. But they had held all these years so there was no use thinking that they would suddenly break now.

For a while they just lay there, getting their breath back. Then Chang spoke.

"That's the worst," he said. "There's one more bad spot, but not as bad as that. One thing is sure"—he chuckled—"Jensen can never follow us through here. He's too big."

As they rested, Chang told them something of the history of the network of mine tunnels they were finding their way through. The mines had first been worked around 1849, when gold was discovered in California. After the first rich gold was gone, many miners moved on, but some stayed, working hard, digging into the mountain for the gold that wandered in thin veins through the rock. Little by little the mines had been extended.

The valley, however, had depended on its grapevines and the wine it made, and after the death of old Mathias Green, Miss Lydia Green's mother had been able to buy it and start building up the vineyard and winery. But then, in 1919, had come Prohibition, when it was illegal to sell wine or any kind of alcoholic beverage.

The vineyard had almost collapsed then. But the workers, with nothing else to do, had turned gold miners, and tunnelled deeper and deeper searching for the elusive metal. The next hardship had been the Depression, beginning late in 1929, when no one had any money, and the gold mines had been used frantically by every able-bodied man in the region as one source of cash.

When things began to get better, around 1940, the gold mining was abandoned. By then Prohibition had been repealed and the vineyard was flourishing again. But all that digging for so many years had left quite a network of abandoned mines and tunnels under the mountain ridge.

"Is there any gold now?" Bob asked eagerly.

"A little, but it would take a pickaxe and probably

dynamite to get it," Chang told them. "Well, let's get going. It must be pretty late by now. Aunt Lydia will be worrying."

Bob kept marking their trail with question marks, mixed with fake arrows, as they went. Only once did Chang seem puzzled, at a point where three galleries stretched away from the same point. He finally picked the right-hand one, but it ended in a cave-in after about three hundred yards.

"Wrong way," he said and pointed his light at the tunnel floor. "Look."

They looked. White bones gleamed in the light. For a startled moment Bob and Pete thought it was a human skeleton. Then they saw the bones belonged to some animal who had been caught by the roof cave-in.

"A donkey. Some miner was using it to move ore out," Chang said. "Lucky he wasn't caught himself. Or maybe he was. Nobody has ever dug in there to see."

Bob glanced down at the white skull of the donkey and shivered a little. He was glad to hurry after Chang as the other boy led them away.

After selecting the right passage, Chang seemed to have no trouble. He led them rapidly past many branching passages, until he stopped so abruptly Bob bumped into him.

"We've come to The Throat," he explained.

"The Throat?" Pete asked. "What's that?"

"It's a natural rock fault that goes through to the mines on the other side of the ridge," Chang said. "But it's pretty rough and narrow."

101

He shone his light into a passageway that seemed to be a mere slit in the rock. Just high enough for a boy to stand erect, it was too narrow for him to enter, unless he slipped in sideways.

"That's it," Chang said, reading their thoughts. "We have to ease through sideways."

"Are you—are you sure it goes through?" Bob asked. The longer he stayed down here underground, the less he liked it. And the idea of easing through that narrow slit did not appeal to him in the least.

"Sure," Chang said. "I've been through it. Besides, feel the air current? There's air coming from that side."

It was true. They could feel the air on their cheeks.

"We've got to get through," Chang said. "It's the only connection between the two sides of the mountain, and only a boy or a small man can make it. I just hope I haven't grown too much in the last six months! Well, I'll go first. You two wait until I'm all the way through. Then I'll flash my light three times, and you, Bob, follow. Pete and I will shine our lights in from each end to help you see. When Bob is through, I'll flash my light three times more and you come, Pete."

They agreed. Chang slipped into The Throat, holding his light in his right hand. Carefully he began to sidestep his way along, making no sudden movement that might get him jammed in the narrow, uneven space.

Pete and Bob, watching, saw his light move jerkily along, his body hiding it most of the time. Chang had said that once through The Throat, they would be almost at the section where the wine casks were stored for ageing, and would be back at the house in an hour.

Chang actually made pretty good speed, but to the two boys waiting it seemed forever before they saw three spaced flashes of light announcing he had got through.

"Okay, Bob," Pete said, "It'll be easy for you, you're smaller than either of us."

"Sure," Bob said, his throat somewhat dry, "It'll be a cinch. Just give me some light."

He slid sideways into The Throat. Pete shone his light after him, holding it close to the floor, and from the other end came a faint gleam which was Chang's torch.

Pete watched his friend move away slowly. Presently Bob's body, filling most of The Throat, cut off the light from the other end. Pete kept his light on a little longer, then, figuring Bob must be much closer to Chang now, shut it off.

He waited tensely for the three flashes of light that would be the signal for him to start. For some reason they were delayed.

Then he heard a faint yell, followed by words. "Pete! Don't——"

It was Chang's voice, muffled by the narrow Throat. And it sounded as if it had been cut off abruptly, maybe by a hand over his mouth.

Pete could guess, though, what Chang had been trying to say. *Don't come!*

He waited for some other sound or signal. Presently

he saw the light flash three times. Then, after a pause, three times more.

But the flashes were jerky and were shorter than Chang had made them.

Pete knew they were a trap. Someone else—not Chang or Bob—was signalling him to come through The Throat.

That, and the yell, gave him a pretty good idea of what had happened. Chang and Bob had been captured!

11

A Fortune in a Skull

BACK AT ROCKY BEACH, at just about this same moment, Jupiter Jones was talking on the telephone with Miss Lydia Green. "Bob and Pete and Chang have *disappeared*?"

"They're just *gone*!" The woman's voice sounded terribly distressed. "They started out on horseback to explore the valley, and said they'd be gone all day. We were so terribly busy here, with the sheriff and reporters and everything, that we didn't miss them until supper.

"Then we discovered they weren't anywhere in the valley. We haven't even found their horses yet."

For once Jupiter's mental machinery didn't seem to work. All he could do was say helplessly, "But where could they be?"

"We think they're in the mines," Miss Green told him. "There's a network of old mines under the mountain here, and we use part of it for a wine cellar in which to age our wines. We believe Chang may have taken them in there to explore, and we have men starting now to search the mines and look for them."

Jupiter pinched his lip. His mental gears were starting to revolve. The Ghost Pearls had disappeared. Now his partners and Chang had disappeared. There might not be a connection but he suspected there was.

He thought as fast as he could. This was an emergency and emergency measures were called for.

"You have all of the men available looking for them?" he asked.

"Of course," Miss Green told him. "All the field workers—those who haven't deserted us—and the winery workers, and even the household staff. We're exploring the mines where the wine casks are. We've also sent men out into the desert beyond Verdant Valley to see if the boys could have ridden out there."

"Tell them to look for question marks," Jupiter said. Knowing his two partners, he knew, that wherever they were, they'd try to leave the mark of The Three Investigators somehow.

"Question marks?" Miss Green sounded puzzled.

"Interrogation marks," Jupiter said. "Probably drawn in chalk. If anyone finds a question mark, or several question marks, have him report it immediately."

"But I don't understand!" Miss Green said helplessly.

"I can't explain over the telephone. I'm coming up there right away. I'll bring someone with me—Bob Andrews's father. I know he'll come. Can you have a car meet us at the airport?"

"Yes—yes." The woman's voice fluttered. "Of course. Oh, I do hope they haven't been hurt."

Jupiter thanked her and hung up. Then he called Bob's father, who, after his first astonishment, arranged to meet him at the airport, and hung up again. Jupiter hurried out to tell Konrad to take care of the salvage yard next day the best he could, and right now to drive him to the airport in the salvage yard's smaller truck.

Jupiter was on the job, but what he could do remained very uncertain. He doubted that Bob and Pete and Chang were merely lost in the mines and would be found so easily.

Nor was he wrong. A short time later, Bob and Chang were whisked through the ring of men searching the mines on the Verdant Valley side of the ridge, and driven away totally unseen and unsuspected. They were unseen because they were inside large wine casks, and wine casks were such common objects around the vineyard that no one gave them a second thought, even when they were loaded on a truck and driven away.

So, even as they were being hunted, Bob and Chang were on their way in the hands of their captor, Mr. Jensen, to an unknown destination. And Pete, bearer of the fabulously valuable Ghost Pearls, was wandering through the complex network of mine galleries, on the other side of The Throat, where no one was searching because no one—except Jensen and his henchmen—knew either that the boys had ridden over the ridge into Hashknife Canyon, or that there was a way from the mines on that side into the area where the wine casks were stored.

Pete, as soon as he realised that Bob and Chang must have been caught by someone waiting for them at the other end of The Throat, backed away in the darkness and watched intently. He was looking for a sign that someone was coming through The Throat after him.

But no light appeared. Pete guessed that whoever had caught his friends were men, too big to risk getting stuck in The Throat. That meant they wouldn't be coming after him, at least not unless they could round up someone small enough to slip through the narrow crevice in the rock.

As he couldn't stay in there and wait, his only hope was to retrace his path, back into Hashknife Canyon, and then hide among the rocks there until next morning. There were sure to be men hunting for them by then, and he could help Bob and Chang best by staying free until he could tell all he knew.

He made sure the old torch holding the Ghost Pearls was still fast under his belt. Then, saying a silent prayer that his good torch would hold out, he started back the way they had come.

Now Bob's insistence on marking their trail paid off. A little hunting picked out one question mark after the other, chalked in green on the rocks. He ignored the arrows Bob had put up to mislead any possible pursuers.

Even so, he went astray once. When Chang had led them up the gallery which ended in a cave-in, Bob had marked it as if it were the right route, and Pete followed the marks. He was brought up short by the closed passage, blocked by tons of rock, and the white bones of the little donkey that had perished when the cave-in happened.

As Pete turned to retrace his steps, a thought stopped him. Had he better keep the pearls? He might get caught. Then if he didn't have the pearls, at least Jensen wouldn't get them.

He thought fast. To hide the pearls under a rock could be risky. All rocks looked alike down here, and if he marked the rock, maybe with his own blue chalk, the mark might be found. If there was only something distinctive that no one would pay any attention to——

His light shone on the white skull of the donkey. That was it! Something that seemed so natural that no one would pay any attention to it, yet something he could always find again.

It took him only a moment to slide the Ghost Pearls in their tissue paper wrapping out of the old torch. He stuffed them inside the hollow skull and put it back in place just as it had been. Now he could easily find the gems once more.

He started back to get on the right track again. As he paused where the three galleries intersected, another thought occurred to him. There was no use lugging the empty, fibre-cased torch with him. Just why the thought came to him, he didn't know, but he decided to put some pebbles in it and hide it. He had some

Quickly he slid the package into the skull.

remote idea that it might come in handy as a decoy if he were captured.

He put a few pebbles in his handkerchief, stuffed it into the fibre-case, then dropped the torch behind a rock. A few feet away he carelessly arranged some smaller rocks so that when viewed closely they made an arrow indicating the large rock. That would help him identify the rock if the necessity ever arose.

With that done, Pete made more rapid progress backwards until he came to the very low stretch where he and the others had had to crawl on their stomachs to get through.

By now he had been underground a great many hours, and he was starting to feel both hungry, and sick of the darkness. But he couldn't hurry. Hurrying would get him wedged in, maybe forever. Slow and easy in a tight spot was the only way.

He shifted the torch in his belt round to the side, where it would be out of the way, got down on his knees, then his stomach, and started to inch his way along.

Once a small rock fell directly in front of him, almost hitting him. He had a terrible moment when he feared the whole section of roof was going to collapse. Under him, as he lay full length, he felt the tiniest quivering of the earth. He lay breathless, expecting everything to fall, but nothing else did. The tiny trembling ended. He reached forward and rolled the rock to one side.

Breathing hard with relief, Pete took several minutes to pull himself together. He had a pretty good idea what had happened. Somewhere there had been a very small earthquake, of which this ridge had felt only a distant quiver.

As Pete, and everyone else living in California knew, the famous San Andreas fault—a vast crack in the earth's rocky crust—runs down beneath western California. The San Andreas fault caused the famous San Francisco earthquake of 1906. It caused the great earthquake in Alaska in 1964, when the land in some places was lifted or sunk more than thirty feet. Every year it caused hundreds of tiny tremors, some so slight only instruments would record them.

What Pete had felt was only the slightest quiver of earth slipping somewhere along the great length of the famous fault. Fortunately, a few minutes' uneasiness was all it caused him.

Elsewhere it had bigger consequences, but he could have no knowledge of that.

Breathing hard, Pete negotiated the rest of the distance until he could stand erect. Then he made all the time he could, following Bob's trail back to the cave from which they had entered the mines.

The cave was empty. All was silent. Outside the cave mouth the blackness of night was like a curtain.

Pete eased slowly through the cave, stopping after each step to listen. He heard nothing. He wasn't using his torch, so he could see the cave mouth only as a slightly lighter spot in the darkness.

Step by step he approached the cave mouth. Again he stopped to listen, and heard nothing. He moved outside, inch by inch, reassured that the cave entrance hadn't been found.

When he was fully outside, he stopped for a moment

to try to adjust his vision to the faint starlight of the night.

That was when someone leaped from behind the rocks outside the entrance.

Strong arms grabbed him and a big hand went across his mouth.

12

Meeting with Mr. Won

BOB AND CHANG were in a room. It was a room with solid plaster walls, no window, and only one door. The door was locked—they had tried it.

The two boys' clothes were very much the worse for wear from crawling around underground. However, most of the dirt had been brushed off, and they had washed.

They had also eaten. In fact, they were just finishing a large tray full of Chinese food that was strange to Bob, but delicious.

Until now they had been too hungry to talk much. Now, comfortably full, they relaxed.

"I wonder where we are?" Bob said. With his stomach full, it was hard to feel quite as worried as he had been for the past few hours.

"We are in an underground room in a large city. Probably San Francisco," Chang told him.

"How do you figure that?" Bob asked. "We had blindfolds on. We could be anywhere."

"I have felt the floor quiver as big trucks went by outside. Big trucks mean a big city. Chinese servants put us in here and brought us food. San Francisco has the biggest Chinatown in the United States. We are in a secret room in the home of some very wealthy Chinese person."

Bob shook his head. "How do you figure *that*?"

"The food. It was cooked in genuine Chinese style, and cooked superbly. Only a very fine cook could have cooked it. Only a rich man could afford such a chef."

"You and Jupiter Jones would get along great," Bob told him. "I wish you lived down in Rocky Beach so you could join The Three Investigators."

"I would like that," Chang said wistfully. "Verdant Valley is quite lonely. In Hong Kong, there were always many other people around, many boys to talk to and play with. Now—— But I shall be a man soon and I shall take charge of the vineyard and the winery as my honoured aunt wishes me to." Then he added, after a moment, "If I am permitted to do so."

Bob knew what he meant. If they ever got out of this mess. Jupe had certainly been right about one thing—there was obviously a lot more to the mystery than just the appearance of a ghost at a deserted house.

The boys' thoughts were interrupted by the sound of the door opening. An elderly Chinese man, wearing the garments of old China, stood there.

"Come!" he said.

"Come where?" Chang asked boldly.

113

"Does a mouse ask where he goes when an eagle's claws seize him?" the man asked. "Come!"

Squaring his shoulders, Chang marched out of the door. Bob, standing as straight as he could, followed.

They followed the old Chinese down a corridor and into a tiny elevator. The elevator took them far up and stopped before a red door. The old man slid back the elevator door, opened the red door, and pushed Bob.

"Go in!" he said. "Speak truth or the eagle will eat you."

They were alone in a large, circular room, hung with a multitude of red drapes on which beautiful scenes had been embroidered in gold thread. Bob could see dragons, Chinese temples, even willow trees that seemed to sway in the wind.

"You admire my draperies?" a voice that was thin and old but very clear spoke. "They are five hundred years of age."

They looked across the room and saw that they were not alone after all. An old man sat in a great carved arm-chair of black wood, thickly padded with soft cushions.

He wore flowing robes, like those worn by the ancient Chinese emperors. Bob had seen pictures of them in books. His face was small, thin, yellow like a badly withered pear, and he peered at them through plain gold-rimmed spectacles.

"Advance," he said quietly. "Sit down, small ones who have caused me so much trouble."

Bob and Chang crossed the room on rugs so thick they seemed to sink into them. Two small stools were arranged as if waiting for them. They sat down, staring in wonder at the old man.

"You may call me Mr. Won," the ancient Chinese said to them. "I am one hundred and seven years old."

Bob could believe that. He was certainly the oldest looking man Bob had ever seen. Yet he did not seem feeble.

Mr. Won looked at Chang. "Small cricket, the blood of my nation flows in your veins also. I speak of the old China, not of the China of to-day. Your family has had much to do with the old China. Your great-grandfather stole one of our princesses for a bride. Of that I do not speak. Women follow their hearts. But your great-grandfather stole something else. Or bribed an official to steal it for him, which is the same thing. A string of pearls!"

Mr. Won showed the first sign of excitement.

"A string of priceless pearls," he said. "For more than fifty years their whereabouts were unknown. Now they have reappeared. And I must have them."

He leaned forward slightly. His voice became stronger.

"Do you hear that, small mice? *I must have the pearls!*"

By now Bob was feeling extremely nervous, for he knew perfectly well they didn't have the pearls to give Mr. Won. He wondered how Chang felt. Sitting beside him, Chang spoke boldly.

"Oh venerable one," he said, "we do not have the pearls. They are in the possession of another. One who is fleet of foot and stout of heart has them, and he has escaped with them to return them to my aunt. Return us to my aunt and I will persuade her to sell them to you. That is, if the letter she received from someone who claims to be a relative of the bride of my great-grandfather does not turn out to be true."

"It is not true!" Mr. Won said sharply. "It was sent by another, whom I know, to confuse things, for he, too, wishes to buy the pearls. I am rich, but he is richer. He will buy them unless I get them first. Therefore—*I must have them.*"

Chang bowed his head.

"We are small mice," he said, "and we are helpless. Those who captured us did not capture our friend. He has the pearls. He has courage, he will escape."

"They bungled!" Mr. Won's fingers drummed on the arm of his teakwood chair. "They will pay for letting him escape!"

"They almost caught him," Chang replied. "Somehow they guessed my plan. They were waiting in silence as first I, then my friend, slipped through a narrow passage no man could travel. Then I heard a pebble roll. I swung my light, saw someone, and shouted to my friend just as Jensen and his men seized us. So my friend escaped. The passage was too narrow for Jensen or his henchmen to get through."

"They bungled!" Mr. Won said. "When Jensen telephoned me last night to say he had the pearls and would bring them to me to-night, I warned him there must be no slip-up. Now——"

He paused. A silvery bell sounded somewhere. Mr. Won reached beneath the cushions of his chair and to Bob's surprise he brought out a telephone. He placed it to his ear and listened. After a moment he put it away again.

"There has been a new development," he said. "Let us wait."

They waited in silence. The silence seemed to grow bigger and bigger to Bob, though he knew it was just his nerves. What was going to happen next? The day had been full of so many surprises that almost nothing could seem surprising now.

Yet what did happen, somehow, was the one thing he hadn't expected.

The red door opened.

Dirty and mussed up and looking very pale and stubborn, Pete Crenshaw walked into the room.

13

"I Must Have the Pearls!"

"PETE!" Bob and Chang jumped to their feet. "Are you all right?"

"I'm hungry mostly," Pete said. "Outside of that I'm okay, though my arm hurts where Jensen's men twisted it trying to make me tell him where I hid the Ghost Pearls."

"Then you did hide them?" Bob asked excitedly.

"You did not tell where. I am sure of that," Chang added.

"You bet I didn't," Pete said grimly. "They were wild. If they knew——"

"Careful!" Chang said. "One listens."

Pete was suddenly silent. For the first time he saw Mr. Won.

"You are not a small mouse," Mr. Won said, looking at Chang. "You are a small dragon, cast in the same image as your great-grandfather." He paused, thinking. "Would you like to be my son?" he asked, nearly bowling the boys over with surprise.

"I am rich, but I am heavy of heart for I have no male offspring. I will adopt you. You will be my son. With my wealth you will become a very powerful man."

"I am honoured, venerable one," Chang said politely. "But in my heart I fear two things."

"Name them," Mr. Won requested.

"The first is that you wish me to betray my friends and obtain the Ghost Pearls for you," said Chang.

Mr. Won nodded. "Of course," he said. "As my son-to-be, that would be your duty."

"The second fear," Chang said, "is that, though you mean the words now, you would forget them when you had the pearls. However, that is of no importance, for I do not betray my friends."

Mr. Won sighed. "If you had accepted," he said, "I would indeed have forgotten. Now I know that I would truly adopt you as my son if you were willing. But you are not willing. Yet, I must have the pearls. They mean life to me. And they mean life to you."

Mr. Won reached beneath the cushions. He brought out from some secret recess a tiny bottle, a thin crystal glass and a round object which he held on his palm.

"Approach and observe," he said.

Chang, Bob and Pete edged up close to him and stared at the thing that rested on the shrunken, shrivelled, claw-like hand.

It had a curious, dead grey colour and might have been a badly made marble.

It was Chang who recognised it.

"It is a Ghost Pearl," he said.

"A foolish name for it," Mr. Won stated. He dropped the priceless pearl into the small bottle. In the liquid inside it fizzed and bubbled until it was all gone—dissolved.

"The true name for these pearls," Mr. Won said, as he poured the liquid from the bottle into the crystal glass, "is pearls of life."

He drank the liquid, draining the last tiny drop from the glass. Then he replaced glass and bottle in the secret place from which they had come.

"Small dragon of the blood of Mathias Green," he said, "and your friends. I shall tell you something only a few men know, and those who know it are either very wise, or very rich, or both. The world calls them Ghost Pearls. The world knows they are priceless. Yet why are they priceless? Not because they are beautiful—as pearls, they are ugly. They look, if I may say so, dead. Is that not true?"

Not having any idea what Mr. Won was leading up to, the boys nodded. The man continued.

"For centuries a few, a very few, have been found at one spot in the Indian Ocean. Now, for some reason, no more can be found. Barely half a dozen strings of Ghost Pearls—I use your name for them—

exist in the world. They are treasured under guard by the richest men of the Orient. Why?"

"Because"—he paused dramatically—"when swallowed as I have just swallowed the one you saw, the last one I own, they confer the priceless gift of prolonging life."

The boys listened with popping eyes. They could see that Mr. Won believed everything he said. Mr. Won drew a deep breath.

"This was discovered hundreds of years ago in China," he said. "The secret was kept by kings and nobles, later by wealthy businessmen such as myself. I am one hundred and seven years old because in my lifetime I have swallowed more than one hundred of the pearls of life, which the ignorant call Ghost Pearls."

He fixed his small, dark eyes on Chang.

"You see, small dragon, why I must have the necklace at any cost. Each pearl prolongs life for about three months. There are forty-eight pearls in the necklace. To me they mean twelve more years of life. Twelve more years!"

His voice rose. "I must have the pearls. Nothing can stop me. You small ones are but dust in my path if you interfere! Twelve years of life—and I, one hundred and seven! Surely, small dragon, you see how important this is to me."

Chang bit his lips.

"He means it," he whispered to Pete and Bob. "He won't stop at anything. I'll try to bargain with him."

"Bargain with me, by all means," said Mr. Won, who obviously had keen hearing. "That is the way of the Orient. An honourable bargain will be kept with honour on both sides."

"Will you pay my aunt for the pearls if Pete tells you where they are?" Chang asked.

Mr. Won shook his head.

"I have already said I will pay the man Jensen. I keep my word. But"—he paused, studying Chang—"there is a matter of difficulty with the mortgage payments on your honoured aunt's vineyard and winery.

"It is I who own those mortgages. I give my word there will be no trouble. Your aunt shall have time to pay them. Also, the ghost who has terrorised the workers will vanish, and the workers will return."

All three boys blinked.

"Then you know whose ghost it is?" Chang cried. "How can you know that?"

Mr. Won smiled slightly.

"I have a large store of small wisdom," he said. "Lead Jensen to the pearls and your aunt's troubles will be over."

"That sounds good," Chang declared. "But how do we know we can trust you?"

Unconsciously, Pete and Bob nodded. That was the thought in their minds, too.

"I am Mr. Won," the old man said sharply. "My word is stronger than bands of steel."

"Ask him how we can trust Mr. Jensen!" Bob blurted out.

"Jensen would promise anything and do the opposite!" Pete chimed in.

Mr. Won raised his voice.

"Have the man Jensen sent to me," he said.

121

They all waited. For a long two minutes, nothing happened. Then the red door from the elevator opened and Jensen strode in. He came insolently towards Mr. Won and the boys, his dark features set in a scowl.

"Did you make them talk?" he growled.

"You do not speak to an equal!" Mr. Won said sharply. "You are a crawling thing of the night, fit only to be stepped on. Act like one!"

All three boys saw rage show on Jensen's face, then fear—deadly fear.

"Sorry, Mr. Won," he said in a choked voice. "I just wondered——"

"Be silent and listen. If these boys place the necklace in your hands to-night, you will see they are unharmed. You may tie them up, if necessary, so they will need an hour or so to get loose, but not too tightly. If they give you the necklace, any harm you do to them you shall receive multiplied one hundred times. If you do not heed my warning you shall enjoy the Death of a Thousand Cuts."

Jensen swallowed several times before he could speak.

"Look," he said, humbly now, "all of Verdant Valley will be crawling with people looking for them. So far I've managed to divert suspicion from Hashknife Canyon, where they left their horses. My men have reported it to be empty. But if I take them back there——"

"Perhaps you will not have to take them back there. Perhaps they can tell you where to find the necklace. I hope so. It will make things simpler."

Mr. Won rose. Standing up in his flowing robes, he was a very small man, hardly more than five feet tall.

"Come," he said. "They wish to talk this over among themselves. As it is a matter of life or death, they have the right to make a free decision."

They went from the room, Mr. Won taking slow, deliberate steps, and vanished behind a crimson hanging.

14

A Fateful Decision

"DON'T SAY ANYTHING you don't want heard," Chang whispered to the others as the two men vanished. "There may be a dozen ears listening. Let's talk a lot, kill time. Time is on our side."

"I'm glad something's on our side," Pete said gloomily. "Right now somebody else seems to have all the marbles. What I want to know is how you two got caught."

"I flashed my light around," Chang said, "and I got a glimpse of a man's face. I shouted to you, Pete. Then about five of them jumped us. They had us tied up and gagged in no time."

"Then they tried to fool you into coming after us," Bob put in. "Lucky you were smart enough not to fall for it. Jensen was really mad when you didn't come. He wanted someone to go through The Throat after you, but they were all big men and afraid to try."

"What I can't figure is how they came to be there," Pete said.

"Jensen said he got to the top of the rise just in time to see us turn the wrong way down Hashknife Canyon," Chang answered. "He boasted he was smarter than any kids, and guessed right away we'd try to make it home through the mines and ageing caves. Somehow he knew all about the connection between the two valleys through The Throat. He went straight to the other end of it to wait for us. And he left several men in the cave in Hashknife Canyon to grab us if we came back that way."

Chang shook his head disgustedly. "I thought I was so smart!" he said. "And I just played right into his hands."

"It was only bad luck Jensen saw us before we were able to hide," Pete told him. "Anyway, now you know a lot of your workers were really working for Jensen, and that he's a crook. That certainly explains all the accidents and damage you told us about."

"Yes," Chang agreed. "Jensen and his men must have caused them. But I can't figure out why. It all started more than a year ago, when no one knew a thing about the Ghost Pearls."

"Well, anyway, after we were tied up," Bob said, "one of Jensen's men came rushing in to say we'd been missed and Chang's aunt had ordered the valley, the mines, everywhere to be searched for us. Jensen was fit to be tied himself. But then he had an idea.

"We had come to a section where some old wine

vats were stored, big ones. He put Chang and me into two wine vats and hammered them shut. Then they just put those vats on a cart, pulled them outside, and loaded them on a truck. I guess nobody thought it strange to see two wine vats loaded on a truck."

"It was a clever idea," Chang admitted. "Inside the vats we were helpless. I could even hear someone ask Jensen if he had seen us, and he said no, but that he was going to look in the pass that leads north from the valley to San Francisco. He said we'd been seen riding in that direction. He said he wouldn't come back until he'd found us. That gave him a very smart reason for being absent from the hunt, you see."

Pete nodded. Jensen might be a crook, but he certainly wasn't any fool.

"The truck took us several miles, I guess"—Bob took up the story again—"then stopped. The wine casks were unloaded and they let us out. We were in an awfully deserted spot."

"It was several miles up the pass leading to San Francisco," Chang interjected. "There was a station wagon waiting. Jensen put us into the back, covering us with a blanket, and told the other men to hurry back and join the search, but to do everything to keep anybody from looking into Hashknife Canyon where we left the horses. And he told them that if they caught you, Pete, they were to bring you and the pearls to a certain address in San Francisco."

"Well, they caught me, but they didn't get the pearls," Pete said with satisfaction.

"Jensen made that station wagon fly," Chang went on. "I guess we beat all records between Verdant

Valley and San Francisco. When we got here, we drove into some kind of underground garage. Then some Chinese servants untied us, let us wash up, gave us a big meal, and that's the whole story until we were taken to talk to Mr. Won."

"I wish someone would give me a big meal," Pete groaned. "And let me wash up. Look at my hands! Well, my part of the story is that I heard you yell, and knew those flashes Jensen made were fakes. The only thing I could think of was to get out the way we came. I headed back. Luckily Bob had marked the trail. That helped."

Bob held up his hand. Then, in the air with his finger, in such a way that their three bodies hid it, he made a "?", the mark of The Three Investigators.

"I also marked the cask I was in," he said, almost soundlessly. "I was able to get at my chalk. But who'll look inside one wine cask among thousands, and if they do, what will our mark tell them?"

"Even Jupe couldn't tell anything from that," Pete whispered back. "But we'd better talk normally or they'll think we are plotting something."

Chang pretended Pete had been about to tell them something important, putting on a little act for the benefit of any unseen watchers.

"No, Pete!" he said loudly. "Don't tell us about the pearls. Just tell us how you got caught."

Pete told them his story. He knew Chang didn't want him to say anything about where the pearls really were—inside the skull of the donkey—so he said he'd hidden the torch behind a rock and crawled out, only to be grabbed.

126

The men who grabbed him had twisted his arm, but when he told them the torch was back in the mine in a section they couldn't get to, they had blindfolded him, led him out of Hashknife Canyon to a waiting car, and driven him here to the same hiding place to which Jensen had brought the others. From their conversation he gathered that the search for all three was centering in the desert beyond Verdant Valley. Apparently the lies told by Jensen's men had kept anyone from finding the three horses in Hashknife Canyon.

Chang looked serious as he spoke.

"My aunt and Uncle Harold are probably frantic, looking for us," he said. "We can't hope to escape from Mr. Won. Whoever he is, he is a man of tremendous wealth and power and can do just about anything he wants. There's only one thing we can do. That's to give him the pearls."

"You mean just hand them over?" Pete asked, thinking of all he had been through and the pains he had taken to hide the necklace.

"I trust Mr. Won," Chang said. "He has said we will be unharmed. He has said Aunt Lydia's difficulties will cease. I believe him."

"Do you suppose he really believes those pearls prolong his life?" Pete asked. "I mean, it sounds crazy."

"I'm sure he believes it," Chang answered. "It may even be so. It does not seem likely, but remember, the lore of China is centuries old. Only recently has western science found that the skin of a certain toad contains a valuable drug, yet this was known in China hundreds of years ago."

"And rich Chinese have always believed in the medicinal value of tiger whiskers and the ground-up bones of giants."

"I've read about that," Bob put in. "The giants' bones were really the bones of mammoths, from Siberia or somewhere."

"So who can say if the grey pearls really prolong life?" Chang asked. "Mr. Won believes it, and sometimes belief alone is medicine strong enough to cure the ill or save the dying."

"I wonder just what he knows about the green ghost," Bob said aloud. "Funny, the way the ghost and the pearls both showed up at the same time and in the same place."

But Chang was not listening. He raised his voice.

"Mr. Won!" he said. "We have decided."

The draperies parted. Mr. Won came towards them. He was followed by Jensen, and three slippered servants.

"And your decision, small dragon?" Mr. Won asked. He had probably overheard everything they said, except the whispers, but Chang did not mention this.

"We will give Jensen the pearls to give to you," he said. "The pearls are back in the mine."

"Jensen can go to fetch them," Mr. Won purred. "You will remain my guests until then. Later you will be released. You do not know my name, or my whereabouts, and you are free to say anything you wish. If you are believed, none can find me. Even to the

Chinatown of this modern day which exists around me, I am a mystery."

"It isn't that easy," Pete blurted out. "Jensen is too big to crawl through the spot where the roof has partly collapsed. Only a very thin man or a boy can get through!"

"I'll find a man——" Jensen began. Mr. Won clapped his hands in anger.

"No!" he said. "You must fetch them. We can trust no one. Let me question the boy. Look at me, boy!"

Pete found Mr. Won's small black eyes fixed on his. He couldn't have looked away even if he had wanted to.

"This is true?" Mr. Won asked. "Jensen cannot get through to the spot where you hid the pearls?"

"Yes, sir." Somehow Pete knew he couldn't lie. With Mr. Won looking at him that way his mind couldn't think of anything but the truth.

"The pearls were in an old torch?"

"Yes, sir."

"And you hid the torch. Where?"

"Under a rock."

"Where is this hiding place of the torch?"

"I can't describe it exactly," Pete said. "I can find it again, but I can't draw a map or anything."

"Ah." Mr. Won seemed to think. Then he spoke to Jensen. "The way is clear. You cannot send a man. Only the boy can find the torch. You must take him, he must regain the torch and the pearls, and give them to you. You will take all the boys."

"But the danger!" Jensen's swarthy face was sweat-

"Look at me, boy!" he croaked threateningly.

ing. "If they are searching in that canyon by now——"

"You must risk the danger. You must get the pearls. Then the boys go unharmed."

"But they'll talk! They'll have me arrested."

"I shall protect you. I shall pay you well and get you safely out of the country. They do not know the faces of your assistants. So they can tell nothing damaging. As for me—no one can find me. Do you understand?"

Jensen was breathing hard. "Yes, Mr. Won," he said at last. "I'll do it your way. But suppose they double-cross me? Suppose they don't give me the pearls?"

A long silence held the room. Then Mr. Won smiled.

"In that case," he said, "I am not interested. Dispose of them as you wish and make your way to safety as best you can. But I think they will try no tricks. They, too, love life, even as I do."

Bob felt himself shivering. He certainly hoped Pete could find those pearls again.

As for Pete, he was thinking that actually Mr. Won had just asked him about the torch, and he had told the truth. It hadn't occurred to Mr. Won that the pearls weren't in the torch any more. What good this would do, Pete couldn't see, but at least it meant he and Bob and Chang were being sent back to Verdant Valley, or anyway to Hashknife Canyon.

"Now haste," Mr. Won said. "It grows late."

"I'll tie them up and——" Jensen began.

"No!" Mr. Won said. "They will sleep until they reach the spot. Simpler, easier, and for them, more comfortable.

131

"Small dragon, look at me!"

Unwillingly, Chang looked into his eyes. Mr. Won stared at him fixedly.

"Small one, you are weary—very weary. You are longing for sleep. Sleep grips you in its soft arms. Your eyes close."

Bob and Pete, watching, saw Chang's eyes flutter shut for a moment. Then with an effort he opened them again.

"Your eyes close!" Mr. Won said again, softly, insistently. "You cannot resist me. My will is your will. Your eyes are heavy. They droop . . . they close . . . close tightly."

And indeed, now Chang's eyes did shut as if he could not control his eyelids. Mr. Won's voice continued its soft, insistent tone.

"Now you are sleepy," he said. "You are so very sleepy. Sleep descends on you like a wave of darkness. You are sinking into sleep. Sleep overwhelms you. In a moment you will sleep, and stay asleep until you are told to awake. Sleep, small dragon . . . sleep . . . sleep . . . sleep . . . sleep. . . ."

His voice continued repeating the word until suddenly Chang went limp and toppled over, fast asleep indeed. One of the waiting servants deftly caught him as he fell, and carried him out. Chang did not waken.

"And now you, hider of my precious pearls. Look at me!"

It was Pete's turn now. He tried to avoid looking at Mr. Won, but Mr. Won's eyes drew his gaze as if they were magnets. Despite himself, Pete could not look away. Desperately he tried to fight the sleepiness that overwhelmed him as Mr. Won's whispered words went on and on, but in vain. Weariness such as he had never known before overcame him. After a few moments his eyes closed tightly and he, too, toppled into the arms of a waiting servant.

Bob realised Mr. Won was using hypnotism, which is often used to put people to sleep—in fact, he had read of it being used to make patients having an operation feel no pain. So he was not frightened when Won turned his gaze upon him.

"Smallest of all, yet stout of heart," Mr. Won said, "you, too, are weary. You would sleep like your friends. Sleep. . . ."

Bob closed his eyes. He toppled forward but was caught before he struck the floor. The third servant carried him out.

Mr. Won detained Jensen for one last word.

"It is well," he said. "They will all sleep soundly until you reach your destination. Then simply tell them to awaken, and they will awake. After that, the pearls—and the boys go free. Otherwise——"

He paused, then finished.

"Otherwise, you may slit their throats."

15

Jupiter finds a Clue

"BUT HASN'T *anyone* seen any question marks?" Jupiter Jones asked in a baffled manner. He and Bob's father had just arrived at Verdant House in Verdant Valley after their hurried plane trip.

Miss Green shook her head. She seemed very weary.

"No one," she said. "I have the whole valley searching for any such marks. Even the children are being asked. No chalked question mark has been seen."

"What's all this fuss about question marks?" demanded Harold Carlson. His suit was wrinkled and he, too, looked very tired.

Jupiter explained that a question mark was the special symbol that he, Pete and Bob used to mark trails or to tell each other they had been at some spot. If Pete or Bob were free anywhere, they would leave a question mark, or even a trail of them, to mark their whereabouts.

"They rode through the pass, out into the desert, I'm sure," Harold Carlson said. "We'll find them to-morrow. I'm having an airplane search made as soon as it is light. If they were anywhere in or near Verdant Valley, their horses would have been found."

"Perhaps." Mr. Andrews, Bob's father, spoke now. His voice was grim. "Miss Green, Jupiter here has something to tell you, something he wants you to hear."

The woman and Harold Carlson waited. All four of them were sitting in the big living-room of Verdant House.

"Miss Green." Jupiter said, making his round face look as adult as he could, "I like to try to figure things out and—well—I've been busy trying to figure out about the green ghost and that scream my partners heard. I figured out the scream didn't come from inside

135

the house—it wouldn't have been heard. The house is too well built. I tested that. The scream had to come from outside the house.

"No ghost would have gone out in the garden to scream, would he, just supposing there are ghosts? So it had to be a living person. The people who were there that night weren't sure how many were in the party. Some said six and some said seven. I decided they were both right.

"Six men started into the house after the scream. The seventh man, the one who screamed, just stepped from behind some bushes and joined them. It was the easiest way to remain unnoticed. It's the only answer that fits the facts."

"The boy's right," Mr. Andrews said. "I can't imagine why Chief Reynolds and I didn't think of it."

Miss Green frowned. Harold Carlson looked impressed.

"It does sound logical," Mr. Carlson said, his brow wrinkled. "But why would anyone do such a thing? I mean, stand behind some bushes and scream?"

"To attract attention," Jupiter said. "A weird scream is a great attention-attracter. And it just happened there was a group of men coming up the driveway to hear it. Only it didn't just happen. Those men had been especially persuaded to go there. At least five of them had."

"Otherwise it would be entirely too much of a coincidence," said Mr. Andrews. "That becomes obvious when you think of it."

"There's just no other answer," Jupiter said. "Somebody walked through the development and suggested

136

to different men he met that they go over and see the old Green mansion before it got torn down. He made it sound like a kind of adventure, so a little group joined him. Some of them didn't know each other so they didn't know he was a stranger.

"When his partner, hiding in the garden, saw them coming up the driveway, he screamed."

Mr. Carlson blinked at Jupiter, as if trying to understand. Miss Green looked puzzled.

"But—but why?" she asked. "Why should two men do such a thing?"

"To get the group into the house." Mr. Andrews spoke now. "To get them inside so they would see the ghost and report it. I'm afraid it makes very good sense, Miss Green."

"Not to me it doesn't," Mr. Carlson objected. "To me it sounds like nonsense."

"Jupiter," said Mr. Andrews, "play the tape that Bob made that night."

Jupiter had the portable tape recorder ready. He pressed the *Play* button. A weird scream filled the room. Miss Green and Mr. Carlson jumped.

"That's just the beginning," Mr. Andrews said. "The recorder stayed on at full volume and picked up some of what the six men said. Tell me if you recognise any of the voices."

Jupiter let the tape run on. They heard the deep-voiced man speak, and Miss Green sat up, her eyes wide and horrified.

"That's enough," she said, and Jupiter turned off the recorder. The woman looked at Harold Carlson. "That was *your* voice, Harold!" she said. "You

137

deepened it, the way you used to when you played villains in college plays. But I know it was yours!"

"After I played it a few times, I was pretty sure I recognised it," Jupiter said. "Not right at first. But the accent is similar to the way Mr. Carlson talked when we met him at the old house. For a disguise that night, he used a deep voice and wore a false moustache. In the darkness that was all that was necessary."

Harold Carlson seemed to have collapsed like a bundle of old clothes.

"Aunt Lydia," he gasped, "I can explain."

"Can you?" Miss Green's voice was icy. "Then do so."

Harold Carlson gulped a few times, then started to talk.

The trouble had begun, he said, a year and a half before, when Chang had been discovered living in Hong Kong, and Lydia Green had brought him to America and announced that, since he was the great-grandson of Mathias Green, the vineyard and the winery really belonged to him and she was going to give them to him.

"But I always expected to inherit the property," Harold Carlson groaned. "After all, until Chang arrived, I was your only living relative, Aunt Lydia. And I worked hard here, building it up. Then I realised it was all about to be taken away from me!"

"Go on." Miss Green's voice was toneless.

"Well"—Harold Carlson mopped his forehead—"I conceived a plan. I would buy a lot of new machinery, borrow money from friends, put the place in debt, and have it foreclosed by my friends. I did that. I hired

Jensen as an overseer and he brought some of his men along to help make trouble—damage equipment, spoil wine—things like that. Well, then you did something you had sworn you would never do. You agreed to sell the property down in Rocky Beach."

"Yes." Miss Green's voice was very low. "My mother promised Mathias Green, before he died, that that property would never be sold even if it collapsed in ruins. But I—I was desperate. So I agreed to sell it. To pay the debts you incurred, Harold."

Jupiter listened with eager interest. He had figured out about the scream, and deduced that Harold Carlson was guilty in some way, but he hadn't been able to figure out why. Nor had he entirely figured out the ghost.

"I thought my plan to get the property away from you for the debts, and share it with my friends, was doomed," Harold Carlson said. "Then—then I received a message."

"A message?" Mr. Andrews spoke curtly. "What was it?"

"To go to San Francisco to see someone. I did. He was a very old man named Mr. Won. I was blind-folded, so I don't know where we met. He told me he had bought up the mortgages on the vineyard and winery, paying my friends a bonus to sell them to him and not tell me."

"But why should he do that?" Miss Green asked.

"I'm coming to that," Harold Carlson sighed. "He had something to tell me. There is a very old servant in his house who was a lady's maid for the wife of Mathias Green. She had been told by someone who read it in the papers that the old house was sold and would be torn down. So she revealed a secret she had kept for all these years.

"She told Mr. Won that Mathias Green's bride had been buried in the house, in a room later sealed up, and all the servants had been sworn to secrecy. But now the house was being torn down, and she did not want the body of her young mistress of so long ago to be disturbed.

"Mr. Won also told me that the servant believed the young bride was buried with the famous string of Ghost Pearls round her neck."

Harold Carlson paused, mopping his face.

"Well, Mr. Won seemed to know everything. He knew I wanted this property. He knew the sale of that house would enable you, Aunt Lydia, to save it. So he had a plan for me.

"I was to make the house seem haunted. That might hold up the sale. At the same time it would give me a chance to search the house thoroughly, by myself. He told me just where the hidden room was. I was to break into it, get the pearls, then announce the discovery of the body of the wife, and say I really believed the house was haunted."

"Mr. Won seems to have thought of everything!" Bob's father commented grimly.

"He had it all worked out. I was to sell him the necklace for a hundred thousand dollars. I was to make sure a ghost was seen in the old house. Then when the ghost 'came' to Verdant Valley, it would make the grape pickers here flee and ruin this year's wine production.

140

"This would bankrupt the winery. Won would fore-close the mortgage, and later on he would sell the business back to me for the hundred thousand dollars he gave me for the pearls. That way I would have the vineyard and winery and he would have the pearls, which for some reason he seemed terribly eager to obtain."

"Did he tell you how to fake the ghost?" Jupiter asked with keen interest.

"Yes. I'll come to that later. Anyway, the whole scheme as he outlined it seemed simple. I made my plans. I got Jensen all set to do the screaming. Then something we hadn't expected happened. The con-tractor started to tear down the house a whole week ahead of schedule.

"He'd already started demolishing it when I learned of it. I was frantic. I rushed to Rocky Beach with Jensen by a special plane, afraid the bride's skeleton would be found before I got there. Then the Ghost Pearls wouldn't be mine to sell. They'd belong to Aunt Lydia, and she would surely be able to pay the mortgage then.

"Well, I got to Rocky Beach before the demolishers had made much progress. When it got dark, I stationed Jensen in the bushes. Then I strolled through the neighbouring development and I persuaded several men to come with me to the old house. Jensen screamed. We investigated. The ghost appeared.

"Some of the men informed the police. Jensen and I slipped away. He returned here to Verdant Valley, while I stayed in Rocky Beach. I slipped around town, making the ghost appear in a number of spots so that the stories in the newspapers would be sensational and exciting.

"I didn't return here to Verdant Valley that night. I stayed in a motel under an assumed name, and next morning I rented a car and drove out to the mansion to search for the hidden room and the pearls.

"Unfortunately, the demolishers got a glimpse of the secret room from the outside and the chief of police had men guarding the house. I couldn't get in until you, Mr. Andrews, and the chief and the boys all arrived and we went in together.

"So when I did find the pearls, I couldn't quietly put them in my pocket without telling anyone and later sell them to Mr. Won. I returned here and received a telephone call from Mr. Won. He had read the stories and guessed my predicament. He told me to stage a fake robbery of the pearls."

Jupiter's round face bore a look of satisfaction.

"I figured you'd faked that robbery," he said. "As soon as I realised it was you making the ghost appear. After Bob spoke to me on the phone, telling me about Miss Green seeing the ghost and then about the pearls being stolen, it occurred to me that you were involved both times. You and Miss Green were alone upstairs when she saw the ghost, or whatever it was. If someone was making it appear, you had to be that someone. There wasn't any other possible suspect.

"And if you were making the ghost appear," Jupiter continued, while the others listened intently, "then whatever the scheme was, you were behind it and the theft of the pearls was part of it. Thus I deduced you faked the robbery. I thought Jensen might be in it with you, since you and he returned to the house together and he had plenty of time to tie you up before he went back to where he had left Bob and Pete and Chang."

"Yes," Harold Carlson admitted glumly. "I made the ghost appear in Aunt Lydia's room again to get the talk started once more. Then I took the pearls out of the safe to show them to the boys.

"It was all arranged for Jensen to rush in with news that the ghost had been seen down in the vineyard. In fact, he had carefully rehearsed three men to pretend they saw it and spread the word, so that all of our pickers would be terrified and leave.

"I rushed out, leaving the safe unlocked. When Jensen and I came back alone, he tied me up and took the pearls. He was supposed to give them to me to-day, but he didn't."

Harold Carlson looked very indignant.

"He told me he was going to sell them to Mr. Won himself. He said I wouldn't dare complain because then my part in the scheme would come out. He's double-crossed me! He's been away almost all day. I suspect he's driven up to San Francisco with the pearls!"

"It's no more than you deserve, Harold." Miss Green's tone was sharp. "You certainly have been acting like a common criminal. But just now the pearls do not matter. We must find the boys. Where are Chang, Pete and Bob?"

Harold Carlson shook his head.

"I don't know."

Jupiter had a flash of inspiration.

"Maybe they suspected Jensen!" he exclaimed. "Maybe he grabbed them to keep them quiet!"

Bob's father nodded grimly. "That sounds to me like a very good theory," he said. "After all, Jensen is missing. You say he's been away almost all day."

"I can see how Jensen might hide three boys," Harold Carlson said. "But how could he hide their horses? I tell you, dozens of people have searched the entire valley and part of the desert beyond it."

"If only someone had spotted a question mark!" Jupiter said. "Bob and Pete would certainly mark their trail if they could."

They were all staring at each other when the door opened without a knock and the old servant, Li, bustled into the room.

"Sheriff here, missy," she said. "Sheriff have news."

"He's found the boys?" Miss Green cried, rising to her feet. But the grizzled, elderly man with a star on his faded blue shirt who followed Li in shook his head.

"No, ma'am," he said. "You offered a reward to anyone who found one of those question marks, and I got a kid here, named Dom, who says he saw one."

From behind the sheriff emerged a small, shy-looking boy in ragged overalls and shirt.

"Yesterday afternoon I see a mark like this." He traced a "?" in the air. "I do not know it mean anything. I go to bed. I wake up to hear my father and brothers talk about reward of feefty dollars Miss Green offer to first person who find funny mark. I remember."

He looked hopefully at Miss Green.

"I get feefty dollars?" he asked.

"Yes, boy, yes!" the woman snapped. "If you're telling the truth. Where did you see this mark?"

"Inside a barrel. Out along the road in the desert," the boy said. "We all drive out to look in desert and I see barrel and I look inside. I see mark but nobody say anything about it yet so I do not know it means anything."

"In a barrel in the desert!" Mr. Andrews's voice sounded disappointed. "I can't see how that could be any help."

"I think we should go and look at it, sir," Jupiter said, with restrained eagerness. "It could be important."

"I'm going with you!" Miss Green announced resolutely. "Li, get my coat."

"I'm going, too," Harold Carlson said.

"You will remain here!" the woman said firmly.

They hurried out and climbed into the sheriff's old sedan. It took ten minutes to drive to the end of the valley and out into the desert beyond.

Several miles from the house, in a desolate section, their headlights showed two wine casks beside the road.

"There!" the boy Dom said, pointing. "First barrel!"

The sheriff played his light over the outside of the large casks, which stood upright. "Those are old, worn-out casks," Miss Green said. "They would never hold wine. I wonder what they are doing out here."

But Jupiter, Mr. Andrews and the sheriff were all trying to peer into the cask to which Dom had pointed.

145

They all saw clearly a wobbly question mark scrawled on the bottom of it.

Only Jupiter, however, realised it was in green chalk, and he knew what that meant.

"Bob was in that cask!" he said. "He left that mark for a clue!"

"Now I understand!" Miss Green cried. "Wine casks are such common objects, no one would notice them on a truck. But they could have had boys inside them!"

"By Jimminy!" the sheriff muttered. "Means they were nabbed, huh?"

"Probably taken out of the casks here and driven off!" Mr. Andrews said. "Very likely to San Francisco. And by that man Jensen, of course. It means we have to get the San Francisco police looking for him. Let's get back to the house and telephone."

They all re-entered the car and the sheriff backed it to make a wide turn. As he did so, they saw in the headlights a piece of paper fluttering beside the road, caught in a ball of tumbleweed. Only Jupiter sensed it could mean anything. At his insistence, they waited for him to climb out and get the piece of paper. He brought it back and they all examined it by torch.

"It's from a notebook," the sheriff said. "And there's writing on it."

"That's Bob's handwriting!" Mr. Andrews cried. "It looks as if it were done in the dark, but I'd know it anywhere."

The note said, in very large, straggly letters:

39
MINE
HELP
? ? ?

"Thirty-nine—mine—help—and three question marks." Mr. Andrews frowned. Jupiter, however, had no trouble getting the general meaning of the note.

"Bob wrote that," he said tensely. "And he's telling us to look in a mine for him somewhere."

"Well, mebbe," the sheriff agreed slowly. "But what's that thirty-nine? Thirty-nine miles?"

"I don't know what the thirty-nine means," Jupiter admitted.

"There is no mine thirty-nine miles away," Miss Green said. "All the mines are in Verdant Valley or in Hashknife Canyon. None of them has a number and I've been assured by the men that both the valley and Hashknife Canyon have been thoroughly explored."

They stared at each other, deeply puzzled and upset.

"Bob's note means he and Pete and Chang are somewhere around here," Jupiter said slowly. "And they're in trouble. But how can we hope to locate them?"

16

A Disastrous Discovery

BOB AND CHANG sat side by side with their backs
against the wall of the cave that was the entrance
into the mine where Pete had hidden the pearls. Very
close on either side of them sat two men—Jensen's
men—in case they tried to escape.

As their feet were tied together, there wasn't much
chance of them going anywhere.

It was pitch dark and very late. They had lain under
blankets in the back of a station wagon all the way
back here to Hashknife Canyon. Then, when the car
could go no farther, they had been roused and forced
to walk through the darkness here to the cave.

Pete and Jensen were now inside the mine, after
the hidden pearls.

"Do you trust Mr. Won?" Bob asked. "Did he mean
it when he said we'd be all right if he got the pearls?"

"I trust him." Chang's tone was thoughtful. "He is
a very clever old man. He lives there in Chinatown in
the old way, in secret, even though Chinatown itself
has all changed and is really very American. I suspect
most of his house is underground. And it may even
be true that he is a hundred and seven years old.

"I saw how afraid Jensen was of him. I guess we're
safe if Pete gives Jensen the pearls."

"But suppose Pete can't find them again?" Bob asked.

"Pete will find them," Chang said. "Pete is smart."

"I sure hope so," Bob answered, still in the same whispering voice so the two drowsy guards wouldn't shut them up. "You know, they put everything back in our pockets—my chalk, my notebook, pencils, knife, everything."

"That means they intend to set us free," Chang declared.

"Provided Pete can find the pearls again," Bob muttered. He remembered how much alike all the rocks inside the mine looked. It wouldn't surprise him a bit if Pete couldn't find the right rock again. He didn't know Pete had hidden the pearls inside the skull of the donkey. That was Pete's secret.

Bob had an important secret of his own. He itched to tell it to Chang, but he didn't dare lest the two guards hear it.

They sat and waited. Only a mile or so away, in Verdant Valley, Jupiter and Miss Green and the others were desperately trying to figure out where to look for them, but without success.

They did not think of investigating Hashknife Canyon because it had been searched and found empty. However it was Jensen's men who had "searched" it, and reported it empty, and Jensen was now deep inside the mine with Pete.

"You try any tricks on me, boy, and you're a gone gopher!" Jensen growled as their torches made crazy shadows along the narrow mine passages. "We have your horses penned in a little natural rock corral

149

down by the water hole at the end of Hashknife Canyon.

"If you don't come across with the pearls, all three of you go into the water hole. It'll look like a terribly sad accident, and I'll be the saddest mourner of them all."

Pete shivered. He believed the big, burly man would do that. All he wanted was to get those pearls into Jensen's hands and have it over with.

"You kids!" Jensen snorted. "Thinking you could outsmart me! I figured out your trick of going through the mines the minute I saw you head down Hashknife Canyon the wrong way. I know all about these mine tunnels. When I move into a neighbourhood, I always learn everything there is to know, just in case I have to make a fast getaway. I know every ridge and canyon for ten miles around here."

They came to the place where the collapse of the roof had squeezed the passage down to mere inches. Jensen gave Pete a last warning and Pete began to wriggle through on his stomach.

Having done it twice before, he was able to make good time. Soon he could stand erect again, and now he almost trotted through the mine galleries, following the trail of question marks Bob had left.

He came to the triple fork, took the right-hand passage, and was at the place where the skeleton of the donkey lay before he realised what had happened.

Then, as he stood and stared, an icy sweat broke out all over his body. The skull of the donkey was gone!

Where it should have been was a rock as big as a

wheelbarrow. A broken roof timber, and a gaping hole showed where the rock had plunged from the roof to fall on the white skull, crushing it into dust.

And the pearls had been inside the skull. They were delicate gems, easily crushed. Now they, too, were dust, mixed with the dust of the ancient bone.

17

The Mysterious 39

PETE, when he could think, knew what had happened. He remembered that very faint tremor, that uneasy quiver of the ground caused by an earthquake somewhere along the San Andreas fault line, which he had felt earlier that night when crawling out of the mine.

That echo of a distant earthquake had dropped the great rock on the Ghost Pearls and demolished them!

Now, no matter how much he wanted to, he couldn't give the pearls to Jensen.

Half-heartedly he tried to push the rock aside, but it was far too heavy. In any case, he knew it would be no use. There was rock under it, and when rock falls on rock, anything delicate in between is ground to bits.

Pete tried to think. It occurred to him he could keep going until he reached The Throat. He could slide through The Throat and try to find his way out of the mines that way.

But once on the other side of The Throat, he had no idea of the way. He would probably get lost and might wander for days.

In any case, he couldn't save Bob and Chang that way. Long before he could hope to find his way out and get help, Jensen would realise he wasn't coming back, and take drastic action.

Then Pete remembered the torch he had hidden, with pebbles in it.

With the faint hope in his mind that he could use the torch to trick Jensen, he walked back down the passage. At the point where the three galleries all separated, he found the line of casually placed rocks that made a kind of arrow, pointing to a bigger rock.

Behind the big rock was the torch.

He wished now he had left the pearls in the torch. But the skull had seemed like a good idea at the time. Who could predict an earthquake?

He shoved the torch inside his belt and started back. He wasn't hurrying so fast now. He was trying to think of how to trick Jensen.

The only possibility was that Jensen would take the torch and not open it. On that Pete pinned his hopes.

He came to the low section and started to wriggle through it on his stomach. At the far end the man saw his torch beam moving and called to him.

"Hurry it up! I think you're stalling! You'd better get here fast!"

Pete kept crawling, his heart heavy. He wriggled out and stood up, brushing the dirt off himself. Jensen interrupted him.

"Give me that torch!" he growled. He saw the end of it and wrenched it from Pete's belt. He hefted it, felt the weight of the pebbles, and thrust it into his pocket.

"Now let's move!" he said. "I want to get out of here."

He started with long strides back towards the cave entrance. Pete hardly daring to hope, followed.

After about ten steps, Jensen stopped and whirled.

"How do I know you're not trying to put something over on me?" he growled, glaring at Pete. "I don't trust you kids. You're too big for your britches."

He jerked out the torch, twisted off the bottom cap, and poked a finger in.

As he did that, Pete's feet moved of their own accord.

He started running past Jensen, hoping to get beyond his reach.

As he went by, the burly man thrust out a foot and tripped him. Pete went sprawling headlong, lay for a moment dazed, then slowly and painfully picked himself up.

By now Jensen had found that the torch held only some pebbles wrapped in a handkerchief, and his fury was so great he could hardly speak. He growled some unintelligible words at Pete, then whipped out his knife.

Even by the light of a torch, the blade gleamed wickedly.

Jensen grabbed Pete's collar, planted the point of the knife against his back and said, "Walk!"

Pete walked, with the raging man behind him.

"You know what this means!" Jensen said, when his fury allowed him to talk intelligibly. "Mr. Won gave me the go-ahead if you tried any tricks. The sun will rise in a few hours now, but none of you will see it!"

Pete didn't even try to explain what had happened. Jensen wouldn't care. He was only interested in the fact he didn't have the pearls.

Presently they came out into the cave that was the entrance to the mine. Pete's torch picked out the dim figures of Bob and Chang, huddled against the wall, as if asleep.

Beside them were the figures of the two guards.

"On your feet!" Jensen barked. "We have to move fast—get rid of these nuisances and get out of here while we can!"

The two men stood up slowly. Then abruptly they had guns in their hands and Pete and Jensen were enveloped in the glow of half a dozen torches. Behind them barked the voice of Sheriff Bixby.

"Don't move, Jensen! You're covered from all sides!"

Jensen did move. He grabbed Pete, swung him round, and ran for the entrance dragging Pete behind him.

So sudden was his action, that no one had time to tackle him. No one dared shoot for fear of hitting Pete.

At the mouth of the cave, Jensen let Pete go and plunged out, past two men who were standing there not expecting anything like this to happen. Almost flinging himself down the rocky canyon wall, Jensen was lost in the darkness before anyone could do more than fire a few aimless shots.

"We'll get him to-morrow," Sheriff Bixby predicted. "By Jimminy, I'm glad to see these three sprouts safe and sound."

Pete, Bob, Chang, and Jupiter Jones, who had emerged from the rear of the cave with Sheriff Bixby's men, were staging a wild reunion, in the middle of which Pete thought to ask how they had got there. It was Mr. Andrews, his hand proudly on Bob's shoulder, who answered.

"Jupiter solved the mystery of the ghost," he said, "and after we found the mark Bob left in the wine cask, Jupiter also saw the message Bob had thrown out of the car telling us to look for you in a mine. We didn't have any idea what mine, but Miss Green remembered that you, Chang, used to explore these mines with an old prospector named Dan Duncan. He's sick in a nursing home up in San Francisco, but she telephoned him and he said that if we hadn't found you anywhere else, to look in the mine in Hashknife Canyon that has a cave for an entrance.

"He was sure that if we had looked in the other mines, and found nothing, this would be the one Chang might have headed for. The sheriff got some men and we slipped into the canyon, had a scuffle with the men guarding Bob and Chang—fortunately Jensen was too deep in the mine to hear it—and laid a trap for him when he came out."

Then he turned to Bob.

"Son," he said, "there's one question we'd like you to answer. Even Jupiter can't figure it out."

"Yes, Dad?" Bob asked.

Mr. Andrews looked at Jupiter Jones and nodded. Jupe unfolded the note they had found, the note that said in large, ragged printed letters:

39

MINE

HELP

? ? ?

"Bob," he said, "we got all the message except the number. I suppose I should know, but—well, what does the thirty-nine stand for?"

Bob grinned. He brought out his notebook and opened it. It was just two covers now. All the pages had been torn out.

"Pete and Chang and I were all under blankets in the rear of a station wagon," he said. "Pete and Chang were asleep, but I was just pretending.

"When I figured we ought to be somewhere near Verdant Valley, I slipped my notebook and pencil out and started writing messages for help. I had to do them in the dark, under a blanket, so I couldn't write much.

"As I finished each one, I slipped it out through a crack where the tail-gate of the station wagon hinges to the rear. I hoped somebody would find one and be able to figure where we were. As I wrote out each one, I numbered it, so if anybody found more than one, he could tell he was following our trail in the right direction. That message was number thirty-nine. I guess the rest blew away."

Mr. Andrews started to laugh. The other men joined in. After the tension of the last few minutes, the mysterious thirty-nine and the simple answer to it seemed very funny.

Finally even Jupiter managed to grin. But it wasn't easy. After all, he was thinking, if he had realised the note was numbered, they could have looked hard for more notes and so found Bob's trail that way. He should have known Bob would be methodical. Wasn't Bob in charge of records and research for the firm?

But luckily the one note had done the job, after all.

18

Jupiter calls up a Ghost

JENSEN WAS NOT captured the next morning. Either he made good his escape, through his boasted knowledge of the territory, or he came to grief in some obscure canyon. In any case, he was never seen again. As for Harold Carlson, Miss Green, unwilling to prosecute a relative, sent him away with orders never to return.

Bob's father, with his son safe and a story to write for his paper, hurried back to Los Angeles. He exposed the green ghost as a hoax and told many of the details of what had happened, including the theft of the pearls and their destruction under a rock in the mine.

However, he played down the part of the boys in the adventure to spare them too much publicity, and he left out Mr. Won altogether, because he could learn nothing whatever about Mr. Won. Evidently the aged Chinese's boast that he had kept himself a mystery to the world was true.

Titus Jones phoned Jupiter to say that The Jones Salvage yard could remain closed for a day or two, so Bob, Pete and Jupiter stayed on to enjoy a visit with Chang Green. Now that the ghost scare was over, the workers returned and the ripe grapes were picked and crushed on schedule. The boys had a good time with Chang, exploring the country, though Bob had to spend a couple of days resting because his leg was rather tired from the strenuous activity.

He spent his time writing up his notes of the case.

Jupiter wanted to see the mine tunnels, but when he saw The Throat and the low spot through which the others had crawled, he admitted it was just as well he hadn't been along. With his rotund, stocky build, he might have got stuck for good in either of the spots.

Eventually The Three Investigators returned to Rocky Beach. Soon after they arrived, Police Chief Reynolds took the trouble to see the boys personally and praise them for exposing the green ghost hoax.

"I can't tell you how glad I am to know I wasn't seeing things," he admitted. "Any time I can give you boys a hand, call on me. Just to show you I mean it, here's a little something that might come in handy."

He handed each of them a small green card. Each card said:

"Gosh!" Bob and Pete said. Jupiter turned pink with pleasure.

"Might come in handy some time," the chief said. "Anyway, it'll show my men you aren't just snoopy kids if you start doing something they think looks suspicious."

He left with their thanks ringing in his ears. The following day, when Bob's notes were completed, they went to call on Alfred Hitchcock, who took keen interest in all their cases since he had agreed to introduce them—if he thought they were well handled.

In the big office, the boys sat upright waiting while the famous motion picture and television producer read over the details of the case. From time to time he nodded and a couple of times he chuckled.

Finally he put the sheaf of papers down.

"Well done, lads," he said. "Quite an adventure."

"I'll buy a double helping of that!" Pete said fervently.

"The outline of the matter seems clear to me," Mr. Hitchcock told them. "Harold Carlson wanted to get the property for himself, so he borrowed money from friends, intending to see to it that the money was not repaid. In this scheme Jensen aided him. Then Mr. Won, learning of the Ghost Pearls in the old house in Rocky Beach, bought the mortgage notes from Mr. Carlson's friends and applied pressure on Mr. Carlson to obtain the Ghost Pearls for him."

He leaned forward, tapping the papers.

"What of Mr. Won?" he asked. "He is a character who intrigues me. One hundred and seven years old, drinking pearls to stay alive, and living in the old style! Did you hear nothing more from him?"

They admitted they had. Bob told Mr. Hitchcock that a couple of days after his dad's story appeared in the newspaper, two small Chinese men had arrived in Verdant Valley. They came from Mr. Won. They wished permission to try to find the last of the crushed pearls under the rock that had smashed them. In return, Mr. Won would agree to give Miss Green as long as she needed to pay off the mortgage notes on the vineyard.

Miss Green had agreed. The two men had crawled into the mine with crowbars, and had come out bearing some kind of dust in a small leather bag. Whether it was pearl dust or bone dust, or what, no one knew. They went away without saying anything.

Mr. Hitchcock pursed his lips.

"I suppose," he said, "that the dust would do as well as the pearls themselves, if his men could actually recover it. Well, well, an interesting idea, that drinking dissolved Ghost Pearls can keep you alive. Perhaps mere superstition. Yet—perhaps not. We'll never know."

He fixed a keen eye on Jupiter Jones.

"Young Jones," he said, "though you were not along on most of the adventure, you seem to have

160

been responsible for solving it. However, two questions nag at me."

"Yes, sir?" Jupiter asked politely.

"In these pages"—Mr. Hitchcock tapped Bob's notes—"I see reference to the small dog one man carried into the Green mansion the night the ghost appeared. Apparently this dog helped you solve the mystery. What I wish to know is—how? What did that dog do that gave you any clues?"

"Well, Mr. Hitchcock," Jupiter told the director, "when I thought about that dog, I remembered a dog in one of the Sherlock Holmes stories. You'll remember that Sherlock Holmes told Dr. Watson to think about the curious incident of the dog in the night-time."

"Of course!" Understanding spread over the man's features. "To which Dr. Watson replied that the dog did nothing in the night-time. And Sherlock Holmes told him that that was the curious incident!"

"Yes, sir," Jupiter agreed.

Mr. Hitchcock leafed through the pages and found a spot. He re-read it.

"That's it!" he exclaimed. "The dog which one of the men carried didn't do anything. He just whined a little, probably because he didn't like being carried. Young Jones, my hat is off to you for spotting that bit of evidence."

Pete and Bob were goggle-eyed. What could you tell from a dog that did nothing?

"I don't get it," Pete said. "So the dog didn't do anything. So what?"

"My dear young man," Alfred Hitchcock told him,

"dogs and cats are universally considered to be very uneasy and frightened in the presence of the supernatural. Cats snarl and spit. Dogs howl and run. In any case, they kick up a fuss. So if this dog did nothing, it was because there was nothing there to frighten it.

"The deduction that follows is, whatever it was you and the men were seeing was not a real ghost, and so the dog paid no attention to it."

"Gosh!" Pete said. "That's right. And we missed that completely!"

"Never mind," Mr. Hitchcock told him. "You all behaved with great credit. You showed courage and determination, Pete. You, Bob, showed good sense in leaving clues that your friend Jupiter could find."

Mr. Hitchcock's brows creased slightly.

"Which reminds me," he said. "Mr. Won put you all to sleep by hypnotism. Yet on the trip down from San Francisco, Bob, you were busy writing notes for help and slipping them out under the tail-gate of the station wagon. Why were the others asleep, and not you?"

"I fooled Mr. Won." Bob grinned. "When I saw Chang and Pete topple over asleep, I knew what was coming. So as soon as Mr. Won started on me, I just toppled over as if I'd gone to sleep instantly. Only I hadn't. I was awake all the time.

"That's how I was able to write the notes. Just about all of them blew away, though, in the desert wind. It was lucky one got caught in a tumbleweed so Jupe could find it."

"Luck," Mr. Hitchcock said, "has to be aided by
162

ability. I feel all three of you showed great ability in this case. I will be happy to introduce it."

"Thank you, sir," Jupiter said, and they rose. They were almost out of the office when Mr. Hitchcock called to them.

"Wait!" he said. "I forgot the most important question of all."

He glared at them.

"Since there was no real ghost, what did all of you see?" he demanded. "Floating down hallways, disappearing through walls—what was it? And don't tell me it was cheese cloth covered with luminous paint because I know better."

"No, sir," Jupiter told him. "It was much cleverer than that. I didn't even suspect until I realised that, as the dog hadn't smelled anything or sensed anything there couldn't really be anything there. May I darken your office?"

The director nodded. Jupiter closed the Venetian blinds and pulled shut the rich drapes that framed the windows. The office was now in a deep twilight.

"Watch on that wall," he said.

Mr. Hitchcock watched. Unexpectedly a greenish blob of light appeared against the white wall. It looked like a ghostly Jupiter Jones in a white sheet. It glided slowly towards a closet door, then faded from sight as if melting away through the door.

"Amazing," Mr. Hitchcock said as Pete and Bob opened the curtains. "Under the right circumstances, that would be a very convincing ghost."

"With a weird scream and a haunted house to help

along, it was too real for comfort," Pete declared. "Wasn't it, Bob?"

Bob agreed, as Mr. Hitchcock examined the object Jupiter handed him. It looked like a slightly oversized torch. But it had a special type of reflector and lens inside.

"It's really a miniature projector," Jupiter said. "It'll project a slide. But if you make the slide of a ghostly figure, out of focus, against a black background—well, when you project it on the wall of a haunted house, you get a mighty convincing ghost."

"And a beam of light could be made to glide slowly along a wall and up a flight of stairs," Mr. Hitchcock agreed. "Very ingenious. I judge that Mr. Won gave this to Mr. Carlson?"

"Yes, sir," Jupiter agreed. "When Mr. Carlson, wearing the false moustache and deepening his voice for a disguise, brought those men to the house to see the ghost, he just carried this in his hand. It looked like an ordinary torch to everybody.

"Some of the others had real torches, so they never noticed that his one didn't give off any light. Instead, Mr. Carlson used it to project the ghost image on the walls or the door. By turning a little button, he could make the image fade out as if it were melting through a wall.

"Up in Verdant Valley, when he took Miss Green up to her room, he just stood outside while she went into the dark room. He projected the ghost image into her room, from behind her. Then when she screamed and turned the light on, he just put the projector in his pocket, rushed in and caught her, and was rubbing her wrists when the others got there.

"It was a very convincing ghost, though, until I realised that somebody had to be at the Green mansion to do the screaming, that the little dog hadn't felt any supernatural presence, and that Mr. Carlson was alone with Miss Green when she saw the ghost, so he had to be the one really causing it."

Jupiter put the small projector back in his pocket.

"We're keeping this as a souvenir of the case," he said, and he and the others turned and filed out.

As he watched them go, a smile played round the director's lips. Sherlock Holmes himself might not have been able to solve the mystery of the green ghost any better!

THE VANISHING
TREASURE

Introduction

THIS VOLUME is another case of my young friends, Jupiter Jones, Pete Crenshaw and Bob Andrews, who call themselves The Three Investigators. In it they become involved in a baffling museum robbery, assist a lady troubled by a bad case of gnomes, find themselves on the way to the Middle East to become slaves, and otherwise engage in adventurous exploits that make my hair stand on end.

If you have read any of their previous cases, of course you know all about them. You know that First Investigator Jupiter Jones is stocky, almost fat; that Pete Crenshaw is tall and muscular; that Bob Andrews is slighter and more studious. You know that Headquarters for their firm is a carefully hidden, mobile home trailer in the super junk yard called The Jones Salvage Yard, owned by Jupiter's aunt and uncle, with whom he lives.

You know that Headquarters is entered by certain secret entrances and exits known only to the boys, and bearing such code names as Tunnel Two, Easy Three, Green Gate One and Red Gate Rover.

You know they live in Rocky Beach, California, a town on the shores of the Pacific, a few miles from that strange and glamorous place, Hollywood. In fact, you know all you need to know, and therefore you could have skipped all this. If it happens that you haven't previously met the boys, let the foregoing words be an introduction to them.

And now, forward! The case begins!

ALFRED HITCHCOCK

1

To Steal the Rainbow Jewels

"I WONDER," said Jupiter Jones, "if we could steal the Rainbow Jewels."

His question took his two companions by surprise. Pete Crenshaw almost dropped a soldering iron, and Bob Andrews did drop the composing stick he was using to set up type for their old printing press.

"What did you say?" he demanded, looking in dismay at the spilled type.

"I said I wonder if we could steal the Rainbow Jewels," Jupiter repeated, "if we were thieves, that is."

"Which we are not," said Pete firmly, "Stealing jewels is dangerous. People shoot at you and chase you. Anyway, I believe in that old stuff about honesty being the best policy."

"Agreed," said Jupiter. But he continued to stare thoughtfully at the newspaper he had been reading.

The three boys, who called themselves The Three Investigators, were in Jupiter's secluded workshop section of The Jones Salvage Yard. Here, out of doors but under a six-foot roof that extended from the Salvage Yard's tall fence, they worked on rebuilding junk that came into the yard. The part of the profits they received from Jupiter's Uncle Titus kept them in pocket money and helped them pay for such luxuries as a telephone in their hidden Headquarters.

It had been quiet around the Salvage Yard for the last few days. The Three Investigators had had nothing to investigate, not even a missing pet. So the boys had nothing more on their minds than fixing the small antique radio Pete had found in the yard's latest batch of junk.

At least Bob and Pete didn't. Jupiter preferred to keep his mind, rather than his hands, working. When he didn't have a good problem to think about, there was no telling what he would come up with on his own.

Bob looked up from the type case. "I'll bet you're talking about the jewels in the Peterson Museum," he said, remembering the newspaper story his family had been discussing the night before.

"Peterson Museum?" Pete looked blank. "Where's that?"

"On top of a hill in Hollywood," Bob told him. "A great big old house that used to be owned by Mr. Hiram Peterson, the oil millionaire. He left the house as a museum, open to the public."

"And right now it has on exhibition a special display of fabulous jewels," Jupiter said, "sponsored by the Nagasami Jewellery Company, of Japan. It is touring round the United States as a means of getting publicity for its cultured pearls. Many of the items on exhibit are pearls or made from pearls.

"However, two other items are of special interest. The main attraction is the Rainbow Jewels. It is a group of gems—diamonds, emeralds, rubies, and stones of other colours—so arranged that they shimmer with all the colours of the rainbow. Some are very large, and even one of them would be worth thousands of dollars. Altogether, they are worth millions."

"There's also a belt," Bob chimed in. "Something made out of huge gold links and set with square emeralds. The paper said it weighs fifteen pounds. It once belonged to the ancient emperors of Japan."

"You're crazy, Jupe," Pete said. "No one could steal jewels like those. I bet they're guarded like a bank."

"Slightly better than most banks," Jupiter said. "There are several guards always in the room with the jewels. A closed-circuit television set trained on the Rainbow Jewels is watched at all times from the main office. At night the room is criss-crossed by beams of invisible light. If anybody broke a beam, it would set off a loud alarm.

"In addition, the glass in the cases has fine wires set into it, which also work the alarm system. If the glass is broken, the alarm goes off. It has its own special electric system so even if a big storm, for instance, knocked out all the power, the alarm would still work."

"Nobody could steal those jewels!" Pete said positively.

"But it does offer a challenge, doesn't it?" Jupiter asked.

"Why is it a challenge?" Bob asked. "We solve crimes, we don't figure out how to commit them."

"But we haven't any to solve right now," Jupiter pointed out. "I was hoping Alfred Hitchcock would write us about some interesting problem. But he hasn't, and an investigator should use his time profitably. If we try to figure out whether or not the Nagasami jewels *could* be stolen, we will be gaining valuable experience for solving future jewel robberies. And we'll be getting the criminal's viewpoint."

"We'll be wasting our time," Pete said. "We'd be a lot better off to go and take some more skin-diving and scuba lessons. We still have a lot to learn about handling the diving gear."

"I vote with Pete," Bob declared. "Let's practise our diving. As soon as we're good at it, Dad has promised us a camping trip in lower California, where we can catch live lobsters in the rocks."

"That's two to one, Jupe," Pete pointed out. "You're outvoted."

"The newspaper says," Jupiter answered, as if he hadn't heard them, "that this is Children's Day at the museum. All children under eighteen get in at half-price, and all scouts in uniform and their leaders will be admitted free. That means any Boy Scouts, Girl Scouts, Cub Scouts or Brownies."

"We haven't any uniforms," Pete said. "That lets us out."

173

"But we have earned some extra money from helping Uncle Titus all week," Jupiter reminded him. "Also, I have time off coming to me. It is an ideal opportunity to go over to Hollywood and inspect the Rainbow Jewels in the Peterson Museum. At least we should see what real jewels look like. Some day we may be called upon to recover some."

"I have a feeling," Bob muttered to Pete, "that we're going to be outvoted, one to two."

"Hey, I have an idea!" Pete had suddenly become interested. "I know how a robbery could be worked. Jewels are stones, aren't they? Well, what do you do with stones?"

"Study them under a microscope," Jupiter said.

"Throw them at tin cans," Bob answered.

"Sure," Pete agreed. "But there's something else you can do if they aren't too big. You shoot them from catapults.

"So that's how the jewels could be stolen. Someone breaks the glass case that holds the Rainbow Jewels. He takes out a catapult, shoots the gems through the open window, and his accomplices catch them in baskets. Then they make a fast getaway."

"Great!" Bob said.

Jupiter looked thoughtful. Then, slowly, he shook his head.

"There are two weaknesses in the scheme," he said. "First, the accomplices might get away with some of the jewels, but the other thief would certainly be captured by the guards. And," he went on, "there is an

174

even greater weakness. The jewels could not be sent by catapult through a window of the museum because——"

He paused dramatically.

"Well, why?" Pete asked impatiently.

"Yes, why?" Bob chimed in. "It seems like a good idea to me."

"Because," Jupiter told them, "the Peterson Museum doesn't have any windows."

2

Excitement at the Museum

AN HOUR LATER, Bob, Pete and Jupiter arrived at the foot of the little hill on which stood the Peterson Museum. The hill was across the street from Griffith Park, where the boys had often gone on picnics. Several acres of green grass sloped up to an immense stucco house with two wings, each having a domed roof. A winding two-lane road led to the rear of the house, and another came down farther off as an exit.

Cars and station wagons were moving slowly up the entrance drive. The three boys hiked up, keeping well out of the way of traffic. They saw that the parking lot was liberally sprinkled with cars. More were arriving, and more people getting out all the time.

175

Most of the crowd were children, many in scout uniforms.

Dozens of little Cub Scouts, in blue uniforms with gold neckerchiefs, ran around wildly while their Den Mothers tried to calm them down. Troops of Girl Scouts, looking very lady-like, watched them disapprovingly. There were a good many little Brownies, and a few tall Boy Scouts carrying knapsacks, each with a hatchet fastened to his belt.

"I want to study the layout of the land," Jupiter told them. "First we'll examine the outside of the museum."

They walked slowly past the rear of the big building. Bob noticed that what Jupe had said about windows was true. There had once been windows in the building, but those on the ground floor and in the domed wings had been filled in. He was staring so hard at the building that he failed to notice a group of small Cub Scouts and their Den Mother. "Oops! Sorry," he said, bumping into one of them and sending him sprawling on the grass. The boy scrambled to his feet, a gold tooth gleaming in a sunny smile and ran to catch up with his troop.

"Oh, oh!" Jupiter said. "Look at that!"

"Look at what?" Pete said, "I don't see anything but the back of the building."

"Look at those wires," Jupiter said. "See? All the electric light wires come from a pole down to that corner and go inside the house in a cable. That could easily be cut."

"Who would want to cut it?" Bob asked.

"Burglars," Jupiter said. "Of course that wouldn't affect the alarm system, which we know is separate. However, it is a weakness."

Now they finished circling the building and approached the front entrance. As they were not in uniform, they each paid twenty-five cents admission.

Inside, a guard directed them to the right. "Follow the arrows, please," he said.

The three went down a hall and found themselves in the right wing, in a big room with a domed ceiling at least three stories high. There was a balcony round one half of the room, and on it was a sign: "Closed".

Many large pictures in ornate carved frames decorated the walls. These were part of the permanent museum exhibition. However, The Three Investigators were not much interested in the pictures. They had come to see the jewels.

"Notice how the pictures are hung" Jupiter said, as they walked slowly past the paintings. "Each one has an invisible support holding it to the wall. In the old days people hung pictures on long wires from mouldings near the ceiling. You can still see the wide mouldings which they used when this was Mr. Peterson's house."

Pete looked, but he was more interested in the way the tall windows had been blocked out.

"Why'd they get rid of the windows?" he asked. "You're right, nobody could shoot any jewels out of this place, but I can't figure out why they did away with the windows."

"Partly," Jupiter said, "to give more wall surface to hang pictures on. But mostly, I expect, so they could install good air conditioning. Notice how cool it is? Keeping the temperature and moisture always the same helps preserve the valuable pictures."

Slowly they circled the room, then went down a hallway at the back of the building following a crowd of giggling, pushing youngsters. They came out in the left wing of the museum, where the jewels were on exhibition. Like the other room, it had a balcony running round half of it, but the steps were roped off.

The Rainbow Jewels were in the exact centre of the room. A velvet rope prevented anyone from getting close enough to touch the glass case.

"Very good precautions," Jupiter said, as they filed past. "It prevents any thief from smashing the case and running."

They lingered as long as they could, staring at an enormous diamond that flashed blue fire, a glowing emerald, a ruby that burned like red ember, and a huge shiny pearl. These were the most valuable jewels, but there were others, of all colours of the rainbow, arranged around them and sparkling in the light.

A guard at the corner of the case told them the jewels were valued at two million dollars, and asked them to move on. A giggling bunch of Girl Scouts took their place.

The boys now found themselves in front of a case nearer the wall, just beneath the balcony, where an impressive jewelled belt was displayed. It was more than three feet long and made of great gold links set with enormous, square emeralds. Pearls edged the links, and diamonds and rubies sparkled from the buckle. The whole belt looked as if it would have taken a big man to wear it.

"This is known as the Golden Belt of the Ancient Emperors," a guard standing nearby told them. "It dates back more than one thousand years. The total weight of gold and jewels is nearly fifteen pounds. It is very valuable, but its historic value is much greater than the value of the precious jewels in it. Now please step along so that others may view it."

They went on to look into other cases which held some really amazing things made out of Nagasami pearls—swans, doves, fish, antelope and other creatures—all made of pearls glued together or set into transparent glass frames. The Girl Scouts ooh-ed and aah-ed over them.

The room was quite full now, and Pete, Jupe and Bob stood in an out-of-the-way spot to converse.

"The room is full of guards," Jupiter said. "So obviously no one could plan a daylight theft. It would have to be executed at night. But then the big problem would be how to get in the front door and how to disconnect the alarm wires in the glass cases." He shook his head. "It is my conclusion that the jewels are safe, except from a gang of experienced, well-organized men. That being the case——"

"Ooops, pardon me!" said a man who had bumped into Jupiter. He had been backing up, looking at his watch, and hadn't seen the three boys.

"Oh, hello, Mr. Frank," Jupiter said.

"Do I know you?" the man asked good-naturedly.

"Baby Fatso," Jupe said, using the name by which he had been known when he was a very small boy in a television comedy series. "You appeared with us on a lot of the old shows, remember? You were always the poor fellow who was blamed for the mischief we kids did."

"Baby Fatso! Sure thing!" the man exclaimed. "Only the name doesn't fit any more. I'd like to talk to you, but I can't. It's time for my act."

"Act?" Jupe asked.

"Watch!" Mr. Frank chuckled. "You'll see some fun. There's a guard. I have to get his attention." He raised his voice. "Oh guard, guard!"

The uniformed guard turned, looking hot and irritated.

"Yes, what is it?" he growled.

Mr. Frank pretended to stagger.

"I'm feeling faint," he whispered. "I need water."

Mr. Frank pulled his handkerchief out of his breast pocket to mop his brow. As he did so, something fell on the floor. It was an enormous red stone, like the ruby in the exhibition case.

"Oh, my!" Mr. Frank looked confused and guilty. The guard was instantly suspicious.

180

At the sound of the whistle everyone froze . . .

"What's this?" he growled. "Where'd you steal that? You've got some questions to answer, buddy!"

He reached out to grab Mr. Frank's shoulder. Mr. Frank started to protest. Instantly the guard put his whistle to his mouth and blew shrilly.

The sound of the whistle seemed to freeze everyone in the room. Every eye turned towards the guard and Mr. Frank. In a moment the other guards had closed in and made a ring round Mr. Frank, who looked more confused and guilty than ever.

"Now mister——" began the head guard.

He never finished what he was saying. At that instant the museum was plunged into total darkness.

There was a second of silence. Then a dozen voices said excitedly, "Lights, lights! Turn on the lights!"

But the lights didn't come on. The head guard blew his whistle.

"Two guards stand by the centre case!" he shouted. "The others, see that no one leaves this room!"

Suddenly the room was in an uproar. Small boys and girls began to cry, mothers called their children, and everyone milled around in the dark.

"Chief!" shouted a guard. "There are kids all around me! I can't get near the centre case!"

"Try!" a voice shouted back. "This is a robbery!"

At that moment came the crash of glass, as one of the jewel cases was broken into. Then the clang of an alarm turned the already noisy room into a bedlam of sound.

"The jewels!" Pete gasped into Jupe's ear. "Someone's after them!"

"Naturally." Jupiter sounded as if he were enjoying this. "This is a well-planned jewel robbery. We must get to the front door and see if we can spot the criminals as they try to leave."

"Maybe there's a back entrance!" Bob shouted.

"We'll have to risk that!" Jupe replied. "Follow me!"

Jupe moved like a small tank through the forest of excited children. But as they got to the door they realized that the guards at the outer door were not letting anyone out. A dangerous situation was building up. The hall was already full of frantic people, pushing and shoving to get out. Soon some of the children would fall and be stepped on.

The boys heard a voice shouting, even above the alarm. Then the alarm abruptly shut off, as someone turned the emergency switch that controlled its special electric supply. The voice now sounded very close. It was a man's, and he had a Japanese accent.

"Guards! Outside!" he cried. "Help people out but do not let them leave the area. All must be searched before leaving!"

At this the guards moved aside and a wave of people surged outside. Jupiter, Pete and Bob followed. They saw that the guards were keeping people together on the big front lawn, trying to calm the women and children. A moment later several police cars pulled up, sirens wailing, to take charge.

The crowd at the door was jammed together, as too many people tried to go through at once. "Let's help," said Jupiter, and the boys held back a troop of Girl Scouts until some of the smaller children had filed out. Among the last to emerge was Mr. Frank. He looked flabbergasted as he approached the boys.

"What's going on?" he asked. "There must have been a robbery. But I——"

At that moment a guard pounced on him.

"You're under arrest!" he shouted and hauled Mr. Frank off, protesting.

"I bet he didn't do anything," Jupiter said, "but naturally he will have to answer a lot of questions. I wonder what the thieves stole and how they made their getaway. It doesn't seem likely they came out this way."

Pete looked over the crowd on the lawn. "It's mostly just women and kids," he agreed.

"Of course they'll probably search everybody," Jupiter went on.

At that moment a small Japanese man, who seemed to be in charge, plunged past them into the pitch-black museum, holding a large flashlight.

A minute later he came back, looking stunned.

"They didn't steal the Rainbow Jewels!" he called to the guards, who were keeping everyone together on the lawn. "They stole the Golden Belt! The case is smashed at the top and the belt is gone! Everyone will have to be searched!"

Jupiter's eyes lit up.

"Golly!" he said. "Why do you suppose they stole that huge old belt when the Rainbow Jewels were so much easier to get away with? It would be difficult for anyone to hide the belt under his clothes. It is too long and lumpy."

"Those Boy Scouts!" Bob pointed to two tall scouts. "They could have smashed the case with their hatchets and put the belt in one of their knapsacks. They're jewel thieves in disguise!"

"That's too obvious," Jupiter said. "They'll be the first ones searched. I'll bet—" he was puffing a little with excitement—"I'll bet they don't find the Golden Belt at all."

As so often happened, Jupiter's prediction proved correct. The Boy Scouts willingly allowed themselves to be searched. Their knapsacks contained only food —they were heading for Griffith Park for a hike and a cookout. They were allowed to go. One by one the others were searched and released. Mr. Frank had been taken away by the police for questioning, and finally only Bob, Pete and Jupiter were left.

The guards dug up flashlights from somewhere and entered the dark museum. The three boys silently followed them.

Inside, the top of the glass case which had held the Golden Belt was shattered. The belt was gone. The jewels in the other cases were intact.

At that moment the small Japanese man saw them and rushed over.

"You boys!" he cried. "What you do here? Why

not you go home? Not wanted here!"

"Excuse me, sir." Jupiter whipped out one of The Three Investigators' business cards. "We're investigators. It's true we're rather young, but we might be able to help you in some way."

The man looked puzzled as he read the card. It said:

```
THE THREE INVESTIGATORS

    "We Investigate Anything"

         ?    ?    ?

  First Investigator – JUPITER JONES
  Second Investigator – PETER CRENSHAW
  Records and Research – BOB ANDREWS
```

"The question marks," Jupiter explained, "are our symbol, our trade-mark. They stand for questions unanswered, riddles unsolved, mysteries unexplained. We attempt——"

"Foolishness! Silly American boys!" the little Japanese man shouted, flinging the card on the floor. "I, Mr. Saito Togati, in charge of security for the Nagasami Jewellery Company, have allowed the Golden Belt of the Ancient Emperors to be stolen. I am disgraced. And three foolish boys wish to add to

186

my troubles by intruding themselves in my way. Go! This is work for men, not for children."

Well, that seemed to be that, as far as Pete and Bob could see.

They turned and trudged out. After a moment, Jupiter Jones followed them, leaving the small white business card lying on the dark floor.

This was one case they weren't going to get to work on.

3

A Call from Alfred Hitchcock

THE NEWSPAPERS next morning were full of the strange riddle of the vanishing Golden Belt. Bob, as official keeper of records, clipped stories about the case and pasted them in the firm's scrapbook. While this wasn't actually one of their cases. Jupiter was taking an intense interest in it, reading every word that was printed.

The newspapers told them some facts they already knew, and a few they didn't. The lights in the Peterson Museum had been blacked out by a man wearing mechanic's overalls. He had been observed strolling towards the back of the museum carrying a heavy wire-cutter.

A few minutes later he was seen driving off in a black panel truck. No one thought anything of it at the time but shortly after that the alarm sounded inside and the excitement began. It was obvious he had been working with the gang of thieves inside, on a carefully timed schedule. His accomplices had promptly set to work when the room was plunged into darkness.

The great riddle, however, was who had been the gang inside? No one had slipped out of the back entrance, for the papers said it had been sealed immediately after the alarm sounded, and a guard posted outside. No one had gone out of any windows for there were no windows to go out. Everyone had gone out through the front door, and everyone had been searched.

The paper said that Mr. Edmund Frank, an actor, had been questioned and released.

"I wonder what Mr. Frank's story was?" Jupiter murmured, pinching his lower lip. "He pretended to lose a jewel the guard thought he had stolen. Obviously it was just a joke of some kind, perhaps for publicity, and the jewel was just glass."

Jupiter frowned in concentration. "This was certainly the work of a professional gang, working to split-second plans," he said. "That much we can tell from the way the crime was executed. But I confess, I am in the dark as to who they were, where they went, and how they got the Golden Belt out."

"Maybe it was the guards!" Bob exclaimed. "Maybe they got their jobs at the museum just to do this robbery."

Pete and Jupiter looked at him with respect.

"That's not a bad idea, Bob," Pete said. "But I have one too. Maybe the criminals hid in the museum and didn't come out until after everyone else had gone."

"No." Jupiter shook his head. "The papers say the museum was searched thoroughly and no one was found who shouldn't have been there."

"Those old houses sometimes have secret rooms," Pete said. "Remember the secret room we saw in the Green mansion." He was referring to their adventure, *The Mystery of the Green Ghost.*

"No," Bob butted in. "It was the guards. It just had to be."

Jupiter sat silent, thinking.

"There seems to be no reason for stealing the belt in the first place," he said. "It would be hard to hide, hard to sell, and worth much less than the Rainbow Jewels. Why didn't the thieves take the Rainbow Jewels? Those could have been put right in their pockets, and later sold with no trouble. I bet if we knew the answer to that question we'd be able to solve the robbery."

Jupiter leaned back in a rebuilt swivel chair in their tiny office in Headquarters. He was obviously thinking hard. They could almost hear his brain spinning round.

"Let us add up what we do know," Jupiter said. "First, the lights went out. An accomplice outside

189

attended to that. The guards were hampered by frightened women and children. We can take it for granted that the gang picked Children's Day at the museum on purpose, just because they figured that would happen."

"Right," Pete said.

"Then, as the guards were surrounding the Rainbow Jewels, someone smashed in the top of the case holding the Golden Belt, and lifted out the belt. It would take a tall man to do that."

"Some of the guards were tall," Bob reminded him.

"True," Jupiter agreed. "Well, when the alarm went off, everyone ran for the door. There was a big crush. When everyone finally got outside, they were searched by Mr. Togati, that Japanese detective in charge of security, and the guards. Then we were all allowed to go home."

"We were *told* to go home!" Pete said indignantly. "And after you offered to help them solve the case, too."

Jupiter looked a trifle miffed, but he only said, "Undoubtedly they thought we were too youthful to be of much help. Too bad Alfred Hitchcock isn't a director of the museum. I'm sure he could get us an opportunity to solve the case."

"I'm not sure we want one," Peter argued. "So far we're as much at sea as the police."

"There is one very suspicious circumstance," Jupiter said solemnly. "Mr. Frank may know more than he was telling."

"Mr. Frank!" Bob and Pete stared at him. "What do you mean?"

"Remember what happened?" Jupiter leaned forward and lowered his voice. "Mr. Frank told us he was going to do his act. Then he pulled out his handkerchief and dropped a piece of fake jewellery on the floor. That attracted the attention of the nearest guard. He blew his whistle. Then what happened?"

"What happened?" Bob repeated. "Why everyone in the room looked his way. And the guards all surrounded him."

"Exactly!" Jupiter's manner was triumphant. "It was a diversion. I deduce that under cover of that diversion, the actual criminals did something no one noticed."

"Something such as what?" Pete asked.

"I don't know," Jupiter confessed. "Just the same, the timing was perfect. Mr. Frank dropped the imitation jewel. A guard blew a whistle. The other guards rushed over. A second or two later all the lights went out. In those two seconds the gang was executing some important manœuvre."

Bob looked thoughtful. "Jupe, I think you have something there," he said. "But what? Nobody knows still who the gang was or how they got the Golden Belt out of there. So we're no further along than we were."

They were all silent, pondering this.

At that moment the telephone rang.

After the third ring Jupiter reached for it, switching on the little radio loudspeaker, which enabled them all to hear what was said.

"Jupiter Jones?" asked a woman's voice. "Alfred Hitchcock calling."

"Maybe he has a case for us!" Bob yelled. Since Mr. Hitchcock, the famous motion picture director, had become interested in The Three Investigators, he had steered them to several exciting cases.

"Hello, young Jones!" It was Mr. Hitchcock speaking. "Are you busy on a case just now?"

"No, sir!" Jupiter said. "That is, we offered to help the Peterson Museum solve the Golden Belt robbery, but they said we were too young."

Mr. Hitchcock chuckled.

"They should have let you try," he said. "Judging by the papers, you couldn't do any worse than the police. However, I'm glad you are not busy. You may be able to help an old writer friend of mine."

"We'd be glad to try, Mr. Hitchcock," Jupiter said. "What is your friend's trouble?"

Mr. Hitchcock paused, as if trying to think of the right words.

"I'm not quite sure, my lad," he said. "But on the telephone she told me she is being bothered by gnomes."

"*Gnomes*, sir?" Jupiter's tone was baffled. Pete and Bob, listening, were equally perplexed.

"That's what she said, my boy. Gnomes. Little people, relatives to dwarfs and elves, who wear leather clothes and live underground and dig for treasure."

192

"Yes, sir," Jupiter answered. "I mean we know what gnomes are—if there actually are any, that is. They're supposed to be mythological and imaginary."

"Well, my friend says they're real! They sneak into her house at night and change all her pictures and books around. They have her very worried, and she wants someone to help her chase them away. She mentioned them to the local policeman and he gave her such a funny look that she refuses to say anything more to anyone she can't trust."

There was a brief silence.

"So what do you say, my boy? Can you help her out?"

"We'll certainly try, sir!" Jupiter said excitedly. "Just give me her name and address."

He wrote down the information Mr. Hitchcock gave him, promised they would report all progress as soon as possible, and hung up. He looked at Bob and Pete triumphantly.

"Well, maybe we haven't got the Golden Belt case," he said. "But I'll bet we're the only investigators who've ever been called upon to solve a case of gnomes!"

4

Something at the Window

MR. HITCHCOCK'S FRIEND, who was named Miss Agatha Agawam, lived quite a distance away in downtown Los Angeles. Jupiter had to get permission from his Aunt Mathilda for Hans, one of the two Bavarian yard helpers, to drive them down in the small salvage-yard truck.

Jupiter's aunt made no objection, for the boys had worked hard around the yard lately. She fed them all —they all ate wherever they happened to be when meal times came—and as they ate, they discussed the museum robbery some more.

Jupiter urged them to try to think of any suspicious things they might have seen.

"I saw a Girl Scout leader wearing a big bunch of hair that looked like a wig," Pete offered. "Maybe she was hiding the belt under the wig."

Jupiter groaned. Then Bob said:

"I saw an old man walking with a cane. Maybe he had the belt hidden inside a hollow cane."

"You two aren't being very helplul," Jupiter complained. "Wigs and canes! Those would have been good hiding places for the Rainbow Jewels, but not for the belt. It is too big and heavy. Think of something else."

"I can't think of anything," Pete told him. "I'm all thought out."

"So am I," Bob said. "The riddle of the Golden Belt is too tough for me. Let's talk about our new case. I looked gnomes up in the encyclopedia and——"

"Tell us as we drive," Jupiter interrupted. "I see Hans waiting in the truck."

They hurried out and piled into the front seat with Hans. Jupiter gave him the address, in a commercial district of Los Angeles some miles away, and they set out.

"Now tell us what you learned about gnomes, Bob," Jupiter suggested.

"A gnome," Bob said, "is one of a race of little creatures supposed to inhabit the interior of the earth and guard its treasures.

The dictionary also says that gnome can be used to mean a dwarf or a goblin," Bob went on. "They're all little people who live underground. Except that goblins are uglier and nastier, and dwarfs are skilled blacksmiths who work precious metals into beautiful jewellery for the gnome queens and princesses."

"And they only live in fairy tales," Pete put in. "They aren't real. They're imaginary. They're miss—mith——"

"Mythological," Jupiter said. "Legendary. Creatures of fable."

"Just exactly the words I was going to use," Pete said, with a certain sarcasm. "So what are mythological, imaginary, unreal, and impossible gnomes doing around Miss Agawam's house?"

"That is what we are going to try to find out," Jupiter told him.

"But nobody believes in gnomes any more," Pete repeated.

Now Hans spoke up. "You are wrong, Pete," he said. "In the Black Forest of Bavaria there happens to

195

be many gnomes. Also trolls and goblins. Nobody sees them, but everybody knows about them. Very spooky place, the Black Forest."

"See?" Jupiter said. "Hans believes in gnomes. So does Miss Agawam."

"Well, this isn't the Black Forest," Pete answered. "This is Los Angeles, California, U.S.A. What I want to know is why gnomes are fooling around here, just supposing there might possibly be any gnomes."

"Maybe they're digging for gold," Bob said, with a grin. "Gold was discovered in California in 1849. May be they've just heard about it and have come here to find some. After all, they are the guardians of underground treasure."

"Whether there are gnomes or not, something mysterious is going on. Very soon we will have more facts to work with," said Jupiter. "I believe we are almost there."

They had reached a very old and rundown section of Los Angeles.

Hans slowed the truck, searching for the street number. They stopped in front of a big boarded-up building. From the outside it looked rather like an Arabian castle, with steeples and domes and lots of gold paint, most of which had tarnished and was peeling away. A faded sign said it was the Moorish Theatre, and a newer one said that soon a twelve-story office building would be built on that site.

Next they passed a high hedge, behind which they could barely see a dark, narrow building. Then they came to a bank, one of the old-fashioned type made out of cut stone, but with a new front that made it seem more modern.

In the next block, they could see a supermarket, then a line of rather shabby stores. It was obviously a business district.

"We've passed it," Jupiter said, reading the street number chiselled into the stone front of the bank.

"I'll bet it was behind that hedge," Bob spoke up. "That's the only building that could be a private residence."

"Back up and park, Hans," Jupiter directed.

Hans obligingly backed up a few feet. They were now opposite the hedge, which was six feet high and shaggy. Behind the hedge they could glimpse an old house which seemed to be hiding from the busy world outside.

It was Pete who spotted a small sign on a white wooden gate that led through the hedge.

"*A. Agawam,*" he read. "This is the place, all right. But why anyone would want to live here beats me. I'll bet it's dark and spooky at night."

The boys piled out, and Jupiter led the way to the gate in the hedge. It was locked. An old, yellowing card under glass was fixed to the gate. In spidery handwriting it said: "Please ring bell. Gnomes, elves and dwarfs, whistle."

"Gnomes, elves and dwarfs, whistle!" Pete exclaimed. "Golly, Jupe, will you please tell me what that means?"

Jupiter Jones wrinkled his brow. "Well, it sounds as if Miss Agawam really believes in these fairy-tale creatures. We're not gnomes, elves or dwarfs. Still, we may as well start finding out what this is all about. Pete, you're a good whistler. Whistle."

Pete looked puzzled. "Why do we have to do everything the hard way?" he grunted. But he puckered up his lips and whistled like a mocking-bird.

They waited. Then they all jumped as a voice spoke from the bushes.

"Yes, who is it, please?"

Jupiter understood at once. Hidden in the bushes was a little loudspeaker. Through it the occupant of the house could speak to anyone at the gate before letting him in. Such devices were common in apartment houses, and he had heard of their being used on large estates.

Peering into the bushes, he could see a little bird house. Undoubtedly it held the speaker, and protected it from the weather.

"Good afternoon, Miss Agawam," he said politely to the bird house. "We're The Three Investigators. Mr. Hitchcock asked us to call to discuss your problem with you."

"Oh, of course. I'll unlock the gate." The voice was sweet and light, rather like a bird's.

A loud buzzing sounded, as the locking mechanism of the gate was worked by a button inside the house. The gate opened and they stepped inside.

For a moment they paused. It was almost as if they had left the city behind them. The tall hedge, higher than their heads, hid the street. On one side the blank brick wall of the old, abandoned theatre rose several stories high. On the other side was the granite side of the bank. The two buildings boxed the old house in completely. The house itself was three stories tall and very narrow, its redwood boards peeling from long exposure to the California sun. A small front porch held several boxes of flowers, the only touch of brightness in the yard.

They all had the same thought at the same time. It was like an old house in a story book. More like a witch's house than anything else.

But Miss Agatha Agawam, who opened the door for them as they climbed upon the porch, was no witch. She was tall and thin with dancing eyes, white hair and a sweet voice.

"Come in, boys," she said. "It was very good of you to come. Let me show you to my study."

She led them down a long hall to a large room, full of overflowing bookcases. The walls were crowded with paintings and photographs of children.

"Now, boys," Miss Agawam said, indicating three chairs, "please sit down and let me tell you why I called my old friend Alfred Hitchcock. I've been bothered for several days by gnomes. I mentioned it to the local policeman a few days ago and he gave me such a peculiar look that I—well, I'm just not going to say anything about gnomes to the police again!"

She paused. And just then Bob let out an unexpected yell.

While settling himself in an armchair, he had happened to look towards a window. There, gazing in at them, was a small creature—it certainly didn't look human—wearing a peaked cap. It had a dirty white beard, carried a tiny pickaxe over its shoulder, and was scowling ferociously.

5

A Story about Gnomes

"A GNOME!" Bob shouted. "Spying on us!"

But before the others could turn round, the little man had vanished.

"He's gone!" Bob cried, leaping up. "But maybe he's in the yard."

He rushed to the window, followed by Pete and Jupe. The window was in a dark recess between two bookcases. He tried to raise it and found his hands touching smooth, unbroken glass. Bewildered, Bob blinked.

"It's a mirror," Jupe said. "You saw something in a mirror, Bob."

Bob turned round, puzzled. Miss Agawam was rising. She pointed in the opposite direction.

"The window is over there," she said. "It does re-

It had a dirty white beard and carried a tiny pick-axe . . .

flect in the mirror, of course. I like that because it makes the room seem larger.

The boys ran towards the open window on the opposite side of the room. Jupe leaned out and peered into the yard.

"Nobody in sight," he said.

Pete joined him. "The yard's totally empty," he reported. "Are you sure you saw something, Bob?"

Baffled, Bob studied the hard ground under the window, the empty yard, the high brick wall of the abandoned movie theatre. Nothing was stirring. Certainly there was no little bearded gnome in sight.

"Maybe he ducked round the side of the house," he said. "Because I'm positive I saw him. We ought to search the yard. With the gate locked he can't get out."

"I'm afraid you won't find him, if it was a gnome," Miss Agawam said. "After all, they have magical powers."

"I think we should search," Jupiter told her. "Is there a rear entrance?"

Miss Agawam led them down the hall to a door that opened on to a small back porch. The three boys ran out into the yard.

"Pete, you go left!" Jupe shouted. "Bob and I will go right."

There wasn't much to search. The yard held a few straggly bushes. At the rear was a high board fence, behind which was an alley. There were no holes in the fence, and only one rear gate, which was locked. An iron emergency-exit door was set into the side of the old Moorish Theatre at one side of the yard. But the door proved to be solidly locked, and very rusty, as if it had not been opened in many years.

"He didn't go through there," Bob said.

Bob and Jupiter peered into the bushes, then studied the cellar windows of the house. They were all locked, and very dirty. Next they moved to the front hedge. There were no breaks in the hedge. No place a small, bearded figure could have scooted out of the yard.

The strange little creature Bob had seen had evaporated, as far as they could tell, into thin air.

Pete joined them. He had found exactly what they had found—nothing.

"Let's look for footprints," Jupiter said. "Under the window."

They trooped round to the side of the house where the study was. Beneath the window the ground was packed hard and dry—much too hard to show marks of any kind.

"No footprints," Jupiter said, disappointed. "However, another mystery."

"What mystery?" asked Bob.

Jupiter stooped and picked up something. "Look at this. A little blob of fresh earth that might have fallen from someone's shoe."

"Or out of one of Miss Agawam's flower boxes!" Bob retorted.

"Perhaps," Jupiter answered. "However, look up at

the window. The bottom of it is above our heads. You say you saw a very small figure at the window, Bob?"

"A gnome about three feet tall," Bob answered. "He wore a peaked cap and a long dirty beard and carried a little pickaxe. I saw him from the waist up. He was looking at us and scowling as if he was very angry."

"How," Jupiter asked, "could a gnome three feet tall stand out here and look in a window at least six feet above the ground?"

The question stumped them, until Pete spoke up.

"A ladder, of course. He was standing on a ladder."

"A folding, collapsible ladder?" Jupe asked with rich sarcasm. "That he put in his pocket before he scooted into a hole in the fourth dimension?"

Pete scratched his head. Bob frowned.

"Gnomes can work magic," Bob said finally. "It must have been some kind of magic."

"Possibly you didn't really see anything, Bob," Jupiter suggested. "You do have a very strong imagination."

"I saw it!" Bob said hotly. "I could even see his eyes! They were fiery red."

"A gnome with fiery red eyes." Pete groaned. "Oh, oh! Couldn't you change your mind and say you imagined it, Bob?"

Bob began to feel doubtful. After all, he had only had that one quick look.

"Well, I don't know," he said. "I think I saw it but I suppose you're right. I was thinking of the picture of a gnome I saw in the encyclopedia and—well, probably I did imagine it."

"Well," Jupiter said, "if you imagined it, we certainly can't find it. And if you really saw it, whatever you saw, it must be able to make itself invisible, for it certainly isn't in the yard."

"And there's no way out of the yard," Pete added.

"We'd better go back in and find out what Miss Agawam has to tell us," Jupiter suggested.

They went back up the front steps. Miss Agawam opened the door for them.

"You didn't find him, did you?" she asked.

"No," Bob told her. "He just vanished. There was no place for him to go but he disappeared."

"I was afraid of that," Miss Agawam said. "That's how gnomes are. It's very rare, though, to see one in the daytime. Well, let us have some tea and then I'll tell you what has been happening.

"I am sure you boys are going to be able to help me with this strange mystery," she said, pouring from a china teapot. "Mr. Hitchcock said you have solved some very unusual cases."

"Well, we have had some pretty interesting ones," Pete agreed, accepting a cup of tea to which he added a lot of sugar and cream. "Jupe has done most of the solving, though, hasn't he, Bob?"

"About eighty per cent of it," Bob agreed. "Though I guess Pete and I helped some, didn't we Jupe? Jupe!"

Jupiter, who had been looking sideways at a newspaper lying on a nearby couch, jumped slightly.

"What?" he asked, and when Bob repeated the question, he said to Miss Agawam, "We work together. I couldn't have done anything without Pete and Bob helping."

"I noticed you were reading the headline about that strange affair at the museum yesterday," Miss Agawam said, offering cookies, of which Jupiter took several. "My, the world is full of mysteries, isn't it?"

Jupiter took time to swallow a cookie. Then he said, "We were actually at the museum when the Golden Belt was stolen, and we are totally baffled by that particular case. We offered to help, but—well, the man in charge thought we were too young."

"He told us to go home!" Pete said indignantly.

"I'm sure he made a mistake," Miss Agawam said. "But to be very selfish about it. I'm glad you aren't busy on something else. But before we start to talk about my problem, let's enjoy our tea. I never believe in talking about something serious while one is eating."

She poured more tea for them and passed round the cookies. Bob and Pete would have preferred a soft drink, but the tea wasn't bad with plenty of cream and sugar, and the cookies were delicious.

"Oh, my, this reminds me of the old days," Miss Agawam said happily as they ate. "Why, not a week passed that I didn't have a tea party for my very own gnomes and elves and dwarfs."

Bob choked slightly on a cookie. Then Jupiter spoke up.

"Do you mean that you invited the neighbourhood children in for tea?" he asked. "And called them your gnomes, and dwarfs and elves?"

"Why, of course!" Miss Agawam beamed at him. "You are clever to guess. I'm sure I don't know how you did it."

"Deduction," Jupiter said. He pointed to the photographs on the walls. "You have many pictures on your walls of children dressed in clothes such as were worn a good many years ago. Most of them are signed, 'With love to Miss Agatha', or something like that.

"Also, you have a whole shelf of books right beside the door which you wrote yourself—Mr. Hitchcock said you were a writer. I noticed several of the titles, such as *The Gnomes' Happy Holiday* and *Seven Little Gnomes*. I deduce therefore that you used to write about such imaginary creatures, and that you probably called your young friends gnomes and dwarfs and elves for fun."

Pete and Bob looked at Jupiter open-mouthed. They had seen the pictures and books but hadn't paid any attention to them.

"Why, you have it exactly right!" Miss Agawam clapped her hands in delight. "Except for one thing. You said gnomes are imaginary creatures. They aren't. They're real. I'm sure of it.

"You see, when I was small my father was well-to

do, and I had a governess from Bavaria. She knew all the wonderful stories about gnomes and the other little people who live in the Black Forest. Later, when I began to write stories, I wrote about the things she had told me. She gave me a big book she had brought with her. It's in German, but you can understand the pictures."

She stood up to get a book off the shelf, a big old book bound in leather.

"This book was printed in Germany about a hundred years ago," Miss Agawam said, turning the stiff pages as the boys crowded round. "It was written by a man who lived for months in the Black Forest. He made drawings of gnomes and dwarfs and elves to illustrate the book. Look at this drawing."

She turned to a full-page picture of a rather terrifying little man in a peaked leather hat. He had large hairy ears, hands and feet, and carried a short pickaxe in his hand. His eyes had a fierce, glaring expression.

"That's like the one I saw peeking in at the window —I think!" Bob said.

"The writer calls this 'The Wicked Gnome King'," Miss Agawam told him. "Some gnomes are wicked and mischievous, but others aren't. The wicked ones, this writer says, have fiery red eyes."

"Ulp!" Bob choked, remembering the glimpse of red eyes he had seen. Well, anyway, thought he had seen.

Miss Agawam turned some more pages, and showed them pictures of ordinary gnomes, who were dressed the same but didn't look quite as mean as the wicked gnome king.

"These pictures look exactly like the gnomes I've been seeing," she said, closing the book. "So that's how I know they are gnomes, and are real. In a moment I'll tell you just what happened. But first let me tell you about the old days when I was a well-known writer of books about the Little People."

She sighed. It was obvious she remembered the old days with great pleasure.

"After my father and mother died, my stories became very popular and I made a good deal of money from them. Of course it was a long time ago—many years before any of you were born—but children often came to visit me and have me sign copies of my books for them. I like children very much and all the children in this neighbourhood were my friends.

"Then, the whole neighbourhood changed. All the old houses and nice trees were torn down, and shops went up instead. All my old friends, the children, grew up and moved away. Many people wanted me to sell, and move away too, but I wouldn't. I had always lived here and, no matter how things changed, I intended to keep on living here. You can understand my not wanting to leave my old home, can't you?" she asked.

They nodded.

"Things kept changing," Miss Agawam sighed. "A few years ago even the motion picture theatre next door had to close. There were so few people around here to visit it. I put up a card telling my gnomes and elves and dwarfs to whistle to be let in, just for old time's sake. And do you know—once in a while one does come back to visit me. But my goodness! They've grown up now. They're grown up with children of their own, and even grandchildren! That tells you how long ago it was."

She paused. They could easily understand how it had all happened.

"Perhaps I should move now," Miss Agawam said at last. "Mr. Jordan, who is going to tear down the theatre next door and build an office building, wants me to sell to him so he can make his building bigger. But goodness—I was born here and I am determined to stay here, no matter how many office buildings they build around me!"

She looked very spunky and determined. The boys could well imagine her defying anybody to make her sell her house.

Miss Agawam poured herself a last cup of tea.

"Well, now I've talked about the past enough. It's time to come up to date. After all these years of writing about gnomes, I didn't really expect to see any. But I did. A few nights ago."

"Please tell us about it," Jupiter requested. "Bob, take notes."

Bob whipped out his notebook. He had taken typing and shorthand in school and was very good at both. Eventually he planned to be a newspaperman like his father.

"I usually sleep very well," Miss Agawam said,

"but several nights ago I woke up about midnight and heard an odd sound. It was the sound of someone using a pickaxe to dig, deep underground!"

"A pickaxe? At midnight?" Jupiter asked.

"Exactly. At first I was sure I was mistaken. No one digs anything at midnight. No one except——"

"Gnomes!" Pete finished her sentence.

"Yes, gnomes," Miss Agawam said. "I got up and went to my window. Out in the yard I saw four tiny figures playing. Little men, dressed in what looked like leather clothes, were playing leapfrog and doing somersaults in my yard. I couldn't see them too clearly, of course. I opened the window and called to them. And they vanished!"

She looked at the boys, frowning.

"I was sure it was no dream, and the next day I told the patrolman who covers this neighbourhood. Officer Horowitz. You should have seen the look he gave me. Well!"

Her blue eyes flashed indignantly.

"He told me to take care of myself. And he asked if I was going away on vacation soon. I swore then and there I certainly wouldn't say another word about gnomes to the police!"

After a moment, Miss Agawam laughed.

"My pride was hurt," she said. "Anyway, the next two nights I woke up and heard them again. But I pretended to myself I just imagined it and I said nothing to anyone. The third night, however, I knew they were really there.

211

"I went to the telephone and phoned my nephew Roger. He lives in an apartment a few miles away—he's a bachelor and my only relative. I begged him to come right over, and he agreed to get dressed and start at once.

"While I waited for him, I decided to look into the cellar where the noise seemed to come from. I crept down the cellar stairs without making a sound or turning on the lights. As I went, the noise got louder. Then I turned on my flashlight and—do you know what I saw?"

All of the boys were keyed up by Miss Agawam's story. Bob burst out, "What?"

Miss Agawam lowered her voice. She looked at each of them in turn. Then she said:

"Nothing. I didn't see anything at all."

Bob let out his breath in disappointment. He'd been so sure Miss Agawam must have seen—well, he couldn't guess what. But something.

"No," Miss Agawam told them, "I didn't see anything. I turned to go back upstairs and wait for Roger. And then I saw something.

"I saw a little figure only three or four feet tall. He wore a peaked cap, leather coat and trousers and pointed leather shoes. He had a dirty white beard, and in one hand he carried a little pickaxe. In the other he held a candle. By the light of the candle I could see his eyes glaring at me. They were fiery red eyes!"

"Just like the one I saw peeking in at the window!" Bob exclaimed.

"Oh, it was a gnome all right," Miss Agawam agreed.

Jupiter was pinching his lower lip and looking puzzled.

"What happened then?" he asked.

Miss Agawam's hand trembled a little as she drank her tea. "The gnome snarled at me. He raised his pickaxe in a threatening way. Then he blew out the candle, and I heard the door at the top of the steps slam. When I got up courage enough to climb the stairs and try the door, it was locked.

"I was trapped in the cellar!"

They stared at her, their eyes round. Suddenly, at the far side of the room, there was a tremendous crash. All of them, even Miss Agawam, jumped.

6

Strange Talk Overheard

"GRACIOUS!" Miss Agawam gasped. "What was that?" Then she answered her own question.

"Why," she said, "my picture just fell off the wall!"

The three boys ran over to where a large painting in a gold frame lay on its side on the floor. As Pete and Jupiter set it upright, they saw that it was a fine picture of Miss Agawam as a young woman.

213

"The artist who illustrated my books did it many years ago," explained Miss Agawam.

The portrait showed her sitting on the grass reading from a book while many strange little creatures, probably meant to be gnomes and elves, crowded round to listen.

A wire hung from a moulding near the ceiling had supported the picture, and this wire had obviously broken. Jupiter examined the break. He looked solemn.

"This wire didn't just break, Miss Agawam," he said. "It was filed almost through, so it had to break sooner or later."

"Oh, dear!" Miss Agawam touched her face with her handkerchief. "The gnomes! They must have done it. The other night when—oh, but I haven't come to that yet."

"I think we can fix the wire for you, Miss Agawam," Jupiter said. "And hang the picture up again. You tell us while we work."

They carefully turned the picture over and Pete, who was very handy at fixing things, knotted the broken wire.

Bob took notes as Miss Agawam continued her story. She had only been locked in the cellar a few moments when her nephew Roger arrived, letting himself in with his own key. She had called out and pounded on the door, and he had released her. But when she told him her story, though he was very nice, she could tell he didn't believe a word of it. Miss

Agawam was sure he thought she had been walking in her sleep and dreamed the whole thing.

"Excuse us a moment, Miss Agawam," Jupiter requested, "and we'll hang up the picture again."

Pete stood on a chair, and Jupiter handed the portrait up to him. As he did so, Bob saw Jupe's eyes suddenly gleam with excitement. Bob knew what that meant.

Jupe had had an idea!

"What is it, Jupe?" Bob whispered, as Pete climbed down.

Jupe was looking rather self-satisfied.

"I believe I have solved the riddle of the Golden Belt!" he whispered back.

"You have? Golly, what's the answer?" Bob had to stop himself from yelling the words. "How could you solve it now, here, anyway?"

"A clue is a clue, wherever you find it," Jupe said under his breath. "We will talk about it later. Right now we have a duty to help Miss Agawam."

Bob sighed. He knew Jupe wouldn't say another word until he was good and ready. He tried to imagine what clue Jupiter might have come across, but he couldn't. So he gave his full attention to Miss Agawam as she took up her story once more.

"Roger wanted me to come to stay at his apartment, but I wouldn't," she said. "He waited a while, but we heard nothing more so he left.

"Well, nothing more happened that night. But the next night I heard strange noises again. I suppose I should have phoned Roger, but his attitude that first night—telling me I must have had a bad dream—well, I didn't like it. I didn't want him thinking I was hearing and seeing things.

"I slipped downstairs very carefully, just in time to hear the back door close. In the library here some of my pictures had been thrown on the floor. All my books had been taken out of the shelves and pages had been torn out of some. As if the gnomes wanted to be nasty and unpleasant. That must have been when they filed the wire of my picture.

"I was very upset. I did phone Roger in the morning and he came over. But he wouldn't believe that gnomes had done it all. He very tactfully told me I must have done it myself, and he thought I should go away somewhere for a good rest. I practically ordered him out of the house. Because I know it really happened! I am definitely not walking in my sleep and having delusions!

"But what does it all *mean?*" Miss Agawam asked, wringing her hands. "It's all so mysterious. I can't understand a single bit of it!"

Neither could Pete or Bob. Looking at Miss Agawam, they found it hard not to believe that every word she spoke was the truth. At the same time, her story seemed too preposterous to be true.

"The first thing to do," Jupiter said finally—for it was obvious he didn't have any handy answers either —"is to get evidence that these gnomes really do exist and are bothering you, Miss Agawam."

216

"Yes, of course!" she clasped her hands. "Then we can learn why."

"What we have to do is set a trap for them," Jupiter told her.

"What kind of trap?" Pete asked.

"A human trap," Jupe replied. "One of us will spend the night here and try to catch one of them."

"Oh we will, will we? Which one of us?"

"You, Pete. You're the one I had in mind."

"Now wait a minute!" Pete protested. "I don't want to be a human gnome trap. It's a line of work I don't care for. Even though I don't believe in gnomes, I don't believe in taking chances, either."

"We have to station someone here who is strong, swift, and courageous," Jupiter said. "I'm strong and fairly courageous, but I'm not very swift. Bob is fast, now that his brace has been taken off his leg—" he was referring to a brace Bob had worn for some years on a leg badly broken when he was a small boy— "and he has the courage of a lion. But he is not as strong as we are.

"No, Pete, the only one of us who is strong, fast and courageous is you."

Pete swallowed hard. What do you do when someone tells you you're courageous but you don't feel a bit courageous yourself?

"Why don't we all stay?" he asked. "Three heads are better than one. We can take turns staying awake."

"I'm supposed to go with my mother and father to

217

visit my aunt to-night," Bob said. "That lets me out."

"You haven't any excuse, Jupe," Pete told him. "Tomorrow is Sunday so the salvage yard won't be open. Suppose you and I stay?"

Jupiter pinched his lip.

"Well, all right," he said. "Perhaps that is a better idea. No doubt two of us can handle the situation better than one. Will it be all right, Miss Agawam, if Pete and I spend the night here with you?"

"Oh, would you?" Miss Agawam exclaimed in delight. "I'll be so pleased. There's a room at the head of the stairs you can have. You're sure you don't mind? I don't want to get you into any danger."

"The gnomes haven't hurt you, Miss Agawam," Jupiter said. "I don't think they plan any harm. But we must see them, and capture one if possible, to find out what's going on. To-night, after dark, we will come back and wait. We will try to slip in unseen so no one will know that reinforcements have arrived."

"That'll be wonderful," Miss Agawam said. "I'll be waiting for you. Just press the bell and I'll open the gate lock."

When they were out in the street again Pete burst out, "Well, is she just imagining things, Jupe? That's what I want to know."

"I don't know," Jupiter said, thoughtfully. "She might be. But she doesn't act like a lady who imagines things. Maybe she really has seen some gnomes."

"Aw, come on!" Pete scoffed. "Nobody believes in gnomes any more."

"Some people do," Jupiter told him. "Just as some people believe in ghosts."

"Just a few years ago, in 1938," Bob piped up, "some scientists discovered a strange fish that was supposed to have been extinct for a million years. It's called a coelacanth. Now scientists know there are thousands, maybe millions of them in the seas.

"Why—" Bob was just getting warmed up—"suppose there really is a race of little people who are called gnomes or goblins or elves. Suppose a long time ago they had to hide underground because bigger people wanted to kill them and eat them. Then they really could exist just as the coelacanth did, only nobody's caught one yet."

"Excellent thinking," Jupiter said. "A good investigator must take every possibility into account. Tonight we will come prepared for anything."

He stood looking down the street. Pete was getting restless.

"Come on," he said. "Let's get in the truck and get back home. It's dinner time and I'm hungry."

"I think we should walk round the block first," Jupiter said. "We inspected the hedge and fence from the inside, but not from the outside."

"You mean to see if there is any place a gnome could get out?" Bob asked.

"Certainly," Jupiter answered. "Perhaps closer inspection will reveal something we missed."

They started towards the old movie house on the corner, Pete still grumbling that he was hungry.

The doors to the theatre were boarded over and covered with tattered advertising signs. They walked round the corner and down one long side of the building until they came to an alley.

"This alley runs behind Miss Agawam's house," Jupiter said. "We'll go down it and inspect her fence."

A few feet down the narrow passageway, they passed a metal door set into the back of the old theatre. In faded letters it said "Stage Door." It was open a couple of inches and, unexpectedly, they heard a rumble of voices inside.

"That's odd," Jupiter said. "The signs out front say 'Closed' and 'Positively No Admittance'."

"I wonder what it's like inside?" Pete was beginning to get interested. "I bet it's pretty spooky."

Jupiter sat down on the stone step outside the door and began to tie and untie his shoelaces, trying to hear what was being said inside. All he could make out was a rumble of voices, as of two men talking.

"Listen!" Pete began.

"Sssh!" Jupiter said tensely. "I just heard someone say the words 'Golden Belt'."

"Golden Belt! Golly!" Bob whispered. "Do you suppose——"

"Quiet!" Jupiter was listening intently. "I just heard the word 'museum'."

"Gosh, maybe we've stumbled on the thieves' hide-out!" Pete whispered, eyes round. "Wouldn't that be something!"

"We must try to hear more before we call the police," Jupiter murmured.

All three boys moved nearer the door. Clearly they heard the word "museum" spoken again. Almost bursting with eagerness, they crowded closer. The door, not really shut, swung open and all three boys sprawled headlong into the hall inside.

As they tried to get to their feet, large hands grasped their collars and a deep voice bellowed in their ears.

"Trespassers!" it roared. "Mr. Jordan, send for the cops! I've nabbed some kids breaking in!"

7

Inside the Old Theatre

A HEAVY-SET MAN with dark eyebrows and a ferocious scowl on his face hauled Pete and Bob to their feet.

"I've got you!" he growled. "Don't try to get away! Mr. Jordan, there's one more. You grab him!"

"Run, Jupe!" Pete gasped. "Get Hans!"

Jupiter, however, stood his ground.

"You're making a mistake," he said in his most adult manner. "Hearing voices within a supposedly empty and abandoned structure, we were under the

221

Large, heavy hands grabbed Pete and Bob.

impression that there were trespassers inside, and we were endeavouring to make sure of our suspicions before contacting the authorities."

"Huh?" The heavy-set man stared at him, mouth open. "What'd you say?"

It was a trick Jupe sometimes used, which almost always gave adults a jolt of surprise.

Now another man appeared behind the first one. He was younger, thinner and light-haired.

"Relax, Rawley," he said, looking amused. "The boy simply said he heard our voices and thought we were trespassers. They were trying to make sure before calling the police."

"If that's what he meant, why didn't he say so?" demanded Rawley, who seemed to have a bad disposition. "I hate smart-aleck kids who talk like dictionaries."

"I'm Frank Jordan, owner of this theatre," the other man told them. "That is, I bought it in order to tear it down and build a new office building. I was just checking with Rawley, here, my night watchman. Why did you boys think our conversation sounded suspicious?"

"The building is supposed to be all locked up——" Jupiter began, but Pete, indignant about the way he had been grabbed, burst out, "We heard you talking about the Golden Belt! That's why we were suspicious. Especially when you mentioned the museum too!"

Rawley's face darkened again.

"Mr. Jordan!" he said. "These kids are screwballs! Troublemakers. I say we call the cops!"

"I'm in charge here, Rawley," Mr. Jordan told him. He looked puzzled, however, by Pete's statement. "Golden Belt?" he said. "I don't remember mentioning any such thing."

Then his face cleared and he smiled.

"Oh, so that's it!" he said. "Now I remember. As I said, I'm going to tear this old theatre down. I was telling Rawley that the inside is so elaborate, with so much gold and gilt, that it's like a museum. I said I really hated to tear it down.

"You see? 'Gold and gilt', if not heard clearly, could easily sound like 'Golden Belt'. You boys have been reading too much about that museum robbery."

He chuckled. Rawley, however, still looked menacing.

"They got too much imagination," he muttered.

"Lucky you don't have any imagination," his employer told him. "You aren't bothered by any of those mysterious noises that made my last two night watchmen quit."

"Mysterious noises?" Jupiter asked, suddenly interested. "What kind of noises?"

"Mysterious knocks and muffled groans," Mr. Jordan said. "But there are logical explanations. It's certainly spooky enough inside, I admit, but that's because it is so big and dark. When it was new it was a very beautiful place.

"Maybe you boys would like to look around inside

and see the gold and gilt I was talking about?" he asked, smiling.

Eagerly, they said they would.

"Turn on the main lights, Rawley," Mr. Jordan directed, and led the boys down a dark narrow hall, lit by just a single bulb.

The farther they went, the thicker the darkness grew. Something brushed past Bob's face and he let out a yell.

"A bat!" he cried.

"I'm afraid so," Mr. Jordan's voice came out of the darkness. "This theatre has been empty so long it has many bats in it. Rats, too. Enormous ones."

Bob gulped but kept silent as he heard the whir of leathery wings in the air over his head. Then he heard strange creakings and groanings ahead, and he felt as if his hair was standing on end.

"Those noises," Mr. Jordan said, "are just the old ropes and pulleys once used to hang the scenery. Besides being a movie theatre, this place presented vaudeville shows. Ah, I see, Rawley has found the light."

A dim light relieved the darkness as the boys emerged on the stage of the theatre. From here they could look out over what seemed miles of empty seats. Overhead, an enormous chandelier of coloured glass —green and red and yellow and blue—shone dustily.

Red plush curtains, heavy with gilt fringe, hung at the side windows. The walls were liberally decorated with scenes of knights and Saracens fighting, all in

225

gold armour. As Mr. Jordan had said, there was lots of gold and gilt around, and the inside did have a museum-like atmosphere.

"This theatre was built during the nineteen-twenties," Mr. Jordan said, "when people felt a movie theatre should look like a palace or a castle. This one was made to look like a Moorish mosque. You should see the funny stairways, and the minarets on the roof. Ah well, times change."

He turned to lead them back to the alley. A shadowy grey form scampered across the stage in front of them.

"One of our resident rats," Mr. Jordan said. "They've had the place all to themselves for years. They won't like being evicted. Well, here you are, boys. Now you know what the old Moorish Theatre looks like. Come and watch us tear it down in a few weeks."

He ushered them out into the alley and the door closed behind them. Firmly. They heard it lock.

"Wow!" Pete said. "Bats and rats! No wonder night watchmen wouldn't stay."

"Presumably they are responsible for the mysterious knocks and groans," Jupe said. "I admit that when I overheard what sounded like 'Golden Belt' I felt sure we had stumbled on an important clue to the museum case. However, Mr. Jordan's explanation is very logical and I believe it."

"It would have been nice if we could have nabbed the museum robbers after being chased off the case,"

226

Pete sighed. "But I guess that's asking too much."

"I'm afraid it is," Jupiter agreed. "Let's not forget we're trying to help Miss Agawam. So come on and we'll finish our inspection of the alley."

They walked on down the alley, testing the boards of the high fence which walled off the rear of Miss Agawam's property. Every one was solid. The gate was tightly locked.

"Nobody could have got in or out this way," Jupiter remarked, pinching his lip. "It's all very curious."

"I'm more hungry than I am curious," Pete said. "Can't we go home now?"

"Yes, I guess there's nothing more we can do now," Jupiter agreed.

They walked back to the truck, where Hans was patiently reading a newspaper, and piled in.

As the truck moved through the city traffic, Bob wanted to ask a question. He wanted to ask Jupiter what clue he had suddenly found, or remembered, back in Miss Agawam's house that had made him say he had solved the riddle of the Golden Belt.

But Jupiter had settled back with his "thinking look" on his face, and Bob knew he wouldn't want to be interrupted now with questions.

So he didn't ask.

8

An Unexpected Visitor

WHEN THE TRUCK got back to Rocky Beach and The Jones Salvage Yard, Pete hopped out.

"Got to get home," he said. "I just remembered. It's Dad's birthday and Mom is having a special dinner. I'll be back as soon as I can."

"Try to be here by eight," Jupiter told him. "And be sure to get permission to spend the night with me at the home of a friend of Mr. Hitchcock's. Say we expect to be back to-morrow morning."

"Right." Pete got on his bike and pedalled off.

As Bob and Jupiter climbed out, Jupiter's aunt came out of the neat little cabin that served as an office for the yard.

"You have a visitor, Jupiter," she said. "He's been waiting for half an hour."

"A visitor?" Jupe repeated, surprised. "Who is he?"

"His name is Taro Togati and he's a Japanese boy. But he speaks quite good English. He's been telling me all about how they make cultured pearls. They use trained oysters, or something!"

She gave a deep laugh. She was a cheerful, good-natured woman, though she did have a peculiar fondness for seeing Jupiter and his friends working hard.

"I'll see him in a moment, Aunt Mathilda," Jupiter said. "May I have permission to spend the night with Pete at the home of a friend of Mr. Hitchcock's? She's a lady writer who has been hearing peculiar noises at night."

"Peculiar noises? Well, I guess it will be all right if it makes her feel better to have two, big, strong boys in the house." Mrs. Jones laughed again. "All right, Jupiter, you can go down in the truck and call Hans to pick you up in the morning."

She raised her voice. "Jupiter and Bob are here, Taro," she called. Then she added to the boys, "Supper in half an hour," and started off towards the Jones's home.

A small boy, no bigger than Bob, but dressed very neatly in a dark blue suit and tie, came out of the office. He wore gold-rimmed eyeglasses and his hair was combed straight.

"So happy to meet you, Jupiter-san," he said, with a slight accent. "And Bob-san. I am Taro, humble son of Saito Togati, chief detective for Nagasami Jewellery Company."

"Hello, Taro," Jupiter said, shaking hands. "We met your father yesterday."

Taro Togati looked unhappy. From his pocket he took a business card, slightly crumpled.

"Yes, I know," he said. "I am afraid my honourable father was rude. But he is very upset, very distracted. I pick up your card, learn your name. I saw

229

you help people out of the door, and I told my father. He asked me to come and give you thanks and many apologies."

"That's all right, Taro," Bob put in. "We know he was upset. And I suppose we are pretty young to be chasing jewel thieves. Right now we're working on a case of mysterious gnomes."

"Gnomes?" Taro Togati's eyes widened. "Oh, I know what you mean. The Small People who dig for treasure underground. I have never seen one, but in Japan we have legends about them. They are most dangerous. Do not let them catch you."

"We would like to catch one of them," said Jupiter. "To see if they actually exist, as the legends say."

As they talked, Jupiter pulled out some rusty iron garden chairs, and they all sat down.

"Tell me, Taro," Jupiter said, with suppressed eagerness, "has your father found the Golden Belt yet?"

"Alas, Jupiter-san," Taro Togati sighed, "my father, guards and police do not yet catch thieves or find Golden Belt. No—what is the word?—no clues. My father is deeply ashamed. Under his nose Golden Belt was stolen, and if he does not get it back, he is dishonoured and must resign his job."

"That's tough, Taro," Bob said sympathetically.

Jupiter was pinching his lip, as his mental machinery moved into high gear. "Tell us what actually has been learned, Taro," he said.

Taro described the police's extensive questioning of

everyone who had seemed in any way suspicious. All this had not come up with a single likely suspect, nor could they discover how the belt had been removed from the museum. Taro's father and the police had decided that the thieves had taken the Golden Belt, rather than the Rainbow Jewels, because it was in a side case, while the Rainbow Jewels were out in the middle, and had been surrounded at the first alarm. Of course, it was less valuable than the Rainbow Jewels, and much harder to get out of the museum, but it was easier to steal.

"But who the thieves were, or how they got the belt out of the museum, no one can guess," Taro said unhappily.

"The guards!" Bob burst out. "One of them could be the thief. He could easily have hidden the belt by letting it hang down inside the leg of his trousers and holding it with his own belt."

"All guards especially hired," Taro said. "My father questioned each. Unless he was deceived. It is possible. I will mention it to him."

"What about Mr. Frank, the actor?" Jupiter asked. "The one who dropped that imitation jewel."

Taro told them that at first the police had been sure Mr. Frank was in on the robbery plot. However, the actor's story was very simple. A woman had hired him by telephone to appear at the museum, and, at exactly noon, drop a large imitation stone from his pocket and look guilty.

She had told him it was a publicity stunt. Of

course everyone in Hollywood was familiar with stunts to get publicity, and accepted them as a matter of course. The woman had promised Mr. Frank that if he could get his name in the papers, together with the fact that he was soon to start work on a movie called "The Great Museum Robbery", he would actually get an important part in the picture.

Mr. Frank had agreed. The large fake jewel and a fifty-dollar bill had come to him by mail, and he had just carried out his assignment. It was obvious, Taro said, that the thieves had hired Mr. Frank to provide a moment's distraction just before the actual robbery. But apparently he was innocent of being part of the gang.

Jupe had the slightly smug look he sometimes got when he felt he had a good idea.

"As I thought." He nodded. "And, of course, the police and your father deduced that the thieves purposely chose Children's Day as an ideal time to stage their daring robbery?"

"Ah, so." Taro nodded. "But my father is still much puzzled about how belt was taken outside."

Jupiter looked important.

"It wasn't taken out," he said, exploding a small bombshell of surprise. "It's still in the museum!"

"Still in the museum!" Bob yelped.

"But museum was searched, bottom to top!" Taro protested. "Belt was not found. Offices searched, washrooms searched, every place! Please explain idea, Jupiter-san."

232

"To-day," Jupiter said, "while working on another case, I came across a clue that I think explains the riddle of the disappearance of the Golden Belt. Given the facts as we know them, it seems to me the answer must be——"

He paused. Bob and Taro waited breathlessly.

"Bob," Jupiter said, "you remember when Miss Agawam's picture fell down? Pete and I hung it back up."

Bob nodded. "Sure," he said. "Go on, Jupe."

"As I held the picture, which was quite a large one," Jupiter said, "I noticed that in the back there was a space a couple of inches deep between the actual painting and the outer frame. Now there are many large pictures hanging in the Peterson Museum. I deduce——"

Seeing what he was getting at, Bob finished for him: "Some of those pictures probably have big crevices between the picture and the carved frames!" he said. "Someone could have slipped the belt behind one of them in the confusion and darkness!"

"Or it could be a gang working together," Jupe said. "We know that a woman phoned Mr. Frank. She may have been an accomplice of the actual thief."

Taro Togati leaped excitedly to his feet.

"I am sure men did not look behind pictures when museum was searched!" he said. "I will tell my father this idea at once."

"Whoever hid it probably intends to go back and get it when things have quietened down," Jupiter said.

"But as the museum has been closed, it couldn't have been retrieved yet. Tell your father not to skip the balcony, either."

"But the balcony was closed," Taro objected.

"Only by a rope anyone could step over. A picture on the balcony would be an ideal hiding place, as it would seem the least likely."

"Thank you, Jupiter-san!" Taro cried, his eyes shining. "I believe your idea is most excellent one. Excuse me now, I go back at once to tell my father of your thoughts."

They exchanged rapid good-byes and Taro ran out to a waiting car.

Bob turned to Jupe admiringly.

"Golly, that was sharp thinking, Jupe," he said. "Maybe you've solved the theft of the Golden Belt even though Mr. Togati wouldn't let us work on the case."

For a moment Jupiter looked doubtful. "There may be another answer," he said. "But—no, given all the facts as we have learned them, that is the only explanation which fits. Since the belt wasn't taken outside, it must still be in the museum. The only unsearched spot is behind a picture. I can't find any flaw in my logic."

"It's good enough for me!" Bob said loyally.

"Well, we'll know in the morning," Jupiter said. "Now I have to get together a kit of gnome-catching equipment to take to Miss Agawam's house. Tomorrow morning I will telephone a message to your home. You can come down with Hans to pick us up."

Bob shook his head in perplexity.

"Do you really think you're going to catch a gnome, Jupe?" he asked. "Or do you think Miss Agawam's nephew was right, that she's been walking in her sleep and imagining it all?"

"I'm keeping an open mind," Jupiter told him. "People have done strange things in their sleep. One man who was worried about some jewellery in his safe is known to have walked in his sleep, opened the safe, taken out the jewellery and hidden it where he couldn't find it himself when he woke up the next morning.

"If Miss Agawam is doing something like that, Pete and I will be witnesses and will be able to convince her of the truth in some way. On the other hand——" and Jupe's eyes gleamed as he spoke—"if she has been seeing gnomes, or something like gnomes, we'll be all set to catch one!"

9

Start of a Gnome Hunt

THE GNOMES were digging busily. Far down at the end of the rocky underground tunnel, Bob could see tiny forms swinging pickaxes.

He crept forward, wishing Pete and Jupiter were

235

with him. He didn't want to go any deeper into that tunnel, where the darkness was so black, but now that he was this close, he couldn't let The Three Investigators down.

His heart pounding, he moved closer, until he was crouching just outside the cave-like room where the gnomes were working. Then, because of the dust in the air, he sneezed.

Instantly, every gnome stopped working exactly as he was, some with pickaxes raised over their heads. They all turned slowly, very slowly.

Bob wanted to run, but the instant their eyes were on him, he was rooted to the spot, as if by some kind of magic. He couldn't utter a sound.

They stared at him without moving. Then he heard footsteps behind him. Something very strange and scary was sneaking up on him. He tried to turn and look—but he couldn't move.

A big claw dropped on his shoulder and shook him.

"Bob!" a voice boomed, hollow and echoing in the cave. "Bob! Wake up!"

The sound broke the spell. Bob squirmed and started to shout.

"Let me go!" he yelled. "Let me go!"

Then he blinked. He was lying in his own bed and his mother was looking down at him.

"Why, Bob, were you having a dream?" his mother asked. "You were wriggling around and muttering strangely in your sleep. So I woke you."

236

"Golly, yes. I guess it was a dream, all right," Bob said thankfully. "Jupiter didn't call, did he?"

"Jupiter? Why should Jupiter call at this time of night? You've only been asleep a few minutes. Now go back to sleep and please try not to dream."

"I will, Mom."

Bob turned over to sleep again, wondering how Jupiter and Pete were making out.

At that moment, the two boys were riding in the pick-up truck on their way to Miss Agawam's home. As they rode, Jupe showed Pete the equipment he had assembled in his gnome-catching kit.

"Most important, the camera," he began. It was Jupe's pride, a special camera that developed a picture within ten seconds. It was a rather expensive make, but Jupe had obtained it in a broken condition from a boy at school, trading him a repaired bicycle for it.

"For taking instant pictures of gnomes or anything else we meet tonight," Jupe explained. "Here's the flashbulb attachment."

He replaced the camera and took out two pairs of work gloves with leather palms.

"Gloves for handling gnomes," he said. "They are supposed to have strong teeth and sharp nails. These will help protect our hands."

"Golly," Pete said, "you act as if you really expect to catch some gnomes."

"It always pays to be prepared," Jupiter told him "Now the rope.

"A hundred feet of light nylon, very strong. In fact, almost unbreakable," Jupe said. "It should be enough to tie up any gnomes we can catch."

Next he brought out two home-built walkie-talkies that had been added to their equipment some time before. Though their range was short, these instruments enabled the boys to keep in touch while on a case. They were especially proud of this professional touch.

"Flashlights," Jupiter said, taking out two powerful ones. "And finally the tape recorder. For recording any sounds of digging," Jupiter said. He studied the kit and nodded.

"All seems to be complete," he said. "Do you have your special chalk?"

Pete produced a stick of blue chalk from his pocket. Jupiter took out his white chalk. Bob's stick was green. By simply scrawling ? or ? ? ? somewhere in green, blue or white, the boys could let each other know they had been there, or were inside, or had found something at the spot worth investigating.

The rest of the world would think nothing of scrawled question marks in chalk, considering them the work of children at play. It was one of Jupiter's most ingenious devices.

"I believe we are now all set," Jupiter said. "Did you bring a toothbrush?"

Pete held up a small zipper bag.

"Toothbrush and pyjamas," he said.

"I don't think we will need the pyjamas," Jupiter said. "We will remain fully clothed, ready to catch a gnome."

Hans looked sharply across at the two boys.

"You are still chasing gnomes, Jupe?" Hans asked. "Konrad and I, we think you should not mess around with gnomes. Many bad stories about them are told in the Black Forest of Bavaria. Stay away from them, that is what Konrad says. That is what I say. That is what we both say. Or else you will, perhaps, be turned into rocks!"

Hans sounded so positive that Pete couldn't help feeling a little uneasy. Of course there weren't any gnomes, but just the same, Hans and Konrad believed in them, Miss Agawam believed in them, and who could tell, just maybe——

Jupiter spoke, interrupting Pete's thoughts. "We have promised to assist Miss Agawam in her present difficulties," he said. "I don't know whether she is really being bothered by gnomes or not but, in any case, you remember the motto of The Three Investigators."

" 'We Investigate Anything'," Pete muttered.

Secretly he wondered if that didn't include just a little too much territory!

10

Trapped!

IT WAS dark and still on Miss Agawam's block. The closed bank and the deserted theatre were pitch-black, and only a single light burning in the house told them Miss Agawam was waiting for them.

As Pete and Jupiter started to climb out, Hans looked at them with a worried frown.

"I still say you should not try to catch gnomes, Jupe," he said. "In the Black Forest where I grow up are many strange rocks and stumps that once were people. It is because they look at a gnome, eye to eye. You better watch out!"

Pete didn't care for this line of conversation. Hans sounded so positive. His feeling of nervousness came back. Something told him the night ahead was going to bring some very unexpected surprises.

Jupe said good night hastily, promising that he would phone Hans in the morning, and the truck pulled away.

Keeping to the shadows along the fence, the boys made their way down the pavement to Miss Agawam's gate. No one, as far as they could detect, was watching them.

Jupiter gave the bell at the gate three short pushes.

Instantly the lock buzzed. They slipped quickly inside and Jupiter paused to listen. Pete was puzzled. The way Jupe was acting you would think he was on a secret mission involving the fate of great armies. But then, Jupe never was careless on a case.

Also, Jupe liked to make things dramatic.

Inside the gate, the yard was in darkness. Silently they stole up on the porch, the door opened, and they slipped inside.

Miss Agawam, a bit pale, greeted them.

"I'm so glad you're here," she said. "The truth is, for the first time in my life I was feeling very nervous. I do believe that if anything more should happen, I would just run out of here and never come back! I'd sell the house to that Mr. Jordan who wants it so badly."

"We are here, and we will take charge, Miss Agawam," Jupiter said politely.

Miss Agawam smiled, a bit shakily. "It's still quite early," she said. "I never have noticed any digging or other activities before midnight. Would you like to look at television?"

"I believe we will take a short nap until eleven-thirty," Jupiter said. "That way we will be refreshed for the night's vigil."

"What's a vigil?" Pete asked.

"It means we stay awake and watch for whatever happens. Miss Agawam, do you have an alarm clock?"

Miss Agawam nodded. She showed Pete and Jupiter to the small room at the head of the stairs where two beds were made up. The boys took off their shoes, made sure their equipment was ready, and stretched out.

In spite of his uneasiness, Pete fell asleep easily. Sleeping was one thing he never had trouble doing. But it seemed no time at all before a small bell roused him.

"What's 'at?" he muttered, still half asleep.

"It's eleven-thirty," Jupe whispered. "Miss Agawam has retired to her room. You can sleep. I'll keep watch."

"Vigil," Pete muttered and was asleep again.

Unlike Bob, Pete almost never dreamed. But now he began to dream it was hailing and the hail was tapping on the windows.

He woke up, this time quite alert, and lay still for a moment. The tapping continued. Pete realized someone actually was tapping on the window. It had a curious rhythm: one—three—two—three—one. Like a code. Or like a magical formula.

With that thought he sat bolt upright, staring at the window. His heart did a double flip-flop and seemed to lodge in his throat.

There was a face peering in at the window!

It was a tiny face, with small, glaring eyes, hairy ears, and a long pointed nose. Small lips drew back and fanglike teeth snarled at him.

The room all around him suddenly was lit by a flash of lightning, and Pete jumped.

But there was no thunder. The face at the window instantly vanished, and Pete realized the light had come from a camera flashbulb.

"Got him!" Jupiter exclaimed in the darkness. "You awake, Pete?"

"Sure I'm awake!" Pete exclaimed. "That was a gnome looking in at us!"

"And I have a photograph of him. Now let's see if we can catch him."

Both boys crowded to the window. They blinked, trying hard to see. Out in the yard, four tiny figures in tall peaked caps were dancing around crazily. They turned somersaults. One stood on another's shoulders and turned a backward somersault. They played leapfrog. They looked like children playing some wild game.

As his eyes grew accustomed to the dark, Pete could even see their tiny white faces, their pointed shoes, their leather clothing.

"Golly, Jupe!" he whispered. "There are four of them! But why are they doing tricks in the yard like that?"

"I think the answer is clear," Jupiter replied, pulling on his shoes. "They are hoping to scare us and Miss Agawam."

"Scare us?" Pete said. "Well, they've made me nervous, if that's what they want. But why should they want to scare us and Miss Agawam? What about the digging?"

243

Four tiny figures were dancing crazily.

"Merely an extra added detail. I deduce, Pete, that the gnomes have been hired by Miss Agawam's nephew, Roger."

"Hired by Roger!" Pete repeated, lacing on his shoes. "What for?"

"To scare her into selling this house and moving away. Remember, she told us Roger was very anxious for her to sell and move into a little apartment. She also told us Roger is her only relative. That means he's her heir—some day he will inherit all her money."

A great light burst in Pete's mind.

"I get it!" he said. "If she sells now she'll get a lot of money which he'll inherit some day. He wants her to sell to Mr. Jordan—sure! So he hired the gnomes to scare her. Jupe, you're a genius!"

"In order to prove anything," Jupiter said, "we have to catch at least one of these creatures and make him talk."

Jupe grabbed the rope from the emergency kit and thrust it through his belt. He pulled on a pair of work gloves, tossed a pair to Pete, and slung his ten-second camera over his shoulder. They both attached flashlights to their belts to keep their hands free.

"How could the gnome look in the window? It's on the second floor," Pete asked as they hurried.

"Figure it out, Pete. You need the experience in simple deduction," Jupiter said. "Come on. Miss Agawam must still be asleep. That's good. We don't want to alarm her."

They slipped down the stairs and out of the front

door. Silently as shadows, they eased off the porch to the corner of the house. On their knees, they peeked round.

The four strange little men were still doing wild acrobatics in the yard—turning somersaults and cartwheels, playing leapfrog.

"Here!" Jupe gave Pete one end of the rope. The other end he tied around his wrist. "Rush them. Get the rope around one and wrap it tight. Come on!"

They made a dash for it. As they burst from cover, Jupiter's camera strap caught on the branch of a bush, and the camera was ripped from his shoulder. But Jupiter did not pause.

The gnomes saw them coming. With a shrill whistle, they scattered and ran headlong towards the deeper darkness of a shadow along the brick wall.

"After them!" Jupiter gasped. "Catch at least one!"

"I'm trying!" Pete panted. His fingers almost closed on the shoulder of one tiny figure. But the little man ducked, and Pete went headlong on the ground. Jupiter fell over him. As they picked themselves up, they saw the four little creatures disappearing into a dark opening in the wall of the theatre.

"The door!" Jupe gasped. "It's open now."

"They went inside. Now we've got them!" Pete cried. "Come on, Jupe."

He ran headlong for the open door.

"Wait, Pete!" Jupiter yelled, holding back. "I've had time to think some more and now I deduce——"

But Pete wasn't listening. He had already rushed through the open emergency door. He held tight to the rope Jupe had tied to his own wrist, and his speed pulled Jupe along behind him.

Jupiter, running as fast as he could to keep from falling on his face, ran through the door and into the pitch darkness inside the great building.

The instant they were both inside, the door closed with an iron bang. They were trapped!

And a second later small creatures with sharp nails were attacking them from all sides.

11

A Wild Chase

"HELP!" shouted Pete. "The gnomes have me!"

"They've got me, too!" Jupiter grunted, trying to brush off the small creatures who seemed to be swarming all over him. "They trapped us!"

He swung his arm. The rope was still tied to his wrist and Pete still held the other end. It caught some small creature in the neck. They heard a gurgle and a shrill scream and the tiny man went flying.

Jupiter was free. But the gnomes would return to the attack. He could hear Pete grunting and thrashing around nearby. Jupiter reached out, got a good hold

247

of a leather jacket and pulled. The little man came loose and Jupiter swung him through the air and let him go.

He came down with a satisfying thud and a high-pitched squeal.

With Jupiter's help, Pete tossed off his other attacker and the two boys pressed close together in the darkness, panting. Jupe untied the rope and put it in his pocket.

"What do we do now, Jupe?" Pete gasped.

"Try to find the door we came in and go back out," Jupe said. "It's behind us—this way, I think."

They backed up until they bumped against a wall. Jupe felt around and found the handle of the iron door. He rattled it but the door wouldn't budge. They were locked in!

"We're trapped all right," Jupe's voice was glum. "Why did you have to rush in so fast, Pete? You should have guessed that's what they wanted us to do."

"I thought I had them," Pete confessed. "And I just pulled you along after me, didn't I?"

"Yes," Jupe answered. "And that's what they wanted. To get us inside. And now—listen!"

In the darkness, they heard shrill whistles to the right and left of them.

"They're getting ready to attack again!" Pete exclaimed.

"We have to get out of here!" Jupiter said. "Maybe we can force our way out at the front of the theatre."

248

"How can we find it in this darkness?"

"Our flashlights. In our excitement, we have been forgetting them. That is one effect of fright—it clouds the thinking processes."

Pete slapped his leg. His flashlight was still clipped to his belt. He thumbed it on, and a beam of light shot out, cutting the darkness. A second later Jupiter's light was added to his.

Tiny figures tumbled for cover as the light hit them, and small voices chattered in a shrill, strange language. Apparently the gnomes were more wary now. They knew Pete and Jupiter were not to be overcome so easily.

The two boys were in the backstage region of the movie house. Here, large rectangular canvas "flats" were stacked in rows, left over from the days when the theatre had shown vaudeville and even an occasional play. A sagging couch, an old spinning wheel, and a step-ladder stood just where they had been left when the building had closed many years ago.

And there was the whisper of wings in the air. Something dark flashed past their heads and was gone.

"Bats!" Pete yelled.

"Never mind the bats. We're going to be attacked," Jupiter said. The little men were creeping up, now armed with pieces of wood for clubs. "Where shall we go?"

"This way. Follow me."

Pete dashed off. He was an expert at finding his way, even in strange surroundings. He had an instinct

249

like a built-in compass for going in the right direction.

Pete ran along between two rows of stacked canvas flats. Jupiter followed, kicking over the step-ladder behind him.

Shrill squeals told him one of their pursuers had got tangled in the ladder. But an instant later Pete stopped so suddenly Jupe ran into him. Down at the other end of the narrow alley, two tiny men armed with clubs were waiting for them.

"We're cornered," Pete gulped. "They're behind us and in front of us."

"Then we have to go sideways," Jupiter said. "Make a hole in the canvas."

He kicked. The old rotted canvas gave way like paper and Jupiter and Pete ducked through. More scenery flats were in their way. Now they just put their heads down and rammed through like bulldozers, leaving ragged, flapping canvas behind them.

Soon their pursuers were lost in the canvas scenery behind them. Jupiter and Pete, still running, came out on the big wooden stage of the theatre.

They beamed their lights outwards. Beyond the hundreds of empty, dusty seats, far in the distance, were the doorways that might lead to the outside. That is, if they could get through the barricades they knew nailed the outer doors shut.

As they were studying the situation, light footsteps sounded behind them. Pete swung his flashlight. The gnomes were creeping up on them.

"Keep going," Pete yelled. "Up the centre aisle."

He dashed for the steps which led to the main floor of the theatre. At that moment the lights overhead came on—someone had pushed the main switch.

The big green and red chandelier glowed dimly. As he followed Pete down the stairs, Jupe saw two tiny figures coming for him. One of them grabbed a rope hanging down from overhead. Like an acrobat, he sailed through the air and dropped squarely on Jupe's shoulders. Jupiter went down, losing his flashlight, fighting for dear life to pull loose the gnome who now sat on his shoulders.

Pete ran to Jupiter's aid, grabbing the tiny man round the waist and pulling him loose from the First Investigator. He dumped him head first between the first two rows of seats, where he got stuck and squealed for help.

The other little men stopped running long enough to pull him free, and Jupe and Pete used that chance to dash up the main aisle into the lobby.

They ran full force against the big main doors. But the doors did not budge.

"They're nailed shut with boards across the outside," Pete gasped. "We'll have to try to find a window or something. Come on, Jupe."

He dashed down a side corridor and up a dark flight of steps. With Pete's flashlight as their only light, they went up one flight of stairs. then another. Stopping to rest, Pete shut off the flash and they peered between some decaying velvet curtains.

251

Apparently they had climbed up to the level of the balcony. They could see, far below them, four tiny figures huddled in consultation.

As they watched, another figure came down from the stage into the auditorium. He was an ordinary man, heavy-set, and there was just enough light for them to see who he was.

"Rawley!" Pete gasped. "He's working with them!"

"Yes." Jupiter sounded very gloomy. "I made a serious error, Pete. But we haven't time to discuss it now. Listen."

"Hey, Small Fry!" Rawley was bellowing to the four gnomes. "Scatter and find those kids. We have to get them, you hear? They can't go far—every door is nailed shut!"

The four little men below started off obediently in different directions.

"They've lost our trail for the moment," Jupiter said. "If we can find a hiding place, sooner or later Miss Agawam will wake up. Then——"

"Golly, yes!! She'll find we're missing and she'll send for the police. The police will search for us! They're bound to look here," Pete said, his spirits suddenly rising.

"They'll find my camera there on the bush," Jupiter said. "They'll pull the film out and know something strange is going on. If we can just hide until Miss Agawam reports us missing, we'll be safe."

"Then let's hunt for a hiding place fast!" Pete said. "I hear voices coming up the stairs."

12

Pete Climbs for His Life

Miss Agatha Agawam awoke with the sound of digging in her ears. She lay quietly in bed for a moment, listening. Yes, there it was, far underneath her—the gnomes were at it again.

Had the boys heard them? So nice of them to offer to stay with her. There was no sound from their room. Perhaps they were still asleep. Perhaps they had slept right through the alarm.

"Boys!" she called. "Jupiter! Pete!"

There was no reply. She would have to wake them so they could hear the gnomes, too.

Miss Agawam slipped out of bed and put on a woolly robe. She hurried down the hall to the door of their room.

"Boys!" she called again. Still no answer. She opened the door and found the light switch. As the light illuminated the room, Miss Agawam gasped.

The boys' beds were empty!

Her heart pounding, Miss Agawam looked around. Their pyjamas, unused, were still neatly folded on a chair. That leather kit they had brought with them was still there.

She jumped to the first conclusion that came to her.

253

Pete and Jupiter had heard the gnomes, been frightened, and had gone home. They had abandoned her.

"Oh, dear," Miss Agawam whispered to herself, "what shall I do now?"

She couldn't stay in that house any longer. She just couldn't. Not after such fine boys as Jupiter Jones and Pete Crenshaw had been so frightened they had run away.

She'd go to her nephew Roger's apartment. He'd invited her to come any time she wanted.

She slipped downstairs to the telephone. Her fingers were shaking so much that she had to try three times to dial his number. When at last his welcome voice answered, she gasped, "The gnomes! They're back. I can hear them plain as plain. Roger, I can't stay here another moment. I want to come to stay with you tonight. To-morrow—yes, to-morrow I'll sell the house to Mr. Jordan!"

"Auntie dear," Roger boomed, "I think you should sell the house, but we can talk about that to-morrow. You get dressed now and pack a little bag and I'll start right away for you in my car. Be ready in ten minutes and I'll be there."

"All right, Roger dear, I'll be ready," Miss Agawam promised.

Feeling better, but with her heart still fluttering, she began to dress. Her nervousness didn't really start to go away until she had left the house, not even checking to make sure the door was locked, and was safely in Roger's car.

Meanwhile, Jupiter and Pete's nervousness was growing stronger.

The boys were still searching for a hiding place in the upper part of the theatre. They used the flashlight only when they had to. Mostly they felt their way down dark corridors which smelled of age and dampness and old carpeting.

Behind them, every so often, they could hear the voices of their pursuers. Rawley's bellow seemed to be getting closer.

They came to a door and shoved on it. Jupiter shone his light around. Two very old motion-picture projectors stood in the middle of a dusty little room.

"This was the projection room," Pete gasped. "Let's hide here."

"Too obvious," Jupiter was beginning to look worried. "We'll have to try somewhere else. If Miss Agawam doesn't wake up soon and call the police, we may be in trouble."

"We *may* be in trouble?" Pete repeated. "We *are* in trouble. We'll just be in worse trouble if she doesn't wake up and find us missing."

"Let's keep going," Jupiter said.

They went down the hall and climbed another flight of stairs. These ended on a small platform, against a closed door that said: "Minaret—Do Not Enter".

"What's a minaret?" Pete asked. "Some kind of monster, I bet."

"You're thinking of a minotaur," Jupiter told him.

"A minaret is sort of an open tower. Let's try it. I have an idea."

The door was rusted shut, but a good push opened it. Very narrow, steep steps lay behind it. They closed the door, wishing they could lock it, and climbed up the ladder-like steps.

A minute later they came out in a little square tower, open on all four sides, high above the street. Below, everything was dark and deserted, lighted only by the glow of a street lamp.

"Well, we've found the minaret all right," Pete said. "And there's no place to go from here. If you ask me, we're trapped but good!"

"At least we aren't locked in," Jupiter said. "There's the street and safety. All we have to do is reach it. It's only about seventy-five feet away."

"Only seventy-five feet. Straight down. Ha ha!" Pete laughed hollowly.

"We have a rope." Jupiter pulled the coil of light rope from his pocket. "I have here a hundred feet of nylon rope. This will easily hold twice your weight."

"Twice *my* weight?" Pete protested. "Why twice *my* weight? Why not twice your weight?"

"Because I am no good at athletics. You are," Jupiter told him. "We'll tie the rope round this corner post, then you will let yourself down and run for the police. We can't wait for Miss Agawam. The pursuit is getting too close."

Pete pulled the rope through his hands.

"It's too thin and slippery," he said. "I couldn't

hold on to it. It would cut right into me."

"You have gloves with leather palms. They will help. Wrap the rope round each hand and let it slide slowly through your palms."

Pete tried it. The gloves did help him get a grip on the thin nylon. At last he nodded. It could be done.

"All right," he said. "I'll do it. If you'll tell me just one thing."

"What is that?" Jupiter asked, busily tying one end of the rope to the corner of the minaret.

"We found some genuine gnomes, didn't we?"

"Genuine little people, yes," Jupiter said. "But I was wrong when I said their main purpose was to scare Miss Agawam into selling her house. They really were digging for treasure all along. It was very dense of me not to realize that from the first."

"Realize it?" Pete exclaimed. "How could you? I mean, why should anyone be digging for treasure under Miss Agawam's house?"

"They weren't. Not underneath the house, really." Jupiter sounded as if he thought Pete should have it all figured out for himself by now. "Where is the nearest treasure to here?"

"Oh, some place up in the mountains, I suppose."

"You're not thinking. The nearest treasure is in the bank just on the other side of Miss Agawam's house."

"In the bank?" Pete stared at him. "What do you mean by that?"

"You'd better get started quickly, or they'll find us," Jupiter said impatiently. "Go down as fast as you dare but don't take any chances."

"Don't worry, I won't," Pete said and lowered himself over the side of the narrow minaret.

He had decided to walk himself down—that is, to plant his feet against the wall, lean back, and walk down a step at a time, letting the rope move slowly through his gloved palms.

He tried not to look down at the hard, dark pavement far below. He concentrated on planting his feet against the rough stucco surface of the theatre.

One step at a time he eased himself down. He had progressed nearly half-way to the bottom when he heard shouts up above him. Jupiter yelled, a deep voice grunted, then there was silence. Pete's heart thudded. Had they found Jupiter up there? If so he had better hurry and get down. He'd——

Suddenly something shook the rope, nearly knocking him loose. Rawley's deep voice growled above him.

"You down there! You kid!"

Pete gulped. The rope shook again. Pete clung tight.

"Y-yes?" Pete said. "I'm here."

"Come back up."

"I'm going down," Pete said stubbornly.

"You'll go down all of a sudden!" growled the man. "I'll cut the rope if you don't come back."

Pete looked down. The ground was still thirty feet below him. If it had been deep grass, he might have risked the drop. But a cement pavement—he knew a couple of broken legs would be the least he'd get.

"Okay, kid." The voice came again. "I'll count three. Then I cut the rope."

"Wait a minute, wait a minute!" Pete shouted. "I'm coming. Give me time to get this rope tight round my hands. It's slipping."

"All right, but no tricks."

Pete had had an idea. It might not work, but it was the only thing he could think of. Hanging on by his left hand, he pulled his right glove off with his teeth. Then he reached in his pocket for his blue chalk.

Working swiftly, Pete made an enormous blue question mark, at least a yard high, on the dirty white face of the theatre. It was the only clue he could leave. Then he dropped the chalk and jammed his glove back on.

"Okay, kid!" The voice above sounded impatient. "Come on up, or down you go!"

"I'm coming! I'm coming!"

Hand over hand, Pete struggled upwards. As he got level with the opening in the minaret, strong hands reached out and dragged him in.

There were three men in the tower with Jupiter. Two of them were holding the First Investigator tightly. Jupiter looked scared and angry and indignant. Pete knew how he felt. He felt that way, too.

But what was it all about? First the gnomes, now these three men——

Pete started to ask a question. But Rawley interrupted him by shoving him forward.

259

Hand over hand, Pete struggled upwards.

"Get moving, kid," he said. "All right, Chuck, Driller, let's get these kids down into the cellar. We've got to get back to work and they can watch us."

The three men hustled Pete and Jupiter down the narrow stairs, then down some more stairs, until they found themselves in an extensive, concrete-lined cellar beside a couple of big, rusty boilers. Pete guessed they had once been used for heating the theatre.

On one wall were several closed doors. In faded lettering, they said, "Coal Bin No. 1", "Coal Bin No. 2" and "Coal Bin No. 3."

Rawley opened the door to Coal Bin No. 1, and pushed them inside.

Pete gave a grunt of astonishment. The four little men were sitting in a far corner playing cards. They showed little interest in the boys now, barely glancing up from their game. Several wheelbarrows, pickaxes and shovels and some large electric lanterns were strewn on the floor. But what surprised Pete most was a hole in the concrete wall, which must be the foundation of the theatre. Through it he could see a long dark tunnel.

Pete figured rapidly. The direction the tunnel was going would lead it to Miss Agawam's house. No, it would go underneath Miss Agawam's house to something beyond it.

And then at last Pete realized what Jupe had meant by saying the nearest treasure was in the bank.

The three men, and the strange little creatures

assisting them, were bank robbers. He and Jupe had stumbled on a brilliantly daring bank robbery!

13

A Sinister Plot is Revealed

PETE AND JUPITER sat on a pile of burlap sacks, leaning back against a concrete wall. Their hands and feet were tied, but they could talk. Except that Jupe didn't seem to feel much like talking.

Pete could see that he was annoyed at himself for not having figured out in the beginning what was happening. But how could you figure you were butting in on a bank robbery when you were only looking for some gnomes reported by an elderly lady who might actually be imagining them?

While he sat there, Pete had been working the whole thing out.

In the first place, Rawley was obviously in charge. The other two men took orders from him—the short, stocky one named Chuck and the small, wiry one called Driller. Driller had a thin moustache and a gold front tooth, and looked at the boys in a very ominous manner.

"Jupe," Pete whispered, "Rawley is really a bank robber, isn't he? He got the job as night watchman here so he could have a chance to rob the Third Merchants' Bank."

261

"That's it, Pete," Jupiter answered in a low voice. "I should have guessed something like this from the beginning. I had two essential facts. A bank on the corner—and someone digging very close to it. That should have told me all I needed to know. And instead I let myself be distracted by thoughts of gnomes."

"Even Sherlock Holmes might not have thought of it," Pete told him. "Those gnomes sure kept us from thinking of a bank robbery. But one thing I don't figure, Jupe—why are the gnomes just sitting around and not helping?"

"Because they aren't really part of the gang," Jupiter muttered, still sounding gloomy. "Obviously they were hired to frighten Miss Agawam and keep people from taking any talk of digging seriously."

"Oh." Pete pondered this. "I get it—I think. But how did Mr. Rawley get hold of the gnomes? Did they come all the way from the Black Forest?"

"Pete," Jupiter sighed, "I'm disappointed in you. Those gnomes never saw the Black Forest. They came straight out of those children's books Miss Agawam used to write. I deduced that as soon as I saw them in the yard."

He seemed to expect Pete to understand him, so Pete chewed on the statement for a while. The gnomes came out of Miss Agawam's books? It might be simple to Jupe, but Pete just couldn't figure it.

Meanwhile, preparations for the bank robbery were going ahead. The three men were busy digging at the other end of the tunnel, hauling the loose dirt out in

262

wheelbarrows. They dumped it outside, apparently into one of the other empty coal bins. Then they went back for another load.

"Only ten feet more, Driller!" Pete heard Chuck say as the two men passed in front of the boys.

"Then I can get to work with my tools, eh?" Driller said, and rubbed his hands. "I'll drill into that concrete vault like a dentist going into a tooth."

They kept on working, extending the tunnel the last few feet to the waiting bank vault. Meanwhile, the little men just took it easy, their share of the work done.

Another question occurred to Pete. He turned to Jupiter.

"Jupe——" he began. Then he stopped. Jupe was stretched out on the burlap bags, asleep!

Pete almost woke him up. What business did the First Investigator have going to sleep at a time like this? They needed his brains to get them out of this mess!

Then Pete realized that they had a long night ahead of them. They would need their energy for the critical moment when the bank had been robbed and the gang started to leave. So Jupiter had done the most sensible thing he could think of. He'd gone to sleep.

Just thinking about it made Pete sleepy. After all, it was pretty late. And since there wasn't anything else he could do——

Pete fell asleep, too.

How long he slept Pete didn't know, but when he

woke up he felt well rested. He was stiff, and his wrists and ankles hurt where they were tied, but his mind was alert again. He heard voices close to him.

He wriggled around and saw that Jupe was sitting up, holding a cup of soup in his tied hands. Mr. Rawley sat on a box beside Jupiter, looking in a very good humour.

The digging seemed to have stopped. The gnomes were sitting in a corner, eating sandwiches. Chuck and Driller were not in sight. Then Pete noticed a heavy electric cable snaking its way into the mouth of the tunnel. Very faintly he could hear grinding noises. That must be Driller, boring into the concrete side of the bank vault.

Jupiter noticed Pete sitting up and said, "Good morning, Pete. I hope you had a good sleep."

"Oh sure, fine and dandy," Pete grumbled, wriggling to get the stiffness out of his back. "The mattresses here are super. Can't be beat."

Mr. Rawley threw back his head and guffawed.

"You kids!" he said. "You give me a kick! I was pretty annoyed at you for butting in, but now that I have you safe and sound where you can't do any harm, no hard feelings."

"You had us fooled, all right," Jupiter told the man. "When I saw your gnomes playing games out in the yard, I thought Roger Agawam had hired them to scare his aunt. Then when I realized they had lured us into this old theatre, it finally came to me what the plot had to be."

"You sure did," Rawley said. "A little more luck on your side and you'd have had the cops down on us by now."

He turned to Pete.

"You got a mighty smart partner here," he said. "Even if he looks stupid most of the time. But that's good, that would help him in my business. People would never suspect him. If he'll throw in with me, I'll train him. In ten years he'll be the smartest criminal around."

"No thank you," Jupiter said politely. "A life of crime is hazardous and leads to ultimate disaster."

"Wow!" Rawley said. "Listen to that language. Kid, you could work right now with the biggest brains in the country. The idea is to plan everything ahead of time, like I did on this job. I'll live like a rich man for the rest of my life, and you—well, since you won't throw in with me I'd rather not say where you will be."

The words gave Pete a very crawly sensation.

"Pete has a lot of questions he'd like to ask," Jupiter said quickly. "Why don't you tell him how you came to figure out this bank robbery, Mr. Rawley?"

"Sure, kid," Rawley said. "Here, have a drink of soup."

He took the aluminium cup Jupe had been drinking from, filled it with hot soup from a vacuum bottle, and handed it to Pete.

"It's like this," Rawley said. "I was born and brought up right in the next block to this one. Forty years ago I was one of Miss Agawam's gnomes."

He chuckled. "Imagine me a gnome!" he said "But that's what she called us. Once a week she'd have a party for all the kids around, and serve ice cream and cookies, and read us her books."

Mr. Rawley went on with his story. When he was a boy, his father, a construction worker, had actually helped build the Moorish Theatre and the Third Merchants' Bank.

One day his father had happened to mention the bank's big underground vault. It had an enormous steel door, but the walls weren't steel at all—just concrete. They had never been strengthened, because the vault was considered to be too far underground for any bank robbers to get to it.

"But me," Mr. Rawley said, "I've been thinking about what my dad said all these years. I figured that if somebody started in Miss Agawam's cellar, they could dig right up to that bank vault and drill in through the concrete side.

"But Miss Agawam never moved. When the theatre shut down, I had a new idea. I figured a fellow could start digging from this building, dig right under Miss Agawam's house, and get to the bank vault with only a little more trouble.

"But then I got into some trouble with the law. As soon as I got out, I went to work on my scheme. I rounded up the gang I needed. Then I had to get into this theatre. I scared away two night watchmen by making strange noises. Finally, Mr. Jordan hired me

266

and I was ready to go."

Rawley related how he and Driller and Chuck had cut through the concrete wall, then begun tunnelling directly beneath Miss Agawam's house. The dirt they excavated had been stored in the locked empty coal bins, so that even if the new owner, Mr. Jordan had looked, he wouldn't have seen anything suspicious.

"So Mr. Jordan isn't in on this scheme?" Jupiter asked. "I thought he might be."

"No. I've played him for a sucker, just like I've played everyone else. Miss Agawam, for instance. I knew if she heard digging, she'd report it to the police. But Miss Agawam has this thing about believing in gnomes. So I brought around some gnomes to slip into her place at night and mess up her books and stuff. I had them dress up like those pictures in one of her books.

"I hoped to scare her into moving away. But suppose instead she reported to the police that gnomes were bothering her and digging under her house. Why, they might have taken her away to a hospital. Then I wouldn't have had a thing to worry about."

Rawley rocked with laughter.

"As it is," he said, "she stayed scared, but she got hold of you kids. You were more of a nuisance. But luckily we were able to nab you in time."

"Suppose Miss Agawam's nephew Roger had believed her?" Jupiter asked. "Suppose he'd stayed in the house and heard digging, too? The police might have believed him."

Rawley winked at him with elaborate slowness.

"I said I played everyone for a sucker, didn't I? I got the job here from Jordan. I fooled Miss Agawam. Well, I made a deal with Roger."

"A deal?" Pete exclaimed.

"Sure. I told him that Jordan had hired me to make Roger's aunt a little nervous, so she would sell the property. I said I wasn't going to hurt—just let her see some gnomes and hear some digging. Then she might sell out to Jordan in a hurry.

"Roger wanted her to sell and take the money while she could get it. So he agreed, as long as I promised not to hurt her. So naturally when she talked about gnomes and digging sounds he pretended he didn't believe a word of it."

Rawley looked pleased with himself.

"Golly, Jupe!" Pete said. "You were partly right about Roger, anyway. He was in on the scheme all along."

"You figured that?" Rawley asked Jupiter. "Kid, you're even smarter than I said. Throw in with me and we will stand the police of this country right on their heads. You have the brains for it."

"Well——" Jupiter looked thoughtful. Pete had an idea the notion of being a super-criminal rather attracted Jupiter. "Let me think about it a little more."

"Sure thing, kid. Well, I'm going to see if Driller and Chuck have bored through the cement wall into the vault yet."

268

As he turned to go, Pete stopped him with a question.

"I guess I understand the plot, and it's a pretty smart one," he said. "But where did you find the gnomes and how did you get them to co-operate?"

Rawley grinned. "They'll tell you," he said. He called to the group of little men. "Hey, Small Fry," he said. "Come here and talk to these two."

He disappeared into the tunnel. A gnome with fiery red eyes and dirty white beard came over and squatted on his heels, looking up at the boys.

"You boys gave us a lot of trouble," he said, in a high voice. "Nearly broke my arm, too. But I won't hold any grudges, because as soon as this is over you're going on a long sea voyage you won't come back from."

The little creature spoke good English, though with a certain European accent. Pete studied him in the dim light. The red eyes, the pointed ears, the big hairy hands—he couldn't imagine how such a creature could have gone around unnoticed. Except maybe by living underground.

"Listen," Pete said. "Are you a real gnome? Or what are you, anyway?"

The little man sniggered.

"Boy, have we had you guessing!" he said. "Watch!"

Deliberately, he tugged at one hairy ear. Pete felt a moment of horror as the ear came loose from his

269

head. Then he saw it was just a big, artificial ear that had been attached over a small, normal pink one.

Next the "gnome" pulled off a big hairy hand to reveal a tiny hand, smaller than a boy's. He pulled some false fangs out of his mouth. Finally, he carefully felt at one eye, twisted something loose and stared at Pete with a smirk.

"Look, kid, one red eye and no fangs!" he said. It was true that now he had only one red eye. The other was a normal blue.

"Tinted contact lenses," he said. He touched his nose. "Plastic nose," he said. "Artificial beard. Everything modelled right after those pictures in the old lady's books. I'm really a midget, kid, and if you call me a gnome again, I'll put a magic spell on you and turn you into a turnip."

"About the time I saw the midgets dart into the open door," Jupiter said. "Then it all came to me in one big flash. The bank—the digging—the gnomes—it all finally made sense."

"But it's too late," the midget said smugly. "You see, we only had to keep the old lady quiet, and things under control, until to-day. To-day we grab the loot and make our getaway. And it's Sunday, so nobody will know what's happened until to-morrow."

"Miss Agawam will miss us," Jupiter said, trying to sound confident. "She'll call the police."

"She won't. She's already beat it in her nephew's car. Probably thinks you ran away or something. We have everything worked out like a breeze, kid. We'll have twenty-four hours before the bank even knows it has been robbed."

Pete felt his heart drop. Jupiter started to say something, but at that moment Mr. Rawley emerged from the tunnel.

"Driller is through into the vault," he said. "We need some help in getting the money out. A couple of you midgets come along to give us a hand."

"May I come, too?" Jupiter spoke up. "I'd like to watch your technique, Mr. Rawley."

"Sure, kid," the big man said. "I still hope you'll throw in with us when you see how smooth we operate."

He cut the rope around Jupe's feet, leaving his hands tied. Jupiter followed Rawley and three of the midgets into the tunnel, leaving Pete alone with the one he had been talking to.

"We sure made suckers out of you!" the midget snickered. "Standing on each other's shoulders to tap on the window and make sure you saw us. Doing acrobatics on the lawn until you chased us. Then leading you in through the door, so we had you trapped. I have to hand it to you, though. You came pretty close to making a getaway."

"Thanks for nothing," Pete replied. "But why did you need to catch us?"

"Because this is the big night, like I said. If you'd heard digging, your partner would have tumbled and called the cops. We had to get you out of the way until we lifted the loot and made our getaway."

Pete was puzzled. "But look," he said. "How can you hope to avoid being caught by the police? Midgets are easy to find. The police will come straight to you when we tell them our story."

"If you *could* tell them your story!!" the little man retorted. "You won't be around to do any talking. But, supposing you did, and the police came after us. This is Hollywood, U.S.A., where they make all the movies, remember?"

"What of it?" Pete asked.

"Why, there are as many midgets in Hollywood as in the rest of the world put together. We are all hoping for jobs in the movies, or TV, or at Disneyland. About thirty of us live together in a special boarding house. Some of us have a little sideline—we sneak through skylights and open windows and lift stuff. Or we help out on a job like this one. Our size makes it easy for us to do things no ordinary man can.

"But us midgets are one big happy family, understand? None of us would tell on another. If anybody asks us, we don't know anything, didn't hear anything, and can't guess anything about any other midget."

"Besides," the tiny man went on, slipping on his artificial ear, "you can't identify any of us. Even if you ever get a chance to try. Which isn't very likely."

With that ominous remark, he got up and disappeared into the tunnel.

Jupiter meanwhile was standing in an enlarged space outside a concrete wall. A hole had been drilled through the concrete—a hole big enough for a small

272

boy to get through. Chuck and Driller, weary from their labours, were mopping their foreheads.

"We could make the hole bigger," Chuck told Rawley. "But it would take time. The midgets can climb through and hand out the loot."

"Right." Rawley boosted the tiny men one by one through the neatly drilled hole. Inside, their flashlights illuminated a large square room. Cash and securities were neatly stacked on shelves. Sacks of silver coins lined the floor.

"Quarter of a million!" Rawley gloated. "Pay day is Monday—end of the month. Big aeroplane factory down the street banks here."

With keen interest Jupiter watched the midgets pass the bundles of cash and securities through the hole. The three men loaded them into burlap bags. Finally everything of value was taken, except the bags of coins.

"Leave the coins," Chuck suggested. "Too heavy. We have enough."

"Right," Rawley said. "No, hand out two sacks of coins."

With much huffing and puffing, the little men managed to push two heavy bags of silver through the hole. Then they climbed out.

When they had trundled everything in wheelbarrows back to the coal bin, Rawley cut open one bundle and handed a sheaf of bills to each midget.

"There you are, ten thousand dollars apiece," he

said. "Be careful how you spend it. Now get out of those gnome outfits. We're almost ready to leave."

"Not any too soon," Driller muttered. "We're running behind schedule."

Rawley ignored him and turned to Jupiter.

"Well, kid?" he asked. "Now that you've seen how we operate, are you going to throw in with us? You'll be a rich man—you have the brains to make a big-time criminal."

Pete wondered what Jupiter would say. He couldn't believe Jupiter would agree, but——

"I'd like to think about it a little more," Jupiter said. "After I have seen how you organize your getaway. After all, commission of a crime is only half the job. Getting away is equally important and it's where most criminals fall down."

Rawley laughed.

"I told you he had brains," he said to the others. "Okay, we'll take you with us on our getaway. Only you'll have to travel in disguise, sort of. Chuck—Driller—dress 'em up."

At that the two men suddenly pounced on the boys. They slid two large burlap sacks over their heads, down to their feet, where they tied the ends of the bags securely.

"We'll load 'em on the truck and take 'em with us," Rawley said. "Let's get busy."

Driller objected. The kids would be a nuisance. Why not just leave them where they were and. . . . His voice dropped so Pete, inside the bag, couldn't hear the rest of what he said. But he heard Rawley laugh.

"No need for that," he said. "Why do you think I took those two bags of silver? Any time we want to get rid of them we just tie the bags round their feet and drop them over the side of the ship.

"They'll be the two richest kids in Davy Jones's locker!"

14

Bob Hunts for His Friends

BOB ANDREWS woke slowly to Sunday morning sunshine pouring in his window. For a moment he lay still, lazily enjoying that moment when you aren't quite awake and have nothing on your mind.

Then a thought hit him like a bumble-bee sting and he leaped out of bed. Jupiter and Pete! What had happened during the night? Had they discovered anything? Had they left a message?

He slipped into his clothes. Automatically pushing his walkie-talkie into a pocket, he went downstairs. His mother was cooking pancakes in the kitchen, and the aroma of maple syrup tickled his nose.

"Any message from Jupiter, Mom?" Bob asked.

"No, he hasn't phoned anything about Green Gate

One or Purple Gate Eight or anything like that. So you can just sit down and eat these nice pancakes I've fixed, and not hurry over to that junk yard."

"It's a salvage yard, Mom, and we don't have any Purple Gate Eight," Bob corrected, loading a plate with pancakes.

As long as Jupiter hadn't phoned, things must be all right. Maybe they had had a quiet night and were still asleep. Or maybe they had left a message at the salvage yard.

He ate without hurrying, and then biked over to The Jones Salvage Yard. The main gate was open and Hans was in the yard washing the small truck.

"Any phone call from Jupe?" Bob asked.

"No call, all is quiet I guess," Hans said.

"He ought to be up by now." Bob's forehead furrowed. "I better call, then we'll go down and get him. We're going to take more lessons in scuba diving today."

He entered the little office and dialled Miss Agatha Agawam's number. It rang and rang but, to his amazement, there was no answer. He tried again. Still no answer. Bob began to feel the first sensations of alarm.

"They don't answer," he told Hans. "Where could they be? I mean, Miss Agawam ought to be home. If she's gone, too——"

Hans looked suddenly very serious.

"They went to catch gnomes. I think gnomes have caught them!" he said grimly.

276

"We'd better go down and see what's happening," Bob said. "Let's get there as fast as we can."

"You bet your shoes!" Hans said.

At that moment the telephone rang loudly.

"Maybe that's Jupiter now!" Bob cried. He raced inside and scooped up the phone.

"Hello?" he said. "Jones Salvage Yard."

"Excuse, please, is Jupiter-san present?" asked a boy's voice, and Bob recognized it as Taro Togati.

"No, he's out on a case. This is Bob Andrews."

"Please give Jupiter-san message. Message is this. My father and guards search museum all last night for Golden Belt. They look behind pictures and in every place possible."

"And they found it?" Bob asked excitedly.

"Alas, no. They found nothing. My father is again angry at himself for listening to the foolishness of boys. I am in disgrace, too. But I still thin! it a very good idea Jupiter-san had. Tell him, though, belt was not found."

"I'll tell him when I see him," Bob said. He hung up and went out and climbed into the truck. This news would really make Jupiter gloomy. Well, it *had* been a good idea that the belt was hidden in the museum all along. Jupe wasn't wrong often, but this time it certainly seemed he had been.

They started downtown with a roar. Traffic on the Los Angeles freeways was lighter than usual, and they made such speed that the old truck rattled and groaned. Forty-five minutes later they pulled up outside Miss Agatha Agawam's old house in the downtown district.

Before the motor stopped, Bob had hopped out of the truck and was ringing the bell.

He pressed a long time, without getting an answer.

By now Bob was very much alarmed.

He called to Hans. As Hans climbed out of the truck, Bob noticed that the gate was not quite shut. He pushed it open, and he and Hans hurried up to the porch.

They rang the doorbell long and loudly. Silence answered them.

"Try the door," Hans suggested. "Maybe they are inside turned to rocks."

Hans couldn't seem to get over the idea that the gnomes had turned Pete and Jupe into rocks. But Bob tried the door. To his surprise it opened. He called out several times.

Only a faint echo of his own voice replied.

Desperate with anxiety, Bob and Hans searched the whole house, including the cellar. There was no trace anywhere of Pete and Jupiter. Or Miss Agawam either. The only things they found were the zipper bags and the open leather kit in the room upstairs.

"Jupe and Pete saw something and they went to investigate!" Bob said, thinking swiftly now. "Maybe Miss Agawam followed them and got caught, too! We have to look for them!"

"Gnomes have caught them all," Hans said. He sounded very gloomy. It was obvious Hans had a great

278

respect for gnomes and their powers.

"We have to look!" Bob said worriedly. He didn't actually believe Pete and Jupe had been turned into rocks, but on the other hand, something pretty serious must have happened to them. "First we search the outside yard."

They searched the outside yard without finding a clue until Bob saw Jupiter's camera dangling from a bush at the corner of the house. He pounced on it.

"Jupe was out here!" he said. "He took a picture of something. Let's see what he photographed!"

It took only seconds to pull the developed picture out. But when they saw it they both gulped.

It was a picture of a wild-eyed gnome, with hairy ears and fanglike front teeth, peering in at a window!

"Wow!" Hans said. "What did I tell you, Bob? Gnomes have got Pete and Jupe for sure."

"Maybe," Bob said, not knowing what to think now. "Just the same we have to hunt for them. We'll get the police and——"

But the thought of showing that picture to the police made him hesitate. No, he and Hans would look first, he decided.

"Listen, Hans," Bob said swiftly. "They aren't in the house or the yard. But they went out last night to catch something and didn't come back. Maybe they left a clue, or maybe someone saw them. First we'll go all round this block. Then the next. We'll ask anyone we see if they saw or heard anything in the night."

Bob led the way to the street. The theatre end was

closest so he started that way. The street was quiet, and they didn't see any people around to ask nor any signs of a clue. As they came opposite the front of the Moorish Theatre, Bob stepped on something that crunched under his shoe.

He looked down. Then he gave a yell. He had stepped on a piece of broken blue chalk.

"Pete's special chalk!" he told Hans. "Pete was around here somewhere last night."

"Look here!" Hans said. Close to the wall lay the other half of the broken blue chalk.

"It was all one piece and it broke," Bob said. "Hans, look at this. See? There is a mark on the sidewalk where it fell and broke!"

"Fall? Where did it fall from?" Hans asked.

But already Bob was backing away, staring upwards. No open windows, no places where a boy Pete's size might be hiding——

Then he saw it. It was almost invisible, because of the dirt that had accumulated on the white front of the theatre. But it was there:

?

An enormous question mark in blue chalk. Pete's special sign!

It meant that somehow, sometime last night Pete had been half-way up the front wall of the closed theatre!

For the life of him, Bob couldn't figure out how this was possible, but the mark meant a lot just the same. It meant that there was a chance Pete and Jupiter might be inside now.

"Hans, we have to get inside the theatre!" Bob said tensely.

"Okay, I will pull boards off and break in the door," Hans said. He started to pull loose the boards that sealed up the main entrance. Bob stopped him.

"If they're inside, there's probably a door open," he said. "I think I know where it is."

He led Hans round the buidling and almost to the alley that ran behind the theatre and Miss Agawam's house.

"Shhh!" he said. "Now we have to take security measures."

From the breast pocket of his jacket he took a small round mirror. It was a piece of new equipment Jupe had issued to The Three Investigators just that week.

Bob lay down on his stomach on the pavement and wriggled up to the corner where the alley began. Very cautiously he thrust the mirror out beyond the corner and angled it so that he could see the length of the alley.

There was something there. A green truck stood just outside the stage door where he and the others had been the day before!

Bob watched in the mirror with growing excitement. He was surprised to see a big man come out of the theatre, lugging a large, heavy canvas sack. It was Mr. Rawley.

"Bob, you see something?" Hans asked.

"I see the night watchman doing something mighty peculiar. I think he's stealing something," Bob whispered, still flat on the pavement. "Anyway, I'm positive Pete and Jupiter are inside."

"Well, what do we wait for? We will go and get them." Hans flexed his powerful muscles.

"No, we need the police. There might be a whole lot of them in there—yes, here come two more men carrying burlap bags. Find some policemen and hurry back, Hans. I'll stay on watch."

"Okay," Hans grumbled, obviously sure he could do a better job by himself. He hurried away. Bob kept watch.

From time to time the men glanced sharply up and down the alley. But they did not notice the small mirror held just above the pavement. The three—one thin and wiry, one short and squat, and the big, heavyset Mr. Rawley—continued carrying out burlap sacks and stowing them in the truck.

Bob began to fidget. Time was running out. Why didn't Hans come back with a policeman?

Now the three men seemed to have finished loading the truck. They held a brief consultation. Then they went back inside and this time two of them emerged with a bigger burlap sack.

The burlap sack wriggled! It tried to tear itself loose.

The man was carrying a heavy canvas sack.

The men shoved it into the truck and went back for a similar sack, even stouter and heavier. This one also wriggled as it went into the truck.

Bob felt frustrated. He was positive Pete and Jupiter were in those last two sacks, and he couldn't do a thing to help them. If Hans had been there, they could have rushed the men and possibly freed his friends. But he'd sent Hans away to find a policeman. And Bob knew that if he tried to help by himself, he'd just be caught, too.

One of the men swung the rear door of the truck shut. All three got in the front seat. An instant later it was moving away down the alley.

Jupiter and Pete were in it and he'd lost his chance to rescue them!

15

The Trail is Lost

JUPITER AND PETE were very uncomfortable. Hands and feet tied, burlap sacks scratching their faces, they lay on bundles of money and securities stolen from the Third Merchants' Bank.

Pete could feel Jupe moving beside him. Jupe was testing his bonds.

"Jupe," Pete whispered through the sack. "Where do you think they are taking us?"

"A ship was mentioned," Jupe whispered back. "Probably they are going to flee by water."

"Did you hear what Mr. Rawley said about tying sacks of silver to our feet and dropping us overboard?"

"I heard," Jupiter answered. "However, remember that the famous magician, Harry Houdini, used to let himself be manacled with handcuffs, sealed in a milk can, and tossed into the water. He always came out alive."

"That would make me feel a lot better if I was Harry Houdini," Pete growled. "But I'm Pete Crenshaw and I haven't had any practice. I don't want to be the richest kid in Davy Jones's locker."

They were interrupted by a giggle. The four midgets had put on the clothing of small boys and were riding in the back of the truck with the two captives. Now one of them spoke.

"Maybe you'll be lucky," he said in his high, childlike voice. "Maybe Mr. Rawley will sell you for slaves somewhere in Asia. They still have slaves back in the deserts of Arabia."

Pete was silent, mulling this over. Did he want to be a slave to some faraway Arabian sheik? Or would he rather be the main course for a school of fish? Neither alternative appealed to him in the slightest.

Now the midgets were silent. The truck full of stolen money jolted along. Then it slowed for a moment.

"All right, Small Fry, hop out and catch your bus!"

285

came Rawley's booming voice from up front. "You've been paid. Remember, don't let anyone see you spending the money for a long time."

"We'll hide it, don't worry," one midget promised.

"And don't talk! Keep your lips buttoned!" snapped Chuck.

"We never talk to police," said the midget. "Us midgets stick together. They'll go crazy trying to pin anything on us."

With that the truck slowed still more, the rear door opened, and one by one the midgets hopped out. The door slammed shut. The truck picked up speed. In a moment it went up a slope and turned on to a smoother road. Its speed increased. Obviously they were now on a freeway, probably leading to the shore of the Pacific Ocean, a few miles away. There, no doubt, a ship was waiting for the bank robbers.

"A slave, or a meal for fish," Pete groaned. "Jupe, we're done for. Why did we ever start this investigation business anyway?"

"For excitement," Jupiter answered, his voice muffled. "And to use our wits."

"I've had enough excitement for a thousand years, and my wits are frozen solid," Pete complained. "The bank robbers have got away free and clear. I did hope Bob would see the only clue I could leave, but it was a pretty far-fetched hope. Well, say something!" he urged, irritated by his friend's silence. "At least tell me we have a chance!"

"I can't," Jupiter said honestly. "I was just thinking that Mr. Rawley has really been very clever."

At that moment, a car's length behind, Bob Andrews and Hans were grimly following them.

Hans had returned, unable to find a policeman anywhere, just as Bob saw the green truck drive down the alley. Bob started to tell Hans he should have found a telephone and called the police. Then he realized that in such a quiet neighbourhood, with everything closed for Sunday, a telephone was probably as unlikely to be found as a policeman.

So he grabbed Hans and led him to the waiting salvage-yard truck. They hopped in and started off.

The green truck had a blue rear door, apparently a replacement after an accident, making it easy to follow. Sunday morning traffic was light, and there was nothing about the salvage yard's ramshackle old truck to arouse suspicion.

"Don't lose them, Hans!" Bob urged. "Pete and Jupiter are in that truck!"

"I could ram it," Hans said hopefully. "Knock it off the road. That would stop it for sure."

"And maybe kill Jupe and Pete!" Bob said. "You know that wouldn't work. Follow it until it stops."

So they drove slowly along, following the truck. After five minutes it slowed down and they hoped it would stop. Instead, the rear door opened and four small boys hopped out and marched to a bus stop.

"By Jiminy!" Hans muttered grimly. "Little boys up to mischief. What shall I do, Bob? Grab them, and make them talk?"

287

"No, no!" Bob replied. "Then we'll lose the truck."

An instant later the green truck pulled on to a freeway and started roaring west, in the direction of the ocean.

Startled, Hans just barely got on to the freeway in time to avoid losing them. Now, the truck ahead was going so fast that Hans could hardly keep up.

"I wonder if Jupe or Pete can use their walkie-talkies," Bob said, remembering a previous occasion when these devices had come in handy. "I'll listen in and see."

He tugged his walkie-talkie from his pocket, pushed the *On* button, and held it to his ear. For a moment he just heard humming.

Then to his surprise he made out a man's voice, very loud, which he recognized as Rawley's. Apparently Rawley was using a powerful walkie-talkie, operating on the Citizen's Band like Bob's.

"Hello, Harbour!" he was saying. "Hello, Harbour! This is Operation Tunnel calling. Can you read me? Come in. Come in."

Bob listened intently. In a moment a fainter voice answered.

"Hello, Operation Tunnel. This is Harbour, standing by. Did Operation Tunnel go off successfully?"

"Hello Harbour!" That was Rawley's voice again. "Couldn't be smoother. Except that we picked up a couple of passengers. We can decide what to do with them when we get aboard. That is all. Will broadcast again when we reach dock. Over and out."

With that the walkie-talkie went dead.

Immediately there was a loud bang. Bob ducked. The men ahead must have seen them and fired at them!

The salvage-yard truck was wobbling. Hans steered it on to the safety strip alongside the road.

"We go too fast," he said. "Bob, we have a blow-out. We must stop."

An instant later the green truck with the blue door, carrying Pete and Jupiter, had disappeared into the distance.

16

Desperate Chances

HANS PUT ON the spare tyre as swiftly as he could. But it took at least ten minutes and by then, of course, the green truck was miles away.

They had lost Jupiter and Pete. Bob had a funny sinking feeling he would never see them again.

"What do we do now, Bob?" Hans asked when they were back in the front seat. "Go for the police?"

"I forgot to write down the licence number of that truck," Bob confessed, feeling very sheepish. "We were so busy following it. There's nothing much we could tell the police."

"Well, they go this way, so we must go this way," Hans said. He let in the gears and the truck moved back on to the freeway, heading west.

Bob was thinking furiously. The road they were on led to the Pacific Ocean. One branch, farther on, would take them to the charming seaside town of Long Beach. Another branch would take them to San Pedro Harbour, the official shipping port for the city of Los Angeles.

On the walkie-talkie the voice had mentioned a harbour. Long Beach wasn't a harbour. San Pedro was. And it was the only one in that direction.

"Hans, head for San Pedro," he directed.

"Okay, Bob," Hans agreed.

They continued roaring along at the greatest speed the old truck was capable of. Bob meanwhile was wracking his brains trying to figure out what could have happened.

Pete and Jupiter had set out to watch for gnomes. They had wound up in burlap sacks in a truck driven by Mr. Rawley, the night watchman of the Moorish Theatre. The strange series of events which had caused all this was impossible to imagine.

He only knew that his friends were in serious trouble and there was no one who could rescue them except himself. The thought made him feel extremely helpless.

Presently they came into the outskirts of San Pedro, its fields dotted by great derricks pumping up oil from far underground. They drove quickly through town to the harbour. It was not a very scenic spot, being mostly man-made, but it was crowded with freighters at the piers and at anchor in the dingy grey water.

Some fishing boats were also anchored in the harbour, and a few small craft were moving back and forth.

Hans stopped the truck and they both stared helplessly about.

Pete and Jupiter were destined for one of those ships, or maybe one of those fishing boats. They'd be taken aboard and never come back. If only there was some way to know which ship it was!

"I guess we are licked, Bob," Hans said. "There is no way to find that truck now. I look in every street and do not see it."

"It's at some pier," Bob said. "The walkie-talkie told us that much. But there are a lot of piers in San Pedro. By the time we examined them all——" Then he jumped as if stung.

"The walkie-talkie!" he said. "We heard them say they'd communicate again when they got here!"

He was in such a hurry it took him an extra couple of seconds to get the little instrument turned on. At first he heard nothing. Breathing hard, he held it close to his ear. Then a voice spoke.

"Operation Tunnel!" it said. "We have lowered boat and will pick you up at Pier 37 in five minutes. Have all luggage including passengers ready for immediate loading."

"This is Operation Tunnel," answered Rawley's

voice. "We have you in sight. All luggage and passengers are waiting in truck, ready for loading."

"Very good," said the other voice. "No more communication. As we approach, wave a white handkerchief three times to indicate all is clear. Over and out."

The voices ended. But Bob was quivering with excitement.

"The truck is at Pier 37," he told Hans. "We have just five minutes, that's all. Where's Pier 37?"

"I do not know," Hans admitted. "I am not acquainted with San Pedro."

"We have to find someone to ask!" Bob panted. "A police officer if we can find one. Start up, Hans, and keep a sharp eye."

Hans started the truck and they moved slowly down the street, looking for someone to ask directions of. But it was Sunday morning and pedestrians were remarkably few. Then they saw a police patrol car turn into the street ahead of them.

"Pull up beside that car, Hans!" Bob yelled. "Honk like anything!"

Hans gunned the motor. The old truck rumbled up, alongside the sleek little police car, its horn going *grr-waaah*! *grr-waaah*!

"Please, officer!" Bob yelled. "Where is Pier 37? It's a matter of life and death!"

"Pier 37?" The officer at the wheel pointed behind them. "Three blocks that way, then down the street towards the harbour. No, that's a one-way street. Go

292

four blocks, turn down to the harbour, come back a block and——"

"Thanks!" Bob shouted. "Follow us! Two boys are in terrible danger!"

The truck roared away, leaving the officer still speaking. He blinked as the truck made a U-turn in the middle of the street, practically on two wheels, and roared away.

"Hey! That's illegal!" the officer said to his partner. Then he started the car, made a U-turn also and raced after them.

Hans sped down three blocks.

"Turn here!" Bob yelled. "It's a one-way street, but it's the quickest way, and our time is almost up!"

A small sign said "Pier 37", and an arrow pointed down the street. They went a block, then with a groan of dismay Hans brought the truck to a squealing stop.

Pier 37 was ahead of them, all right. But the entrance to it was blocked by a heavy iron-and-wire gate. The gate was padlocked.

Beyond it they could see the green truck with the blue door. A heavy-set man leaned against the front bumper, casually waving a white handkerchief. Only a hundred yards out in the water a dilapidated motor launch was churning towards the pier.

"We are locked out, Bob!" Hans said. "They have Pete and Jupe for sure!!"

At that moment the police car roared up beside them.

"You're under arrest!" shouted the officer at the wheel. "You made a U-turn, you were speeding, and you went down a one-way street the wrong way! Let me see your licence."

"We have no time!" Hans yelled. "We must get out on Pier 37 quick!"

"They're not loading to-day," the other officer said. "And you've broken the law. Now let's see your licence."

"Officer, you don't understand! The men in that truck are kidnapping two boys!" Bob yelled, poking his head around Hans. "Please help us to stop them!"

"Fancy stories won't help you get out of this one!" the officer growled. "Now, mister, let me see your licence."

With every second that passed, the launch drew closer to the pier.

"Hans!" Bob shouted with a sudden inspiration. "Drive fast! Break the gate down!"

"Okay, Bob, good idea!" Hans grunted. He stepped hard on the gas pedal and the truck shot ahead, leaving the policemen shouting after them.

As the big bumpers hit the middle of the locked gate, there was a noise like a shrill scream. Then gate and fence collapsed. The truck went forward a few feet, then the wire of the fence wrapped round the wheels, and it stalled, still fifty feet from the green truck.

"Come on, Bob!" Hans roared. He leaped out and dashed forward, Bob at his heels.

Hans bore down on Rawley like a runaway bull. Startled, Rawley saw him coming, and reached for something in his pocket, probably a gun. But before he could get it out, Hans had wrapped powerful arms round him, picked him up like a child and thrown him into the harbour. Rawley went under and came up spluttering. The oncoming launch stopped, and the men on it hauled him aboard.

Now Chuck and Driller, armed with a wrench and tyre-iron, jumped down from the truck, and rushed at Hans. Hans deftly ducked their blows, spun them round, and caught each by the collar. He marched them to the edge of the pier and threw them into the water.

Meanwhile, Bob was busy at the rear door of the truck. He got it open and yelled inside, "Pete! Jupe! Is that you?"

"Bob!" It was Jupiter's muffled voice. "Get us out of these bags!"

"Rah for Bob!" said Pete, more faintly because Jupiter was partly lying on him.

Meanwhile, the launch picked up Chuck and Driller and turned at high speed, heading for a fishing boat out in the harbour.

Having seen Han's strength, the two police officers approached him cautiously, waving revolvers.

"You're under arrest!" one of them shouted. "I don't know how many laws you've broken, but it's plenty, I know that."

"Ha!" Hans snorted. He pointed to the departing

295

launch. "You catch that boat. Then you have the right fellows.

Unnoticed, Bob was busy with his knife, cutting the burlap bags off Jupiter and Pete, then freeing their hands and feet. The two boys stood up and stretched, looking very tousled. They blinked their eyes while getting used to the light..

The second police officer noticed the boys emerging from the sacks, and he came over looking puzzled.

"Say, what's going on here, anyway?" he asked. "What were you kids doing in those sacks? Is this some kind of stunt?"

Jupiter drew himself up and mustered all of his dignity. He reached inside the truck for a burlap sack and, taking Bob's knife, cut a slit in it. Bundles of bills tumbled out on the pier. Then he took out one of The Three Investigators' business cards. He handed it to the officer.

"The Three Investigators have just finished solving a bad case of gnomes," he said in a grand manner. "They have also saved the loot from a daring bank robbery. The men who committed it are now trying to escape," he told the flabbergasted officers, "so we are turning the case over to the proper authorities. I think that covers everything."

Pete and Bob and Hans gazed at him in admiration. They had never seen Jupe look more impressive.

When it came to being dignified, you couldn't beat Jupiter Jones!

17

Surprise Attack

SIX DAYS had passed since that exciting Sunday. After Jupiter had said, "I think that covers everything," the boys had had to answer about a million questions.

Eventually the police agreed that they had indeed successfully prevented the thieves from getting away with the loot from the Third Merchants' Bank. They were sceptical at first about the part involving the "gnomes", but were finally convinced when Miss Agawam came forth to back up their story.

However, the police did not succeed in capturing the criminals. Rawley, Chuck and Driller got away by boat in a light fog that sprang up while the police were still questioning The Three Investigators. As for the midgets who impersonated gnomes, the wily little men simply denied everything. The police went to the theatrical boarding house where most midgets stayed in Hollywood. Every one of them had several friends who swore he hadn't been out of the house during the time of the bank robbery. No one could shake their stories, and it was impossible to make any arrests.

During most of the six days that had passed, Jupiter had moped and acted grumpy. The fact is, he was angry at himself.

While it was true Jupe had finally deduced that the gnomes were disguised midgets, and then had guessed a bank robbery was in progress, he had done so only moments before he had been captured.

It was Pete who had left the clue on the outside wall of the theatre. It was Bob who had found the clue. It was Bob and Hans who had saved Jupiter and Pete.

The truth was that Jupiter Jones, First Investigator, had not shone brightly in the case of Miss Agawam's "gnomes", or at least he didn't think so. And just to make things worse, his solution of the disappearance of the Golden Belt had also been wrong, in spite of his excellent logic. For Jupiter, this was a hard pill to swallow. Even the warm praise Miss Agawam had given them all only softened Jupiter's mood a little.

Something had to happen to get Jupiter back to feeling his normal self, and Bob and Pete hoped it would happen soon.

The following Saturday afternoon, after the three boys had put in a hard morning rebuilding some damaged junk, Bob, Pete and Jupe were taking it easy in the hidden workshop section of the salvage yard. Hard work with his hands had helped make Jupe a bit more cheerful, and he and Pete were filling in added details for Bob of their adventures in the old Moorish Theatre.

"I'm surprised the police haven't located Rawley, or at least that fellow Driller by now," Pete commented. "Sooner or later Interpol will spot him. After

298

all, that gold tooth of Driller's should make him pretty conspicuous."

"Lots of people have gold teeth," Bob said. "Even a little Cub Scout I bumped into at the museum had a gold tooth. Why, Jupe, what's the matter?"

Jupiter was acting very strangely. He had leaped to his feet and was staring at Bob as if he had never seen him before.

"You saw a little Cub Scout with a gold tooth?" he asked, his face pink with excitement. He leaned over and beat his fists on their printing press. "Bob!" he groaned. "Why didn't you tell me at the time? *Why didn't you tell me?*"

"About seeing a Cub Scout with a gold tooth?" Bob asked, rather startled by Jupiter's actions. "I didn't think it was important . . . and I never thought of it again until right now."

"But don't you realize?" Jupiter said. "If you had told me, I could have——"

At that moment Mrs. Jones's powerful voice interrupted them, announcing a visitor. It turned out to be the Japanese boy, Taro Togati, looking very downcast.

"Jupiter-san," he said, making a little bow. "Bob-san. Pete-san. I come to say good-bye. My father is in disgrace. We return to Japan."

"What's the matter, Taro?" Jupiter asked. "Is the exhibition of the jewels being abandoned?"

"Ah, no." The small Japanese boy shook his head. "But you know the Golden Belt has never been found.

It was not, alas, inside the museum as you so cleverly suggested. The guards have been proved innocent. And no new suspects were found. So the Nagasami Jewellery Company dismisses my father as chief detective. He is much disgraced. He is a man half dead."

The boys were sorry to hear this news. They liked little Taro. They knew his father had done the best he could—the gang that had robbed the Peterson Museum was just too smart.

However, Jupe was acting peculiarly. He was pinching his lower lip, setting his mental machinery in motion. His eyes were bright. All of his gloominess of the past week seemed gone.

"Taro!" he said. "To-morrow is the last day of the exhibition, right?"

"Ah, so," Taro nodded. "Sunday night it closes. Sunday night my honourable father and I fly back to Japan. So I come to-day to say good-bye to my only American friends."

"Didn't I read in the paper," Jupiter asked, "that tomorrow is going to be Children's Day? All children under twelve admitted free, the rest at half fare?"

"Yes," agreed Taro. "Last time it was, what you call big bust. So they decide to have another Children's Day."

"Then we have no time to lose! Taro, I have an idea. Will your father give me some co-operation?"

"Co-operation?" Taro did not quite grasp the word.

"Will he work with me on my idea?"

"Oh, yes!" Taro bobbed his head vigorously. "My

300

father desperate. He say police not solve case, he willing to try boys now."

"Then let's go!" Jupe leaped up. "You have a car?"

"My father send me in car with driver."

"Good. Bob, Pete—you wait for us. I may be gone all afternoon. Bob, keep writing up your notes so we can give this case to Mr. Hitchcock to read. Pete, keep on rubbing down that rusty power mower. We'll make ten dollars out of that. Get permission to stay here all night, if necessary."

With that, leaving Bob and Pete with their mouths hanging open, Jupiter was gone, tugging Taro Togati behind him.

It took Bob and Pete a minute to recover their voices.

"Well!" Pete said. "What was that all about?"

"Darned if I know," Bob answered. "All of a sudden something seemed to bite Jupe. I guess all we can do is wait until he gets back."

The mystery became greater when they received a telephone call from Jupiter in the latter part of the afternoon.

"Test all secret entrances and exits, except Emergency One and Secret Four," he ordered, referring to their escape and entry routes for use only under the most desperate conditions. "Use Green Gate One, Tunnel Two, Red Gate Rover, and Easy Three. Go in and out several times. Make sure they are all working smoothly."

That was all he would say. He hung up before they could ask questions.

What Jupiter had in mind was certainly beyond Pete and Bob. But they obeyed. They went in through Green Gate One—two boards of the fence painted green—and crawled in through the corrugated pipe of Tunnel Two.

Next they tried Red Gate Rover. This one consisted of three boards painted red as part of a scene of the San Francisco fire of 1906. A little dog sat watching the fire, and by pressing his eye they made the boards swing up. Once through, they crawled round and between and under junk stacked with seeming carelessness, until they reached the side of Headquarters. Here a panel admitted them.

Easy Three was the simplest entrance. A big oak door, still on its hinges, leaned against some timber in the yard. A big rusty key, hidden in a barrel filled with rusty metal, opened the door. Behind it, a short passageway led to the original side door of the mobile home trailer that had been turned into Headquarters. Easy Three was used only when the yard was deserted and no one was looking.

Neither Bob nor Pete was happy about following Jupe's instructions, but he was head of the firm and they did what he said. They tested each entrance three times. Then they waited again.

It was not until Mrs. Jones had held up supper almost an hour that Jupiter returned, looking hot but triumphant. Surprisingly he came in a taxicab. The

302

cab drew up directly in front of the Jones's cottage and Jupe got out and paid the driver with a flourish. Bob and Pete were startled to see the cab then stop around the corner and little Taro creep up and scuttle into the house by the back door.

"Mercy and goodness and sweetness and light!" Mrs. Jones exclaimed as Jupiter came in. "What in the world are you up to now, Jupiter? You're wearing your best jacket and it will hardly button around your waist. You're positively fat."

Being called fat was one thing Jupiter disliked. He didn't mind being called stocky or muscular, but fat —no. However, now he just grinned.

"If you're getting mixed up in another bank robbery, Jupiter my boy," said Mr. Jones, a small man with a large black moustache, who liked to talk in flowing English, "let me say that I am unalterably opposed. In other words, I disapprove. To put the matter simply, I forbid it."

"I'm just trying to help out Taro here," Jupiter said, putting a hand on the Japanese boy's shoulder. "His father is in a little trouble. He's misplaced a belt and I want to help him find it."

"Hmm." Mr. Jones thought about the remark until he finished serving the roast beef and mashed potatoes. "Misplaced a belt. I have turned that remark over in my mind several times and I can find no sinister aspects to it, so you may proceed."

The rest of the meal went swiftly. Jupiter and Taro both seemed distracted, and Jupiter didn't give Pete

303

and Bob any clues as to what was in his mind. Also, he kept his jacket tightly buttoned, though it was a hot evening.

As the sky started to darken, Jupiter got up.

"If you'll excuse us, Aunt Mathilda and Uncle Titus," he said, "we're going to have a meeting in the yard."

"Oh yes, your club," his aunt said vaguely. She still clung to her original notion that the investigation firm was a club. "Go right ahead, boys, Titus and I will do the dishes."

"I hope you can help this lad's father find his lost belt," Titus Jones said, putting his hand on Taro's shoulder. "Well, run along."

"Er—for special reasons," Jupiter said, "we don't want anyone to know we have a guest. So I'm going to get Hans and Konrad to carry Taro over in a cardboard box."

This seemed peculiar to Bob and Pete, but Mr. and Mrs. Jones merely nodded. They were used to the odd things Jupiter sometimes did.

So presently Bob, Pete and Jupiter, followed by Hans and Konrad carrying a large box, assembled in the workshop area inside the yard. The men put the box down, and Taro crawled out.

As soon as the two yard helpers had left, Jupiter led the three boys into Headquarters through Tunnel Two.

Once they were all inside, Jupiter asked, "Did you carry out my orders?"

Pete and Bob said they had.

"But we didn't want to," Pete grumbled. "Some kids were flying a kite across the road and they may have seen us going in and out of our secret entrances."

"It was probably some of Skinny Norris' gang spying on us," Bob explained. "But you said to do it, so we did."

"Excellent." Jupiter seemed pleased. "No organization can function unless orders are obeyed. I have had a very interesting afternoon, about which I will tell you later. Now let us tell Taro about some of our adventures."

Jupe's orders seemed to make less and less sense. However, Pete and Bob obeyed. Taro Togati sat silent, listening to their accounts of various cases they had solved. He was especially intrigued by *The Mystery of the Stuttering Parrot*, for he had a trained parrot at home, he told them.

It got darker and darker outside. Through the overhead skylight they could see the night sky turn a deep black.

Then, and only then, did Jupiter unbutton his jacket. They could see what had made him look so fat.

Jupiter was wearing the Golden Belt of the Ancient Emperors!

The great gold links, the huge emeralds, shone richly as, with relief, he took it off and laid it on the table.

305

"I've been wearing it all day," he said. "It's quite heavy."

Bob and Pete hurled excited questions at him. Where had he found it? Why was he wearing it? Why hadn't he given it back?

Before Jupiter could answer, the trap-door from Tunnel Two heaved up under their feet. A tiny man, grimacing horribly and waving a knife, glared up at them. At the same instant the panel from Red Gate Rover swung open and another little man, also armed, appeared.

Timed to coincide exactly, the main door from Easy Three burst in. Two little men, looking fierce and determined despite their size, pointed sharp knives at the boys.

"Okay, kids, we've come for it!" one of them shrilled. "Hand over the belt!"

No adults could have come through the secret entrances to Headquarters. That is, no normal adults. But these were not fully-grown men; they were midgets.

As the four midgets swarmed into the little office, Jupiter moved into action.

"Red Alert! Top emergency! Exit instant!" he shouted.

He grabbed the Golden Belt and was on top of the desk even as he spoke. He thrust up the skylight, and from outside pulled down a rope with two loops in it for footholds. Taro went up it like a monkey, and Jupe passed him the belt. Pete and Bob, slightly dazed, reacted to automatic training and clambered after him. By the time the angry midgets filled the little office, Jupiter had joined the others on the roof.

It seemed they were trapped there. The midgets, acrobats themselves, were already swarming after them. They shouted exultantly, for there seemed no way for the boys to get down. But Jupiter had provided for just such an emergency.

An old chute from a school play yard stood against the side of the trailer. Beams of steel seemed to block it.

But one by one the boys flung themselves on to the chute and, flat on their stomachs, plummeted on to the saw-dust-covered ground below. They dodged round piles of junk, heading for the exit gate.

On the roof of Headquarters, the first midget tried to follow them down the chute. However, he went down sitting, instead of lying flat, and was brought up with a jolt against a jagged steel beam. His squeal of outrage pierced the night.

"Go back!" he yelled. "Inside and out that way! We've got to catch them!"

There was a scramble on the roof and the midgets swiftly lowered themselves into the office and out through Easy Three.

"We have to find them!" one screeched in a high voice. "They've still got the belt."

The boys, who were hiding in the dark space behind a pile of timber, felt a shiver of fear as four tiny

Waving a knife, he glared up at them . . .

shadows, long knives glittering in their hands, came towards them.

Then Bob and Pete received their second surprise of the night. Somewhere a whistle blew loudly. An instant later, half a dozen large figures raced through the main gate and threw themselves on the midgets. The little men twisted and squealed, but they were no match for the policemen and Mr. Saito Togati, who had been waiting outside.

There was a brief, ferocious struggle, and then the midgets were being tightly bound and carried off to a waiting police car. Bob, Pete, Jupiter and Taro crawled out of their hiding place. Little Taro was almost beside himself with joy.

"You see, Father!" he cried. "Plan of Jupiter-san work with brilliance. Belt is recovered and little criminals are caught, also."

"Ah, so!" Mr. Togati said. "Truly, from small books may come large words of advice. Jupiter-san, my humble apologies for rudeness in beginning."

"That's all right, sir," Jupiter said, almost stuttering because he was so pleased with the way things had worked out. "Naturally, you figured the police could do a better job."

"With usual criminals, yes," Mr. Togati agreed. "But not with very unusual criminals such as these. My son, I am pleased with you that you persuaded me to listen to these American friends of yours."

Little Taro almost burst with pleasure at his father's praise.

"Now I take good care of belt." Mr. Togati reverently touched the golden links. "It is worth much money. You boys save my honour. I shall not forget. Again many thanks. Come, Taro. We must go. But in our memories we remain with you."

Mr. Togati and his son bowed low and then left, taking the Golden Belt with them. Chief of Police Reynolds stayed a few minutes more, asking Jupiter questions.

Bob and Pete stood open-mouthed, trying to figure out what it had all been about. Jupiter's mysterious actions—his sudden revelation that he had the Golden Belt, the invasion of Headquarters by armed midgets, their flight, the appearance of Chief Reynolds and Detective Togati—it was more than Bob and Pete could grasp at once. But Bob finally got the correct idea.

"Jupe!" he said, when the police chief had finally gone, "those midgets who came here after the Golden Belt! Why, I'll bet they were the same ones who helped Mr. Rawley rob the bank, weren't they?"

"Yes, they were," Jupiter agreed. "They're really very complete criminals, and it's time they were caught. They've been getting away with too many crimes disguised as children."

"But——" It was coming to Pete now. "But—hey, wait a minute? Are they also the gang who took the Golden Belt in the first place?"

"They certainly are. I said at the time it had to be the crime of a gang of well-organized men. The

310

midgets are men all right—they're just *little* men. They were disguised as Cub Scouts, of course, which is why they never were suspected. Who'd have thought of child criminals? I might have guessed sooner if Bob had mentioned the gold tooth. But as it is I was able to recover the Golden Belt and the midgets were captured, so no harm is done."

There was still a lot Pete and Bob didn't understand, but they had no doubt Jupiter would explain everything in his own good time. Right at the moment Jupe was looking slightly smug, as he sometimes did when things had worked out the way he planned.

Certainly he had every reason to be pleased. Once again Jupiter Jones had demonstrated his right to be First Investigator!

18

Mr. Hitchcock Demands Some Answers

MR. ALFRED HITCHCOCK, the motion picture director, sat back in his swivel chair. Facing him across his desk in his luxurious Hollywood office sat Pete, Bob and Jupiter. Each of them was scrubbed to shining pinkness and wore his best slacks and shirt.

In his hand Mr. Hitchcock held the bundle of

papers which told the story of the riddle of the Golden Belt, and the story of Miss Agawam's gnomes, as Bob had written them up. The boys waited anxiously for Mr. Hitchcock's reaction to the stories.

"Well done, lads," Mr. Hitchcock rumbled at last. "Well done indeed. So you rid my friend Agatha of her gnomes, I see. Of course, in doing so you had to solve a bank robbery, recover the loot, find a missing golden belt of fabulous worth and bring the thieves into the hands of the police. But these are mere trifles. I expect something like that to happen when The Three Investigators get started on a case, no matter how trivial it may seem on the surface."

Bob grinned. So did Pete. Jupiter looked pink with pleasure.

"So dear Agatha's gnomes were midgets in disguise," Mr. Hitchcock murmured. "The only possible answer, of course. But tell me—how did she feel when she learned that her nephew Roger knew about Rawley's plot to frighten her with fake gnomes?"

"She was very angry at first," Jupiter said. "But of course, Roger didn't know it was part of a criminal plot to rob the bank. He was very ashamed, so Miss Agawam forgave him. In fact, she actually has decided to sell her home and move to a small apartment by the sea. She says that she'll be more comfortable there."

"I am happy to hear it," Mr. Hitchcock answered. "She is a very fine lady. Well, I believe that clears up all mysteries surrounding the bank robbery. A most ingenious scheme it was—to become night watchman of an abandoned theatre in order to dig a tunnel into the vaults of a nearby bank. Perhaps I can work that into a motion picture some time.

"But now—" Mr. Hitchcock tapped the manuscript—"we come to a part which baffles me greatly. I confess I do not understand about the Golden Belt. How it was stolen. Where it was hidden. How you, Jupiter, enticed the criminal midgets into attacking you so that the police could seize them. Please give me a full explanation of these mystifying matters."

"Well, sir—" Jupiter took a deep breath, because he had a lot to tell—"I should have seen it all much sooner, just as soon as we discovered that Miss Agawam's gnomes were midgets in disguise. I should have realized that if midgets could look like gnomes, they could also look like children.

"But I was too slow to put two and two together. Until Bob told me about seeing a Cub Scout with a gold tooth at the museum."

"Ah!" Mr. Hitchcock leaned forward, greatly interested. "The gold tooth. I've been waiting for that. Pray tell me what even a Sherlock Holmes would deduce from a Cub Scout with a gold tooth?"

"Well," Jupiter said, "small boys lose their teeth and grow new, permanent ones. Everyone knows that. Nobody gives a small boy a gold tooth, because it'll just fall out when the tooth behind it comes through."

"Of course!" Understanding spread over the director's face. "Only a grown boy or a man would have a gold tooth. Exactly. So you realized the little Cub Scout was really a full-grown man!"

"A full-grown little man, a midget, wearing a Cub Scout uniform," Jupiter said. "He and his friends, surrounded by dozens of other small Cub Scouts, went totally unsuspected."

"Astounding," Mr. Hitchcock said. "Such ingenuity should be used for better purposes."

"These particular four midgets are acrobats from Central Europe," Jupiter said. "Work for midgets in Hollywood has been scarce lately, and these four decided to pull a robbery. The Nagasami jewel exhibition came to town. It was announced that there would be a Children's Day, with all children in Scout uniforms admitted free. This gave the midgets a terrific opportunity, for they had often dressed up as children. It was a perfect set-up for them.

"At almost the same time, Mr. Rawley came looking for some midgets to impersonate gnomes for him, to help him in the bank robbery.

"The midgets made a deal with Mr. Rawley. Mr. Rawley got a woman friend to dress up like a den mother, and take the midgets inside the museum, dressed as Cub Scouts. The woman hired Mr. Frank, the actor, to create a diversion inside the museum. When all eyes were turned towards him, the four midgets started up the stairs leading to the balcony. No one noticed them there.

"An instant later the lights went out. I'm sure Mr.

Rawley did that, in return for the favour the midgets were doing him. He cut off all the electricity and drove away. The midgets were now on the balcony. Meanwhile, down below, children were running around like crazy and everything was in confusion."

"I'll buy that!" Pete chimed in.

"The midgets," Jupiter continued, "had a short piece of nylon rope which the woman with them probably had worn around her waist, under her blouse. Three midgets held the rope, while one climbed down it, kicked in the glass case, grabbed the Golden Belt, and was pulled back up to the balcony."

Mr. Hitchcock looked thoughtful.

"Mmm, yes," he said. "They could manage such a feat, being acrobats, in about thirty seconds. Now I understand why they stole the Golden Belt rather than the Rainbow Jewels. The case holding the Rainbow Jewels was out in the middle of the room, beyond their reach. They took what they could get. No doubt they intended to sell the belt back to the Nagasami Jewellery Company for a very large sum."

"They won't talk," Jupiter told him. "But that's what Mr. Togati, the detective, thinks. Well, after they stole the belt, they knew they had to hide it because they couldn't carry it out without being seen. So they hid it, very quickly, then hurried downstairs to the main floor in the darkness. Then, in the tremendous confusion, they all left. No one suspected their disguise, and of course they couldn't be caught with the belt because they didn't have it."

"Mmm!" Mr. Hitchcock said. "You say they hid the belt in the museum. Yet, following your suggestion, the museum was thoroughly searched, even the spaces behind the pictures. The belt was not found. Why was it not found?"

"Because the detectives and the guards looked every-place but the right place," Jupiter said. "The midgets had figured out that hiding place very carefully. They were sure the belt wouldn't be found and they could go back some other time to get it. Actually, they were busy with the bank robbery, so they planned to go on the next Children's Day, when no one would notice them in their Cub Scout uniforms."

"Precisely," Mr. Hitchcock agreed.

"The police hadn't been able to arrest them for the bank robbery. Their friends gave them alibis. It occurred to me that if I could get them to attack me and have the police waiting when they did, they would be caught red-handed for that crime."

"You could at least have told us what you were up to!" Bob said at this point. "Pete and I were scared stiff when those midgets broke into Headquarters, waving knives at us!"

"Our emergency exit worked perfectly, as I was sure it would," Jupiter told him. "So all was well. You see, Mr. Hitchcock, I hurried to the museum and found Taro Togati, the son of the Japanese detective in charge of guarding the exhibit. He and I and his father found the belt, and I put it on under my jacket——"

316

"But where did you find it?" Pete couldn't help interrupting.

"I'm coming to that," Jupiter told him. "Anyway, I put the belt on under my jacket and then went to the boarding house where the midgets lived. I seemed to be alone but of course I was followed by plain-clothes men because the Golden Belt is worth probably a million dollars.

"I talked to the midget with the gold tooth, as I knew he had to be one of the gang. He pretended not to know what I was talking about, but he knew perfectly well I had helped break up Rawley's bank robbery.

"I told him I was sorry now I hadn't accepted Rawley's proposition to become a member of the gang. That I wanted to make a lot of money fast. He understood that all right."

"All criminals feel that way," Mr. Hitchcock agreed. "So of course they think everyone else does, too."

"I told him I had the Golden Belt, but didn't know how to get rid of it, and I was willing to sell it for the amount Rawley paid the four of them—forty thousand dollars. I opened my coat and let him see the belt and his eyes almost popped out. He knew it was real, all right, and he knew I must be a crook or I would have reported it to the museum authorities."

Jupiter looked pleased at having been thought a big-time crook.

"I said I'd give him and the others until midnight to think it over. Until then I'd be in my Headquarters

317

in The Jones Salvage Yard with my friends. If they wanted to make a deal, they could come, bringing the money, and we would give them the belt for the money. I knew they wouldn't dare pull anything at the boarding house. There were too many people around."

"Aha!" exclaimed Alfred Hitchcock. "Knowing they were crooks, you felt sure they would try to take the belt from you rather than buy it."

"Yes, sir. But even if they had come to buy it with the money stolen from the bank, that would have been evidence against them."

"So that's why you had us go in and out our secret entrances so much that day!" Bob exclaimed. "Those kids watching us were midgets in disguise. You wanted them to learn all about how to attack us better!"

"Yet, I'll bet they even photographed us from that kite!" Pete said. "Next time you risk our lives, please let us know about it!"

Jupiter Jones squirmed a little in his chair.

"I had perfect faith in Emergency One," he said. "And it was necessary for the midgets to know how to get in. I had Taro with me so that he could win his father's approval. But I couldn't let the midgets know or they would have been suspicious.

"Anyway, I alerted Detective Togati and Chief Reynolds and they were waiting outside, carefully hidden. The midgets attacked us on schedule. We fled, and they were captured. The case was brought to a successful conclusion."

"Indeed it was!" Mr. Hitchcock said. "However—" and he fixed his gaze severely on Jupiter—"you sidestepped my question. So I'll ask it again. Where did the midgets hide the Golden Belt so that no one else could find it?"

"Where no one else would look for it," Jupiter said. "I had trouble figuring it out until I remembered they were acrobats. At Miss Agawam's house they stood on each other's shoulders so they could rap on the window. That made me think that maybe in the museum——"

"One moment, young Jupiter!" Mr. Hitchcock boomed. "Light is beginning to dawn for me. Let me see if I can figure out the rest the way you did."

He turned back to the bundle of papers on his desk and leafed through them. He found the one he wanted, read it over again, and nodded.

"Ah, yes," he said. "The clues are all here. On page 18. Everything is clear now."

Bob and Pete tried hard to remember what was on the page he had mentioned. Something about the inside of the museum and the way the pictures were hung. That was all they could remember.

"Yes, indeed," Mr. Hitchcock went on. "In the narrative, it is clear that a broad moulding runs round the wall just under the ceiling of the two rooms with domed ceilings. Such mouldings were once used to hang pictures. Also, in large, older houses, mouldings were put up as a decoration, to keep the walls from seeming too high.

319

"Such a moulding, large enough, could have a deep crevice in it, or possibly a flat place on top. Now as I imagine it, the midgets noticed this moulding at the museum. They knew no one would ever suspect it as a hiding place. So after they had stolen the belt, they made a human ladder, and the midget on top placed the belt either in the crevice of the moulding or along the top, where it could not be spotted from below."

"This took only a moment. An instant later they were ready to flee as four frightened Cub Scouts. Later, no one looked at the moulding because it would have taken a ladder to reach it and everyone knew there was no ladder in the room at the time of the robbery. Is that correct, Jupiter?"

Bob and Pete were mentally kicking themselves for not having figured it out for themselves. After all, they had seen the moulding. Of course, it was pretty dark up near the ceiling, with no windows.

Jupiter's answer gave them a jolt of surprise.

"No, sir," he told Alfred Hitchcock. "Your answer isn't quite correct, sir."

Mr. Hitchcock's cheeks puffed out. He frowned at Jupiter. His voice deepened.

"Indeed, young man!" he said. "If I had been making a movie of this story, that's the hiding place I'd have chosen. Just where, then, was the belt?"

"I figured it out just as you did, sir," Jupiter said. "But when I got to the museum and climbed up on a ladder, I found the moulding was curved. There was no flat place to hold the belt. That stumped me."

"I should think it would," Mr. Hitchcock said.

"Then," Jupiter said, "as I stood there on the ladder feeling pretty foolish, I felt a current of cool air blowing in my face. That immediately told me the truth——"

"Aha!" Mr. Hitchcock rumbled. "The air conditioning!"

"Yes, sir," Jupiter agreed. "There was an opening just underneath the moulding for the special air conditioning installed in the museum. I tried the grillwork on the front, and it came loose. The Golden Belt was hung down inside the air-conditioning duct by a black string. But as you said, the opening was up so high it needed a ladder to reach it, so it hadn't been searched previously."

"Excellent!" Mr. Hitchcock said. "Now everything is clear. You solved two cases, actually, which were connected by the four larcenous midgets involved in both. That was quite an achievement, even for The Three Investigators."

The boys looked at each other and grinned. As they got up to leave, the director asked, "And what is on the agenda now, lads?"

"Skin-diving lessons," replied Pete promptly, and Bob nodded.

Jupiter looked thoughtful. "I wonder," he said, almost to himself, "if further practice in deduction would be more valuable."

Mr. Hitchcock laughed. "Well, whatever you boys

321

take on, I know it will be interesting," he said. "I shall await your next report."

The boys left, and the movie director turned back to Bob's notes on his desk. "Gnomes and a vanishing treasure," he said with a chuckle. "What a movie that would make!"

SKELETON ISLAND

Skeleton Island was first published
in the USA in 1966 by Random House Inc
First published as a single volume in the UK
by Armada in 1970

WARNING! Proceed with Caution!

THE ABOVE WARNING is meant for you if you are of a nervous nature, inclined to bite your fingernails when meeting adventure, danger and suspense. However, if you relish such ingredients in a story, with a dash of mystery and detection thrown in for good measure, then keep right on going.

For this is the sixth adventure that I have introduced for The Three Investigators, and I can only say that never have they been in any tighter spots than they encounter here. You don't have to take my word for it—read the book and see!

Just in case you haven't met The Three Investigators before, they are Jupiter Jones, Pete Crenshaw, and Bob Andrews, all of whom live in the town of Rocky Beach, on the Pacific Ocean a few miles from Hollywood, California. Some time ago they formed the firm of The Three Investigators to solve any riddles, enigmas or mysteries that might come their way, and so far they have done well.

Jupiter Jones, the First Investigator, is the brains of the firm. Pete Crenshaw, the Second

Investigator, is tall and muscular and excels at athletics. Bob Andrews, the most studious of the three, is in charge of Records and Research.

Now on with the show! Turn the page and travel with the Three Investigators to Skeleton Island!

ALFRED HITCHCOCK

1

A Case for The Three Investigators

"How ARE you lads at Scuba diving?" Alfred Hitchcock asked.

Across the big desk from him in his office at World Studios, The Three Investigators—Jupiter Jones, Pete Crenshaw and Bob Andrews —looked interested. It was Pete who answered.

"We've just been checked out on our final tests, sir," he said. "Our instructor took us down to the bay day before yesterday and okayed us."

"We're not exactly experienced, but we know what to do and all the rules," Jupiter added. "And we have our own face masks and flippers. When we do any diving, we rent the tanks and breathing apparatus."

"Excellent!" Mr. Hitchcock said. "Then I think you are definitely the three lads for the job."

Job? Did he mean a job investigating some mystery? Mr. Hitchcock nodded when Bob asked him the question.

"Yes, indeed," he said, "and doing some acting, too."

"Acting?" Pete looked doubtful. "We're not

actors, sir. Although Jupiter did some acting on TV when he was a very small kid."

"Experienced actors aren't needed," Mr. Hitchcock assured them. "Natural boys are what they want. I'm sure you know, Pete, that your father is at the moment in the East working with director Roger Denton on a suspense picture called *Chase Me Faster*."

"Yes, sir." Pete's father was a highly experienced movie technician and his job took him all over the world. "He's in Philadelphia right now."

"Wrong." Mr. Hitchcock seemed pleased at Pete's astonishment. "Right now he's on an island in Atlantic Bay, down on the south-east coast of the United States, helping rebuild an old amusement park for the final scene of the picture. The name of the island is Skeleton Island."

"Skeleton Island! Wow!" This came from Bob. "It sounds like a pirate hangout."

"It was indeed once a pirate hangout," the director told them. "Skeleton Island—a strange and sinister name! A ghost is said to haunt it. Bones are still uncovered in its sands. Sometimes when the sea is stormy, a gold doubloon washes up on its beaches. However, before you get your hopes up, let me say there is no treasure on the island. That has been proved. There may still be small bits of treasure scattered on the bottom of the bay but none on Skeleton Island."

"And you want us to go there?" Jupiter Jones asked eagerly. "You say there's a mystery to be solved?"

"It's like this." Mr. Hitchcock put the tips of his fingers together. "Your father, Pete, and a couple of other men are camped there, using local workmen to fix up part of the park for the final scenes of the movie, most of which is being shot in Philadelphia.

"They're having trouble. Pieces of equipment have been stolen, and their boats have been tinkered with at night. They have hired a local man as a guard, but the nuisance hasn't stopped, just slowed down.

"Skeleton Island is picturesque and the waters of Atlantic Bay around it are shallow. Roger Denton thought that as long as he is working on the island, his assistant, Harry Norris, could direct a short subject about three boys on a holiday who dive for pirate treasure for fun."

"Yes, sir, an excellent idea," Jupiter said.

"It would cost very little more, and the company has a man, Jeff Morton, who is an expert diver and underwater photographer. That's where you come in. You boys could be the three actors, do enough Scuba diving to qualify, and on your time off wander round the town, hunting for clues to this mysterious thievery. We will keep your identity as investigators secret, so no one will suspect you."

"That sounds great!" Bob said with enthusiasm. "If our families will let us go."

"I'm sure they will, with Mr. Crenshaw there, too," Mr. Hitchcock said. "Of course, the mystery may not amount to anything, but in view of your past record, you may discover more than any of us suspect."

"When do we start?" Pete asked.

"As soon as I can make the arrangements with Mr. Denton and your father, Pete," Alfred Hitchcock said. "Go home and pack and be ready to fly East tomorrow. Here, Bob, since you are in charge of Records and Research, you may want to look at these articles about Skeleton Island—how it was discovered, the pirates who once made their headquarters there, and other interesting data. Familiarize yourself with it. The trip should be an interesting experience for you."

2

An Unexpected Meeting

"THERE'S Skeleton Island!" Bob Andrews exclaimed.

"Where? . . . Let me look!" Jupiter and Pete exclaimed. They leaned over Bob to peer out of the window of the sleek silver airliner.

The plane was gliding down over a long narrow bay—Atlantic Bay. Bob pointed to a small island almost directly below them. Its shape bore a curious resemblance to that of a skull.

"I recognize the shape from the maps Mr. Hitchcock gave us," Bob said.

They stared at the island with eager curiosity. Skeleton Island had once, more than three hundred years before, been a pirate hangout. Although Mr. Hitchcock had said there was no pirate gold buried there, maybe he was wrong. Maybe there was still some treasure to be found. They hoped so. In any case, the island held a mystery which they would attempt to solve.

Another island, much smaller, came into view.

"Then that must be The Hand!" Jupiter said.

"And those are The Bones," Pete added, pointing to a scatter of narrow reefs between Skeleton Island and The Hand. "Golly, think of it! We left Rocky Beach after lunch and here we are in time for dinner."

"Look," Bob said. "The Hand *does* look sort of like a hand. The fingers are rocky reefs that are under water most of the time, but from up here they're very clear."

"I hope we get a chance to explore The Hand," Jupiter said. "I've never seen an actual blowhole before. That magazine article Mr. Hitchcock gave us said that in a storm, water spouts out of the blowhole just like a whale."

Now the islands fell behind them. So did the small village on the mainland called Fishingport which was their immediate destination. A room was waiting for them there at a boarding house.

As the plane slid down out of the sky, a fair-sized city appeared on their right. This was Melville, where the airport was. A few moments later the boys were unfastening their seat belts as the plane rolled to a stop in front of the air terminal building.

They climbed down the stairs and stood looking around them at the small crowd which waited behind a wire fence.

"I wonder if your dad will meet us, Pete," Bob said.

"He said he'd try to, but he would send someone else if he couldn't," Pete answered. "I don't see him."

"Here comes someone who seems to be looking for us," Bob said in a low voice as a short, pudgy man with a red nose approached them.

"Hi," he said. "You must be the three kid detectives from Hollywood. I was told to pick you up." He stared at them with small, shrewd eyes. "You don't look much like detectives to me," he said. "I thought you'd be older."

Bob felt Jupiter stiffen. "We're supposed to act in a picture," he said. "Why do you think we're detectives?"

The man gave them a broad wink.

"There isn't much I don't know," he said with a grin. "Now follow me. I have a car waiting. There will be another car to pick up your baggage—got a lot of stuff coming in from Hollywood on this plane, too much for my car."

He turned and led them out of the gate to an old station wagon.

"Hop in, boys," he said. "It's a good half-hour's ride and by the looks of it, we're in for a storm."

Bob looked up at the sky. Although the sun still shone, low on the horizon, black clouds were whipping towards them from the west. A flicker of lightning played along the front of the clouds. It did look as if a storm was coming, a real whopper.

The boys climbed into the back seat, the man got in behind the wheel, and the station wagon started away from the airport, heading north.

"Excuse me, Mr. ——" Jupiter began.

"Just call me Sam," the man said. "Everybody calls me Sam."

As he spoke, he stepped on the gas and the car hurtled along at a high speed. The sun had gone behind a cloud, and suddenly it was almost dark.

"Excuse me, Mr. Sam," Jupiter asked, "but do you work for the movie company?"

"Not regularly, boy," Sam answered. "But I agreed to pick you up as a favour. Say, look at that storm coming. This will be a good night for the phantom of the merry-go-round to show

333

herself. I wouldn't want to be out on Skeleton Island tonight."

Bob felt little prickles of excitement go up his spine. The phantom of the merry-go-round! The magazine articles they had studied so carefully had told them all about the ghost that supposedly haunted Skeleton Island. According to legend, it was the ghost of lovely but headstrong Sally Farrington, a young woman who had been riding the old merry-go-round one night twenty-five years before.

A sudden storm had blown up and the merry-go-round had stopped. Everyone else had got off, but Sally Farrington refused to climb down from her wooden horse. According to the legend, she cried out that no storm was going to stop her from finishing her ride.

As the operator of the merry-go-round was arguing with her, a bolt of lightning had crackled down from the sky and struck the metal pole in the middle of the carousel. To the horror of everyone, Sally Farrington was killed.

Her last words had been, "I'm not afraid of any storm and I'm going to finish this ride if it's the last thing I ever do!"

Everyone agreed that the tragedy was her own fault. But no one was prepared for what followed. A few weeks later, one stormy night when Pleasure Park was closed down and empty, people on the mainland saw the lights of the merry-go-round blaze up. The wind brought the sound of carousel music to their ears.

Mr. Wilbur, the owner of the park, had taken some men in a boat to investigate. They got close enough to the island to see the merry-go-round spinning and a white-clad figure clinging to one of the painted horses.

Then the lights had abruptly gone out and the music stopped. When the men reached the scene a few minutes later, they found the park utterly deserted. But lying on the ground beside the carousel they found a soaking wet handkerchief, tiny and feminine, with the initials "S.F." embroidered on it. It was easily recognized as one of Sally Farrington's handkerchiefs.

A wave of superstitious fear spread among the townspeople. It was said that Sally's ghost had come to finish her interrupted ride. The amusement park soon had a reputation for being haunted. Many people stayed away from it, and the following year it had not reopened. The roller coaster, the Ferris wheel, the merry-go-round—everything had been left to rot and decay as the years passed.

But the legend of Sally Farrington's ghost did not die. Fishermen claimed to have seen it, especially on stormy nights, wandering about the island. In the last few years it had been reported a dozen times, sometimes by two or more men. The popular belief was that Sally Farrington was doomed to haunt the island, waiting to finish her fatal ride on the merry-go-round. And now that the merry-go-round was no longer able to run, she would wait for ever.

Therefore Skeleton Island had been deserted for years. There was no real reason to go there, with the amusement park closed, except perhaps to have a picnic in the summer. And picnickers were few and far between because of the island's reputation.

"I hear," Sam called back to the three boys, "that these motion-picture fellows are fixing up the old merry-go-round again. Sally's ghost will be mighty happy about that. Maybe if it gets running again she can finish her ride."

He chuckled. Then, as the first wind from the approaching storm struck them, he devoted himself to driving.

They were driving through what seemed to be marshy, empty country. After half an hour, they came to a fork in the road. The main road turned left and in the headlights the boys could see a sign pointing in that direction: *Fishingport: 2 miles.* To their surprise, Sam turned the car down the unmarked road to the right, which soon became two sandy ruts.

"The sign said Fishingport was the other way," Pete spoke up. "Why are we going this way, Mr. Sam?"

"Necessary," Sam said over his shoulder. "Been a crisis. Mr. Crenshaw wants you to come straight out to the island instead of going to Mrs. Barton's in town tonight."

"Oh, I see." Pete subsided. They all wondered what the crisis was. Had something very serious happened?

After bumping along the sandy road for a couple of miles, the car stopped. The headlights showed a rickety pier. Tied to the pier was a small, rather dilapidated fishing boat. "Out you get, boys!" Sam cried. "Lively now! That storm's ready to bust loose."

They climbed out of the car, a little surprised that the movie company didn't have better transport than this. But probably it was Sam's own boat.

"Will our baggage follow us?" Jupiter asked as Sam joined them.

"Your baggage is safe and sound, boys," Sam said. "Climb in now. We've got a ride ahead of us."

They climbed into the boat. Sam bent over the motor. He turned a switch and the heavy flywheel began to spin. Soon they were chugging out into the choppy water, all three boys hanging on for dear life as the small craft pitched and plunged.

Then the rain came. First it was a fine pelting spray mingled with tiny hailstones. Next came the big drops. The boys, crouched under a thin canvas cover, were soon soaked.

"We need raincoats!" yelled Pete to Sam. "We'll be the first boys to drown above water in Atlantic Bay!"

337

Sam nodded and lashed the wheel. He went to a locker and pulled out four yellow plastic slickers with hoods. He put one on himself and handed the others to the boys.

"Get into these," he yelled. "I keep 'em for fishing parties."

Jupiter's was too tight to button and Bob's was much too long. But they kept out the rain.

Sam went back to steering. Now the sky was a bombardment of thunder. The tiny boat tipped dangerously in the high waves, and the boys were afraid that any moment they would overturn.

After what seemed a long time, they could see land ahead, lit by lightning flashes. They saw no dock or pier, and were surprised when Sam pulled the boat alongside a flat rock that projected out into the water.

"Jump ashore, boys!" he yelled. "Lively now!"

Puzzled, The Three Investigators leaped from the boat to the rock.

"Aren't you coming, Mr. Sam?" Jupiter called as the boat started drifting away.

"Can't," Sam yelled back. "Follow the trail to the camp. You'll be all right."

He gunned the motor. In a moment the boat had vanished into the stormy night.

The boys bent their heads against the pelting rain.

"We better try to find that path!" Pete shouted. Jupiter nodded.

Then Bob heard a strange sound, like a great beast breathing hoarsely.

"Whooooo-*whish!*" it went. "Whooo-*whish!*"

"What's that sound?" he shouted. "Listen!"

Again came the strange noise. "Whoo-*whish!* Whoo-*whish!*"

"Something on the island," Jupiter answered. "Let's see if we can see it when the next lightning comes."

They all stared inland. Then came a vivid bolt of lightning. By its brilliant light they could see they were on a rather small island, certainly not big enough to be Skeleton Island.

This one was all rocks, with a hump in the middle and a few straggly trees. There was no path, and no camp. And just before the sky darkened again, they saw a plume of water shoot upward from the centre of the hump. It went up like a spouting geyser, and as it did so they heard the "Whoo-*whish!*" sound again.

"A spout!" Jupiter called. "It must come from a blowhole in the rocks. We aren't on Skeleton Island at all. We're on The Hand."

They looked at each other in dismay.

For some unknown reason, Sam had marooned them on The Hand, at night in a storm. And they had no way to get off or call for help.

The Phantom is Seen

JUPITER, Bob and Pete crouched beneath an overhanging rock. It wasn't completely dry, but it provided some shelter from the wind and rain. During the last few minutes, they had scrambled over enough of the little island to convince them it had to be The Hand, and that there was no one else on it, and no boat.

They had taken a close look at the curious spout, which shot up from the middle of a flat place on the rocky hump. Jupiter, whose scientific curiosity never flagged under any circumstances, explained that there must be a crack in the rock that went deep under the island. The waves of the storm forced water into it, to be expelled up the blowhole.

However, they hadn't lingered to study the spout. They had to find shelter. After more stumbling around, they had found the rocky crevice that protected them now.

"Sam's marooned us!" Pete said indignantly, wiping rain from his face. "Why did he do it, that's what I want to know?"

"Maybe he made a mistake and thought this really was Skeleton Island," Bob suggested.

"No." Jupiter shook his head. "He brought us here on purpose. I confess I am baffled as to his reason. I am also baffled by the fact that he knew we were investigators. There's something queer going on."

"I'll buy a double helping of that," Pete grumbled. "I only hope we don't starve to death on this island before someone finds us!"

"We'll be found in the morning," Jupiter said. "Some fishing boat will spot us. We'll just have to stick it out tonight."

"But there aren't any fishing boats up at this end of Atlantic Bay," Bob put in anxiously. "Don't you remember those articles we read? Some tiny red parasite has got into the oysters in this part of the bay. All the fishing boats have moved down to Melville, at the south end, where the shellfish are still safe to eat. Fishingport is almost a ghost town because of the sickness of the oysters."

"Someone will spot us," Jupiter said. "There will be a search on for us when it is learned we have disappeared. And at least we have seen the spout actually working."

There didn't seem much more to be said. Fortunately it was not too cold on the island, and the storm seemed to be letting up. The only thing they could do was wait for morning. When they had decided that, they relaxed. Soon they found themselves dozing off.

Suddenly Pete awoke. It took him a few

seconds to remember where he was and what had happened. Then he saw that the storm had passed. The stars were out. And out on the water a hundred yards away a light was flashing.

Pete leaped up and started to yell. In a moment, Bob and Jupiter were awake and struggling sleepily to their feet.

The light turned in their direction, like a probing finger trying to find them. Pete ripped off his yellow raincoat and waved it madly.

"Here, here!" he shouted.

The light caught the billowing raincoat and held. Whoever was out there had seen them!

The powerful beam of light pointed upwards, illuminating the sail of a small boat. Then it flickered along the shore and picked out a little beach. It held on that spot, bobbing as the boat moved.

"He'll land there," Pete said. "He wants us to meet him there."

"Luckily there is some starlight now," Jupiter observed. "Even so, we'll practically have to feel our way."

"Look!" Bob exclaimed. "He's trying to help us."

The flashlight was now flicking over the ground between the boys and the shoreline, showing them the way in brief glimpses.

They made the best time they could. Even so, they each fell down and Pete skinned his knee. By the time they reached the beach, a small sailing-boat was drawn up in the sand, the sail down. A boy in a windbreaker jacket and trousers rolled up to the knees stood on the sandy shore.

He flashed his light briefly over their faces, then reversed it to shine it on himself. They saw a tanned, smiling face topped by dark curly hair. Merry black eyes glinted at them.

"Ahoy!" he said, in a voice with a foreign accent. "You are the three detectives, yes?"

It seemed that everyone knew who they were.

"We're The Three Investigators," Jupiter said. "We're certainly glad you found us."

"I think I know where to look for you," the boy said. He was almost as tall as Pete, but skinnier, though he had powerful chest and arm muscles. "I am Chris Markos. Christos Markos, in full, but call me Chris, okay?"

"Okay, Chris," Pete said. They took an immediate liking to this smiling, cheerful boy who had come to their rescue. "How'd you know where to look for us?"

"Long story," Chris told them. "Climb in my boat, and we will sail to town. Movie people are very upset. We will make them feel better to see you."

"Aren't you part of the *Chase Me Faster* company?" Bob asked as they clambered into the tiny boat.

"No, not me," Chris said, shoving the boat off and wading after it. He climbed in the rear and

343

settled himself by the tiller. Soon the little sail had caught the breeze, and the boat began to cut through the water. In the distance the boys could see the lights of the little town of Fishingport.

Once the boat was under way, Chris Markos told them about himself. He had grown up in Greece, on the shores of the Mediterranean, where he had lived with his father, a sponge fisherman. His mother was dead. Greek sponge fishers went down great depths to gather sponges from the ocean bottom, using no diving apparatus except a heavy stone to take them down swiftly.

Chris's father, one of the most daring divers, had one day been afflicted by an attack of the bends, the dread of every diver. As a result he was partially disabled and had been unable to continue diving. But a cousin who was an oyster fisherman in Fishingport had sent money for him and Chris to come to the United States.

"For a few years, fishing goes well," Chris said. "Then oysters get sick. Little red bug gets into them. Oyster fishing around here is all finished. My father's cousin, he has to sell his boat. He goes to New York to work in a restaurant. But my father is not well enough. He gets worse from worrying. Now he is in bed almost all the time. I try to take care of him, but I have trouble getting a job. I hear movie company is coming to town, they maybe need a diver. I am a good diver. When I was a little boy,

I start practising to be a sponge fisher like my father. But movie people, they say no. They do not like me. Everybody is suspicious because I am a foreigner. Oh well, maybe luck will turn soon."

They were sailing along briskly now. The boys could hear the mutter of breaking waves, and see splashes of whitecaps off to their left.

"Where are we now?" Pete asked. "How can you find your way when you can't see what's ahead? You may crash on one of those rocks."

"I tell by the ears," Chris said cheerfully. "I hear waves break, and know reefs are off there. They are what some people call The Bones. Skeleton Island is off ahead, to the left."

The boys all peered ahead, trying to see Skeleton Island. They knew its history by heart, from studying the papers Alfred Hitchcock had given them.

Skeleton Island had been discovered in 1565 by an English sea captain, Captain White. He had explored the island briefly, discovering that it was used as a sacred burying ground by Indian tribes on the mainland. As the Indians did not bother about digging very deep graves, many skeletons had been found. Because of this, and its skeleton-like shape, Captain White had named it Skeleton Island. At the same time he had visited The Hand, noticed the reefs which made it seem like a hand, and so given it its name. Then he had sailed away.

In the years that followed, pirates had infested the whole south-eastern sea coast. They had used the island for winter quarters, and come to the mainland to spend their gold. Blackbeard himself had spent one winter there.

But gradually the British authorities began to crack down on the pirates. By 1717, after Blackbeard was dead, the only buccaneer left in the region was the notorious Captain One-Ear. One night the British troops had made a surprise attack on his quarters on Skeleton Island.

While his crew was being slaughtered, the captain himself had escaped with his treasure chests in a longboat. The British commander, as anxious to recover the gold as to exterminate the pirates, gave chase.

Captain One-Ear, finding he could not escape, made a final stand on The Hand. Here his remaining men were killed and he was captured, badly wounded. But the chests that the British had been so anxious to recover turned out to be empty. The treasure had disappeared. The Hand was too rocky for him to have buried the gold there, and the British could find no other hiding place. To all questions, Captain One-Ear gave only one laughing answer:

"Davy Jones has my gold doubloons in his grasp now, and he'll hold them tight until he decides to give them back. And that won't be until the crack o' doom!"

Even when he was hanged, he would say no

more, and the British commander was cheated of his spoils. It was obvious Captain One-Ear had dumped the treasure overboard, just to disappoint his pursuers. It was scattered over the sea bottom now, and no one could ever find it again.

The boys peered through the darkness, hoping to see the outline of the fabled Skeleton Island. It was too dark, however, to see anything.

"You must sail these waters a lot," Jupiter said to Chris, "if you can tell where you are by sound."

"Sure thing!" Chris agreed. "I sail all round here. Sometimes I dive, too. I look for gold— you know gold scattered over the bottom of bay."

"Yes, we know," Bob said. "Over the years quite a few doubloons have been found that way. Probably from the treasure Captain One-Ear dumped overboard."

"Have you found anything?" Pete asked.

Chris hesitated. Then he said, "Yes, I find something. Not a big something. But something."

"How did you find it, Chris?" asked Jupiter.

"I find it just last week," Chris said. "Only a little something, but who knows, maybe I will find more. Can't tell you where, though. Secret one person knows is a secret. Secret two persons know is no secret, Secret three persons know is knowledge shouted to the world. That is an old saying. Duck your heads, we come about on a new tack."

They ducked. The sail swung from one side to the other. The boat heeled the opposite way and started on its new tack, straight towards the lights of Fishingport.

"Skeleton Island is right behind us now," Chris said. "But we head for town."

Again the boys peered through the darkness, trying to see the island. Then Bob gasped.

"Look!" he yelled. "Lights!"

Suddenly in the darkness lights had appeared. They made a circular pattern, like the lights on a merry-go-round. Music — carousel music! — floated over the water. The lights started to revolve, slowly, then faster and faster. A moment later, a pale figure appeared, moving among the merry-go-round's painted horses.

"The phantom of the merry-go-round!" Pete cried. "It has to be—it's a girl in a white dress!"

"Chris, turn round!" Jupiter begged. "We have to investigate this."

"Not me!" Chris exclaimed. "That is the ghost all right. She is back to take her ride on the merry-go-round now the movie people have it fixed. We get away from here. Wish I had a motor, so we go faster!"

He kept the boat headed straight for Fishingport. Bob and Pete were rather glad, but Jupe was obviously disappointed. He itched to see a real phantom at close range.

Behind them the merry-go-round kept spinning, a blaze of lights in the darkness. Sally Farrington trying to finish her last ride, twenty-five years after she had died! Bob shivered at the thought.

Then, unexpectedly, the music stopped. The lights went out. The carousel and the white figure were gone. For some reason poor Sally Farrington had been unable to finish her last ride.

Jupiter sighed in disappointment. Half an hour later they were safe at Mrs. Barton's boarding house in Fishingport, and Mrs. Barton was spreading the news by telephone of their being found. She made Pete, Bob and Jupe take hot baths and get straight into bed.

They were glad to do so. But, just before he dozed off, Jupe murmured out loud, "I wish I could have got closer to the phantom!"

"That remark," replied Pete sleepily, "does not reflect the sentiments of the rest of The Three Investigators!"

Faster and faster went the merry-go-round.

4

Skeleton Island at Last

AS BOB AWOKE, he was puzzled to see a slanting ceiling with striped wallpaper over his head. Then he remembered. He wasn't at home. He was three thousand miles from Rocky Beach, in a town called Fishingport, on Atlantic Bay.

He sat up and looked round. He was in the upper half of a double bunk. Below him Pete was fast asleep. In a bed a few feet away Jupiter Jones was also sleeping.

Bob lay back again, thinking over the strange events of the previous night.

There was a rap on the door. "Boys!" It was Mrs. Barton, the plump, cheerful landlady. "Breakfast is waiting, and Mr. Crenshaw is downstairs. Be down in five minutes or we'll throw it out!"

"We'll be there!" Bob leaped down to the floor. Pete and Jupiter, awakened by the voices, were soon dressed, and they all hurried downstairs. In a bright yellow dining room, decorated with various nautical objects, breakfast was waiting. Two men sat at the table, conversing in low tones and drinking coffee.

Pete's father, a large, ruggedly built man, jumped up as the boys entered. "Pete!" he exclaimed, putting an arm round his son. He shook hands with Bob and Jupiter. "I certainly was glad last night to hear you'd been found and were safe. By then you were asleep, so I hurried back to Skeleton Island. We have to guard our supplies and equipment every minute these days. But we'll come to that later. Right now I want your story."

As The Three Investigators ate, they took turns telling what had happened the night before. The other man, who was introduced as Police Chief Nostigon, nodded and puffed on a stubby pipe as he listened. While the boys got to the part about the man named Sam, Mr. Crenshaw turned to the police chief.

"This fellow Sam?" he asked. "Can you place him?"

"Sounds like Sam Robinson to me," the chief said, a trifle grimly. "Know him well. Been in jail a few times. Do anything for money, and likes to play practical jokes. Wonder if he could have been trying some crazy joke last night? Expect I'll have to ask him a few questions."

"That was no practical joke!" Mr. Crenshaw exploded. "I want to ask that fellow some questions myself. One, how he knew the boys were coming. Two, how he knew they were amateur investigators. And three, why he marooned them on that island. Why, we might

352

not have found them until today or tomorrow if that boy Chris hadn't rescued them!"

"That's a fact," the chief agreed. "When we learned you lads had got off the plane and then vanished into thin air, we were looking on land for you. Stopped cars for miles around to ask questions."

"What I want to know," said Mr. Crenshaw, "is how this kid Chris was able to find you so easily. What's his story?"

The three boys were forced to confess they had forgotten to ask him. They had meant to—then they had seen the merry-go-round and the ghostly figure of a woman on it, and in the excitement the question had slipped their minds.

"You saw the ghost?" Mr. Crenshaw exclaimed. "But that's impossible. The phantom of the merry-go-round is just a local superstition!"

"Now hold on a minute," Chief Nostigon said. "Folks around here believe in that phantom pretty strongly. The last few years, more'n one fisherman has seen it on a stormy night out on Skeleton Island. Hardly a soul will go near that island now.

"What's more, the whole town is buzzing about the phantom riding the merry-go-round last night. Lots of folks heard the music, and a few got out spyglasses and could see a white figure just like these boys describe it. I'm not saying I believe in ghosts, but you can't get a soul in these parts to believe poor Miss Sally Farrington's spirit wasn't trying to ride that merry-go-round last night."

Pete's father shook his head. "This whole part of the picture is jinxed! I'll bet not a single workman shows up today."

"And maybe not tomorrow either," agreed Chief Nostigon. "Well, Mr. Crenshaw, I'll pick up Sam Robinson and ask him some questions. But we still don't know just how the boy Chris found these lads last night."

"It's darned suspicious, if you ask me," Mr. Crenshaw said. "That kid has been pestering me for a job, but he's got a bad reputation locally. Plenty of people say he's a clever little thief. I wouldn't be surprised if he had a hand in all the trouble we've been having."

"Chris didn't seem like a thief to us, Dad," Pete put in. "He seemed like an all-right kid. He has a sick father to help, and he sails round looking for washed-up treasure, but that's nothing against him."

"The boy's right," Chief Nostigon agreed. "I know Chris has a bad reputation, but he's a foreigner and most folks in this town are pretty clannish. They're ready to believe anything bad of a foreigner."

"Just the same, I have my suspicions of him," Mr. Crenshaw declared. "Now that I think of it, it could easily be a boy stealing our equipment. Maybe he's hoping to sell it to help his father."

He stood up. "All right, boys, let's get going. Mr. Denton himself is waiting out on the island for us. Chief, I'll be seeing you later. Meanwhile, I hope you can find this Sam Robinson and clap him in jail."

A few minutes later, Jupiter, Pete and Bob were in a fast motor-boat speeding to Skeleton Island. They would have liked to look round Fishingport more, but they didn't have time. They saw many docks and piers, but few boats— they understood that most fishermen had gone to the south end of Atlantic Bay where oystering was still safe and legal. All in all, Fishingport looked like a small and very poor fishing village.

Now, as the speedboat raced through the water, they eyed the island ahead with interest. It was a mile long, well wooded, and had a small hill towards the north end. They could barely see the remains of Pleasure Park through the trees. Across this mile of water, boats had once ferried gay crowds of merrymakers, but that day was far in the past.

They coasted in to an old pier at the south end of Skeleton Island, and Pete made a line fast. Another motor-boat was tied up there, a wide craft with special steps over the side—the kind of boat often used for Scuba diving.

Mr. Crenshaw led the boys up a well-marked trail. They soon reached a clearing where two trailers and several large, army-style tents had been set up.

355

"There's Mr. Denton," Pete's father said. "He drove down from Philadelphia yesterday for a conference and is going right back."

A young man wearing horn-rim glasses came towards them. Behind him three other men waited, one with greying hair who the boys soon learned was Harry Norris, the assistant director; a blond young man with a crew cut, who was Jeff Morton; and a big, barrel-chested man with a stiff left arm and a gun strapped to his waist who was Tom Farraday, the guard.

"This is our camp for now," Mr. Crenshaw went on. "We ferried the trailers and equipment over on a barge. The tents are all right until the main company gets here, then we'll need more trailers."

He pointed out and identified the other men, then spoke to Roger Denton, the director.

"Sorry to be a little late, Mr. Denton," he said. "I stopped to get the boys."

"Good," Roger Denton said. He looked rather upset. "Harry Norris has just been telling me about all the delays and I'm not happy about them. If you find you can't get the roller coaster working in a week, we'll forget Skeleton Island altogether. It's a great place for the scenery we want, but we may be able to save money by renting a roller coaster back in California and artificially ageing it. We can take back groundshots here that will give us the wonderful old, dilapidated effect."

"I'm positive we can get the roller coaster fixed," Mr. Crenshaw said. "I've got a call out for carpenters now."

"I doubt if you'll get them," Roger Denton said grimly. "Not since the whole town knows the ghost was seen riding the merry-go-round last night."

"That ghost!" Pete's father exclaimed. "I wish I could figure that out."

Tom Farraday, standing a few feet away, coughed apologetically.

"I'm very sorry, Mr. Crenshaw," he said. "I guess—well, I'm afraid I was the ghost folks saw last night."

5

The Skull Talks

"IT'S LIKE THIS," the guard explained as everyone stared at him. "Last night, I was here alone on guard when you all went to the mainland to look for the boys. When the storm hit, I took cover in a trailer. After the storm I heard a motor-boat, and I went out to see if maybe some thief had landed. I thought I saw a dark figure lurking behind the merry-go-round. As I started that way, I saw someone run away.

"I was worried that he'd been fooling with the motor, right after you got it fixed. So I turned on the lights and started it up. Of course the music started playing and the merry-go-round started turning. I walked round it, making sure there was no damage, then I turned it off."

"But the ghost, man, the ghost!" Mr. Crenshaw exclaimed.

"Well, sir—" Tom Farraday seemed embarrassed—"I was wearing a yellow storm slicker. And from a distance me in a yellow slicker probably looked enough like somebody in a white dress so that folks thought—well, you know."

"Oh, no!" Pete's father groaned. "Tom, you've got to go ashore later and tell everybody exactly what happened."

"Yes, sir," the guard said.

"As if we didn't have enough troubles already," sighed Mr. Crenshaw. "Well, we'll hire two more guards. Tom, look for two good men. None of these no-good fishermen who'll pretend to guard our equipment and then steal it—get honest men."

"Yes, sir."

"The idea of these boys doing a little private sleuthing for us on the quiet is no good now," Mr. Crenshaw said to Roger Denton. "Everybody in town seems to know they're boy detectives. That fellow Sam Robinson for one, though I'm blamed if I can figure out how."

"I think I can explain that, too, sir," Tom Farraday spoke up. "You see, when you and Mr. Denton were discussing the whole idea on the telephone with Mr. Hitchcock in Hollywood —well, most phones in this town are still on party lines. Other people can listen in. You know how it is in small towns. People snoop. It was probably all over town as soon as you hung up."

Mr. Crenshaw groaned. "That's what we're up against!" he said. "I'll be happy to get back to Hollywood. This Skeleton Island idea is turning into a jinx."

"We can get some beautiful shots here," Roger Denton said, "if you can get the roller coaster fixed up. Well, I have to get back to the mainland and start for Philadelphia. Jeff, suppose you ferry me over."

"Sure thing, Mr. Denton," the younger man said, and they started for the pier.

Mr. Crenshaw turned to the boys.

"Why don't I show you round while Jeff is gone?" he said. "As soon as he gets back, he'll see how well you boys can dive."

"Great, Dad!" said Pete.

A short walk brought them to a tumbledown fence. They walked over it and were in the abandoned amusement park. Pleasure Park really did look decayed. Refreshment stands were half caved in. The rides were rusty and falling apart. The Ferris wheel had toppled over in a storm and lay in pieces on the ground. An ancient roller coaster still stood upright, but with some timbers of its foundation dangling loose.

But the boys were most interested in the huge, old merry-go-round. Even in daylight, it had a spooky look, its paint peeling and new wood showing where Mr. Crenshaw's men had repaired it.

Mr. Crenshaw told the boys how it was to be used in the movie. "The way the picture is going to end is this: It's about a man who is falsely accused of a crime and is trying to find the true criminal. That's where the title comes from— *Chase Me Faster*. Finally the criminal hides on Skeleton Island here. Some young people row out for a picnic. They try the old merry-go-round, while the criminal secretly watches them."

"Golly, that sounds pretty exciting," Pete said.

"Where does the roller coaster come into it, sir?" Jupiter asked.

"The hero tracks the criminal here and starts to close in on him. The criminal abducts two girls from the picnic party and forces them into a car of the roller coaster. As the police surround him, he threatens to throw the girls over the side. The hero manages to get into the same car and there is a terrific fight at the end, as the old roller coaster swoops up and down and around."

"Terrific!" Bob said. "And in this spooky old

park it'll be the most! I can hardly wait to see it."

"If we shoot it here," Mr. Crenshaw said gloomily. "Well, we'll see. You boys can look round. Come back in half an hour. Jeff Morton ought to be back from the mainland by then."

He started away, then paused.

"Whatever you do," he said, with a look half worried and half humorous, "please don't find any treasure! Repeat, don't find any treasure! This was once a pirate hangout, you know."

"Yes, sir," Bob answered. "We've read all about the pirates and the treasure and the capture of Captain One-Ear."

"People never seem to give up," Mr. Crenshaw shook his head. "This island must have been dug up by large expeditions at least twenty times since then. Luckily, during the last fifty years not a doubloon has been found, so the treasure fever has died out. But knowing you boys, nothing would surprise me—not even your finding treasure where there isn't any!"

"Will it be all right, sir, if we explore the cave?" Bob asked. He pointed to the one hill on the island. "The old maps show a cave up at the top of that hill. The stories say it was used by the pirates to hold prisoners for ransom, but no treasure was ever found there."

"Yes, you can explore the cave," Mr. Crenshaw agreed. "But be back in half an hour."

He turned and walked away. The boys stood

staring round them at the ruins of Pleasure Park.

"It sure is creepy here all right," Pete said. "But that roller coaster scene will be terrific. It's scary just to think about."

"Jupe, you haven't said much," Bob said. "What're you thinking about?"

The First Investigator was looking very thoughtful.

"Your dad, Pete, and the others," he said, "seem to think that some of the fishermen are responsible for the thefts that have been going on, either for mischief or to steal something valuable. But I don't think so."

"You don't? What do you think?" Pete asked.

"The sabotage of the boats and the thefts of equipment," Jupiter said, "seem designed to get the movie company so fed up with Skeleton Island they'll move away and shoot the end of the picture somewhere else. This island has been deserted for twenty-five years and it is my deduction that someone wants it to stay deserted, and is deliberately trying to annoy Mr. Denton into abandoning the project."

"Want the movie company to leave!" Pete said blankly. "Why would anybody care if they left or not?"

"That is the mystery," Jupiter acknowledged. "Now let's go and see the old cave."

Ten minutes trudging uphill through scraggly trees brought them to a cave near the top of the rocky hill. The entrance was small, and the interior dark. However, once they were inside, there was light enough to see that they were in a roomy cave that went back quite a distance, narrowing towards the rear.

The soil of the cave was loose. It looked as if it had been dug up many times. Jupiter picked up a little of the sandy dirt and nodded.

"Many people have dug here for treasure," he said. "I daresay every inch of this cave was examined several times in the past hundred years. However, no sensible pirate would ever hide his treasure here. He'd look for a place less noticeable."

"Yeah," Pete agreed. "Wish we'd brought our flashlights. I'd like to look around in the back there."

"You're not as much of an investigator as I thought, Pete," Jupiter said, grinning. "You either, Bob. Look at me."

They looked with surprise as Jupiter unclipped a flashlight that was hanging from his belt.

"Primary equipment for any investigator," Jupiter said loftily. "However, I'll admit I remembered the cave, too, and planned on looking into it if we got the chance. Otherwise I might not have thought of it either."

He beamed the light towards the low back part of the cave. Some flat rocks looked worn smooth, as if imprisoned men had once lain on them as very hard beds. Jupiter's flashlight flicked over other rocky crevices and ledges until, at a point about six feet above the ground, it stopped suddenly.

Something white rested there on the ledge of a rocky shelf. Something white and round. Bob gulped. It was a human skull.

It seemed to grin at them. And then, just as Bob was reminding himself that it was only a bony memento of the bad old pirate days of long ago, the skull spoke to them.

"Go 'way," it sighed, with a strong accent that sounded Spanish to Bob. "Let me 'ave my rest. No treasure is here. Only my tired old bones."

6

Gold Doubloons

BOB FOUND that his feet had automatically turned to take him out of the cave. In another moment he and Pete were racing each other for the outside, with Jupiter not far behind. Bob and Pete collided and sprawled headlong at the entrance.

Jupiter, however, had turned back. He picked up the flashlight he had dropped and shone it on the skull.

"Skulls can't talk," he informed the aged death's head, "because to talk you need a tongue and larynx. Therefore logic tells me you did not speak."

Bob and Pete, picking themselves up outside the cave, suddenly heard whoops of laughter. Puzzled and a little embarrassed, they went back inside.

Chris Markos, the boy of the night before, was climbing down from a niche in the ricky wall.

"Hi," he said, tossing the old skull behind him. "Remember me?"

"Of course we remember you," Jupiter said. "In fact, I had already deduced it was you because earlier I saw a sailing-boat ahead of us that looked like yours. Besides, the voice that spoke was too youthful to be anything but a boy's."

"I scare you, yes?" Chris grinned. "You think dead pirate is talking to you."

"You startled me," Jupiter corrected him. "You scared Pete and Bob, though."

Bob and Pete looked sheepish.

"You didn't scare *me*," Bob said. "You scared my legs. I didn't know they were going to run until they did."

"Me, too," Pete agreed. "When a skull starts talking, my legs want to be some place else."

"Good joke!" Chris still radiated merriment.

"I hope you will not be mad, though. It is just for fun."

"No, we're not mad. We've been wanting to talk to you. Let's go outside in the sun." Jupiter led the way outside and all four boys stretched out, their backs against a rock.

"How did you happen to be here?" Jupiter asked the Greek boy. "I mean in the cave and everything, waiting for us?"

"Easy," Chris said. "I am sailing, and I see boat take you to the pier. I sail round the island and pull up my boat on the beach. I slip through trees, and see you at the old merry-go-round. I hear you say you are going to explore the cave. I know a short-cut, so I get there first. Then I think of this good joke with an old skull I know is up on one of the rocks. I climb up and hide and wait for you."

That explained everything, but Bob wanted to know why Chris had hidden. Why hadn't he come out and said hello earlier?

"The guard," Chris said simply. "That Tom Farraday always chases me away. Everybody chases me away."

His cheerful grin was suddenly gone.

"I have a bad name in town," he said slowly. "People think I am a thief, because my father and I are poor. And different. From a foreign country. In town are some people who are not good. They steal things and say Chris the Greek does it. But I do not do it!"

They believed him. It was an old trick, they knew, to blame things on an outsider.

"We believe you're honest, Chris," Pete said. "One thing puzzles us, though. How did you find us so quickly last night?"

"Oh, that," Chris said, grinning again. "I do some work in a place called Bill's Tavern. I sweep, wash dishes, get two dollars a day. My father and me, we live on that. Mr. Bill is a nice man."

"Two dollars a day!" Bob exclaimed. "How can you live on that?"

"Live in an old, abandoned fishing shack, no rent," Chris explained soberly. "We eat beans and bread and I catch many fish. But father, he is sick. He needs good food. So all the extra time I have, I sail around the bay, hoping to find big treasure. But I am foolish, I guess. Some treasure lies on the bottom of the bay. But what chance has Chris Markos to find lots of it?"

"You have as much chance as anybody!" Pete said. "But you were going to tell us how you knew where to look for us."

"Oh, sure. Yesterday I am washing dishes. I hear men talking in the last booth of tavern. One says, 'Three kid detectives, huh? Well, I'll hand them a surprise. I'll hand them something they won't forget!' Then they all laugh."

Jupiter pinched his lip thoughtfully. "Tell me, Chris, when this man spoke the word 'hand' did he do it with special emphasis?" he asked.

"He means did he say 'hand' in some special way?" Bob interpreted as the Greek boy looked puzzled.

"Oh, yes he does!" Chris exclaimed. "Each time he says 'hand' he makes the voice deeper and louder. So when I hear three boys are missing, I think to myself, where could anyone hide three boys? Then I remember the funny way that man says 'hand'."

"And you deduced that he was referring to the island called The Hand!" Jupiter exclaimed.

"That is just what I think. So I sail out as soon as the storm is over. And I find you right there, on The Hand. Only—" and Chris's face clouded again—"now movie people think that I had something to do with it. Nobody believes good of me."

"We believe in you, Chris!" Bob said stoutly.

Chris smiled. "You believe in me, I show you something."

His hand went beneath his pullover and out came a little well-oiled leather sack. Chris loosened the draw string.

"Hold your hands out," he said. "Close your eyes. Do not look until I say."

They obeyed. Something warm and heavy was placed in each boy's palm. When they opened their eyes, each was holding an antique gold piece!

Bob examined the worn, but still shiny coin. "Sixteen fifteen!" he exclaimed.

"Spanish doubloons!" Jupiter said, his eyes shining. "Real pirate treasure!"

"Golly!" Pete said in awe. "Where'd you find them?"

"In the water, lying on sand. There is plenty of treasure in bay — Captain One-Ear, he dumped his whole treasure overboard a long time ago. But now it's all scattered, a little here, a little there. Very hard to find any. I dive and dive. One piece I find off the other end of Skeleton Island, near wreck of nice yacht. But I find two right together in one special little bay where I think maybe——"

At that moment a loud, angry voice interrupted them.

"Hey! You, Chris! What're you doing here?"

Startled, they looked up. Tom Farraday, the normally good-natured guard, was puffing up the path towards them, his face dark with anger.

"I told you if I caught you hanging round any more, I'd give you a whaling!" Tom Farraday cried. "Those are my orders and—"

He stopped. The boys turned and followed his gaze. But Chris Markos had disappeared behind a rock as silently as a shadow.

7

Danger Underwater

"WHAT DID that kid want?" Tom Farraday demanded. "Why did he bring you boys up here?"

"He didn't want anything special," Jupiter told him. "And he didn't bring us up here. We came up to look at the cave."

"Well, let me tell you, that Chris is no good!" the guard said. "If nobody's actually caught him stealing anything yet, it's because he's too smart. Take my advice and stay away from him. Now come along. Jeff Morton is back and wants to do some diving with you."

As they started down the trail, Tom's manner became more friendly.

"I suppose you were hoping to find some treasure in that cave," he said. "Well, there isn't any and never was. What's left is scattered over the bottom of the bay. Once in a long while a piece turns up on a beach, but people have got tired of even hunting for it any more, it happens so seldom."

He chuckled.

"When Davy Jones takes something, he doesn't often give it back. Did you know that he took a hundred thousand dollars in good American cash only ten years ago? Yes sir, he took it and kept it. And because of that hundred thousand dollars my left arm got crippled and I've been this way ever since, only able to do odd jobs."

He moved his stiff left arm to show what he meant. The boys clamoured for the story, and Tom willingly obliged.

"Well, boys," he said, "I used to be a guard on an armoured car for the Dollar Delivery Company. One of our jobs was to pick up cash from the local banks and take it to the big national bank in Melville.

"Never had any trouble and didn't expect any. You see, we never followed the same route twice or went to the banks at exactly the same time. Just the same, one day—"

What had happened was that one day, about ten years before, they had stopped to pick up money from the bank in Fishingport. Then they had parked the armoured car to eat lunch. Naturally it was tightly locked, and they sat where they could see it.

However, as Tom and the driver left the restaurant, two men wearing Hallowe'en masks had stepped out of an old sedan and shot the driver in the leg. Tom had lunged at the men, but they had smashed him over the head and shoulder with the barrel of the gun, knocking him unconscious.

Then they had taken the keys of the armoured car from his pocket, and driven off. But Chief of Police Nostigon, then a patrolman, had heard the shot and came running in time to fire at the two as they climbed into the stolen truck. He hit one of the robbers in the arm.

The alarm went out promptly, of course, and all nearby roads were bottled up. At nightfall the armoured car, bloodstained and empty, was found in an abandoned boat-house some miles away. It became apparent that the thieves had made their escape by water.

During the night a Coast Guard patrol boat sighted an old motor-boat drifting helplessly in the bay. As they closed in on it, two men were seen to dump several bundles overboard. They sank immediately.

When the Coast Guard boarded the boat, they found two men, Bill and Jim Ballinger, ready to give up. Their engine had broken down, and one of them, Jim, had a bullet wound in his arm. But not a scrap of money from the hold-up was found, then or later.

"You see, boys," Tom Farraday said, "they just chucked it overboard. Same thing old One-Ear did hundreds of years ago when he saw the British were going to catch him. It went to the bottom, sank in the mud, and no one could find it. Being paper money, it rotted away mighty fast."

"Golly!" Pete said. "That was quite an experience, Mr. Farraday. Did the Ballingers go to jail?"

"Oh, sure," the guard replied. "With the bullet from Chief Nostigon's gun in Jim's arm, they never had a chance. They went up for twenty years, but it was reduced to ten for good behaviour. They just got out a couple of weeks ago. I'd certainly like to pay them back for crippling my left wing, boys," Tom said fervently. "Haven't been much use since then— just odd jobs for me. Well, here we are and there's Mr. Crenshaw."

Pete's father and Jeff Morton were on the pier, stowing some gear into the big motor-boat. Mr. Crenshaw straightened as the boys came up.

"Hi, boys," he said. "Jeff is ready to check you out on your skin-diving. He's an expert diver and we have the very latest equipment here. He'll explain everything."

With that, Mr. Crenshaw left them, and the three boys climbed into the broad, roomy motor-boat.

"Okay, fellows," Jeff said. "Tell me what diving you've done."

Pete described the lessons they had had at a local swimming pool at home. They had become very familiar with snorkelling, and had been

373

checked out by their instructor in Scuba diving just before coming East.

"So far, so good," Jeff said with an encouraging grin. "Now let's *see* how much you know."

He started the motor and ran the boat well out into the bay. Near a small yellow buoy, he dropped anchor.

"There's a wreck underneath us," he said. "No, it's not a treasure ship. Any old Spanish ship would long ago have disintegrated in these waters. This is a small yacht that went down in a storm several years ago. It lies in twenty-five feet of water, which means we can dive down to it without worrying about decompression problems."

He inspected and approved their face masks and flippers. Then, from a well-stocked equipment locker, he got out tanks of air, hose connections, and weighted diving belts.

"This is the latest equipment, and as nearly foolproof as it can be," he said. "We won't use wet suits because the water here is nice and warm. Get into your trunks, Bob, you'll take the first test dive with me. Remember, we'll be using the buddy system at all times—always two divers together."

The boys got into their swimming trunks, and Bob carefully put on the equipment Jeff handed him. Last of all he buckled on the weighted belt that would come off if he had to make a fast ascent.

Jeff inspected him critically, nodded his approval, and got ready to go over the side. Bob followed, using the special steps.

In the water, Bob kicked his flippered feet and shot downwards. He liked swimming. Over the years he had done a lot of it to build up strength in the leg he had broken as a small boy. Now, able to go down like a fish and breathe without difficulty, he felt wonderfully light and free, part of a new universe.

Below him a dark shape loomed up. It was the sunken yacht, and with Jeff at his side he swam slowly towards it.

The yacht lay on its side, a gaping hole near the bow. As they got closer, Bob could see that it was covered with seaweed. Small fish swam around it in swarms.

Jeff swam ahead. Using only his flippers to propel him, as he had been taught, Bob followed. Jeff swooped gracefully over the stern of the sunken yacht.

As Bob started to follow, his attention was caught by two large lobsters retreating beneath the stern. He swam closer to the sunken vessel.

Suddenly he was jerked to a stop.

Something had him firmly by his right ankle!

8

"Don't Tell Anyone!"

IT WAS the first time Bob had run into any trouble underwater. A pang of alarm shot through him and he kicked his leg to free it. The grip on his ankle tightened. He was sure he could feel himself being pulled backwards.

He turned frantically to see what had grabbed him, and as he did so, his arm brushed his face mask. The next thing he knew he was blinded. Water had fogged the mask and for a second he couldn't remember how to clear it.

Then something gripped his shoulder. For a moment he was sure the monster, whatever it was, was attacking him. But three light raps on his air tank told him Jeff Morton had come back to his rescue.

Jeff's hand gripped his shoulder, calming him. Gradually Bob relaxed, though it did not release him.

Forcing himself to breathe calmly, he turned his head to the right, reached up, and cracked the left side of his mask ever so slightly. Then he breathed out through his nose. The air was forced out of the mask, taking the water with it, and he could see again.

The first thing he saw was Jeff Morton, shaking his head. He pointed, and Bob looked down to see what had caught him. A loop of rope!

He doubled over and eased the rope off his flippered foot. Angry at himself for panicking, he shot ahead a few feet and waited for Jeff, expecting him to end the dive immediately. However, Jeff formed a circle with his thumb and forefinger, a sign everything was okay. Then he swam ahead again and Bob followed, carefully keeping clear of the wrecked ship.

They swam the length of the ship, then all round it, the fish moving aside for them as if they were just two harmless larger fish.

Bob saw more lobsters sheltering themselves under the yacht. If he had brought a spear gun, he was sure he could have bagged a lobster or two.

They swam until Bob was relaxed again and enjoying himself, then Jeff headed for the surface at an unhurried pace. They could see the bottom of the anchored motor-boat. A moment later they came up beside it, their masked faces popping from the water like the snouts of some strange monsters.

Jeff swam to the steps at the side of the boat and climbed it. Bob followed.

"How was it?" Pete said eagerly, helping him in the boat. Bob shook his head.

"I didn't do so well," he said. "I got snagged on a rope, and got panicky."

Jeff Morton agreed that he hadn't done so well. He gave them all a brief lecture on getting too close to tangled wreckage, and followed it with one on losing your head in an unexpected situation—the most dangerous thing a diver could do. Then he relented and smiled.

"Maybe it was a good thing it happened now," he said. "A harmless but helpful lesson. Bob recovered himself well and next time I'm sure he'll keep calm. All right, Pete, now it's your turn."

Pete got ready swiftly. In a moment the two divers were gone beneath the water, leaving Bob and Jupiter alone in the gently bobbing motor-boat.

Bob told Jupiter of his experience in more detail, adding, "I think next time I go down I'll have more confidence. Now I know I can make myself act calm and clear my face mask if I have to."

Jupiter was about to reply when they heard a voice hailing them. A hundred yards away, the tiny sailing-boat owned by Chris Markos was gliding silently towards them.

Chris came up beside them and swung round, letting his sail flutter down. His white teeth

Fearfully he glanced behind him.

gleamed against his tanned face as he grinned at them.

"That fellow Tom Farraday tells you bad things about me, I guess," he said, his smile vanishing. "I hope you don't believe him."

"No," Bob said stoutly, "we don't believe him. We think you're all right, Chris."

"I am glad to hear that," Chris declared. He reached out and caught the side of the motor-boat to steady his craft.

He looked at the variety of diving gear in the motor-boat with some longing, but said airily, "Why do you need all that stuff to dive down to sunken yacht? I can go down that far just in my own skin. I'm a real skin-diver!"

"Is it true that Greek sponge fishers can go down more than a hundred feet without any diving apparatus?" Bob asked.

"Sure, easy," Chris boasted. "My father when he is a young man, he goes down two hundred feet with just a stone to make him sink fast, and a rope to pull him up again. He stays under three whole minutes without breathing."

Chris's face clouded. "But he dives too long," he said. "And he gets sick. But some day I find treasure, take my father home, get a little boat in Greece and be a fisherman myself."

Chris's smile came back. "Got to get busy. Keep looking if I wish to find treasure," he said. He hesitated, then added, "Maybe I take you with me tomorrow if you like to go? Nice fun even if we find nothing."

"That would be great!" Bob said. "If we aren't needed, that is."

"We might have to do something for the movie company," Jupiter added. "Or practise diving some more."

Then he surprised them, and himself, by giving a mighty sneeze.

"Are you catching cold, Jupe?" Bob asked.

"Do not dive if you have cold!" Chris warned. "Ears hurt fierce. Well, so long, I must get busy. See you tomorrow, maybe."

He let go, hoisted his sail, and in a moment the little boat was skimming across the sunlit surface of the bay.

A few minutes later, Pete and Jeff Morton surfaced and climbed aboard. Pete shucked off his gear, grinning widely.

"It was terrific," he said. "Had a little trouble clearing my eustachian tubes, but I swallowed hard and that fixed them up. Now it's your turn, Jupe."

Jupe got ready a little less eagerly than the others. Jupe was not naturally athletic, and though he liked swimming all right, he was not really keen on it. When he was ready and had passed Jeff Morton's inspection, he and Jeff slipped over the side.

"Bob!" Pete said excitedly as the other two vanished under the water. "Guess what?"

"What?" Bob asked.

"I think I saw something. Just as we were turning to come up, I saw something gleaming on the sand about fifty feet from the sunken yacht. I'll bet it's a gold doubloon. If we dive again I'm going to try to find it!"

"Wow, are you sure?"

"Not positive. I just got a glimpse of something bright. But it could be. Everybody says there's treasure scattered loose all over the bottom of this bay."

Bob started to reply, then stopped. Jeff Morton and Jupiter were already coming back up! In fact, Jeff was helping Jupiter, who was swimming blindly, his face mask twisted to one side of his face.

"What happened?" Bob asked.

"Nothing to be alarmed at," Jeff said. "Somehow Jupiter knocked his face mask loose. I don't know how but we weren't down far and he didn't lose his air hose."

The two climbed aboard, Jupiter looking miserable.

"My ears hurt as we went down," he said. "I tried to swallow to open the eustachian tubes. Then I had to sneeze. I pulled out my mouthpiece and held it, but I had to move my face mask to sneeze and I couldn't put it back again and—well, I guess I didn't do too well," he finished miserably.

He sneezed again.

"You're catching a cold," Jeff said sternly. "You should never have tried to dive today. Lucky we were only down a few feet. No more diving for you, my boy, for the next few days!"

"No sir, I guess not," Jupiter said humbly. "The air conditioning on the plane yesterday was pretty chilly and then being out in the storm last night—well, I guess I'm catching a cold all right."

"Never dive unless you're in excellent health," Jeff said. "Especially not if you have a cold or cough. Well, I'm supposed to give you kids practice in diving and I'll go ahead with Bob and Pete, but if you're going to be laid up, we may have to change our plans."

For the next couple of hours, Bob and Pete alternated in longer and longer dives. By the end of the afternoon they felt weary, but were sure they could handle any simple underwater diving that might be required of them.

On each dive, Bob kept his eyes open for the shiny thing Pete said he'd seen, but he didn't spot it. On the last dive of the day, though, Pete came up with his right hand tightly clenched. He scrambled aboard and hastily removed his face mask and mouthpiece.

"Look!" he said exultantly.

He opened his fist. On his palm lay a worn but shiny round coin, large and heavy.

"Holy cats!" Jeff exclaimed. "A doubloon!" He examined it carefully. "Dated 1712, and

Spanish, all right. Pete, whatever you do, don't let anybody know about this. I mean, besides us and your father."

"Why not?" Pete asked, puzzled. "You mean someone would try to take it away from me?"

"No, it's yours all right, you found it on the open sea bottom. But the people around here are treasure happy! They know in their hearts that there isn't any gold on Skeleton Island, but if word got round that you'd found something, the treasure hunters would be swarming over the island in no time. They'd ruin any chance we have of ever getting that movie finished!"

9

Mrs. Barton has Suspicions

THE BOYS were ready for bed early that night. Pete and Bob were weary from their diving, and Jupe was feeling very droopy because of the cold he was catching.

Mr. Crenshaw came to Mrs. Barton's home and had dinner with them. He was worried about the progress of the work on Skeleton Island.

"That story of the phantom of the merry-go-round is all around town!" he exclaimed angrily. "Tom Farraday has been telling people the truth, but they'd rather believe in a ghost than the truth. Oh, well, we'll make out somehow. I'll see you boys in the morning. Have to go now and try to line up a couple of new carpenters."

After he had left, they went to their room. They examined the gold doubloon repeatedly. It was very exciting to have a piece of pirate treasure in their hands, even knowing they'd probably not see any more. Then Pete put it under his pillow and they turned in.

They all slept soundly until Mrs. Barton called them for breakfast.

"Come and get it, boys!" she sang out up the stairs. "Pete, your father is here. He wants to see you all before he gets started."

They scrambled into their clothes and hurried downstairs. Mr. Crenshaw was waiting, looking rushed.

"Boys," he said, "you'll have to be on your own today. I have some workmen coming so I'll be very busy. And there can't be any more diving until we get our plans straightened out. Anyway, Jeff tells me you have a cold, Jupiter, and can't dive for several days."

"Yes, sir," said Jupiter and sneezed explosively. "I'm sorry, sir." He blew his nose, which was red. "I couldn't help it."

"No, of course not." Mr. Crenshaw examined

385

him keenly. "Boy," he said, "you stay quiet for a day or so. Go over this morning and see the doctor. Name's Doctor Wilbur. Fine fellow. In fact, he's the owner of Skeleton Island. While you're eating, I'll phone him."

The boys sat down at the table, and Mrs. Barton bustled in with pancakes and sausages. Mr. Crenshaw went off to the phone and came back to tell Jupiter that Doctor Wilbur would see him at lunch-time, when he'd have a few minutes free. He wrote down the address of Doctor Wilbur's office and hurried off.

"Gosh, Jupe, it's too bad you're going to be laid up," Pete sympathized. "I was thinking maybe we could borrow the motor-boat and go exploring."

"It will give me time to think," Jupiter said, trying not to act sorry for himself. "There is much to think about. The secret of Skeleton Island, for instance. I'm sure it does have a secret, but I cannot quite fathom what it is."

"Skeleton Island!" Mrs. Barton exclaimed, as she came in with more pancakes. "That horrible place! Did you know the ghost was seen riding the merry-go-round again just night before last?"

"Yes, ma'am," Jupiter answered. "Except that there is a perfectly natural explanation." He told Mrs. Barton what had really happened.

"Well, maybe," she conceded, but she didn't look convinced. "But everybody says there's a ghost and I say, where there's so much smoke, there's bound to be some fire."

With that she went out again. Jupiter sighed.

"Mrs. Barton is a good example of the difficulty of convincing people to give up a cherished belief," he said.

Just then there was a tap at the window. They turned. A tanned face was peering in at them.

"It's Chris!" Bob exclaimed. He hurried to the door.

"I'm getting ready to go hunting again," Chris said. "You want to come with me?"

"You bet!" Bob exclaimed. "Pete and I can. Jupiter has a bad cold."

"Too bad," Chris said. "But boat is pretty small for four anyway. I see you down at the waterfront. Bring swim trunks!"

He hurried off. When Bob told the others what Chris had wanted, Pete's face lit up.

"Great!" he said. "Maybe I'll find another doubloon! Let's go and get our trunks, Bob."

"Sure," Bob answered. "Golly, Jupe, it's too bad you can't go."

Jupe's face said he thought so, too, but the First Investigator just said stoically, "Well, if I can't, I can't. You two go on. I'll see you later."

"We'll be back for lunch."

Bob and Pete got their swimming trunks from their room. Then they hurried down to the waterfront where Chris had his sailing-boat tied to an old sagging pier. They jumped in, and they

387

were off on their first hunt for pirate treasure!

Left alone, Jupiter sighed a couple of times. Then, deciding to make the best of it, he went up to look again at Bob's notes and the magazine articles about Skeleton Island.

Mrs. Barton was in their room making the beds.

"Just thought I'd slip up and straighten your room while you boys were eating," she said. "I—land's sake, what's this?"

She had picked up Pete's pillow, and there was the gold doubloon.

"Land's alive!" the woman exclaimed. "It's an old Spanish gold piece. Treasure!"

She looked at Jupiter with wide eyes. "You boys found it out on Skeleton Island yesterday, I'll be bound. Didn't you, now?"

"Pete found it," Jupiter said. He remembered that Jeff Morton had warned them not to let anyone know of the find. But now the cat was out of the bag.

"He didn't find it on the island, though, but in the water. Quite a way from the island," Jupiter added.

"My, my!" Mrs. Barton clucked, finishing the bed. "On his very first day here, too."

She gave Jupiter a shrewd glance.

"You know," she said, "lots of folks are saying this business about making a movie out on Skeleton Island is just—well, just a big story. They say you folks are really hunting for old

Captain One-Ear's treasure that was never found. They say you have a new map and everything."

"That might explain why the company is being bothered," Jupiter said thoughtfully. "If people think there is a treasure map, they might be prowling around hoping to find it. And they might be trying to drive the movie company away in order to look for the treasure themselves.

"But really, Mrs. Barton, we don't know a thing about any treasure. All we want to do is get a few scenes of a new movie shot. You can tell everybody that."

"Well, I'll do that," Mrs. Barton answered. "But I don't know as they'll believe me. Once they get an idea in their heads it's a sightly job to shake it out again."

"Yes," Jupiter agreed. "Like they keep on believing in the ghost. Do you mind if I ask you some questions, Mrs. Barton? You've lived here all your life, and you can probably tell me a lot."

"Lands, I don't mind." The woman laughed. "Let me finish this room, then I'll come downstairs and have a cup of coffee and you can ask me any questions you like."

Jupe took Bob's bundle of notes downstairs and read them until Mrs. Barton joined him, sipping a cup of black coffee.

"Now ask away, boy," she said.

"Tell me how Skeleton Island came to be

haunted in the first place, Mrs. Barton," he requested, by way of getting started. Of course, he had read the story already, but he wanted to see if the local version agreed.

With great animation Mrs. Barton started talking. What she said tallied closely with what Jupe had read. However, the woman had more to add. After Pleasure Park had been abandoned, she said, the ghost stopped appearing. Then suddenly, some years back, it had appeared again—not just once, but several times a year.

"These fishermen who saw it," Jupiter asked, pinching his lip, "were they reliable men? People you could believe?"

"Well, now." Mrs. Barton frowned slightly. "I don't know as they were exactly that. We have some pretty rough elements among our fishermen. But lands, why would anyone make up stories about seeing a ghost?"

Jupiter had no idea. Yet he couldn't help wondering if someone hadn't done just that—made up stories.

"About when did this happen?" he asked.

Mrs. Barton couldn't remember exactly. Ten years ago, or maybe fifteen. Somewhere along there. She only knew that ever since, the island had had a very bad reputation, and people rarely went there.

"Until you Hollywood folks turned up, right out of the blue," Mrs. Barton finished, eyeing

Jupiter shrewdly. "And the phantom rides the merry-go-round again and one of you boys finds a gold piece and your people talk of thieves taking their equipment and—everything. If you ask me, there's something mighty strange going on that we don't know about."

Jupiter agreed with that. All his instincts as an investigator told him something strange was going on. But for the life of him he couldn't figure out what.

10

Disaster!

THE LITTLE sailing-boat moved briskly along, heeling over under a nice breeze. The boys had the bay to themselves, with no other boats in sight except far to the south.

Soon they were docking at the pier on Skeleton Island. It was Pete's idea to ask Jeff Morton for permission to borrow two sets of Scuba equipment. They would have borrowed a set for Chris, too, but they knew Jeff wouldn't have agreed. Besides, Chris wasn't experienced in using Scuba equipment.

Jeff said they could take some equipment for practice diving, warned them not to try anything dangerous, and hurried off in the direction of Pleasure Park.

Pete and Bob got their face masks, flippers and other equipment from the locker in the motor-boat. As an afterthought they added two underwater flashlights. Then they rejoined Chris in the sailing-boat. Chris had his own face mask and was confident he could dive as well with it as they could with all their aqualung equipment.

The boys relaxed in the warm sunshine, lulled by the gentle bobbing of the boat. After a time Bob saw they were heading towards the small island known as The Hand, where they had been so mysteriously marooned on their first night.

The Hand was about a quarter of a mile long and several hundred yards across. Now by daylight they could see that it was rocky and barren, uninhabitable. Bob looked for the spout of water they had seen that first night, but there was no sign of it.

He mentioned it to Chris. The Greek boy explained that the water was too quiet today. It only happened when the wind was blowing and the waves were rolling across the bay.

"Some kind of hole under island," he said. "Waves rush in there, blow out spout. Like whale."

He sailed up to within a hundred yards of the mid-part of the island. Then he dropped sail and flung a small anchor overboard.

"Have to anchor out here," he said. "Low tide

now, rocks are too close to surface. Only at high tide boat can sail right up to the island."

With the boat bobbing at anchor, Pete and Bob put on their Scuba equipment and Chris produced an old but serviceable face mask. They eased themselves into the water. Chris swam about fifty feet, then stood up. The water was only knee-deep.

"See?" he said. "Rocky reef here. Come on."

They swam over, found rock under them, and stood on a ledge about five yards wide. On the island side was a little bay with a sandy bottom, about twenty feet deep where they were. The bright sun showed the bottom quite clearly.

"In this bay I find two doubloons at one time last week," Chris said. "The other one I find near where you dive yesterday. Maybe we are very lucky today, find some more here."

They lowered themselves off the reef and Bob and Pete inspected the bottom, while Chris swam on the surface, peering down. They saw seaweed-covered rocks, starfish, and schools of small fish. There were lots of crabs going about their business in curious sideways motion. But nothing that looked like any treasure.

Pete signalled and he and Bob rose to the surface.

"This water isn't very deep," Pete said, removing his mouthpiece. "I don't think we should waste our air here. We may want to try somewhere else later. Let's take off the tanks and just use face masks, like Chris."

Bob agreed. They paddled to shore, stowed their Scuba equipment among the rocks, and swam back out to Chris. Then the three of them covered the entire length of the small bay, peering sharply down for the glint of gold.

They were not rewarded by any exciting discovery, however, and after a time they paddled in to shore to rest, warm themselves in the sun, and talk.

"Today no luck, I guess," Chris said, a bit disheartened. "I sure hope we find something. Father, he is more sick, needs care. Well, I know another place, I find gold piece once a long time ago. We go there and—"

He paused, staring at something offshore. Then all three of them became aware of the sound of a powerful motor in the distance.

A large dark-grey motor-boat, old and rather shabby, was heading towards the little cove at high speed.

"Somebody sees us, they come to hunt, too," Chris said.

Then, as the boat did not slacken speed, he leaped to his feet.

"They crash on the reef!" he cried. "Hi!" he shouted, waving his hands. "Sheer off! You hit the rocks!" Bob and Pete joined him, waving and yelling.

They could see a man in the stern of the boat,

"Sheer off!" they cried, signalling desperately.

an old hat pulled down over his face. Whether he understood their warning or not, they couldn't tell. But abruptly the roar of the motor changed. The boat slowed as if the motor had been thrown into reverse.

At the same time the bow swung round. Still with plenty of speed, the turning boat crunched into the side of Chris's anchored sailing-boat.

The heavy prow of the motor-boat cut into the smaller boat as if it were made of cardboard. For an instant the two boats were locked together. Then the man in the motor-boat gave his engine a surge of power. It reversed and pulled free.

The next thing they knew the motor-boat was heading back into open water.

The three boys stopped yelling. With sinking hearts they watched Chris's sailing-boat settle deep into the water and go under, disappearing from sight.

"Golly!" Pete groaned. "There go our clothes, our watches, everything!"

"There goes our ride home!" Bob said in dismay. "We're stranded here. Stranded again!"

Chris said nothing. Only his clenched hands and anguished face said what it meant to have lost the only thing he owned, the little sailing-boat with which he had been desperately hunting for treasure to help his father.

11

A Warning to Jupiter

JUPITER was still engrossed in Bob's notes about Skeleton Island when Mrs. Barton came to tell him lunch was ready.

"My gracious, where are Pete and Bob?" she asked. "I've fixed lunch for them, too, and they aren't anywhere in sight!"

Jupiter blinked. Bob and Pete had said they'd be back for lunch. But they'd probably got interested in searching for doubloons and forgotten the time.

"They'll be along any minute," he said. "I'll eat now. I have to go and see Doctor Wilbur soon."

Jupiter had a sandwich and a glass of milk at a scrubbed pine table in the kitchen. His nose was running badly and he still wasn't very hungry. Mrs. Barton told him how to get to Doctor Wilbur's clinic, which was only a few blocks away.

Not many people were on the streets. He walked past rows of colonial-style houses, many of which needed paint badly. He also passed a number of vacant stores with "For Rent" signs in the windows. Empty stores are usually a good sign that a town is having hard times, and business in Fishingport seemed very bad indeed.

Doctor Wilbur's clinic was a neat brick building, fairly new. In the waiting room was a woman with two small children, and two elderly men who sat patiently looking ahead of them at nothing.

The nurse behind the desk sent Jupiter straight in. He found himself in a combination office and examination room, with a desk at one end, and an examining table and white cabinet full of medicines at the other.

Doctor Wilbur, a tall man with greying hair, sat at his desk eating a sandwich.

"Hello, Jupiter," he said, eyeing the stocky First Investigator keenly. "I'll be right with you."

He took a swallow of coffee from a thermos and stood up. Rapidly and efficiently, he examined Jupiter's nose, throat and ears, listened to his heartbeat, tapped his chest, and took his blood pressure.

"Mmm," he said a few minutes later. "You seem to have a bad cold. Probably the sudden change of climate from California."

He got some white pills from the medicine cabinet, put them in an envelope and handed them to Jupiter.

"Take two of these every four hours for the next two days," he said. "Get plenty of rest and stay out of the water. I'm sure you'll feel a lot better soon."

"Excuse me, sir," Jupiter said, "can you spare me enough time for a few minutes' talk? I mean, if you're not too busy——"

"Have to finish my lunch," the doctor said, giving him another sharp look. "We can talk until then." He crossed to his desk and sat down again.

"All right, shoot," he said. "What do you want to talk about?"

"Well, I'm just trying to get all the information I can," Jupiter said. "Since you own Skeleton Island, where the movie company has been having so much trouble——"

"Skeleton Island!" Doctor Wilbur exclaimed. "I'm getting sick of hearing the name! That poor Sally Farrington was too nice a girl ever to become a ghost!"

"Then you don't believe in the ghost these fishermen say they've seen?" Jupiter asked.

"I do not. Those fishermen are an ignorant, superstitious lot. The ghost was seen just exactly once, and I can tell you the truth of that occasion. It was a silly practical joke by some very foolish pranksters. I was a young man at the time—the island belonged to my father— and I made it my business to find out. I know who it was—three boys who have since moved away.

"They rowed out to the island, started up the

merry-go-round, and one of them put on a white sheet. They waited until the lights and music had attracted investigators from town, then they left, rowing away in the darkness on the far side of the island.

"However, they never would admit it and I couldn't prove it. I told people it had been a prank, but everyone preferred to believe in the phantom. Ghosts are much more exciting to believe in than practical jokers!"

Jupiter nodded. Doctor Wilbur's story sounded like the truth.

"Once a wild story like that gets started," the doctor said, "you can never kill it. From time to time thereafter people claimed to have seen the phantom. The story was partly responsible for Pleasure Park's closing, but only partly. The truth is, another amusement park was built near Melville, and it was newer and more convenient. My father didn't have the money to compete with it, so eventually he had to close.

"When he died, I inherited the island. I couldn't sell it and there was no point in re-opening the park, so I've simply let it sit there.

"It's never made me a cent, all these years, until you people came along and offered to rent it for your movie. If—" and Doctor Wilbur looked at Jupiter from beneath bushy eyebrows —"you really *are* making a movie. People seem to think you have a clue to a vast pirate treasure hidden on the island, and are hunting for it."

"No, sir." Jupiter shook his head. "That's just a story, like the story about the ghost."

"Hmph! I rather hoped it was true, because if you found any treasure it would probably belong to me, being on my island."

"No, sir. We're not looking for treasure. Everybody says any treasure hidden there was found years ago."

"Of course it was. And I believe you. But people aren't rational about treasure. They'll believe anything."

"Doctor Wilbur," Jupiter asked, "why do you think some of the local people are trying to keep us from making a movie on your island? Because that's what I think is happening."

"Hmph!" the doctor said again and poured himself some more coffee. "If they think there's treasure, they're trying to chase you away before you find it. Or they may just be trying to steal some of your equipment—you know, many folks around here are terribly poor since the oyster fishing went bad. Or, it might be the mean streak some of the fishing people have. They may think it fun to plague you Hollywood people. Three possible reasons—take your choice."

"It seems hard to understand," Jupiter said, frowning.

"Trying to solve the mystery, eh?" The doctor smiled. "Understand you're sort of a whiz of a boy detective."

"I wouldn't say that, sir," Jupiter answered modestly, though he did have a pretty good opinion of himself. "My friends and I have done some detection. Here's our card."

He handed Doctor Wilbur one of The Three Investigators' business cards. It read:

```
┌─────────────────────────────────────┐
│                                     │
│       THE THREE INVESTIGATORS        │
│                                     │
│        "We Investigate Anything"     │
│                                     │
│            ?    ?    ?               │
│                                     │
│   First Investigator - JUPITER JONES │
│   Second Investigator - PETER CRENSHAW│
│   Records and Research - BOB ANDREWS  │
│                                     │
└─────────────────────────────────────┘
```

"The question marks," Jupiter explained, "are our symbol. They stand for questions unanswered, mysteries unsolved, enigmas of all sorts that we attempt to unravel."

Doctor Wilbur smiled.

"Pretty highfalutin'," he remarked. "But I like to see a boy with confidence in himself. Tell me, why do you suppose Sam Robinson deliberately marooned you on The Hand when you got here?"

"To scare us, I think," Jupiter said. "To make us want to go back to Hollywood. Because somebody is afraid we might find out the reason why the movie company is being bothered so. That makes the mystery even bigger, sir. It can't be mere mischief."

"Mmm." Doctor Wilbur shot him another keen glance. "You have a point there, son. You're smarter than you look."

"Thank you. Tell me, sir, I understand that stories about the ghost of the merry-go-round died out for many years, then suddenly began again ten or fifteen years ago. Can you tell me just when?"

"Let me see now—" the doctor stroked his chin—"I began to hear them just after I moved into this building. That was about ten years ago. Yes, that would be it. The ghost stories started up ten years ago and have been pretty thick ever since, at least among the more uneducated people in town. Why do you want to know?"

"I'm not sure," Jupiter confessed, "but anything might be important, sir. Thank you very much. I guess I've taken up enough of your time."

"Not at all." The doctor stood up. "Going to be very interested if you find any answers. And," he called after Jupiter, "if there's any treasure on that island, remember it belongs to me!"

Jupiter went out in a thoughtful mood. He had learned some things but he wasn't sure yet just what they meant. It would take a lot of thinking.

As he stepped out on the street, a passing car stopped and backed up. Chief Nostigon was driving it.

"Hello, boy," the chief said. "Thought you'd like to know we traced that scoundrel Sam Robinson. He's skipped."

"Skipped?" Jupiter asked.

"Got a job as a deck hand on a freighter, sailed out this morning. Won't be back for months, if ever. Did say, though, one friend reports, he did it just for a joke. Because you lads came here with such big reputations. Can't say I swallow that."

"I don't either," Jupiter answered.

"Well, that's all we've learned," the chief said. "I'll be in touch with you folks if we get anything more." And he drove off.

Jupiter continued towards Mrs. Barton's boarding house in a thoughtful frame of mind. He felt sure he should be able to guess the answer to the curious mystery of Skeleton Island, but so far it eluded him.

He hardly noticed his surroundings until, as he was passing a tavern, a tall, thin man stepped out in front of him and barred his way. Jupiter had to stop to avoid bumping into him.

"Hold on a second there, kid," the thin man said, his face twisting in an ugly grin. "I want to give you some advice."

"Oh? Yes, sir?" Jupiter recognized that the man was unfriendly, and he let his round face go slack so that he looked—as he could when he wanted to—very stupid.

"Just take a tip from me. Go back to Hollywood where you belong if you want to keep a whole skin. And take the rest of those movie fellows along with you. None of you are wanted here in Fishingport."

The man continued to grin nastily and Jupiter saw a tattoo mark on the back of his hand. It wasn't too clear, but it looked like a mermaid. He felt a little shiver of fear run down his spine.

"Yes, sir," he said, keeping a dull expression. "I'll tell them that. Who shall I say gave me the message?"

"Never mind the wise stuff, kid!" the man snapped. "Just vamoose if you know what's good for you. That's my helpful hint for today!"

Abruptly he stepped back into the tavern.

Jupiter's heart stopped beating quite so fast. Slowly, he walked on towards Mrs. Barton's. It certainly seemed he'd been right about one thing. Someone was very determined to drive the movie company away from Skeleton Island.

12

An Exciting Discovery

"MY BOAT!" Chris was fighting hard to keep back tears. "It is gone. No more boat. No more chance to find treasure."

"Gosh, yes," Bob said, realizing Chris's loss was much greater than theirs. "What got into that guy anyway? Was it an accident or did he do it on purpose?"

"On purpose!" Chris said angrily. "Or else he would stop, see who owned boat, say he is sorry!"

"I suppose so," Bob said. "But why on earth would anybody want to wreck your boat, Chris?"

"Keep me from hunting treasure," Chris said. "Lots of fishermen don't like me. Don't like any strangers. Think the bay, the whole place belongs to them."

They stood there a moment longer, unable to decide what to do. They were hungry, there were no other boats in sight, and no way to signal. How long would they have to stay there?

"Well, anyway," Bob said at last, "we didn't lose the Scuba equipment. It's pretty valuable and I'd hate to have to pay for it."

"Gosh, yes!" Pete said. "This kind of equipment costs hundreds of dollars and—wait a minute!"

He and Bob looked at each other, the same idea coming to them in the same instant.

"Why, we can dive down for our clothes!" they exclaimed together.

Chris grinned, shaking off his gloom.

"We all can dive!" he said. "I am the son of

406

Greek sponge fisherman. I bet I can dive better than you, even if I don't stay down so long."

Now excitement spurred them on. Bob and Pete got swiftly into their Scuba diving gear, and they all waded out into the bay. They swam to the reef and walked over it, then lowered themselves into the deep water beyond.

The sunken sailing-boat was a glimmer of white on the bottom, seeming to sway gently as small waves washed the surface. Bob and Pete began to propel themselves downwards with their flippered feet.

Chris had picked up a rock from the shore and, clutching it in his arms, he sank rapidly past them. He reached the sand beside the wrecked sailing-boat before they were halfway down. He rummaged inside the boat, which lay on its side, for the clothes they had stowed neatly under the seat. With his arms full, he shot upwards. They could see him grin as he went past.

In the peacefulness of the ocean depths, Bob and Pete for a moment forgot their plight. They were Scuba divers doing a real salvage job, even if only on a tiny sailing-boat.

Close together, they kicked down to the boat and grasped the side. The sail rippled in the water and they had to take care to avoid being caught in it. They examined the interior of the boat. Chris had missed a pair of pants—Bob's pants—and Bob swam a few feet to rescue them.

Pete had to dive for one of Chris's shoes that slipped away from him and began to move away along the bottom. In fact, a fairly strong current seemed to be moving the whole boat, and when they let go of the side, they had to swim to get back to it.

After five minutes, they figured they had everything that could be rescued, and Bob nodded to Pete. They kicked upwards. They broke water to see Chris standing on the reef waiting for them. He grinned as they climbed up on the rock with their salvage.

"We do not do so bad, yes?" he said. "I guess we got everything."

He took his clothing from Pete and examined the soggy bundle. Then his face fell.

"My compass is not here," he said. "Nice one. I go back down and look."

He dived into the water.

"I guess we might as well take our stuff ashore and spread it out to dry," Pete said.

"I sure wish we had some way of signalling," Bob said. "Your dad will think we were mighty careless, getting stuck on this island again."

"It wasn't our fault, or Chris's fault either," Pete said. He picked up the two heavy-duty underwater flashlights they had rescued from the sunken boat. "I'm sure glad we got these back. They're expensive. And if we have to stay until dark we can signal with them."

"Golly!" Bob looked at the sun. "It's quite a

while to dark. I hope we don't have to stay here until then. I'm starved!"

"Let's get our clothes dry, then see what we can think of," Pete suggested.

They slid their face masks into place, then eased into the water and swam to The Hand. Wringing out their clothes, they spread them flat on the warm rocks, which promised to dry them in no time. They had removed their face masks and were starting to get out of their Scuba equipment when they suddenly realized that Chris had not reappeared. They had been busy for at least ten or fifteen minutes, and Chris was still underwater.

That could only mean trouble.

"Golly!" Bob blurted out. "Something must have happened to Chris!"

"Maybe he got caught down there." Pete went pale at the thought. "We have to try to rescue him!"

Without another word they got back into their diving gear, and started paddling for the reef.

They stood on the rocky ledge a moment, staring down into the sunlit green water. No moving form that could be Chris caught their eye, nor could they see the sunken sailing-boat now. Together they shoved off into the deeper water and started propelling themselves downwards, their hearts beating fast with anxiety.

There were cavities in the base of the reef—hollows formed by the currents. Maybe Chris had been pulled into one of them and got stuck. Or could he be tangled in the sail or trapped beneath the boat?

Soon they located the boat. Underwater currents had sent it bumping along the bottom of the reef for about twenty feet. They headed for it, but Chris wasn't in the boat.

Bob swam down until he could touch the sandy bottom. He peered under the boat fearfully. But Chris wasn't there, either. Whatever had happened to him he had not got caught in the rigging. Bob knew there were no sharks in these waters, or other deadly fish. What other danger could Chris have encountered?

Pete touched his arm. He held up two fingers side by side, then pointed towards a rock formation. Bob understood. He meant they should investigate the rocks together. Underwater you always stayed close to your buddy in case of trouble. Bob nodded and they set out, kicking themselves along vigorously.

The bottom of the reef was irregular. In places, small dark hollows had been cut by the swift current. They peered into each hollow place, wishing they had brought the underwater flashlights. But all they saw were swarms of little fish that swam hastily away at their intrusion.

Seaweed made waving curtains in spots, and

they had to push it aside to peer into the water beyond. At least five minutes passed. They had covered a good hundred feet without a sign of Chris.

They paused and put their face masks close together. Bob could see Pete's eyes, wide and anxious. Bob pointed back in the other direction. Pete nodded. Side by side they kicked rapidly back towards the sunken boat. They had almost reached the sailing-boat when a swiftly swimming figure shot past them.

It was Chris, and he was in a hurry to get to the surface!

How could Chris have stayed under water for twenty minutes without any diving gear?

They headed for the surface. Chris was sitting on the edge of the reef in waist-deep water, gulping great breaths of air into his lungs. He certainly didn't look hurt, and he was grinning broadly.

They came up beside him and shoved up their face masks.

"Good grief, Chris, you gave us a scare!" Pete exclaimed.

"Where were you?" Bob asked, grinning with relief. "What happened?"

Chris threw back his head and laughed merrily.

"I find something," he said, and held up his right fist, tightly closed. "Guess what?"

"Your compass?" Bob asked.

The Greek boy shook his head. "Guess again."

"A gold piece!" Pete cried.

Still grinning, Chris opened his hand. An irregularly shaped, shiny gold blob lay in his palm. It was rather battered, but it was certainly a gold piece.

"You never guess what I find," he said.

"A treasure chest?" Bob said hopefully. "Buried in the sand?"

"No, not that. I find a round opening in the bottom of the reef. Fish swimming in and out. I think, if fish can swim, Chris can swim. I swim in."

He paused dramatically.

"I find an underwater cave under the island! I find this doubloon in it! I bet—I bet there is a lot more treasure down there!"

13

The Secret Cave

SIDE BY SIDE, Bob and Pete floated in the water about five feet from the bottom. Bubbles went up from their breathing tubes in little clusters. A school of sea bass wriggled past them and disappeared into the black opening the boys were staring at.

It was not a big opening, perhaps only twelve feet wide by four or five feet high. It was shaped roughly like an eye—a dark, staring eye without any eyeball. The sides were smooth from the water currents that went in and out with the tides, and though there was seaweed nearby, none grew in the opening of the underwater cave.

Twenty feet to one side, Chris's sunken sailing-boat bobbed a little, but Bob and Pete weren't interested in the sailing-boat at the moment. They were engrossed in this underwater cave Chris had found. Each of the boys now had one of the waterproof flashlights in his hand, and in a minute, as soon as they got up their nerve a little more, they were going to swim into the cave and explore it.

According to Chris's story there was no danger.

He had been unable to find his compass on the sandy bottom of the bay. However, just as he was about to surface, he had seen the mouth of the underwater cave. Thinking of possible treasure inside, he impulsively swam in.

The cave seemed to get bigger as he went. It was dark, but he could look back and see the light spot which was the opening, and he kept that behind him.

He had just decided to turn back when he realized that in his excitement he had gone farther than he should. He didn't have breath enough to get outside and up to the surface.

"I sure am one scared fish then." Chris had grinned when he came to this point in his story. "I know my only chance is to go ahead, maybe cave will get big and I can come up for air. I swim like crazy. Then I see little bit of light ahead of me. I swim that way, then I come up and I have air to breathe! I breathe hard, then I look round. I am in a cave under the island! A hole going up through rocks lets in enough light to show me rocky ledge, covered with seaweed. I climb out to rest. My hand touches gold piece under seaweed. I get very excited. I look under all the seaweed for more gold, but cannot find any. Then I swim out to get you."

An underwater cavern with pirate treasure in it! If Chris could swim into it without any Scuba equipment, Pete and Bob could certainly do it with the modern aqualungs they had borrowed from Jeff Morton. It didn't sound dangerous. They could certainly take a quick look anyway.

As the boys hesitated at the entrance to the cave, a white body swam between them. It was Chris. Waving to them, he shot like an arrow into the dark mouth of the cave. With one accord they followed.

The twin beams of their flashlights gave excellent illumination in the clear water. On either side rose the rocky walls of the cave, heavily fringed with seaweed. Startled fish scurried past. A green moray eel poked its heavily fanged head out of a crevice in the rock, and the boys gave it a wide berth.

Chris was out of sight, swimming much faster than they. They had to be careful not to rub against the side of the passage lest it damage or pull off some of their Scuba equipment.

Pete shone his light upwards. Suddenly the top of the tunnel vanished. The boys swam quickly up—twenty feet, thirty feet. Abruptly their masked faces popped out of the water.

They were in a sizeable cavern with a rough ceiling four or five feet above their heads. Chris was sitting on a rocky ledge, dangling his feet in the water. The two boys paddled over and climbed cautiously up beside him on the slippery seaweed. They pushed up their face masks.

"We are inside The Hand now," Chris said to them. "How do you like my cave?"

"Golly!" Bob said fervently. "I'll bet nobody but us has ever been in here!"

He flashed his light around. The cavern was irregularly shaped, the roof varying from four to six feet above the water. Down towards the far end the cave narrowed sharply. However, there was a splash of daylight there, which puzzled them for a moment.

They shut off their flashlights to study it, and in the gloomy half-light the cave began to seem much bigger, eerie and mysterious. The eddying water made little gurgling noises against the rock, and strands of seaweed rose and fell like the floating hair of some mysterious underwater creature.

"There must be a hole in the rocks, going up to the surface," Bob said, puzzled.

"The spout!" Chris exclaimed. "It's that hole, the blowhole. In storm, water comes in here, rushes against rocks, and shoots up spout. Only nobody knows there is a cave down here. Think it is just a narrow crack some place down deep!"

"Sure, that's it!" Bob cried. He remembered how they had seen the water spouting up from the middle of the island during the storm two nights before. And of course, his notes mentioned the spout as something the very first explorers had discovered. Now they had found what caused it, something no one else had ever done.

"Oh," Bob's face fell, and the others looked at him inquiringly. "I just thought of something," he said. "If we're the first people ever to find this cave, there can't be any pirate treasure hidden in it."

"I didn't think of that!" Pete groaned.

"How do we know?" Chris demanded. "I find one gold piece, don't I? Let me have the flashlight and I dive down and see!"

Bob gave him a flashlight and Chris slipped

into the water. In the darkness they could see a dim glow of light as Chris swam down to the sandy bottom.

"It sure would have been nice if this had been a secret pirate hiding place no one had found before," Pete said. "But you're probably right, Bob."

They watched the glimmer of light below them move back and forth. Chris could certainly stay down a long time! It must have been two and a half minutes before the light went out.

An instant later Chris's head popped out of the water. Pete turned on his light, and Chris climbed up next to them.

"You are right," he said in a gloomy voice. "No treasure down there. Just crabs, fish, shells. Like this."

He opened his clenched fist.

In it lay two gold doubloons!

"Wow!" Pete and Bob whooped together. "Chris! Where were they?"

"In sand," Chris said.

They passed the gold pieces eagerly from hand to hand. They felt wonderfully heavy and valuable.

"Now we got three!" Chris said, eyes shining. "One each."

"No, you found them," Bob said. "They're yours."

"Share equal," Chris said stubbornly. "Now you go down. Maybe you will find more. Maybe enough to buy me a new boat, and take good care of my father!"

Eagerly, Bob and Pete adjusted their face plates, made sure their breathing tubes were in working order, and slid into the water.

The sandy bottom was dotted with shells. As they turned their lights this way and that, they saw nothing unusual. Then Pete spotted a shiny glint at the edge of the rocky wall. It was a gold doubloon, half buried in the sand.

Bob swam back and forth over the bottom with easy kicks of his flippered feet. A few minutes later he spotted a shiny object, partly hidden beneath an empty oyster shell. It, too, was a doubloon.

Excitement overwhelmed both boys. There really was pirate treasure in this underwater cave! Not handily stacked up in a nice, solid chest, maybe, but scattered over the bottom. There must be more and they would find it!

Heedless of the passage of time, they scoured the sandy bottom. They turned over oyster shells, making clouds of sand in the water and then having to wait until it cleared to search some more.

When they had found half a dozen gold doubloons each, their hands were too full to hold any more. Bob tapped Pete and they swam up and clambered out of the water. Exultantly they poured their golden find on to a flat spot on the ledge.

"We found some!" Bob said excitedly. "Chris, you're right, there *is* treasure in this cave!"

Smiling, Chris reached behind him and produced three more doubloons. "I find these on ledge under the seaweed," he said.

"I'll bet there's more!" Bob said. "I don't know where it came from, but if we found this much we ought to be able to find some more."

"You've convinced me!" Pete said. "Come on, let's keep looking."

Treasure fever makes it impossible for a person to think of anything else. And the three boys certainly had treasure fever now. Heedless of time or any other consideration, they began to search the underwater cave. They swam along the bottom inch by inch, and explored every crevice of the rocky cave.

Even as they hunted however, something was happening that they couldn't possibly guess. Chris's sunken sailing-boat, nudged by the underwater currents, was being wedged into the eye-shaped mouth of the cavern. There it stuck, sealing up the entrance like a cork in a bottle.

The three boys were trapped in an underwater cave that nobody knew existed!

A Dangerous Predicament

JUPITER was worried. It was late in the afternoon and still Bob and Pete had not come back from their sail with Chris. What could have happened to them?

He got up from the desk where he had spread out all Bob's papers and the notes he had added to them. He plucked a tissue from the large box Mrs. Barton had provided. Staring out of the window, he inspected the north end of the bay. There was no little sailing-boat in sight.

Mrs. Barton came in, bringing a glass of milk and some cookies.

"Maybe you'd like a snack, Jupiter," she said. "Lands, aren't those two boys back yet? Where can they be?"

"I don't know," Jupiter said, shaking his head. "They said they'd be back for lunch, and they're very reliable. Maybe they're in some trouble."

"Now, it doesn't pay to worry," the woman said. "Maybe they started fishing off one of the rocks and forgot the time."

She bustled out. Jupiter sat down and

munched the cookies while he looked at his notes.

In his mind he tried to sum up the facts. Twenty-five years earlier, poor Sally Farrington's death and a ridiculous joke by some boys had started the legend of a phantom on Skeleton Island. For many years it apparently hadn't been seen. Then, beginning about ten years ago, it had been reported quite often, but always by an unreliable group of fishermen. As a result, no one went to Skeleton Island.

Then the movie company had come to fix up Pleasure Park and shoot some scenes there. They had run into a campaign of theft and sabotage that Jupiter felt sure was intended to drive them away.

Were the stories of the ghost somehow connected with the harassment of the movie company, or weren't they?

Jupiter was still struggling with this question when the door opened. Jeff Morton came in, looking very upset.

"Jupiter," he said, "have you seen Chris Markos?"

"Not since breakfast," Jupiter answered. "Pete and Bob went sailing with him. They haven't come back yet."

"Sailing all day!" Jeff exclaimed, his freckled face pink with anger. "But they borrowed two sets of aqualung equipment from me this morning and said they wanted to practise diving."

His features darkened.

"Do you suppose they're out diving with that crazy Greek kid, looking for treasure?"

He and Jupiter stared at each other in growing alarm.

"We'll have to go and look for them!" Jeff said. "Something may have happened to them. If anything has, on top of what's already happened——" He didn't finish the sentence, but he looked grim. "Come on, Jupiter, let's get going!"

Jupiter forgot about his cold, forgot about the mystery, and everything else but finding Bob and Pete and Chris. He followed Jeff down to the waterfront, where a small boat with an outboard motor was tied to the pier.

They got in, the motor spun to life, and they roared out into the bay.

Jupiter wanted to ask Jeff what he had meant when he started to say "on top of what's already happened, "but he was obviously in no mood for conversation. In any case, the roar of the motor made it difficult to talk.

They sped over to the pier on Skeleton Island where the bigger motor-boat was tied up.

"We'll need more room to bring the kids back when we find them," Jeff explained as they got into the bigger boat. "Also," he added ominously, "I want my gear handy in case I have to do any diving."

That could only mean, Jupiter thought gloomily, that Jeff Morton was afraid something had happened to the boys while they were diving. He tried to put the thought out of his mind.

Bob and Pete weren't reckless. They wouldn't have any crazy accidents. But he knew that not all accidents were due to recklessness. Sometimes something unexpected just happened.

Jeff swung the powerful motor-boat out into the bay and they began their search. First Jeff circled Skeleton Island. Then he skirted up past the rocky reefs between the bigger island and The Hand. Finally he made a circle twice around The Hand.

"Nowhere in sight," he said to Jupiter, cutting the motor to idling. "That sailing-boat isn't in this part of the bay. The only other possibility I can think of is that the boys sailed over to the east side of the bay. We'll just have to go over there and cover every inch of the coastline."

Jupiter nodded. Jeff moved a lever, the motor took hold, and the boat started to roar away from The Hand.

Meanwhile, in the submerged cavern beneath The Hand, Bob, Pete and Chris crouched on the seaweed-covered ledge, dark water eddying round their waists. They didn't know how long they had been in the cave. But at the end where the blowhole was, the light had faded, and the tide had risen at least two feet.

They had been too excited at first to think about anything but the gold doubloons they were finding. They had gathered between forty and fifty gold pieces, which now filled the little canvas sack Chris had brought along for treasure. It wasn't a very big fortune, it was true, but an exciting find all the same.

Suddenly Chris had realized the tide was rising.

"We better get out of here," he told them cheerfully. "Anyway, we find all the gold, I think."

"We haven't found a doubloon for at least half an hour," Pete agreed. "And I'm starved. It must be awful late."

It was Pete, in the lead, who first saw the boat jammed in the entrance. It had slid into the eye-shaped opening on its side, its mast and flapping sail inward. The movement of the water had ground it into place and caught the tip of the mast in a crack in the rock.

Pete's flashlight picked up every detail. Less than a foot of space was left between the boat and the rocks. They couldn't possibly scrape through there. They were trapped!

Together Pete and Bob swam against the boat and pushed. All they did was push themselves backwards in the water. The boat didn't budge.

At that moment Chris came shooting between them. He saw the boat at the last minute, hesitated just long enough to take in the situation, then turned and swam desperately back into the cave. He had to surface and get another breath before the air in his lungs was exhausted.

Pete and Bob suddenly remembered that their own air was running low. They made another effort to push the sailing-boat out of the way, with the same lack of success. Then they followed Chris.

A couple of minutes later they were all crouched on the ledge.

"Golly! We are in a jam!" Chris said. "Tide has that boat wedged in tight."

"It sure has," Pete agreed glumly. "Who'd ever expect a thing like that to happen?"

"I noticed the tide was moving the boat earlier," Bob put in. "But I never expected it to push it into the entrance. What are we going to do?"

There was a long silence. Then Chris said, "Tide is coming in now. Pushing boat in. Maybe when tide goes out, water will push boat out again. We must hope so, I guess."

"But the tide won't turn for hours yet!" Pete groaned. "And when it does, suppose the boat doesn't move?"

"We've got a bigger problem than that," Bob said.

"Bigger problem?" Chris repeated. "What do you mean?"

"Look." Bob flashed his light upward. Just above their heads arched the roof of the cavern, wet and slimy with seaweed.

"See?" Bob said. "When the tide rises, this cave gets full of water. If we wait for the tide to turn, we'll be under water."

The rising water gurgled as it lapped around them. Nobody had anything to say. They knew Bob was right.

At that moment, in the motor-boat that was speeding away from The Hand, Jupiter gave a yell.

"Mr. Morton!" he called. "Turn back! I see something on the shore."

Jeff Morton frowned but swung the boat round. A minute later they were nudging up on a tiny sandy beach. Jupiter was out of the boat and running along the shore towards the rocks where he had glimpsed the boys' clothes. By the time Jeff had secured the boat and joined him, Jupe was excitedly rummaging through the now dry clothing.

"All their clothes!" he told Jeff. "They must still be here somewhere. Maybe they're diving on the other side of The Hand. I'll go and see."

Jeff Morton stared at the clothes in perplexity.

"The boat isn't here!" he exclaimed. "They've left their clothes and gone off in the boat with the diving gear for some reason. We——"

But Jupiter wasn't there to listen. He was hiking up the hump in the middle of The Hand, moving much faster than he usually moved.

He reached the top of the ridge and eagerly looked down towards the other shore. For a moment he couldn't believe there was nothing in sight. He had been so positive he would see his friends, or the boat. But they weren't there.

Dismayed, and realizing now just how badly he was worried, he slumped against a boulder.

Jeff came puffing up beside him.

"We were all round this island," he said. "They aren't here, you should have known that. But where can they have gone?"

Angrily he picked up a small rock and flung it down. The rock landed in a slight hollow in front of them, rolled a bit, and went down a hole about eight inches across. After a second, there was a faint splash down below.

Jupiter hardly noticed.

"You're right," he said, "I guess we just have to try the east shore of the bay. Though I can't imagine why they'd leave their clothes here."

Jeff stood up. "Come on, we'd better get a move on. I think we should call the Coast Guard to come and help us look. It'll be dark and we'll need all the help we can get!"

Jeff started back for the motor-boat and Jupiter followed. He knew Bob and Pete and Chris were in trouble. In his imagination he could hear their voices calling for help, and he couldn't answer because he didn't know where they were. He could almost hear them, as if—

"Golly!" Jupiter whirled around and started back, his legs pumping hard. He ignored Jeff's startled shout as he ran to the little hole in the rock, the blowhole, and flung himself down beside it.

With his face directly above the hole, he shouted, "Bob! Pete! Are you down there?"

There was silence. Jupiter, his heart pounding, realized it was a crazy idea. They couldn't possibly be down under this island.

Then up out of the blowhole, muffled but clear, came Pete's answer.

"Jupe! We're in a jam! If the tide rises a little more, we'll be under water. Get us out of here!"

15

Jupiter Thinks Fast

IN THE CAVE the boys held tightly to the seaweed on the rocky ledge. Otherwise the water that was up around their shoulders would have

428

floated them away. It was rising fast. Soon they'd have to swim and keep swimming, until the rising tide squeezed them right up against the roof.

"I wonder what's taking them so long?" Pete muttered, shivering a little. It seemed like a long time since the stone had unexpectedly come down the blowhole, and he and Bob had started yelling for help.

When they hadn't got any answer, there had been a bad minute in which they figured the rock had just rolled down by itself. But they kept on yelling, and then Jupiter's voice answered them.

After Jupiter, Jeff Morton had called down. It took a couple of minutes of yelling back and forth before they could get him to understand the situation. As soon as he realized the fix they were in, he shouted that he would get help for them fast. Then he and Jupiter went away.

Now the three boys were waiting for the promised help. Bob kept his light turned on, though the batteries were running down, because even the dim glow helped in the darkness.

"Listen!" said Chris. "We do not tell about gold doubloons. We keep that secret for now, yes?"

"Why?" Bob asked. "We'll have to explain what we were doing in here."

"Everybody with diving gear will come to

explore cave," Chris protested. "We do not get the chance to come back and look some more."

"As far as I'm concerned," Bob said, "I never want to see this cave again. I don't care how much treasure is in it. Let somebody else have it."

"I'll buy a double helping of that," Pete agreed. "Anyway, I think we found all there is. Just some doubloons that got washed in by the tide."

"But maybe there is some more!" Chris argued. "It is my big chance to find treasure to take my father back to Greece. What we have, only forty or fifty doubloons, is not nearly enough, especially when we divide up."

"Well," Bob said, "maybe we can keep it a secret. We can try, for your sake. I guess you're right about people coming to search this cave."

"Pete Crenshaw won't be among them!" Pete said fervently. "But if you want to come back, Chris, well, we'll just say we found the doubloons in the water. That's true enough. We won't say where."

"I keep doubloons secret if I can," Chris said. He clutched the canvas sack which held the coins. "I am not afraid to come back. The way we got caught would not happen again in a million years."

"Once will be enough if Jeff Morton doesn't hurry!" Pete groaned. "Golly, do you suppose he's going to have to go all the way to get the Coast Guard?"

"He'll need some help to get that sailing-boat out of the mouth of the cave," Bob said. "I'm almost sure he can't drag it loose by himself."

"But that could take a couple of hours!" Pete exclaimed, grabbing at the seaweed as a surge of water almost washed them from their slippery perch. "The tide will be in and this cave will be full by then!"

"Jupe will think of something," Bob said hopefully. "You can't beat Jupe in an emergency."

"I hope you are right," Chris said, in a very low voice. "But it sure is taking a long time!"

Actually, it had been only fifteen minutes since Jeff Morton and Jupiter had left the blowhole above and hurried back to the motor-boat. Now the boat was idling a hundred feet offshore, with Jupiter handling the controls while Jeff got as swiftly as he could into an aqualung outfit.

"Crazy kids!" he muttered, as he strapped on his weights and prepared to step over the side of the boat. "How in the dickens could they get into such a fix?"

He turned to Jupiter.

"All right, Jupiter, hold the boat steady right here," he said. "I'm going down and see what the situation is. Probably I can ease the sailing-boat out of the way. Anyway, I hope so. I don't want to have to go for the Coast Guard."

He pulled his face mask into place, grabbed an underwater flashlight, and went over the side.

Jupiter felt very much alone. In the distance he could see boats heading for Fishingport from the south end of the bay, but none came anywhere near him. The minutes went by very slowly as he waited for Jeff to come up again. When it seemed like an hour, he looked at his wristwatch and saw that only five minutes had passed. Another five minutes went by. Then Jeff Morton's head popped up right beside the boat. He climbed aboard, looking grey and anxious.

"That boat is jammed in the cave entrance, all right," he said. "As neat as a cork in a bottle. I got a grip on it and pulled but I couldn't budge it. It's a job for the Coast Guard. We'll need divers with crowbars either to break up the sailing-boat or pry it out of there."

Jupiter stared at him.

"Won't that take too long?" he asked tensely. "I mean, a couple of hours, perhaps?"

Jeff nodded slowly.

"All of that," he said. "I know what you're thinking. The cave will be full of water by then. But I don't know what else to do. If that blowhole was big enough, we could lower a line down it and pull them up. But it isn't."

Jupiter was pinching his lip, which always

helped him think. Now an idea was coming to him.

"Mr. Morton!" he exclaimed. "Maybe we could pull the sailing-boat loose!"

"Pull it loose?" Jeff frowned at him. "How?"

"With the motor-boat!" Jupiter said. "It has a powerful motor. We have an anchor and plenty of rope. We could hook the anchor on to the sailing-boat. Then if we give the motor full power straight ahead——"

"I'm with you!" Jeff exclaimed. "By George, it might work. Come on, we have to move fast!"

Working swiftly, he untied the anchor rope from the bow, brought it back and attached it to a ring-bolt on the stern. Then he dropped the anchor overboard, paying out all the rope.

"There!" he said. "A hundred feet of rope should be enough. Now I'm going back down to attach the anchor to the sailing-boat. When I tug on the anchor rope three times, ease the boat forward until the rope is taut. Then slowly give it full power. I'll be down there trying to help ease the sailing-boat out.

"If you feel a give, followed by a slow heavy drag, that'll mean you have the sailing-boat loose. Pull forward a hundred feet or so, then cast loose the anchor rope and reverse to come back to position. I'll swim into the cave and get those kids out.

"If you feel a tug, then suddenly you jerk free, you'll know the anchor came loose. Stop and wait for me to come up. But pray your idea works the first time!"

Jeff climbed over the side and was gone into the depths again. Jupiter waited, his heart beating anxiously, the anchor rope in his hand. He felt a pull on it, but that was only Jeff recovering the anchor and carrying it back to the cave. A minute passed, two—then he felt three sharp tugs on the rope.

Jupiter moved the boat ahead until the anchor rope was a taut, straight line from the stern down into the water. Then, ever so easily, he increased the power.

The motor began to roar. The propeller threw up a wash behind him. But the motor-boat did not move. Jupiter increased power, his heart in his throat for fear the anchor would tear through the side of the sailing-boat.

Very, very slowly, the motor-boat began to move. Sluggishly, as if pulling a whale, it gained distance. It was dragging a dead weight across the bottom, and it had barely enough power to move it. But it did move. Twenty feet—fifty feet —a hundred feet!

Jupiter would have cheered if he had not been so intent on the job. He threw the motor controls into neutral, and with his prized Swiss pocket-knife reached back and cut the anchor rope. The rope slithered down into the water. Jupiter gave the motor reverse power and eased back into position.

He tried to imagine what was happening below. The cave entrance was open now. Jeff was swimming in. He had found the three boys. Now he was instructing them to swim out and surface. In a minute—or two minutes—

A head popped out of the water just behind the boat. It was Chris Markos. He thrust up his face mask and breath exploded from his lungs. He paddled over to the motor-boat, grabbed on to it and pushed something heavy over the side. It dropped at Jupiter's feet with a clink.

"Hide it, Jupe!" Chris gasped. "We find treasure. But we keep it a secret. For now, anyway. Tell you all about everything later."

Jupiter hid the wet bag the best way he could think of. He sat on it.

"Boy!" said Chris when he was safely in the motor-boat. "We are sure afraid you can't get us out in time. Pete and Bob, they will be up any second."

Just then Bob's head appeared, and a second later, Pete's.

"It sure was good to hear your voice down there," said Pete when both boys had clambered aboard. "Yours and Jeff Morton's."

"He's pretty angry at us," Bob said. "I guess he has a right to be."

"When he talks to Dad, Dad will be angry, too," Pete said dolefully. "But anyway, we found some treasure. Did Chris tell you?"

"I'm sitting on it," Jupiter said. "You can tell me all about it later."

"I guess we're going to get a good bawling out," Bob said easing himself out of his gear. "But it actually wasn't our fault. First somebody sank Chris's sailing-boat, then——"

"Here comes Jeff Morton now," Jupiter interrupted him. "He'll want to hear what happened."

Jeff had surfaced at the stern of the motor-boat. In his hand he had the severed end of the anchor line. When Jupiter had grabbed it and attached it to the ringbolt, he swam round to the steps and climbed on board.

He removed his face plate and slowly took off his weights and air tank. Then he looked at the silently waiting boys.

"Well," he said at last, "I'm glad you boys are safe. Plenty glad. But that doesn't alter the fact that you acted recklessly and got into serious trouble."

"But—" Bob began. He was sure that if he could explain just how it all had happened, Jeff Morton would see that there wouldn't have been any danger except for the freakish current that had wedged the boat into the cave entrance.

Jeff held up his hand. "I don't care what your explanations are," he said. "Facts are facts. When I tell Harry Norris and Mr. Crenshaw what's happened, I'm sure they'll agree with me that you kids aren't to do any more diving.

"Hide it, Jupe!" Chris gasped.

"It was a bad idea to begin with—the water in this bay isn't really clear enough to get good underwater pictures. Harry Norris agrees with me, and I'm sure Mr. Denton will when he gets back here. So that idea of a short subject showing you diving for treasure is washed up."

He paused for breath, but it was plain he had more to say.

He turned and faced Chris.

"However," he said grimly, "I think one source of our troubles is ended. We've discovered who's been tampering with our equipment, stealing things, and giving us such a headache. Last night the equipment trailer was broken into through a small window, too small for anybody but a boy to get through. Someone stole two lenses worth almost a thousand dollars. I discovered the lenses missing—and I found something else. Something the thief dropped by accident."

His eyes bored into Chris's.

"I found your knife, Chris," he said. "Where you dropped it when you stole those lenses. Nobody else but you could have slipped through that tiny window.

"I've already reported the facts to Chief Nostigon, and when we get back to Fishingport, I'm marching you down to the police station. I'm very much afraid that you're going to jail!"

16

Jupiter Solves One Mystery

"BOY, we sure are in the doghouse!" Bob sighed.

"We're in the doghouse, but Chris is in jail," Pete said gloomily. "I don't think he stole those camera lenses, do you, Jupe?"

Jupiter didn't answer. He was sitting on the sofa in Mrs. Barton's living room, a far-away "thinking" look on his face. It was the middle of the afternoon and outside a heavy rain was pouring down. The boys had been ordered not to leave the house by Mr. Crenshaw, who had given them a severe lecture about irresponsibility the previous evening.

"Jupe!" said Pete more loudly. "I just said I don't believe Chris stole those camera lenses. Do you?"

Jupiter coughed. His cold was still bothering him.

"No," he said, "I don't. One kid can generally tell when another kid is sneaky and Chris isn't sneaky. It's just that appearances are against him. His knife being found at the scene of the crime is very peculiar."

439

"He lost it two days ago," Bob pointed out. "He said so."

"And of course the men wouldn't believe him," Jupiter said, coughing again. "They want to think the mystery of Skeleton Island is solved, so they believe he did it. That's the way adults often are."

"Well, what *is* the secret anyway?" Bob grumbled. "We're investigators and we ought to be able to at least make a guess."

"The secret is, someone wants to keep everybody away from Skeleton Island, that's all," Jupe told them. "I figured that out yesterday. The mystery is, why?"

Just then Mrs. Barton came into the room to answer the doorbell, and Jupe fell silent. Chief Nostigon came in, his raincoat dripping.

"Hello, boys," he said. "Mrs. Barton, I'd like to talk to these lads if you don't mind."

"Of course not, Chief." She went back out to the kitchen and the chief hung up his raincoat and took a seat. Deliberately he lit a cigar.

"Boys," he said, "I don't mind telling you things look bad for your friend Chris. We made a search and found those stolen camera lenses in a little woodshed behind the shanty where he lives with his father."

"He didn't steal them!" Bob said hotly. "We know he didn't!"

"Maybe not," Chief Nostigon agreed. "But the evidence is all against him. Everybody knows he's trying hard to raise money to get his father back to Greece."

"He doesn't have to steal to do it!" Pete exclaimed. "He has money! And the chances are he'll find some more!"

"Oh." The chief gave them a long look. "Now that's very interesting. He has money, has he? And he may find more. Meaning just what?"

Pete, realizing he had given away the secret of the doubloons, was silent.

"Boys," the chief continued, "I like Chris and I want to help him. Now, nobody will tell me exactly what happened yesterday. Just that you kids got into some trouble and had to be rescued. I think I understand why you're keeping it such a secret. If you found some treasure and the word gets round, Skeleton Island will be swamped with treasure hunters in no time.

"Just the same, I think you ought to tell me. Maybe I can help young Chris. So suppose you give me the whole story."

They hesitated. Then Jupiter made up his mind.

"Yes, sir," he said. "Pete, go and get the canvas bag."

Pete went upstairs. A moment later he returned with Chris's bulging canvas sack. Pete spilled the contents out on the sofa. With a soft clinking sound, between forty and fifty shiny doubloons slid on to the cushions.

Chief Nostigon's eyes widened.

"By Jiminy!" he said. "That's real pirate treasure. And Chris found that?"

"Chris and Bob and Pete," Jupiter said. "In an underwater cave on The Hand. Chris wants to go back and look for some more. That's why we're keeping it a secret."

"Mmm." Chief Nostigon pulled at his chin. "Well, you can count on me. I won't blab."

"So you see," Bob said eagerly, "Chris wouldn't need to steal anything. He has money and may find more."

"Boys," the chief answered, "I'm afraid that doesn't prove anything. You see, these doubloons were found *after* the camera lenses were stolen. So Chris didn't know he was going to have money. That means appearances are still against him."

It was true. Bob scowled as he realized it. Pete jammed his hands into his pockets.

Jupiter coughed again. He blew his nose. Then he spoke up.

"Excuse me, Chief," he said. "I admit Mr. Crenshaw and Mr. Norris and Jeff Morton think the secret of Skeleton Island is solved—that Chris was causing all the trouble. But I'm sure they're wrong. There's someone else, someone we don't know about, behind it. There has to be. Let's look at all the facts from the beginning. Now to start with——"

At that moment Mrs. Barton came in.

"Supper, boys," she said. "Oh, I didn't know you were still talking. Well, talk as long as you like, Chief."

As she started to leave the room, the pile of gold coins on the sofa caught her attention. Her eyes widened and she bustled out. She hurried down the long hall to the telephone, and a moment later was talking in an excited whisper.

"My goodness, Ella May," she said. "What do you think? Those boys staying at my house really are here to help hunt for treasure. Why, I just saw an immense pile of gold pieces they found. Yes, they must have found them out on Skeleton Island. My goodness, I don't know how much there was but it seemed like a lot. It's probably just their share. I'll bet there's lots more out there!"

She hung up and dialled another number.

Unaware that news of their find was being broadcast to the town, the boys were still deep in conversation with Chief Nostigon.

Jupiter was outlining everything that had happened. First he mentioned the ghost scares that had kept people away from Skeleton Island for years. Then he reminded the chief of the troubles the movie company had had ever since it set up camp on Skeleton Island. He told again how he and Pete and Bob had been marooned their very first night in Fishingport.

Finally he brought up his warning of the previous day by the tall, thin man, a man with a mermaid tattooed on his hand. The chief rubbed his chin.

"Could have been Bill Ballinger," he said. "Peculiar, mighty peculiar. Go on, boy."

Jupiter told of the way Chris's boat had been smashed and sunk, and finished up by saying:

"Chief Nostigon, doesn't the pattern seem pretty clear? Because there is a pattern. The pattern is to keep people away from Skeleton Island. First the ghost scares kept the local people away. Then, when the movie company came, someone tried to harass them into leaving.

"When word got out we three were coming to town, somebody must have thought we were more important than we were. They had that Sam Robinson maroon us on The Hand to scare us into going back.

"Then I was warned we weren't wanted and should go back to Hollywood. And almost at the same time, someone was sinking Chris's sailing-boat, to keep him from sailing round Skeleton Island. And if this wasn't enough, someone stole those camera lenses and dropped Chris's knife at the scene to implicate him and put him in jail.

"The whole pattern points to keeping everybody away from Skeleton Island."

"Well now," the chief said, "it does look that way. I'm going to have to turn this over in my mind. As for Chris, I'd like to let him out, and Doctor Wilbur will go bail for him, but Judge Harvey has to sign the papers and he's away on business. Can't do anything until he comes back. But I'll sure work to get him loose."

With that he said goodbye and left. Pete hurriedly put the gold doubloons back into their sack and carried them upstairs to hide under his mattress.

When he came back down again, supper was on the table. Mrs. Barton served them with a funny little knowing smile. Finally, as she brought out custard for dessert, she could keep quiet no longer.

"Aren't you naughty boys," she said reproachfully, "telling me you folks weren't on Skeleton Island to hunt for treasure."

They looked at her in surprise.

"But really, Mrs. Barton——" Jupiter began.

"I saw!" she said. "I saw the great heap of gold pieces you were showing the chief. I didn't mean to spy, but when I came into the room, there it was on the couch. I think it's very exciting."

The boys looked at each other in dismay.

"Did you tell anyone, Mrs. Barton?" Jupiter asked.

"Just my three best friends," Mrs. Barton said. "I couldn't help it, it was so exciting to see all that treasure. How much was it?"

"Not nearly as much as you think, Mrs. Barton," Jupiter said. "And it wasn't found on Skeleton Island at all."

"Now you can't fool me, young man!" She

wagged a finger at him. "Tomorrow come sun-up you're going to have company out on that island. I do think quite a few people will sail over and try their luck at digging for treasure. Oh my, yes. I'd go, too, if I were a little younger and spryer. I'm sorry to say it, but local folks are a little bit peeved that you outsiders should come in and find treasure on Skeleton Island when the town is so poor and needs it so badly."

She started collecting the dishes.

"But I mustn't talk so much," she said. "Goodness, I'm just a chatterbox when I get started."

She went to the kitchen, leaving the three boys very upset.

"That does it!" Pete exclaimed. "Why, half the town will be out on Skeleton Island tomorrow. They'll never be able to finish the movie now. And I guess it's our fault."

"I guess it is, all right," Bob said. "Your father will be stopping in to see us soon, Pete. What shall we tell him?"

"We'll have to tell him the truth," Pete answered. "Won't we, Jupiter?"

"I guess we will," Jupiter agreed. "But I'm having an idea. Let me think about it for a while."

He continued thinking as Pete and Bob listlessly turned the pages of some old magazines in the parlour.

Shortly after dark Mr. Crenshaw and Harry

Norris arrived. They announced that Roger Denton would be back the following morning and shooting would begin in a day or so on the island. However, they had decided against making the short subject about the boys diving for treasure. The incident in the underwater cave was only one reason. The cloudiness of the water and Jupiter's cold also had helped them make up their minds.

Normally the boys would have been deeply disappointed, but now they had too much on their minds to give it much thought.

They told Mr. Crenshaw and Mr. Norris what had happened and the two men uttered exclamations of dismay.

"That ruins everything!" Mr. Crenshaw cried. "Why, treasure hunters will swarm all over us like locusts. We'll never convince anybody we aren't here to hunt for pirate gold."

"I have an idea," Jupiter said slowly. "I mean, it might help save the situation. Why not film all these people sailing out to the island and racing around looking for treasure? You could get a short subject out of it, called maybe, 'Treasure Fever'. You could never hire so many people, but they'll be coming of their own accord and it might make a swell picture."

Harry Norris thought for a moment.

"It's coming to me," he said. "Sure, this is a disaster, but maybe we can turn it into an asset. Say we show somebody finding some treasure,

447

and the word gets round, and the whole town sails out to look, and we photograph them all digging . . . Yes," he turned to Pete's father, "I think we can swing it. The thing to do is to organize this treasure hunt. Now here's my idea—"

Swiftly he outlined his plan for keeping the digging under control.

"Instead of trying to keep people off the island," he said, "we'll invite them to come and dig! We'll get Doctor Wilbur to go on the local radio and invite people to dig for treasure on Skeleton Island tomorrow. We'll say we don't believe there is any treasure, but they're welcome to look. And we'll offer a prize of five hundred dollars, to be won by a draw held in the evening. That will convince them we don't believe in any treasure.

"The conditions will be that everybody who comes to dig registers with us for the prize draw, and that they don't damage the merry-go-round or the roller coaster. Then in the evening we'll be hosts for a big clambake for everyone, and hold the draw for the prize. We can shoot pictures of all the frenzied digging and we'll get an interesting short subject we can call 'Treasure Fever,' as Jupiter suggested. Then, when it's all over, people will be convinced there's no treasure and leave us alone and we can finish off the scenes for *Chase Me Faster* without being bothered."

"I think it'll work," Mr. Crenshaw said. "Let's get over to the hotel and phone Mr. Denton in Philadelphia. You boys—" he turned to The Three Investigators—"stay put. Go to bed soon. You can come out to the island tomorrow to see the fun. But for now don't get into any more trouble!"

"But Dad, about Chris——" Pete began.

"That boy can stay in jail a few days to teach him a lesson," his father replied. "Come on, Norris."

The men went out in a hurry. The boys slumped back into attitudes of despondency.

"Gosh, I was hoping we could persuade them Chris didn't do anything," Pete said. "But they won't even listen."

"Adults don't like to listen to kids when their minds are made up," Bob observed. "Anyway, Jupe, you sort of saved the day with your idea for making a short subject about the mob of treasure hunters."

Jupiter didn't answer. He was thinking again. His mind was buzzing round, going over and over the facts they had.

"Don't overdo the thinking," Pete advised him, trying to sound humorous. "You might burn out a bearing."

Jupiter coughed loudly. Then a look of satisfaction came over his round face.

"What is it, Jupe?" Bob asked alertly. "You've actually thought of something?"

"I believe I have deduced a logical reason why you found gold doubloons in that hidden cave underneath The Hand," he said.

"You have?" Pete almost shouted. "What? And use short words. This is no time for long ones."

"Bob, let's go and look at your notes," Jupiter said. "I want to read that part about Captain One-Ear and his last stand against the British again."

The three of them trooped upstairs. Swiftly Bob found the place. He read about how the old-time pirate had been surprised at night by British troops. He had fled with his chests of treasure, been chased, and landed on The Hand. In the darkness he had eluded his pursuers, but when daylight came they surrounded him and captured him.

But his treasure chests were empty, and the British realized he had emptied all the treasure overboard to keep them from getting it. And just where in the mile of water he had emptied the chests he refused to answer. All he would say was, "Davy Jones has the doubloons in his grasp and nobody will see them again until Davy Jones decides to give them up."

"Well?" Bob asked.

"Don't you see?" Jupiter replied. "If he had just dumped the doubloons overboard, he'd have said they were in Davy Jones's *locker*. But he said 'grasp.' Now what do you grasp with?"

"Your hand, of course!" Bob said excitedly. "Golly, Jupe, you mean——"

Jupiter nodded. "It's the only logical answer," he said. "After he saw he couldn't escape, Captain One-Ear emptied all his stolen treasure down the blowhole. Then he teased the British by saying it was in Davy Jones's grasp, meaning it was inside The Hand. Even if they had figured out what he meant, they wouldn't have been able to get it. So it stayed hidden down in that underwater cave all these years."

"Then there must be lots more!" Pete exclaimed. "Chris was right! There may still be a fortune down in that cave!"

"I don't think so," Jupiter said. "Remember, it was loose coins he poured down the blowhole. Three centuries of tides and waves have had time to bury most of them pretty deep or to carry them out into the bay. There might be a few more doubloons under the sand there, but I doubt if there are many. You found just what the ocean left."

Pete sighed. "You're always so logical. But I suppose you're right. For Chris's sake, though, I hope he finds a lot more so that he can take his father back to Greece."

The mention of Chris reminded them of his plight, and they became gloomy again. But there was nothing they could do, and soon they went to bed.

Pete and Bob fell asleep right away. Jupiter,

however, couldn't sleep. His mind was turning over with special sharpness now. There was still another mystery to be figured out. He had all the facts, he was sure, if he could only put them together correctly.

He thought about old Captain One-Ear, fooling the British by dumping his treasure down the blow-hole. Then, abruptly, a bit of conversation he had heard and almost forgotten came back to him. And all of a sudden everything clicked into place.

"That's it!" he exclaimed, sitting up suddenly. "Ten years! That's what happened. It has to be. Bob, Pete, wake up!"

The other two awoke and yawned sleepily.

"What is it, Jupe?" Pete asked. "A nightmare?"

"No!" said Jupiter excitedly. "You two have to get your clothes on and row out to Skeleton Island. I've just deduced the real secret of the island."

Rapidly he explained to them what he had just figured out. They listened with mouths open, and when he had finished, Pete said, "Jupe, you're a genius! You have to be right— it's the only answer that makes everything fit."

"I don't know why it took me so long," Jupiter said. "Anyway, I'm sure that's the answer. You get out to the island and check on my deductions. Then go down and wake up your father, Pete, and the others. Show them what you find. Then let them take over."

He looked wistful.

"I'd go with you," he said, "but I ache all over."

"You've done enough, Jupe," Bob said. "This will get us out of the doghouse, all right. It'll be nice to be a hero for a change. But why not wake up the men and have them help us hunt?"

"Because," Jupiter said, "I might be wrong. They'd be very angry at us for waking them up. If I'm wrong, you can just row back here and nobody will be the wiser."

"Well, okay," Pete said. "Though I would like to tell Dad. But we'll do it your way."

In five minutes he and Bob were dressed and had their flashlights. They tiptoed downstairs and let themselves out of the house.

Jupe lay back in bed, feeling terrible. Why did he have to catch a cold, anyway? But it couldn't be helped and there wasn't any danger—

There wasn't any danger!

A new thought hit him like a wallop from a baseball bat. Of course there was danger! There was terrible danger, if only he hadn't been so pleased with himself he'd forgotten to think about it. Why, Pete and Bob might be killed!

17

Bob and Pete in a Tight Spot

PETE PULLED HARD at the oars of the small rowing-boat, which they had been lucky to find tied up at the movie company's pier. By the dim light of the stars, they were heading for Skeleton Island.

"There it is," whispered Bob, as the island suddenly appeared like a black blob in the darkness in front of them.

Pete had a keen sense of direction. He rowed them towards the little bay near the amusement park. The land grew closer and then was on both sides of them, and Pete eased quietly forward until the bow of the rowing-boat nosed up on the sand. Bob jumped out and pulled the boat up on the beach.

"Now we have to go through the amusement park," Pete said in a low voice. "Then up the path to the cave. I wish Jupe hadn't said not to wake up Dad."

"So do I," Bob agreed. "I wouldn't mind some company now. Do you think you can find the way in the dark, Pete?"

"Sure," Pete answered. He hesitated a

moment. It was very dark, and silent, except for the little noise of water lapping up on the beach. "Well," he said, "we better get going."

He led the way, using the flashlight just long enough to get a glimpse ahead. In a moment they were inside the ghostly ruins of Pleasure Park.

The roller coaster was a big skeleton against the sky. It gave Pete a landmark, and he skirted round it and past the merry-go-round. At the rear fence of the park, he stopped.

"Darn it," he said in a low voice. "I'm going to wake up Dad. It's not because I'm nervous, although I am, but Dad ought to know what we're doing. After all, he told us to stay at Mrs. Barton's and—well, I think he ought to know what Jupe figured."

"Okay," Bob agreed, almost whispering. "Let's do that. I'll feel better, too."

They turned round. And then they stopped dead in their tracks, their hearts beating fast.

Somebody was behind them. Somebody big. Somebody who now flashed a brilliant light in their faces and growled, "All right, stand still! I've got you dead to rights!"

Both boys froze. They couldn't see a thing with the light shining in their eyes. Then a surprised voice said, "Thunderation! It's Bob and Pete! What do you think you're up to, sneaking round on the island like this?"

The man lowered the light to the ground.

Now the boys could see him, but they had already recognized his voice. It was Tom Farraday, the guard.

"You could have got hurt," he said. "I thought you were somebody out to damage the rides that've been fixed up. Come on now, explain yourselves."

"Jupiter figured out the secret of this island," Bob said. "We came out to see if he's right."

"The secret of the island?" Tom Farraday sounded puzzled. "What are you driving at?"

"There really is treasure hidden on it," Pete told him. "At least, Jupe is sure there is."

"Treasure?" The guard obviously didn't believe them. "What treasure?"

"Well, you see——" Pete began. But Bob interrupted.

"You helped Jupiter figure it out," he said. "You gave him the clue he needed."

"Now wait a minute!" the guard rumbled. "I don't know what you're talking about."

"The other morning," Bob said, "you were telling us how the Ballinger brothers held up your armoured truck ten years ago, stole a hundred thousand dollars, and crippled your left arm."

"Yes? What about it?"

"Well," Pete put in, "you also told us how the Ballingers were captured by the Coast Guard in a disabled boat, and how the Coast Guard saw

456

them dump some packages overboard. The stolen money, everybody thought."

"Sure it was. What else?"

"Well," Bob went on, "it was just ten years ago that someone started scaring people away from this island by starting up the story of the ghost on the merry-go-round again. Jupiter said it couldn't be a coincidence that the hold-up was ten years ago and the campaign to keep people off the island also started ten years ago. He said they had to be connected."

"I don't get what you're driving at." Tom Farraday sounded puzzled.

"Don't you see?" Pete said importantly. "The Ballinger brothers tried to make a getaway by boat and their engine broke down. They must have managed to get here to Skeleton Island and hide the stolen money. Then they pushed off again, determined that if they did get caught, everybody would think the money was lost. That way, when they got out of jail, they could come and get it and slip away quietly.

"You said yourself they got out of jail just a couple of weeks ago. But obviously they haven't come for the money yet, because with the movie company on the island they've been afraid to risk getting caught."

"Jumping fishhooks!" Tom Farraday said. "Say, you make it sound true! But supposing the Ballingers did hide the money on this island,

457

does your friend have any idea where it could be?"

"Jupiter says it would have to be some place high and dry," Bob told him. "Canvas sacks and paper money buried in the ground would rot. The best high and dry place on the island is——"

"The old cave!" Tom Farraday exclaimed. "It has plenty of cracks in the rocks where sacks of money could be hidden."

"That's what Jupiter thinks," Pete agreed. "It's the only place high and dry enough to keep the money safely."

"Except," Bob put in, "that tomorrow hundreds of people will be swarming over this island on a mammoth treasure hunt, so someone is bound to go exploring that cave. That's why we came over right away, tonight, to look for the hidden money."

"By golly, I think you may be right!" Tom Farraday exclaimed. "Think of it, all that money hidden in that cave ten years now and nobody guessing until you kids came here. Why didn't I ever think of it myself? Well, there's only one thing to do. Let's go and see if the money really is there."

"We were going to get Mr. Crenshaw," Bob said.

"No need for that," Tom Farraday told them. "Since they have to be up so early, let them sleep. If we find the money we can lug it down and wake them up. If we don't find it, you kids can slip back home and nobody'll be the wiser."

"Well——" Pete began, but Tom Farraday had already turned.

"Follow me," he said. "I know the path."

Tom Farraday moved rapidly through the trees, the boys close behind him. The whole scene was hushed and spooky, and Bob was glad they had encountered Tom Farraday. It made him feel safer to have the big burly man along.

"Oof!" Bob grunted abruptly. Someone had stepped out from behind a tree and grabbed him. Powerful hands had him in a vice-like grip.

"Mr. Farraday, help!" Bob managed to gasp. Then a strong hand covered his mouth and he couldn't make a sound.

He heard a scuffle behind him, a grunt from Pete, and then silence. But Tom Farraday, ahead of them, was free and he had a gun. He would—

Tom Farraday turned. He didn't seem the least bit surprised. Nor did he draw his gun. "Good work!" he said. "They didn't have time to yell."

"No thanks to you!" said the man holding Bob. "Suppose they had gone to the camp first and woken up those movie people? We'd be in the soup!"

"But they didn't, Jim, and we've got them," the guard said, sounding nervous. "So it's all right."

"It's not all right," said the tall, thin man who

had Pete in his grasp. "Now we've got to get rid of them. But we'll tend to that later. First we get them to the boat. Then we get the money. Then we take care of these snoopy, interfering kids."

"Sure, Bill, sure," Tom Farraday agreed quickly. "Is it true what they said about the money being hidden in the cave?"

"Never mind if it's true or not. That's our business!" growled Bob's captor.

"It's my business, too!" Tom Farraday said. "After all, one third of that money is mine and I've waited ten years for it. Not to mention getting a crippled wing from your clumsiness!"

"Shut up! You talk too much!" the man called Bill said. "You'll be taken care of. Now take off your shirt and tear it into strips. We have to gag these kids and tie their hands."

"But——"

"Move!"

"All right, all right."

Tom Farraday slipped off his jacket, removed his shirt, and rapidly tore it into strips. Bob's stunned mind began to work again. Bill and Jim —those were the names of the Ballinger brothers. And now it was apparent that Tom Farraday was their accomplice! He must have helped them work out the hold-up in the first place. He had let himself be slugged to throw off suspicion, but they had hit him too hard and broken his collarbone. Ever since then he had been waiting for the Ballingers to recover the money they had hidden, so that he could get his share.

Bob's racing thoughts were interrupted as the hand covering his mouth was removed. He opened his mouth to yell, and as he did so, Tom Farraday shoved a wadded-up piece of shirt into his mouth. Another strip was tied round his head to hold the gag in place. A moment later Bob's arms were twisted behind him and Tom Farraday was tying a strong strip of cloth round his wrists. He was effectively tied and gagged.

When Pete was also bound and gagged, the two Ballinger brothers gripped them by their jacket collars.

"Now, kids," Bill Ballinger rasped in their ears, "march ahead of us. Don't try any tricks or you'll be very, very sorry!!"

Bob stumbled along over rough ground. He could hear Pete being forced along behind him. How far they stumbled through the darkness, neither Pete nor Bob could tell. But after what seemed a long time, they came out at a pebbly beach. Dimly they could see a large motor-boat drawn up on shore.

"Get aboard, you two!" growled Bill Ballinger. Awkwardly the boys climbed over the bow of the motor-boat into the open space in front of the engine.

"Now, down!" Ballinger growled and gave them a shove that sent them toppling in a heap.

"Jim, get me the fishing-line. I'm going to make sure these kids don't escape while we're busy."

A moment later Bob felt himself being wound in the heavy fishing-line, until he was tied up like a well-wrapped bundle. Then the two men rolled him to one side and proceeded to tie Pete just as securely.

As they worked, the brothers conversed in low, angry tones. They were furious at the boys for finding treasure that afternoon, and so setting the scene for a big treasure hunt. Bob gathered they had planned to wait quietly, not going near their hidden loot until it was perfectly safe. But the prospect of the island swarming with treasure seekers had forced them to take immediate action, despite the risks.

"There!" Bill Ballinger said finally. "These two little eels aren't going to give us the slip now! Come on, Jim, let's get the cash. We've lost too much time as it is."

The two men climbed out of the boat.

On shore, Jim Ballinger said in a low voice, "You stay here, Tom, and keep an eye on the boat. Give an owl hoot if you need to warn us."

"What are you going to do with them?" the boys heard the guard ask uneasily. "They'll talk, they'll implicate me——"

One of the Ballingers laughed in an ugly tone.

"They won't talk," he said. "We're taking them with us. Never mind what we plan. But after we're gone you turn their rowing-boat over and shove it out into the bay. Tomorrow it'll be found floating and folks will think they overturned and got carried out to sea."

"Well—okay. I guess that's how it has to be," the guard answered. Then there was silence as the footsteps of the two Ballingers faded away.

They heard Tom Farraday muttering to himself. "So that's why all their friends and relatives gave out phony stories about seeing the ghost! So no one would come prowling round this island! If I had only guessed I could have had all the money to myself!"

Bob lay on his side next to Pete. He tried to speak but could manage only a muffled sound. His fingers strained to reach the knots that bound his wrists, and then gave up.

18

Something Very Unexpected

THEY WERE in a real jam, Bob thought glumly. Just about the worst jam they could have got into. Jupiter had guessed correctly that the armoured car money was hidden on Skeleton Island. But he hadn't guessed that Tom Farraday was in with the men who had stolen it, and he hadn't figured that the Ballingers would be coming to get it tonight because of the big treasure hunt the next day.

Bob wouldn't let himself think of what would happen next.

He lay still and listened to the tiny ripples of water breaking against the stern of the motorboat. Then a bigger ripple made the boat bob up and down a bit. Bob opened his eyes and saw a dark figure slipping on board over the stern.

The figure was crouched down so that Tom Farraday, on shore, could not see him. He started crawling carefully past the engine towards the two boys.

For a moment all Bob could hear was the sound of breathing. Then a low whisper reached his ears.

"Hi!" it said. "Don't be afraid. It's just me, Chris."

Chris! How in the world could Chris be here? Chris was in jail!

"I untie you," Chris whispered in his ear. "You hold very still."

Bob could feel Chris working at the fishing-line that was wound round him, then at the strips of shirt that tied his wrists and gagged him. It seemed like hours that the Greek boy struggled with Bill Ballinger's knots—but then he was free, cautiously stretching his cramped arms and legs.

"Chris——" he started to whisper.

"Shhh!" the Greek boy hushed him. "Slip back to stern, be ready to slide into water. I get Pete free."

On hands and knees Bob crawled to the stern. He wrenched off his sneakers. If they had to swim, he didn't want anything weighing him down.

A few moments later, making hardly a sound, Pete and Chris joined him.

"Over the stern!" Chris whispered. "Hold on to rudder."

There were about a million questions Bob wanted to ask, but they would have to wait. He eased himself down into the water, followed by Pete.

"Gosh!" Pete gasped in his ear. "Where did he come from?"

"I don't know, but I'm sure glad he came," Bob whispered back fervently.

Chris slid like an eel into the dark water. "Now we swim," he said. "If you swim on your side, make no splash. Follow me."

Without a ripple, he moved away, following the shoreline. Bob swam after him, wishing he had taken off his trousers and jacket as well as his sneakers.

They swam silently, their heads close to the dark water. After about ten minutes, they rounded a tiny point of land and were out of sight of the boat and Tom Farraday.

Now Chris led them ashore. They followed

him to a spot where the scrub trees came down near the water. Chris got down low and wriggled up until he could peer between two boulders. Following his lead, Pete and Bob found they could see, very dimly, the shape of the motorboat about three hundred feet away.

"Now we can talk if we keep voices low," Chris said. "They do not find us here."

"How did you get here?" both boys asked together. Chris chuckled. In whispers, he told them. Chief Nostigon had returned to the jail that afternoon pretty well convinced of Chris's innocence. He had managed to find the judge and the judge had set fifty dollars bail for Chris, which Chief Nostigon himself had put up. Then, after giving Chris a good dinner, he had turned him loose.

"I go home," Chris said. "I find my father pretty good. Neighbour lady looks after him. But I start to think. How does my knife get at scene of robbery on island? Somebody put it there, that's how, after I lose it. But where did I lose it? Then I think, I must have lost it in front of the cave yesterday when I have fun with you. Only person around to find it is Tom Farraday. I think Tom Farraday finds my knife and plants it at scene of robbery to make me look like a thief. Tom Farraday is up to something.

"I decide to watch Tom Farraday. Borrow boat from friend of my father's and row out after dark very quiet."

Chris had watched Tom Farraday set out on his nightly patrol of the island, and had seen him stop where the motor-boat was now beached, and flash his flashlight three times. The Ballinger brothers had paddled their boat in and come ashore. Then the noise of Pete and Bob rowing to the island had reached them.

"You do not row so good, Pete," Chris chuckled. "Make a splash. Ballinger fellows hide, Tom Farraday meets you and leads you into trap. I do not know what to do. Maybe I should go to camp, get men, but I think, suppose they do not believe me? Suppose they think I'm back to steal some more? Maybe I better stick around, see if I can help you.

"I see you put in boat and Ballingers go up to cave. I slip into the water, come and untie you. Now we watch the fun."

"You were great, Chris!" Pete said. "But what do you mean, watch the fun?"

"Shhh, Ballingers come back. Watch!" Chris whispered.

Dimly they could see the dark shapes of the Ballinger brothers join Tom Farraday. Each of them carried two big sacks across his shoulders.

"Everything all right?" Bill Ballinger asked, his voice coming clearly across the water.

"Everything's fine," Tom Farraday answered. "Listen, I want my share of the money now."

"You'll get it when we're ready," the other

man growled. "Come on, Bill dump the cash in the boat and let's get going."

They shoved past the guard and dumped their sacks into the beached motor-boat.

"The kids! They're gone!" Bill Ballinger shouted. "Tom, you cut them loose!"

"I did not!" the guard answered angrily. "They can't be gone!"

He flashed his light into the boat and saw the fishing-line that had bound Pete and Bob.

"They *are* gone!" he said, sounding bewildered. "But they couldn't be! Not right under my nose!"

"They're gone, and we're getting out of here!" Jim Ballinger growled. "Get in, Bill!"

"But what about me?" Tom Farraday objected. "For ten years I've been waiting for my share of the money. Ten years! Even if I got all of it it wouldn't pay me for the arm you crippled. And besides, if those kids are free, they'll blab and I'll go to jail!"

"That's your lookout," Jim Ballinger retorted brutally. "There's a tramp freighter waiting for us, and it's sailing for South America. Shove off, Bill."

Bill Ballinger pushed the motor-boat out into the water and hopped on board. Jim Ballinger pressed the starter button. The starter whirred but the motor did not catch. He tried again, but nothing happened.

"The motor!" Jim Ballinger exclaimed, a note

of fear in his voice. "It won't start! Tom, what did you do to the motor?"

"Not a thing," called back the guard. "But I'm glad it conked out. I only wish I could get my hands on you!"

"Keep trying, Jim!" the other Ballinger urged. "We've got to get going. We have to get out of here!"

Again and again they pressed the starter, but the motor refused to catch.

Chris chuckled with merriment.

"I pull wires off spark plugs," he said. "I fix them. They will not go any place. Now we go get men from camp and they take care of these fellows."

But before the three boys could move, they heard the sound of motors roaring towards the island. Two boats came racing towards them, searchlights stabbing through the darkness.

The Ballingers acted with panicky speed. Using oars as paddles, they moved the motorboat close to the shore. They leaped out and started running, directly towards the hidden boys.

Chris stood up.

"We stop them!" he yelled excitedly. "They do not get away!"

Chris picked up a length of driftwood and scrambled behind a big rock. As the first of the fleeing criminals came opposite him, Chris thrust out the stick and Jim Ballinger went sprawling on the beach.

Bill Ballinger tripped over him and fell, too. Chris pounced on them like a small whirlwind.

"You get me put in jail!" he shouted. "You make people think I am thief! I show you!"

He wrapped his arms round Jim Ballinger, preventing him from rising. Bill Ballinger hauled Chris off and threw him to one side. He fell against Bob and Pete, who were just coming to his aid.

But as the three boys sprawled on the ground, another element entered the fight. Tom Farraday came charging up and hurled himself at the two Ballingers. All three went down in a furiously fighting mass.

"Cheat me out of my share, will you!" the guard was shouting. "Leave me to face the music alone!"

Despite his disabled arm, Tom Farraday was as strong as a bull. The Ballingers could not get away from him. The three men rolled down the beach and into the water with a great splash. After a few moments of frenzied struggle, Tom Farraday had forced the Ballingers' heads beneath the water. They went limp.

"Let them up!" a voice roared. "You'll drown them!"

The boys had been so engrossed in the fight they had not seen the two boats run up on the beach a few feet away. Several men leaped ashore. Chief of Police Nostigon played the beam of a powerful flashlight on the three men in the water. In his other hand he held a revolver.

"Let them up, Tom, you hear me?" he shouted again.

But the guard seemed intent on drowning his two accomplices. It took four men to pull him loose from Bill and Jim Ballinger, who were hauled out of the water gasping weakly for breath.

When all three men had been handcuffed, Chief Nostigon flashed his light round and saw Chris, Pete and Bob.

"Well, you boys are all right, praises be!" Chief Nostigon said. "But Chris, how the dickens do you happen to be here?"

"He saved us and kept the Ballingers from escaping, Chief," Bob said quickly. "But golly, how did you get here? Did you guess the Ballingers would be coming after their hidden money tonight?"

"I'm afraid not," Chief Nostigon said. "I never dreamed they'd stashed away their hold-up loot on Skeleton Island. You can thank your friend Jupiter Jones. He came down to the police station about forty minutes ago with a wild tale about hidden money and the Ballingers probably going after it tonight because tomorrow would be too late.

"I don't know why I listened to him, but I did.

Down he went on all fours.

Rounded up some men and came out here—and by gosh, he was absolutely right!"

He turned. "Jupiter? Where are you? Here are your friends, safe and sound."

Jupiter climbed out of the motor-boat on to the shore. He came trudging towards them.

"It was stupid of me to send you out here without stopping to think that the Ballingers would be coming for the money tonight," he said. "It didn't occur to me until half an hour later. Then I went to get the chief."

"But you did think of it," Pete said loyally. "That's what counts."

"You'd have thought of it sooner if you didn't have a cold," Bob added. "Colds always slow a fellow down."

"I——" Jupe began. "I——Achoo!"

"There's enough credit for everybody," Chief Nostigon said firmly. "Between the four of you, you've solved the secret of Skeleton Island, recovered the stolen money, and got the criminals captured. That's not a bad night's work. Now you can leave the rest up to us. It's time you all got back to the mainland and into bed."

Jupiter let out another great sneeze. It sounded as if he agreed.

19

Report to Alfred Hitchcock

ALFRED HITCHCOCK looked down at the little pile of gold doubloons on his desk.

"I see you found it, after all," he said with a chuckle. "I said there was no pirate treasure left, yet you found some."

"Only forty-five doubloons," Jupiter said regretfully. "It really isn't a very big treasure."

"But treasure nonetheless, and a very interesting souvenir," Mr. Hitchcock said. "Now tell me, young Jupiter, how did you deduce that the stolen money from the Dollar Delivery hold-up was hidden on Skeleton Island?"

"Well, sir," Jupiter said, "it seemed obvious someone wanted everybody to stay away from Skeleton Island. That was why the stories of the phantom were spread around. I deduced there was something there someone was afraid might be found. The only thing of value that had been mentioned was the Dollar Delivery hold-up loot.

"The story of how the Ballingers apparently dumped it at sea was remarkably similar to the method Captain One-Ear used to fool the British. I concluded that the Ballingers had actually hidden the money and then fooled people into thinking it had been lost for ever."

"Excellent thinking!" Mr. Hitchcock said. "I suppose that after the Ballingers were sent to jail they instructed their friends and relatives to keep on spreading false stories of seeing the phantom."

"Yes, sir. Meanwhile Tom Farraday was hanging around, waiting for the Ballingers to be released. One third of the loot was his for helping set up the hold-up, and they had told him that when they got out they would pay him off. But he didn't know where it was."

"Or he might have taken it all." Mr. Hitchcock chuckled. "When the Ballingers got out of jail, they must have been very shocked to find the movie company actually camping on Skeleton Island."

"Yes, sir, they were," Jupiter said. "They didn't dare go for the money while someone was around. So they tried to drive the movie company away by thievery and sabotage at night. When Mr. Norris hired Tom Farraday, Tom just carried on the work—he did the mischief while pretending to guard the equipment."

"Including planting young Chris's knife and trying to frame him, eh?" the director said.

"Yes, sir. Also starting up the merry-go-round that first night we arrived to help spread the idea that the phantom was around."

"A point I would like to clear up. Exactly why were you marooned on The Hand by that fellow Sam Robinson as soon as you arrived? Not really to scare you into going home again, apparently."

"No, sir. I was wrong on that point. Bill Ballinger figured that everybody in the movie company would go hunting for us and the island would be deserted except for Tom Farraday. Then they could hurry out and get the hidden money.

"But the storm prevented them from starting for the island right away. Then Chris rescued us, and the search party returned before the Ballingers could go out and get their money. So that foiled their scheme that night."

"I see," the director murmured. "Then, of course, when it became known that hundreds of people would converge on the island to dig for treasure, the Ballingers had to take the risk of coming for it immediately. That's how Pete and Bob got caught."

"Yes, sir," Jupiter said humbly. "I should have realized that first thing. But Bob and Pete were gone before it came to me, so I hurried to the chief of police."

"That seems to clear up almost everything," Mr. Hitchcock said. "However, I have two more questions. How did the movie turn out, and what became of young Chris and his father?"

"The movie turned out fine. Mr. Crenshaw

got the roller coaster fixed up as soon as everyone learned the ghost was just a hoax. The final scene of *Chase Me Faster* was very exciting.

"Also, Mr. Denton got a good short subject from the treasure hunt. He used Chris in it instead of us, and showed Chris diving for treasure to help his father. The part with the townspeople digging on the island was very comical.

"But the best part of all is that the Dollar Delivery people paid a reward for the return of the money. Chief Nostigon and Mr. Crenshaw said that it should go to Chris, because he was the one who saved Bob's and Pete's lives and kept the Ballingers from getting away with the money. That and the money he earned from the movie was enough to have his father treated by some very good doctors, and take him back to Greece to live.

"He let us keep his share of the doubloons. Skin-divers did rush to explore the cave Bob and Pete and Chris found, but they only got a few more doubloons. Most of what Captain One-Ear poured down that blowhole had been washed away, I guess."

"Hmm," said Alfred Hitchcock. "Well, lads, you have justified my faith in you and I will be glad to introduce your account of this adventure. If any other investigation of an unusual nature comes up, you may be sure I'll get in touch with you."

"Thank you, sir."

The boys stood up. Pete gathered the doubloons on the desk and put them in a sack.

"We're saving these for our college education fund," he said. "But we all thought that since you sent us to Skeleton Island, you might like one for a souvenir."

He handed Mr. Hitchcock the best preserved of the doubloons. The director took it with a smile.

"Thank you, my boy," he said. "I'll treasure it."

As the three filed out, he tossed the doubloon in his fingers.

"Real pirate treasure," he said to himself with a smile. "Who would have thought they'd find it? I can't help wondering—what kind of mystery are those boys going to find themselves involved with next?"

The Hardy Boys Mystery Stories

Frank and Joe Hardy are superb crime-fighters. See how they solve these brilliant mysteries, all available in Armada.

Order Form

To order direct from the publishers, just make a list of the titles you want and fill in the form below:

Name ....

Address ....

....

....

....

Send to: Dept 6, HarperCollins Publishers Ltd, Westerhill Road, Bishopbriggs, Glasgow G64 2QT.

Please enclose a cheque or postal order to the value of the cover price, plus:

UK & BFPO: Add £1.00 for the first book, and 25p per copy for each additional book ordered.

Overseas and Eire: Add £2.95 service charge. Books will be sent by surface mail but quotes for airmail despatch will be given on request.

A 24-hour telephone ordering service is available to Visa and Access card holders: 041-772 2281

Exotic Heat

Passion in paradise…

Praise for three bestselling authors –
Anne Mather, Sandra Field
and Sharon Kendrick

About Anne Mather
'Anne Mather unfolds…romance with her own
brand of special enchantment.'
—Affaire de Coeur

About BEYOND REACH
'Sandra Field blends a beautiful setting with a
passionate conflict.'
—Romantic Times

About Sharon Kendrick
'Sharon Kendrick's [story] bursts with strong
sexual chemistry.'
—Romantic Times

Exotic Heat

SINFUL PLEASURES
by
Anne Mather

BEYOND REACH
by
Sandra Field

SAVAGE SEDUCTION
by
Sharon Kendrick

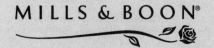
MILLS & BOON®

*MILLS & BOON and MILLS & BOON with the Rose Device
are registered trademarks of the publisher.
Harlequin Mills & Boon Limited,
Eton House, 18-24 Paradise Road, Richmond, Surrey, TW9 1SR*

EXOTIC HEAT
© by Harlequin Enterprises II B.V., 2002

Sinful Pleasures, Beyond Reach and *Savage Seduction*
were first published in Great Britain by Harlequin Mills & Boon Limited
in separate, single volumes.

Sinful Pleasures © Anne Mather 1998
Beyond Reach © Sandra Field 1995
Savage Seduction © Sharon Kendrick 1995

ISBN 0 263 83159 0

05-0802

*Printed and bound in Spain
by Litografia Rosés S.A., Barcelona*

SINFUL PLEASURES
by
Anne Mather

CHAPTER ONE

IT HAD been snowing when she left London. Great fat flakes that brushed against the aircraft's windows and covered the runway in a feathery coat of white. She had wondered if the plane would be able to take off in such conditions; or perhaps she had hoped that it wouldn't, she reflected tautly. Then she would have had a legitimate excuse for staying at home.

And it wasn't as if she didn't like the snow, she assured herself. It was much more the sort of weather she was used to at this time of the year. A blazing sun and blue-green seas were out of place in January, even if the shops back home were already anticipating the holiday season ahead.

Not everyone would agree with her, of course; she knew that. Indeed, most people would consider the opportunity to spend four weeks in the Caribbean a godsend. Particularly in her circumstances, she conceded. After a miserable Christmas spent in a hospital bed.

But most people were not her, Megan reminded herself impatiently, shifting somewhat uneasily in the comfortable aircraft seat. She didn't want to be going to the Caribbean, in good health or in bad. She had no incipient longings to see her so-called stepfather and his family again. Since her mother died, she had had little or no contact with the Robards, and that had suited her very well. Very well indeed.

Below the aircraft, the turquoise waters mocked her feelings. Whether she wanted it or not, she was now less than an hour from her destination. Already the huge jet was beginning its descent towards Cap Saint Nicolas, and the island of San Felipe would soon be beneath them. However reluctant she might be to renew her acquaintance with her

5

mother's second family, it was no longer an option. By stepping aboard the aircraft, she had taken any alternative out of her hands.

It was a small consolation that it had not been entirely her decision. The fact that her stepsister had phoned while she was still in the hospital had been pure chance. Simon had answered the call, knowing nothing of the rift that had developed between herself and the Robards. He had had no hesitation in telling Anita that Megan was ill; had probably exaggerated her illness, in fact, as he was prone to do; and he had thought Anita was being kind when she had suggested Megan might like to spend a few weeks with them to recuperate. It had never occurred to him that she might not want to go.

And, of course, Anita was being kind, Megan acknowledged ruefully. Anita had always been kind, and in other circumstances their friendship might have survived. Anita was much older, but she had always treated the younger girl with affection. After all, if it hadn't been for Anita and Remy, Megan would have found those holidays spent with her mother and the man who was to become her stepfather very lonely indeed.

But, even so, she would never have accepted Anita's invitation in the ordinary way. Her stepsister might have issued the invitation, but Megan knew she wouldn't have done so without her father's consent. Ryan Robards probably controlled his daughter now, just as he had done all those years ago. If Megan was coming to San Felipe, it was because it suited Ryan Robards that she should.

The trouble was, it didn't suit her, Megan thought frustratedly. And now that she was actually nearing her destination she couldn't imagine how she had allowed herself to be persuaded to come. But her illness, and the weakness it had engendered, had left her susceptible to Simon's inducements. She needed a break, he had told her firmly. And where better than with people who cared about her?

Only they didn't care about her, she protested silently. Not really. Not the grown-up woman she had become. They remembered Meggie, the child, the fifteen-year-old adolescent. The girl who had been naïve enough to think that her parents would never get a divorce.

Megan sighed, and adjusted the pillow behind her head yet again, drawing the attention of the ever vigilant stewardess. 'Can I get you anything, Ms Cross?' she enquired, her smile warm and solicitous, and Megan forced herself to answer in the same unassuming tone.

'No, thanks,' she replied, wishing she could ask for a large Scotch over ice, with a twist of lemon for good measure. But the medication she was still obliged to take denied any use of alcohol, and she was sufficiently considerate of the tenderness of her stomach not to take any risks.

The stewardess went away again and Megan tried to relax. After all, that was what she was here for. To relax; to get away from phones and faxes, and the never-ending demands of the designer directory she and Simon Chater had founded almost eight years ago. Work had become her life, her obsession. Nothing else had seemed so important. Not possessions, not people, and most especially not her health.

The ironic thing was, she didn't honestly see how coming to San Felipe was going to help her to relax. On the contrary, even the thought that they'd be landing shortly set her nerves on edge. Nothing Anita had said had convinced Megan that her stepfather would be pleased to see her. So far as Ryan Robards was concerned, she had betrayed her mother by choosing to live with her father. And even though Giles Cross was dead, too, the bitterness he'd suffered lived on.

The only optimistic note was that Anita had phoned without being aware that Megan was ill. After years, when their only contact had been through Christmas and birthday cards, she had called totally out of the blue. Even now, Megan wasn't precisely sure why Anita had phoned. Unless the goodwill of Christmas had inspired a sudden need to renew old ties.

But it was going to be difficult even so. Megan had no idea what she would say to someone she hadn't had a

proper conversation with for more than sixteen years. How
could she share her problems with a virtual stranger? She
didn't even know if the other woman was married, let alone
what might have happened to her son.

Remy.

Megan tilted her head against the cushioned rest and
sighed. It was strange to think that Remy would be grown
up, too. He'd been—what? Five? Six?—when she'd last
seen him? A dark-haired little boy, who'd run around half
naked most of the time, and who had taken a delight in
teasing his older playmate: herself.

She hadn't asked Anita about Remy when she'd spoken
to her. She'd been tense and uncommunicative, too intent
on trying to find excuses why she shouldn't come to show
any interest in Anita's affairs. Not that that had deterred
her stepsister, she acknowledged. Anita had probably
thought that Megan's attitude was the result of the weeks
she'd spent under medication. She'd been adamant that
Megan should come to San Felipe to regain her strength.
It was what Megan's mother would have wanted, she'd
insisted, and Megan couldn't argue with that.

She was getting more and more edgy, and, deciding she
needed to reassure herself that she didn't look as sick as
she felt, she took herself off to the toilet. In the narrow
confines of the cubicle, she examined her pale features critically. Lord, she thought ruefully, it would take more than
a re-application of her lipstick to give her face any life.

The truth was, she had been neglecting herself recently.
But with Simon spending so much time in New York, or-
ganising the launch of the directory there, she had naturally
had a lot more work to cope with. She should delegate
more; she knew that. Simon was always telling her so. But
she liked to feel that she was needed. A hang-up from her
childhood, she supposed.

She leaned towards the mirror. Was that a grey hair? she
wondered anxiously. Certainly, the fine strand glinted silver
among the corn-silk helmet of hair that framed her face.

She shook her head and the offending hair disappeared, absorbed by the bell-like curve that cupped her chin.

Did she look too severe? she fretted, smoothing damp palms over the long narrow lines of her jacket. The trouser suit, with its fine cream stripe, was navy blue and not really a holiday outfit. She'd known Simon didn't approve of her choice from the minute she'd come downstairs that morning.

But she couldn't have worn something light and feminine, she told herself, not in her present state of mind. The navy suit was smart, if a trifle impersonal, and it was certainly more in keeping with her mood.

Someone tried the toilet door, reminding her that she was spending far too long analysing her appearance. What did it matter what she looked like, after all? She grimaced. She could be stopping someone from keeping an intimate assignation. As unlikely as it seemed, such things did go on.

Outside, the purser gave her a searching look. 'All right, Ms Cross?' he asked, his cheeky grin proving that he was not above having such thoughts about her. 'We'll be landing in a few minutes. If you'll take your seat and fasten your seatbelt, we'll soon have you safely on the ground.'

'Oh—good.' Megan managed a polite smile in return, and groped her way back to her seat. The aircraft was banking quite steeply now, and it was difficult to keep her balance. She put the sudden sense of nausea she felt down to a momentary touch of air-sickness.

Yet she guessed her feelings was mostly psychosomatic. The prospect of seeing the Robards again was what was really causing her concern. She wondered if her stepfather would come to the airport to meet her. What on earth was she going to say to him that wouldn't sound abysmally insincere?

Her stomach dropped suddenly, but this time it really was the effects of the plane levelling out before landing. The pilot lowered the undercarriage as they passed over the rocky promontory of Cap Saint Nicolas, and then they dipped towards the runway that ran parallel to the beach.

It was beautiful, she thought reluctantly as memories of the holidays she had spent here sent a painful thrill through her veins. She had been so naïve in those days; so innocent. Which was why she'd been so hurt when the truth had come out.

But she didn't want to think about that now. That period of her life was dead and gone—like her parents, she reflected bitterly. It was no use believing that her father would still be alive if her mother hadn't betrayed him; no good wondering if Laura—her mother—would have developed that obscure kind of skin cancer if she'd continued to live as his wife...

The plane landed without incident and taxied slowly towards the airport buildings. Megan remembered that when she'd first come here the formalities had been dealt with in a kind of Nissen hut, with a corrugated-iron roof that drummed noisily when it rained. And it did rain sometimes, she recalled unwillingly. Heavy, torrential rain that left the vegetation green and the island steaming.

But now, when the plane door was opened, and her fellow passengers began to disembark, Megan felt the heat almost before she stepped out onto the gantry. She was immediately conscious of the unsuitability of her clothes, and her skin prickled beneath the fine cashmere.

Consequently, she was glad to descend the steps, cross the tarmac, and step into the arrivals hall. Gladder still to discover that air-conditioning had also been installed, and the debilitating heat was left outside.

All the same, for once she wished she hadn't travelled first-class. On this occasion, being at the front of the queue that was forming had little appeal. She would have preferred to hang back, to let the rest of the passengers disperse before she collected her luggage. She was uneasily aware of how ill-prepared for this meeting she was.

Beyond Passport Control, the building opened out into the customs area. Two carousels were already starting to unload luggage from the British Airways plane. She saw, to her dismay, that her suitcases had already been unloaded, and, realising she was only delaying the inevitable, she went to claim them as hers.

She didn't know whether to feel glad or sorry when she emerged from the customs channel to find that neither Ryan nor Anita was waiting for her. She had acquired a porter to transport her luggage to where taxis traditionally touted for fares, but she hadn't considered that she might have to hire one herself.

She didn't know what to do. Her formal clothes set her apart from the regular holidaymakers, most of whom were dressed in lightweight summer gear. She looked more like a returning resident, she reflected. If only she'd had her own car in the car park.

The heat was really getting to her now. Even beneath the canopy that jutted out over the taxi rank, the moist air was sapping what little strength she had. On top of which, the porter she'd hired was beginning to get restless. Megan guessed he was thinking of all the gratuities he was missing, hanging about with her.

'Megan.'

The voice was unfamiliar, but he evidently knew her name, and she turned to give the man an enquiring look. Perhaps Ryan Robards employed a chauffeur these days, she reflected, regarding him with some reserve. In faded jeans and a skin-tight vest, with a single gold earring threaded through the lobe of his left ear, he didn't look the type of person to win anyone's confidence.

'Are you speaking to me?' she asked, somewhat stiffly, wondering if he was some kind of beach bum who haunted the airport looking for gullible tourists to fleece. Her eyes dropped to the suitcases on the porter's cart, suspecting he had got her name from the labels, but all her secretary had done was put 'Ms M Cross' on the tabs.

'It is Megan, isn't it?' he asked, tawny eyes mirroring his slight amusement at her formal response, and she realised he wasn't about to go away. On the contrary, he was watching her with intense interest, and she suddenly wished that Ryan Robards would appear.

'What if it is?' she asked now, glancing somewhat impatiently about her. For God's sake, she thought, where was Anita? Didn't she know what time the plane was due to land?

'Because I've come to meet you,' the man said coolly, and a look of consternation crossed her face. He handed the porter a couple of notes and plucked her cases from the trolley. 'If you'll come with me, the car's parked just along here.'

'Wait a minute.' Megan knew she was probably being far too cautious, but she couldn't just go with him without knowing who he was. 'I mean—I still don't know who you are,' she added uncertainly, licking her lips. 'Did Mr Robards send you? I expected—Anita—to come herself.'

The man sighed. He was still holding her cases, and she knew they must be heavy for him. Not that it seemed to bother him. His arms and shoulders looked sleekly muscular, the sinews rippling smoothly beneath honey-gold skin.

'I guess you could say they—sent me,' he agreed, at last, inclining his head with its unruly mane of night-dark hair. For a moment there was something vaguely familiar about his lean features, but she would still have preferred to send him on his way.

He started along the walkway and she had, perforce, to follow him. Either that, or say goodbye to her luggage, she decided, with some resignation. Besides, although it was after four o'clock, the sun was showing no signs as yet of weakening, and she was longing to get out of her formal clothes.

She was hot and sticky by the time they reached the car, though the fact that it was a long, low estate car, the closed windows hinting of air-conditioning, was some consolation. 'You get in,' the man suggested, a quick glance in her direction ascertaining that she was already wilting with fatigue. He flipped up the tailgate. 'I'll be with you in a minute. Mom guessed you'd prefer the Audi to the buggy.'

Megan blinked. 'Mom?' she echoed, gazing at him in

disbelief, and her companion permitted her a rueful grin. 'You're—Remy?' she gasped weakly, feeling in need of some support. 'My God!' She swallowed. 'I'm sorry. I had no idea.'

'No.' There was a faintly ironic twist to his lips as he responded. 'Welcome to San Felipe, *Aunt* Megan. I hope you're going to enjoy your stay.'

Megan blinked and then, realising she was staring at him with rather more curiosity than sense, she hastily folded her length into the car. But, 'Remy!' she breathed to herself, casting an incredulous look over her shoulder at the young man loading her suitcases into the back of the vehicle. She'd expected him to have grown up, but she'd never expected—never expected—

What?

She shook her head a little impatiently. What had she expected, after all? That the boy she remembered should have lost that lazy teasing humour? That he couldn't have turned into the attractive man she'd just met?

Nevertheless, she wouldn't have recognised him if he hadn't spoken. It was hard to associate the child she remembered with the man. He'd been little more than a baby when her mother had first brought her to San Felipe. It made her feel incredibly old suddenly. He'd called her 'Aunt' Megan, and she supposed that was what she was to him.

She wondered what he did for a living. Whether he worked for his grandfather at the hotel. There was the marina, too, of course, and an estate that grew coffee and fruit. He could probably have his choice of occupations. Just because he dressed like—like he did, that was no reason to assume he spent his time bumming around.

The tailgate slammed and presently Remy swung open the driver's door and got in beside her. Megan permitted him a rueful smile as he started the engine, but she was uncomfortably aware that her feelings weren't as uncomplicated as his.

'I recognised you,' he remarked, checking his rear-view

mirror before pulling out. 'I did,' he averred, when she
looked disbelieving. 'You haven't changed that much.
Apart from your hair, that is. You used to wear it long.'

So she had. Megan had to steel herself not to check her
reflection in the vanity mirror. Her hair had always been
straight, and in those days she'd used to curl it. By the time
she was a teenager, it had been a frizzy mop.

'I don't know whether to regard that as a compliment,'
she remarked now, grateful for the opening. 'God, I used
to look such a fright in those days. And I was about twenty
pounds overweight.'

'But not now,' observed Remy, his tawny eyes making
a brief, but disturbing, résumé of her figure. 'Mom told us
all about the operation. Imagine having ulcers at twenty-
eight.'

'I'm almost thirty-one actually,' said Megan quickly, not
quite sure why it was so necessary for her to state her age.
'And it wasn't ulcers, just one rather nasty individual. I'd
been having treatment for it, but it didn't respond.'

'And it perforated.'

Megan nodded. 'Yes.'

'Mom said it was touch-and-go for a few hours.' He
paused. 'Your boyfriend gave her all the gory details.'

'Did he?' Megan was about to explain that Simon wasn't
her boyfriend, and then changed her mind. They did share
a house, because it was convenient for both of them to do
so. But anything else—well, that was their business and no
one else's.

'Yeah.' Remy pulled out into the stream of traffic leaving
the airport, his lean hands sliding easily around the wheel.
'I guess your job must stress you out. You need to learn to
relax.'

Like you?

Megan pressed her lips together, turning to look out of
the window to distract her eyes from his muscled frame.
Dear God, she thought, who'd have thought that Anita's
son would turn out to be such a hunk? If he ever got tired

of island life, she could get him a modelling job in a minute.

Yet that wasn't really fair, she acknowledged, noticing that the road from the airport into the town of Port Serrat was now a dual carriageway. Remy might be a hunk, but he didn't possess the bland good looks of the models she'd dealt with. There was character in his lean features, and a rugged hardness about his mouth. The camera might love him, but she doubted he'd give it a chance.

In fact, he looked a lot like his grandfather, she thought with tightening lips. Ryan Robards had possessed the same raw sexuality that was so evident in his grandson. Of course, Remy might resemble his father, too, but that was something that had never been talked about, not in her presence anyway. She only knew that Anita had been little more than a schoolgirl herself when he was born.

'So what do you think of the old place?' he asked now, casting a glance in her direction, and Megan forced her disturbing memories aside. She hadn't come here to speculate about his parentage, even if her father had used that in his arguments more than once.

'It's—beautiful,' she said, and she meant it. The blur of white beaches and lush vegetation she had seen from the air had resolved itself into the colourful landscape she remembered. Between the twin carriageways, flowering shrubs and vivid flamboyants formed an exotic median, and away to her left the shimmering waters of Orchid Bay glistened in the sun. 'I always loved coming here.'

'So why have you stayed away?' asked Remy flatly, and then, as if realising that was a moot point, he went on, 'I know Mom's looking forward to seeing you again. She's talked about nothing else for days.'

'Hasn't she?' Megan caught her lower lip between her teeth. 'Well, I'm looking forward to seeing her, too.' She moistened her lips. 'Um—how—how is your grandfather?' There, she'd said it. 'I suppose he must be ready to retire if he hasn't done so already.'

Was it her imagination or did Remy consider his words

before replying? 'Oh—Pops is still around,' he said
vaguely, but it was obvious he didn't want to speak about
him. Why? she wondered. Because he wasn't part of this
package? Oh, God, she wasn't strong enough to handle
Ryan's recriminations right now.

There was silence for a while, and Megan stared at the
road passing under the car's wheels without really seeing
it at all. She was hot, and even in the air-conditioned comfort of the car she felt uncomfortable. And she was nervous.
Why had she agreed to put herself through this? she wondered. She had the feeling she was going to regret it, after
all.

The speeding tarmac made her feel dizzy, and she cast
a surreptitious look at her companion as he concentrated on
the road. His profile was strong, despite the softening effect
of thick dark lashes, and the moist hair that curled a little
at his nape.

He was attractive, she thought wryly, aware that it was
a long time since she had been affected by any man. Not
that she was attracted to him, she told herself, except in a
purely objective way. He was her 'nephew', after all. All
he did was make her feel old.

'What's wrong?'

He was perceptive, too, and Megan hoped all her
thoughts were not as obvious to him. She was going to have
to get used to being around him without showing her feelings.

'Um—nothing,' she said, forcing a lighter tone. 'It's
just—strange, being here again. It's quite a relief to see the
island has hardly changed at all.'

Remy's straight brows ascended. 'Unlike me, you
mean?' he queried, and she nodded.

'Well, of course.' She shrugged. 'We've all changed.
I've only to look at you to see how much.'

'Don't patronise me, Megan—'

'I wasn't—'

'It sounded like it to me.' Remy's tawny eyes had darkened now, and she experienced an involuntary shiver. 'I

guess it is hard for you to accept that we can meet on equal terms these days. You were always so conscious of your couple of years' superiority when we were young.'

Megan gasped. 'You make me sound like a prig.'

Remy's lips twitched. 'Do I?'

'And it wasn't—isn't—just couple of years' *seniority*—' she emphasised the word '—between us.' She moistened her lips. 'You were just five or six, the last time I saw you. I was nearly fifteen!' She grimaced. 'A teenager, no less.'

'I was nearly nine,' declared Remy doggedly. 'I'm twenty-five, Megan, so don't act like I'm just out of school.'

Megan swallowed. 'I didn't mean to offend you...'

'You haven't.' Remy's lips twisted. 'But stop making such a big thing about your age.' He slowed at the inter-section before taking the turning towards El Serrat instead of the island's capital. 'Still—as you're practically senile, haven't you ever felt the urge to get married?'

Megan felt a nervous laugh bubble up into her throat, but at least it was better than sparring with him. 'Not lately,' she confessed. 'I've been too busy. Being your own boss can be a pain as well as a pleasure.'

'Yeah, I know.'

His response was too laconic, and she gave him a curious look. 'You know?'

'Sure.' His thigh flexed as he changed gear. 'I work for myself, too. I guess it's not so high-powered, but it pays the rent.'

Megan looked at him. 'I suppose you run the hotel now?'

'Hell, no.' He shook his head. 'I guess you could say I have more sense than to work for Mom. No,' he said again, 'I'm a lawyer. I've got a small practice in Port Serrat.'

'A lawyer!' Megan couldn't help the incredulity in her tone.

'Yeah, a lawyer,' he repeated. 'A grown-up one as well. I actually defend naughty people in court.'

Megan could feel the colour seeping into her throat. 'There's no need to be sarcastic.'

'Then quit acting like my maiden aunt.'

'Well—that's what I am,' said Megan, with a rueful smile. Then, 'All right. I apologise. I guess I've got a lot to learn about—about all of you. So—how's your mother? She does still work in the hotel?'

Remy expelled a resigned breath, as if her words had hardly pacified him at all. Then, 'Yeah,' he said. 'She practically runs the place these days.'

'And she's never married?' asked Megan, hoping to keep their conversation on a less—personal level, but the look Remy levelled at her was hardly sympathetic.

'To make me legitimate, you mean?' he asked, and she wanted to kick herself. 'No, I guess you could say Pops is the only father-figure I've ever known.'

'That wasn't what I meant, and you know it,' said Megan defensively. 'Only she's still a—a comparatively young woman. I thought she might have—fallen in love.'

'Perhaps she loved my father,' said Remy sardonically. 'However unlikely that might seem. Besides—' his lips adopted a cruel line '—I wouldn't have thought love meant that much to you.'

Megan's jaw sagged. 'I beg your—'

'Well, you did abandon the woman who loved you for a man without any perceptible emotions that I could see,' he continued, with some heat. 'Your mother loved you, Megan. Or have you conveniently forgotten that? How can you talk about love when you broke her heart?'

CHAPTER TWO

Now why had he said that?

Remy's hands clenched on the wheel, and he couldn't bear to look her in the face. It wasn't as if what had happened was anything to do with him, after all. He had no right to criticise her when she'd been too young to understand what was going on either.

She seemed to be speechless, and he was uneasily aware that the colour had now drained from her cheeks. For a moment there he'd forgotten how seriously ill she had been, and he felt as guilty as hell for upsetting her this way.

'Look—I'm sorry,' he began harshly, wishing they were still on the wide airport road where he might have been able to stop and apologise properly, instead of on the narrow road to El Serrat. He dared not stop here, not on one of these bends, where he'd be taking their lives into his hands. He'd done enough without risking an accident as well.

'My—my father loved me,' she said, almost as if she hadn't heard him. 'He loved me, and he'd done nothing wrong. How do you think he felt when he found out my mother had been cheating on him with your grandfather? My God! He'd made a friend of the man! How would you feel if it happened to you?'

Remy's mouth compressed. 'Like I said—'

'You're sorry?' Megan appeared to be trembling now, and he hoped he hadn't ruined everything by speaking his mind. 'Well, I'm sorry, but that's not good enough. And if your mother feels the same way I suggest you turn around and take me back to the airport.'

'She doesn't.' Remy swore. 'Ah, hell, she'd be furious with me if she knew what I'd said. Okay, you have your memories of what happened, and I accept that. But I lived with your mother for almost six years. Believe me, she was devastated when you wouldn't come to see her. You were the only child she had.'

Megan slanted a cool look in his direction. She looked like the Megan he remembered, even if the plump, pretty features she'd had as a child were now refined into a pale beauty, but she wasn't the same. The softness had gone, replaced by a brittle defensiveness, and he wondered if he had been naïve in thinking he might be able to change her mind.

'Was I?' she asked pointedly, and he had to concentrate for a moment to remember what he'd said.

He blew out a breath. 'You're talking about the miscarriage,' he intimated at last. 'She was devastated when she lost the baby. And it didn't help when your father wrote and told her she deserved it, too.'

Megan gasped. 'He didn't do that.'

'No.' Remy conceded the point. 'His actual words were, "God moves in mysterious ways." He didn't say that he was sorry for what had happened. That he understood how she must be feeling or anything like that.'

'He was hurt—'

'So was she.'

Megan's hands were clenched together in her lap, he noticed, but her voice was dispassionate as she spoke. 'Well, I don't know why she bothered to let Daddy know what had happened. It wasn't as if—as if it mattered to him.'

'Perhaps she hoped for some words of comfort,' said Remy flatly. 'Your father was supposed to be a man of God, after all.'

'He was also human,' retorted Megan tightly. 'Would she have expected him to congratulate her if the baby had lived?'

Remy silenced the angry retort that rose inside him. It wasn't fair to blame her for her father's sins. And who knew what he might have done if he'd been in the same position? It was easy to see both sides when you weren't involved.

'I believe your work is in the fashion industry,' he forced himself to say at last, in an attempt to change the subject. 'Mom said something about a catalogue. Do you sell mail-order or what?'

'Do you really want to know?'

Megan was terse, and he couldn't altogether blame her. His mother was hoping to heal old wounds, but all he'd done was exacerbate them.

'Look,' he said, feeling obliged to try and mend fences before they got to the hotel, 'forget what I said, okay? What do I know anyway? Like you said, I was only a kid. Kids see things in black and white. I guess you did, too.'

Megan glanced at him again, her eyes shadowed beneath lowered lids. She had beautiful eyes, he noticed; they shaded from indigo to violet within the feathery curl of her lashes, and glinted as if with unshed tears. He knew a totally unexpected urge to rub his thumb across her lids, to feel their salty moisture against his skin. Her face was porcelain-smooth, and so pale he could see the veins in her temple, see the pulse beating under the skin. He knew a sudden urge to skim his tongue over that pulse, to feel its rhythmic fluttering against his lips. To taste it, to taste her— He fought back the thought. Megan hadn't come to San Felipe because of him.

He dragged his eyes back to the road, stunned by the sudden heat of his arousal. For God's sake, he thought, was he completely out of his mind? What the hell was he doing even thinking such things? This woman wouldn't touch him with a bosun's hook.

'You didn't want me to come here, did you, Remy?'

Her question, coming totally out of the blue, startled him. In his present state of mind, that was the last thing he'd have said. But then, she didn't know how he was feeling, thank God! She couldn't feel the tight constriction of his jeans.

'That's not true,' he got out at last, feeling his palms

sliding sweatily on the wheel. It irritated him beyond belief
that he'd betrayed any bias to her, but it irritated him still
more that he couldn't control himself.

'So why are you giving me such a hard time?' she asked,
and he was aware of her watching him with a wary gaze.

'I'm not,' he said tensely, giving in to his frustration. 'I
just don't think you're entirely even-handed when it comes
to your parents. Your father was a vindictive bastard.' He
paused. 'I should know.'

Megan had been given the penthouse suite, which, in island
terms, meant that her rooms were on the sixth floor of the
hotel. None of the hotels that had sprung up along the coast
was allowed to build beyond six floors and these days, she
had noticed, there were quite a number of new ones.

Which meant, Megan assumed somewhat uneasily, that
the Robards were sacrificing quite a large slice of their income by accommodating her in such luxurious surroundings. This was, after all, their most lucrative time of year,
when the island was flooded with visitors from North
America and Northern Europe escaping the cold weather
back home.

Yet, despite her anxieties—and the fact that by the time
they'd reached the hotel she and Remy had barely been on
speaking terms—Anita had made her feel welcome. The
other woman had behaved as if it were sixteen weeks—not
sixteen years—since she had last come here. She had
greeted her stepsister with affection, and dispelled the apprehension Remy had aroused.

Anita had been waiting on the verandah of the hotel
when the estate car had swept down the drive. Megan had
barely had time to admire the hedges of scarlet hibiscus
that hid the building from the road before her stepsister was
jerking the door open and pulling Megan out into her arms.
There had been tears then, tears that Megan couldn't hide
even from Remy. She was still so weak, she'd defended
herself silently. Any kind of emotion just broke her up.

Blinking rapidly, she'd been grateful for the cooling

breeze that swept in off the ocean. Apart from the immediate area surrounding the hotel, where artificially watered lawns and palm trees provided the guests with oases of greenness, the milk-white sands stretched as far as the eye could see. But she hadn't been able to ignore the fact of the car door opening behind her, or Remy getting out and walking around to the back of the vehicle to unload her bags.

'Oh, Megan,' Anita was saying as she hugged her in her protective embrace, 'it's been far too long. It's a sad thing if you have to be at death's door before you'll accept our invitation.'

Our invitation?

Megan wondered who Anita included in that statement. Not Remy, surely. But she could only shake her head, unaccountably moved by her stepsister's welcome. After the way Remy had behaved, she'd been dreading this moment.

And Anita had hardly changed at all. She'd been pleasantly plump as a teenager, and she was plump still, with round dimpled features that could never disguise her feelings to anyone. As before, she was wearing one of the loose-fitting tee shirts and the baggy shorts she had always favoured, her curly dark hair scooped up in a ponytail.

Yet, despite her welcome, Megan sensed that Anita wasn't quite as carefree as she'd like her to think. She noticed as the other woman drew back that there were dark lines around her eyes, and a trace of more than wistfulness in her tears.

But perhaps she was being over-sensitive, Megan considered, and, avoiding Remy's eyes, she allowed Anita to lead her into the hotel. She found some relief in admiring the changes that had been made and consoled herself with the thought that this was the most difficult time for all of them. No matter how accommodating they might try to be, they couldn't ignore the past.

A fountain now formed a centre-piece in the newly designed foyer, with the lounges and reception area moved to the floor above. 'I suggest I show you your room and let you freshen up before dinner,' Anita declared, leading the way across to the bank of lifts. 'I imagine you could do with a rest. Did you have a pleasant journey?'

The lifts were new, too, much different from the grilled cage that Megan remembered. Would her mother have become so enamoured with the place if it had always been as impersonal as this? she wondered. Laura had always said it was the informality of Robards Reach that made it so unique...

'There's so much I want to tell you,' Anita continued as they went up in the lift—not with Remy and the luggage, Megan was relieved to find. 'So much time we have to make up. I want to know all about what's been happening in your life. Your boyfriend—partner—' She coloured. 'Simon, isn't it? He sounds really nice. I'm glad you've found a decent man to care for you.'

'He doesn't—that is—' Megan pressed her lips together and didn't go on. As with Remy, she was loath to deny that she and Simon were an item. She didn't know when it might be useful to have that excuse to turn to, and, hoping Anita would put the colour in her face down to the heat, she finished, 'It was good of you to—to invite me here.'

'Well, it's not as if it was the first time,' declared Anita, with a trace of censure, but with none of the aggression her son had shown. 'Anyway, it's so good to see you.' She took a breath. 'You're so like—so like Laura when I first knew her.' She touched Megan's face. 'It's going to be hard for—for my father.' Her lips tightened. 'But you're so pale. We'll have to try and put some colour into those cheeks before you leave.'

Anita left her alone in the luxurious suite then, ostensibly to allow her to relax for a while before dinner. Megan was grateful for the respite, grateful that she was going to have a breathing space before meeting Ryan Robards, but she doubted she'd relax in her present mood.

A bellboy brought her luggage. When the polite tap sounded at her door, she was apprehensive for a moment, expecting Remy to bring her suitcases in. But she should have known better. As he had told her, he was a lawyer, not a hotel employee.

Although she was tempted to step out onto the balcony, where a cushioned lounger and several wicker chairs were set beneath a bougainvillaea-hung awning, Megan decided that a shower might liven her up. It would be too easy to get disheartened, particularly as her body clock was still on European time, and she determined to concentrate on the positive aspects of her trip. Who wouldn't like to recuperate in such surroundings? She had four whole weeks to get completely well.

Which was part of the problem, she acknowledged, when she stepped into the mosaic-tiled shower and turned on the gold-plated taps. At this point in time, four weeks seemed like a lifetime. She'd never have committed herself to such a long stay if it had been left to her.

But it hadn't been left to her. Simon had made all the arrangements while she was still too weak to protest. It was too long since she'd taken a real holiday, he'd told her. She needed plenty of time to recover her strength.

By the time she went downstairs again, Megan was feeling considerably better.

When she'd emerged from the bathroom, wrapped in one of the soft towelling robes the hotel provided, it was to find a tray of tea and biscuits awaiting her. While she'd been taking her shower, someone—Anita, she guessed—had let herself into the suite and deposited the tray on the round table by the window. There was milk and cream, and several kinds of home-made biscuits. Although she'd been sure she wasn't hungry, she'd sampled all the biscuits, and drunk three cups of tea as well.

Afterwards, she'd rested on the square colonial bed that was set on a dais, so that its occupants could see the sea. Megan had watched the darkening waters of the Caribbean until the sun had disappeared into the ocean, and then she guessed she'd dozed for perhaps another hour after that.

She'd awakened to a darkened room and for a few moments she'd felt a sense of disorientation. But then she'd switched on the lamps, and the memory of her arrival had come back to her. She hadn't felt much like resting after that.

Still, after unpacking her suitcases, there'd been plenty of time to get ready for dinner. Anita had told her to come down at eight, but not to worry if she was late. There were often problems associated with the hotel that required her attention, and if she wasn't there Megan should just make herself at home.

As if she could do that! Going down in the lift, Megan had to admit that such an instruction was probably beyond her. Besides, what if Ryan Robards was waiting for her? What on earth was she going to say to him?

The apartments the family used were on the first floor, immediately behind the reception area. Megan was familiar with them, of course. Before the ugly break-up of her parents' marriage, the Crosses and their daughter had often had drinks with Ryan Robards and Anita. In those days, Megan and her parents had rented one of the cottages that stood in the grounds and belonged to the hotel. Her father had always preferred self-catering to the blandness of hotel food, but because of his love for sailing he and Ryan had become good friends...

Now, Megan stepped out of the lift feeling decidedly self-conscious. It was some time since she had taken as much trouble with her appearance, but for some reason she had felt the need to make an effort tonight. But although the black silk leggings and matching beaded top were perfectly presentable she was intensely aware that they exposed the narrow contours of her bones.

A belief that was made even more apparent when she entered her stepsister's sitting room to find only Remy waiting for her. He was standing at the open French doors that led out onto a private terrace, one hand supporting himself against the screen, the other wrapped around a glass.

The indrawn breath she took upon seeing him attracted his attention, and he swung round at once, surveying her

with cool shaded eyes. What was he thinking? she wondered as his brows arched in a silent acknowledgement of
her presence. After what he had said earlier, she wasn't sure
what to expect.

His appraisal of her appearance was deliberate, she
thought. Was he trying to intimidate her, or was he simply
waiting to see what her reaction would be? He was far too
sure of himself, she thought, stiffening her resolve not to
let any of them upset her. Yet, as she felt her features hard-
ening, his unaccountably softened.

'Feeling better?' he enquired, before swallowing the remainder of the liquid in his glass with one gulp. 'Let me
get you a drink. You can probably use one.'

Could she not?

Megan linked her hands together at her waist and con-
templated the advantages that alcohol could bring. It would
certainly make this interview easier, smooth the rough
edges of her tension, so to speak. But her doctor had been
quite specific, and she had no desire to fall ill again.

'Um—do you have a mineral water?' she asked at last,
and he regarded her with narrowed eyes.

'A mineral water?'

'I'm still on medication,' she explained, moving further
into the room, even though she would have preferred to
keep her distance from him. She swallowed. 'Where's your
mother? She asked me to join her here.'

'She won't be long,' replied Remy, depositing his empty
glass on the small bar that was recessed into the wall. He
examined the row of small bottles that occupied one shelf
in the refrigerated cabinet. 'Mineral water, you said,' he
murmured thoughtfully. 'Yeah, here we are. Will sparkling
water do?'

'Fine,' said Megan quickly, moving across the room and
taking up his former position by the French doors. Beyond
the terrace, the sound of the sea was a muted thunder, the
warmth of the night air scented with spice and pine.

'There you go.'

He was behind her suddenly, his reflection visible in the

glass door, his height and darkness disturbingly close. Once again, she was made aware of how the years had changed him. It was difficult to remember now exactly what she had expected.

'Oh—thanks,' she said, half turning towards him to take the glass, her efforts to avoid brushing his lean, tanned fingers almost causing an accident. Only a swift recovery on his part prevented the glass from ending up on the floor, and a splash of ice-cold liquid stung her leg.

'Dammit!' Remy stared down impatiently at the damp spot on her leggings, and Megan felt like a fool. 'What the hell did you do that for?' he demanded. 'I'm not contaminated, you know.'

'I didn't do it on purpose!' she exclaimed, even though she doubted he believed her. 'I—I wasn't thinking. You startled me, that's all.' She brushed her leg almost dismissively. 'Anyway, there's no harm done.'

'Isn't there?'

She wasn't sure what he was referring to, so she chose to say nothing, relieved when he walked back to the bar. But he was back a few moments later, holding a napkin, and, squatting down on his haunches in front of her, he pressed the white linen against her leg.

'Oh—please.' He was really embarrassing her now, and she attempted to take the napkin from him. 'Let me,' she said. 'Let me do that.' But he merely tipped his head back and cast her an ironic look and carried on.

She glanced down, her eyes unwillingly drawn to his bent head. His hair was glistening with moisture, she noticed, tiny drops of water shining on the dark strands. He had either taken a shower or a swim while she'd been resting, she reflected, the images her thoughts were evoking causing a moistness in her palms.

She sighed. Why couldn't she ignore him? Yet, crouched in front of her as he was, she would have had to be numb as well as blind not to notice the straining seam between his legs. Despite her irritation with him earlier, she couldn't deny his sexuality. It was as natural to him as breathing. Just like his grandfather's had been...

'Will—will Mr Robards be joining us?' she asked stiffly—anything to distract herself from what he was doing—and as if her words had diverted him, too, he rose abruptly to his feet.

'I guess I owe you an apology, don't I?' he said, without answering her question. 'I was an ignorant lout before. I'm sorry.'

Megan was confused. 'Oh—well, I—it was my fault really—'

'I don't mean for spilling your drink,' he contradicted her drily. 'I mean for the way I spoke to you in the car. I guess I had no right to criticise you or your father as I did.'

'Oh.' Megan let her breath out slowly. She was finding it difficult to keep abreast of his changes of mood. Or at least that was the excuse she gave herself. But there was no denying that he disturbed her, and it would be fatally easy to respond to his charm. 'Let's forget it, shall we?'

'I'm forgiven?'

'Of course.' She was abrupt.

'Is your drink all right?'

Her glass was still more than half full, and she hurriedly took a sip. 'It's delicious,' she said, hoping she sounded more controlled than she felt. 'Um—will your grandfather be joining us?'

Remy hesitated for a moment, and then he shook his head. 'Not tonight,' he said, his tone flatter now. 'And I've got to be getting back to town myself.'

'You don't live here?'

Megan realised at once that her response had been far too revealing. Dammit, she should have guessed he'd have his own place as soon as he'd told her he worked in Port Serrat.

'I have an apartment near the harbour,' he said, his eyes assessing her. 'It's handy for the office. Like tonight, I sometimes have to work in the evenings.'

She swallowed. 'You're working this evening?' she asked, managing to sound less daunted, and he smiled.

'I've a client who works in one of the hotels,' he explained. 'It's difficult for him to keep sociable hours.'

'So you accommodate him?'

'I'm an accommodating fellow,' he remarked mockingly, and she realised how easily he could disconcert her. How did he do that, when she was usually so at ease with men? It was as if he had a conduit to her soul.

'So,' she persevered firmly, 'do you often work long hours?'

'When I have to.' He shrugged. 'Otherwise I'd like nothing better than to join you and Mom for dinner.' His eyes held hers with deliberate provocation. 'I can't wait to hear what you've been doing with yourself. Apart from nearly killing yourself, that is.'

Megan shook her head. 'It was hardly that.'

'I heard it was,' he contradicted her gently. 'Is that why you're so edgy? Or is it just me?'

Megan coloured then. She couldn't help it. She could feel the heat spreading up her neck, darkening the exposed hollow of her throat, and seeping into her hairline.

'I'm not edgy,' she denied, producing a smile that probably gave her words the lie. 'I'm tired, I suppose, but that's understandable. It's been a long day.'

'Yeah, I guess it has,' he said, his tone softening. He lifted one hand and to her dismay he rubbed his knuckles along the curve of her jawline. 'You'll feel better in the morning. All you need is a good night's sleep.'

Megan drew her chin back automatically. His warm knuckles were absurdly sensual, hinting at an intimacy she couldn't begin to cope with.

She didn't say anything, but she knew he was aware of her withdrawal. His hand fell to his side, and his eyes narrowed on the way her chest rose and fell in a nervous display.

'Relax,' he said. 'What are you afraid of? I'm not going to hurt you.'

'I never—I don't know what you mean—'

Megan stumbled to deny his mocking accusation, but before she could get coherency into her words Anita's voice interrupted them.

'I'm sorry, Megan—' she was saying as she came into the room, before breaking off in some surprise when she saw her son. 'Why, Remy!' she exclaimed, not without some asperity. 'I thought you were leaving half an hour ago.'

There was an awkward pause, when Megan wondered if what had gone before was visible on their faces, and then Remy seemed to find his voice. 'Well, as you can see, I'm still here,' he remarked tersely. 'I wasn't aware I had to report my whereabouts to you.'

Anita flushed, as stung by his words in her turn as Megan had been earlier. 'You don't, of course,' she said. 'But I could have done with your assistance. The air-conditioning went out in one of the bungalows, and I couldn't get in touch with Carlos.'

'Have you fixed it?'

Remy was slightly less aggressive now, and his mother took a steadying breath. 'At last,' she said. 'It was only a fuse, thank goodness. But—but—your grandfather's rather fractious this evening, and I didn't really have the time to go charging about looking for spares.'

'I'm sorry.'

There was still an edge to Remy's voice, and, realising she should say something in his defence, Megan chipped in. 'Um—Remy's been keeping me company, I'm afraid,' she said apologetically. 'I probably delayed him, or he would have been gone.'

Anita managed a faint smile. 'Don't give it another thought. Either of you,' she added, looking at her son. 'I'm sorry if I sounded harassed. It's just one of the joys of running a hotel.'

Remy straightened his spine. 'Then I guess I will get going.' He looked at Megan. 'Now that you've got my mother to entertain you, you won't need me any more. Enjoy your evening, won't you? I'll think of you while I'm earning my lonely crust.'

'Oh, don't be silly, Remy.' Anita evidently thought her son's manner was due to what she'd said, but Megan wasn't so sure. 'Naturally, if I'd thought you had the time to stay and have a drink with us, I'd have suggested it. It was you who said you had work to do this evening.'

'And I do,' said Remy flatly, arching a mocking brow in Megan's direction. 'I'll see you—both—later, though maybe not tomorrow. I've got to go to the Beaufort plantation in the afternoon.'

'All right, darling.' Reassured, Anita gave her son's arm a squeeze. 'Give my love to Rachel when you see her, won't you? Tell her it's been far too long since she's come to visit.'

CHAPTER THREE

MEGAN slept fitfully, even though she was tired, waking the next morning before it was really light. Even the lingering effects of her illness were not enough to counter her body's rhythms. It was obvious her system was still running on London time.

She lay for a little while mulling over the events of the previous evening. She knew now that Anita's invitation had not been as spontaneous as it had at first appeared. Oh, her stepsister was pleased to see her, and she had been concerned when she'd learned Megan had had an operation. But she had had another reason altogether for making the call that had brought her stepsister to San Felipe.

Not that Megan had learned that immediately.

After Remy's departure, they had both felt the need to get their relationship back on an even footing, and while Anita had a martini, and during the course of their dinner—which was taken on the candlelit terrace—they had talked about less personal things.

Then, at Anita's instigation, Megan had told her how she had come to be in the hospital. Her stepsister had seemed to find it incredible that Megan should have developed an ulcer at her age. She didn't seem to understand the stresses and strains involved in trying to start a business, and Megan had been loath to tell her that the specialist had intimated that she might have had the ulcer since she was in her teens.

'And are your rooms comfortable?' Anita asked at last, clearly eager that Megan should have every opportunity to relax while she was here.

'They're perfect,' Megan assured her. 'I just don't think I should be taking up such luxurious apartments. This must be the busiest time of the year for you.'

'You're family. Where else would I put you?' Anita retorted firmly. 'And it's not as if you haven't always been
welcome. I told you when—when your mother died that
you had an open invitation. Any time you'd wanted to
come for a visit, you had only to pick up the phone.'

Right. Megan nodded politely, wondering somewhat
cynically how often she had said those same words herself.
In business, people often offered hospitality without meaning it. And contacting the Robards had never been on her
list of priorities.

'Anyway,' went on Anita, as if sensing the other
woman's reservations, 'you're here now, and that's what
matters.' She gave a rueful smile. 'I bet you were surprised
to see Remy at the airport. He told me that you thought he
was some toy-boy trying to pick you up.'

Hardly that, thought Megan indignantly, feeling somewhat hurt that Anita should feel the need to tell her exactly
what Remy had said. Besides, it was not what he had said
to her, though perhaps his assertion that they could meet
on equal terms had been meant to flatter her, after all.

'I didn't recognise him,' she admitted, and Anita gave a
short laugh.

'I don't suppose you did,' she said. 'He was just a boy
the last time you saw him. Did he tell you he got a law
degree? He's started his own practice in town.'

'Yes.' But Megan was aware that her stepsister's explanation had caused a sudden tightening in her stomach. It
was Anita's persistence in treating Megan like an equal that
disturbed her. Which was silly after the way she'd reacted
to what Remy had said.

'We're very proud of him,' went on Anita, clearly taking
Megan's silence as a cue to elaborate. 'Even his grandfather
sings his praises, when he isn't grumbling about him neglecting the hotel. I think we were all afraid when he went
to college in the States that he wouldn't come back.'

'But he did.'

Anita nodded. 'Despite—well, despite everything, this is
still his home. I don't think he'd be happy living in Boston

or New York, even though he could have earned a lot more money there.'

'I'm sure.'

Megan was impressed in spite of herself, understanding a little of Anita's pride in her son. After all, he was her only child. And because she'd never got married their relationship was that much more special.

'Of course, Rachel probably had something to do with it,' added Anita, pulling a wry face, and Megan was reminded of her stepsister's remark when Remy was leaving. She'd said, 'Give my love to Rachel,' but Megan hadn't paid much attention to it then. She'd been too relieved that Remy was leaving after the tenseness of their exchange, and she supposed she'd assumed the woman worked for him or something.

'Rachel?' she said now, faintly, hoping her tone didn't imply anything more than a casual interest, and Anita nodded.

'Rachel De Vries,' she said comfortably. 'Her family own the De Vries plantation that adjoins the land we own on the other side of the island. Her father sits in the local legislature. Remy and Rachel have been dating one another since they were in their teens.'

'I see.'

Megan was impatient at the feeling of emptiness this news engendered. For heaven's sake, she thought, what did it matter to her? Despite what Simon had said she intended to stay here as short a time as possible. She'd find some excuse for leaving, and then their lives would go on as before.

'Of course, I live in hope,' continued Anita ruefully, and Megan forced herself to respond.

'In hope of what?'

'Of him getting married, naturally!' exclaimed Anita, reaching across the table to tap Megan's hand. 'I want to be a grandmother, before I'm too old for it to be any fun.'

Megan sought refuge in her wine glass at that point. Despite her medication, she'd decided that one glass of wine

wouldn't hurt her, and she was grateful now for the diversion it offered. For all the room was air-conditioned, she
was feeling uncomfortably hot suddenly. This was harder
than she'd expected, and she hadn't even met Ryan
Robards yet.

'Anyway, I'm sure you must be tired of me going on
about Remy,' Anita concluded, possibly putting Megan's
restlessness down to the fact that she was bored. She shook
her head. 'Tell me about your job. What is it you do exactly?'

'Oh—I'm sure you're not really interested in my work,'
said Megan hurriedly. 'I believe Simon told you about the
directory, and that's all it is. My role is fairly simple; I'm
just the gofer. I coordinate the designs, and deal with the
printers and so on.'

'I'm sure it's not as simple as all that,' declared Anita
reprovingly, but, as if sensing that Megan didn't really want
to elaborate, she chose another topic. 'I know your—father
would have been very proud of you. You always were the
apple of his eye.'

'Perhaps.'

Megan wasn't at all sure that Giles Cross would have
approved of his daughter getting involved in a business that
was so trivial—in his eyes, at least. He'd expected so much
of her. Without her mother to mediate, it hadn't been easy.

'Well, whatever.' Anita's lips tightened. 'It's not as if he
could have expected you to follow in his footsteps.'

'No.'

'There are so few women in the ministry—none at all
here—and his work was very demanding.' Anita frowned.
'He put so much of himself into his work. Your mother
said you were often on your own.'

Megan caught her breath. 'We didn't mind.'

'*You* didn't.'

'Are you saying that my mother did?'

Anita sighed. 'Laura was a wonderful, vital woman,
Megan. Of course she minded.' She paused. 'Particularly
as your father didn't have to do as much as he did. All

those missions to African countries, for example. Why didn't he ever take your mother along?'

Megan stiffened her back. 'She didn't want to go.'

'That's not true. To begin with, she'd have gone any-where with him to try and make their marriage work. The trouble was, he wouldn't let her leave the parish. You must know your father preferred to travel alone.'

Megan swallowed. 'What are you implying?'

'I'm not implying anything, Megan. I'm telling you that your mother was not wholly to blame for what happened. If it hadn't been my father it would have been someone else, can't you see that? She needed company; companion-ship; love.'

'She seemed happy enough until she came here.'

Anita gave a wry smile. 'Oh, Megan, you're a woman now. Can't you understand what I'm trying to tell you? Your mother wasn't—wasn't the evil woman your father tried to make her. She was just lonely, that's all.'

'And your father took advantage of that!' exclaimed Megan bitterly. 'Oh, Anita, we're never going to agree on this. Can we just—change the subject, please?'

'If you insist.' But Anita looked a little disappointed now, and Megan wished she'd been a little more forthcom-ing about her work. At least that was a safe subject, despite what she thought about her relationship with Simon.

'Anyway,' Megan continued, 'Remy said you practically run the hotel single-handed these days. I think he said your father had retired.'

'Oh, God!' Anita took a deep breath, and then, as if she couldn't sit still any longer, she got to her feet and paced about the room. 'If only that was true.'

'What do you mean?'

Megan was confused now, and Anita turned to give her a strangely bitter look. 'You don't know, do you? Remy never told you? Well, of course, he couldn't. He doesn't know the truth himself.'

'Told me what?'

'That his grandfather's very ill?'

Megan shook her head. 'No.' She moistened her lips. 'I—I'm sorry to hear that.'

'Are you?' Anita's tone hadn't altered, and Megan wondered why she was looking at her with such a wealth of emotion burning behind her eyes. 'Yes. Maybe you mean it. For his sake, I hope you do.'

'Anita!' Megan's hands gripped the arms of her chair. 'What is it? What's the matter? Why are you looking at me like that?'

'He's dying, Megan,' replied the other woman tremulously. 'That's why I rang you, why I begged you to come. I've been carrying the burden alone for so long, and I—I need someone to talk to, to share the pain.'

'But Remy—'

'I've told you, he knows his grandfather is ill, but that's all. I—I couldn't tell him the truth. He and his grandfather are so close. He's going to be devastated when he finds out.'

'Oh, Anita!' Megan got up from her chair then, and almost without thinking how her stepsister might react she went to her and put her arms around her. 'Anita,' she said again as the older woman clutched at her with desperate fingers. 'I'm so sorry. If there's anything I can do, you only have to ask.'

It was little wonder she had slept fitfully, thought Megan now, throwing back the sheet and sliding her legs out of bed. Such sleep as she had had had been punctuated by dreams of her father and mother, and her own encounters with Remy, who apparently was unaware of how ill his grandfather really was.

Biting her lower lip, Megan crossed the floor to the windows and, unlatching them, stepped out onto the balcony. Even at this hour of the morning the temperature was warm, and a little sultry, too, the clouds hanging over the horizon a lingering reminder of the rain that had come in the night. Megan had heard it pattering against the panes, and it had reminded her of how she and Remy used to go hunting for

crabs after a storm when they were children. The pools that
had dotted the shoreline had been a source of all sorts of
exciting mysteries, with seashells and other flotsam capturing their attention.

Propping her elbows on the wrought-iron rail, Megan
gazed out now at a view that was still disturbingly familiar.
Beyond the paved walks and exotically planted gardens of
the hotel, white coral sand edged an ocean that was fringed
with foam. Seabirds swooped along the beach, always scav-
enging, and in the distance the tide turned to mist against
the rocks. It was all inexpressibly beautiful—a tropical
paradise that was no less magical than she remembered.

Or was it?

Certainly, her father would have said it had its serpent.
The wonderful holiday island he had found had turned into
a nightmare for him. She knew he would not have approved
of her coming here, consorting with the enemy. Even if
Ryan Robards was a very sick man. That didn't excuse his
behaviour of years before.

Yet she couldn't deny feeling a certain compassion for
the man. She was not a vindictive creature by nature, and
although she would not have chosen to see her mother's
husband again she did have sympathy for him. And, after
all, before her parents had separated, she had regarded
Remy's grandfather as a kind of surrogate uncle. He had
been kind to her in those days. Had his affection only been
a means to get close to her mother, as her father had said?

Whatever, in the beginning, Megan had looked forward
to their holidays in San Felipe with great excitement. She
remembered the girls at the exclusive day school she had
attended had all envied her those yearly trips to El Serrat.
She hadn't even been too upset when her father hadn't always been able to accompany them, though later on she'd
realised that that was when her mother's affair with Ryan
Robards had begun.

She'd been eight years old when she'd first come to the
island, and almost fifteen when her parents had divorced.
She had no idea how long her mother and Ryan Robards

had been conducting their relationship; she only knew that her father had been the one who had been badly hurt.

What had always amazed her was how her mother could have allowed herself to become involved with someone like Ryan in the first place. All right, he was fun to be with, but compared to her father he was brash and insensitive, and lacking in any formal education. Indeed, in the early days of their relationship, Megan could remember her father laughing about some expression Ryan had used in error. He'd described the other man as a philistine, although Megan hadn't understood then what he had meant.

Looking back, she conceded that there must have been more to what had happened than she'd imagined. No one gave up almost twenty years of marriage on a whim. She'd been far too defensive of her father to listen to any explanation her mother might have given her. She'd been totally prejudiced, she acknowledged, not prepared to give her mother a chance.

After the divorce, Megan had never gone back to San Felipe. She'd seen her mother from time to time, but always at some neutral location. Then, six years after Laura had married Ryan, she had developed an obscure form of cancer that was incurable. Although she'd been treated in a London hospital, and Megan had spent a lot of time with her, the looming presence of her new husband had prevented any real reconciliation being made.

Not that Megan had seen Ryan then, nor afterwards at her mother's funeral service. She had been too distressed herself, too concerned about her father, who had taken his ex-wife's death very badly, to pay any attention to either Ryan or Anita. Afterwards, after the cremation, she'd learned that Ryan had taken his wife's remains back to San Felipe to be scattered in a garden of remembrance there. It had been the final bereavement so far as Giles Cross was concerned—the realisation that there was nothing left of the woman he had loved.

His death some six months later, in what could only be described as suspicious circumstances, had left Megan com-

pletely alone. She had been in her final year at college, and
to learn that her father had died from an overdose of the
painkiller he'd been taking for some time, and with whose
properties he was perfectly familiar, had been the final
straw. She'd dropped out of college after his funeral, and
rented a cottage on the Suffolk coast, spending several
weeks in total isolation. She'd been trying to come to terms
with her life, trying to understand how a man who had
loved God, and to whom he had professed such allegiance,
should have become so depressed that he'd taken his own
life.

Eventually, loneliness—and the need to get a job—had
driven her back to London. The vicarage, where she had
lived for most of her young life, had now been occupied
by another incumbent, and the few possessions left to her
had had to be rescued from storage. What little money her
father had left had been used to furnish a small, rented flat
in Bayswater, and she'd initially got a job in an advertising
agency to try and put some order back into her life.

It was soon after that that she'd run into Simon Chater
again, and their eventual collaboration had led to her leaving the flat and sharing a house with him. It suited both of
them to project a united image, and the fact that they both
had their own rooms was no one's business but their own.

The sun had risen as she'd been musing, and, straightening, Megan stretched lazy arms above her head. There
was no doubt she was feeling better this morning, but it
was time to remove her scantily clad figure from public
view.

She decided to have a shower and get dressed, and then
take a pre-breakfast stroll along the shoreline. Anita was
taking her to see Ryan at ten o'clock, but that gave her
plenty of space. She refused to admit she was looking for
a diversion. Good Lord, Ryan wasn't a monster, he was a
very sick man.

By the time she had had her shower and dressed in cream
silk shorts and a matching vest it was still barely seven
o'clock. Slipping her feet into soft leather loafers, she sur-

veyed her appearance critically. She didn't really want to
wear make-up, but a touch of blusher and some lipstick
seemed mandatory. She looked so pale otherwise, and she
had no wish for her stepsister to suspect she hadn't slept.

The lift hummed silently to the ground floor, and when
she stepped out into the marble foyer she was surprised to
see that there were already guests about. Obviously, judging
by their attire, they belonged to the indefatigable band of
joggers who insisted on taking their exercise whatever the
weather. For her part, Megan preferred to confine her activities to the gym.

Continental breakfast was being offered in the lobby in
a small bar divided from the rest of the area by a vine-
hung trellis, and, grateful to be anonymous for once, Megan
helped herself to a warm Danish pastry and a cup of black
coffee. Carrying them across to a small table, she settled
herself by the window, deciding there were advantages to
being here, after all.

She garnered a few interested glances from the men who
passed her table, but for the most part she was left in peace.
And it was pleasant sitting in the sunlight, with air-
conditioning to mute the heat, munching on her apricot
Danish and watching the world go by.

'I see you couldn't sleep.'

She hadn't seen him come into the lobby, if indeed he
had just arrived at the hotel, and his lazy greeting caught
her unawares. Child-like, she had torn the pastry apart and
saved the apricot until last, and Remy discovered her sa-
vouring the juicy item, her lips moist and her fingers sticky
from the fruit.

'Um—jet lag,' she mumbled, stuffing the rest of the apricot into her mouth and licking the tips of her fingers rather
guiltily. 'Where did you come from anyway? I thought you
said you lived in town.'

'I do.' Remy glanced behind him, then raising a hand,
as if to impress her to stay where she was, he strode across
to the buffet table and helped himself to a coffee. He was
back almost before she had swallowed the remains of the

apricot, swinging out the wicker chair opposite and straddling it, its back to the table. 'I thought I might join you for breakfast.'

Megan's eyes widened, but she tried not to let him see how his words had affected her. It was hard enough coming to terms with his appearance. In a beige silk shirt and the trousers of a navy suit, the jacket looped carelessly over one shoulder, he looked vastly different from the beachcomber she had met the day before. He looked—unfamiliar, she thought fancifully: dark, and enigmatic, and mature. And he was watching her with disturbing closeness, as if those tawny eyes could actually read her thoughts.

'I'm flattered,' she said, trying to keep her tone noncommittal. 'But how did you know I'd be up?'

'Jet lag?' he suggested, turning her words back on her before taking a mouthful of his coffee. And when her brows arched in disbelief he gave a grin. 'I hoped,' he added, with rather more diffidence. 'Of course, I didn't think I'd be lucky enough to find you here.'

Megan grimaced. 'Well, I admit, I never can adjust to the time change. I doubt I ever will.'

Remy folded his arms along the back of the chair and regarded her with a wry look. 'Any minute now you're going to tell me you're too old to change. Come off it, Megan, anyone knows a five-hour time lag takes some getting used to.'

Megan shrugged. 'If you say so.'

'I do say so.' He propped his chin on his wrist. 'Did you have a pleasant evening after I left?'

'Very pleasant, thank you.' Although that wasn't quite the description she would have used. 'Your mother and I are old friends. It was good to see her again.'

'I bet.' But Remy's expression was suddenly guarded. Then, as if overcoming some inner conflict, he said, 'I wished I could have stayed.'

'Yes.' But Megan didn't make the mistake of saying, So do I. She had no wish to rekindle those disturbing moments from the night before.

'Believe it or not, I enjoyed our conversation,' he continued evenly. 'I guess you're not what I expected, after all.'

'Why?' Megan was intrigued. 'I thought you said I'd hardly changed.'

'Physically, you haven't, but I've decided you're much nicer than you used to be. You were quite a little prig when you were younger.'

'I wasn't.'

'You were.' She suspected he was teasing her now, but she didn't quite know how to deal with him in this mood. 'You always thought you knew everything,' he insisted. 'I thought you were a smartarse, if you want the truth.'

Megan gasped. 'Well, thank you.'

He grinned. 'It's my pleasure.' He paused. 'Of course, as I said before, you've much improved. You're much more feminine for one thing. I'll never forget those khaki shorts you used to wear.'

Megan flushed. 'They weren't khaki. They were fawn. And all the church Scouts wore them.'

'Not the girl Scouts, I'll bet,' retorted Remy, laughing. 'Of course, you always wanted to be a boy.'

'I did not!'

Megan was defensive, but she couldn't deny that she had been a bossy creature in those days. It came from being an only child, she defended herself. And the suspicion that her father had wanted a son.

'Well, you weren't exactly a little angel,' she declared now. 'You practically frightened the life out of me when you put that frog in my bed.'

Remy chuckled reminiscently. 'It was only a little frog,' he protested, but Megan wouldn't have it.

'When it jumped out of the sheets, I nearly died.'

Remy grimaced. 'Well, thank goodness you didn't. I dread to think what your father would have said if he'd known. Which reminds me, I never did thank you for not telling him. And you were a lot nicer to me after that,' he added irrepressibly.

'I wonder why?' Megan pulled a face at him. 'I'd forgotten what a disgusting little boy you were.'

Remy's eyes darkened. 'Have I changed?' he asked with sudden seriousness, and Megan coloured.

'I hope so,' she said, trying to keep the conversation lighthearted, but Remy chose to put her on the spot.

'I mean it,' he said. 'Have I changed a lot? I'm interested to hear what you think.'

Megan sighed, suddenly aware of the dangers of getting too close to him. 'Of course you've changed,' she said hurriedly. 'You're sixteen years older to begin with.' She paused. 'Your mother's very proud of you, you know.'

Remy regarded her through narrowed lids. 'Is she?' he said carelessly. 'Well, that's some consolation, I suppose. But it doesn't really answer my question.' He grimaced. 'I doubt your father would have been so reticent about what he thought.'

Megan doubted it, too. Although Giles Cross had made time for Ryan Robards, he had had little patience with Anita and her young son. In private, he'd expressed the view that as soon as Anita had discovered she was pregnant she should have arranged to have the baby adopted. He would never have allowed his daughter to be a fifteen-year-old mother.

Of course, Anita's circumstances had been different from those of the girls in his parish in England. Megan remembered her mother making that argument very well. Although Ryan Robards had been born in the United States, he and his wife had moved from Florida to the island of San Felipe when Anita was little more than a baby. He'd sold up his business in Miami and opened the hotel at El Serrat.

In consequence, Anita had been brought up with the local girls, many of whom were married by the time they were fifteen years old. And perhaps she would have got married, too, if her mother hadn't been killed in a plane crash when Anita was just a schoolgirl. As it was, she'd stayed to take

care of her father and had always seemed an integral part
of the hotel…

'Anyway,' Remy went on after a moment, 'despite
everything, I was sorry to hear that Mr Cross had died. It
was just after Laura's death, wasn't it? It must have been
hard for you at that time.'

'It was.' Megan looked down at the dregs of coffee in
her cup. 'It was daunting to feel completely on my own.
My parents were only children, you see, and their parents
were dead. For a time, I didn't know what I was going to
do.'

'You could have come here,' pointed out Remy gently,
and Megan realised it had been a real option for them.

'Perhaps,' she said now, aware of him watching her. 'But
at the time I wasn't thinking very coherently, I suppose.'

'And you knew your father wouldn't have approved,' put
in Remy, putting his hand across the table and capturing
her wrist. 'Don't worry. I'm coming to terms with your
loyalty. I guess that's what I really wanted to say.'

Megan's throat felt tight. His fingers gripping her wrist
were strong and strangely comforting, and for the first time
she acknowledged to herself that perhaps she hadn't made
a mistake in coming here. Maybe this was what she
needed—this feeling of family. This awareness that people
cared about her, in spite of everything.

And then she permitted herself to meet his eyes and
changed her mind again. However appealing it might seem,
she was not here to share her problems with him. Apart
from anything else, he was far too familiar, and much too
disturbing to her peace of mind.

She was about to draw her hand away, when Remy blew
out a breath and said, almost casually, 'I guess Mom told
you that Pops is dying, didn't she?' He watched her eyes
widen, and then added flatly, 'I know. I'm not supposed to
know.'

Megan stared at him. 'But then how—how did you—?'

'Mom thinks it's a big secret,' he went on, without answering her. 'But I'm not as dumb as all that.' He grimaced.

'Goddammit, Megan, that's why they invited you here. He wants to ask your forgiveness. Why else would he want to do that?'

CHAPTER FOUR

'HE WANTS to ask my forgiveness?'

Megan was stunned. Anita hadn't even suggested that her father might be having a crisis of conscience, and she wasn't altogether sure she believed it. After all, Ryan hadn't considered her feelings when he'd destroyed her parents' marriage, so why should he care whether she forgave him now?

'I guess he never did get over the guilt he felt about your mother losing her daughter,' Remy offered gently. 'He's not a bad old guy really, whatever you may have been told.'

'Whatever *my father* told me,' Megan said tightly, pressing her shoulders back against the chair. She shook her head, and looked down at his hand clasping hers. 'Remy, I don't think—'

'Don't think,' he advised her softly, massaging her knuckles with his thumb. 'I find it's better not to pre-judge a situation. That way, you can't be accused of being partisan.'

'But aren't you being partisan?' she protested, only too aware of the faint roughness of his skin abrading hers. 'Obviously you're more prepared to see your grandfather's side of things than me.'

'Why?' Remy sighed. 'Because I'm trying to persuade you that there are two sides to every situation?'

Megan took a steadying breath, intensely conscious of the fact that her sensitivity to his touch was in danger of colouring her judgement. How easy it would be, she thought, to turn her hand and link her fingers with his, to feel the heat of his palm hot against her own...

'Things aren't always that simple, Megan,' he persisted, and she forced herself to concentrate on what he was say-

48

ing. 'You should know that. I mean—who'd have thought you'd be holding my hand like this when only yesterday you were accusing me of giving you a hard time—?'

'Why, you—'

Megan would have withdrawn her hand then, but as if anticipating her reaction he only laughed and held it even tighter. 'That's better,' he said, as her eyes sparkled with resentment, and then his expression altered, and he muttered, 'Oh, hell!' before letting her go.

His sudden exclamation and the scowl that accompanied it were so unexpected that even though he had released her hand she didn't immediately take it back. It was obvious that something, or someone, was responsible for his sudden change of mood, but when he abruptly swung himself to his feet she could only stare at him with bemused eyes.

'My mother,' he explained in an undertone, and Megan barely had time to absorb that information before Anita herself appeared from behind the trellis.

'Why, Remy!' she said, much as she had done the night before, and Megan was uneasily aware that she wasn't pleased. 'I didn't realise you two had arranged to meet for breakfast.' She gave Megan a determined smile. 'Did you have a good night?'

'I didn't—that is—' Megan caught Remy's eye and revised her explanation. 'I slept very well, thank you,' she said instead, even though she hadn't really. 'Um—it's a beautiful morning, isn't it? Too nice to stay in bed.'

'All our mornings are beautiful mornings here,' said Anita crisply, and Megan had the feeling it was her standard response to that kind of remark. She turned to her son. 'What time did you arrive? I didn't hear the car. You might have told me you were here. This is my home, you know.'

Remy's mouth turned down. 'Gee, and I was treating it like a hotel,' he said drily, earning another reproving look from his mother. 'I didn't intend to go without seeing you. But—well, Megan was already here, and we got talking.'

'What about?'

Anita's tone was clipped, and Megan wondered if her

stepsister had sensed the disturbing air of intimacy between them. But who was she kidding? she asked herself, a few moments later. Remy had been friendly, that was all. She shouldn't read too much into his words.

'This and that.' Remy was annoyingly oblique. 'How's the old man this morning? Have you seen him? I thought I'd drop by and see how he is before I go.'

Anita's expression slackened. 'He's—as well as can be expected, I suppose. But I'd rather you didn't disturb him this morning, Remy. I don't want him to get too excited before he meets Megan.'

Remy's lips twisted. 'Since when did seeing me excite him?'

'Well, I don't want to take the risk,' declared his mother firmly. 'You can see him later. You and Rachel are joining us for dinner this evening, aren't you?'

'Maybe.'

'There you are then.' Anita was struggling to be pleasant. 'And your grandfather's looked forward so much to Megan's coming. You never know, it might make all the difference.'

'I doubt it.'

Remy was laconic, and Anita's eyes glittered with obvious irritation. 'We don't know,' she insisted, her dark head tilted at an impatient angle. 'He's frail, I know, but he's stable. The doctor says—'

'That he could have a relapse at any time,' Remy finished for her. 'Don't give me platitudes, Mom. I know.'

'You know?' Anita made a valiant attempt to appear nonplussed. 'What do you know?'

'I know the old man's dying,' Remy stated flatly. 'What did you think? I couldn't see what was happening for myself?'

Anita's eyes turned to Megan now, and Megan felt as if she was being accused of betraying a sacred trust. 'He—he did know,' she offered lamely, but she had the feeling that Anita didn't believe her.

'How did you find out?' she asked her son abruptly, and

Megan was glad she was still sitting, and didn't have to confront her stepsister on her feet.

'I asked the doctor,' replied Remy without flinching. 'Unlike you, he treated me as an adult.'

Anita's shoulders sagged then, and, casting a half-apologetic glance in Megan's direction, she pulled out a chair from the table and sank into it. 'I wish you'd told me,' she said, looking up at him, and Megan remembered what she'd said about bearing the burden alone.

'You should have told me,' retorted Remy, straightening the lapel of his jacket.

'But you're so young,' his mother murmured, biting her lower lip. 'I didn't think it was fair to put it on you. You've got problems of your own. I didn't want you to have to worry about your grandfather as well.'

Remy's nostrils flared. 'Well…' It was obvious he would have liked to say more, but a glance at his watch provided an alternative escape. 'I'd better go. What time do you want us tonight? About seven?'

Anita nodded. 'Seven, yes. We'll eat about seven-thirty, if there are no hold-ups.' She turned to Megan, and forced a smile. 'I always cross my fingers. As I said last night, it's one of the joys of running a hotel.'

Ryan Robards occupied one of the hotel's bungalows.

Set in the grounds, some distance from the hotel proper, the single-storey villas provided families with the alternative of either using the hotel's facilities or catering for themselves. Each bungalow contained a living room and kitchen, with either one or two bedrooms. Self-catered meals were generally taken on the verandahs that wrapped around three sides of the bungalows, where guests could enjoy the view of the beach and the ocean beyond.

On their way there later in the morning, Anita explained that it was easier to take care of her father away from the noise of the hotel itself. 'I suppose he should be in the hospital,' she said, 'but I know he'd hate that. He does have full-time nursing care, and his nurse can reach me any time of the day or night.'

'It sounds like the ideal solution to me,' said Megan, grateful of anything to distract her thoughts from the prospect of the interview ahead. 'Um—so have you—have you spoken to him this morning? Are you sure that he wants to see me?'

'I'm sure.'

But Anita didn't elaborate, and Megan could hardly confront her stepsister with what Remy had said. She still couldn't believe what he'd told her in any case. Her memories of Ryan Robards did not encourage her to take a sympathetic view.

Her first impressions were overlaid with the pervasive odour of the sickroom. It was a distinctive smell, a combination of medication and disinfectant which, even with the air-conditioning, still created a kind of enclosed atmosphere. The sense of airlessness was enhanced by the oxygen mask covering Ryan's face. Obviously he had difficulty breathing, and in spite of herself Megan was disturbed.

He had changed so much. He'd lost an awful lot of weight, and when he saw them and dragged the mask away from his nose she was shocked by the gauntness of his features. She remembered a big man, strong and muscular, whose boisterous laugh had made everyone want to join in. This man was just a shadow of the man her mother had fallen in love with, a pale reflection of the individual her father had declared had ruined his life.

The arms lying on the sheet were thin and lifeless, the folds of skin evidence of the flesh that had melted away. Even his hands were thin and bony, the nails unexpectedly long and curved like talons.

But the eyes that sought her face were anything but lifeless. They burned in his wasted features with an unexpectedly vivid fire. 'Meggie,' he said, gazing at her almost hungrily. 'I'm so glad you agreed to come.'

Megan didn't know what to say. The male nurse, who had been tidying the room when they arrived, had disap-

peared, and when Megan glanced around, seeking Anita's
support she found she had left her, too. She was alone with
Ryan Robards, alone with the man she had never allowed
herself to regard as her stepfather—the man her father had
taught her to hate.

She swallowed. 'Mr Robards.' She acknowledged his
greeting politely. 'How—how are you?'

It was an unnecessary question, perhaps, but it was hard
to think of anything else to say. She could hardly thank
him for inviting her, when he must know she had come
here under duress.

He coughed before answering her, a thick, wheezing
cough that had him seeking the relief of the oxygen mask
before he was able to go on. 'I've been better,' he croaked
at last, with a trace of humour. 'But thank you for asking.
Even though I guess you don't really give a damn how I
feel.'

'That's not true—' began Megan quickly, and then halted
at the cynical expression that crossed his face. 'I mean, I'd
feel sorry for anyone who—who—'

'Was dying?' he suggested drily, and Megan felt the heat
of embarrassment flooding her cheeks.

'Who's ill,' she corrected stiffly, even if he patently
didn't believe her. 'I had no idea—that is, Anita didn't tell
me that—that you weren't—still—running the hotel.'

'Oh, bravo!' His response was vaguely mocking, and he
made a gallant effort to applaud. 'It's hard to find the right
words, isn't it?' he got out hoarsely, before once again taking refuge in the mask. Then, after a moment, he said, 'I
guess it took a lot of spunk to come here.'

Spunk? Megan considered the word carefully. Spunk
meant courage, and she would never have regarded herself
as courageous. On the contrary, she thought of herself as
something of a moral coward. After all, she'd really only
come because Anita had invited her, and she hadn't been
able to think of a convincing excuse.

'It's been a long time,' she said, moving a little closer
to the bed. Then, because his intent gaze disturbed her, she

added awkwardly, 'It's been good to see Anita and—and Remy again.'

'Good for them, too,' he assured her harshly, before another spasm of coughing racked his narrow frame. His lips quivered. 'Did anyone ever tell you you're the image of your mother at the same age?'

Megan blew out a breath. 'Anita said that.'

'She would.' He pressed a fist against his chest, and for a moment she thought he had forgotten she was there. 'We had so little time together,' he breathed unsteadily. 'I loved her so much...' He swallowed convulsively. 'I miss her still.'

Megan's hands came together, her fingers linking and unlinking as she tried to reconcile her memories of this man with the broken individual she saw before her. She watched as a tear escaped from the corner of his eye and trickled slowly down his cheek, and in spite of herself she felt as if a hand was squeezing her heart. Whatever her father had thought, whatever he had said, there seemed little doubt in her mind that Ryan really had loved her mother, and their relationship had not just been the result of a reckless passion that had destroyed lives without thought or conscience.

But, as if assuming that he was embarrassing her, Ryan smudged a hand across his eyes and forced another smile. 'I'm sorry,' he said. 'I'm not usually so maudlin. It's all the drugs they pump into you these days. I doubt if there's any part of my system that hasn't been artificially resuscitated.'

Megan's lips parted. 'Well, at least you have a beautiful place to recuperate in,' she ventured at last, wishing Anita would come back. 'I think the improvements you've made to the hotel are excellent. And—and my rooms are—terrific.'

'You're comfortable?'

'Very.'

'That's good.'

But Ryan's voice was much fainter now, and Megan guessed that talking so much was exhausting him. Perhaps she should just go, she thought uneasily. What more could he say, after all? He'd told her how much he'd loved her mother, and she was amazed to find that she believed him. It didn't excuse what he'd done, but it did give her a new perspective on the whole affair.

'You'll stay?' he asked, his voice barely audible over the sound of his laboured breathing, and Megan wondered for a moment whether he expected her to stay with him until...until... 'I mean—you'll stay for a few weeks, won't you?' he elaborated weakly. 'I know Anita would appreciate it.'

Megan nodded somewhat jerkily. 'I—of course,' she said quickly, instantly jeopardising any thought she might have had about curtailing her visit. 'If I can.'

'Good. Good.'

He closed his eyes then, his breathing deepening, and, realising she could leave, Megan turned somewhat blindly for the door. It wasn't until she got outside that she realised there were tears on her cheeks, too, and she scrubbed at them with an impatient hand. Heavens, she thought, and she had been so sure that nothing Ryan Robards said or did could affect her. How wrong she had been.

'All right?'

It was Anita at last, appearing from the direction of the kitchen, her sharp eyes missing nothing of Megan's distress. What had she expected? Megan wondered. That she wouldn't be moved by Ryan's condition, or that, like her father, she'd be unable to forget the past?

'He's asleep,' she said obliquely, and Anita's shoulders sagged a little.

'You spoke to him?'

'Briefly,' Megan conceded. She took a deep breath. 'Do you think we could go now?'

'Oh, yes.' Anita took a moment to check that her father really was sleeping, and then led the way out onto the sun-drenched verandah. 'I forgot how harrowing his condition must seem to someone who hasn't seen him for such a long time.' She gave a wry grimace. 'I'm used to it and actually he's a little better this morning, believe it or not.'

Megan shook her head. 'I'm so sorry,' she said, not knowing what else to say. 'But it must be some relief to know now that Remy understands.'

'Do you think so?' Anita sounded doubtful. 'The doctor says he has only a few weeks left.' They started back towards the hotel, and her lips twisted ruefully. 'You've no idea how hard it's been to hide my feelings. Remy's my son, and I suppose I still regard him as a child.'

Megan bit her lip. 'You should have called me sooner.'

Anita turned to look at her. 'You don't mind?'

Megan shook her head. 'How could I mind?' She put aside her own misgivings. 'And you should have told me why—why your father wanted to see me.'

Anita's eyes darkened. 'He told you?'

Megan coloured, realising she had almost betrayed something Remy had told her in confidence. 'Um—who?' she asked innocently, and Anita's eyes narrowed.

'Why, Pops of course,' she said, and Megan swallowed.

'He told me he was pleased to see me,' she said awkwardly, aware of the guilty colour in her cheeks. She hesitated. 'Is that what you mean?'

Anita frowned, and then, as if thinking better of probing deeper, she returned her attention to the path ahead. 'I suppose so,' she said a little tightly. 'I know it must have been hard for him, seeing you, in spite of what he said. It must have brought back so many memories of your mother.'

'Yes.' The lump was back in Megan's throat. 'He said—he said he'd loved her very much.'

'He did.' Anita's tone was almost bitter. 'More than—more than you will ever know.'

Megan had the feeling that that wasn't what she had wanted to say, but she'd avoided any reference to Giles Cross. 'So,' Anita added as they approached the entrance to the hotel, 'I hope you'll feel able to visit him again.'

Megan was tempted to ask, Why? but she didn't. She would wait and see whether what Remy had intimated was true. Despite what she'd said, she wasn't absolutely sure that Anita trusted her. And why should she? Megan was her father's daughter, after all.

'Well...' Anita halted in the airy foyer and made a concerted effort to behave normally. 'Have you any plans for the rest of the day?'

Megan glanced at her watch. 'Oh—I thought I might have a rest this afternoon,' she offered. 'I think the time change is getting to me. I am—rather weary.'

'Of course. You must be.' Anita seized on the idea with obvious relief. 'And this evening you'll join us for dinner, won't you? I know Remy will want to introduce you to Rachel. And I'll be glad to have someone of my own age to talk to. So often with those two I feel like the skeleton at the feast.'

Megan pressed her lips together. 'Oh, I'm sure that's not true,' she protested, aware that once again Anita was making a distinction between them and her son. 'Anyway—' she forced a smile '—I'll look forward to it.'

'So will I,' Anita agreed, and then, as one of the hotel employees came purposefully towards them, added, 'You'll excuse me now, Megan? This looks like trouble.'

CHAPTER FIVE

'WHAT'S wrong?' Rachel De Vries nestled closer to Remy's shoulder, the solid console of the open-topped buggy preventing her from getting any nearer. She tilted her head, and her long curly hair swung against the sleeve of his shirt, a dark contrast to the cream silk. 'Is it your mother?'

'Nothing's wrong.' Remy glanced affectionately down at her, hoping she wouldn't press him all the same. 'I was thinking, that's all.'

'You've been thinking all the way from Port Serrat, then,' said Rachel drily, lifting her head and sitting up straighter in her seat. 'If I've done something wrong, tell me. I don't want to spend the evening wondering what it is.'

'It's nothing, I've told you,' declared Remy shortly, aware that his tone was sharper than it should be. 'I've got a lot on my mind at the moment, Rachel. What with the Rainbird trial and Pops' illness.'

'I know, I know.' Rachel gave a placatory wave of her hand, and smoothed the skirt of her dress. Short, like most of the clothes she wore, the lemon-yellow print flared about her thighs, exposing her slim legs, of which she was justifiably proud. 'I'm just nervous, I suppose. I'm not looking forward to meeting this—surrogate aunt of yours.'

Remy's lips tightened. 'She's not a surrogate aunt.'

'All right, your step-aunt, then. What does it matter?' She made a sound of impatience. 'I just think it's kind of morbid. Turning up here when your grandfather is dying.'

'She didn't just turn up here,' declared Remy doggedly. 'You know very well that my mother invited her. And Pops wanted to see her, too. It's really down to him that she's here at all.'

'Mmm.' Rachel's lips curled unpleasantly. 'All the same, it's funny that she's accepted your mother's invitation now, after all these years. Is she hoping he'll remember her in his will?'

'I doubt it.'

Remy was abrupt, and he couldn't help wondering why the things Rachel was saying irritated him so much. When he'd first heard that Megan was coming here, he'd been sceptical, too. Only the knowledge that she'd been seriously ill had persuaded him to keep his comments to himself.

And then, when he'd met her…

'So what's she like?' Rachel persisted. 'You've not said very much about her, I must say. All I know is that she's half a dozen years or so younger than your mother, and that she nearly died from a perforated ulcer.'

Remy sighed. 'What do you want to know?' he asked patiently. 'She's fairly tall—taller than you, anyway—and she's very thin. She's a blonde, so naturally she's pale-skinned, and her eyes are blue. Is that good enough for you?'

Rachel grimaced. 'That's not what I meant, actually.' But, as if realising she was being less than charitable, she took a more optimistic tone. 'I just wondered if I'd like her, that's all.'

'I'm sure you will,' said Remy tersely, cursing as a reckless motorcyclist cut across him at a junction. 'Now, can we talk about something else?'

Rachel gave him a curious look. 'If you say so,' she agreed, pleating the hem of her skirt. 'What?'

Remy was impatient. 'What—what?'

'What do you want to talk about?'

Remy blew out a breath. 'I don't know, do I? Anything; everything.' He paused. 'Has your sister heard yet how she did in her exams?'

'Now, I'm sure you're not really interested in how Ruth did in her mid-term exams,' declared Rachel mildly. And then, at his hard stare, she said, 'She did all right as it happens. Nothing to worry about. Okay?'

'Okay.'

'What is it with you?' Remy was unhappily aware that his attitude was not helping his case. 'Come on, Remy. I know you too well.'

Remy was ruefully coming to the conclusion that she didn't know him at all. Unfortunately, he had the same feeling about himself, and he realised he might have stretched his own credibility by coming here tonight.

'I've told you,' he said, his smile grim even by his own standards. 'I'm tired, I guess.' He hesitated, and then continued honestly, 'I'm not looking forward to this evening either.'

He bit back the words 'But for different reasons,' and was relieved to see that Rachel seemed to take what he'd said at face value.

'Your mother,' she murmured sympathetically, leaning towards him again and squeezing his muscled forearm. She dimpled. 'Doesn't she know we're practically living together? All she ever talks about is when we're going to get married. I know she wants grandchildren. I want children, too. But not yet.'

Remy's mouth tightened. 'She's old-fashioned,' he said flatly. 'And we haven't exactly set up house together.'

'But we will,' said Rachel impatiently. 'Eventually. I'll be twenty-one in six weeks' time, and then Daddy won't have any say in where I choose to live.'

'Perhaps not.'

Remy knew he sounded unsympathetic now, but he'd been having some misgivings about Rachel's idea of moving in together. He liked her a lot; dammit, he was very fond of her; but she was still very young, and he didn't just mean in years. As the youngest member of the De Vries family, she was used to getting her own way in everything, and that, combined with her youth, often created friction between them.

'You don't sound very enthusiastic!' she exclaimed petu-

lantly, flinging herself back in her seat again. 'Honestly,
sometimes I wonder why I put up with your moods!'

'With my moods?' Remy was sardonic. 'Oh, please.'

'Well—' Rachel sniffed. 'It's not my fault if your
mother's always on your case. Usually it's the hotel she
wants you for, but now it's this—woman. This long-lost
relative who's getting up your nose.'

'Megan is not getting up my nose,' retorted Remy
grimly, annoyed at how much he resented her words. 'For
heaven's sake, I'm tired. How many more times do I have
to say it? I need a break, for God's sake. I've been working
flat out since Thanksgiving.'

Rachel looked for a minute as if she might take exception
to his tirade, but then his outburst seemed to remind her of
something else. Snatching up her purse, she rummaged in
the pocket for a few moments, uttering a triumphant cry
when she found the scrap of paper she'd been looking for.

'Talking of breaks,' she said delightedly, waving the paper in his face, 'I got that information you wanted about
Orruba. The next charter boat leaves two weeks from
Thursday, and, as you expected, they supply all the equipment. How does a couple of weeks' treasure-hunting appeal
to you?'

Megan sat on her balcony as long as she dared, putting off
the moment when she would have to go in and get changed.
She'd had her shower earlier, and all she had to do was put
on some make-up and get dressed, but the prospect of the
evening ahead was not appealing. Despite Anita's kindness
to her, she was very much aware of being the outsider here,
and she suspected she would have preferred to recuperate
among people she didn't know.

Or was that being entirely honest? Was it not more to
the point to say that she would have preferred not to spend
the evening with Remy and his fiancée? It wasn't that she
had anything against the girl. On the contrary, she was prepared to accept Anita's word that Rachel was one of the
sweetest young women you could meet. But she—

Megan—didn't belong here, whatever the Robards said, and she was sure it would have been easier for all of them if she'd maintained the status quo.

Of course, she knew she was being ungrateful. But by accepting their invitation she had put herself into their hands. Or rather by Simon's accepting on her behalf, she thought wryly. She would have a few choice words to say to her business partner when she got back.

The phone rang at that moment. The distinctive sound carried easily onto the balcony, and, guessing it was Anita, making sure she wouldn't be late for dinner, Megan got unwillingly to her feet and padded indoors.

'Hello,' she said, instantly aware of a certain hollowness on the line, and then, as if her thoughts had conjured the man, she heard Simon Chater's voice.

'Hi, Megs,' he said, using his own affectionate name for her. 'I hoped I'd catch you before you went down for dinner. I'm just on my way to bed myself.'

Megan caught her breath. 'Simon!' she exclaimed, the warmth of her tone in direct contrast to the thoughts she'd been having earlier. 'Oh, gosh, I promised to ring you, didn't I? But there's been so much going on, I'm afraid I forgot.'

'No problem.' Simon was unperturbed. 'But I'm glad to hear you arrived safely. So—how are you? How are you feeling? Has the long-awaited reunion taken place?'

'I don't know what long-awaited reunion you're referring to,' said Megan tartly, 'but yes, I've met all my step-relatives again.'

'That's good.' Simon sounded pleased. 'I told you you'd enjoy it once you were there.'

'Did I say I was enjoying it?' countered Megan drily. But then, half afraid that someone might be listening in, she amended her words. 'It's a beautiful place,' she agreed, without committing herself. 'And—and Anita and her family have been very kind.'

'Anita? That's the woman I spoke to, isn't it?'

'That's right.' Megan did her best not to allow her own

misgivings to show. 'And there's her son, Remy, and—and my stepfather, Ryan Robards. Only unfortunately he's very ill.'

'Your stepfather?'

'Yes.' Megan was amazed at how quickly she had adapted to a relationship that she'd always denied existed. 'It's been very hard for Anita coping alone.'

'But she has a son, doesn't she?' Simon pointed out. 'And however young he was when you last saw him he must be in his twenties now.'

'Yes, he is.' Megan bit her lip. 'But—well, I suppose it's different having someone of your own generation to talk to. I'm more Anita's age; Remy isn't.'

'You're not old enough to have a son of that age!' exclaimed Simon, with a short laugh. 'I know you've been looking pretty grim lately, Megs, but get a grip.'

Megan felt a rueful smile tugging at her lips. It was good to talk to Simon again, she reflected. At least he could be relied on to put things into perspective.

'Anyway, you still haven't told me how you're feeling,' he continued. 'I hope you're taking it easy. I expect you to have an all-over tan when you get back.'

Megan chuckled. 'I'll do my best.' She shook her head. 'It's so good to hear from you, Simon. I didn't realise how much I'd missed your sarcastic voice.'

They spoke a little longer about business matters: how the launch was going in New York, for example, and the tentative enquiry they'd had from Australia. Megan felt a brief wave of homesickness sweep over her as they talked about the new season's designs and the feedback they'd had from the public. This was her world, she thought impatiently. She'd soon be bored living here with nothing to do.

Indeed, in spite of what she'd told Simon, as soon as he rang off she wondered how she was going to face the next four weeks. She simply wasn't a hedonist; she couldn't remember when she'd last taken a holiday. And with only Anita for company the days were going to seem awfully long.

But, as she prepared for dinner, she admitted that taking a break hadn't exactly been an option. Going back to work too early could easily wreck her recovery. She needed to rest; to recuperate. To regain her strength for the taxing months ahead.

She examined her appearance critically before going downstairs. The bronze Chinese silk shirt, with its bands of black and gold and red, was loose enough to draw attention away from the narrowness of the matching ankle-length skirt. It, too, was banded around the hem, and she slipped her feet into a pair of black heel-less court shoes. They added to her height, and she was glad of that. She was used to being on eye-level terms with most of the men of her acquaintance, and Remy topped her by some half a dozen inches.

She still looked pale, even after the careful application of some blusher, but she doubted anyone would notice. The advantages of eating by candlelight were not just nostalgic, she thought as she went down in the lift with a group of American tourists who were apparently on their way to the Harbour Bar.

Megan got out of the lift at the mezzanine, and walked across the reception area to the door leading into Anita's private apartments. A couple of the young women on the reception desk gave her a friendly smile, and she guessed they had already been told who she was. She closed the door behind her, and then, squaring her shoulders, she started down the corridor to the sitting room. She just hoped Anita was already there tonight. It might be awkward meeting Remy if she wasn't.

She was. Dressed in a navy taffeta cocktail dress, Anita was seated on the sofa beside a very pretty dark-haired girl wearing a yellow floral mini-dress. Remy was lounging in an armchair opposite, and they all looked towards the door as Megan made her entrance.

Despite her determination not to let them disconcert her, it was an awkward moment. Whether it was the perceptive glance Remy cast his fiancée, or the significant way both women stopped talking and studied her appearance, Megan didn't know, but there was no doubt that her arrival had created a vacuum.

Remy was the first to recover, getting easily to his feet and bidding her to sit down. 'Mineral water?' he suggested, proving he'd remembered their encounter of the night before, and Megan nodded gratefully as Anita made the introductions.

Megan had the feeling her stepsister had expected Remy to introduce the two younger women, but his offer of a drink was deliberate. Consequently, it was left to Anita to do the honours, and Megan shook hands with Rachel before taking a seat.

'How are you feeling now?' Anita asked, as if Megan's health had been under discussion. She turned to the girl beside her. 'I expect Remy told you it was touch-and-go for a while.'

'Oh, I—' Megan started, but before she could say anything in her own defence Rachel chimed in.

'Oh, yes,' she said, sympathetically. 'He said you'd come here to recuperate after an operation. I can't imagine what it must be like to have an ulcer!' She gave a delicate shudder. 'I hope it's a long time before I find out.'

'I hope you never find out,' declared Anita firmly, patting Rachel's hand in a proprietorial way. She smiled. 'Thankfully, we don't have the pressures here that Megan has, do we, dear?'

'Well—' began Megan again, but this time Remy intervened.

'You make it sound as if everyone who lives in London is living on a knife-edge,' he remarked drily, handing Megan a glass containing ice and mineral water before resuming his seat. 'As I understand it, ulcers can be caused in various ways. Stress isn't always the reason.'

'It usually is,' declared his mother, but Megan had heard enough.

'Do you think we could talk about something else?' she asked, not enjoying being the centre of attention. She looked at Rachel pleasantly. 'Have you lived on San Felipe all your life?'

'I'm afraid so.' Rachel's words were innocent enough but she didn't sound apologetic. 'Remy and I are both native islanders. I don't think either of us could bear to live anywhere else.'

'No.'

Megan acknowledged the truth of that as she sipped some of the chilled water in her glass. Anita had said much the same thing when she had spoken so proudly of the opportunities Remy had rejected on the mainland. Even when she was dying, her mother had said that San Felipe got into your blood.

'Anita was telling me that you run a fashion catalogue,' Rachel put in now, and Megan schooled her features into a polite mask.

'It's a directory, actually,' she said. 'We don't sell the clothes ourselves. We just provide a showcase for amateur designers—college graduates and the like.'

'It sounds fascinating,' said Anita, but Megan sensed she wasn't really interested in that side of her life. 'But haven't you ever wanted to get married? To settle down and have a family of your own?'

'Not yet,' replied Megan evenly, and the older woman shook her head.

'Well, you're not getting any younger, my dear,' she declared. 'The old body clock is ticking, as they say.'

'Mom!' Remy's impatience was evident, and his mother gave him a defiant look.

'Well, this young man Megan lives with sounds very nice, I must say,' she retorted. 'If I were her, I wouldn't wait much longer to tie him down.'

'Simon and I—' Megan found herself on the brink of disclaiming their association, and then once again decided not to say anything more. After all, what did it matter what the Robards thought about her relationships? In a few weeks' time, they'd have forgotten all about her. 'We're good friends.'

Anita snorted now. 'Good friends!' she exclaimed. 'I've heard that before. Well—' she acknowledged her son's glowering face with a defensive shrug '—I suppose you know your own business best.'

'Yes, she does,' said Remy, finishing his drink and getting up to get himself another. 'And she isn't on the verge of senility either.'

'I never said she was—'

'Tell us how you started the catal—the directory,' said Rachel hurriedly, before her fiancé and his mother could come to verbal blows. 'How did you know where to look for designers?'

'Oh—' Megan's face was uncomfortably hot, but she forced herself to go on. 'It was Simon's idea. He—er—he was working for one of the tabloid newspapers, and during the course of a feature he was writing he visited several art colleges and saw the work they were producing. He realised there was an awful lot of talent going to waste. We decided to provide a showcase for that talent, that's all.'

'But it is clothes we're talking about, isn't it?'

'Mostly.' Megan once again found herself the cynosure of all eyes. 'Occasionally we add a small household section. There's quite a market for soft furnishing fabrics and so on.'

'And who chooses what goes into the—the directory and what doesn't?' asked Anita, with a frown, and Megan sighed.

'We both do,' she replied carefully. 'It's very much a personal point of view.'

'But you've obviously been successful,' pointed out Anita. 'Is that because you and Simon have similar views?'

'It's more because we share a similar eye for colour,' Megan amended quietly. 'Apart from our work, we have very little in common.'

'Oh, I can't believe that.'

Anita was patently disbelieving, and Megan knew she had to change the subject before she said something she'd regret. 'It's true,' she affirmed, and then turned deter-

minedly to the young woman sitting beside her. 'What do
you do—er—Rachel? Do you work in Port Serrat, too?'

'What do I do?' Rachel looked at her now as if she'd
used a dirty word. 'What do I *do*?' She glanced at Remy,
as if expecting him to answer the question for her. 'I
don't—do—anything, if you mean as a way of earning
money. Daddy wouldn't allow it.' She cast a helpless
glance at Anita. 'He's terribly old-fashioned, as you know.'

'He's a dinosaur,' agreed Remy laconically, earning himself another warning look from his mother. 'Well, he is,'
he persisted, coming back to his chair to sit with his legs
splayed, the glass suspended from both hands between
them. 'He's still living in the nineteenth century. He thinks
women were born to breed and nothing else.'

'Remy!'

'Oh, Remy!'

Anita and Rachel spoke together, the former with re-
proval, the latter with a coy little laugh. For her part, Megan
was beginning to wish she had confessed to having a headache and got out of this dinner party. She wasn't enjoying
herself, and she suspected no one but Anita was either.

To her relief, the uniformed waiter who had served them
the night before appeared at that moment to advise her stepsister that the meal was ready to be served. Finishing her
sherry, Anita got immediately to her feet, and, tucking her
arm through Rachel's, she led the way out onto the terrace.

Megan put down her own glass and followed them, the
distinctive sound of a steel band becoming audible as she
stepped outside. A barbecue was taking place on the beach,
and she could smell the spicy food and see the torches that
illuminated the scene. If only she could join that anonymous crowd, she thought wryly. This was supposed to be
a holiday, not an endurance test.

'Bored?' asked a lazy voice far too close to her ear, and
she realised that she had halted for a moment and Remy
had come up behind her. 'Cheer up,' he added. 'It'll soon
be over. You'll have to forgive my mother. She doesn't

realise that dinner guests are supposed to have something in common.'

Megan's lips twitched, but happily the darkness hid her guilty humour. 'I don't know what you mean,' she insisted, moving quickly towards the candlelit table. She admired the pretty centre-piece of ivory orchids and crimson hibiscus. 'This looks lovely, Anita.'

Her stepsister was pleased and the food, as always, was delicious. A light consommé was followed by tender medallions of pork in a sweet and sour sauce, served on a bed of flaky rice, with a delicate fruit terrine to finish. Megan realised as the plates were cleared that despite her reservations she had enjoyed the meal. Probably because Rachel and Anita had done most of the talking, she acknowledged drily. Her contributions had been few and far between, which suited her very well.

It was as Anita was pouring cups of aromatic Colombian coffee that once again Remy chose to disrupt her mood. 'You saw Pops this morning?' he enquired, cutting across his mother's dissertation on what a mischievous little boy he used to be, and there was a moment's awkward silence before anyone spoke.

And then it was Anita who chose to answer him, her eyes sparkling impatiently, as if she'd hoped to avoid this discussion. 'Of course she saw your grandfather,' she declared tersely. 'What kind of a question is that?'

Remy shrugged his shoulders, and Megan looked away from the sleek muscles moving under brown skin. He was wearing a cream shirt this evening, and his tan showed darkly beneath the fine silk. 'I was talking to Megan actually,' he said, his tone bordering on insolence. 'Well?' He fixed her with a taut gaze. 'What did he have to say?'

Megan was again glad of the darkness to hide her blushes. What was wrong with her, she wondered, that he should have the ability to embarrass her without any apparent effort on his part? 'He—said he was glad to see me,' she answered at last, exchanging an apologetic look with

Anita. 'He said I was like—like my mother. I think seeing me was—was rather painful for him.'

'I'll bet.' To her relief Remy seemed content with her answer. He bit his lip. 'I'll look in on him myself before I leave.'

'Can I come, too?'

Rachel, who was seated at right angles to Remy, covered the hand that was playing with the stem of his wine glass with her own, but he shook his head. 'I don't think so,' he said, raising the glass to his lips so that her fingers were forced to fall away. 'Doc O'Brien's orders are only family.' His smile was faintly malicious. 'And you're not that—yet.'

Rachel's response was to thrust back her chair and leave the table. As Megan and Anita exchanged helpless glances, she rushed indoors and out of their sight. No one was in any doubt that Remy's words had upset her, and as soon as she was sure the girl was out of earshot Anita turned on her son.

'There was no need for that!' she exclaimed, screwing up her napkin and thrusting it to one side. 'You know perfectly well that what Dr O'Brien meant was that your grandfather shouldn't have a lot of visitors. Allowing Rachel to accompany you would have done no harm at all.'

Remy tilted his chair onto the two back legs and gazed carelessly at the star-studded heavens. 'Perhaps I didn't want her to go with me,' he declared, and his mother made a sound of impatience.

'You're being deliberately unpleasant, Remy,' she retorted, almost as if he were still the small boy she had been speaking about earlier. 'Now for goodness' sake go and tell the girl you're sorry. I can hear her sniffling away in the sitting room and I know it's not because she's coming down with a cold.'

Remy's chair legs dropped with ominous speed, and Megan wished she were any place but here. But her only obvious exit was through the room where Rachel was hiding, and she had no wish to embarrass the girl any more than she already was.

'I'm not a child, Mom,' Remy stated now, his eyes meeting his mother's bleakly across the table. 'And I object to you behaving as if my relationship with Rachel was a *fait accompli*.' He paused. 'It's not. All right?'

Anita's lips quivered. 'You're just saying that to punish me.'

'No, I'm not.' Remy caught Megan's eyes upon him, and she quickly looked down at her cup. 'And I suggest you tell Megan why she's really here, instead of pretending it's just because of the old man's health!'

CHAPTER SIX

MEGAN put down her book and reached for the tube of
sunscreen lying on the low table beside her. Although the
lounger she was occupying was shaded by a striped umbrella, as the sun moved round, her legs were becoming
exposed, and she could feel the heat of the sun prickling
her skin.

Uncapping the tube, she squeezed a circle of the cream
onto her palm and applied it to her ankle. She felt an immediate sense of relief as the cream did its work, and she
paused a moment to look about her, reluctantly admitting
that she was lucky to be in such delightful surroundings.

She was sitting by the hotel pool, another innovation
since the days when she and her parents had visited the
island. Anita had told her that having a pool was almost
mandatory these days. Not all their guests enjoyed getting
sand between their toes or combating the flies that occasionally plagued the beach area. Many people, women particularly, only wore a swimsuit for sunbathing. They never
went into the water, and although they enjoyed being
photographed beside the pool it was more of a decoration
than a resource.

For her part, Megan enjoyed both locations. It was true
that she preferred to swim in the sea, but so far she hadn't
swum at all. She was still very chary about doing anything
that might upset her recovery, which was why she was so
protective of her skin.

Of course, she had developed a slight tan. Because she
endeavoured to spend as much time as possible out of the
hotel, it had been impossible to remain totally immune from
the effects of sun. She was sure she must have walked miles

in her efforts to rebuild her strength—and try to avoid Anita, she admitted with a pang.

Not that she'd been very successful with the latter, she acknowledged ruefully. Apart from anything else, her step-sister insisted that they have their evening meal together, though, thankfully, there'd been no repeat of the disastrous dinner party she'd given five days ago. On the whole, Megan's days had been fairly uneventful, with only her visits to see Ryan Robards making this any different from an ordinary holiday.

Still, just thinking about the evening Remy had brought Rachel to dinner brought an uneasy feathering of her skin. She should have stuck by her instincts and made some excuse not to attend, she reflected wryly. Although she hadn't said anything, Megan was sure Anita blamed her for at least a part of the unpleasantness that had occurred. And it wasn't as if she had wanted to be there. She would have much preferred to eat in the restaurant.

The evening had ended as inauspiciously as it had begun. After Remy's outburst, Anita had gone to attend to Rachel, and Megan had followed her and made good her escape. Neither she nor Anita had mentioned it since, even though it would have been more natural to do so.

Which meant she was no wiser now as to the reason Ryan had wanted to see her than before. There had been no mention of there being another reason why he had wanted her here. Megan sometimes wondered if Remy had made the whole thing up. Or was Anita hoping that no more need be said?

For her part, Megan was inclined to the same view. Although she and Ryan had spoken more in the last few days than they had ever done, their exchanges tended to be more reminiscing about her mother than anything else. How he felt now, what he thought during the long hours he spent alone in his room, seemed of less importance to him than what had gone before. And his memories of Laura were precious—more precious with every hour they spent together.

Feeling the sting of tears behind her eyes, Megan determinedly reached for her sunglasses. She was not going to cry, she told herself. She had done all her crying years ago. But there was no doubt that Ryan had given her a new perspective on the woman who had borne her, and although she still sympathised with her father she was beginning to see that his view had been decidedly biased.

She sank back against the lounger, picking up her paperback again and trying to stimulate some interest in the story. But the characters she was reading about were so two-dimensional, and her mind refused to concentrate on the plot.

She wondered what Remy was doing at this moment, and then swiftly dismissed the thought. The less she saw of her 'nephew' the better, she decided. He'd been around the hotel twice since the evening of the dinner party, but happily she hadn't seen him. He visited his grandfather regularly, but she'd been out both times he'd made the trip from town.

She sighed now, gazing up at the canopy above her head, watching the shadows of the nearby palm trees moving against the cloth. This was a heavenly place, she thought reluctantly. She didn't want to admit it, but she was beginning to understand why her mother had said it got into your blood.

She closed her eyes, only to open them a few seconds later when it seemed as if the sun had been blocked from her view. Despite the sunglasses, she could sense the darkness beyond her eyelids, and she blinked at the man who was standing beside her chair.

It was Remy. Somehow, she'd known it would be, and she wondered if the thoughts she'd had a few moments ago had been inspired by his presence in the hotel. But he was alone; his mother wasn't with him; and Megan was immediately conscious of how unattractive she must appear.

'Hi,' he said, moving her legs aside and perching on the end of the lounger. 'You look hot.'

Megan struggled into a sitting position. 'I am hot,' she

agreed, aware of the layers of sunscreen giving her skin a greasy shine. 'What are you doing here? I thought you'd be working. Or don't lawyers in Port Serrat keep office hours?'

'I neither know nor care what hours other lawyers keep,' declared Remy carelessly, loosening the buttons on his shirt. He pushed back his dark hair with a lazy hand and briefly scanned the poolside area. 'I thought I might keep you company for a while.'

Megan determined not to overreact. 'Is that wise?' she asked, leaning forward to massage an errant drop of cream into her leg. 'I'm sure if your mother knows you're here she'll find something for you to do. She was saying she was having a problem with the coffee machine last night.'

Remy's mouth compressed. 'I'm not an electrician, Megan, and if it's mechanical I'm not an engineer either. My mother knows a perfectly adequate firm of technicians she can call on in an emergency. If she chooses not to use them, that's her problem, not mine.'

'Nevertheless—'

'Nevertheless—what?' Remy stared at her, and she wished she weren't so aware of the muscled expanse of his body visible in the open V of his shirt. 'What is your problem?' he countered. 'Do you object to me being here? I thought you might be glad to see me. It can't be much fun holidaying alone.'

Megan moistened her lips. 'I don't mind what you do,' she protested, not altogether truthfully, but he was not to know that. 'Um—how long are you staying? Is—is Rachel with you?'

Remy gave her a speaking look. 'No, she's not,' he answered at last, though his expression had said it all. 'Rachel and I don't live in one another's pockets, whatever my mother may have told you. She has her friends, I have mine.'

Megan absorbed this. 'But you live together, don't you?' she ventured, needing to know where the younger woman stood.

'Not yet,' replied Remy. 'She lives with her parents. Did my mother tell you otherwise?'

'No,' Megan answered hurriedly. She couldn't let him think Anita had said any such thing. She didn't want him to think they had been talking about him at all. He was far too presumptuous as it was.

'Good.'

Remy got to his feet now, loosening the button at the waistband of the black jeans he was wearing and pulling the ends of his shirt free. Taking it off, he dropped it onto the empty chair beside her, then, leaving her for a moment, he went to take a couple of the courtesy towels from the rack.

He sauntered back casually, dropping the towels beside his shirt before peeling down his jeans. She found herself holding her breath as he disrobed in front of her, but the boxers he was wearing under his jeans were as conventional as shorts.

After spreading the towels, he subsided onto the lounger beside her, and for a while there was silence. The pool deck was only thinly patronised at this hour of the morning, most guests taking advantage of the cooler mornings to go sightseeing or into town. In consequence, the only sounds were the gentle shushing of the water against the sides of the pool and the occasional whisper of the breeze through the palms.

Megan knew she should have been able to relax again, but she couldn't. Her eyes were irresistibly drawn to the length of the legs residing on the lounger next to her. The fringe of her umbrella hid all but the lower half of his body from her, but what she could see was disturbing and far too interesting for comfort.

She picked up her book again, but it was no use. She read the words over and over again, but they didn't mean anything to her. She actually found herself wondering what it would be like to have a relationship with someone like Remy. She'd never been attracted to young men before, but there was no doubt he was different from the norm...

But he shouldn't be, she reproved herself irritably. For God's sake, what was wrong with her? She was acting as if she'd never seen a man in the nude before. And Remy wasn't nude; he was wearing a perfectly adequate pair of boxers. The fact that they exposed the impressive mound between his legs was purely incidental.

Or it would have been if she hadn't been so curious about him, she realised. He was probably totally unaware of the fact that she was fascinated by his sex. As for Anita— Megan's throat dried. She would be positively appalled if she guessed what Megan was thinking. She'd already made it clear that she considered her her contemporary, not his.

Which was as it should be, Megan told herself, pushing her sunglasses up into her hair and shifting onto her side so she didn't have to look at him. She hitched up the top of her swimsuit, glad that she wasn't wearing anything as revealing as a bikini. But her scar hadn't made that an option, and the terracotta-coloured maillot was happily loose across her taut breasts.

'How are you getting on with the old man now?'

Her restlessness must have communicated itself to him for when she glanced over her shoulder she found he had swung his feet to the ground and was sitting on the edge of his chair.

'Um—we talk,' she said, turning back to the pool again. 'He's easily tired, but I think he likes to see me. We talk a lot about my mother. Sometimes I think he mistakes me for her.'

'Laura.' Remy's voice was low and affectionate, and it did unwelcome things to Megan's senses. 'She was quite a special lady.'

Megan didn't attempt to answer that. She'd changed her mind about a lot of things since she'd been here, but she still felt an instinctive loyalty to her father. Nevertheless, she could see how she might have been mistaken. At fifteen she must have been so naïve.

'How about Mom?' Remy asked. 'How are you getting on with her?' And against her better judgement Megan shifted onto her back.

'We get along fine,' she said, sliding her dark glasses over her eyes, and Remy gave her a knowing look.

'Has she been honest with you yet?' His eyes were intent. 'I know what she's like. She's very good at avoiding awkward subjects.'

'I suppose we all are.'

Megan had spoken carelessly, but now Remy's eyes narrowed. 'What's that supposed to mean?'

Megan's lips parted. 'Nothing.'

'You're not by any chance getting at me?' he countered, and she gave a hurried shake of her head.

'No. Why would I?'

'Who knows?' Remy scowled. 'Something the old man said, perhaps.' He paused. 'Has he mentioned my grandmother to you?'

Megan frowned. 'You don't mean my mother?'

'No. I mean my grandmother,' said Remy flatly. 'His first wife.'

'I'm afraid not.' Megan wondered if that was why he was so irritable suddenly. 'I'm sure he must have loved her, too. But—people get lonely, I suppose.'

Remy's expression was droll. 'I'm not looking for sympathy, you know.'

'I never said you were.' Megan tilted her head. 'I just don't know what you're getting at, that's all.'

'You don't? You mean your father never told you?' Remy's lean features were sceptical. 'I'd have thought that man would have done anything to spite this family.'

Megan stiffened. 'If you're going to start insulting my father again—'

'I'm not.' Remy interrupted her. 'And I promised I'd keep my opinions to myself. But he hurt my mother a lot, and that's not easy to forgive.'

Megan expelled her breath slowly. 'I suppose you mean because he didn't approve of her—keeping you.'

'That was only part of it,' said Remy bitterly. 'But, hey—' his lips tightened '—it's not your concern, is it? I just wanted to know what you were thinking. Whether you felt the same.'

'Felt the same about what?' She frowned.

Remy stared at her. 'It doesn't matter.'

Megan felt confused. 'Is this something to do with *your* father?' she asked cautiously, and then wished she hadn't when his expression grew bleak. 'I don't know what you mean.'

'It doesn't matter,' he said again shortly, and pushed himself to his feet. 'I've disturbed you long enough. I'd better get back.'

'Remy…' Uncaring what he thought of her appearance now, Megan scrambled off the lounger and pulled off the protective glasses. 'Please,' she said, touching his arm, which was rigid with muscle beneath the hair-roughened skin. 'Can't we forget about the past if that's what you're talking about? Or at least not let it influence what happens now?'

Remy looked down at her hand gripping his arm, and then, when she awkwardly withdrew it, he stepped away from her. 'If only we could,' he said drily, stepping into his jeans and pulling up the zip. 'Look, I'd better go and show my face. It wouldn't do for the old lady to think I was avoiding her again.'

Megan knew he was right, but she wondered why that hadn't bothered him earlier. Until she'd implied that everyone had something to hide, they'd been getting along just fine. All right, she'd had her reservations when he'd first appeared, but that was understandable in the circumstances. She was so afraid of betraying herself; so afraid of revealing how attracted to him she was.

Megan chose to have lunch in her room.

She insisted to herself that because she was feeling rather tired she would have done so anyway, but in all honesty she didn't want to intrude on Anita and her son.

It wasn't cowardice, she defended herself, when her conscience pricked her. After her conversation with Remy, she was quite sure he'd be glad not to see her again. For some reason she had offended him when she'd spoken of his father. Why was it such a secret, for heaven's sake? These days being a single mother didn't mean a thing.

Perhaps it was the man himself, she reflected thoughtfully. Perhaps he had treated Anita badly, or refused to accept responsibility for his son. Whatever, it was too long ago now to matter. Surely Remy didn't think it made any difference to her…?

Two more days passed without incident. Simon phoned again to say that all was well in London. He also said he'd met a young man who had some great ideas about next year's directory. He'd suggested that they should consider expanding into the ethnic market. There were so many good Afro-Asian designers with no obvious showcase for their work.

Megan's enthusiasm was lukewarm at best, but she couldn't help it. Despite her determination not to do so, she was becoming involved with the Robards, almost against her will. Ryan's illness and Remy's attitude seemed infinitely more important than next year's fashions. She wouldn't have believed it could happen, but she was no longer counting the days to going back.

Realising she was in danger of stagnating, she decided to ask Anita if she could borrow a car to go into town. She hadn't visited the island's capital since she'd returned to San Felipe, and she also wanted to see the Garden of Remembrance where her mother's ashes had been spread.

She found it wasn't easy, broaching the topic with Anita. Since her arrival, they'd tended to skirt round the details of her mother's death. But her stepsister was quite willing to tell her where the cemetery was, and even offered to go with her if she'd prefer not to risk straining her stomach by driving.

'Oh, I'm sure I'll be fine.' Megan hadn't really considered that possibility, but she'd done so much walking, she was sure she'd be all right. 'And I'd like to go on my own, if you don't mind. It's something I want to do, something I should have done sooner. I hope you understand?'

'Of course.'

Anita didn't argue, and Megan guessed she was hoping it would help her to see Ryan Robards in a more sympathetic light. As far as Megan was concerned, she couldn't wait to get behind the wheel again. It was six weeks since she'd felt in control of her life.

The vehicle Anita lent her was an open-topped buggy, one of several that were available for hire to guests staying at the hotel. Anita also lent her a hat, a floppy-brimmed straw one with a wide scarlet ribbon around the crown, which Megan was rather chary of, but which did a good job of protecting her from the sun.

For the rest, she wore a short pleated skirt in navy, and a short-sleeved shirt. The shirt was a soft lemon silk that accentuated her slight tan, a pair of gold hoops swung from her earlobes, and a matching handful of bangles encircled her wrist.

She was actually feeling much better in herself, she acknowledged with some relief as she drove towards Port Serrat. The weakness she had been suffering when she'd come here was dissipating, and the rest, and the fact that she was eating proper food, instead of just grabbing a sandwich or a takeaway when she could, was bringing the glow of health back to her cheeks. So long as she didn't put on too much weight, she appended. She wanted her clothes to fit her when she got home.

When she got home…

Pausing to allow a man leading an ox-cart that was laden with a wobbly load of green bananas to pull out in front of her, Megan was dismayed to find how reluctant she was to anticipate her return. Like her mother, she was beginning to understand that the island could grow on you, but when had she stopped looking for excuses to leave?

Dismissing such disruptive thoughts, she began to realise how familiar she still was with her surroundings. Although she hadn't been allowed to drive in those days, the holidays she had spent here had given her a comprehensive knowledge of the island. Her father—or her mother—had always hired a car to get about, and they'd often taken Remy with them on their expeditions.

Or at least her mother had, she amended honestly. Giles Cross had not encouraged her friendship with the younger child. Perhaps even then he'd sensed the effect the Robards were going to have on his family, she reflected ruefully. She couldn't believe he had blamed Remy for his mother's sins.

Still, she would never know now, and, putting such thoughts aside, she looked about her with delight. The flowering hedges that defined the road were giving way to clusters of small houses, each with its own garden, and at the bottom of the sloping high street she could see the bobbing masts of the yachts in the harbour.

The small town of Port Serrat clung to the hills around the harbour. It was a quaint place, much of it very old, and she remembered Ryan used to entertain the tourists with tales of its disreputable past. In the eighteenth and nineteenth centuries, it had been a haunt for pirates and buccaneers, and according to him they accounted for the number of bars and inns that thronged its streets.

Megan parked the buggy in a chandler's yard, and then sauntered down towards the quay. A fish market occupied one corner of the quayside, with every kind of seafood imaginable. There were shrimps and crabs, and wriggling lobsters, and shark and salmon and grouper. Many of the varieties of fish Megan hadn't tasted since she was last here, and she guessed Anita had no problem in varying the menu.

Beyond the fish market, the quay opened out into a marina, where the tall-masted vessels she had seen as she'd driven into town jostled prettily on their moorings. Like Barbados and Antigua, San Felipe attracted sea-going yachts, but many of these vessels were privately owned or charters.

Ryan used to own a yacht, she remembered, which was

how her parents had got to know him so well. He used to enjoy ferrying his guests around the island, or on longer expeditions to other islands in the group.

She was beginning to feel thirsty, and, finding a small café, she seated herself outside, beneath a huge striped umbrella. When the waiter appeared, she ordered a glass of sweet lemonade, and sat there, sipping the ice-cold liquid with genuine enjoyment.

Glancing at her watch, she discovered it was only a little after half-past ten. She'd left the hotel early, to make the most of the less oppressive heat of the morning, and now she was very glad she had. She had lots of time to do a little window-shopping before visiting the cemetery Anita had described to her, and then she'd drive back to the hotel for lunch.

When she left the café, she couldn't help wondering where Remy's flat was situated. He'd said he lived near the harbour, but there were no obvious pointers as to whereabouts. There were no modern apartment blocks here, just a wealth of colourful housing, and she guessed his home was hidden amongst them.

Of course, his office was something else, she reflected, glad she had kept her hat on as she slogged up the busy main street. This area of town was famous for its shops and boutiques catering for the rich tourist market, and her eyes were drawn to the colourful displays of designer goods.

It was possible he worked at home, she mused, but she didn't think that was likely. A lawyer would need to be accessible to his clients, and she thought Remy would want to keep his public and private lives separate.

And then she saw him. He was several yards ahead of her, walking with another man, and she thought it said something about her state of mind that she recognised him at once. Even from behind, his broad shoulders and lean, muscled thighs were unmistakable. He moved with such a lithe, easy grace, his identity was not in any doubt to her.

But what should she do? Despite the fact that he wasn't wearing a jacket today, his shirt and trousers were formal, evidence surely that he was working. Besides, the last thing she wanted was for him to think she was looking for him. However innocent her curiosity, she'd rather keep it to herself.

She halted uncertainly, glancing back towards the harbour, but when she looked round again she found he and his companion had halted, too. Remy appeared to be saying goodbye to the other man, his hand raised to push open a nearby door. Was that where he had his office? she wondered. Over one of the shops that lined the street?

And then he saw her.

Despite the hat, despite the incongruity of finding her here, in Port Serrat, alone, his recognition of her was just as immediate. Before she could move, before she could turn and hurry down the street and pretend she hadn't recognised him, he bid his companion farewell and came striding towards her, and Megan could only stand and wait for him, her stomach quivering in anticipation.

CHAPTER SEVEN

To HER relief, he seemed pleased to see her. She'd been rather apprehensive that after their previous conversation he might be holding a grudge. But she should have known better, she admitted. She wasn't that important to him.

'How did you get here?' he asked now, by way of a greeting, and Megan wondered if he thought she'd come with his mother. His mobile mouth tilted. 'Nice hat!'

'Yes, isn't it?' Megan tugged the brim around her cheeks and pulled a face at him. 'And, believe it or not, I came by buggy.' She nodded up the street. 'Is that where you work?'

'Alone?'

Megan frowned, pretending to misunderstand him. 'Yes, I know. You told me you worked alone.'

'No, I mean—' Remy started to explain, and then caught her smiling. 'You knew what I meant,' he accused good-naturedly. 'I thought Mom might have brought you. Are you supposed to drive?'

'I do have a licence,' she declared sweetly, enjoying their exchange much more than she should. She sobered. 'And it is almost six weeks since I had the operation. I'm feeling pretty good, as a matter of fact.'

'Yes, I can see that.' Remy's eyes made a disturbing résumé of her slender figure, lingering longest on her bare legs. 'And as you are here—and alone—perhaps we could have lunch together?'

'Well...'

Megan's tone mirrored her hesitation and Remy was quick to give her an escape. 'Of course, you've probably got other things to do,' he said. 'I'm sorry. I wasn't thinking. Perhaps you want to get back to the hotel and rest.'

'Oh, please!' Megan couldn't let him think that. 'Apart from visiting the cemetery, I've got nothing planned.'

'So?'

'So—yes. I would like to have lunch with you.' She paused. 'Where shall we meet? You know this place much better than me.'

Remy considered. 'Why not come back here, and I'll show you round the office?' he suggested. He gestured towards a sports shop set further up the street. 'Use the side door and come straight up.'

'All right.'

Megan beamed, and Remy stared at her for a moment before turning away. Then, as she was heading back down the street, he hailed her. 'I'm glad you came,' he called, and she hugged the words to herself all the way back to the car.

The Baptist cemetery, where Laura Robards' ashes had been scattered, was on the outskirts of the small town. It was set on the cliffs, overlooking the harbour, and Megan guessed Ryan must have come here often before his illness had confined him to the hotel. Within the Garden of Remembrance she found a small plaque with her mother's name engraved on it, and the words 'I Miss You' half hidden behind an enormous vase of orchids and lilies.

It was immensely poignant and immensely moving. Megan was alone in the garden, and she groped blindly for the stone bench that allowed visitors to sit for a while and share the garden's peace. And after a while a little of that peace crept over her, too, assuring her of her mother's forgiveness, and giving her a sense of completion.

It was after twelve when she walked up the high street again, and despite what she had said to Remy earlier, she was beginning to feel weary. After all, she'd only taken fairly undemanding walks since her illness, and although she had felt all right when she'd accepted his invitation now she half wished she'd headed straight back to the hotel.

She pushed open the glass door to one side of the sports shop he had indicated, noticing the name outlined on the

glass beneath her hand. 'Jeremy Robards,' she read.
'Attorney at Law.' Funny, she reflected ruefully, she'd
never realised that Remy wasn't his full name.

The stairs were steep, and by the time she got to the top
she was panting. She stood for a moment on the landing,
trying to get her breath before entering the office, and then
started in surprise when the door was opened and a young
black woman emerged.

She was a pretty woman, small and rather voluptuous,
and her eyes were kind and they immediately darkened with
concern. 'Are you all right?' she exclaimed, slipping an arm
about Megan's waist and leading her back into the office.
'Do you feel faint? Would you like a glass of water? Let
me tell Remy you're here.'

'No, really—' began Megan, sinking down weakly onto
the worn leather sofa that ran along one wall of what she
now realised was a kind of waiting room. Across the room,
a desk occupied by a word processor seemed to indicate a
secretary, though at the moment there was no one else
about. 'I'll be fine.'

The young woman ignored her, hurrying across the
rubber-tiled floor to an inner door. She tapped once and
then opened it with the familiarity of long usage, and
Megan realised she must work here, too.

For herself, Megan wished the floor would open up and
swallow her. She had never felt so helpless in her life. Except maybe the afternoon when her ulcer had perforated,
she acknowledged. And at least she wasn't in pain at the
moment.

Her head was buzzing, and she had no idea what the
woman said to Remy. But presently he was there, squatting
down in front of her, his expression full of the kind of
sympathy she couldn't cope with. 'Dammit, Megan,' he
said, sweeping off her hat, 'what the hell have you been
doing to yourself now?'

Megan drew a breath. 'Your stairs are steep, that's all.'

'Oh, right. And that's why you're as pale as a ghost.'

'I'm tired,' she defended herself. 'Perhaps I've tried to

do too much. I'll be all right as soon as I get my breath back.'

'Will you?' Remy didn't sound convinced, though he got abruptly to his feet. 'A glass of water, please, Sylvie,' he requested politely. 'Then you can leave Miss Cross to me.'

Sylvie got the water, smiling sympathetically, and Megan drank thirstily from the glass. Perhaps she was just dehydrated, she thought. That was why she felt so wobbly. But her legs were still like jelly when she got to her feet.

'Where are you going?' Sylvie had departed after delivering the water, and now Remy stepped between her and the door.

'I thought we were going for lunch,' protested Megan, making a vain attempt to appear enthusiastic. 'Oh, yes.' She remembered. 'You were going to show me your office.'

Remy's nostrils flared. 'You don't seriously expect me to take you to a restaurant when you're shaking like a leaf.'

'I'm not shaking.' But she was. 'Oh, I'll be all right in a few minutes. It was hot up at the cemetery, and I suppose I'm not used to hill-walking.'

Remy's mouth compressed. 'All right,' he said, and she was surprised at how easily he had given in. 'We'll have lunch. But not at a restaurant.' Which explained his compliance. 'My apartment's not far from here. We'll eat there.'

Megan's mouth rounded to make an objection, but the warning look in his eyes deterred her. Why not? she thought, pushing aside the suspicion that it really wasn't a good idea to go to his home. She had been dreading the possibility of making a fool of herself in public. And what was she afraid of, after all? She had been curious to see where he lived.

Lifting her shoulders in a gesture of acceptance, she followed Remy across the room and into his office. A square sun-lit room, with long windows overlooking the harbour, it was much more attractive than her own office at home. She would swop her steel and chrome technology for a view like that, she thought enviously, and Remy's ancient

mahogany desk and leather chair matched their antique surroundings.

'This is where you work?' she murmured, observing the
bulging filing cabinets and the desk that was loaded down
with briefs.

'When I have the time,' he answered, shoving his wallet
into his pocket. 'That's it. I'm ready.' He glanced around
with some resignation. 'I've got a court appearance this
afternoon so I've got to be back by two.'

'Oh.'

Megan wondered if he was regretting offering the invitation as much as she was regretting accepting it, but she
met his eyes and decided not to ask. She had the feeling
her appearance had caused enough aggravation as it was.

It was easier going down the stairs, though Megan clung
to the handrail, just in case. She'd snatched up her hat again
before leaving, and now she tugged it back onto her head,
uncaring of what Remy might think.

Outside, the midday heat was enervating. Megan felt herself wilting, and hoped Remy's apartment wasn't far away.
She didn't object either when he gripped her arm just above
her elbow to guide her, though the feeling of those hard
fingers against her flesh was far too disturbing.

'It's not far,' he said, his voice only marginally less
clipped than before, and Megan forced a grateful smile.

'What a state to be in,' she said. 'Falling apart just because I've done a bit of sightseeing. You must think I'm a
complete idiot.'

'What I think is best not stated,' retorted Remy shortly,
matching his steps to hers. 'I should have gone to the cemetery with you. Or my mother should, anyway. It was too
long a journey to make alone.'

'That's not true.' Megan couldn't allow him to think that.
She bit her lip. 'And your mother did offer to come with
me, as a matter of fact. But I wanted to come on my own.'

'Why?'

They had turned down a side street, where the jutting
balconies of old buildings provided a blessed escape from

the sun, and before Megan could think of an answer Remy
had paused beside a narrow opening. A brick passageway
led into a kind of inner courtyard, and he ushered Megan
ahead of him into the square beyond.

'Welcome to Moonraker's Yard,' he announced drily,
glancing about him. 'I'm afraid you're going to have to
climb a few more stairs.'

Megan shook her head, too bemused by the charm of her
surroundings to worry about something as ordinary as
stairs. They were in a kind of mews, with the sun beating
down upon their heads from between a circle of tall houses,
with narrow wooden steps giving access to the floors above.

'This is where you live?' she asked, and Remy nodded.
'It's not as decrepit inside as it appears.'

'Oh, no.' Megan was vehement. 'It doesn't look decrepit
at all. I was just thinking how delightful it was.'

'You're obviously a romantic,' said Remy, with a wry
grimace. 'Come on. My pad's just up here.'

They climbed one of the flights of wooden stairs to a
studded wooden door, and after Remy had used his key
they stepped into a long corridor. At the end of the corridor,
light flooded from a stained-glass window, covering the
floor with prisms of light in a hundred different colours and
shades.

'Oh!'

Megan barely had a chance to exclaim at the unusual
design of the window before Remy had closed the door and
was striding away to open a door on their right. 'Come in,'
he said, gesturing for her to follow him, and she moved
almost dreamily into a room that seemed both ancient and
modern.

It was obviously his living room, and although it was
fairly large the low ceiling, with its dark oak beams, gave
it a cosy appearance. The walls, two of which were panelled
and gleamed with the patina of age, were hung with several
impressive oil paintings, and a huge urn of flowers filled
the wide stone hearth.

The furniture was eclectic: wide squashy sofas existing

cheek-by-jowl with cabinets from another age. There were Victorian bookshelves, and an eighteenth-century captain's table, and various tubs and planters filled with climbing plants.

The windows were long and narrow, like the hall, but the view was expansive. From here, it was possible to see the whole sweep of the harbour and the bay. One of the windows was ajar, and a slight breeze moved the long curtains—curtains which were almost transparent, and reflected the colours of the sea.

Megan drew a trembling breath and gazed all about her. 'It's fantastic,' she said. 'I never expected anything like this.'

'What did you expect?' he enquired lightly, tilting back the brim of her hat. 'That I probably lived in a loft somewhere, without any running water?'

'Well, no.' She moistened her lips. 'But this is so—so—'

'Rustic?'

'Tasteful,' she insisted firmly. She lifted her shoulders. 'You're very lucky to live in a place like this.'

'Am I?'

His tone was sardonic, but Megan chose not to answer him, approaching the windows instead, and resting one knee on the low sill. 'What a marvellous view!' she exclaimed. 'You must never tire of looking at it. I bet it's pretty at night when all the lights are lit.'

'You'll have to come and see for yourself,' remarked Remy evenly, opening a door at the far side of the room. 'Will cheese and salad do? I'm afraid I don't have anything more sophisticated. I wasn't expecting to have a guest for lunch.'

'Of course.' Megan felt guilty. 'Please—don't put yourself out for me. Anything will do—a sandwich or some fruit, even. I'm really not very hungry at all.'

Remy pulled a face and disappeared though the door, and after depositing her hat on one of the winged armchairs Megan followed him. She found herself in a small kitchen which was surprisingly well equipped, with pans and bunches of herbs hanging from the beams. There was a dresser lined with dishes in a cream and gold design, and a tiny window looking out onto a terrace.

Remy was in the process of taking a dish of crisp lettuce from the fridge, along with some of the tiny cherry tomatoes that Megan knew were so sweet. A loaf of crusty French bread rested on a wooden board, beside a huge chunk of cheese and a dish of creamy butter.

'You're supposed to be taking it easy,' he declared at once when he saw her, and she pulled a face.

'I feel much better now,' she insisted, and she did. The thick walls of the old building kept the apartment delightfully cool, and although she still felt a little flushed she had stopped shaking.

'Well, why don't you go and sit at the table?' he suggested, gesturing towards an archway she hadn't noticed before. Beyond the fronds of greenery that hung from the ceiling she now saw a tiny dining area, with a square mahogany table and four ladder-backed chairs. 'Here—' he handed her two place mats and some cutlery '—take these with you. And there are some glasses in the cabinet right behind you. I know you don't want anything alcoholic, but I've got some mineral water in the fridge.'

Megan laid the table, and then did as he suggested and sat by the window, which, like the living room, looked out over the harbour. She might be feeling a little guilty, not having let Anita know what she was doing, but if she was honest she would admit that she had seldom felt so happy in her life.

The food, when it came, was simple and delicious. As well as the lettuce and tomatoes, there were tangy radishes and sweet peppers and thin slices of cucumber. The bread was cut into crusty chunks, which she spread with some of the yellow butter, and the cheese was ripe and crumbly, and full of flavour.

'So,' said Remy, circling the rim of his glass with a lazy finger, 'why did you want to come alone? Is Mom getting on your nerves already?'

'No!' But Megan wondered at his perception. 'Your mother and I get along—very well.' She paused. 'I just wanted a little time on my own, that's all.'

'So what are you doing here?' he countered, and she coloured.

'Well—this wasn't planned to happen.'

'Wasn't it?'

'No.' She forced herself to meet his knowing gaze. 'It wasn't. But that doesn't mean I'm not glad it did.'

His eyes darkened. 'Good.'

Megan drew a trembling breath. 'Anyway, I doubt your mother would approve.'

He didn't argue. 'No.'

'I think she's afraid I'll be a bad influence on you,' added Megan, attempting to lighten the mood. 'I'm not sure she entirely approves of me. Not being married and so on.'

'You could be right.' He smiled. 'And you like the apartment?'

'Mmm.' Megan nodded, taking a sip of iced water before replying. 'What I've seen of it anyway,' she said. She moistened her lips. 'Will—will you and Rachel live here after you're married?'

Remy's tawny eyes darkened. 'Who says we're getting married?'

Megan shrugged. 'Well, aren't you?'

'Not to my knowledge,' he retorted shortly. 'When are you marrying Simon?'

'I'm not. That is—' Megan looked down at her plate. 'It's not something we've ever discussed.' Which was true, she told herself defensively, though perhaps not for any reason Remy might assume. 'We're friends, that's all. And—and business partners.'

Remy moved his broad shoulders. 'Well, so are Rachel and I—friends, at least. As she doesn't have a job, we could hardly be business partners.'

Megan pressed her lips together and then, lifting her head, she looked him squarely in the eye. 'That's not exactly true, is it?'

Remy's stare was daunting. 'Isn't it?'

'No.' Megan hesitated. 'I've assumed that Rachel and you—well, that you're lovers,' she said hurriedly. 'Friends don't usually sleep together.'

Remy gave a snort. 'Don't they?' His tone was disparaging. 'You sound like my mother.'

Megan endeavoured not to show any reaction, but his words stung. 'Well, I suppose I am your aunt—your *step-*aunt, at least,' she reminded him crisply. 'I didn't think you'd mind me showing some interest in your future. I didn't mean to pry.'

'Didn't you?' Remy, who had eaten very little, she noticed, pushed his plate aside and got abruptly to his feet. 'I think you were being honest for once, and now you're trying to rationalise it. Don't pretend you feel like my aunt, because I don't believe it. You're concerned because you're becoming attracted to me, and you know your father would never have approved.'

'No!' Megan was horrified.

'Yes.' Remy came round the table and pulled her roughly to her feet. His hands massaged her shoulders. 'That's why you came looking for me today. Because we never have any privacy at the hotel.'

'You're wrong—'

'Am I?' Patently, he didn't believe her, and she could hardly blame him when her insides were churning and her heart was thudding erratically in her chest. He bent his head and rubbed his mouth against hers in a light, taunting caress. 'Stop kidding yourself, Megan. You might not like it, but you knew what was happening that first evening when you spilled your drink.'

'That's not true.' Despite the fact that the brush of his lips had started a fire that spread wantonly throughout her body, Megan fought to be free of him. She could not allow him to think she had come here with some wild notion of starting an affair. Until he'd accused her of being attracted to him, she'd thought she'd done a good job of hiding her emotions. To discover her feelings were so transparent was

humiliating, apart from creating a situation she couldn't
deal with. 'Will you let go of me?'

Remy held her for a few seconds longer, his breath cool
against her hot forehead. Then he spread his fingers wide,
enabling her to move out from under their restraint, and she
stumbled back instinctively, putting the width of her chair
between them. But she could tell from his expression that
he still didn't believe her; that he had only let her go because he'd chosen to do so.

Megan was breathing rapidly. Where before she had regarded the confines of the dining room as cosily intimate,
now she was only conscious of its limited space. To get
out of the room she was forced to squeeze past him, and it
didn't help to know that her embarrassment was as evident
as her indignation.

She hurried through the kitchen, pausing on the threshold
to the living room because she found her head was spinning. Oh, God, she thought, she surely wasn't going to
make a fool of herself again. She had to remember she was
still convalescing and not go charging about as if she were
fit and well.

'What are you doing?'

Remy was behind her now, his voice low and full of
resignation. But when she would have moved away his
hand at her waist prevented her, sliding beneath the loosened hem of her shirt and stroking her skin.

'What do you think you're doing?' she countered, stiffening automatically away from him. She took a breath. 'I'm
leaving. Thank you for lunch. It was—well, it was—interesting.'

'Megan—'

'What?' Unable to bear the caress of his cool fingers or
the heat of his body behind her, she swung away from him
then, feeling her balance tilt and then right itself as the
dizziness attacked her again. 'Look, Remy, I'm sorry if I've
given you the wrong impression. I was curious about where
you lived and worked, I'll admit it. But anything else is
purely in your head.'

'Really?'

'Yes, really.' She looked about for her hat. However much she wanted to get out of here, she dared not go without it.

'Okay.' Remy's sigh was weary. 'If that's how you want to play it.'

'Play it?' Megan found her hat and jammed it onto her head with a shaking hand. 'I don't know what you're talking about. I'm not playing. I like you, Remy. I like you a lot. But I can't see you as anything more than the boy I used to play with.'

'Bullshit.'

Megan caught her breath. 'I beg your pardon?'

'I said—'

'I know what you said, but you had no right to say it.' She swallowed. 'I'm sorry if you don't believe me, but that's the way it is.'

'I don't believe you.' He was scathing. 'You've just had second thoughts, that's all.'

'No.' Megan couldn't believe she was having this conversation with him. 'Please—you know your mother would be so upset if she knew what was going on—'

'My mother!' Remy said the words almost contemptuously. 'Of course. We mustn't forget my mother's part in all this, must we? What's wrong? Are you afraid we're going to offend her? My God, it's been a long time since I allowed my mother to make any decisions in my life.'

Megan moved her head from side to side. 'Remy—'

'What?'

She edged towards the door. 'This is crazy.'

'I agree.' But instead of abandoning the argument he closed the space between them. Cupping her hot face between his palms, he looked down at her with dark intent. 'Don't you get it, Megan? I don't care why you came here as long as you stay.'

Megan's lips parted. 'I can't.'

'Why can't you?' His fingertips probed the soft contours of her ears. 'This isn't anything to do with anyone else. It's to do with us, that's all. With the fact that you want me as much as I want you.'

'No!'

Megan would have moved away from him then, but the closed door was at her back and there was no place to go. Her mouth was dry, but when his thumb rubbed sensuously across her lower lip she felt wet in other places. He was playing with her emotions, she thought, in a panic, and there was nothing she could do to stop him.

She couldn't believe this was happening. Any minute now Remy would let her go and admit that he'd just been teasing her. But deep inside her she knew it was no game. Remy was actually preventing her from leaving.

And, to add to her distress, she knew that everything he'd said was true. She didn't understand all of it, but she couldn't deny that she was attracted to him, and beneath his hands the blood was rushing hotly to the surface of her skin. She wanted him to touch her; dammit, she wanted to touch him, and rivulets of fire seemed to be attacking every nerve in her body.

He was removing her hat now, bending his head to stroke the sensitive skin behind her ear with his tongue. She felt weak, and she tried to tell herself it was a hangover from her illness, but when he wedged his knee between her thighs she was more concerned he'd feel the dampness between her legs.

'You're trembling again,' he said huskily, his anger dissipating at the knowledge of her vulnerability, and she wondered if he'd believe her if she pretended she was going to faint. But then his mouth moved across her cheek and found her parted lips, and such strategies were no longer an option.

CHAPTER EIGHT

ALTHOUGH it was the last thing she would have chosen to face, Megan wasn't really surprised to find Anita waiting for her when she got back.

'Oh, so there you are!' Anita exclaimed, when Megan had parked the buggy outside the hotel. 'I was beginning to get anxious. You didn't tell me you intended to have lunch in town.'

'It—was a spur-of-the-moment thing,' began Megan, wondering if Remy could have phoned his mother and told her she'd been to his apartment, but before she could incriminate herself Anita made it plain that he hadn't.

'I've been trying to get in touch with Remy,' she declared. 'I wondered if you might have called at his office. But Sylvie—that's his secretary, you know—she said he'd gone out with a client at twelve o'clock and hadn't come back.'

A client!

Megan wondered if that was Sylvie's interpretation of who she was or Remy's. She had the feeling it was the former. From the little she had seen of her, Sylvie had appeared to be a very shrewd assistant.

'So did you go to the cemetery?' asked Anita, inadvertently letting Megan off the hook. And at her stepsister's nod she said, 'It's a pretty place, isn't it? Pops used to spend hours sitting in the garden.'

'I guessed as much,' Megan murmured. 'I sat there for a while, too.'

'Did you?' Anita hooked her arm through hers and led her into the hotel. Then she gave Megan a thoughtful stare. 'You look tired. Are you sure you haven't done too much?'

'Of course not.' But Megan could feel her colour rising

in spite of her efforts. 'I am a little tired, though. You're right about that. If you don't mind, I'll have a rest before dinner.'

'You don't feel up to visiting with Pops, I suppose?' Anita ventured hopefully. 'He asked for you this morning, and I had to tell him you'd gone into town.'

Megan gave an inward groan, but she turned to Anita with a determined smile. 'Why not?' she said. 'I'd like to tell him where I've been.'

'Thank you.'

Anita squeezed her arm and then let her go, and Megan restored her hat before stepping outside again. Although it was after three o'clock, the sun was still as hot as ever, and the wide brim gave some protection to her eyes as well.

It only took a few minutes to reach Ryan's bungalow. It was the one furthest from the beach and therefore in the quietest position. As always, the nurse on duty was pleased to see her. It enabled him to relax for a few minutes, knowing his patient was not alone.

Ryan appeared to be asleep, but Megan had learned not to be deceived. During the course of their many conversations, he had told her that he seldom slept for long, day or night. He closed his eyes and dozed sometimes, but he never got what she would have called a good night's sleep.

'You're back,' he said as she approached the bed, pulling off the oxygen mask so that he could speak. His voice was harsh and often laboured, but she'd got used to that, too. She no longer felt like running for assistance if he appeared to be short of breath.

'Yes,' she said now, sinking down into the chair the nurse had placed beside the bed for her. 'How are you?'

'What is it they say? As well as can be expected,' he muttered humorously. 'Did you enjoy your outing? Anita said you might be going to the cemetery.'

'Yes. I did.' Megan nodded, looking at his thin wrist which lay beside hers on the sheet. 'It's a very peaceful spot, isn't it? I think it did me good.'

'Good, good.' He echoed the word, his lips twitching

involuntarily at his own thoughts. 'Laura and I used to spend a lot of time together, when I could still walk from the car to the bench.'

Megan pressed her lips together. 'I'm sure she misses your visits,' she said, before caution could silence her tongue. 'That is—I think it's where she'd have wanted to rest.'

'Do you?' His eyes bored into hers. And then, as if what he wanted to say required some effort, he pressed the mask briefly to his face. 'You don't know how grateful I am to hear you say that, Meggie.' His hand groped for hers. 'Does that mean you've forgiven me at last?'

Megan breathed deeply, allowing him to enfold her soft fingers within his dry flesh. 'I suppose it does.'

'Thank you.' He sighed. 'You've made me very happy. Remy said you didn't bear grudges and he was right.'

Remy...

Megan would have preferred not to think about Remy at that moment. Indeed, she'd been trying to stop thinking about him ever since she'd left Moonraker's Yard. Not that she'd done anything wrong, she assured herself firmly. She had nothing to be ashamed of, and she should stop blaming herself for his mistakes.

'You like my boy, don't you?' the old man continued now, and Megan attempted not to betray her fears.

'We're—old friends,' she said, wanting to withdraw her hand before he sensed her apprehension. She licked her lips. 'I'm not tiring you, am I?'

'I'll survive,' he said sardonically. 'For the present anyway.' His lips twisted. 'Tell me what you think about him. His mother's proud because he's become a lawyer.'

'And you're not?' The words slipped past Megan's lips once again, and hot colour bathed her cheeks at her audacity.

'Of course I'm proud of him,' Ryan said unevenly, resorting to the oxygen mask once more. 'But Remy knows where his real loyalties lie. The hotel will eventually be his responsibility.' He coughed. 'He knows that as well as me.'

Megan absorbed his words, realising that he regarded Remy's career as nothing more than a stop-gap, a way to fill his time until he was needed. She could see that in his way Ryan was as single-minded as her father had been. They both believed they knew what was best for their children.

'I'll have to be going,' she said, hoping to avoid an answer, but Ryan's fingers tightened round her hand for a moment.

'Has he told you?' he asked succinctly. 'Has he told you about his father?' He swallowed with some difficulty. 'If he hasn't, it's important that he should.'

'Told me what?' Megan was confused. She'd assumed that was a topic that was never broached.

'Your father never told you?' he wheezed, clearly getting agitated. 'Why would he? He despised us for it.'

'Mr Robards—'

'Ryan.'

'Ryan, then.' Megan paused. 'I'm afraid I don't know what you're talking about.'

'No.' Another harsh cough tore through his narrow frame, and this time he had to release her hand to grope for the box of tissues lying on the bed beside him. 'I'm sorry,' he said when he was able, obviously tiring. 'We'll have to discuss this at some other time.'

'Of course.'

Megan got to her feet at once, hoping that Ryan would have forgotten this conversation the next time she came. Anita had told her that he was inclined to be forgetful, the drugs he was being given for the cancer acting as a sedative as well.

It was good to be outside again, but for once she didn't hurry back to the hotel. Her mind was buzzing with thoughts of what he might have been trying to tell her, and she wondered why he thought Remy's parentage would mean anything to her.

It wasn't as if she had any lasting role to play in his life. Despite what had almost happened that afternoon, their relationship to one another was unlikely to change. And she didn't want it to, she told herself, even if she was attracted to him.

Reaching the foyer, she crossed to the lifts and, finding one vacant, stepped inside and pressed the button for the penthouse floor. Leaning against the fabric-covered wall, she felt an overwhelming sense of relief that she hadn't done something foolish when she was with Remy. If she'd submitted to her baser instincts, how could she have faced Anita again?

Once inside her room, she shed her hat and shoes and padded wearily into the bathroom. Turning on the shower, she stripped off the rest of her clothes and then stepped under the cooling spray. Tilting back her head, she let the fall of water revive her for a few moments, before reaching for her favourite brand of soap.

However, although the shower was supposed to rid her mind of thoughts of Remy, and the sinful pleasures thinking of him evoked, she found the simple task of cleansing herself inspired images she couldn't ignore. As she soaped her breasts, she couldn't help but remember the way Remy had held her, how his hands had slid up beneath her shirt and found the taut nipples that had surged against his palms…

She took a deep breath, trying not to recall the hungry passion of his kiss. But once the idea was seeded it couldn't help but take root, and she sank against the tiled wall of the cubicle, shaking uncontrollably.

It shouldn't have happened, she told herself. She shouldn't have gone to Remy's office, and she most definitely shouldn't have gone to his apartment. It was all very well telling herself that she had had no hidden motives for accepting his invitation, but if she was brutally honest she'd admit that she hadn't been entirely impartial either.

So what had she expected? she asked herself. It was too easy to excuse her behaviour on the grounds that she hadn't had a lot of choice in the matter. In actual fact, as soon as she'd felt unwell, she should have headed straight back to the hotel.

Whether Remy would have allowed her to do that was another matter, of course, and the fact that she hadn't felt ill until she'd reached his office would have complicated the situation, she supposed. But she was pretty sure he wouldn't have propositioned her if she'd kept him at a distance. It had been stupid to ask him all those personal questions. He must have thought she was checking out the competition.

A shudder of revulsion swept over her, and, pushing herself away from the wall, she started to soap her legs. It wasn't the first time she'd felt the need to get things into perspective, but she hadn't realised she was quite so transparent before.

His accusation had caught her completely unawares. She wasn't used to men—or women, for that matter—who voiced their feelings so openly. It wasn't just that he was good-looking; she'd known good-looking men before. It was something about him personally that had such a devastating effect on her hormones.

Yet there'd been something vaguely scornful about the way he'd challenged her. Almost as if he'd despised her for the very feelings he'd attempted to expose. Perhaps he thought she'd come on to him to liven up her holiday, and whatever she might regret about that afternoon he had certainly done that.

Her breathing quickened. Soaping her legs had reminded her of how reckless she had been. When he'd pushed his thigh between her thighs and chafed that most sensitive part of her anatomy, she'd almost lost control. It would have been so easy to give in to him, so easy to ignore the outcome at that moment. For the first time in her life, she'd discovered what it was like to actually want a man. And she'd wanted him so badly, she'd been dizzy at the thought.

But somehow she hadn't given in. Despite the fact that the sensual heat of his mouth had burned her senses, she'd clung onto her sanity. Perhaps her swimming head had been her saviour; perhaps the groan she'd uttered had pierced his

sensual haze. Whatever, he'd let her escape from him, and
she hadn't waited to find out what he really thought.

She remembered that walk back to where she'd left the
buggy only vaguely, but she did remember how relieved
she'd been to find it was still there. Even the scorching
leather of the seats had been preferable to the anguish she
was feeling, and she'd driven away from Port Serrat with
no intention of ever going back.

She was half afraid Remy might appear at dinner. She
wasn't at all sure what she'd do if she found him waiting
for her in his mother's sitting room, but to her relief she
didn't have to find out. Only Anita was there, scanning a
sheaf of bills the office manager had given her, but she
thrust the papers aside when Megan came into the room.

'How are you feeling now?' Anita asked, ever the courteous hostess, and Megan knew a moment's irritation at the
enquiry.

'Much better,' she answered, remembering Anita hadn't
shown such concern for her earlier. 'Thank you.'

'Good.' Anita paused, and then, as if her thoughts had
moved onto the same wavelength, she asked, 'Did you
spend long with my father?'

'Not long.' Megan was noncommittal, accepting the
other woman's mimed offer of a mineral water with a nod.
'He seemed pleased that I'd been to the cemetery.'

'I'm sure he would be.' Anita handed her a glass. 'It's
good you could share that with him.'

'Yes.' Megan took a tentative sip of her drink. 'Mmm,
this is lovely.'

'Did he talk about your mother at all?'

Clearly Anita wanted to know everything, and it was true
that Megan had suffered several of these debriefings after
spending time with Ryan. 'He wanted me to forgive him,'
she said quietly. 'I think it's been preying on his mind. I
think we've made our peace with one another at last.'

'I'm glad.' Anita resumed her seat. 'I suppose you realise
that's why he wanted to see you.'

Megan hesitated. 'Remy hinted as much,' she said at last, taking the bull by the horns, and Anita frowned.

'He did?' she asked tersely. 'I don't think it was his place to tell you anything. I must have a word with him the next time I see him.'

'Oh, no—' Megan broke off, wishing she hadn't been so indiscreet. 'That is, he thought I knew,' she offered lamely. 'And of course you didn't know he knew how ill his grandfather is.'

Anita frowned again. 'You didn't tell Pops that Remy had said—'

'No. Oh, no.' Megan was adamant. 'We hardly mentioned Remy at all.'

Anita's eyes narrowed. 'But you did speak of him?'

'A little.' Megan felt as if she was getting into deeper and deeper water.

'In what connection?' Clearly, Anita saw nothing wrong in being so inquisitive. 'I suppose he complained about the hotel.'

'About the hotel?' Megan shook her head in confusion. 'I don't think he complained about the hotel.'

'But I assume he told you he expects Remy to take over when—when it's necessary.' Anita nodded. 'That is one of his hang-ups, I'm afraid.'

Megan said nothing, afraid to voice an opinion in case she was wrong. 'I wonder what we're having for dinner?' she ventured instead, hoping to change the subject, but Anita fixed her with a calculating gaze.

'You didn't suggest that Remy should be allowed to lead his own life, did you?' she persisted. 'When I saw Pops earlier this evening, he seemed a bit restless to me. I thought at first it was because he'd had a bad day, but it wasn't so. According to his nurse, he was all right before your visit.'

Megan's jaw sagged. 'Do you think that I—'

'I don't think anything,' said Anita hurriedly. 'But as you'd been discussing Remy...'

'We hadn't been discussing Remy.' Megan was indignant.

'So what were you talking about?'

'This and that.'

'So what did he say?'

'Who?' Megan was confused. 'Remy?' Which she realised said more about her train of thought than Anita's.

'No, not Remy,' said her stepsister shortly. 'You haven't been talking to Remy, have you? I meant what did my father say about my son?'

Megan was glad of the shadows in the room which hid her expression. She'd already regretted not being honest with Anita—about meeting Remy, at least—and now she felt as if she'd been snagged on the horns of her own dilemma. It suddenly occurred to her that Anita might mention Megan's outing to her son, and he might admit quite openly that he'd seen her.

Oh, God!

It seemed the lesser evil to be frank about this situation anyway and, after taking a drink, she viewed her stepsister warily over the glass. 'Your father asked if Remy had told me about—about his father,' she said, somewhat defiantly. 'I don't know why. It's nothing to do with me.'

'No, it's not.'

Clearly, Anita was irritated now, and Megan guessed she didn't like the idea of her father discussing family business with a virtual stranger.

'Well, he hasn't,' Megan offered, hoping to placate her. 'Remy hasn't spoken about his father at all.' She bit her lip. 'It's not something we'd talk about.' She hesitated. 'I imagine it's as painful to him as it obviously is to you.'

'Why should you assume that talking about Remy's father would be painful to me?' Anita countered. She sucked in a breath. 'What else has my father said?'

'Nothing.' Megan gave an inward groan. 'Honestly, nothing. I wish I'd never mentioned it.'

Anita regarded her narrowly. 'Did your own father talk to you about me?' she asked suddenly.

'No.' Megan was defensive. 'We never talked about you or Remy after—after the divorce.'

'You're sure about that?'

'Of course I'm sure.' Megan was feeling indignant again now. 'If you're ashamed of how it happened, as I said before, it's nothing to do with me.'

'Ashamed!' Anita looked horrified, and despite her own resentment Megan wanted to curl up and die at the look on Anita's face. It wasn't her nature to upset anyone, and particularly not someone who had been kind to her.

'You really don't understand, do you?' Anita exclaimed wonderingly. 'For all you said your father hadn't said anything, I couldn't believe you didn't know the truth.' She waved a dismissive hand at the waiter who had appeared in the doorway. 'Later,' she said firmly, leaving him in no doubt as to who was in charge here. And then, to Megan, she said, 'Obviously he never discussed my mother with you either.'

'Your mother?' Megan shook her head. 'No. Why would he?'

'Because she was the reason Daddy moved to San Felipe in the first place.' Anita paused. 'My mother was black, Megan. And people weren't as—enlightened in the fifties as they are today.'

CHAPTER NINE

MEGAN was stunned. Of all the things she might have expected Anita to say, she had never thought of anything like this. And yet, when she thought of it, it made a cruel kind of sense. But it was her first brush, however distant, with racism, and she didn't like the ugly images it had inspired.

'I've shocked you, haven't I?' Anita's tone was flat, and Megan realised how her silence must seem to her stepsister. 'But perhaps now you can appreciate why your father was so antagonistic towards me and towards Remy.'

'No!' Megan was appalled, but not because she sympathised with her father's prejudiced views. And then, because even now her tongue was inclined to act independently of her brain, she said, 'But you look—you look so—'

'White?' Anita got up from her chair and moved towards the open windows, tilting her head to gaze up at the arc of black velvet above. 'Or sufficiently so to pass as white on an island like San Felipe?' she queried. She turned towards Megan again. 'I don't know whether that's a compliment or not.'

'It wasn't meant to be a compliment!' Megan exclaimed forcefully. 'But, Lord, Anita, you can't drop something like that into the conversation and not expect me to react.' She shook her head. 'I'm sorry if I'm being clumsy. What I meant was, I never would have guessed.'

'No.' Anita's smile was sardonic. 'You and Remy's father both.' She took a deep breath. 'When he found out what I was, he couldn't wait to get out of here. He hightailed it back to New York on the next flight.'

Megan came to her feet. 'You mean—he abandoned you and Remy?'

108

'No.' Anita was honest. 'To give him his due, he didn't know I was pregnant when he left. But until then he'd been planning to take me back to meet his parents. He was a student, you see. He'd been working at one of the bars in Port Serrat during his summer break.'

'Oh, Anita!' Megan crossed the room and captured the other woman's hands and held them tightly. 'I'm so sorry. I know I keep saying that, but I don't know what else to say.' She bit her lip. 'Did you love him? Were you terribly distressed when he walked out?'

'I survived.' Anita grimaced. 'Pops was a great support, and when Remy was born I thought I was the luckiest girl in the world.' Her eyes glistened suddenly. 'I love that boy, Megan. I love him so much. I don't want anything like that to ever happen to him.'

Megan swallowed. 'Of course not.'

'Which is why I was so glad when he decided to come back to San Felipe when he'd finished college,' Anita continued. 'And now he has Rachel, and I don't have to worry any more. Her family—like most of the families on the island—has a mixed heritage. There's no danger of her accusing him of trying to ruin her life.'

Megan nodded, but she had the feeling there was a hidden message there for her, too. Anita might not know what had happened, but she had perhaps sensed a certain affinity between her son and her stepsister. Had Ryan sensed the same? Was that why he had wanted her to know the truth?

After a little while, Anita released herself, and, moving back to her chair, she extracted a tissue from her purse. 'So now you know all our little secrets,' she said, blowing her nose briskly. 'I hope it won't make any difference to the way you feel about us.'

'As if it could.' Megan was vehement. 'Anita, I'm ashamed of the way my father behaved. How could he, when he had spent so much time in Africa?'

'It's not important now.'

'It is to me.'

'Well…' Anita lifted her shoulders. 'I suppose he knew

there was no danger of becoming intimately involved with his congregation,' she declared drily. 'It may even be one of the reasons why he never took you with him. I imagine it was something he fought against admitting, but when your mother became involved with my father he couldn't avoid it any more.'

'Yet he never said anything to me.'

'No.' Anita shrugged. 'Well, that's some consolation, I suppose. Forget it, Megan. It's all in the past and we can't do anything to change it.' She smiled. 'At least we're friends, and, however your father felt, his prejudice can't affect us.'

Megan hoped she was right, but she thought they were both relieved when the waiter reappeared. 'Yes, Jules, you can serve the meal now,' Anita told him. 'And then perhaps you'd ask Michael to let me know when Dr O'Brien arrives.'

'It's a bit late for the doctor to be making house calls, isn't it?' Megan queried, after they were seated at the table on the terrace, and Anita nodded.

'It's not exactly a house call,' she explained. 'Pops and Doc O'Brien are old friends. Pops asked me to call him earlier this evening. Like I said before, he was a little feverish when I looked in on him, and O'Brien's visit will calm him down.'

'I see.'

Megan accepted her explanation, but she couldn't help worrying about the part she might have played in the old man's possible relapse. He had shown some agitation when he'd spoken of Remy, and she intended to reassure him about that the next time they met.

In the event, the meal was over before Anita was called away. Coffee had just been served, and Megan was wondering how soon she could make her excuses, when Jules came back to say that Dr O'Brien had just arrived.

Anita departed at once, offering her apologies, and assuring Megan she'd see her again in the morning. 'Don't worry about my father,' she added, as if sensing Megan's ambivalence. 'Believe me, he's tougher than he looks.'

Megan doubted that, but she bid her stepsister farewell, glad that she didn't have to manufacture an excuse for going up to her room. In the present circumstances, it would be so easy to give Anita the wrong impression, whereas her feelings for Remy were still the most troublesome thoughts she had.

Finishing her coffee, she left Anita's private apartments, and then trailed absently down the marble staircase to the ground floor. It was just a week since she'd arrived here, yet it seemed so much longer. So much had happened over which she'd had no control.

Not least, the development of her relationship with Remy, she acknowledged tensely, suddenly aware of his sensitivities as well as her own. Dear God, she thought in horror, did he think she'd known about his grandmother? Was he, even at this moment, labouring under the illusion that that was why she'd charged out of his apartment that afternoon?

She had to tell him, she thought frantically. She had to speak to him, and explain that until his mother had spoken to her she'd known nothing. She didn't know why it was so important that he should understand that she was innocent of any bias, but she was sure she'd never get to sleep until she'd done so.

There were several phones in the foyer, for the use of guests, and Megan stepped inside one of the plastic domes and picked up the receiver. She had no doubt she could have got Remy's number from one of the hotel receptionists, but she had no wish to alert Anita to what she was doing.

Which way why she was using one of the lobby phones instead of dialling from her own room, she admitted honestly, then the operator came on and she asked if she could give her the number of Mr Jeremy Robards' apartment in Moonraker's Yard. Despite the urgency that was driving her, she was not totally convinced that what she was doing

was entirely sensible, and the fewer people who were involved in her madness the better.

San Felipe wasn't a large island, and the four figure number was easily remembered. Finding a coin in her purse,
she dropped it into the slot and dialled the number she had
been given.

It seemed to ring for ages before it was answered and
she was just about to put down the receiver when the call
was connected. 'Yes?' said an impatient female voice that
she instantly recognised was Rachel's. And then, when
Megan didn't respond, she said, 'Remy, there's no one on
the line.'

Whether Remy himself would have taken charge of the
receiver at that point, Megan didn't wait to find out. Hurriedly replacing the hand-set, she stepped back from the
booth. She should have known Rachel would be there, she
chided herself bitterly. Her only consolation was that Remy
hadn't answered the phone himself and allowed her to make
a complete fool of herself.

Remy shifted restlessly between the sheets. It was after two
o'clock already, and he hadn't been to sleep yet. For the
past week, ever since he'd brought Megan to his apartment,
in fact, he'd had trouble sleeping, and he knew he was a
fool for not allowing Rachel to stay over.

But it would have been pointless inviting her to stay
feeling as he did. He could hardly tell her he didn't want
to sleep with her, and although he could make the excuse
that his restlessness would keep her awake that was only
part of the story.

However unlikely it seemed, the truth was that he no
longer wanted to make love with her. Although he'd known
her since before he'd gone away to college, and they'd been
dating constantly since he got back, the attraction was gone.
He'd tried to tell himself it was only a fleeting thing, that
as soon as Megan returned to England he'd get his life back
into perspective, but so far it wasn't working. On the con-

trary, Rachel had begun to irritate him, and he was having the devil's own job hiding his feelings.

Shifting onto his back, he gave up the unequal struggle and allowed the thoughts that were keeping him awake free rein. He was going to El Serrat tomorrow; his grandfather had requested to see him. And that was another source of frustration to him. The old man had never had to ask to see him before.

But what the hell was he supposed to do? If he went to the hotel, there was always the chance that he'd see Megan, and he'd made the decision to stay out of her way. In consequence, it was almost a week since he'd seen his grandfather, and his mother was constantly on his back, wanting to know what was going on.

He sighed and, pushing back the covers, he got out of bed. Perhaps if he made himself a drink it would help to cool his blood. Padding barefoot across the hall, he entered the kitchen via the living room, swinging open the fridge door and pulling out a carton of milk.

He drank deeply, wiping his mouth on the back of his hand when he was finished. Yeah, he thought, that was good. But it hadn't stopped him thinking about Megan, or the possibility of meeting her the following day.

He had to get some sleep. He'd promised to go and see the old man in the afternoon, but he had to work in the morning. The owners of an island cooperative wanted to sue their mainland distributor for undervaluing the weight of the sugar cane they had exported, and Remy was going to court to try and get an injunction to stop the man from moving the goods.

But, back in bed, his mind was as active as ever, and it was getting light before he fell into a fitful slumber. Even so, he was awake again before his alarm went off, and, pushing himself out of bed again, he went to take a shower.

The morning dragged. His client's case was at the end of the judge's list, and it was after two o'clock before he got back to his office. The fact that he'd pleaded his client's

case successfully was some consolation, he supposed, and
the men had been effusive with their thanks.

'You've got a pile of messages,' Sylvie advised him as
he passed her desk on his way into his office. 'And your
mother's called several times since twelve o'clock. Apparently, she was expecting you for lunch; is that right?'

'I said I'd try and make it,' Remy responded wearily,
flicking through the pink slips she'd left on his desk. 'Most
of these can wait, but you might ring a couple of the more
urgent ones and explain the situation. Tell them I'll get
back to them tomorrow.'

'Okay.' Sylvie had left her desk, and now stood with her
shoulder against the door jamb. 'You look tired,' she commented drily. 'You should try an early night. At this rate,
you'll be an old man before you're thirty.'

Remy regarded her sardonically. 'All I have are early
nights,' he told her, dropping the pink slips back onto his
desk.

'Then Miss De Vries must be stronger than she looks,'
declared Sylvie irrepressibly, and, raising both hands, palms
outwards, to ward off his retaliation, she shrugged her
shoulders and went back to her desk.

If only it was that simple, thought Remy ruefully later
that afternoon as he drove the few miles to El Serrat. He'd
never had any real problem dealing with Rachel. They argued from time to time, but that was as far as it usually
went. She'd certainly never disturbed his sleep, he reflected
wryly as he swung round a bend in the road and the whole
sweep of the bay lay ahead of him. Perhaps he took her for
granted, he admitted honestly. Perhaps he always had, and
that was why their relationship seemed so fragile now.

The russet-tiled roof of the hotel appeared below him,
the road curving down in a delicate arc to the open gateway
of Robards Reach. Avoiding meandering guests, he drove
smoothly to the car park at the back of the building. Then,
tossing his keys in one hand, he strode through the rear
door into the foyer, acknowledging the porter's greeting
before mounting the stairs to the first floor.

His mother was behind the reception desk, handling one of the guest's complaints personally. One of the reasons for the hotel's success was its boast that it gave a personal service, and there was no doubt that his mother was skilled in political diplomacy after all these years.

She registered his arrival with a faintly approving nod, but continued speaking to the man who had brought the complaint. She could have passed him over to one of the two female receptionists who were also present, but she didn't. In true Robards style, she herself made sure he was satisfied before he departed.

'Problems?' queried Remy as they passed through the door marked 'Private' and started down the hall towards his mother's sitting room.

'Just a misunderstanding,' she replied shortly. 'Room Service failed to deliver the exact meal he'd ordered last evening, and when he complained he felt the response was offhand. I'll have to speak to Lovelace. He'll know who was responsible. We can't have waiters who act as if they're doing the guests a favour by serving them.'

'Ah.'

Remy nodded, and, as if remembering why he was here, his mother gave him a disapproving look. 'You're late,' she commented as they entered the sitting room. 'You know lunch was at one. If you're hungry now, you'll have to make do with a sandwich, or have you already eaten?'

Remy went to help himself to a cool beer, twisting off the cap and taking a thirsty drink before replying. 'I haven't eaten,' he said at last, feeling grateful for having missed a possible family gathering. 'But don't worry. I'm not hungry. I just got out of court.'

'But it's almost three o'clock,' she protested, pausing in the doorway to the terrace. 'You must be hungry, Remy. You know it isn't wise to neglect these things. I hope Rachel will take more care of you when she moves in.'

Remy was glad she'd moved out onto the terrace as she was speaking and he wasn't obliged to make any reply. He dreaded to think what she'd say when he told her Rachel wasn't moving in with him. He knew she had her heart set on him settling down.

He followed her to the door, and found her hovering beside a pair of rattan chairs. 'Shall we sit out here?' she suggested. 'Your grandfather's asleep at the moment, and I haven't had a chance to talk to you for ages.'

'Okay.'

Remy took another swallow of his beer, and then sauntered across to join her in the shade of a striped canopy. From here it was possible to watch the activities on the beach, and admire the sails of the yachts that plied across the bay.

'So,' she said, when he'd stretched his length beside her, 'what have you been doing with yourself all week? I can't believe you've been so busy that you couldn't find time to visit your grandfather. He's a dying man, Remy, or have you forgotten?'

Her words stung. 'Of course I haven't forgotten,' he retorted. 'Dammit, Mom, I do have a job to do, you know.'

'And you've got a duty to your grandfather,' she countered. 'Without his help, you wouldn't be a lawyer. Don't you think you owe him a few minutes of your time?'

'But it's not just a few minutes of my time, is it?' Remy answered. 'It takes me a half hour to get out here to begin with, not to mention the time it takes to go back.' He sighed, because he knew he was only looking for excuses. 'I'm sorry, right? I'll do better from now on.'

'I'm pleased to hear it.' His mother looked a little less tight-lipped now, viewing his long, dark-suited legs with some sympathy. 'You came straight from the office,' she said, as if that had just occurred to her. 'I'm sorry, son. I don't mean to be so grumpy, but Pops has been driving me wild.'

'To see me?'

Remy was surprised, and his mother gave an impatient shake of her head. 'No, not that,' she said. 'That's a more recent demand. But he's had Doc O'Brien coming and going all week.'

'Why?' Remy was anxious. 'Has his condition deterio-
rated?'

'No, that's the annoying thing. Well, not annoying.' His
mother was embarrassed. 'I just mean he's seemed brighter
in recent days.'

'Well, that's good, isn't it?'

'Of course.' She gave him a chiding look. 'I suppose
I've gotten used to letting Michael bear the burden. I suppose if it wasn't for Megan I'd have gotten no work done
at all.'

Remy took another swig of his beer. 'Megan?' he said,
when he was sure he had himself under control. 'Where
does Megan come into it?'

'Oh, she's been helping me. It was your grandfather's
idea to let her give me a hand in the office.'

'In the office?'

'Yes.' His mother looked rueful. 'I told him she's supposed to be relaxing, but there has been a lot to do. And
what with Phoebe being sick and Tina leaving to get married—'

'I see.' Remy arched a dark eyebrow. It seemed as if his
staying away hadn't meant a thing to Megan. Had she even
noticed his absence? Or had she been far too busy playing
the angel of mercy to give a thought to him?

'Anyway, I've no doubt she's been wondering why you
haven't been around,' his mother continued, and he wondered somewhat guiltily if she'd read his thoughts. 'I told
her that your evenings are usually tied up with Rachel, so
I don't suppose she's been too concerned. And, of course,
that young man of hers rings every other day.'

Remy's stomach muscles tightened. 'Simon?'

'Yes, that's his name.' His mother pulled a wry face.
'She insists he's just ringing about business matters, but I
don't believe that.'

'Why not?'

'Why not?' She looked at him a little impatiently now.
'Remy, it's obvious the man's in love with her. Why else
would he worry so much about how she is?'

'But is she in love with him?' murmured Remy thought-fully, and then adopted an innocent expression when his mother gave him a troubled look. 'Well,' he said defen-sively, 'she might have agreed to come out here to get away from him. Have you thought about that?'

'What disturbs me more is that you obviously have,' she retorted sharply. 'It's nothing to do with us, Remy. She'll be gone in a couple of weeks and I doubt if we'll see her again.'

'Why?'

'Why what?'

'Why do you doubt that we'll see her again?' He paused. 'I thought your inviting her here was to create a family reunion. Now you're talking as if you'll be glad when she leaves.'

'Well, perhaps I will.' His mother looked a little uncom-fortable now. 'I know I was eager to see her again, but it hasn't worked out exactly as I'd planned. Your grand-father's getting far too attached to her, for one thing, and for another I don't think she's happy here.'

'Why not?'

She frowned. 'Oh, I don't know.' She lifted her shoul-ders. 'She spends a lot of her time on her own. She went into Port Serrat last week and she wouldn't let me go with her. I was half afraid she'd gone there looking for you.'

Remy controlled his features with an effort. 'For me?' he echoed, managing to sound suitably surprised. 'Why should you think that?'

His mother sighed. 'Well—you must have noticed that she treats you more like her contemporary than me. That evening Rachel was here, I was quite embarrassed. Megan didn't say a lot, but she was watching you all the way through the meal.'

Remy's palms felt damp. 'You're imagining things,' he said, even as he acknowledged the fact that Megan had apparently kept their meeting to herself.

'I don't think so.' His mother was unconvinced. 'I think if you gave her the slightest encouragement she'd be happy to have an affair with you. But that's all it would be, believe me. She's her father's daughter as well. We mustn't forget that.'

Remy stared at her. 'What are you talking about?'

'I told her,' said his mother stiffly. And as Remy continued to hold her gaze she added, 'About your father; about your grandmother. Your grandfather wanted her to ask you about your father, but I thought it would be easier if I told her everything.'

Remy's throat felt dry. 'I see.' He stood his empty beer bottle on the ground beside him with exaggerated calmness. 'And what did she say?' he asked, with forced politeness, wondering if that was why she'd come looking for him in Port Serrat.

His mother shrugged. 'She was—surprised, I think. Shocked, even, though she didn't show it. But, as I said before, she is her father's daughter. Who knows what she's really thinking beneath that cool façade?'

Remy blew out a breath. 'But you think it upset her? That maybe that's why she—wanted to go to Port Serrat?'

'Oh, no.' His mother shook her head then, confounding him. 'She went to visit the cemetery, or so she said.'

Remy shifted forward in his seat, drawing up his knees and splaying his legs. 'So, when did she ask you about my father?' he enquired levelly. 'Was that before or after she made the trip?'

'Does it matter?' His mother looked at him strangely, and then, as if sensing his impatience, said, 'It was that evening, actually. The evening after she'd been to town. Your grandfather had been asking to see her all afternoon, and, as I say, it was he who told her to speak to you.'

Remy breathed deeply. 'She told you that, did she?'

'More or less.'

'What's that supposed to mean?'

'It means I asked her what your grandfather had said to her, if you must know. Pops was in quite a state when I went to see him. I was afraid she'd said something to upset him.'

Remy heaved a sigh. 'I see.'

'Anyway, it's as well to have these things out in the open,' declared his mother firmly. 'And I mean, I wasn't to know her father had never told her the truth. So far as she was concerned, she thought he'd taken exception to the fact that I was a young, unmarried mother. She had no idea there might be more to it than that.'

'And she was shocked,' said Remy flatly, watching her.

'Well, it was quite a surprise, I suppose.' She bit her lip. 'She was very sympathetic—about your father. But she couldn't really be anything else, could she?'

Couldn't she? Remy pressed his hands down on the sides of the chair, and got heavily to his feet. It wasn't unexpected, he supposed. He'd been anticipating her mentioning his background ever since she'd returned to the island. But, like his mother, he'd thought her father would have told her about his grandmother. He wondered how she'd react towards him now.

'How's Rachel?'

His mother's words forced him to answer her, though he doubted she'd like what he had to say. 'She's okay, I guess,' he replied. 'I haven't seen her for a few days.'

'Why not?'

'Because I haven't,' he said briefly, trying not to let his feelings show. He squared his shoulders. 'I guess it's time I went and saw the old man.'

CHAPTER TEN

MEGAN almost walked into Remy.

She'd been for a walk and her eyes were still dazzled from the glare of the sun on the water as she followed the shady path that led back to the hotel. It was quite late in the afternoon, but since she'd been giving Anita a hand with the bookkeeping it was often after four o'clock before she set out.

She hadn't known he was coming this afternoon, or she wouldn't have been out there. Anita hadn't told her he was expected, and he was the last person she'd anticipated meeting in the grounds of the hotel. This time she'd had no warning of the encounter, and it was an effort to meet his gaze with a neutral face.

'Hi,' he said softly, but there was something in his eyes that made her think he had been as reluctant to acknowledge her as she was him. There was constraint in his voice and a certain amount of resignation, as if he expected her to be nervous, and he wasn't disappointed.

'Hello,' she responded, her hand going automatically to her throat. Not that the scoop-necked vest was particularly revealing, apart from exposing a three-inch-wide band of flesh between its hem and her shorts. 'Are you here to see your grandfather?'

'Who else?' He was sardonic, and she wondered what he was thinking. Was he remembering what had happened at his apartment? Or had Rachel put such thoughts out of his head? 'It looks pretty hot out there.'

'It is.' Megan caught her lower lip between her teeth. 'I've been for a walk.'

'No sweat.' He acknowledged her admission without enthusiasm. 'Well, you be careful, Megan. We both know how debilitating the heat can be on pale skins.'

'Yes.' Megan felt her pulse quicken. 'I suppose you've been talking to your mother.'

'Right.' His eyes narrowed. 'But don't worry. I didn't tell her about your visit. As soon as I realised you hadn't mentioned it, I kept my big mouth shut.'

'Well, thanks. But that wasn't what I meant,' said Megan uncomfortably, aware that she shouldn't have said anything. 'Um—but it's probably just as well. In the circumstances.'

'Oh, yeah, the circumstances.' Remy's lips twisted. 'We mustn't forget them. D'you want to remind me which circumstances we're talking about? Just so I don't make a mistake.'

He was making fun of her. She knew it. And not gentle fun either. His was of a much more serious kind. She suspected he hadn't forgiven her for walking out of his apartment, but what else could she have done without losing her self-respect?

'Your mother wouldn't understand,' she declared now, aware that they were attracting unwelcome attention. 'You know how she feels about Rachel. I don't want to lose her friendship again. I don't want her to think I went to Port Serrat to—to see you.'

'You didn't?'

His brows arched, and Megan didn't know how to deal with him in this mood. 'No,' she insisted firmly. And then, she said, 'I never should have gone to your apartment.'

'Why not?' Remy regarded her enquiringly. 'We had lunch. What could she possibly object to about that?'

Megan's lips drew in. 'You're being deliberately obtuse.'

'Am I?'

'Yes.' She tilted her head defensively. 'You know your mother would never have approved of—of us being alone there.'

'Why not?'

'Because—because she wouldn't.' Megan lifted her

shoulders. 'I don't think she trusts me, if you want to know.'

A strange expression crossed Remy's face, and then he slumped back against the broad bole of the palm tree behind him. 'Perhaps it's you who doesn't trust me,' he suggested flatly, crossing his arms over the impressive width of his chest. His skin was dark against the white fabric, reminding her of what else his mother had said. Had Anita really told her because Ryan Robards had advised her to talk to Remy? Or was it just another attempt to drive them apart? 'That's why you don't want to talk about it.'

'There's nothing to talk about,' she said now, and would have moved past him if his hand hadn't closed about her arm.

'Perhaps you're ashamed of letting me touch you,' he commented harshly. 'Admit it, Megan, you're Giles Cross's daughter and we all know how he felt about my mother and me.'

Megan didn't even stop to consider her words then. Dragging her arm away from him, she faced him with contempt. 'That's a rotten thing to suggest!' she exclaimed, not even tempted to pretend she didn't understand. 'And it's not true.' She rubbed the red marks on her arm with trembling fingers. 'You're the one who should be ashamed. I hope Rachel realises what a faithless—oaf you are!'

It was hot in the sickroom; or perhaps it was only him, thought Remy disgustedly. He deserved to suffer the fires of hell—and probably would, he admitted—for behaving in the way he had. Dammit, he'd sworn to keep away from her, to avoid the kind of confrontation they'd just had. But seeing her again had seemed to addle his brain, and he hadn't been able to prevent himself from trying to make her squirm.

Only it hadn't worked that way. Instead of getting some satisfaction out of baiting her, all he'd done was frustrate himself. And destroy whatever communication there had been between them, he conceded bitterly.

Which didn't stop him wanting her at all...

His grandfather was awake and restless, his bony hands clenching and unclenching against the sheet. When he saw Remy, his eyes glittered with impatience, and he patted the bed beside him with obvious intent.

'Where've you been, boy?' he grunted, his breath whistling hoarsely in the still air. 'Don't tell me you haven't had time to come and see your old grandpa, 'cos I won't believe it.'

Remy perched on the side of the bed, loosening another button at his collar and pulling his tie partway down his chest. 'I have been working,' he said mildly, noting that the old man did seem more animated than usual. 'But I guess I've been neglecting you, too.'

'You better believe it.' Ryan Robards spoke with a surprisingly sharp edge to his voice. 'And you've been neglecting Laura—I mean Meggie,' he corrected himself hurriedly. 'I thought you liked the girl. Or is that useless hussy keeping you to herself?'

Remy doubted Rachel would appreciate being deemed a 'useless hussy', but his grandfather had always deplored the fact that she didn't have a job. He had worked all his life, and so had Remy's mother, and in Ryan's eyes a woman should want to help her man.

But it was the revealing use of Megan's mother's name that gave Remy most pause. His mother was right; his grandfather was becoming dangerously attached to Megan. So much so that he was beginning to confuse their names, and Remy was apprehensive of what would happen when she went back to England.

'I haven't seen much of Rachel, as it happens,' he remarked now, reminding himself that there had been nothing any of them could do for him before Megan arrived. 'Mom said you'd been asking to see me,' he added, avoiding her name. 'Was it just my pretty face you've been missing or have you got a problem?'

Ryan sighed. 'Did she tell you? Meggie, I mean. She comes and visits me every day.'

'That's good.' Remy endeavoured to sound enthusiastic. He forced a smile. 'I'm glad you get on so well.'

'Mmm.' His grandfather sought the relief of the oxygen mask, and breathed shallowly for several seconds before going on. 'I like her, Remy,' he wheezed at last. 'I like her a lot. She's exactly what this place needs: new life, new blood, new ideas—'

'Hold on—' Remy's hand closed over the old man's wrist in sudden consternation. He waited until he had his grandfather's attention, and then said carefully, 'She doesn't live here, Pops. I don't know what she's told you, but she's planning on going back to London in a couple of weeks.'

'I know that. Do you think I'm stupid?' The old man shook off his grandson's hand with unexpected strength. 'But perhaps she doesn't want to; perhaps she doesn't *have* to. Why shouldn't she have a stake in the hotel? It was her mother's home after all.'

Remy's jaw dropped. 'You're not serious!'

'Why not?'

'Why not?' Remy sought desperately for an answer. 'I—Mom would never go along with it. She's worked too hard for all these years to share it now.'

His grandfather fixed him with a milky gaze. 'Must I remind you that this is still *my* hotel?' he grunted harshly. 'I'm not dead yet, boy.'

Remy suppressed a groan. 'I know that,' he muttered awkwardly. 'But, dammit, Pops, the Crosses wanted no part of us.'

'Giles didn't,' agreed the old man grimly. 'He hated me, and I guess that's what killed him in the end. He couldn't bear the thought that he never forgave his wife. When she died any hope of his own redemption died with her.'

'Even so—'

'Meggie's not like her father,' Ryan persisted hoarsely, as if his grandson hadn't spoken. 'I know that. Anita's told her about your grandmother and she understands what Anita went through with your father. When we're talking together, I can almost pretend I've got Laura back again. Oh, I know what you think—what your mother probably thinks—that I'm getting senile. But I do know who Meggie is, and I think I know what she needs.'

'What she needs?' Remy stared at him. 'Pops, Megan doesn't need anything. She's a successful businesswoman in her own right, with a partner who might—' or might not, he chided himself mockingly '—be her lover as well.'

'He's not her lover,' said Ryan weakly, and Remy despised himself for the sudden leap of his pulse.

'How do you know?' he asked, belatedly realising how revealing his question was, and his grandfather's lips parted.

'Because he's not,' he declared doggedly. 'D'you think I wouldn't know? She's like her mother. She's open. She couldn't hide something like that from me.'

Remy's blood cooled. He should have known better, he thought disparagingly. For a minute there, he'd imagined Megan must have discussed her feelings with the old man. And he'd been stupid enough to expose his interest on the strength of nothing more than a hunch.

'Yeah, right,' he said now, getting up from the bed and pacing over to the window, forcing the slats of the blind apart and peering onto the verandah outside.

'You don't believe me, do you?'

The old man's voice was definitely frailer now, and Remy swung round with a determined smile. Dammit, what did it matter what he thought? His grandfather was dying. If it pleased him to leave a small share in the hotel to Megan, then why should his mother object?

But she would…

'If you say it's so, I believe you,' he said, approaching the bed again. 'But don't get your hopes up about Megan. She doesn't know squat about running a hotel.'

'She doesn't need to.' As his grandson's brows drew together Ryan panted, 'In any case, I told your mother to let her help out in the office. Anita's had to admit she's got a good head for figures.'

Remy blinked. 'Mom knows about this?'

'About what?' The old man could hardly get the words out, and Remy knew he shouldn't persist.

'About you—leaving Megan a share in the hotel?'

'Hell, no.' Ryan tried to laugh, but it came out as a winded chuckle. 'This is just between you and me, boy. What your mother doesn't know won't hurt her.'

Remy walked back to the hotel feeling uneasy. Not just because of what Ryan had told him, but because he was now obliged to face the consequences of what had happened earlier between him and Megan. It would be too much to hope that she'd stay out of his way until he was leaving. She despised him; he knew that. But she wouldn't back down from a fight.

He wondered if she knew what the old man was planning, and then immediately dismissed the thought. Whatever else Megan was, she wasn't dishonest. If she'd suspected what his grandfather had in mind, she would have mentioned it to his mother, he was sure.

In any case, it wasn't likely to happen. If the old man had asked to see his lawyer, he'd have been told. And his mother would have known and brought the subject up with him. His grandfather was probably playing a game with them all.

All the same, Remy couldn't help wondering what Megan would do if she inherited a part of the hotel. Would she keep it as an investment, or would she be prepared to sell it back to Anita if she asked? There was no way she would want to live on the island. Apart from anything else, she had another business to run.

His mother was in the lobby when he strolled into the hotel. She wouldn't admit that she'd been waiting for him, but it was obvious from her expression that she was expecting some explanation for the old man's insistence on seeing him.

'Well?' she said, when he joined her beside the flower-rimmed fountain. 'Is—is everything all right?'

'I guess.' Remy bent to pick a velvety-skinned magnolia from the display, smoothing its soft petals between his fingers. 'What do you think?'

'What do I think?' His mother set down the watering-can she had been wielding to give him an impatient look. 'You know what I think. I think he's becoming far too maudlin about the past. Encouraged—encouraged by Megan.'

Remy's lips thinned in resignation. 'You've really got it in for her, haven't you?' he protested. 'What grounds do you have for making an accusation like that?'

His mother snapped her fingers, ostensibly to get rid of the dampness that clung to their tips, but Remy sensed her frustration. 'I don't need grounds,' she declared irritably. 'I know your grandfather. I know what he's thinking. He thinks Megan is like her mother, but she's not. I loved Laura, you know I did, but Megan's *that man's* daughter. I thought it wouldn't matter, but it does. I should never have let your grandfather persuade me to get in touch with her. She doesn't belong here.'

Remy found himself shredding the magnolia, and thrust it back amongst the greenery. 'He doesn't think so,' he said shortly, looking with some distaste at his hands. 'Do you have a tissue?'

His mother supplied one almost automatically so that he could wipe the moisture from his fingers, but her mind was fixed on the remark he had made. 'He doesn't think so?' she echoed, and Remy cursed himself for giving her the opening she needed. 'What's that supposed to mean?'

Remy sighed. 'It doesn't matter.'

'It does matter.' Her eyes narrowed. 'Has he been saying something to you?' She stared at him suspiciously. 'You might as well tell me. I'll find out sooner or later.'

'Why don't you ask him?' retorted Remy, wishing he'd done as he'd told Megan he would and kept his big mouth shut. 'What he does is nothing to do with me—or you, for that matter.'

'You are joking.' His mother was incensed, and he

wished he could just turn away and leave. 'Let me guess,' she said harshly. 'He's trying to think of some way to keep her here, isn't he?'

Remy shrugged. 'I wouldn't know,' he said flatly, but his mother wasn't listening to him.

'That's it, isn't it?' she exclaimed, her eyes boring into his. 'He's going to try and bribe her, isn't he? How? By making you the prize?'

Remy was sickened by the suggestion, but his mother was triumphant. 'He thinks if he can dangle you like a carrot in front of her she'll stay—'

'No!' Remy couldn't let her go on thinking that. It was far too tempting a prospect. 'It's nothing to do with me. All right, I admit he wants her to stay. But I'm not the prize.'

'Then what is?' She swallowed convulsively. 'Not—not the hotel?'

Remy groaned. 'I don't want to talk about this—'

'So it is the hotel!' His mother's face had grown pale. 'No.' She shook her head. 'No, he wouldn't do that to me.'

'God, Mom—'

'I've worked too hard; I've sacrificed too much—'

'Stop it!' Remy couldn't stand much more of this. 'We all know how much you've given to the hotel, not least Pops, but is it so inconceivable that he should want to give the daughter of the woman he worshipped a small piece of it?'

His mother's mouth opened and closed, like a fish that had been too long out of water, and Remy was beginning to fear that she was having some kind of seizure when he saw Megan coming down the curved staircase. She obviously didn't expect to find them in the lobby, but it was the impetus he needed to bring his mother to her senses.

'Here's Megan,' he said, taking her arm, but as if his words were the final indignity she snatched her arm out of his grasp and hurried away towards the staff quarters, leaving him to offer whatever excuse he thought fit.

Perhaps Megan wouldn't have noticed them, he speculated later, if his mother hadn't made such an obvious exit. As it was, her hurrying footsteps were a dead give-away, and Megan's eyes registered her stepsister's departure with apparent concern before switching back to him in unmistakable accusation.

She seemed to hesitate, and he held his breath for a moment, willing her not to approach him, but when she reached the bottom step and turned in his direction he expelled his breath on a heavy sigh.

'What's wrong with Anita?' she asked in a puzzled voice, and he wondered if she had forgotten their altercation earlier.

'Who knows?' he responded, looking anywhere but at her. As if he didn't have a mirror-image of her slender, chemise-clad figure imprinted on his subconscious...

'You haven't—said anything to upset her, have you?' she ventured, and although he had warned himself not to let her provoke him the injustice of her words caught him on the raw.

'Such as what?' he enquired icily. 'What could I have possibly said to upset her?' He paused, and then added, unforgivably, 'Perhaps it wasn't me she was running away from.'

Megan's face paled. 'What do you mean?'

Remy fought back the urge to reassure her, and merely shrugged his shoulders. 'You tell me.'

Megan moistened her full lower lip, and for a moment he was mesmerised by the tantalising glimpse of her tongue. 'I can't,' she said unsteadily. 'I don't know what I've done.'

'Apart from looking like your mother, you mean?' he countered mockingly, and then, realising he was being unnecessarily cruel, he shook his head. 'Forget it,' he advised carelessly. 'She'll get over it. She always does.'

'Get over what?'

Megan was staring at him imploringly, and, realising he was in danger of saying too much, he looked ostentatiously at his watch. 'I've got to be going,' he said flatly. 'I've got someone to see at six o'clock.'

He turned away, but her voice arrested him. 'Remy.'

He stiffened without looking at her. 'What?'

'We need to talk,' she said, but he couldn't take any more.

'No, we don't,' he assured her harshly, and strode away through the swinging glass door.

CHAPTER ELEVEN

MEGAN decided to talk to Anita at dinnertime.

She wasn't looking forward to it, but she had to know what she was supposed to have done wrong. She'd spent the time since Remy's departure worrying about what he'd said and wishing she knew what was going on.

But when she arrived at Anita's apartments later that evening she discovered her stepsister wouldn't be joining her for dinner, after all. 'Mrs Robards has a headache,' the waiter who usually served them told her apologetically. 'Perhaps you'd eat in the restaurant this evening, Ms Cross. Mrs Robards says she'll see you in the morning.'

Megan sighed. She had no choice but to accept this explanation, but a headache sounded mightily convenient to her. She was fairly sure Anita was avoiding her, and she was tempted to storm into her bedroom and demand to know why she was being punished.

As she went down the stairs to the patio restaurant, however, she had to admit that during the last few days her relationship with Anita had changed. The warmth and affection she'd felt when she'd first arrived had been replaced with an impersonal politeness, and whenever she said she was going to see Ryan Anita often found an excuse why she shouldn't. He was sleeping, she'd say, or he'd just taken his medication—events that previously hadn't seemed important, but which now were offered as a reason why she should stay away from the sickroom.

But—foolishly, perhaps, she acknowledged now—she hadn't thought anything of it until that afternoon. Ryan had soon kicked up a fuss if Megan hadn't been to see him, and Anita had usually had to back down. She'd even attributed Anita's coolness to the worries she had about her father, remembering how anxious she had been about her own father when her mother died. Until that incident in the foyer, she'd assumed everything was all right.

After all, she hadn't hesitated in offering her help when Ryan had mentioned how overworked Anita was, and, working together in the office, she'd felt they'd found a certain rapport. It was only now she questioned her naïveté; in fact, Anita hadn't treated her any differently from any other of her employees. And there was no doubt that without Ryan's encouragement she would never have asked Megan for help.

Megan was given a table by the low wall overlooking the beach and the ocean. It was an excellent table, indicative of her status as stepdaughter of the proprietor, but she wasn't in the mood for such obsequious attention. She ate little—just a couple of shrimps and some grilled chicken—making her escape without waiting for coffee, and retreating to a stool in the Harbour Bar.

But even there she couldn't avoid the unwelcome advances of a man in striped biker shorts and a tank top, who evidently thought she had had a row with her boyfriend and was looking for company. Picking up her glass of mineral water, she sought refuge on the terrace, breathing a sigh of relief when her companion took the hint.

If only she knew what Remy had meant when he'd made that crack about her looking like her mother, she thought unhappily, sipping almost absently from her glass. One thing was certain, however—she couldn't ask his grandfather something like that. Despite the fact that she'd become surprisingly close to Ryan in the past couple of weeks, she wasn't foolish enough to think you could wipe away the effects of more than fifteen years in a few hours.

Nevertheless, it seemed obvious now that Anita resented it. But would that explain her behaviour this afternoon? What *had* Remy said to upset her? Why had he implied that his mother was running away?

Could he have told Anita about her visit to his apartment? she wondered. Although he'd denied having done so earlier, after their contretemps, she doubted he felt he owed her any favours. And he had seemed to imply that what she'd learned about his grandmother had affected her attitude towards him. He didn't seem to realise that her concerns lay in another direction entirely.

God! She shivered. If Anita resented her friendship with Ryan, she couldn't imagine how she'd feel if she discovered Megan was having a relationship with her son. And there was Rachel to consider as well—the young woman who evidently thought they were a couple. What the hell was Remy playing at? she fretted, feeling her eyes smarting with unshed tears. And why the hell did she care?

She'd go and phone Simon, she decided, finishing her mineral water. What she needed was his common sense right now. But then she remembered it was the middle of the night in England. Much as he cared for her, she doubted he'd appreciate being woken up because she felt blue.

She turned and rested her elbows on the rail behind her. Dinner was over now, and the terrace was becoming the haunt of romance-seekers, all wanting to enjoy the view. To see, but not be seen, she reflected enviously. It would be nice to share the rest of the evening with—with a friend.

She pushed away from the rail, and, depositing her empty glass on a nearby table, she left the terrace to the lovers. It was nearly nine o'clock; she supposed she could have an early night. The trouble was, she knew she wouldn't sleep, and her suite of rooms had never seemed less attractive.

She sauntered along the path that led round to the back of the hotel. It was quieter here, the people who were enjoying an after-dinner constitutional being bent on exercise and nothing more. The car park loomed ahead of her, mostly occupied by the vehicles used by the hotel staff. Few of Anita's employees actually lived in the hotel. Most of them drove in from the surrounding villages every morning.

An area at one end of the car park was used to accommodate the buggies. The small open-topped vehicles were a popular resource of the hotel. The one Megan had hired was there along with all its fellows, and as she approached the first she saw the keys still sitting in the ignition.

Her lips parted, and she glanced about her. It was a mistake, obviously. None of the other buggies had keys, as far as she could see. One of the guests must have borrowed the buggy, and forgotten to return the keys to Reception. Would anyone know if she took the car for a ride?

She didn't stop to find out. It was too good an opportunity to miss. She felt like a prisoner who'd just discovered her cell door was open. Being able to go out without first consulting Anita was too good to be true.

It wasn't until her headlights picked up the signpost that said 'You are now entering Port Serrat. Please drive carefully' that she paused to wonder exactly what she was doing. Until then, it had been enough to drive through the soft night air, with a velvety breeze brushing her temples, and the muted roar of the ocean in her ears. But now she had to face her own intentions; to acknowledge to herself precisely why she was here.

She'd just come for the drive, she defended herself. Where else could she have driven at this hour of the evening? If she'd taken one of the mountain roads that led to the interior of the island, she would have been foolhardy. Apart from the fact that they were narrow, she had no way of knowing whether they were made up or not.

She drove down towards the harbour, passing small houses where televisions flickered behind undrawn drapes. There were plenty of people about, but she guessed they were mostly tourists. There was a cruise ship in port, and its inhabitants were taking advantage of the duty-free shops.

She saw the narrow street she and Remy had taken to reach his apartment, and before she knew what she was doing she had turned into it and accelerated towards the alleyway that led to Moonraker's Yard. There were lights glittering in the archway and lamps burning in the courtyard beyond. She wondered if Remy was home, and if he was there with Rachel.

Stopping the buggy, she got out, still not acknowledging

to herself that this was really why she'd driven to Port Serrat. For heaven's sake, she chided herself impatiently, she was just curious about the area. Of course Rachel was with him. Where else was she likely to be?

But what if she wasn't?

The thought came out of nowhere, and although she tried to put it aside it was impossible to ignore. And who else could tell her why Anita was behaving so strangely? she asked herself reasonably. Even if Rachel was there, what did she have to lose?

Her dignity?

Her integrity?

Her self-respect?

The list was endless, but she refused to listen to any doubts. If Rachel was there, then she'd ask him to tell her what was going on and leave. If she wasn't... If Rachel wasn't there... Megan wet her lips. Oh, Lord, what did she really want?

Before she could change her mind, before she could get back into the buggy again and drive away, Megan hurried through the stone passage into the courtyard beyond. The steps were there, just as she remembered them, and she gripped the hand-rail as she climbed to the upper floor.

The studded wooden door was absurdly familiar. She'd only been here once before, yet she had no hesitation in identifying Remy's apartment. There was no bell, so she knocked, not without some trepidation, squeezing the buggy's keys between her fingers because she had nowhere else to put them.

Standing there, she made a bargain with her conscience. If Remy didn't answer at the first attempt, she'd go away. But he didn't, and she knocked again, bruising her knuckles. So much for her integrity, she thought, chewing her lower lip.

She was actually considering the merits of going away and finding a phone and ringing him when Remy opened the door. And, in consequence, although she'd believed she was prepared, she found she wasn't. Just seeing him again had the most profound effect on her, and the fact that he was only wearing a silk dressing gown caused an actual ache low in her stomach.

'Hello.' She spoke first, finding some relief for her emotions in breaking into words. 'Um—is Rachel here?'

It was a stupid question; she knew that at once. Of course Rachel was here. That was why Remy was only wearing a dressing gown. She had probably interrupted them, which was why he'd taken so long to come to the door.

Remy regarded her blankly. 'You want to see Rachel?' he said at last.

'I—why—no.' Megan was horribly embarrassed. 'I just thought she might be here. She—she was the last time I—I—'

She couldn't finish the sentence. How on earth could she explain that abortive call? But Remy wasn't so scrupulous. 'The last time you what?' he enquired silkily. 'Don't tell me you've come here before.'

'No! No, of course not.' Her face was flaming. 'Oh—if you must know, I phoned you. One evening.' She shifted uncomfortably. 'When Rachel answered, I disconnected the call.'

Remy's eyes darkened. 'So it was you,' he remarked. 'I wondered.'

'Well, you don't have to wonder any more,' said Megan, stepping back towards the staircase. 'I—er—I'm sorry I bothered you. Goodnight.'

'Wait!' Remy stepped forward, and she noticed he was barefoot, too. 'Rachel's not here, as it happens. I'm alone. As you've come so far, you might as well come in.'

Megan swallowed. 'She's not here?'

There was scepticism in her tone, and Remy's mouth turned down. 'No,' he said flatly. 'Why did you think she would be?' He glanced down at his robe-clad figure and grimaced. 'Oh, I see. Well, actually, I was taking a bath.'

'Oh!'

The relief in that small exclamation was revealing, but Megan was unaware of it. She was too busy noticing the

damp patches that spotted his gown. She saw now that the
cloth was clinging to his damp skin in places, and her
nerves prickled pleasantly as she stepped past him into the
hall.

Remy closed the door behind her, and because the hall
was too confining for them to conduct any kind of conversation there Megan did as she'd done before and walked
along to the living room.

Lamps were lit about the room giving it a warm ambi-
ence that was different from the last time she'd been here.
The curtains were not drawn, and she could see the lights
from the harbour below them, but it was dark tonight, and
the intimacy of her surroundings was enhanced.

Or perhaps it was only her, she thought ruefully. Certainly, there was nothing in Remy's expression at the moment to give her any hope that he might be pleased to see
her. On the contrary, he seemed suspicious of her appearance, and she surmised he wasn't making any guesses as
to why she'd come.

There was a pregnant silence while they each summed
one another up, and then Remy said, as if the invitation
was dragged from him, 'Can I offer you a drink?'

Megan licked her dry lips. 'Um—a Coke would be nice,'
she accepted gratefully, and he went past her into the
kitchen.

While he was gone, she looked about her, wondering
again what she was really doing here. What did she want
from him? What did she want from herself? A chance to
redeem their friendship, perhaps, but was that all?

'There you go.'

Remy had popped the cap on the can and poured half its
contents into a glass. He handed them both to her, his cool
fingers brushing lightly against her hot flesh, then he gestured to one of the squashy sofas, indicating that she should
sit down.

Megan didn't sit down. She took a thirsty gulp of the
ice-cold liquid, and then set both the can and the glass on
the stone rim of the hearth. 'That's good,' she said, straight-

ening and rubbing the palms of her hands together. 'Thanks.'

Remy folded his arms, his shoulders moving in a dismissive shrug. 'My pleasure.'

It was obvious he wasn't going to make this easy for her, and she wished she'd had a clearer idea of what she was going to say before she'd got here. To give herself time to think, she waved a hand towards the harbour lights behind her, and said, 'Doesn't it look pretty at night?'

Remy's lips took on a sardonic slant. 'Is that why you came?'

'What do you mean?'

'Well, I did suggest that you should come and see the view after dark,' he reminded her cynically. 'And I can't imagine any other reason why you might come here.'

'Can't you?'

It was an inflammatory thing to say, but Remy didn't take her up on it. 'No,' he replied flatly. 'I can't.' He waited a beat, and then continued with a twist of his lips, 'Does my mother know you're here?'

'Of course not,' she replied, and he arched a sardonic brow.

'Why "of course not"?' he queried drily. 'As I recall it, it was her opinion you were most concerned about this afternoon.'

'No one knows I'm here,' declared Megan, without answering him. 'I didn't even know I was coming here myself until I reached Port Serrat.'

Remy regarded her from beneath lowered lids. 'Is that supposed to be an excuse?' he enquired sardonically, and she gazed at him in sudden frustration.

'No,' she said. 'I'm just being honest with you, that's all.'

Remy snorted. 'That'll be a first.'

'I've never lied to you,' she protested.

'Haven't you?' Remy shrugged. 'Well, not in words, perhaps.'

Megan sighed. 'I didn't come here to argue with you,

Remy. And you should know that I could hardly ask your mother's permission to do anything. She's not even talking to me.'

'That's an exaggeration.'

'No, it's not.' Megan swallowed. 'She didn't even appear at dinnertime. She told Jules to tell me that she had a headache, but I don't believe she did.'

Remy shrugged. 'She does suffer from migraines from time to time,' he murmured mildly, but Megan wasn't having that.

'And I suppose it just came on as I was coming downstairs this afternoon,' she said sceptically. 'Come on, Remy; I wasn't born yesterday. I've done something—or she thinks I've done something,' she amended, her eyes flickering with unknowing hunger over his lean frame, 'and she's avoiding me. Isn't that the truth? You know it's so, so why don't you tell me what I'm supposed to have done?'

Remy lowered his arms, pushing his hands into the pockets of his robe. 'Have you considered that she might be jealous of you?' he asked, after a moment, and Megan's lips parted in sudden disbelief.

'Jealous of me?' she echoed. 'Why?'

Remy hesitated. 'Perhaps because the old man has taken such a fancy to you?' he suggested quietly. 'He has, you know.'

'Only because I remind him of my mother,' said Megan tersely, turning away so he couldn't see the pained expression in her eyes. 'Surely she doesn't begrudge me that?'

'Perhaps that's only a part of it,' murmured Remy softly, and she wondered if it was her imagination that made her think she could feel the warmth of his breath on the back of her neck.

'Only part of what?' she asked, chancing a glance over her shoulder, only to discover he had indeed closed the gap between them. 'I don't know what you mean.'

'Maybe the old man is hoping you'll change your mind about going back to London,' Remy offered lightly, and she was ashamed of the way her spirits plunged at his explanation. She realised she had been hoping for a more personal reason, and the knowledge that despite the fact that he was standing right behind her he had no intention of touching her caused her heart to plummet alarmingly.

'You must be wrong,' she said, turning sideways to avoid the impulse to lean back against him. 'It's like you said—he wants us to be friends. And we are. End of story.'

'What if he doesn't see it that way?' persisted Remy huskily, and he did touch her now, lifting a hand to tuck the silky strand of hair that had fallen across her cheek and hidden her profile from him behind her ear.

Megan shivered; she couldn't help herself. 'Well, he knows I've got to go back to London,' she said, a little breathlessly, and Remy's hand dropped to his side again.

'Because of—Simon?' he ventured evenly, and this time she didn't hesitate before giving her answer.

'No. Well—not in a personal way, anyway. He's my business partner.'

'Hmm.' Remy absorbed this, and she was intensely conscious of his eyes watching her. Then, without warning, he asked, 'Why did you phone me?'

Megan's breathing quickened. 'I—I can't remember now...'

Remy's mouth compressed. 'And you said you didn't lie,' he mocked.

'I don't—' Megan darted a glance sideways, and then wished she hadn't when she saw the resignation in his face. 'Well—it wasn't important,' she prevaricated. 'I just wanted to talk to you, that's all.'

'What about?' He was insistent and Megan closed her eyes.

'Oh—about what your mother had told me,' she admitted at last. She sighed. 'I wanted you to know that I hadn't known about your father before I—before I—'

'Walked out on me?' he suggested, and her eyes opened again.

'I suppose so.' She bent her head then, unknowingly exposing the vulnerable curve of her nape to his gaze. 'It was a stupid thing to do.'

'Walking out?' He gave a wryly amused laugh. 'Oh, I'd agree with you there.'

'No, I—' She turned to look at him, colouring at the sensual look in his eyes. 'That's not what I meant.'

'So you don't think it was stupid to walk out?'

Megan sighed. 'I meant it was stupid to phone you.'

'Why?'

'You know why.'

'Do I?'

'Rachel was here.'

'So?' He lifted his hand again and allowed his forefinger to trace a path from just below her ear to the corner of her mouth. 'Would it make any difference if I told you she left just after your call?' His thumb invaded her lips, tugging on the sensitive flesh. 'I wish I'd answered the call myself.'

Megan quivered. 'Why didn't you?'

'Well, it wasn't because I was struggling to get my clothes back on, if that's what you're thinking,' said Remy huskily, and she wondered if he could read her thoughts. He shrugged. 'Rachel beat me to it, that's all.'

'So what was she doing here?' asked Megan, and then realised it was really nothing to do with her.

But Remy didn't seem to mind. 'We'd had supper together,' he replied, his hand moving down to her throat and encircling the nape of her neck. 'We'd been talking about you, actually.'

Megan was amazed she could still get air past the tight muscles in her throat. 'What about me?' she asked thickly, aware of how easily this situation could get out of hand. 'I'm sure Rachel's not interested in me.'

'Did I say she was?' He caressed the soft flesh that bracketed the bony ridge of her spine, before allowing his hand to curve about her shoulder and draw her against him. He bent his head and kissed the skin exposed by the narrow straps of her dress, his tongue moving sensuously against her. 'But I think she realised how I felt.'

'Remy—'

'What?' His free hand tipped her face up to his. 'You want me to stop?' His hands fell away. 'Okay.'

Megan's tongue appeared between her lips. 'This isn't why I came here.'

'Isn't it?' His eyes darkened. 'I thought it was.'

Megan stiffened. 'You're making fun of me.'

'Of myself, perhaps,' he conceded tightly, taking one of her hands and bringing it to the heavy arousal that swelled against his robe. 'See what I mean?'

'Oh, Remy…' She couldn't help herself; she turned towards him, and his hands cupping her buttocks brought her fully against him. His thin dressing gown was no adequate barrier to the raw strength of his sex, and her legs went weak when he bent his head towards her.

He kissed her gently at first, lips parted, his tongue pushing wetly into the moist hollow of her mouth. There was an aching inevitability about it, she thought, as if he, as much as she herself, had no control over what he was doing. It seemed that ever since she'd come back to San Felipe they'd been heading for this moment, and this time Megan knew there was no turning back. She was past making excuses for what she now recognised was an irresistible attraction, and the possible outcome of what she was about to do was not something she was prepared to consider right now.

The kiss deepened and lengthened, his mouth seeking a more passionate connection as he felt her instinctive response. With something suspiciously like a groan, his hands spanned her waist, and she lifted her arms to wind them about his neck.

All she could think about was that he wanted her just as much as she wanted him. The powerful heat of his body wrapped itself around her, making her quiveringly aware of his need and hers, and of how much she wanted him inside her.

A steel band was playing somewhere down at the quayside, and the wild rhythm of the drums mingled with the

erratic beat of her heart. A film of heat was making her
whole body slick and unknowingly sexy, but it was nothing
compared to the damp heat between her legs.

Remy kissed her many times, his mouth slanting across
hers with ever increasing hunger, his teeth fastening greedi-
ly on her lower lip and reducing her to a helpless suppli-
cant. Megan had never experienced such an onslaught on
her emotions before, and she realised her relationships with
other men had only been a poor imitation of the real thing.

When he drew back a little, she almost moaned in protest, but it was only to allow him to slip the straps of her
chemise dress off her shoulders. The soft cotton pooled
about her waist, exposing the lace-trimmed cups of her bra,
and she felt a moan escape her when he bent to suck one
of her nipples through the material.

Then, with a frankly sensual expression twisting his lips,
he brought her hands down to release the catch of the bra
before palming the swollen peaks. 'Does that feel good?'
he asked huskily, and she could only nod rather frantically
when he bent to suckle them again.

A feeling not unlike a shaft of pain shot from her breasts
down into the pit of her stomach. A pulsing, tingling need
spread down into her thighs, creating an actual ache between her legs, and as if sensing this Remy pushed her
dress down over her hips and put his hand there.

Megan was trembling. She knew he must be able to feel
how wet she was even through her silk panties, and she
closed her eyes so he wouldn't be able to see the blatant
hunger in them. She would never have believed she could
come so close to losing what little control she had just
because he was touching her, but she was.

His fingers were inside the leg of her panties now, inside
her, and she couldn't help herself; she put her hands down
and covered his. 'Please,' she begged, not knowing what
else to say, and as if he understood how desperate she was
he took his hand away, and swung her up into his arms.

His bedroom was across the hall, although she could not
have described how they got there. With her arms tight

around Remy's neck, and her face buried in his shoulder, she was only conscious of him and nothing else.

The quilt on his bed was cool at her back, but she hardly noticed. She felt as if her whole body was burning up, and when Remy peeled off his dressing gown and stretched his length beside her she moved convulsively into his embrace. Against her stomach, the throbbing heat of his erection was all she was aware of, and he slid her panties down her legs before raising himself to straddle her thighs.

She caught her breath then at the powerful length of him, rearing from a nest of curling dark hair, and as if sensing her sudden apprehension he paused. Keeping an admirable control on his own emotions, he smoothed the silky strands of hair back from her damp face, and brushed her lips with his thumbs.

'Are you sure about this?' he asked softly, and she marvelled at his sensitivity.

'I'm sure,' she breathed, not knowing how to tell him it was her own ability to please him that she was worried about, nothing more. 'Are you?'

'Oh, baby, I've never been so sure about anything in my life,' he assured her huskily, and, parting her legs, his fingers brought her to the brink of a climax she could only guess at.

Finally, his hands spread the blonde curls that marked the junction of her thighs, and then, with an ease of movement that was an innate part of his sexuality, he buried himself inside her. Her muscles swelled and expanded to accommodate him, but she was still half afraid she wouldn't be able to take all of him. Yet, somehow, she did, and the feeling of him filling her was like nothing she had ever felt before.

'Okay?' he asked in a hoarse voice, and she reached up to cup his face in her hands.

'Okay,' she agreed, pulling his mouth down to hers, and as he began to move she felt the ripples of her climax sweeping irrevocably over her. Her voice broke. 'I'm sorry…'

'Don't be.'

His thrusts quickened, and almost before the devastating effects of her first climax had ebbed she felt another coming right after it. This time, Remy joined her, and she was dizzily aware of his cry of release before his shuddering body collapsed in her arms...

CHAPTER TWELVE

MEGAN drove back to El Serrat in the early hours of the morning.

Remy had offered to drive her back but she'd insisted on going alone. The fewer people who knew where she'd been the better, she thought, and until she knew what they both wanted from this relationship she would rather keep it to herself.

'Besides,' she'd added huskily, when he'd protested that it was too late for her to be out alone, 'I'm already in enough trouble with your mother as it is.' She'd bestowed a soft kiss on the corner of his mouth. 'Can you imagine what her reaction would be if she discovered we'd been—together?'

'I don't particularly care,' said Remy thickly. 'She's going to find out sooner or later. But, if you insist—'

'I do.'

'Then when am I going to see you again?'

Megan caught her breath, her hands lingering on the hair-roughened skin exposed by the carelessly drawn lapels of his dressing gown. 'Soon, I hope,' she confessed, leaning towards him, and when Remy covered her open mouth with his it took an enormous effort of will on her part to pull herself away.

'You could always stay,' he said as she picked up her car keys and started for the door. He followed her down the steps to the courtyard in his bare feet. 'I'll phone my mother and tell her where you are. She can hardly change a *fait accompli.*'

Megan wished she felt as certain, but instead of answering him she tried to block his way. 'You'll get cold,' she said, pointing to his bare feet, but as the temperature still

147

lurked somewhere in the mid-seventies Remy just gave her an old-fashioned look.

'You'll ring me when you get back?' he said, holding her upper arms in a possessive grip, and Megan nodded.

'I will,' she said, suddenly absurdly reluctant to leave the security he represented. She reached up to kiss him again. 'Until tomorrow, hmm? I'll be counting the hours.'

'I'll be counting the minutes,' Remy retorted roughly, letting her go with equal reluctance. 'Drive carefully.'

It was nearly two o'clock when Megan reached the hotel, but to her surprise the foyer was as brightly illuminated as it had been when she'd left. A station wagon she didn't recognise was parked at the door alongside another vehicle that she thought belonged to Dr O'Brien, and her guilty conscience immediately interpreted this as meaning that Anita had discovered her absence and had suffered some kind of collapse.

But then the more likely reason for Dr O'Brien to be here occurred to her, and her knees, which were already shaky, turned to water. Ryan, she thought sickly. Oh, God, was Ryan all right?

Instead of parking the buggy at the rear of the hotel where she'd found it, Megan abandoned it beside the other two vehicles and charged into the hotel. But despite the lights there didn't seem to be anyone about, and she was considering making the trek to Ryan's bungalow, to see if there were any lights on there, too, when Anita and two men, one of whom she didn't know, appeared at the top of the stairs.

Megan didn't know what to do. Anita's behaviour earlier that evening did not lead her to believe that her stepsister would be glad to see her, whatever the circumstances, and she half wished she could disappear as swiftly as Anita had done.

But to her surprise Anita didn't hesitate. As soon as she realised it was Megan who was standing in the foyer, she left the two men and hurried down the stairs towards her. 'Oh, Megan,' she choked, the tears streaming down her cheeks, 'he's gone. Pops is gone.' She enfolded the younger woman in her arms. 'He's dead! I just can't believe it's true.'

Megan could hardly believe it herself, but she was relieved that Anita didn't ask where she'd been. Nevertheless, she couldn't help feeling guilty. She should have been here, she thought unhappily. She should have been here for Anita's sake, if nothing else. Instead of which, she had been with Remy. She and Remy had been—

'Remy...'

She was hardly aware she had spoken his name out loud until Anita drew back to look at her. 'Oh, God, yes,' she said, dabbing her eyes with a tissue. 'I've got to tell Remy. He's going to be devastated when he hears the news. He and Pops—well, you know how close they were. If only he'd been at home when I phoned him earlier. I tried to reach him at his apartment and at his office, but I'm afraid he and Rachel must have been out with friends.'

Megan took an involuntary step backwards. 'You— phoned Remy?' she echoed faintly. 'When—when was that?'

'Does it matter?' Anita sniffed unhappily. 'It was earlier on, as I said. Half-past ten, maybe. What does it matter?'

Megan swallowed. Anita had not phoned at half-past ten. At half-past ten, she and Remy had been making love in his bedroom, with an extension of his phone on the table beside them...

But she couldn't tell Anita that, even though Anita's words troubled her quite a bit. Why would Remy's mother claim to have phoned her son when she hadn't? What could she possibly hope to gain by it?

'So—so when—?' Megan was amazed at how difficult it was to ask about Ryan's death. Yet, in the short time she'd known him, he had become incredibly important to her, and she knew his absence was going to make a difference.

'About eleven, I think.' Anita's breath caught in her throat. 'Sam—he was the nurse on duty tonight—called me

about a quarter-past ten, when he noticed the monitor
was—was—' She broke off, shaking her head helplessly.
'He tried, but there was nothing he could do; nothing anyone could do,' she added, giving way to another bout of
tears, and Megan put a comforting arm about her shoulders.

The two men who had followed Anita down the stairs
now approached, and Megan gave Dr O'Brien a sympathetic look. The doctor, who was not a young man himself,
had known Ryan for a lot of years, and she guessed he
must be feeling pretty bad about it himself.

'Megan,' he said, patting her shoulder, death creating a
familiarity between all the participants somehow. 'This is
a sorry occasion.'

Megan nodded. 'I know it sounds silly, but it—it was so
sudden.'

'Hardly that,' said Anita sharply, recovering her com-
posure. 'We've all been expecting it.'

'I think what Megan means is that Ryan had seemed a
little better during the past few days,' declared O'Brien
soothingly. 'I must admit, I was beginning to wonder if he
wasn't going to confound us all.'

'You're not serious!' Anita dabbed her eyes with an impatient hand. 'You may have thought he was improving,
but I thought he was trying to do too much.'

'Why?' O'Brien looked at her a little grimly now, and
Megan wondered if she was only imagining the edge in his
tone. 'You know Megan's being here had made a difference. Even you can't deny he gained a new lease of life
when she arrived.'

'And much good it's done him,' retorted Anita coldly,
causing the younger woman to catch her breath in sudden
disbelief. She squared her shoulders, causing Megan's hand
to fall to her side. 'I'm sorry. I can't help how I feel.'

Megan glanced at the doctor, the pain evident in her pale
face, and he quickly drew the other man forward. 'This is
Superintendent Lewis, Megan,' he said, to fill the awkward
silence. 'From the Port Serrat Constabulary. He and I were

having dinner together when I got Anita's call. Frank, this is Megan Cross. Mrs Robards' daughter.'

'How do you do?'

Megan managed to find the appropriate response, and the swarthy policeman gave her a rueful smile. 'Better than you at this moment, I should think,' he assured her gently. 'I'm so sorry we had to meet in such unhappy circumstances.'

'Megan's only been here a couple of weeks,' went on O'Brien, giving Anita time to compose herself. 'But you remember her mother, I'm sure.'

'Laura?' Superintendent Lewis's smile was warmer now. 'Oh, yes. I'm happy to say I knew your mother quite well, Miss Cross. I seem to remember meeting your father on one occasion, too.'

Megan nodded, and as if she'd decided that her stepsister had been the centre of attention long enough Anita intervened. 'An unforgettable encounter, I'm sure,' she said bitterly, and then, making an obvious effort to hide her resentment, she gestured towards the doors. 'And now, gentlemen, if you'll forgive me…'

'Of course, of course.'

It was Superintendent Lewis who instantly took the hint, but Dr O'Brien touched Megan's arm with curiously rueful fingers. 'You'll be all right?' he asked, and, guessing it was a covert reference to Anita's attitude, she gave him a determined nod.

'Someone—someone has to tell Remy,' she ventured, wondering if he might find it easier coming from someone other than his mother, but once again Anita broke in.

'I'm going to tell him,' she declared firmly, successfully dispensing with any offer the doctor might have made. She ushered the two men towards the door. 'He should be home by now. I'm going to drive into Port Serrat and tell him myself.'

'Oh, but—'

Megan started to make a protest, but one look from Anita was enough to silence her. And why not? she thought tensely. It was nothing to do with her. Not really. All right,

she and Remy had become lovers, she couldn't deny that,
but now that his grandfather was dead, who knew what it
would mean to their relationship? What had Ryan said?
That Remy knew where his real loyalties lay, that although
he might rebel a little the hotel was his inheritance.

Tears pricked at the back of her eyes. Two weeks ago
she'd have said that Ryan Robards' death would mean
nothing to her, but it was true no longer. Curiously, he'd
found his way into her affections and she'd miss their little
tête-à-têtes more than she could say.

Because it seemed the polite thing to do, she accompanied the others to the door. She doubted she would get any
sleep tonight anyway. She couldn't help thinking about
Remy and what this was going to mean to him.

As soon as she saw the buggy at the door, she realised
her mistake. Until then, Anita had forgotten to ask her why
she'd been in the foyer at two o'clock in the morning, but
now her eyes turned to Megan with evident intent. What
was she thinking? Megan wondered anxiously. And what
was she going to tell her if Anita asked where she'd been?

She couldn't tell her she'd been with Remy, she realised
at once. Apart from anything else, it would be like charging
Anita with lying about the call she was supposed to have
made. Admitting she'd been at Remy's apartment since just
after nine o'clock would be tantamount to an accusation,
and, no matter how much she wanted to be honest about
her relationship with Remy, now was not the time for con-
fessions of that kind.

Nevertheless, she wasn't foolish enough to think that
Anita wouldn't demand some explanation, and while her
stepsister exchanged a final few words with Dr O'Brien
Megan sought desperately for a solution. Somehow saying
she couldn't sleep wouldn't cut it, and she decided she must
be as honest as the circumstances allowed.

The two men were getting into their respective cars now,
and Megan raised her hand in reluctant farewell. With Dr
O'Brien's departure, the realisation that there really was
nothing more any of them could do for Ryan struck her

anew, and the tears that stung her eyes were as unexpected as they were profound.

She was smudging them away when Anita came towards her, her expression mirroring nothing but contempt. 'You've been out,' she said, and it wasn't a question. 'Where have you been?'

Megan drew a deep breath. 'I went for a drive,' she said honestly. 'I wasn't tired, so I thought you wouldn't mind if I borrowed one of the buggies.' She paused, and then, hoping to avoid any more questions, asked, 'How are you, by the way? If it's not a silly question, is your headache any better?'

'My headache?' If Megan had needed any proof that Anita's indisposition earlier had been manufactured, she had it then, but as if remembering what she'd told Jules to tell the younger woman Anita gave an impatient shake of her head. 'I haven't had time to think about it,' she declared tersely. 'Ever since Sam called to tell me Pops was—well, finding it difficult to breathe, I haven't had a moment to myself.'

'I know.' Megan felt guilty for doubting her. 'I'm so sorry, Anita.'

'I'll bet you are.'

The change in Anita's tone was startling, and Megan, who had been about to take her stepsister's arm in sympathy, stood back aghast. 'I beg your pardon?'

Anita shook her head, as if unwilling to get into any kind of argument now, and started off across the marble floor, but Megan had had enough of her insinuations.

'Anita!' she exclaimed, forcing her own emotions aside and going after her. 'Anita, what are you talking about? Why are you being like this?' She took an appalled breath. 'Are you implying that I had something to do with your father's death?'

Anita's shoulders heaved as she took a deep breath, and then, instead of starting up the stairs, she turned to face her. 'With his *death?*' she said harshly. 'Oh, no. I'm not implying you had anything to do with his death. You didn't want him to die, did you, Megan? He's no use to you dead!'

Megan gasped. 'I don't know what you mean!' she exclaimed in dismay. 'How—how could I—*use* your father?'

Anita snorted. 'To get a share of the hotel, of course,' she retorted contemptuously. 'It never occurred to me when I invited you here that you might see this place as some kind of an investment. Pops wanted to see you, he wanted to make his peace with you, and I, poor fool that I am, only wanted to please him. I never dreamt I might be inviting a—a snake into our midst!'

Megan was horrified. 'You're not serious!'

'Why not?'

'Why not?' Megan swallowed convulsively. 'Because it's not true.'

'You're telling me that you and Pops never discussed the hotel?'

'No.' Megan shook her head a little frantically. 'Of course we discussed the hotel. He—he was very proud of it. Why wouldn't we discuss it?'

'You're telling me you didn't put the idea of him leaving you a share in the hotel to him?'

'Of leaving me a share?' echoed Megan blankly, seemingly unable to do anything but repeat Anita's vile accusations. 'Of course I didn't put such an idea into his head.' She tried to think clearly. 'And it's not true. He hasn't left me a share of the hotel. You—you're imagining things.'

'I'm not imagining anything,' said Anita coldly. 'But you are if you think I'd let either of you get away with a thing like that.'

Megan was taken aback. 'I don't know what you're talking about,' she protested. 'Your father and I were friends. We had a friendship. There was no question of me—using him to get a part of the hotel. It's not mine. It's nothing to do with me. You have to believe me when I say—'

'Then why did Pops ask me to call Ben Dreyer?' demanded Anita fiercely. 'Ben Dreyer is his lawyer. He told me he wanted to speak to him tomorrow when I went to say goodnight.'

Megan's jaw sagged. 'I—I don't know,' she cried unsteadily. 'Did—did he say it was to do with me?'

'Oh, no.' Anita's lips twisted scornfully. 'No, he didn't say anything like that. He wouldn't tell me why he wanted to see him. But I'm not stupid! I knew what he had in mind.'

Megan quivered. 'Then it's just as well he died, isn't it?' she said tremulously, using the only defence she had. 'He's dead now, Anita. He won't be making any more calls on his lawyer. Your precious hotel's as safe as it ever was.'

Anita's face collapsed. One moment she was glaring at Megan, the hate she didn't attempt to hide shining in her eyes, and the next she had slumped down onto the lowest step of the staircase, burying her face in her hands, and giving way to noisy sobs. Rocking to and fro, her sturdy frame seeming to fall in upon itself, she had a pathetic appeal, and although Megan wanted to leave her her conscience was stirred.

'Anita,' she said desperately, sinking down beside the other woman and gathering her shuddering body into her arms. 'Oh, Anita, I wouldn't do anything to hurt you. Surely you know that?'

There was a moment when she thought Anita was going to reject her, when the plump shoulders stiffened, and it seemed as if she would pull away. But then the attraction of comfort apparently got the better of her, and she buried her face in Megan's shoulder and allowed the tears to flow.

CHAPTER THIRTEEN

MEGAN went to bed, but she didn't sleep. Despite the fact that she and Anita had ostensibly made their peace with one another, she knew she'd never forget the accusations her stepsister had made. Anita might have begged her forgiveness, she might have declared that she'd been distraught with grief, and that she hadn't known what she was saying, but Megan felt cold inside, and she doubted she'd ever feel warm again. She was hurt, frozen, numbed with the kind of chill that came from knowing herself betrayed. How could Anita have said those things? How could she have even thought them? Dear God, it was Anita who had invited her here. How could she believe that Megan had had anything more than Anita's father's well-being at heart?

But it was no use worrying about that now. As she crawled out of bed the next morning, Megan knew there were other problems to deal with, not least her relationship with Remy. How had he reacted to the news of his grandfather's death? Oh, Lord, she thought wearily, what was going to happen now?

She deliberately took a shower before getting dressed in an effort to revive her flagging spirits, and then slipped on a simple white tunic whose hem ended a modest couple of inches above her knees. She had become accustomed to not wearing make-up during the day, but this morning she felt obliged to apply a trace of blusher. Her drawn cheeks were waxen-pale, and she was sure she looked every inch her age, but no one could survive the kind of battering she had taken the night before without it showing in her face. She felt mentally, and physically, shattered, and she thought longingly of London and Simon's undemanding company.

Downstairs, the hotel was functioning as efficiently as usual, and Megan reflected, rather cynically, that Anita was unlikely to allow her father's death to interfere with her investment. Or was she being unnecessarily cruel? she wondered, realising that until the night before she hadn't really thought of Anita as being particularly ruthless. But she was, she acknowledged wryly. At least so far as the hotel was concerned, anyway.

Deciding she would rather not invade her stepsister's apartments until she was invited, Megan chose to take coffee in the lobby bar, seating herself by the window as she had done on her first morning here, when Remy had arrived to have breakfast with her.

Remy…

Sipping her coffee, Megan allowed thoughts other than those of her stepfather and stepsister to fill her subconscious, recalling the hours she had spent at Remy's apartment in glorious detail. Whatever the future held she knew she would never regret what had happened, and her memory of the way he had made her feel still caused a tingling sensation to spread throughout her whole body.

But then she remembered what had happened when she'd come back to the hotel, and the tingling sensation vanished. Oh, God, Ryan was dead. Dead! And although she hadn't said as much Megan knew Anita blamed her for that, as well.

She was still sitting there, with her empty coffee-cup in front of her, when she became aware of Remy crossing the foyer towards her. He was wearing a dark silk suit this morning, the whiteness of his shirt contrasting sharply with the tanned column of his throat. He looked heavy-eyed and weary, but so handsome that Megan felt her senses stir in spite of herself.

Yet, despite what had happened between them the night before, she was instantly aware of his relationship to Anita, and of the fact that the accusations his mother had made could just as easily have come from him.

'Hi,' he said, pulling out a chair and seating himself opposite her. 'I thought I might find you here.'

'Did you?' Megan was unaccountably nervous with him. 'I—I'm so sorry about your grandfather.' She caught her lower lip between her teeth. 'You must be devastated.'

'Well, sad, certainly,' he agreed gently. 'The old man was something else.' He lifted his shoulders. 'But it wasn't as if it was unexpected, despite the fact he'd appeared to rally these last few days. O'Brien was amazed he'd lasted as long as he had.'

'Was he?' Anita hadn't said that. 'Well, anyway, you have my condolences. He was a remarkable man.'

Remy's lips twisted. 'Your condolences?' he echoed softly. 'So formal. Why don't you just say we're all going to miss him? I am, and I guess you are, too.'

'What do you mean?'

Megan's response had been unnecessarily sharp, and Remy narrowed his eyes as he looked at her. 'What do I mean?' he asked mildly. 'What do you think I mean? You will miss him, won't you? Or were all those conversations you had with him just so much hot air?'

'No!' Megan was defensive, but she couldn't help it. After what Anita had said, she was sensitive to any hint that she might have had some ulterior motive for visiting Ryan. 'I—I liked your grandfather. A lot. But I realise my association with him can't compare to yours. Or your mother's.'

'Did I say it could?' Remy looked a little confused now. 'Come on, Megan. I know you got on well with the old man, and he was very fond of you.'

'Oh, I don't think—'

'He was,' Remy insisted flatly. He looked puzzled. 'Has someone implied he wasn't?'

'No.' Megan couldn't allow him to think that. To all intents and purposes, she and Anita had mended their differences. She had no desire to cause another rift by telling tales to her son. 'I just don't want you to think that I— well, that I imagine my relationship with him meant more

to him than it did. We were friends. I reminded him of my
mother. But that's all it was.'

Remy frowned. 'That sounds suspiciously like a defence
to me,' he remarked drily. 'So—have I accused you of anything? If I have, then tell me about it. I don't want you to
think I resent the affection that grew up between you and
Pops. Hell, if seeing you made his last few days any easier,
then I'm grateful. Okay?'

Megan swallowed. 'Okay.'

'Right.' Remy took a deep breath. 'So long as we understand one another.'

Megan nodded, but she couldn't help wondering how he
would have felt if Ryan had decided to leave her a share
of the hotel. It was all very well telling herself that Remy
wasn't like his mother, but where money was concerned
people could be surprisingly similar.

And, thinking of Anita, she said stiffly, 'Um—how is
your mother this morning? She—er—she was pretty upset
last night.'

'Yeah.' Remy pulled a wry face. 'I guess she was.' His
eyes darkened. 'I gather she was waiting for you when you
got back to the hotel.'

Now it was Megan's turn to draw a deep breath. 'Did
she tell you that?'

'She said you turned up just as O'Brien was leaving,' he
conceded levelly. 'She also said that you'd told her you'd
been for a drive because you couldn't sleep.'

'That's right.' Megan pushed her cup aside, and, resting
her forearms on the table, she twisted her hands together.
Then, moistening her lips, she said, 'I could hardly tell her
where I'd really been, could I?'

'Couldn't you?' Remy's response was a little more cal-
culated now. But then, as if acknowledging that she had a
point, he shrugged. 'I guess not.'

'Besides, it's not something I'd want to tell her,' went
on Megan carefully, distinctly unwilling to mention the call
Anita had claimed to have made. 'I mean, you know how
she would feel if she knew, and—and until—until—'

'Until what?' Remy's tone had definitely hardened. 'Until the funeral is over? Until you decide what you want to do about it? Until you *leave?*'

'No.' Megan had never expected this kind of reaction. 'But, I mean, in the circumstances—'

'To hell with the circumstances,' said Remy harshly. 'I don't give a damn about the circumstances. Okay, Pops is dead, and no one's going to miss him more than me, but that doesn't mean I have to put my life on hold until my mother decides it's okay to start living again.'

'That's not what I meant.'

'Then what did you mean?' he asked, a dangerous edge to his voice. 'Okay, maybe this isn't the time to talk about it, but I'd like to know what you feel about it. About *us!*'

Megan swallowed again, uneasily aware of how exposed they were here, in the foyer, with his mother likely to come upon them at any moment. She wasn't afraid of Anita, she told herself fiercely, but she was afraid of what her words might do to their fragile relationship, and until Ryan was safely buried she didn't want to be the cause of any more friction between Anita and her family.

'You know how I feel,' she said now, in a low voice, but Remy's expression was not encouraging.

'Do I?'

'Yes.' Her palms were sweating and she pressed them tightly together. 'Last night—last night was—wonderful!'

'That's not exactly what I meant,' said Remy flatly. 'It was good sex—is that what you mean?'

'No—'

'It wasn't good sex?'

Megan sighed. 'You're deliberately misunderstanding me.'

'So tell me,' he urged, reaching across the table and covering her nervous hands with his. His thumbs massaged the vulnerable curve of her wrists. 'Tell me what it meant to you.'

'Oh, Remy—'

'That sounds better,' he approved, hearing the anguish in her voice. 'I like the way you say my name.'

'Remy—' She caught her lower lip between her teeth. 'We can't talk about this now. Not now.' She shook her head. 'I don't want to upset your mother any more than she already is—'

'But it's okay to upset me, right?' Remy smothered an oath and got abruptly to his feet. 'Forgive me; I was foolish enough to think that I was more important to you than my mother, but obviously I was wrong.' And, without another word, he strode away towards the stairs that led to his mother's apartments, taking them two at a time, and swiftly disappearing from her sight.

The funeral was held in the late afternoon.

Megan was amazed at the speed with which the arrangements had been made, but she understood the need for urgency in such a hot climate.

The service was held at the Baptist church in El Serrat, and she marvelled at the number of people who crammed into the small building. Most of the staff from the hotel were there, together with Ryan's sailing and drinking cronies from as far away as St Nicholas, at the north end of the island.

For her part, Megan stayed firmly in the background. Although she and Anita had spoken together briefly, she was still very much aware of feeling the outsider here, and she noticed that Remy kept firmly out of her way.

Which wasn't difficult, she conceded painfully, considering he was constantly surrounded by friends or Rachel's family. That young woman seemed permanently at his side, sharing the proffered condolences, consoling him in his grief.

Megan told herself she was glad. She wouldn't have wanted anyone to take too close a look at her eyes, which were red and puffy from the tears she had shed earlier. In fact, she had spent a good part of the morning crying, she thought tautly. For Ryan; for Anita; but mostly for Remy and herself.

As she stood at the back of the church, watching Remy as he gave his grandfather's eulogy, her heart swelled painfully in her chest. What if she'd caused an irreparable rift between them? she fretted anxiously. What if he refused to listen to her explanations? What if he decided he loved Rachel, after all? How would she survive?

It was dark by the time they got back from the cemetery in Port Serrat. Ryan had been laid to rest in the garden where his wife's ashes had been scattered, and Megan wondered fancifully if they were together again at last.

Anita had arranged for a buffet supper to be laid out on her private terrace, and several people, including Dr O'Brien, Superintendent Lewis, and Ben Dreyer, Ryan's lawyer, gathered about the tables. There was a small bar, and Megan noticed that Jules was on duty tonight, leaving Remy free to circulate among his fellow mourners. As before, Rachel was at his side, and, although Megan knew she could have joined Anita, once again she stayed in the background.

She was standing by the vine-hung trellis when she became aware of someone beside her. For a heart-stopping moment, she thought it was Remy, but a swift sideways glance disabused her of that thought. It was Dr O'Brien, and although she managed to summon up a faint smile she doubted he was deceived.

'I expect you'll be glad when it's all over,' he remarked, passing her a glass of wine. 'I know I will.' He grimaced. 'But it was a fine service. Ryan would have been pleased.'

Megan nodded, not trusting herself to speak, and as if understanding how she was feeling the doctor continued, 'Yes. And if it's any consolation he'd have wanted you to be here, too.'

'Would he?' The words were choked, and Megan cleared her throat before going on. 'I'm going to miss him.'

'Hmm.' O'Brien sipped his own wine with a thoughtful air. 'I know he was so pleased he'd made his peace with you at last. He and your mother—well, they loved you, you know.'

Megan looked down at her wine. 'I know.'

'And I'm sure Laura would have been glad to know that you're going to have a reason to come back to San Felipe now.'

'A reason?' Megan's brows drew together. 'Oh—you mean because the ice is broken at last?' She shook her head. 'It's nice of you to say so, but I doubt if I—'

'No. Not that.' The doctor interrupted her. 'I meant the hotel, of course.' He frowned. 'Ryan told you, didn't he?'

Megan's hand froze halfway to her mouth. 'Told me what?' she asked unsteadily, and O'Brien gave a muffled groan.

'Oh, God, he didn't, did he?' He pushed his thinning hair back with a troubled hand. 'I'm sorry, Megan. Hell, I forgot. He didn't have time to—' He broke off. 'He was going to tell you; he was. Dammit, why did I have to open my big mouth?'

Megan swallowed with some difficulty. 'You're not saying—' She distanced herself from him, mentally if not physically, and gave him a tormented look. 'I mean—Ryan didn't—he wouldn't—he hasn't—'

'Left you a piece of the hotel?' asked O'Brien heavily. 'Hell, yes. Of course he has.' And at her look of horror he added, 'Just a small piece.' He made a frustrated gesture. 'But for God's sake don't let Ben know I told you.'

Megan shook her head. 'But—I don't want it,' she protested, imagining how Anita was going to react when she discovered that her worst fears had been realised. Then, in a strained whisper, she asked, 'Are you sure?'

'Sure I'm sure.'

Megan wet her lips. 'But Anita—I mean, she mentioned that Ryan had—had asked to see his—his lawyer, but he was supposed to come today, wasn't he?'

The doctor snorted. 'I wonder how she came to tell you that?' he remarked drily. And then he said, 'Sure, Ryan had asked Ben to call, but it wasn't to change his will, if that's what Anita thought. He did that through me.' His lips twisted. 'He was a sly old beggar, right to the end.'

Megan felt sick. 'But why?' she asked a little wildly. 'Why would he do a thing like that? He—he doesn't owe me anything.'

'Perhaps because he wanted to,' said O'Brien quietly. 'I wasn't joking, Megan. He was very fond of you. And perhaps he wanted to ensure that you and Remy wouldn't lose touch with one another as you and he had.'

Megan put a trembling hand to her head, feeling the sweat beading on her forehead, the throbbing in her temples that warned of a headache to come. It couldn't be true, she told herself desperately. Ryan wouldn't leave her a share in the hotel. Dr O'Brien must be mistaken; he must have misunderstood. Ryan couldn't be so cruel, not knowing how Anita felt about Robards Reach.

'Are you all right?'

Remy's voice was like a cool breeze against her hot head, and although all day she had been dying for some indication that he had forgiven her for what had happened that morning she couldn't deal with him now.

'I'm—I'm fine,' she said, and she could hear the awful stiffness in her voice. 'Are you?'

Remy's dark eyes narrowed, and had she been watching she would have seen him exchange a speaking look with Dr O'Brien. 'I guess so,' he said evenly, and although she had sworn she couldn't cope with him her gaze darted irresistibly to his. 'I missed you earlier.'

'I think Megan's been keeping out of the way,' put in O'Brien, after a moment's awkward silence, and Remy frowned.

'Oh? Why?'

'Well, I imagine she thought you and your mother had your hands full as it was,' the doctor replied staunchly. 'Um—excuse me, won't you? I want to go and have a word with the Reverend.'

Remy inclined his head, but it was obvious his attention was focused elsewhere, and Megan wanted to weep at the thought of what he would think when he discovered what his grandfather had done. What his grandfather *was reputed to have done,* she amended fiercely, but there was really no doubt in her mind. Dr O'Brien wouldn't have said anything if he hadn't known it for a fact, and the idea that Remy might think she was as guilty of using his grandfather as his mother believed filled her with dread.

'Did you miss me?' he asked softly, and her bones melted at the tenderness in his voice. But she couldn't respond to it. Not now. Not with Ryan's will hanging, like the sword of Damocles, over her head.

'I—I liked the eulogy,' she said instead, seeing the light go out of his eyes. 'It—it was a beautiful service.'

'Yes, it was, wasn't it?' Remy took his cue from her, and adopted a cooler stance. 'I expect you're tired.'

'Pretty much,' she nodded, feeling as if she was dying inside. She glanced about her. 'Where's Rachel?'

She heard the oath he used then, even if it was barely audible. 'What is this, Megan?' he demanded harshly. 'What do you care where Rachel is?' His eyes glittered. 'You didn't give much thought to Rachel last night, as I remember.'

Megan's face flamed. 'I just thought—'

'Yes? What did you think?'

'Well—you have been with her all day.'

'I've been with lots of people,' he snarled angrily. 'And as you weren't willing for us to be together, then I don't think you can blame Rachel if she gets the wrong impression.'

Megan swayed back. 'I couldn't be with you,' she protested.

'Because you were afraid of what my mother might say?' he demanded, and when she gave a nervous little nod he acknowledged it with one of his own. 'Well, okay, I'll accept that. It probably wasn't the moment to get into that can of worms. But the funeral's over, Megan. You can't have any objections if I tell my mother I'm taking you back to town with me now—'

'No—'

She couldn't let him do it. Not until he knew exactly what his grandfather had done. How would she feel if he turned against her? It was not a prospect she even wanted to consider.

'Megan.'

His voice was anguished now, but there was nothing she could do. 'Just give me a little more time,' she begged, still hoping he might indulge her. 'I—I can't just walk out on your mother. If she needs me, I've got to be here for her.'

Remy closed his eyes for a moment, as if the sight of her offended his sensibilities, but when he opened them again all his anger had gone. Unfortunately, so had any emotion, she saw distractedly. His face was as cold as a mask.

'I thought you were different, Megan,' he said, and although the words were crippling there was no condemnation in his voice. 'But I was wrong. You don't want any commitment. What was I? Part of your cure? Or am I flattering myself? I was probably just a holiday romance.'

CHAPTER FOURTEEN

REMY swallowed the remainder of the beer in the bottle he was holding, and then set it down beside its fellows on his mother's coffee-table. There were, he saw with some disgust, at the least half a dozen empty bottles there already, and he was nowhere near as drunk as he wanted to be.

He shouldn't have accepted his mother's invitation to dinner, he acknowledged dourly. During the past month, he'd managed to avoid all her invitations, and although he knew that sooner or later he would have to deal with her for the time being he was better left to himself.

He wasn't in the mood for company—for any company, actually, but his mother's company in particular. His emotions were still too raw, too savage. It would take a lot of time for him to view her objectively again.

He needed another beer—or something stronger. Any minute now, his mother was going to join him. She was going to come into the room and expect him to behave towards her as he had always done, but he couldn't do it. Not without a stiffener, anyway, he conceded. Something to stop him from stuffing her invitation down her throat.

Realising he was getting dangerously maudlin, he got up from his chair and walked out onto the terrace. He had hoped to escape his thoughts in the darkness, but the sounds of music and laughter from the restaurant below only added to his misery. God, when was it going to get any easier? When was he going to accept the fact that Megan wasn't coming back?

He'd been so stupid, he realised bitterly. He'd thought that once the funeral was over, once his mother had come to terms with his grandfather's death, all he had to do was tell Megan how he felt. He had hoped that she'd understand that the anger he'd shown towards her on the day of the funeral had only been frustration. And jealousy, he admitted honestly. He'd been jealous of the fact that she should put his mother's feelings before his.

But it hadn't worked like that, and he had only his mother to blame. As soon as she'd discovered that her father had left a ten per cent share in the hotel to Megan, she'd had hysterics, and by the time she'd calmed down Megan had been making arrangements to leave.

A corrosive pain twisted inside him as he recalled the frozen horror in Megan's face. He would never have believed his mother could behave so violently. She'd accused her stepsister of deception and collusion, and God knew what else besides.

It had all been so unnecessary. Pops had left her a forty-five per cent share of the hotel, for God's sake, so what was all the fuss about? It wasn't as if he'd made Megan part-owner. He'd left Remy the other forty-five per cent, which seemed eminently fair to him.

But his mother had been so blinded to anyone's feelings but her own that she hadn't cared that Megan was hurting. Remy was sure all she'd cared about was getting Megan out of the hotel, and no one would have wanted to stay in those circumstances.

All the same, he hadn't believed that Megan would leave without seeing him. When he'd left the hotel that night to go back to his apartment, he'd had every intention of coming back to see her the following day. But work had intervened, and it had been late in the evening when he'd arrived at El Serrat, only to find that Megan had left on the early evening flight.

Even then, he'd been sure she'd get in touch with him. He'd left word with Sylvie that if Miss Cross rang she was to be put through to him immediately. And if he was in court she'd had orders to get a message to him somehow. He'd had no intention of losing any opportunity to speak to Megan again.

But she hadn't rung, and when, after three agonising

weeks, he'd swallowed his pride and rung her, there'd been no reply. Well, not from her town house, at least, and he had no idea of the name of her company. His mother might have known it, but he'd had no wish to speak to her.

It was four weeks now, and the knowledge was killing him. Which was why he'd given in to his mother's pleas and come here tonight. He intended to ask her if she knew how he could get in touch with Megan. If it caused a row, so be it. After the way she'd screwed up his life, he didn't much care what she thought.

'Remy?'

He heard her voice now in the sitting room, and he guessed she was anxious in case he'd got bored and gone away. 'I'm here,' he said, shoving his hands into his trouser pockets and sauntering to the French doors. 'I was just getting some air.'

'I'm not surprised you need it.' Her voice was sharp at first, but then, as if realising she was walking on shaky ground, she bit her tongue. 'I'm sorry I've been so long. André is frantic. He's got ninety-five reservations for dinner, and he's having problems with two of the ovens.'

Remy shrugged. 'Tough.'

Anita's lips tightened. 'I might have known it wouldn't matter to you.' She squared her shoulders. 'When are you going to start showing some responsibility for the day-to-day running of the hotel? Your grandfather obviously expected us to work together.'

'I wonder if that's why he left Megan a share as a buffer?' Remy retorted, stepping into the room so that she could see his face. 'He knew we'd never agree on anything.'

'Yes.' Anita stiffened. 'Yes, well, that's what I wanted to talk to you about.' She bit her lip. 'I had word today from Ben Dreyer. Apparently, Megan wants to relinquish her share.'

'No!'

Remy's response was automatic, realising that if Megan gave up her share in the hotel he might never see her again.

'I'm afraid so.' His mother delicately pushed the empty

beer bottles aside, and set the vodka and tonic she had poured herself on the table. 'I know you don't want to believe it, Remy, but it does seem to vindicate my opinion. She's obviously had a guilty change of heart.'

Remy's lips twisted. 'You still believe you were right to accuse her of deluding the old man?' He shook his head. 'That's rubbish, and you know it. Pops never did anything without due care and consideration. He knew we'd never be able to work together without a mediator, so he gave Megan the deciding vote.'

Anita evidently didn't want to argue with him. 'Well, whatever the truth is, she doesn't want the responsibility,' she declared, taking a seat on the sofa. She patted the cushion beside her, looking up at him appealingly. 'Come on, darling. Sit down. Your grandfather wouldn't have wanted Giles Cross's daughter to come between us.'

'But she has come between us,' said Remy flatly, making no effort to join her. He moved to the bar and helped himself to another beer, despite his mother's mute look of disapproval. 'You might as well know, we were lovers. Only she was too afraid of offending you to admit it.'

Anita swallowed. 'I don't believe you.'

'It's true.'

'No.' Anita got to her feet. 'You're just saying this to hurt me.' She pressed her hands together. 'How can you be so cruel? You know that you and Rachel—'

'Rachel and I are finished,' Remy told her bleakly. 'We were finished the day I picked Megan up from the airport.'

Anita gasped. 'You're not serious.'

'I'm afraid I am.'

'But—but she's too old for you!'

'She said that, too.'

Anita's shoulders sagged in relief. 'There you are, then.'

'But it's not true,' Remy remarked evenly. 'Age has nothing to do with it.'

'You're saying that's not why she left you?' His mother's lip curled. 'Well, don't say I didn't warn you.'

'It wasn't anything to do with my grandmother either, if

that's what you're implying!' exclaimed Remy harshly.
'She left because you made it too unpleasant for her to
stay.'

'So you say.'

'So I know,' retorted Remy, wishing he felt as certain as
he sounded. 'In any case, that's why I'm here. I want to
know the address of her company in England.'

'Her company?' Anita stared at him. 'Why?'

'Why?' Remy uttered a short laugh. 'Why do you think?
Because I want to get in touch with her, of course.'

'But I've just told you, she wants to relinquish her share
in the hotel.'

'So?'

'So, obviously she wants nothing more to do with us.'

'She wants nothing more to do with *you*,' Remy corrected her grimly. 'Megan and I—we have unfinished business.'

Anita pressed trembling hands to her lips. 'No.'

'Yes.'

'But you can't do this, Remy. Not now. Not now she's
agreed to give up her share—'

'Agreed to?' Remy seized on the words. 'What do you
mean, she *agreed* to give up her share? I thought you said
Ben Dreyer had been in touch with you.'

Anita pushed back her hair with a nervous hand. 'Well,
I did. He has. What I mean is—'

She was at a loss for words, and Remy saw it all now.
Far from accepting the status quo, his mother had either
contacted Megan, or had Ben Dreyer do it on her behalf,
and asked her if she would be prepared to sell her share of
the hotel. He felt sick with loathing. How could she? How
could she do such a thing? To Megan, to his grandfather,
to *him?*

'You—you—'

Words failed him now, and, as if sensing this might be
her last chance to tell him her side of the story, Anita
clutched his sleeve. 'Please,' she said. 'Please, Remy, listen
to me. You know how ill your grandfather was, how frail.

People like that, people in that situation, are easily persuaded. Megan knew Pops confused her with Laura. She played on that, don't you see? Whatever she says about this directory of hers in London, it can't compare to this place. From the minute she got here, she must have been planning—'

'Shut up!'

Remy's words briefly silenced her, but when he pulled his arm out of her grasp she started again. 'You have to believe me, Remy. Goodness knows, everything I've done has been for you, for your heirs, for the children I thought you and Rachel were going to have—'

'I said shut up.' Remy couldn't stand any more of this. 'If you've done anything, it's been for yourself as much as anyone. My God, don't forget I know how devastated you were when I suggested Pops might want to leave Megan some small token—'

'A ten per cent share in a several-million-dollar enterprise is not a token,' snapped his mother angrily. 'I knew he was planning something. I just knew.' She twisted her hands together. 'But he was too clever for me. He knew when he asked to see Ben Dreyer that I'd think it was because he was going to change his will, but he'd already done it. By the time I heard about it, it was too late.'

Remy stiffened. 'Too late?' he echoed faintly. 'My God, you're not saying you had something to do with his sudden relapse?'

'No.' Anita looked horrified now. 'How can you even suggest such a thing? I loved your grandfather. I loved him very much. I'd never have done anything to hurt him.'

'But you have to admit his death was—unexpected.' He shook his head. 'My God, you didn't even have time to call me, to let me know—'

'I did call you,' said Anita at once. 'But you weren't there.'

'When?' Remy stared at her. 'When did you call me?'

'The—the night your grandfather died, of course.' Anita turned away. 'Must we talk about it now?'

'I was home the night Pops died,' said Remy grimly. 'If you'd called I'd have known about it.'

'How do you know?' Anita spread her hands. 'It's weeks ago now. How can you possibly remember where you were the night your grandfather died?'

'Because I was with Megan,' said Remy, not without some relish. 'If you must know, that was the night we became lovers. I wouldn't forget that.'

Anita's lips parted. 'Oh—well, maybe I got a wrong number—'

'Maybe you didn't,' said Remy harshly. 'You didn't phone me, did you? You deliberately didn't phone me. For God's sake, Mom, why?'

Anita seemed to shrink in upon herself. 'There was nothing you could have done,' she said, as she'd said so many times before. 'There was nothing anyone could do.'

'Maybe not, but—hell, Mom, what gave you the right to stop me from seeing Pops before he died?'

'If I'd known you were with Megan, I wouldn't have hesitated,' muttered Anita darkly. And then, as if she was weary of prevarication, she lifted her shoulders in a dismissive gesture. 'Oh, well, you might as well know, I suppose. I was afraid of what he might say to you.'

'To me?' Remy was confused. 'What about?'

'About his will, of course,' said Anita irritably. 'For pity's sake, Remy, I've just told you. I thought he was only *thinking* about changing his will. I didn't know he'd already done it.'

'And you thought if he told me what he was planning to do I might insist on giving Megan a part of my share, right?'

Anita nodded.

'Oh, Lord, Mom, does this place mean that much to you?' He groaned. 'You'd deny an old man's dying wish to ensure that you—'

'It wasn't his dying wish,' protested Anita tearfully. 'All he said was your name—and—and Megan's.'

'And from that you deduced that he wanted to trick you out of your inheritance?'

'Not him.' Anita licked her lips. 'Megan. Oh, Remy, say you forgive me. Say you won't hold this against me. I was only trying to do my best for—for us—'

'Not for us,' Remy told her coldly, feeling sick to his stomach. 'My God, no wonder Megan wanted to get out of here. She must think we're both—mad!'

'Does it matter what she thinks?' Anita went to him then, and in spite of his resistance she cupped his anguished face in her hands. 'Please, Remy, try to understand for my sake. I don't want that woman to ruin your life, as your father did mine.'

Remy couldn't help himself. He dashed her hands away and stepped back as if he couldn't bear for her to touch him. 'You know what, Mom?' he said bitterly. 'You're the only person who's ruined my life. I love Megan, and before all this happened I think she cared about me, too. But you destroyed that, just as surely as you've destroyed the one thing that might have brought her back to San Felipe. I'll never forgive you for that. Never.' He brushed past her then, feeling in desperate need of clean air. 'Excuse me, I think I'll take a rain check on that dinner, after all.'

CHAPTER FIFTEEN

THE plane had been late leaving London so it was after six o'clock when it touched down in San Felipe. Megan would have preferred the earlier arrival, not least because it would have given her some time to check into a hotel in Port Serrat before going in search of Remy, but as it was she was afraid that if she delayed any longer he might go out for the evening.

Of course, common sense told her to check into a hotel anyway—that whatever she had to say to Remy could be said just as easily the next morning—but her nerves wouldn't allow her to do that. Besides, she was very much afraid that if she waited until the next morning she wouldn't have the courage to beard Remy in his office, and once she had seen Ben Dreyer the temptation to leave without seeing him might overcome her instincts.

It probably wasn't the most sensible thing to see him anyway. It was over a month since she'd left San Felipe, and she hadn't heard a word from him since. Surely, if he'd wanted to see her again, if he'd had second thoughts about what he'd said to her the day of the funeral, he'd have made some effort to get in touch with her? But, although she'd waited expectantly for a call or a letter, she'd heard nothing.

It hadn't helped that Simon had been too wrapped up in his new relationship to spend any real time with her. The young man he'd told her about, the one who'd had such original ideas about introducing an ethnic section to the directory, had turned out to be more than a friend, and he and Simon had decided to set up house together.

Which meant Megan had had to find herself a new apartment. Naturally, Simon had wanted to sell his share of the house, and although he'd given her first refusal Megan had

175

decided a completely new start would suit her better. In any case, the house was too big for one person, and Simon and Keith—she was rapidly getting used to the idea that they were a couple now—wanted to buy somewhere new, too. Keith had friends in another part of London, and Megan accepted that from now on Keith's wishes were going to figure large in Simon's plans.

Not that she objected to their relationship. On the contrary, she was glad Simon had found someone he could care for at last. One of the reasons they had decided to buy a house together was that he'd decided, after his last abortive affair, that he was unlikely to fall in love again, and she hoped Keith wouldn't let him down.

For her part, she had been having mixed feelings about her own future. Simon's contacts in Sydney had suggested that she might like to temporarily relocate there to organise an Australian directory, and she'd still been considering that when Anita's letter had arrived.

She shivered now, remembering how excited she'd been when she'd seen the San Felipe postmark, but Anita's missive had been short and to the point: as far as she was concerned, Megan had no real right to the share in the hotel Ryan Robards had left her, and as she was unlikely to find it of any intrinsic value Anita was offering to buy her out.

It was the final insult, but Megan was past caring what Anita thought of her any more. The scene she had created when her father's will had been read had destroyed any lingering affection Megan might have had for her, and gouged a rift between her and Remy that was so deep, she'd felt she had no choice but to leave the island at once.

Of course, when she'd got back to England, the situation hadn't seemed as clear-cut as it had done before. She'd realised then that she hadn't given Remy a chance to tell her how he felt about the situation, which was why she'd spent the last four weeks waiting anxiously for his call. But all that had arrived was Anita's letter, providing her with the opportunity to be free of the Robardses, once and for all.

Only her feelings wouldn't allow her to end it, just like that. She didn't want the share in the hotel, and she certainly didn't want Anita's money, but she did want to see Remy one last time, and a call to Ben Dreyer had given her the ideal excuse. There were papers to sign, papers which could have been dealt with by her solicitor, but which she had chosen to deal with herself. Which was why she was now riding in the back of a rackety cab, on her way to Port Serrat and Remy's apartment in Moonraker's Yard.

'Are you sure this is where you want to be, miss?'

While she had been musing over the circumstances that had brought her here, the taxi driver had stopped at the end of the alleyway that led into Remy's courtyard, and was peering somewhat doubtfully along the lamplit tunnel.

'Oh—yes. This is it,' she agreed hurriedly, pushing open the door and getting out, hauling the haversack, which was all she had brought, after her. 'How much?'

The driver stated the fare, and, using some of the dollars she had saved from the last time she was here, Megan paid him. 'Would you like me to wait?' he asked with a troubled frown, but Megan gave him a reassuring shake of her head.

'No. I'll be fine,' she said, stepping back from the cab. 'Thank you.'

The driver nodded, but she was aware of him waiting until she was safely through the alley before driving off. If only Remy would show as much consideration, she thought uneasily, climbing the stairs to the upper floor. *Oh, God, please don't let Rachel be here tonight.*

It wasn't until she had knocked at Remy's door that it occurred to her that he might be working late. Even though it was dark, it was only a little after seven o'clock, and she remembered how conscientious he had been. But someone was at home. She had barely acknowledged the possibility that Remy might be out before she heard the latch being lifted, and presently the door swung inwards.

Megan's legs went weak. No matter how eager she'd been to see him, the actual appearance of Remy in the open doorway briefly robbed her of speech. She'd anticipated this moment, longed for it, even, but now that she was really here she couldn't think of a thing to say.

It was partly due to the fact that he looked so stunned to see her, as if he'd never expected to see her again, and she didn't quite know what to make of that. Was his reaction due to a pleasurable disbelief, or was she really the last person he had wanted to see?

'Megan!' His use of her name was equally dazed. He gripped the back of his neck with a hand that she noticed wasn't quite steady. 'What—what are you doing here?'

Megan endeavoured to pull herself together. Forcing a lightness into her tone she was far from feeling, she managed to make a casual response. 'What do you think?'

'I don't know.'

Remy was wary, and as he moved into the light of the street lamp outside she saw how tired he looked. He had obviously been over-working, she thought anxiously, wondering if that was his way of dealing with his grandfather's death.

She hesitated, and then, deciding she had nothing to lose, she said, 'Aren't you going to invite me in?'

Remy seemed taken aback. 'Oh—of course,' he muttered stiffly, and, stepping back from the door, he allowed her to precede him down the hall.

The living room was a mess. Files and papers littered chairs and sofas alike, spilling onto the floor in places, and mingling with the various items of discarded clothing that were also strewn about. Significantly, several empty glasses occupied the captain's table, and there was the sweet-sour smell of alcohol in the air.

Megan paused just inside the doorway, appalled at the state of the room, and with a muffled oath Remy pushed past her. 'Sorry,' he said, stooping to gather up his papers from one of the sofas, and bundling several garments into a ball and depositing them in the kitchen. 'I wasn't expecting visitors.'

'No.'

Megan caught her lower lip between her teeth, more concerned by Remy's appearance than by the appearance of the room. Now that she could see him properly, she had noticed the days' growth of stubble that darkened his jawline, and the unfamiliar hollowness of his cheeks.

'I've been working at home today,' he added, gesturing to the sofa he'd cleared. His eyes flickered over the haversack she had dropped onto the floor. 'Can I get you something?'

Megan shook her head. 'Not right now, thanks.' She glanced about her. 'You've been busy.'

Remy's mouth twisted. 'You didn't come here to comment on my working practices,' he declared tersely. 'Did Sylvie send you?'

'Sylvie?'

Megan was confused, but Remy only heaved a resigned sigh. 'I assume you have been to the office first. Well, I have to tell you, it was nothing to do with me. I didn't even know my mother had contacted you until yesterday.'

Megan blinked, and then she realised what he was talking about. 'You think I've come about—about transferring my share in the hotel,' she said weakly. 'Well, no. I could have handled that by phone.'

Remy dropped the pile of files he was holding onto a chair, and regarded her with wary eyes. 'So why have you come here?' he asked. He frowned, and his eyes sought the haversack once more. 'Did you just arrive this afternoon?'

'This evening, actually,' said Megan, smoothing her damp palms down the seams of her jeans. 'The plane was late, so I came here directly from the airport.'

Remy's eyes narrowed, his thick lashes hiding their expression from her. 'To see me?' he said, as if he didn't believe it, and she gave a jerky nod. 'Why?'

Megan swallowed. 'You don't make it easy, do you?'

'What's that supposed to mean?'

'Well—' she lifted her shoulders in a helpless gesture '—I thought—I hoped—we might be able to iron out a few differences between us.'

Remy pushed his hands into the back pockets of the
creased, but formal, trousers he was wearing, causing the
unbuttoned neck of his shirt to gape. 'Like what?' he said,
and although she had no reason to hope he would be any
more understanding than his mother had been she had to
try.

'Well, first of all, I want you to know I didn't have—
have anything to do with your grandfather leaving me a
share in the hotel.'

'I know that.'

Remy's tone was almost indifferent, and she could only
gaze at him with wide, uncomprehending eyes. 'You
know?'

'Sure.' He took a deep breath. 'I think I know you better
than that.'

'Then why didn't you—?'

But she couldn't go on. How could she ask why he
hadn't been in touch with her since she left the island?
After what had happened at his grandfather's funeral, she
had only herself to blame. If only she hadn't cared so much
about Anita's feelings. If only she'd followed her heart instead of her head.

'Then why didn't I what?' he demanded now, and she
realised he was waiting for her to finish. 'Try to persuade
my mother that you had nothing to do with it?' he suggested. His mouth curled. 'Do you really think I didn't?'

Megan linked her hands together. 'But she didn't believe
you?' she said, grateful for the diversion. 'I'm sorry she
feels that way, but at least there's something I can do.'

'Yeah.' Remy took an involuntary step towards her, and
she smelled the scent of alcohol on his breath. 'Reject the
gift the old man wanted to give you,' he said harshly. 'Do
you think that's what Pops would have wanted you to do?'

Megan breathed a little unevenly. 'It's what your mother
wants me to do.'

'That's not what I asked.'

'Well, I—I assume it's what you want, too,' she said,
shifting her weight from one foot to the other. 'But I'm

glad you didn't think I'd—cheated you. And it's only fair that it should stay in—in the family.'

Remy's jaw compressed. 'The old man thought you were family,' he said, and she wondered how two people could stand so close without touching one another. 'He wanted you to have a reason to come to the island. He wanted us to stay in touch.'

Megan trembled. 'Us?' she ventured faintly. 'As in me and your mother?'

'No, *us*,' he muttered, seemingly unable to prevent himself from moving even closer. 'For God's sake, Megan, it was you and me he meant.'

Megan swayed, and, as if he was afraid she might fall, Remy wrenched his hands out of his trouser pockets and bracketed her shoulders between his palms. But he didn't pull her towards him or try to kiss her. He just held her there, as if he didn't trust himself to do more.

And, realising it was up to her to precipitate the situation, Megan lifted her hands and spread them against his chest. 'Don't you want me to give up my share of the hotel?' she asked in a tremulous whisper, and with a groan of anguish he gathered her into his arms.

'What I want...' he breathed against her neck, and she realised he was shaking '...what I want is for you to stop tormenting me.' He heaved a sigh. 'I swore I wouldn't do this. But, God help me, there's only so much a man can stand.'

Megan drew back to look into his haggard face. 'To stop tormenting you?' she breathed, cradling his face between her palms, feeling the prick of his beard against the pads of her fingers. 'Oh, Remy, I don't want to torment you. I'm here because I hoped you might still want me.'

'No.' His denial was harsh.

'No, you don't want me?' Her heart plummeted.

'No, I do,' he groaned, pulling her close to him again. 'But, dammit, Megan, it wasn't me who went away without even saying goodbye.'

'Oh...' The breath left her lungs with dizzying speed,

and she clung to him as if she'd never let him go. 'I—I thought you wouldn't want to see me,' she protested. 'After what your mother said, I—I had to get away.'

A sigh escaped him. 'But you didn't think of contacting me—'

'I'm here now.' She drew back and gave him a faintly defensive look. 'You didn't try to contact me either.'

'I did.' Remy lifted one hand to smooth back the moist tendrils of hair from her forehead. 'I tried to,' he amended. 'Eventually. But you were never at home.'

'Oh, God!' Megan gulped. 'I've moved out of the house I used to share with Simon. It's been empty for the past couple of weeks.'

Remy stared at her. 'You've split up?'

'Yes, we've split up.'

'Because of me?'

'No.' Megan saw the light go out of his eyes, and quickly reassured him. 'Because Simon's met a rather attractive young man called Keith,' she said softly. 'I did tell you we were only friends.'

'You didn't tell me he was gay,' said Remy huskily. 'Oh, God, you don't know the agonies I've suffered wondering if you were sharing a bed with him.'

'Simon and I have never shared a bed,' she assured him gently. 'But—' She coloured. 'I wouldn't say no if you—'

'Like this?' Remy held her face between his hands and glanced down at his rumpled appearance. Then, as if unable to stop himself, he bent and kissed her. 'Don't tempt me. I don't have much resistance right now.'

Megan quivered. 'I was hoping you'd say that,' she breathed, looping her arms about his neck. 'And I don't care how you look.'

'I do.' With slightly shaky hands, Remy put her away from him, and, taking a deep breath, started towards the door. 'Just give me time to take a shower and I'll begin to believe I'm human again.'

Remy had shaved the stubble from his chin, and was soaping his chest and body, when the shower door opened. He turned in amazement to find Megan stepping into the shower beside him, her lips curving into a smile when she saw his expression.

'I need a shower, too,' she said. 'I've just got off a long-haul flight. I didn't think you'd mind sharing. I can always rub your back, if you want.'

Remy shook his head. 'You know what I want,' he said, the sight of her causing an arousal he didn't attempt to hide. 'For God's sake, Megan, what are you doing? I haven't finished with the soap yet.' And then he said, in an anguished whisper, 'Oh, what the hell?'

He took her in his arms then, the soap sliding down unheeded between their wet bodies. Her mouth was moist and parted, her tongue darting to meet his with an eagerness he remembered from before. He'd never known a woman so instinctively attuned to his every need as Megan, and the feel of his erection against her flat stomach was the purest kind of torment he could imagine.

But the sweetest, too, he admitted, his tongue plunging eagerly into her mouth in frank imitation of what another part of his anatomy ached to do. 'God, Megan,' he breathed, 'I've nearly been out of my mind with wanting you.'

'Me, too,' she whispered, standing on tiptoe to nudge his swollen body with hers. She arched against him, and when his hands cupped her breasts, abrading the taut nipples, she groaned in protest.

'Megan,' he moaned, when she wound one of her legs about his thigh, unable to prevent himself from moving against her, and then, when she reached up to bite his lip, he lifted her completely, allowing her to wrap both her legs about his hips.

'This is crazy,' he choked, but already she was guiding his body into hers.

'Wonderfully crazy,' she agreed, covering his mouth with hers, and the feeling of her slick body accepting him was even better than he had imagined it. 'I love you,' she

added, barely audibly, and her admission was all he needed
to know…

Some time later, Megan stirred amid the tumbled covers of
Remy's large bed. After he had made fast and furious love
with her in his shower cubicle, they had retired to the more
comfortable surroundings of his bedroom where, in this
bed, he had made love to her again, this time with all the
tenderness and sensitivity she could have wished.

'What time is it?' she murmured, finding him awake beside her, and he turned sleepy eyes towards the clock on
the bedside cabinet.

'About half-past nine, I think,' he answered drowsily.
'Why? Are you hungry?'

'Only for you,' she answered mischievously, straddling
him with one slim thigh. 'Oh, Remy, I'm so glad I came
back.'

'So'm I,' he said huskily. 'I was beginning to think I'd
only imagined that you felt the same way I did.'

'And how do you feel?' Megan traced the outline of his
mouth with her forefinger. 'You never did tell me.'

'I haven't had a lot of time,' he replied ruefully. 'Besides, I thought I'd shown you.' His lips twisted. 'I love
you. Of course I love you. As I told my mother, I think I
fell in love with you that afternoon when I met you from
the plane.'

Megan caught her breath. 'You told your mother?' She
couldn't believe it.

He nodded. 'I told her we were lovers.'

'You didn't.'

'Yes, I did.' He gave a modest grin. 'She tried to tell me
she'd phoned me the night Pops died, and I was able to
state categorically that she couldn't have done or I'd have
heard her.' He grimaced. 'Whether I'd have answered the
phone is another matter.'

Megan's lips parted. 'She told me that, too.'

'She did?'

'Mmm.' Megan bit her lip. 'It was the night your grandfather died. I like to think I might have told her where I'd been if it hadn't been for the fact that I'd have been virtually calling her a liar.'

'She's called you a lot worse,' said Remy harshly. 'Oh, love! There have been so many misunderstandings.'

'But no more, hmm?' suggested Megan, bending to brush his throat with her tongue. Then she lifted her head, as if the thought had just occurred to her. 'Why did she say that anyway? Why would she say she'd phoned if she hadn't?'

Remy sighed. 'Well, I think the old man was still lucid when she got to him, and, according to her, he said both of our names.'

'So?' Megan frowned.

'Well—' Remy groaned. 'If you must know, the old man had hinted that he wanted to do something for you, and I was stupid enough to let her guess what he was thinking.'

'You don't mean—'

'Nothing disastrous,' he assured her gently. 'Just a fear on her part that if I got to speak to him Pops might tell me what he wanted to do.'

'But what did that matter?'

'She didn't know he'd already changed his will,' explained Remy. 'And she knew that if I'd heard what he wanted I'd have made sure his wishes were granted.'

Megan blinked. 'You'd have given me a piece of your share?'

'I guess,' he said in a low voice, and she snuggled her head into his shoulder.

'Oh, Remy!' She kissed him. 'Well, you can have my share now.'

'I don't want your share,' declared Remy firmly. 'The old man wanted you to have it, and unless you have some other reason for wanting rid of it, then I think you should keep it.'

Megan caught her breath. 'You don't mind?'

'For God's sake!' He was impatient. 'You never thought I did?'

'Well, your mother said—'

'My mother has a hell of a lot to answer for,' said Remy savagely. 'Megan, as far as I'm concerned you can keep your interest in the hotel with my blessing. In fact, I think you should.'

'But your mother—'

'My mother can hardly object if—if my wife owns a piece of the hotel,' he said evenly. 'That is, if this love you say you have for me encompasses marriage as well.'

Megan stared at him. 'You're proposing?'

Remy made a sardonic sound. 'It sounds like it.'

'Then in that case I might just keep my share,' she murmured teasingly. 'As a kind of reverse dowry.'

Remy scowled, pushing himself up onto his elbows. 'Does that mean you're accepting my proposal?' he asked, and she giggled.

'It sounds like it,' she said, turning his words back at him. 'I was looking for a new challenge. Helping to run a hotel sounds just the thing.'

And Remy's hoot of laughter as he bore her back into the pillows was a sign of his approval.

Nine months later, Anita's first grandchild was born.

It had been a busy nine months for Megan. First, there had been her marriage to Remy, and the exotic honeymoon they'd had in Fiji. Then a trip to England with her new husband, to transfer her share of the Chater-Cross Directory to Simon, and last, but not least, the discovery that she was pregnant, with all the excitement that entailed.

It had been a stressful time in some ways. Although Anita had been forced to accept her son's decision or risk losing contact with him altogether, she and Megan had taken some time to mend their differences. She very much resented Megan's involvement in the hotel, and there had been times when Megan feared they'd never come to terms.

Finding Megan was pregnant had made a difference. And Anita had had to concede that Remy had never looked so well. If Megan was responsible for that, she couldn't be all bad, she'd decided. And, as daughter-in-laws went, Megan was probably better than most.

For her part, Megan had found that being pregnant made her excessively tolerant, and now that she and Remy were married she could afford to overlook any little digs Anita might make. And, in time, they'd even come to an understanding, which the arrival of the newest member of the family could only endorse.

Megan's only regret was that Ryan wasn't there to see his great-grandson. And her mother, too, she reflected one sunny afternoon, when she and Remy wheeled their son's pushchair up to the cemetery.

'She'd have been so happy,' she whispered, feeling the security of her husband's arm about her as they sat in the Garden of Remembrance. 'Forgive me, Daddy, but I think the Robardses and the Crosses have made their peace at last.'

Although born in England, **Sandra Field** has lived most of her life in Canada; she says the silence and emptiness of the north speaks to her particularly. While she enjoys travelling, and passing on her sense of a new place, she often chooses to write about the city which is now her home. Sandra says, 'I write out of my experience; I have learned that love with its joys and its pains is all-important. I hope this knowledge enriches my writing, and touches a chord in you, the reader.'

Look out for Sandra Field's next book
PREGNANCY OF CONVENIENCE
out next month in Modern Romance™!

BEYOND REACH
by
Sandra Field

CHAPTER ONE

LUCY BARNES stared at the words on the board as if she was mesmerized, as if someone was offering her precisely what she wanted most of all in the world.

The individual letters were printed forcefully on a square of white cardboard with an indelible black marker. A masculine hand, she'd be willing to bet, Lucy thought with a distant part of her mind, and read the notice again.

> Wanted. Cook/crew-member for four weeks, starting immediately, on chartered 50-foot sloop. Maximum four guests. Apply at *Seawind*.

She raised her head, looking past the bulletin-board where the notice was pinned to the sunlit row of yachts moored along the cement dock. Several of them were sloops. Which one was *Seawind*? As if in response to her question, the wind from the sea lifted her hair, teasing its long mahogany-colored curls against her neck. The trade winds, she thought in pure excitement. The famous trade winds of the West Indies that she had read about in geography class, when she had been a little girl and had thought the whole world open to her... But that she had waited until now to experience. She could sail out of this harbor under their impetus. Sail among the green-clad volcanic islands that rose from a sea so blue that it made her feel like shouting for joy. She took two impetuous steps toward the dock.

5

And then she stopped. Think, Lucy. Think, she ordered herself. You've already landed yourself in one mess by acting on impulse. A royal mess. One that you're not finished with yet. Are you going to compound it by taking another leap into the unknown without considering all the consequences? Let's face it. An hour ago all you wanted to do was get on the first plane out of here and head home. Where at least you know the rules, even if you don't like them very much. Chewing her lip, she stood indecisively, the sun beating down on her face and arms, her flowered skirt blowing against her legs like a sail luffing in the wind.

How she wanted to be on that boat! Four weeks of sailing among the Virgin Islands. Four *weeks*...

Lucy thrust her hands in the pockets of her skirt, looking around her. On the other side of the road that led into the marina there was a wooden bench under a tree adorned with fat clusters of orange flowers. An oleander hedge flanked the road, its sharp-pointed leaves rustling gently, its salmon-pink blooms bobbing up and down. So much color, so much beauty... Lucy marched across the road and sat down, and knew even as she did so that this way she could see if anyone else came along to read the notice and try for the job on *Seawind*.

The slats of the bench were hard under her thighs. The dappled shade of the tree played with the flowers on her skirt. Tame flowers, she thought absently, running her fingernail along the stem of a tidy little rose. Northern flowers. Nothing like the exuberant blossoms of Road Town, capital of Tortola, largest of the British Virgin Islands. Where she, Lucille Elizabeth Barnes, now found herself.

Her money-belt dug into her waist. At least she still had that. Her money, her return ticket and her passport. Even if that was all she had. Her luggage was sitting in the guest bedroom of the villa belonging to Raymond Blogden, who had been—very briefly—her employer. And there it was likely to stay until she went back with reinforcements. Large male reinforcements. Because she wasn't going back alone, that was for sure.

Her two sisters had thought she was crazy to answer the advertisement in the Ottawa paper, while her cool, commonsensical mother had said, 'But what about the clientele you've worked so hard to build up, Lucy? Surely if you leave for a month—especially after you've just been ill for three weeks—some of them will look elsewhere? Had you thought of that?'

But the ad—rather like the printed notice on the bulletin-board across the road—had seemed like a message from heaven.

Family vacationing in British Virgin Islands requires a massage therapist for month of April. Excellent salary and comfortable quarters in hillside villa in Tortola.

The ad had been placed in March, when winter had been at its worst in Ottawa. Dirty snowbanks edging all the streets. Gray, overcast skies. Not a blossom to be seen anywhere…only the dull, dispirited green of pine and spruce trees that had been battered by frigid winds since December. No wonder she had jumped at the chance of warmth and color and sunshine! To top it all off, she'd been ill for nearly a month, miserably ill, with a flu virus that had clung to her as tenaciously as the patches of ice had clung to the front steps of her apartment building. She had craved a change of scene, a break in her routine. Something different and exciting.

Her lips twisted wryly. Well, she'd certainly gotten that. Rather more than she'd bargained for. Shutting from her mind the ugly little scene that had been played out in the spacious hallway of the hillside villa, she firmed her mouth and tried hard to think in a manner of which her elder sister Marcia would approve.

She could go to the police station, explain what a fool she'd made of herself, trust that they would help her get her luggage back and then head for the airport. Her return fare, luckily, was an open ticket, prepaid by Mr Blogden. She could fly out on the first available seat and go back to Ottawa. Because her mother was right. She, Lucy, had worked extremely hard over the last four years to build her reputation and steady list of clients, and it was irresponsible of her to jeopardize everything she had struggled so long to establish.

She got up. The police station was only a few blocks away. The worst part would be the explanation of why she had fled the Blogden villa at high noon minus her luggage. After that, she'd be home free.

She should go home. Of course she should. Even though she'd finally paid off the last of her student debts, she had her eye on a little house in the country outside Ottawa. If she was going to take on a mortgage she had to do everything in her power to ensure a regular income.

She didn't want to live in the city for the rest of her life. Her good friend Sally thought she should stay there so she'd meet more men; the countryside was devoid of eligible males, according to Sally. But, for now, Lucy was through with men. Big blond men who weren't there when she needed them. The only kind she ever seemed to be attracted to.

A woman in a colorful sarong skirt was approaching the bench. Lucy collected her wandering thoughts; this wasn't the time or the place to deal with her problems with the opposite sex. Perhaps this woman could direct her to the police station.

Then, from the corner of her eye, Lucy saw a flock of gulls rise in the sky over the moored yachts. She stood still, her gaze following the graceful curves they were inscribing against the depthless blue of the heavens, where the rays of the sun made the flashing white wings translucent. Their cries were like the cackling of a coven of witches, mocking her decision. Making nonsense of it.

Responsible. Sensible. Should. Ought. Horrible words, Lucy thought blankly. Words that had ruled her life for as long as she could remember.

The woman in the sarong skirt had already walked past her. In sheer panic Lucy made a small gesture with her hand, as though to call her back. Then her hand fell to her side. Feeling her heart pounding in her chest, she knew that somehow she had made a decision. A momentous decision. She wasn't going back. She was going to walk down the dock and find *Seawind* and do her level best to get herself signed on as cook and crew.

Rubbing her damp palms down her skirt, she fastened the image of the gulls in her mind's eye like a talisman and crossed the road. The sign was still there, its black letters every bit as forceful as she remembered them. There was an urgency behind the words, she decided thoughtfully. Whoever had written them was desperate. Good. All the more chance that he'd hire her. That she'd have four weeks at sea. Four weeks to figure out why the job she'd worked so hard to create had swallowed her up in the process. Four weeks to try and understand why she was always drawn to the wrong kind of men—handsome, blond, sexy, undependable men.

Four weeks to have fun?

She suddenly found that she was smiling. Taking a deep breath, Lucy marched down the dock.

She passed *Lady Jane*, *Wanderer*, *Marliese* and *Trident*.

Then she stopped in her tacks, feeling her heart leap in her ribcage. *Seawind* was painted white with dark green trim, her furled headsail edged in green, the bimini awning over the cockpit a matching green. She was beautiful. Wonderfully and utterly beautiful.

'Can I help you?'

Lucy jumped. A bemused smile still on her face, she turned to face the man who had seemingly appeared from nowhere. He was standing on the dock four or five feet away from her, wearing a faded blue T-shirt and navy shorts. For a moment, knocked off balance, Lucy thought she must have conjured him up out of her imagination, for he was big, blond, handsome and sexy—exactly the kind of man who had become anathema to her over the last few months. The kind she was intent on avoiding at any cost. 'Oh, no. No, thanks,' she said. 'I'm looking for the skipper of *Seawind* actually.'

'Are you applying for the job?'

None of your business, thought Lucy. 'Yes, I am.' With a sudden clutch of dismay she said, 'It's not filled, is it?'

'No. What are your qualifications?'

'I think I should leave that for the skipper, don't you?' she said sweetly.

'I'm *Seawind's* skipper.'

Then why didn't you say so in the first place? Lucy thought crossly. And why in heaven's name did you have to be big and blond and overpoweringly masculine? Smothering the words before she could speak them, she held out her hand with her most professional smile. 'I'm Lucy Barnes.'

His grip was strong, his own smile perfunctory. 'Troy Donovan. Tell me your qualifications.'

He had every right to ask; he was, after all, the skipper. She said calmly, 'Would you mind if we went on board?

I'm not used to the sun and I'm not wearing any sun-screen.' Her sunscreen, along with everything else, was back at the villa.

After a fractional hesitation he said, 'Go ahead.'

She stepped from the dock to the transom of the boat called *Seawind*, and without being asked slipped her feet out of her sandals before stepping on to the teak deck. The bimini cast a big square of shade. The wood was warm and smooth under her bare soles. She had to get this job, Lucy thought, determination coursing along her veins. She had to. Waiting until Troy Donovan had positioned himself across from her, she said, 'For nearly four years, as a teen-ager, I spent all my free time sailing. Daysailers, Lasers, and then as crew on a forty-five foot sloop not unlike this in design.'

He said edgily, 'Would you mind taking off your sun-glasses? I like to see the person I'm talking to.'

She pushed her glasses up into her hair. Her eyes were her best feature—thick-lashed and set under brows like dark wings. Beautifully shaped eyes, that hovered between gray and blue and bore tiny rust flecks that echoed the rich, polished brown of her hair. Her face had character rather than conventional prettiness: her chin pointed but firm, her nose with a slight imperious hook to it. To the discerning eye it was a face hinting at inner conflicts, for, while her lips were soft and her smile warm, a guardedness in her eyes hinted that she might withhold more than she gave.

Troy Donovan said abruptly, 'How old are you now?'

'Twenty-five.'

'Haven't you sailed since then?'

Unerringly he had found her weakest point. 'No—I've lived in Ottawa for many years. But I've never forgotten anything I learned, I know I haven't.'

'Where did you do your sailing?'

'Canada. Out of Vancouver.'

'So you don't know these waters at all?'

She tilted her chin. 'I can read charts, and I'm a quick learner.'

'Can you cook?'

Although one of Lucy's favorite haunts was the Chinese take-out across the street from her apartment building, her theory had always been that if you could read, you could cook. Somehow she didn't think that particular theory would impress Troy Donovan. But her mother had always taught her that you could do anything you put your mind to, and not even several flunked physics exams and a failed engagement had entirely destroyed Lucy's faith in this maxim. With a nasty sensation that none of her answers were the right ones, she said evasively, 'I haven't actually cooked on a boat before. But I'm sure the same general principles hold true at sea as on land.'

'What about references?'

His eyes, too, were gray. But unlike hers they were a flat, unrevealing gray, like the slate from the quarry near her old home on the west coast. With a sinking heart she said, 'I'm self-employed. But I can put you in touch with the bank manager where I do all my business dealings, and my physician would give you a personal reference.'

He looked patently unimpressed. 'You can come back tomorrow, Miss Barnes. If I haven't found anyone by then, perhaps I'll reconsider you.'

He was dismissing her. He wasn't interested. She was going to lose out on something that she craved more than breath itself. Lucy said in a rush, 'I don't think you quite understand—I love the sea! I come alive on a boat that's under full sail. I'd give everything I own for four weeks on the water…*please*.'

He had been standing with one hand wrapped around the backstay. Straightening, he ran his fingers through his hair and said, exasperated, 'I've got enough on my mind without taking on someone who's never sailed here before. I'm sorry, Miss—'

'I'll do it for nothing,' she blurted. 'Food and board, that's all.'

'Are you in trouble with the law?' he said sharply.

'No!' Her brain racing, she sought for words to convince him. 'Haven't you ever wanted anything so desperately that you'd sell your soul to get it? You don't really know why—you only know that your whole body is telling you what you want. That you're denying yourself if you ignore it.'

So quickly that she almost missed it, a flash of intense emotion crossed the carved impassivity of his features. He, like her, had pushed his sunglasses to the top of his head, where they rested in hair that was a thick, sun-streaked blond. While Lucy was something of an expert in body language and the long term effects of tension, she didn't need her expertise to realize that Troy Donovan had been under a severe stress of some kind for far too long: the toll was clearly to be seen in his shadowed, deepset eyes, his clenched jaw, the hard set of his shoulders.

He didn't answer her question. Instead he said slowly, 'So you're desperate... Why are you desperate, Lucy Barnes?'

'I—I can't tell you that. I'm not sure I know myself. But I'll work my fingers to the bone and I'll do my very best to please your guests. And I'm certainly strong enough physically for the job.'

His eyes ranged her face with clinical detachment. 'You don't look strong. You look washed out. In fact,' he continued, with almost diabolical accuracy, 'you look as

though you're not fully recuperated from some sort of illness.'

Damn the man! He'd found every chink in her armor.
Worse than that, by telling him how much she wanted the
job she'd revealed to him a part of herself that she would
have much preferred to keep private. 'I've had the flu,' she
replied shortly, and with reckless disregard for the frown
on his face plunged on, 'Why don't you take me out for
a trial run? So I can prove I'm the right person to crew
for you.'

'Give me one good reason why I should bother doing
that.'

She had nothing to lose and everything to gain. Her nails
digging into her palms, Lucy said with false insouciance,
'Your notice said you needed someone immediately.' She
looked around and gave him an innocent smile. 'And I
don't exactly see a huge line-up of other applicants.'

As his facial muscles tightened she felt a thrill of primitive victory. He said flatly, 'The trouble is, it's too early
for college students, and anyone else who's half reliable
has long ago been snapped up by the big charter compa-
nies.' He added, his gray eyes inimical, 'Let's get something straight, Miss Barnes. I'm the skipper, you're the
crew. I give the orders and you take them. Is that clear?'

Refusing to drop her own eyes, Lucy said, 'Those are
the rules on board, yes.'

'Didn't you bring a pair of shorts with you?'

A blush crept up her face. 'No. I—no.'

'Check in the forward cabin—the drawer under the port
bunk. You can borrow a pair of mine.'

In spite of herself her voice shook. 'You mean you'll
take me for a trial run?'

'Yeah…that's what I mean.'

She gave him a dazzling smile that lit up her face and

gave her, fleetingly, a true beauty. 'Thanks,' she said breathlessly. 'You won't regret it.'

Before he could change his mind, she climbed up on the foredeck, her bare feet gripping the roughened fiberglass. The forward hatch was open. With the agility of the fifteen-year-old she had once been, she climbed down the wooden ladder into his cabin. It had two bunks, one unmade; a faint, indefinable scent of clean male skin and aftershave teased her nostrils. Closing her mind to it, as she had closed her mind to the awkward truth that once again she was doing her utmost to involve herself with a big, handsome, blond man, Lucy pulled open the left-hand drawer. She scrabbled among Troy Donovan's clothes, not quite able to ignore how intimate an act this was, and shook out the smallest of the three pairs of shorts there. Dropping her skirt on the bunk, she pulled them on. They might be the smallest pair, but they were still far too big, the waist gaping, the cuffs down to her knees. After grabbing a canvas belt coiled neatly in the corner of the drawer, she cinched in the waistband and let her T-shirt fall over it.

She looked ridiculous. And somehow she wasn't so sure that that was a bad thing.

Not stopping to analyze this, Lucy climbed back on deck. A skipper from another boat had ambled over to help with the mooring lines. Troy said, giving Lucy's attire a single derisive glance, 'The ignition switch is by the radio. Then you can retrieve the anchor—these are the handsignals I'll use.' Briefly he demonstrated them. 'We'll head out under power, and once we're in the strait you can hoist the mainsail.'

She should have been nervous. But, as the diesel engine began to throb beneath her feet, Lucy felt such a purity of happiness rocket through her body that there was no room

for anything else. Again she went forward, pulling on the
gloves she found stowed by the anchor winch and glancing
back over her shoulder to catch all Troy's instructions.

The groaning of the winch and the clanking of the anchor chain made her feel fully alive, every nerve alert,
every muscle taut. As she guided the chain into its berth
she found herself remembering for the first time in many
years how at fifteen she had anticipated in hectic detail the
way such feelings might be deliciously enhanced by that
mysterious act called making love.

How wrong she'd been! Big blond men. Bah! The next
time she fell in love, Lucy decided, it was going to be with
someone short and stout and bald. Then *Seawind* began to
move, and all her concerns, her love-life included, vanished from her mind.

Within minutes she'd hauled in the fenders and stowed
them away. The dock was receding. The channel with its
red and green buoys beckoned them on. Troy said,
'There's sunscreen in the cupboard under the bar. You'd
better put some on before we get out on open water.'

Again Lucy went down the companionway steps. The
cabin was spacious, constructed from highly polished mahogany. Two couches, flanking a dining table inlaid with
marble, two padded swivel chairs, a chart cupboard and a
neatly appointed galley were all fitted in without any sense
of constriction, and again Lucy felt that shaft of unreason-
ing happiness. As she smoothed the cream over her face
and arms the deck began to lift and fall beneath her feet.

When she want back up, Troy said tersely, 'You can
hoist the mainsail now.'

She fastened the halyard to the headboard and began
hauling on the sheet, bending her knees to give herself
leverage, using every bit of her strength. Following Troy's
instructions, she tightened the winch, slotting the handle

and bracing herself against the companionway. Then she unfurled the headsail and trimmed it to a port tack. The breeze had freshened as they left the confines of Road Harbor. Troy turned off the engine and suddenly *Seawind* came to life, her bow rising and falling as she heeled into the wind that was her reason for being.

'Isn't this wonderful?' Lucy cried, giving Troy another of those brilliant smiles that held nothing in it of seduction yet was infinitely seductive.

Her shirt was molded to her body, her hair whipping about her ears. 'Ease off the headsail,' he ordered in a clipped voice.

Lucy knew enough to do as she was told. But, spoiling her exultation, a cold core of dismay had appeared somewhere in the vicinity of her gut. Did she want to sail with a skipper who so plainly hated his job? He had yet to give her anything approaching a real smile. Even now, as he checked the masthead fly and adjusted the wheel, he didn't look the least bit happy to be out on the water.

'We'll change tacks in a few minutes,' he called. 'I'll tell you when.'

This maneuver went without a hitch. Then Lucy took a stint at the wheel, delighted to find that her old intuitive sense of wind and sail had never left her. After they'd changed tacks again, Troy questioned her on the rules of the road and threw a number of hypothetical situations at her to see how she'd deal with them. Then they headed back to the harbor, running before the wind. Finally, Lucy furled the headsail and folded the mainsail on the boom, and before she knew it Troy was backing into the dock. He was, she had to admit, a more than competent skipper.

The engine died, and into the silence Lucy said tautly, 'Do I pass?'

He leaned against the folding table that ran along the

centre of the cockpit and answered her question with another. 'It's ten or eleven years since you sailed, right?'

'Ten.'

'You loved it.'

'They were the best years of my life,' Lucy heard herself
say, and felt her face stiffen with shock as the truth of her
words struck home. 'That's nuts, isn't it?' she said, more
to herself than to him. 'It can't be true…'

'It sure doesn't say much for anything that's happened
since then.'

'No…' she whispered. 'It doesn't.'

Ruthlessly Troy Donovan hurled two more questions at
her. Are you married—or living with someone?'

'No and no.' Fighting to regain control of herself—what
was it about this cold, unfriendly man that made her reveal
herself so blatantly and so unwisely?—she added, 'Are
you?'

'I'm interviewing you, not the reverse,' he retorted. 'If
you're independent, and you so clearly love sailing, why
aren't you living on the west coast again?'

'Mr Donovan,' Lucy said coldly, 'this is a hiring session. Not a counseling session.'

'The name's Troy. Why don't you answer the question?'

'Because I can't!' she flared. 'Because the reasons I live
where I do are nothing to do with you. '*I'm* not asking
you why you never smile, why you have a job that you
seem to dislike so thoroughly. Because it's none of my
business.' Her face changed. 'Please…are you going to
hire me?'

'I don't have much choice, do I?' he said unpleasantly.
'The first guests come on board the day after tomorrow
and there's a pile of work to do in the meantime. However,
I won't make you do it for nothing.' He named a salary

that was more than fair. 'I want you to take my vehicle now, and go to the grocery—'

'You've hired me—for four whole weeks!' Lucy interrupted. 'But that's terrific! Oh, I'm so excited!' Grabbing the extra fabric that flapped around her slender legs and holding it out like a skirt, she did a solemn little dance on the deck. Then she gave him a wide grin. 'I'll do the very best I can, I promise.'

Because Troy was standing in the shade he had pushed his sunglasses up again and there was in the flint-gray eyes an unquestionable, if reluctant, smile. Much encouraged, Lucy said pertly, 'So you do know how to smile. You'd be extremely handsome if you smiled properly, you know.' She bared her teeth in an exaggerated smirk. 'You should try it some time.'

'Lucy,' he said tightly, 'maybe now's as good a time as any to make something else clear. You and I are going to be living and working together in pretty close quarters for the next month. There'll be no male-female stuff between us—have you got that?'

His smile was gone as if it had never been, and the anger that she'd already sensed as a huge part of his make-up was very much in evidence. She stared right back at him. 'You're afraid I might make a pass at you?'

Biting off the words, he said, 'Of course I'm not afraid of you! But the comfort and security of the guests is our only concern for the next four weeks. You and I are co-workers—and that's all.'

She could match his anger with an anger of her own— it would be all too easy—or she could keep her sense of humor. Choosing the latter—because his pronouncement definitely had its funny side—Lucy gave a hoot of laughter. 'No problem! Now if you were five-feet-seven, bald and overweight, then you should worry. But tall, blond and handsome—nope. I'm immune. Thank you very much.'

'I don't see what's so funny,' he snarled.

'I don't think you see anything very much as funny,' Lucy said, with more truth than tact. 'And I swear that's the last remark of a personal nature that'll cross my lips today.'

He said—and Lucy was one hundred percent sure he hadn't meant to say it, 'Immunity implies exposure.'

'Indeed,' she said drily. 'I fell in love with my first blond hunk—the history teacher in school—when I was twelve, and I've been doing it ever since. When I came down here, I'd made a vow—no more blond men. Bald is beautiful. So you're quite safe, Troy Donovan. Now, what was that about groceries?'

'For their sakes, I'm glad none of them married you,' he said nastily.

Lucy flinched. She would have married Phil, who'd had wavy blond curls and had proposed to her among the tulips along the Rideau Canal when she was twenty-three years old. But Phil had met Sarah, chic, fragile Sarah, two months before the wedding, and had gone to Paris with Sarah instead of staying home and marrying Lucy. She said, almost steadily, 'If they had I wouldn't be crewing for you, would I? What did happen to your previous cook, by the way?'

'Her son crushed several bones in his foot last night. She flew to San Juan with him this morning.' His scowl deepened. 'I shouldn't have said that about marriage—I'm sorry.'

Despite her vow, a vow she fully intended to keep, Lucy was already aware that it would be much safer if she disliked Troy. He was taller than Phil, more handsome than the history teacher, and sexier by far than anyone she had ever met. 'Grocery store,' she repeated in a stony voice.

'I'll give you the keys to my Jeep. I want you to cook supper for me tonight, as if I were a guest—an appetizer to go with drinks, then dinner and dessert. This evening you can draw up menus for the next six days and I'll check them over. Our first charter is just one couple, Craig and Heather Merritt, from New York. They'll come on board the day after tomorrow—by then you've got to have the boat provisioned and spanking clean brass and woodwork polished, bathrooms spotless, beds made so they can have their choice of cabin. I'll look after ice, water supplies and the bar, and in the meantime I'll overhaul the engine and the pumps. Any questions?'

She blinked. 'No. But some time today I'll have to get my suitcase.'

'Use the Jeep,' he said impatiently.

It was by now blindingly obvious to Lucy that Troy didn't like her at all and wouldn't have hired her if he'd had any other options. In fact, he thought so little of her that he considered her unmarried state a boon to the male sex. So she might as well confirm him in his dislike; it would beat going to the police. She said in a small voice, 'I need to borrow you as well as the Jeep.'

He frowned. 'Surely you haven't got that many clothes? Storage space is limited on a boat, as you should know.'

Lucy said rapidly, 'I arrived in Tortola this morning, planning to work for a family with a villa in the hills. But when I got to the villa it very soon became plain that the family wasn't about to materialize and that the man of the house and I had radically different ideas about the terms of my employment.'

'He put the make on you?'

She grimaced. 'Yes. So I left with more haste than grace

via the nearest window, and my suitcase is still there.' Her shoulders slumped. 'I'm scared to go back there alone,' she confessed. 'But I could go to the police if you don't want to go with me, Troy. It's nothing to do with you, I do see that.'

'I'll go,' Troy said with a ferocious smile. 'This has been the week from hell, and I don't see much chance of it improving—I could do with a little action. Why don't we go there first?'

Lucy took a step backwards and said with absolute truth, 'I'm not so sure that you don't frighten me more than Raymond Blogden.'

'I almost hope he resists,' Troy said, flexing both fists.

The muscles of his forearms moved smoothly and powerfully under his tanned skin and there was such pent up energy behind his words that Lucy backed off another step, until the teak edge of the bench was hard against the backs of her knees. 'I know nothing whatsoever about you,' she muttered, 'and yet I've agreed to live on a fifty-foot boat with you for a month. Maybe *I* should be asking *you* for references.'

'You can always check with my bank manager and my physician,' he said with another fiendish smile. 'Anyway, if nothing you've done since you were fifteen has impressed you as much as sailing a Laser, you might benefit from throwing caution to the wind. Let's go.'

It was, Lucy thought, not bad advice.

And throwing caution to the winds had brought her to Tortola in the first place, hadn't it?

CHAPTER TWO

LUCY hurried below, changed back into her skirt, and five minutes later was driving west out of Road Town. Troy drove the Jeep as competently as he drove a boat; she couldn't help noticing that the muscles in his thighs were every bit as impressive as those in his arms, and forcibly reminded herself of her vow. Fortunately, in her opinion, to be truly sexy a man had to be able to laugh...

They braked for a herd of goats trotting along the road, and then for a speed bump. 'The turnoff's not far from here,' Lucy said, her pulses quickening.

The driveway to the villa wound up the hill in a series of hairpin turns; all too clearly she remembered running down them, glancing back over her shoulder in fear of pursuit. It seemed like another lifetime, another woman, so much had happened since then. And then the Spanish-style stucco villa came in sight and her heart gave an uneasy lurch. It looked very peaceful, the bougainvillaea hanging in fuchsia clouds over the stone wall, the blinds drawn against the glare of the sun.

Troy drew up in front of the door and pocketed his keys. 'Why don't you stay here?'

She had an obscure need to confront Raymond Blogden again. 'I know where the case is,' she murmured, and slid to the ground.

Troy pushed the doorbell.

The chimes rang deep in the house. A bee buzzed past Lucy's ear, and from the breadfruit trees behind the house a dove cooed monotonously. Troy leaned hard on the bell,

23

and from inside a man's voice said irritably, 'Hold on, I'm on my way.'

Lucy recognized the voice all too well, and unconsciously moved a little closer to Troy. The door swung open, Troy stepped inside without being asked and Lucy, perforce, followed. 'What the—? Who are you?' Raymond Blogden blustered. 'Get out of my—' And then he caught sight of Lucy. His recovery was instant. 'Well, well... I'm glad you came back, Miss Barnes,' he sneered. 'I was about to call the police. Breach of contract and destruction of personal property should cover it, don't you think?'

He was a big man, his black hair slicked back in the heat, his expensive white linen suit dealing as best it could with a figure whose musculature had long ago been subsumed by fat. Rings flashed on his fingers. Lucy remembered how they had dug into her arm and shivered.

Troy said with icy precision, 'I wouldn't do that if I were you, Mr Blogden—you should be thankful Miss Barnes isn't at the police station charging you with assault... Go get your case, Lucy. You're quite safe this time.'

The house was shaded and cool and very quiet. Lucy scurried down the hall to the bedroom that was to have been hers, finding her blue duffel bag exactly where she had left it on the tiled floor. She picked it up and ran back to the foyer. Raymond Blogden's complexion was several shades redder than when she had left. 'Perhaps you wouldn't mind telling me your name, young man?' he was saying, and to her horror Lucy saw his right hand inching toward his pocket.

'Troy, he's got a weapon!' she cried.

In a blur of movement Troy went on the offensive. Three seconds later Raymond Blogden's arm was twisted behind his back and Troy was saying calmly, 'Search his pocket, would you, Lucy?'

As gingerly as if a tarantula inhabited Raymond Blogden's pocket, Lucy inserted her fingers and came up with a pearl-handled knife that was disconcertingly heavy. 'We'll take that,' Troy said cheerfully. 'And since I'm rather fussy about those with whom I associate, Mr Blogden, I think I'll keep my name to myself.'

'She's nothing but a hooker,' Raymond Blogden spat. 'She dresses it up with fancy words, but that's all she is.'

'Shut up,' Troy said, very softly, 'or I'll have your hide for a car seat... Ready, Lucy?'

She was more than ready. She opened the door and heard Troy say, in a voice all the more effective for its lack of emphasis, 'If I ever see you within fifty feet of Miss Barnes again, I'll wipe the floor with that pretty white suit of yours... Goodbye, Mr Blogden.'

The sunlight almost blinded Lucy. Troy gunned the motor and surged down the driveway. He was whistling between his teeth and looked extremely pleased with himself. 'You enjoyed that,' Lucy said shakily.

'Damn right I did.' With casual skill he took the first of the turns. 'What in heaven's name made you think you could work for a man like that?'

'I never met him,' she said defensively. 'The interview was in Toronto, with his personnel adviser.'

'And what do you do that led him to call you a prostitute?'

'I'm a massage therapist,' she said. 'There are certain people who seem to think that massage has everything to do with sex and nothing to do with healing—I get so tired of all the innuendoes and off-color jokes.'

'It's a very useful profession,' Troy said mildly.

She shot him a suspicious glance. 'Do you really mean that?'

'Kindly don't equate me with the likes of that creep up in the villa!'

Only wanting to change the subject, Lucy looked distastefully at the knife in her lap. 'What am I going to do with this?'

'Keep it. In case you're ever silly enough to work for someone like him again. Naïveté doesn't pay in any job, but particularly not in yours, I would have thought.'

Troy had spoken with a casual contempt that cut Lucy to the quick. I won't cry, she thought, I won't. If I didn't cry when it happened, why would I cry now?

But the hibiscus blooms that bordered the driveway were running together in big red blobs, as red as Raymond Blogden's face. She stared fiercely out of the side window of the Jeep and felt Troy slow to a halt as they reached the highway. Then his hand touched her bare elbow. 'Don't!' she muttered, and yanked it away.

'Look at me, Lucy.'

'No!'

'Lucy…' His fingers closed on her shoulder.

She turned to face him, her eyes brimming with fury and unshed tears, her mouth a mutinous line. 'You're only the skipper when you're on the boat,' she choked. 'Let go of me!'

If anything, his hold tightened. Lines of tension scoring his cheeks, his gray eyes bleak, he said, 'I owe you another apology, don't I? You'll have to forgive me, I'm—out of touch with the female sex. You did well to get away from him; he's as nasty a piece of work as I've come across in a long time.'

A tear dripped from her lashes to fall on his wrist. 'I—I was so f-frightened.'

'Of course you were, and rightly so. That charming little object in your lap is a switchblade.' As she regarded it with horror, Troy asked, 'How *did* you get away from him?'

'He has a collection of jade in the hallway. I picked two pieces up and told him I'd drop them if he didn't stay where he was. I g-guess he didn't believe me. So I dropped one on the floor and it s-smashed. I felt terrible, but I didn't know what else to do.' She gave a faint giggle. 'You should have seen the look on his face. He said he'd paid nine thousand five hundred and forty dollars for it. Once I'd climbed out the window I put the other piece on the sill and ran for my life.'

The look on Troy's face was one she hadn't seen before. Admiration had mingled with laughter, and with something else she couldn't name but that sent a shiver along her nerves. She said fretfully, 'Let's get out of here—I want to go back to *Seawind*.'

Troy checked for traffic and turned left. 'The supermarket's going to be an anticlimax after this.'

Knowing her lack of culinary skills, Lucy wasn't so sure that he was right. Although wrestling with menus would certainly beat wrestling with Raymond Blogden. 'I need to blow my nose,' she mumbled.

Troy fumbled in the pocket of his shorts and produced a small wad of tissues. He checked them out, then said, grinning at her, 'No engine grease—I thing they're okay.'

It would be a great deal safer to dislike Troy Donovan, Lucy thought, swiping at her wet cheeks then burying her nose in the tissues and blowing hard. When he grinned like that it not only took years off his age, it put his sexual quotient right up there with Robert Redford's. She blew again, reminding herself that violence was what had put the grin there in the first place. A physical confrontation with another man. She'd do well to remember that.

She put the tissues in her skirt pocket and said, before she could lose her nerve, 'Thank you for going with me, Troy. I was dreading having to explain the whole situation to the police.'

'You're entirely welcome,' he replied. 'Haven't had as much fun in months.'

'You'd have made a good pirate,' she snapped.

'Blondbeard?' he hazarded.

Smothering a smile, she went on severely, 'You *like* violence?'

'Come on, Lucy—that was a situation straight out of a Walt Disney movie. He was the bad guy, I was the good guy coming to the rescue of the beautiful maiden, and because I was bigger than him and, I flatter myself, in better condition, right triumphed. How often in these days of moral ambiguities do we have the chance to participate in something so straightforward?'

She frowned. 'You haven't answered the question, and I don't think the grin on your face is quite as easily explained as all that.'

'Of course it's not,' he said shortly. 'Mind your own business.'

So she wasn't to be told why Troy hadn't had as much fun in months. And his tone of voice had pushed her away as decisively as if he'd strong-armed her.

Women must be after him in droves, she thought, her lips compressed. So, didn't he like women? Certainly he hadn't answered her when she'd asked if he was married or living with someone.

All her warning signals came on alert. Keep your distance. So what if he's a handsome blond? You know your weakness for them and you're not going to fall into that trap again. You're not!

But the sunlight through the windshield was glancing on the blond hair on Troy's arms, shadowing the hollow in the crook of his elbow where the veins stood out blue, and his fingers gripped the wheel with an unsettling combination of sensitivity and strength. Lucy remembered the speed with which he'd pinioned Raymond Blogden's arm behind his back, the strength with which he'd almost lifted the other man off the floor.

The knight in shining armor. The villain. And she herself cast as the beautiful maiden.

A hackneyed story. But—she knew from the languorous throb of blood through her veins—a primitive and still powerful story, nevertheless.

She'd better bring her mind back to the menus. She could handle *Seawind*; she had no fears on that score. But meals for several days for four people, one of them the steel-eyed Troy Donovan? Now that was a challenge.

Not nearly the challenge of keeping her distance from that same steel-eyed Troy Donovan.

An hour later, after paying ten dollars for a driver's license, and having been given Troy's account number at the supermarket and strict instructions to drive on the left, Lucy was on her own. All she had to do was get the supplies for tonight's dinner and come up with ideas for the next few days.

That was all, she thought wryly, standing in front of the meat counter and wishing she'd paid more attention in her grade nine home economics classes. But home economics had taken third place to sailing and the captain of the basketball team: six feet tall, blond and—by the not very demanding standards of a fourteen-year-old—incredibly sexy.

Tom Bentham. Who'd dated her, Lucy, twice and then gone steady for the next two years with petite and pretty Tanya Holiday.

Someone jostled her and Lucy brought her mind back to the present with a bump. She roamed the store, cudgeling her brain for some of her mother's recipes. Her mother combined a career as a forensic pathologist with a reputation as one of the city's most elegant hostesses, whereas Lucy's idea of fun on a Saturday night was a group of friends, a case of beer and pizza ordered from the neighborhood Italian restaurant.

She began putting things in the cart. The couple from New York no doubt had very sophisticated tastes, and Troy, she'd be willing to bet, was on a par with them. A man didn't acquire the kind of confidence he wore like a second skin by doing nothing but chartering yachts in Tortola. She'd got to impress him. She didn't think he'd fire her—he needed her too much for that—but he could make life very unpleasant for her if he chose.

Another forty-five minutes had passed before she was lugging the brown paper bags of food on board. Troy, stripped to the waist, his hands coated with grease, had the various components of a pump spread over the table in the cockpit. He gave her a preoccupied nod as she eased past him. 'I ran the engine while you were gone—so the refrigerator's cold.'

'Thanks,' she said, and disappeared into the cabin as fast as she could. His image had burned into her brain: the dent in his chin, the entrancing hollow of his collarbone, the tangled blond hair on his deep chest. It's not fair, she thought wildly. No man should look that gorgeous.

Not only gorgeous, but oblivious to his own appeal. Because Troy, she was quite sure, wasn't trying to impress her with his physique. Troy was merely oiling the pump and didn't want to get his shirt dirty.

He wasn't interested in her enough to try and impress her.

Scowling, Lucy stepped down into the galley. It was past six o'clock already. She'd better get moving. She'd decided to make a crab and cream cheese dip, chicken Wellington, a sweet potato casserole, broccoli with a hollandaise sauce, and a chocolate fondue with fruit. All of these were tried and true recipes of her mother's that she herself had made at least once. She'd mix the pastry first and put it in the refrigerator to set, then do the two sauces and get the dip in the oven.

An hour later Troy came down the stairs, shrugging into his shirt. 'How're you doing? I'm getting hungry.'

The hollandaise sauce had curdled, so she'd had to resuscitate it in the blender; she'd forgotten to get cream for the chocolate sauce and every inch of counterspace was cluttered with dirty dishes and partially cooked food. 'Fine,' she said, trying to look cool and collected when she could feel the heat scorching her cheeks and wisps of damp hair clinging to her neck.

'I wouldn't want the guests seeing the galley in such a mess,' he commented.

'Troy,' Lucy snapped, 'I haven't figured out where everything is yet, I've had a long and difficult day, and chaos is a sign of creativity. Didn't you know that?'

The anger that was so integral to him flared in response. 'Chaos can also be a sign of disorganization. Didn't *you* know *that*?'

It had been a more than difficult day, and Lucy suddenly realized she was spoiling for a fight. Making a valiant effort to control her temper, she said, 'The crab dip will be done in fifteen minutes, and I'll serve it to you in the cockpit.'

'I'm serious, Lucy… People come on these cruises to relax, to get away from it all. The state the galley's in is totally unacceptable.'

She should count to ten. She should smile politely and ask him if he'd like a drink. Lucy banged a saucepan on the plastic counter and cried, 'You may be the skipper— but I'm the cook! The galley's *my* territory. Not yours. I'd appreciate your keeping that in mind.'

He leaned forward, his voice honed to an edge as deadly as the pearl-handled switchblade. 'Don't think I'm so desperate for crew that I can't fire you.'

'Go ahead!' she stormed. 'I dare you.'

Her eyes, fueled by rage, were the turbulent blue of the sea under gray skies. In her free hand she was clutching a butcher-knife she'd been using to chop onions; her breast was heaving under her blue knit shirt, her whole body taut with defiance.

Troy said scathingly, 'You're behaving like a ten-year-old.'

'At least I'm capable of emotion!'

'Just what do you mean by that?'

'I mean you're as cold as the refrigerator. You're frozen, solid as the block of ice in the—'

A man's voice floated down the companionway. 'Ahoy, *Seawind*… Anyone on board?'

Troy's muttered profanity made Lucy blink. He said furiously, 'Don't think we're through with this—because we're not. I'm the boss on this boat, Lucy, and you'd better remember it.' Then he turned on his heel and took the steps two at a time. She heard a stranger's jovial laugh and then the murmur of masculine conversation.

For two cents she'd follow Troy up those steps, march

down the dock and leave him in the lurch. Let him find another crew-member! What did she care? One of the reasons she'd become self-employed was so she wouldn't have to deal with dictatorial male bosses. Because one thing was clear to her: what she had earlier labeled as Troy's confidence wasn't confidence at all. It was arrogance. Downright arrogance.

High-handedness. Despotism. Tyranny.

The buzzer rang on the stove. The crab dip was as perfectly browned as any her mother had ever made, and smelled delicious. Balancing it on top of one of the gas elements on the stove, Lucy heaved a heavy sigh. Tyrant though Troy was, she still wanted to sail out of the harbor the day after tomorrow. She wanted to hear the slap of waves under the prow and feel the helm quiver with responsiveness. She wanted to swim in the turquoise waters of a coral reef...

She reached for the packages of crackers she'd bought, and five minutes later was climbing the steps with a platter on which the crackers and some celery stalks were artistically arranged around the dip. 'Hello,' she said, with a friendly smile at the man sitting across from Troy.

'Jack Nevil,' he said bluffly, getting to his feet. 'Skipper of *Lady Jane*... Is this for us? You've lucked out, Troy.'

Lucy smothered a smile. Troy said with a dryness that wasn't lost on her, 'I sure have... Want a beer, Jack? Or something stronger?'

'A beer'd be great...and one for the lady?'

'The name's Lucy,' she said limpidly. 'I'd love one; it's been pretty hot in the galley.'

Her eyes, wide with innocence, met Troy's. He was quite aware of her double meaning, she saw with some satisfaction. He said blandly, 'Jack, who was that chemist who won the Nobel prize—Prigogine? His thesis was that at a state of maximum disequilibrium, a system will spontaneously create its own order—I think that's Lucy's theory of cooking.'

'If this dip is anything to go by, the theory works,' Jack said enthusiastically. 'Have a seat, Lucy.'

'Oh, no,' she said sweetly, 'I'd better get back to work. Troy's a hard taskmaster.'

'Only that I have a preference for eating before midnight,' Troy responded equally amiably. 'Thanks, Lucy…see you later.'

And who had won that round? Lucy wondered as she went back to the steaming-hot galley. If she were an optimist she could call it a tie.

But Jack Nevil and her mother's crab dip had probably saved her from being fired.

Two hours later Lucy twirled the last strawberry in the chocolate sauce and took another sip of the German dessert wine in her glass. She'd drunk rather more wine than was good for her in the course of the meal. Maybe to hide the fact that Troy had spoken very little as they ate. Or maybe so she'd have the strength to face all the dirty dishes stashed below. 'What a glorious night,' she said soulfully.

Jack had left before dinner, having demolished the crab dip and three beers. She and Troy were eating on deck, where the smooth black water was illumined by a three-quarter moon and stars glimmered in the blackness overhead. It was blissfully, blessedly cool.

'That was an excellent meal, Lucy,' Troy said brusquely. 'But entirely too elaborate—I can't have you spending all day in the galley when you'll be needed out on deck.'

She took a gulp of wine. 'Is that what's called damning with faint praise?' she said provocatively.

His eye-sockets were sunk in shadow, his irises reflecting the harbor's obsidian surface. 'And that's another thing,' he said, in the same hard voice. 'You and I can fight like a couple of tomcats from sun-up till sundown tomorrow. But when the Merritts come on board there'll be no more fighting. We'll get along even if it kills us.'

To her horror she heard herself say, 'You mean you'll actually be nice to me?'

He banged his clenched fist so hard on the table that the cutlery jumped. 'I've never in my life met a woman as contentious as you! Don't you ever let up?'

'I wouldn't be so cranky if you'd act like a human being,' she retorted. 'It's because you're so—so unreachable.'

'Unreachable is exactly what I am, and what I intend to remain,' he answered grimly. 'I said no male-female stuff and I meant it. And don't, if you value living, ask why.'

Any flip reply Lucy might have made died on her lips, because there was genuine pain underlying Troy's voice and the moonlight lay cold along his tightly held jaw and compressed lips. He had a beautiful mouth, she thought unwillingly. Strongly carved yet with the potential for tenderness. What had made him so unreachable? Had filled him to the brim with suppressed rage?

Whatever it was, it was his secret. Nothing to do with her.

Swallowing the strange bitterness this conclusion caused her, Lucy let her thoughts march on. There was more than an element of truth in everything Troy had said. The meal *had* been too elaborate. And people didn't pay high rates for a charter to spend their time listening to the crew fight all day. She downed the last of her wine and said forthrightly, 'I'll prepare simpler meals from now on. And I'll do my best not to lose my temper again.' She gave him a small smile. 'Or at least not more than once a day.'

His mouth softened infinitesimally. 'I should have told you there's a very good delicatessen on one of the back-streets—you can buy a lot of stuff already prepared and freeze it. Quite a lot of it's West Indian style, so the guests enjoy it. Plus, it would make life much easier for you.'

'Oh. That's a good idea.' And because Troy's voice, like his face, had gentled, and because she was alone on the deck of a yacht in the tropics by moonlight with a hand-some blond man, she babbled, 'I'm going to give the galley a good cleaning tomorrow before I bring in the sup-plies. The brass lamps and fittings are tarnished, so I'll polish them, and then I'll—'

'It's okay, Lucy... If there's one thing I've learned today it's that you're a hard worker. Why don't you go to bed now? You must be exhausted. You can take one of the cabins downstairs and I'll sleep up at the bow.'

'I think you just gave me a compliment,' Lucy said dazedly. 'A real one.'

'I believe I did. Off you go.'

Struggling to collect her wits, Lucy muttered, 'I'm going to do the dishes first, they won't take long.'

He stood up. 'I'll give you a hand.'

As he stretched lazily, a bare strip of skin showed itself between his waistband and his T-shirt. She dragged her gaze away. 'You don't have to do that.'

'Two confrontations with Raymond Blogden today, along with a yelling match with me, is more than enough for one woman. Come on, let's get at them.'

'You can be so darn nice when you forget about being angry,' Lucy blurted, then, before he could reply, ran on, 'I know—I shouldn't have said that. My sisters always tell me I speak before I think, and they're right. They're right about nearly everything,' she added gloomily, 'it's very depressing. But it seems such a waste when you could be nice all the time.'

'You'd be bored,' Troy said. Then he raised one brow in mockery as he gathered the dessert dishes from the table. 'Besides, I was just practising for when our guests arrive.'

And that, thought Lucy, was that. After picking up the leftover chocolate sauce, which now looked sickeningly sweet, she followed Troy down the stairs.

CHAPTER THREE

LUCY woke at daylight. She knew exactly where she was as soon as her eyes opened. On board *Seawind* in Road Harbor. With four weeks ahead of her to cruise the Virgin Islands.

She jumped out of bed, filled with the tingling anticipation she had felt as a little girl every Christmas Eve. Except that this time she was the one who'd given herself a gift. The gift of time, she thought fancifully. What better gift was there?

Although even Christmas Eve hadn't always been trustworthy, she remembered, her hands faltering as she pulled on her darkest shorts. Her father had died when she was three, and confidently, at three, four and five, Lucy had requested Santa Claus to bring him back. Only when her elder sister Marcia had laughed at her efforts had she ceased to hope that she would find him early in the morning under the Christmas tree among all her other presents.

She gave her head a little shake. She rarely thought of her father now. And she had a lot to do today. Reaching up to look out of the open port, she saw that the sun was already glinting on the water, and again she was swept with excitement. When she went to the supermarket today she'd leave a message on her mother's answering machine, explaining her change of plans, then she was free. All she had to do was work hard and have fun.

And keep her temper with Tory Donovan.

She could handle Troy. She was through with big blond men.

Just as everything had gone wrong the day before, today the gods were with Lucy. Before she left for town, the galley, the brass and the woodwork were all gleaming with cleanliness. Near the delicatessen she found a spice shop that sold a series of recipe books with all sorts of suggestions for easy and tasty meals and aperitifs—just what she needed. She bought the first volume and several bottles of mixed spices, had a lemonade in a little restaurant and drew up her menus, then hit the deli and the supermarket.

It gave her great pleasure to stow everything away in her tidy galley. In the tiny microwave over the gas stove she heated *rotis* for lunch—West Indian sandwiches stuffed with curried chicken and vegetables, that tasted delicious washed down with ginger ale. Troy had been scrubbing the deck and polishing the winches; they ate in a silence that she was quite prepared to call companionable. When she'd cleared away the dishes, she tackled the three cabins that led off the saloon.

She was down on her knees wiping the floor of the aft cabin's shower when Troy spoke behind her. 'Let's take a break, Lucy.'

She glanced round, swiping at her hair with the back of her hand. 'How does it look?'

'You've done wonders,' he said.

His praise gave her a warm glow of pride. 'I've had a ball, actually—the woodwork and the fittings are all so beautiful that it's a pleasure to clean them. Much more fun than cleaning my apartment.' She sat back on her heels, stripping off her rubber gloves. 'What was that about a break?'

'I have to run the engine a couple of hours every day to keep the refrigerator and freezer cold. I thought we might head for Peter Island and have a swim. What have you got left to do?'

'The saloon floor. Make the beds and put out the towels.' Lucy tilted her head to one side. 'You did say swim, didn't you?'

She had managed to coax from him one of his reluctant smiles—a smile that, oddly, hurt something deep within her. He looked at her bucket and sponge. 'I hate to tear you away from something you're enjoying so much.'

'For you, I'll make the sacrifice.' She got to her feet. 'Will you show me how to snorkel?'

He looked surprised. 'You don't know how?'

'Troy, I've never been further south than Boston in my entire life. Everything down here's new to me.'

Her forehead was beaded with perspiration and there was a smudge of dirt on her chin, but her eyes were dancing and her smile was without artifice. Troy said slowly, 'You're making up for lost time, aren't you?'

She wouldn't have expected such discernment—or even interest—from him. Her heart beating a little faster, she said, 'I guess I am. These four weeks seem like time out. A break from my normal life. I—I seem to have lost my sense of direction somewhere along the way.'

As though the words were torn from him, he said, 'You're not alone there.' Then he raked his fingers through his hair. 'Let's pull up anchor and get out of here.'

No more revelations, Lucy realized, and knew better than to push. 'I'll dump the bucket and be right there,' she said. But for a moment she stood still, watching him stride across the saloon and up the steps. His leg muscles were those of a runner, but what was he running from? And how had he lost his way?

Once they were anchored off the beach at Peter Island, Lucy went below to put on her swimsuit. She had bought it—acting on another of her impulses—in the middle of a hailstorm in March. It was, in direct consequence, a bright red and quite minimal bikini. If she'd known about Troy Donovan, she thought, trying without success to cover even a fraction of her cleavage, she'd have purchased a staid one-piece. In an innocuous shade of beige. She pulled a white sport shirt over the bikini and went up on deck.

But the wind instantly whipped the shirt away from her body. As Troy turned around, about to say something, his jaw dropped, and he gaped at her as though someone had hit him hard in the chest. She was tall and full-breasted, her hips ripely curved, her long legs tapering to narrow ankles and feet. As an adolescent Lucy had hated her body, for she had shot up at the age of thirteen, towering over the boys in her class yet having to endure their covert and not-so-covert sniggers at her generous breasts. She had wanted to be tiny and delicate and feminine, like Tanya Holliday.

In the intervening years she had more or less made peace with her build. But right now she felt absurdly self-conscious, as though she were fourteen again. Grabbing at the shirt, she yanked it over what felt like an immense expanse of bare flesh.

This gave her something to do. Because if Troy was staring at her, she was struggling hard not to return the compliment. Under his taut belly his dark green trunks sat low on his hips; any attempt to regard his torso as nothing but neatly delineated groups of muscles—like the diagrams in her anatomy text—was a miserable failure. She said weakly, 'Where's the snorkeling gear?'

He snapped his mouth shut, knelt down and began hauling fins and masks out of a storage hatch. The wind played with his thick, unruly hair. Lucy quickly found a pair of fins that fit, then Troy passed her a mask. 'Try this one.

Keep your hair out of the way—when you breathe in through your nose, the mask should stay airtight.'

The first mask was too big. As she pulled on the second Troy came closer, checking the seal. 'That looks good,' he said. 'You put this piece in your mouth and clamp your teeth over it. If water gets in the tube, throw your head back and breathe out hard.'

He was standing so close to her that Lucy was having difficulty breathing at all. Fighting to subdue her pleasure in the way Troy towered over her, she nodded her understanding of his instructions.

'The reef's to our left,' he added. 'I'm going to dive down and check that the anchor's holding, then we'll head over there.'

He pulled on his own fins and slid off the transom of the boat into the water. Lucy shed her shirt and followed with rather less grace; with her fins flapping in front of her and an undignified splash she fell forward into the sea. But she soon discovered that the fins added immeasurably to her speed, and by the time Troy surfaced with a thumbs-up sign she was over the reef. She dunked her mask into the water and gave a gasp of delight.

Below her in the clear turquoise water big purple sea-fans waved in the current, and a coral that looked like nothing so much as ostrich feathers swayed lazily back and forth. Patterns of sunlight danced on the white sand. Through the prongs of a hard coral shaped like antlers a school of fish darted; when they turned as one, their scales flashed with the iridescence of sapphires. Lucy opened her mouth to tell Troy about them, swallowed seawater as bitter as Epsom salts and raised her face, choking.

Immediately, it seemed, Troy was beside her. 'You okay?'

She spat out the water and the mouthpiece. 'The fish—they're like jewels!'

His own mouthpiece was hanging by his ear and he had pushed his mask up. 'Indeed. But when you're underwater you'd better keep your mouth shut—unless you want an early supper.'

'Yuk,' she said. 'I never did like sushi.'

'And, seriously, don't brush against any of the corals. Fire coral can sting you quite badly.'

'I won't.' Flashing him another smile before she adjusted her equipment, she struck out again. There were fish everywhere: black, yellow, silver, red and blue, small and large, striped, spotted and lined. Fascinated, she hovered over the shelves and crenellations of the corals, then Troy gestured to her and she swam over to him, forgetting how little of her body the bikini covered, ignorant of how gracefully she moved, her limbs all pale curves, her cleavage shadowed. Following his pointed finger she saw three small pink squid fluting through the water, their huge eyes, like silver coins, riveting her gaze.

Impetuously she surfaced again, shoving her mask away from her face. 'Thank you *so* much for bringing me here, Troy!' she sputtered. 'It's unimaginably beautiful—like another world.' But then her voice died away. 'What's the matter?'

He said with a savagery that frightened her, 'You're the one who's unimaginably beautiful.' The flat of his hand hard against her back, he pulled her closer, the water swirling between them. Then he bent his head and kissed her wet lips, his mask bumping against hers, his arm heavy across her shoulders.

Her fear vanished. It was as though all the wonders she had just seen, all the brilliant hues of the fish and of the corals, had exploded in her body in a wild kaleidoscope

of color, and for a split second that was outside of time
Lucy was consumed by an all-powerful and all-consuming
happiness. But, as suddenly as he had seized her, Troy
thrust her away, his heavy breathing overriding the splash
and ripple of the sea. He looked as though he hated her,
she thought blankly, and could not, for the life of her, think
of a word to say.

'We'd better go back,' he grated. 'We've still got a lot
to do.' As if he was being pursued by sharks, he began
stroking toward *Seawind* in a strong overarm crawl.

Lucy, barely remembering to tread water, stayed where
she was. She was about as adept a judge of character as
she was a gourmet cook, she decided. Never, in a thousand
years, would she have anticipated that kiss.

Troy hated her. So why had he kissed her?

Or did he hate her because he'd kissed her?

She had no answers to either question, and she could
see him hauling himself up on *Seawind's* stern. She didn't
think he'd leave her behind. But then what did she really
know about the man called Troy Donovan?

Painfully, pitifully little.

Once she'd washed the salt water from her body with the
transom hose, Lucy winched in the anchor and disappeared
below to get changed. She was pegging her wet swimsuit
to the lifeline that ran round the hull when Troy finally
spoke to her. 'You can call that kiss temporary insanity or
insatiable lust or just plain curiosity…I really don't care.
I assure you it won't happen again.'

There was as little feeling in his voice as if he were
discussing the lunch menu. Carefully not looking at him,
because if she did she wasn't sure she'd be answerable for
the consequences, Lucy went below decks and started
washing and buffing the mahogany floor of the saloon.

When they reached the harbor, she went to the forepeak and used the agreed hand signals to anchor *Seawind*. No need for conversation there. Afterward, she finished the floor, made two of the three beds with fresh sheets and threw together a shrimp salad for supper—activities that kept her busy and out of Troy's way, but did nothing to tame the tumult of emotion in her breast.

She was bent over the refrigerator, wondering where she'd hidden the bottles of dressing, when a sixth sense told her Troy had come downstairs and was watching her. Feeling her scalp crawl, not looking at him, she said, 'Ten minutes and we can eat.' As she moved two blocks of cheese to one side she saw the yellow caps on the dressing and pulled the bottles out. 'Good, there they are.'

'What the devil happened to your arms?' he demanded.

She put the bottles on the counter and clicked the hatch shut. 'What are you talking about?' she said, glowering at him.

He stepped on to the narrow strip of floor between the stove and the sinks, crowding her into the corner. 'Those bruises—how did you get them?'

Craning her neck, Lucy for the first time saw the ugly purple blotches high on the backs of her arms. Involuntarily she shivered, knowing exactly how she'd gotten them. 'Blogden—when he grabbed me, his rings dug in.'

Troy's epithet was unprintable. But Lucy wasn't in the mood to be impressed. 'I wonder what *his* motive was,' she said shrewishly. 'Temporary insanity, plain curiosity or insatiable lust?'

There was a small, deadly silence. 'Are you comparing me to him?'

As clearly as if it had just happened Lucy remembered how Troy's kiss had filled her with a joy as many-hued and vivid as the fish, and how everything he had done since then had repudiated that joy. She was honest enough to know she was as angry with herself as with him—for she'd been the one to feel the joy, she who had sworn off tall, blond men. She didn't want to fall in love again, it hurt too much and got her nowhere. She said, 'I am, yes. Although overall I'd have to say he showed more emotion than you.'

'Don't push me, Lucy.'

'Why did you kiss me, Troy?'

'I gave you three good reasons.'

'I want the real one.'

'I already gave it to you,' he said with a wolfish smile. 'Insatiable lust.'

Her knees were trembling. Bracing them against the cupboard door, Lucy said, 'You're the one who said no male-female stuff between us.'

'Haven't you ever wanted something—or in this case, someone—so badly your whole body told you what it wanted?' he quoted mockingly.

Lucy paled. 'You know what's so horrible about all this?' she demanded, with sudden, searing honesty. 'I liked you kissing me. I wanted you never to stop.' She dashed at the tears that had filled her eyes. 'What a stupid idiot I am…because you're nothing but a cold-blooded manipulator. You wouldn't recognize an emotion if you fell over it.'

If her vision hadn't been obscured by tears she might have seen Troy flinch. But all he said was, 'So you're not quite as immune as you thought you were. Maybe we should sleep together, Lucy—then you could add me to your total. One more blond hunk to notch in your belt. Or wherever it is you keep tally.'

There was plenty of emotion in his voice now, and all

of it was anger. 'No, thank you,' she said, as steadily as she could. 'I'm a little more discriminating than that.'

'That wasn't the impression I got.'

That he should so misread her hurt horribly. She wasn't one bit immune, she thought wretchedly, and knew she had to end this. Turning, she cut three slices of bread with a reckless disregard for safety, plastered them with butter, put two on Troy's plate and one on hers, then put the butter back in the refrigerator. How could she possibly have woken this morning feeling as if it was Christmas Day? More to the point, how on earth was she going to get through the next four weeks?

'I'm going to eat in my cabin,' she said, picking up her plate of salad and a glass of water. 'Kindly get out of the way— I already told you the galley was my turf.'

But Troy stayed where he was, blocking the narrow little passageway with his body. 'You said you liked me kissing you. But that wasn't because it was *me*. It was because I'm big and blond and male. Admit it, Lucy—you've stereotyped me from the first minute you saw me.'

With a cold clutch at her heart Lucy knew his words had touched a nerve. Were they true? Was he just one more in the succession of blond men she had fallen in love with? Fruitlessly. Quite often unrequitedly. And most certainly, except for Phil, chastely.

But compulsively. That was the awful part about it. She didn't seem to have any choice.

Taking her courage in her hands, she met his eyes. 'I don't want that to be true,' she said in a low voice. 'I'm trying to break that pattern.'

'I'd say you're a long way from succeeding,' he rasped.

A sudden wave of exhaustion swept over her, the same exhaustion that had so debilitated her while she'd had the

flu. She stared hard at the front of his shirt. 'I'm tired,
Troy. Please move so I can sit down and eat.'

'The only time you call it quits is when you don't want
to face the truth—right, Lucy?'

She bit her lip, and said with sudden fierceness, 'Don't
push your luck! I can leave *Seawind* you know. Anytime.
And then who'll you get to cook for you?'

'You can't leave,' he said levelly, 'anymore than I can
fire you. We're committed to the next four weeks on *Seawind*—and to each other. And don't ask me what I mean
by that because I don't have a clue.' He backed up so that
she could leave the galley and added testily, 'You'd better
go to bed early tonight. It's not much of an advertisement
for a cruise boat if the cook looks like she's on the verge
of collapse.'

He wasn't worried about her, Lucy thought bitterly,
crossing to her cabin and ostentatiously closing the door
behind her. He was only worried about what his customers
would think.

At least she and Troy wouldn't be able to fight while
the Merritts were on board.

Lucy wasn't sure what she'd expected of her first set of
guests. Two city sophisticates in designer cruise wear?
Frazzled by high-powered careers and bored by anything
less than the spectacular?

The reality couldn't have been more different. Heather
Merritt was in her early thirties, a pretty and slightly overweight blonde who was openly delighted with *Seawind*;
her husband Craig, also a little heavier than was healthy
and perhaps ten years older than his wife, was a very or-
dinary-looking man until he smiled at his wife—his face
then was so suffused with love that Lucy was moved.

She and Troy took them down to the saloon, offering

them their choice of the three cabins. 'How beautiful everything is!' Heather exclaimed, taking in the basket of fruit that Lucy had arranged that morning, the neat shelf of paperbacks over the couch and the shiny mahogany fittings that were polished to perfection. 'Isn't it lovely, Craig?'

'Fantastic,' he said, squeezing his wife's hip.

She blushed. 'We'll take one of the two front cabins. Is that all right, darling?'

'Perfect.'

'The aft cabin has a slightly bigger bed,' Lucy said.

Heather's blush deepened. 'Oh, we like to cuddle up,' she said artlessly. 'We're on our honeymoon.'

'Married a week ago,' Craig said fondly, nuzzling his wife's neck. 'Let's take the cabin on the right, honey. You were standing to the right of that table in the library the very first time I saw you.'

Heather wound her arms around her husband's neck. 'I didn't know you remembered that!'

'I've never forgotten anything about you,' he declaimed, and kissed her with more ardor than was perhaps appropriate.

Troy muttered, 'I'll be on deck, Lucy, if you need me,' and made his escape.

When Heather had unwound herself from the embrace, Lucy ushered them both into the cabin, showing them the towels and the storage space and demonstrating how to pump the head and the shower. 'If you want to use both forward bathrooms, you're welcome to...and you might want to keep your bags in the other cabin, too. I think Troy plans to go to Peter Island for lunch, so you could come up on deck anytime you're ready.'

The Merritts did come up on deck, twenty minutes later. Heather's cheeks were rosy and Craig looked very pleased with himself; Lucy was quite sure they hadn't just been unpacking their bags.

Her main job at this juncture, Troy had informed her that morning, was to set their guests at ease; he wasn't planning to hoist the sails until after lunch, so she had nothing else to do. Since part of Lucy's success at massage was her genuine warmth toward people, she enjoyed chatting with the Merritts, pointing out various features of the boat as she did so.

'The agenda's totally up to you,' Troy intervened. 'Night-life, dining at resorts, beaches, swimming, hiking… Whatever you'd like to do most.'

'I want to dance to a steel drum band,' Heather said promptly.

'We can do that on Virgin Gorda—probably tomorrow night.'

'Snorkel,' Craig added.

'Right after lunch. I'll make sure you have the chance to swim with sea turtles, too.'

'I think we'd rather eat on board than go to fancy resorts, wouldn't we, darling?' Heather said.

'Whatever you want, babe,' her husband said, toying with the nape of her neck.

'Have you snorkeled before?' Troy asked smoothly.

'I have,' Craig replied. 'You haven't, have you, Heather?'

'You can teach me,' Heather said.

They exchanged a look so charged with sexuality that Lucy found she was the one who was blushing. She had worried about having to awaken the jaded appetites of a pair of New Yorkers; she hadn't anticipated that their appetites, so obviously carnal, might be more than she could handle. Glad of the cool wind on her cheeks, she remarked, 'Did you meet in New York?'

For the next ten minutes the Marritts regaled them with the story of their romance, from their meeting in a branch library in Manhattan to the first part of their honeymoon in a hotel at the west end of Tortola. 'A pool surrounded by palm trees,' Heather said ecstatically. 'It was wonderful... New York had more snow this winter than the last five years.'

'Remember the snowstorm that marooned us in your apartment for two days?' Craig murmured.

Heather giggled, Craig rested her fingers on his thigh and started playing with them, and Troy kept his gaze on the hills of Peter Island. He anchored in the same spot where he and Lucy had snorkeled yesterday. Where he had kissed her, Lucy thought, suddenly not able to bear watching the Merritts for a moment longer. 'Lunch in ten minutes,' she said briskly, and vanished below.

They ate on deck. Lucy served *rotis* with salad, chutney and hot sauce from the spice shop, following this with sliced mango and melon decorated with strawberries. The Merritts relished everything, and insensibly she relaxed. While she cleaned up the dishes in the galley, Troy fitted their guests with snorkeling gear. 'Are you going swimming, Lucy?' he called down to her.

'No, I'm going to make dessert for tonight.'

'Okay, I'll leave you in charge.'

A few minutes later, after the Merritts had changed, she heard the dinghy chugging away from the stern. She had *Seawind* to herself, she thought, feeling the tension that Troy seemed to cause by his very presence slowly seep from her body. She mixed a crumb crust, pressed it in a pie plate and put it in the oven, then soaked gelatin and began cracking ice to make the filling for a rum chiffon pie—tasks that soothed her further. Because, back home in Ottawa, she had chosen not to share her apartment, she was used to spending time every day by herself. It was nice to be alone now. Humming to herself, she separated four eggs and beat the whites into frothy peaks.

Had Troy been right when he'd accused her of not seeing him for himself? Her hands stilled. Had he—and this hadn't occurred to her before—been hurt that she'd bracketed him with the other men who'd passed through her life? Just another blond hunk? One more to add to the list?

Not hurt. Not Troy.

She added sugar and a generous measure of West Indian rum to the egg whites. The crust was cooked, so she put it to cool, and while she was waiting mixed cream cheese with sour cream and mayonnaise as the base of the crab dip she planned to serve with drinks before dinner. As long as she could stay organized she wouldn't get in a panic, as she had the night of the curdled hollandaise.

What had Troy meant when he'd said they were committed to each other? *Could* she quit?

She wasn't sure she could. And what did that mean?

CHAPTER FOUR

THE next twenty-four hours tested Lucy's fortitude to the limit. While she liked the Merritts, both individually and as a couple, she could cheerfully have wished their sex-lives to the bottom of Sir Francis Drake Channel. They were never more than three feet away from each other, they were frequently entwined, and she was quite sure that if she and Troy hadn't been there they'd have made love in the galley, the cockpit and the dinghy.

The saloon was by no means soundproof. She had gone to bed to the sound of enthusiastic coupling and had woken in the night to hear Heather moaning her husband's name in what was clearly a state of ecstasy. The only one of the blond hunks with whom Lucy had gone to bed had been Phil, when she had been engaged to him; it had been, in general, a pleasant enough experience, but she couldn't for the life of her recall making, or even wanting to make, sounds so redolent of unbridled passion.

If she were to make love with Troy, though… And here Lucy's thoughts had slammed to a stop.

The worst part about having the Merritts aboard was the way it made Lucy achingly and constantly aware of Troy: the breadth of his shoulders in the tank top he had worn all day, the neat set of his ears, the shining cleanliness of his hair, blown dry by the wind, even the way his high-arched feet clung to the companionway steps. His feet, for goodness' sake! When had she ever noticed a man's feet before? When had the sight of a man's pulse beating in the hollow of his wrist made her weak with longing?

Never.

The trouble was, she was almost sure Troy reciprocated every one of her feelings. He'd brushed against her last night when she was serving dinner, and had backed off as if he'd put his hand on the blue flames of the gas stove rather than on her elbow. When they had all been swimming, late yesterday afternoon, she'd caught him staring at the swell of her breasts in her red bikini as though he'd never seen a woman before.

Tonight all four of them were supposed to go dancing. Craig and Heather would no doubt spend the evening wrapped in each other's arms on the dance-floor. What would she and Troy do?

She mixed a rum punch decorated with cherries and pineapple for Craig and a pina colada for Heather and put them on a tray, along with the crab dip and crackers. Up on the deck Craig had his arm around Heather, whose head was resting on his shoulder. Troy had his back to them, lighting the barbecue that was attached to the stern rail; he was going to grill fillet steaks for dinner. 'Beer, Troy?' Lucy asked.

'Sure…thanks.'

She climbed to the cooler near the hatch of his cabin and took out a can of beer, and when she got back to the cockpit, opened it. Heather was feeding Craig a cracker laden with dip, her tongue licking her lips, her gaze locked with his. Lucy's eyes skidded away and met Troy's. As she passed him the can of beer their hands touched, and she felt a jolt of naked desire lance along her nerve-endings. She snatched her hand back and saw the same raw need flare in the slate gray of his irises, lustrous as sunlight falling on the smooth surface of a rock.

She fled back to the galley, to the ordinary demands of baking potatoes and wrapping up onions brushed with curry powder to go on the barbecue. She could hear music playing in one of the boats moored near *Seawind*... Would Troy dance with her tonight at the yacht club? Maybe he was no more prepared to risk that than she was.

She was mixing the salad dressing when Troy came down to get the barbecue sauce. He crouched down to rummage through the cupboard; she could have run her fingers through his hair. She said brightly, 'How long before you're ready?'

'Fifteen minutes.' He gave a grunt of satisfaction and stood up. 'You've got flour on your face,' he added, reaching out one finger to wipe her cheekbone.

Unconsciously Lucy swayed toward him. Very deliberately he put the bottle of sauce on the counter, rested his palms on her shoulders and drew her closer. She knew he was going to kiss her; with the softness of her lips, the pliancy of her body, she welcomed him. And then she was drowning in a host of sensations new to her: his height, the burning heat of his mouth moving against hers, the strong clasp of his fingers and the frantic beating of her own heart.

'Oh...sorry,' said Heather. 'I didn't mean to interrupt.'

Lucy froze, Troy wrenched his mouth free and Heather gave a coy giggle. 'You two are so discreet,' she said admiringly. 'We didn't even realize you were a number.'

'We're not!' Lucy gasped.

'Discretion's my middle name,' Troy drawled.

'There's nothing to be discreet about,' Lucy flared.

'Didn't look that way to me,' Heather said.

'Nor me,' Troy murmured, and with a reckless gleam in his eye laid claim to Lucy's lips again.

She tried to push him away. But his chest was as hard as the teak in the cockpit, and as his tongue flicked against her teeth her traitorous hands crept up to busy themselves in his hair. She had, she thought dimly, been longing to do that for the last three days. From a long way away she heard the stairs creak; Heather, presumably, was leaving. Only then did Troy release her, taking his time about it, drinking in the feverish glitter in her eyes, the patches of pink staining her cheeks. He said, '*That* feels better,' picked up the barbecue sauce and followed Heather up the stairs.

Lucy sat down hard in the nearest swivel chair. She'd done it again, she thought, horrified. She'd fallen under the spell of a big, blond man. How *could* she have?

The scent of grilled meat drifted to her nostrils. After kissing her until she'd thought she'd die with pleasure, Troy was now barbecueing as if nothing had happened. Not sure whether she wanted to laugh, cry, or stamp her bare feet on the polished floor, she somehow, in the next fifteen minutes, managed to mix the salad dressing and lay the table in the saloon with a pretty green cloth and an array of wine-glasses and cutlery. If only to keep thought at bay, she folded flowered napkins into shapes like little sailboats and hibiscus blooms.

Cute, Lucy. Really cute.

Rather to her surprise, all the food was ready at once and it all tasted delicious. Troy poured a more than respectable burgundy and kept the conversation flowing on such impersonal topics as the history, wildlife and music of the Virgin Islands. Afterward Lucy cleaned up the galley, banging the dishes around and splashing the water as much as she could to hide Heather's squeals as she and Craig got changed. Then she went to her own cabin and shut the door.

She could wear a pair of unexceptional beige linen trousers and a loose blouson top, or she could wear her favorite sundress, which did rather cling in all the right places and was a rousing shade of tangerine.

She was in the tropics. She was going dancing with the most attractive and disturbing man she'd ever met, a man who had kissed her and walked away from her without a backward look and hadn't once, during dinner, by word or gesture, remotely referred to that kiss. From experience Lucy knew she attracted attention when she wore that dress—at least Troy would know she was on the same planet.

Last, but by no means least, in three and a half weeks she'd be going back to all the predictabilities and responsibilities of her life in Ottawa.

No contest.

When Lucy went on deck twenty minutes later the others were waiting for her. While her sundress had a flared skirt that went to midcalf it was sleeveless and low-cut in both the front and the back; gold jewelry glittered at wrist and ear and makeup gave her eyes a mysterious depth and her cheeks a soft glow.

Craig emitted a shrill wolf whistle as Heather said unaffectedly, 'How beautiful you look, Lucy! Doesn't she look beautiful, Troy?'

'Very,' said Troy, without a trace of emotion. 'Shall we go?'

All Lucy's pleasure in her appearance evaporated. He thought she was overdressed. He hated orange. He didn't want to go dancing with her.

He probably wished he hadn't kissed her.

She was the last one to get in the dinghy, casting off as she did so. Night had fallen while they ate. The lights of the yacht club glimmered on the waves and the rhythms of the band drifted across the water, exotic and compelling. The moon, a thick, creamy yellow, hung low in the sky.

The wind of their passage flattened Troy's blue shirt against his chest; his tailored cotton trousers were taut over his thighs. Lucy looked away and bent her head to catch something Heather had said. Maybe, she thought hopefully, Craig would tear himself away from Heather long enough to dance with her. She loved to dance, and it sure didn't look as though Troy was going to ask her.

The dance-floor was sheltered by a green and white striped canopy and was surrounded by tables under the rustling sheaves of the palm trees; as the fronds swayed gracefully in the breeze the stars appeared and disappeared. The scent of frangipani hung in the air. Troy ordered drinks and Craig asked Heather to dance. Troy and Lucy then sat, in complete silence, through the next three numbers.

A romantic setting was no guarantee of romance, Lucy decided, watching Craig whirl Heather in a circle and very much aware of what an uncomfortable emotion envy could be. Troy seemed to have his eyes glued to a young girl with straight blonde hair who was gyrating at the far corner of the dance-floor with a burly redhead. He was gripping his glass so tightly his knuckles were white.

The band struck up a lively calypso number. Feeling like the wallflower she had been at the age of thirteen, when she'd been three inches taller than all the boys in her class, Lucy snapped, 'It's obvious you don't want to dance with me—so why don't you ask her to dance?'

Troy's head jerked round. 'Who? What are you talking about?'

'The blonde you've been staring at for the last ten minutes—ask her to dance, Troy.'

She couldn't complain that she didn't have his attention now; he was glaring at her with such concentrated fury that Lucy shrank back in her chair. 'No,' he said with icy calm. 'I don't want to dance with her. Or with you, Lucy. Got that?'

Refusing to back down, she said, 'So you can kiss me any time you feel like it, but I'm not good enough to be seen with you in public, is that it?'

'Don't be an—'

'Craig and Heather are coming back,' she interrupted, giving him a smile of patent falsity.

'Dance with me, Lucy?' Craig asked.

Heather circled Troy's wrist and pulled him to his feet. 'It's a great band and I bet you're a fabulous dancer.'

As Craig jived with her Lucy kept catching glimpses of Troy and Heather, for they were only a few feet away; Troy was indeed a fabulous dancer and was giving every appearance of enjoying himself. Hurt and rage mingling in her orange-clad bosom, Lucy noticed out of the corner of her eye that the blonde girl and her red-headed partner had left. When the dance ended, amid a smatter of applause, Heather pulled Troy over to Lucy and said firmly, 'Your turn to dance with Lucy, Troy... Craig and I never switch partners for more than one dance in a row, do we, darling?'

Short of outright rudeness, Troy had no choice but to dance with her now, Lucy thought, inwardly furious with Heather for her interference. The music started, a much slower song, with a dreamy repetitive rhythm that was so far from Lucy's present state of mind that she didn't know whether to laugh hysterically or run from the dance-floor. Troy solved her dilemma by taking her in his arms. Holding her an impersonal distance from his body, he began to dance.

She wasn't sure which was worse: sitting in silence with him at the table, or dancing with him when he was only doing it to please Heather. Lucy knew a lot about touch, because it was her business. She loved the feel of Troy's hands—the smooth warmth of his palm, the latent strength of his fingers—and hated how that very strength was being used to keep her away. He had said not a word since Heather had foisted her on him.

She said amicably, 'You don't like my dress, do you?'

Troy's eyes slashed to her face. 'Whatever gave you that impression?'

'And you sure were telling the truth when you said you didn't want to dance with me. I don't have any communicable diseases, Troy.'

'You like the truth? Then I'll tell you the truth!' The fingers of his right hand dug into her hip as he scowled down at her. 'I don't scare easy, Lucy Barnes. But I was scared witless to take you out on the dance-floor. In that dress. In which you look ravishingly, gloriously, irresistably beautiful.'

'You *like* it?' she squeaked.

'Of course I do!'

'Oh.' Gaping at him like an idiot, she said, 'You were scared that if we danced together I might rip the shirt from your body?'

'I was probably scared you wouldn't.'

She tripped over his foot, lost her balance and grabbed at his elbows for support. 'I hate sewing on buttons,' she said. 'That's the downside of shirt-ripping.'

His voice thickening, he answered, 'No buttons on that dress of yours—all I'd have to do is haul it over your head.'

Giving up any attempt at dancing, Lucy stood stock-still in the middle of the dance-floor. Fluttering her lashes, she said, 'We might even teach Craig and Heather a thing or two.'

Troy suddenly threw his head back and began to laugh, a deep belly laugh that made him sexier than Robert

Redford could ever have been and gave Lucy an inkling
of what he might look like if only he were happy...
Because, of course, Troy wasn't happy, she thought
slowly. Something was eating at him, robbing him of vi-
tality. Destroying any possibility of the light-heartedness
she was now seeing and that touched her to the core.

Before she could even formulate any questions, he said,
'We're attracting attention. Maybe for now we should stay
fully clothed and attempt a two-step...okay?'

She would have stood on her head to keep that smile
on his face. Which was not, Lucy thought in puzzlement,
the way she had ever felt with Phil. Or Wayne, who'd
taught her to dance last year and had done his best to
inveigle himself into her bed in the process.

She stopped thinking altogether when Troy drew her
closer. Their two bodies moved in perfect unison to the
music, its languorous throbbing an intimate part of the
warm, moonlit darkness. The beat began to quicken. Troy
pulled her toward him then whirled her away, clasped her
by the very tips of her fingers, then held her by the whip-
cord strength of his arms, hard against the wall of his chest.
The beat was intoxicating now, fierce and imperative—
ancient rhythms of the jungle that were far less gentle than
moonlight and intimate in a totally new way. Lucy let her
body move as it would, her hips swaying in outright invitation, her hair swirling around her face.

Finally the song ended. Troy spun her in one last circle,
so that she ended up with her back to his chest, his arms
wrapped around her waist with an unspoken possessiveness that filled her with excitement. Into her ear he muttered, 'Next time I say no male-female stuff, you have my
full permission to call me a liar.'

She loved the clasp of his fingers against her belly, the
warmth of his breath stirring her hair. More than loved

them. Hungered after them with an intensity that shocked her. Phil had made love to her; Wayne had danced with her. But she had never felt in a man's arms this unsettling mixture of utter safety and searing danger. She chuckled, twisting her neck so she could look into Troy's face and widening her eyes. 'Call the skipper a liar? You might maroon me on the nearest island with a keg of rum.'

'I might join you,' he said roughly.

Abandoning herself to a happiness that shimmered in her heart like moonlight on water, Lucy closed her eyes, the better to savor the sweetness of Troy's embrace. She could have wished the band, Heather and Craig, and all the other dancers and onlookers a thousand miles away. She wanted to be alone with Troy. Just the two of them and this growing tension in the soft, seductive night…

But then Troy said, 'Hell, who's that waving at me? It's Jack—you remember Jack. He ate all your crab dip the first night you were on board. We'd better go and say hello. Those must be his guests with him; he said his next charter was fully booked.'

Before she was ready for it, Lucy was plunged into a flurry of introductions that she never did succeed in straightening out. One of the young men asked her to dance. Troy had already settled down between Jack and a rather attractive brunette whose name was either Darlene or Charlene, so Lucy accepted. Action was better than sitting there watching Troy be charming to someone else, and feeling as though she'd just had a limb amputated because he wasn't holding her in his arms anymore.

What was wrong with her? She'd never felt like this in her life.

The young man was a flashy dancer; she had to concentrate if she wasn't going to disgrace herself. She danced two numbers with him, one with the husband of Darlene or Charlene, and then lumbered around the floor with Jack, who suffered from the classic complaint of two left feet. Troy didn't ask her to dance again.

Two rounds of drinks were ordered and consumed. Lucy danced some more. Then Heather yawned widely and said with an endearing laugh, 'Past my bedtime.'

Craig kissed her ear amorously and Troy got up. There was a round of farewells, and in a few minutes the four of them were heading back to *Seawind* in the dinghy.

When they got on board Troy included Lucy in his smile, without singling her out, and said, 'Goodnight, all... See you in the morning.' Craig and Heather disappeared into the saloon and Lucy was left alone in the cockpit.

She felt at once desperately tired and wide awake; she also felt both angry and deeply hurt. How could Troy wrap his arms around her on the dance-floor as if she was his heart's desire and then say goodnight to her as if she was no more to him than Heather?

And what was this male-female stuff he kept talking about? Nothing more than sex?

A profound depression settled like a shroud over all her other emotions. Screwing up her face like a gargoyle at the moon, which was now sailing serenely in the heavens, Lucy went to bed.

When Lucy woke it was still dark. She had been dreaming, a confused dream where she was serving crab dip to Charlene—or Darlene—on board a bright orange dinghy to the strains of a steel band. It's rhythmic thump-thump echoed in her ears. And then she sat bolt upright, instantly awake. It wasn't the steel band she was hearing. It was Craig and Heather.

She switched on the little brass lamp over her bed. Three a.m. They were sex maniacs, she thought, enraged. Didn't they have any consideration for someone like herself, who didn't have a man and who, moreover, had to get up early tomorrow morning to bake pineapple muffins for their breakfast?

She turned off the light, buried her head under her pillow and squeezed her eyes tight shut. But the thudding continued, until, unable to bear it any longer, Lucy picked up her pillow and blanket, opened her cabin door and marched up the stairs, ducking to avoid the closed hatch.

The cockpit was cool, and the slapping of waves against the hull smothered any other sounds. She arranged three padded cushions along the bench and curled up on them with her blanket and pillow, composing herself for sleep.

She was lying in the deep shadow of the bimini. But the moonlight shone white on the hull, and she suddenly felt inexpressibly lonely. She was twenty-five years old. She was hundreds of miles from all her friends, she had a family who loved her without understanding her in the least, and she had a history of choosing the wrong men.

A high percentage of her friends were married with children. Why wasn't she? What was wrong with her?

She might be furious with Heather and Craig for disturbing her sleep, and she might deride them at times as a typical honeymoon couple, but she was quite astute enough to see that they truly loved each other and were very happy in each other's company. She would have liked to know what that felt like.

The wind sang softly in the shrouds. The boat rose and fell on the waves. The first tear crept down Lucy's cheek. She pulled the blanket over her face and read herself a stern lecture on the perils of self-pity.

Something hit her hard on the shoulder. Flung sideways on the bench, Lucy gave a screech of fear utterly unlike Heather's lovesick cries and tried to struggle free of the folds of the blanket. A dark shape thudded on to the deck beside her. For the second time that night she sat bolt upright, her blood pounding in her ears, with fear, this time, rather than rage.

Then the shape cursed in a reassuringly familiar voice and resolved itself into a large blond man clutching at the table for support. Troy.

Who else?

Lucy said shakily, 'What do you do for an encore?'

'I didn't see you—you scared me out of my wits.'

'Not half as bad as you scared me.'

He ran his fingers through his hair. He was wearing a pair of very brief shorts and nothing else. Lucy clutched the blanket to her chin and heard him ask, 'Do you make a habit of sleeping up on deck?'

She lowered her voice. 'Only insofar as those two make a habit of lovemaking half the night.'

He sat down on the bench beside her. 'I know the feeling... How many times is this in the last twenty-four hours?'

'Four?'

'I thought it was five.'

'We could fight over it,' Lucy suggested, realizing that her heart was still racing even though she was no longer afraid. Or, at least, no longer afraid of an unknown intruder.

Troy said forcefully, 'It's like living in a bordello.'

'What I need,' Lucy responded thoughtfully, 'is a swim in the Pacific Ocean. In April, that's cold.'

'A five-mile run.'

'Watch *Psycho* three times in a row.'

'Fifty bench presses at one hundred pounds each.'

Lucy chuckled. 'Or maybe just an undisturbed night's sleep.'

'Yeah...' His eyes narrowed and he leaned forward. 'Lucy, you've been crying. What's wrong?'

She pulled back, wiping her cheeks with the blanket. 'Nothing!'

'Come on, surely we've progressed beyond that?'

She bit back an acid retort. 'Have we, Troy?' Playing with the silk-lined hem of the blanket, she added in a rush, 'Progress implies starting somewhere and ending up somewhere else. In a better place. I don't have any idea if you and I are going anywhere. Or even if there's anything between us.'

'There's sexual attraction for sure,' he said, in a voice raw with feeling. 'At the moment I can't get beyond that.'

It wasn't exactly the answer she had hoped for. But he had been honest with her. 'Male-female stuff,' she said drily.

He nodded. Making no move to touch her, he said with a matter-of-factness that was totally convincing, 'Right now I'd like nothing better than to take you to bed.' He hesitated. 'Would you go with me, Lucy?'

Her heart gave its own answer by leaping in her chest, and somehow the moonlight and the silence that underlaid the soft playing of the sea precluded anything but the truth. In a small voice she said, 'I guess so. Even though a couple of days ago you more or less accused me of promiscuity.'

'All these big blond men that you're so attracted to...didn't you sleep with them?'

'One of them. Phil. We were engaged at the time.'

'Only one? You're twenty-five, Lucy!'

'Only one.'

The breath hissed between his teeth. 'Why?'

She hugged her knees to her chest under the blanket. 'My mother had very strict standards. And I was always falling in and out of love, so I didn't really trust my own emotions… I suppose there's a certain poetic justice to the fact that Phil was the one to leave me. He ran off with one of those tiny, fragile little women who was everything I'm not.'

'I like you exactly as you are, and if you were any more beautiful I don't think I'd be able to stand it,' Troy announced.

'*What*?'

'You heard. Phil, in my humble opinion, was an idiot.'

'I think I've just received the very best compliment of my whole life,' Lucy said.

'I happen to mean it,' Troy replied in a clipped voice.

The very lack of feeling in his voice was what persuaded her; Troy, she was beginning to realize, combined honesty with locked-up emotion in a way that was disconcerting but very much part of him. Had she ever wanted to understand Phil as intensely as she now wanted to understand Troy?

She didn't think so.

She said, casually she hoped, 'Have you ever been married or engaged, Troy?'

'Engaged. Once. Never married.'

As the silence stretched out Lucy added in exasperation, 'Well, you can't stop there!'

'You're very curious, Lucy Barnes.'

'I'm interested, that's all,' she said loftily, trying to subdue what was undoubtedly jealousy at the thought of the unknown woman to whom Troy had been engaged.

'To understand the story of my broken engagement, you'd have to know my parents,' Troy said. His profile, with its strongly hewn nose and cleft chin, was turned to her; he was speaking as much to himself as to her. 'They've lived in Victoria all their lives. Good, law-abiding citizens, with—like your mother—very high standards. Strong emotion—emotion of any kind—they considered rather bad form. When I escaped to university in Toronto at the age of nineteen I sowed considerably more than the usual crop of wild oats. But eventually I got that particular rebellion out of my system and settled down, and then three or four years later Rosamund moved to Toronto. She was the daughter of my parents' best friends and my mother had never made any secret of her hope that Rosamund and I would marry. Rosamund was quiet and gentle and very lovely, and I was run off my feet at the time and in need of a little cherishing, so we started dating. One thing led to another and we got engaged.'

He turned to look at Lucy and said with sudden force, 'It wasn't enough! She wasn't enough. I knew that almost immediately. But I didn't want to hurt her, and I kept hoping that somehow things would change. That my feelings would get out of hand instead of everything being so goddamned placid and low-key.' He grimaced. 'You can probably guess the rest. I started to feel trapped, confined...through no fault of Rosamund's—I never blamed her. I finally broke our engagement. And even though I felt like a louse, I also knew I'd done the right thing. For both of us. I'm not sure my mother ever understood, though. She kept asking what was wrong with Rosamund—and of course nothing was.'

Lucy's hands were cold, even under the blanket. 'What's happened to you since then, Troy?' she asked. 'Because you've taken all your feelings—except anger— and buried them. All those feelings that you wanted to express with Rosamund and couldn't.'

His short laugh was devoid of humour. 'Don't get too curious, Lucy.'

Her lashes flickered. 'You give intimacy with one hand and take it away with the other.'

'That's all I can do right now! And, for Pete's sake, don't ask me why.' He stood up abruptly. 'You're cold, you'd better go back to bed.'

She stood up too, the blanket loose around her shoulders. Her nightgown was made of thin white cotton decorated with old-fashioned lace; it reached only to mid-thigh and more than hinted at the swell of her breasts. She could have covered herself. Instead she waited, seeing the tension gather in Troy's mouth, the torment shadow his eyes.

Like a man who couldn't help himself he took two steps toward her and pulled her into his arms. The blanket slithered to the deck. Lucy circled his neck with her arms and lifted her face for a kiss whose pent up need did away with any vestige of resistance she might have felt. His lips burned into hers with all the heat of the noonday sun; her body melted and with every nerve she possessed she was aware of his hands roaming her ribcage, her waist, her hips. It was as if he couldn't bear for there to be space between them, as if body pressed to body and muscle strained against muscle was what the moonlit night and his own desperation called for.

She opened to the searching of his tongue and felt his hand seek the warm weight of her breast. Shifting slightly in his arms, she gave him what he wanted, and was rewarded, as he stroked the curve of her flesh, by a pleasure so strong as to border on pain. His erection pressed into her groin; her body ached with an emptiness that was more than just physical, and that only he could fill.

He was kissing her cheekbones, her hair, the slim length of her throat, passionate kisses, between which he was whispering her name like a mantra. And then with frantic haste he found her mouth again, imprinting himself on her so that she could know him as the shore knew the waves.

Like a streak of fire she felt his hand slide under her gown, traveling the tautness of buttock, the concavity of spine. Drowning in desire, she moaned his name, her hips of their own accord pressing into his with all her strength, moving back and forth in primitive and instinctual invitation.

The shock ran through his body. His hands grew still. Against her lips he muttered with anguished certainty, 'This is madness, Lucy—we can't do this!'

He cupped her shoulders, pushing her away. Her face was a battleground between bewilderment and desire, while her mouth was soft and swollen from his kisses. 'But I—I want you,' she stammered foolishly.

A pulse was hammering at the base of his throat. 'I want you, too—we both know that.' He took a step away from her. 'Come on, Lucy... You've only slept with one man before, and I outgrew going from bed to bed when I was twenty-one. Neither of us is into casual affairs and neither of us is in love with the other. Time to call it quits, wouldn't you say?'

'You sound so damned logical!'

'Why were you crying a while ago?'

She stooped and picked up her blanket, wrapping it around herself, all her movements short and jerky. 'I was lonely.'

'All the more reason for us not to make love,' he said grimly.

'For you, maybe. Don't speak for me.'

His voice rose. 'By God, you're argumentative.'

The pain of unfulfilled desire had all too swiftly translated itself into fury. Lucy retorted, 'Let me tell you something—I've never noticed you being either placid or low-key around me. Why don't you go to bed—by yourself, of course—and think about that, Troy?'

'Are you trying to tell me I'm in love with you?' he snarled. 'Don't be ridiculous! We've only known each other for four days and all we do is fight.'

Lucy swallowed hard. What she was really afraid of was that she was the one falling in love with Troy. A man she'd only just met, with whom she did indeed spend a lot of time arguing. The rest of the time she spent wishing he was in bed with her, she thought in horror, and prayed that he couldn't read her mind. Gathering her dignity around her, as if it were a blanket, she said with frigid politeness, 'Good night, Troy. I'll see you in the morning.'

'Okay, so you're different from Rosamund—so what?' he said harshly. 'And don't speak to me as if I'm something you found floating in the bilge.'

Lucy had often needed her sense of humor when dealing with a mother and two sisters who regarded her as a changeling. She said flippantly, 'Pardon me, Captain Donovan, sir,' and dropped Troy the best curtsy she could, swathed as she was in the blanket.

The glint in his eye had nothing to do with the moonlight. 'Goodnight, Lucy,' he said. Lightning-swift, he closed the distance between them and brushed his mouth back and forth with tantalizing slowness across her parted lips. 'Pleasant dreams,' he added, letting both hands trace the outline of her breasts under the blanket, watching her face change as he did so. Then lithely he climbed up on the bench and over the nearest hatch. Two seconds later he disappeared into his cabin.

Lucy, now that he was gone, thought of several very clever remarks she could have made. Her breasts were tingling, and as she ran a finger along the lips he had kissed so thoroughly she caught the faintest trace of the scent of his skin.

Heaving a huge sigh, she trailed toward the companionway steps. She felt frustrated, infuriated, upset and off-
balance.

What she didn't feel was lonely.

CHAPTER FIVE

SOMEONE was knocking on Lucy's door, and the voice that had played havoc in her dreams was saying, 'Lucy—time to get up.'

Still half-asleep, Lucy leaped out of bed and yanked the door open. 'What's the matter?'

'Nothing.' Troy looked revoltingly wide awake, surveying her sleep-tousled hair and rumpled bed with a mockery that did nothing for her disposition. 'It's eight o'clock,' he said. 'Heather and Craig have taken the dinghy to go snorkeling in the cove—they'll be hungry when they get back.'

'Eight?' she repeated, horrified. 'It can't be!'

He said, an edge to his voice, 'Did you have pleasant dreams last night?'

It wasn't the moment to remember, with embarrassing clarity, the particularly compromising position she had found herself in with Troy in a dream that was a typical example of wish fulfillment. Lucy blushed scarlet and muttered, 'Go away!'

'So, you're argumentative first thing in the morning as well.'

'Troy,' she seethed, 'I have to make a fruit salad and muffins for our guests. Who also had an active night. Why don't you plug the coffee in? That would be far more helpful than standing there making personal remarks.'

'The coffee's already made,' he said tersely, took her by the shoulders and kissed her on the mouth.

He had used mint toothpaste and a herbal aftershave, and desire leaped rampant upon Lucy, like a tiger that had been lying in wait for its prey. As he pulled free of her she said faintly, 'If you keep that up, you'll be making the muffins—because I'll be taking a long, cold shower.'

'It's going to take more than a shower to get rid of what's between you and me,' he said, with a grimness that she deplored. 'Craig and Heather only just left the boat; you've got lots of time.'

Lucy said darkly, 'They're probably making love under the keel.'

Troy didn't smile; in fact, she wasn't sure he'd even heard her. 'Look,' he said, 'about last night. I think we should treat it as an accident, an aberration. Moonlight on water, altogether too much bare flesh, and our two busy little honeymooners raising our hormone levels to a peak. We should cool it, that's what I'm trying to say. Not get in that situation again.'

'Which is why you kissed me a moment ago,' she flashed.

'I kissed you because my thought processes go out the window when I'm within ten feet of you!'

'Good,' she said.

'Lucy, I'm serious.'

'I hate that word "should",' she said vigorously. 'I'm beginning to realize I've lived most of my life according to other people's "shoulds", and I'm sick and tried of it.'

'We are not going to have an affair!'

'I don't see why you have to fight me every inch of the way,' she cried. 'What is it that's got you so uptight? Why are you angry all the time?'

'Go to hell,' he said, and shut the cabin door in her face.

Lucy stamped her bare foot on the floor, winced from a pain that was entirely self-inflicted, and went into the bathroom to wash her face. Considering how many men she'd fallen in love with, a whole train of them ever since her grade seven history teacher, she knew nothing about men, she thought, glaring at herself in the tiny mirror.

Or, at least, nothing about Troy.

One thing was certain. She was behaving very differently with him than with any of the rest of them. So she wasn't in love with him. If that was any comfort.

It wasn't. She pulled on green shorts and a blouse which was wildly patterned in greens, pinks and yellows and that seemed to match her mood, and yanked her brush through her tangled curls. Big yellow earrings, a generous coating of pink lipstick, and she was ready for the fray.

Appropriate word, Lucy, she thought with a wry grin, and opened her door. To her great relief the saloon was empty. And to her great surprise the muffins, when she served them on deck an hour later, were excellent, as was the fruit salad she'd made to go with them. She sat as far from Troy as she could and made bright and bubbly conversation with Heather and Craig, and when the meal was finished she vanished belowstairs, feeling as though she'd already put in a hard day's work. Washing the dishes was soothing—the froth of suds and the hot water in the sink held no hidden messages, the neatly stacked and rinsed dishes were exactly as they appeared.

By the time she had cleared away breakfast, the Merritts had gone snorkeling again. Troy was sitting with his back to her at the chart table, bringing the log up to date. Wishing he'd gone snorkeling too, Lucy started rolling out a prepared package of puff pastry to make a strudel for dessert. Her hair fell forward in her face and she tucked it behind her ear, leaving a gob of dough stuck to it.

Troy said irritably, 'your hair shouldn't be so long when you're cooking all the time.'

He hadn't complained about it last night, when he'd had his fingers entangled in it and had been kissing her as if she were the only woman on earth. Stretching one corner of the pastry to make a right-angle, in no mood to be conciliatory, she snapped, 'More "shoulds". Is that your favorite word?'

'I'm the skipper; I'm allowed to use it. Get your hair cut when we're back in Road Town, will you?'

Abandoning the puff pastry, Lucy put her hands on her hips. 'And what if I don't want to?'

'The college crowd'll be arriving soon. Don't think of yourself as irreplaceable.'

His words cut through her anger, as perhaps he had intended. If he fired her she'd never see him again, she thought sickly, and was sure she hadn't felt so dead a weight of despair even when Phil had left town with Sarah. Hating the place to which her emotions had brought her, she hauled the cutlery drawer open, picked up the kitchen shears, which were as sharp as any of the knives in the galley, marched over to the chart table, seized a handful of the hair that hung over her left shoulder and cut it off.

Little wisps of hair drifted down on to the open pages of the logbook. Lucy was left with a clump of curls in her hand. Aghast, she said, 'I spent the last eight months growing this.'

Troy got to his feet. Standing very close to her, he said, 'You're like a volcano. One minute you're peacefully rolling out pastry, the next you're wielding a pair of scissors as if they're a machete.'

She tilted her chin. '*Would* you fire me?'

His voice was as sharp-edged as the scissors she was still clutching. 'Heaven help me, I don't think I can.'

'Well, that's a relief,' Lucy said. Gaping at the hank of hair, she added weakly, 'But that means I did this for nothing.'

'I'm not the easiest of bosses—I'd have thought you'd be delighted to be fired by me.'

'Then you'd have thought wrong.'

'Because I'm a big, blond man?'

'No.' She looked him straight in the eye. 'It's a lot more complicated than that, Troy—trust me. What am I going to do about my hair?'

'You infuriate me, you exasperate me, you're keeping me awake at night and on edge all day...and I can't damn well fire you,' Troy said. 'Will someone please explain that to me?'

A rueful smile curved her lips. 'Maybe we should ask our resident experts on male-female stuff—Craig and Heather.'

'I don't think that's a very good idea.' A fugitive smile lightened his features as he looked at the curls that were wrapped around her knuckles. 'You're going to have a hard time gluing those back on.'

'I'll have to try and cut the other side to match.'

'Sit down. I'll do it for you.'

His rare smiles always enchanted her. She glowered at him. 'Have you ever cut anyone's hair before?'

Troy hesitated, an odd look on his face that she was to remember later. 'Well, no, not exactly. But I'm sure I'll do a better job than you.'

'You could hardly do a worse one,' she answered gloomily. 'My mother had a quote, something to do with perverseness being a primitive impulse... Fits me to a T.'

'Why don't you get a comb and a towel from your room?' he said patiently. 'Unless you want to explain how you got such a lopsided hairdo to the honeymooners?'

She didn't. When she came back, Troy pushed her down in the chair and draped the towel over her shoulders. He worked quickly, with a deftness that fascinated her. 'Are you a hairdresser when you're not being a skipper?' she asked suspiciously.

'No. Hold still.'

His hands were warm on the back of her neck, and the small tugs of his fingers felt unbelievably sensual. Lucy closed her eyes, savoring each sensation. Troy said huskily, 'When the light strikes your hair, it gleams like bronze.'

'Your's is like gold,' she said.

'Yoohoo!' Heather called. 'Where are you?'

Lucy jumped and Troy cleared his throat. 'Down here,' he shouted.

Heather came tumbling down the stairs. 'Guess what— we saw three sea turtles. Lucy, you've got to— Oh, your hair looks gorgeous! Troy, you're a marvel.'

Very carefully Troy removed the towel from Lucy's shoulders. 'Where were the turtles?' he asked.

'Way over on the far side of the cove... They were so beautiful, Craig took a whole roll of pictures. I love him dearly but he's not the best of photographers; I do hope we get one decent photo out of all that. Lucy, you must come and see them.'

Lucy scrambled to her feet. 'I've got to change my shirt and finish the strudel.'

'Darn the strudel! We can eat leftover muffins. This is more important, isn't it, Troy?' Shamelessly Heather batted her wet lashes at him.

Troy raised his brow. 'Off you both go—I know when I'm outnumbered.'

So fifteen minutes later Lucy was swimming over beds of wavering green grasses, where conch traced meandering paths along white sand that was dotted with spiny black sea urchins. Then a swifter, surer movement caught her eye. The turtle was stroking lazily over the grass toward the deeper water, its head and flippers speckled dark and light. The sun made flickering patterns of turquoise over its dull green shell.

She followed it at a safe distance, realizing how lucky she was to have entered a world not her own, and how privileged to be seeing an animal behave the way nature and instinct had ordained it to behave. Gradually the turquoise grew more opaque as the ocean floor fell away, until the turtle was lost to sight.

Filled with wonderment, she lifted her head. Heather wasn't ten feet from her. 'Lovely,' said Heather, and the two women smiled at each other. Heather added artlessly, 'That was kind of elemental, wasn't it? Like sex, in a way.'

'Oh?' Lucy said cautiously.

'Mmm... I mean, I almost felt what it was like to be a turtle, swimming with one like that. As though I'd joined with it in some mysterious way. When Craig and I make love—which, when you think about it, is rather a peculiar act; whoever designed it must have had a sense of humour—this magical thing happens. We make love with our bodies but somehow our souls touch. We know each other, sort of like I knew the turtle.'

Any facetious comments Lucy might have made died on her lips. That was what had been wrong between her and Phil: their souls—whatever that word meant—had never touched. 'I see what you mean,' she mumbled, treading water and thinking what a peculiar place this was to be having a discussion about sex.

'You see, I don't think that kind of knowing happens very often. But I'm sure you and Troy could have it. I guess that's all I wanted to say—don't turn your back on something you might never find again.'

Heather was the customer; Lucy couldn't very well tell her to mind her own business. 'Troy and I aren't involved

with each other!' she sputtered, as a wave slapped her in
the chin.

'Piffle,' Heather said, pulling her mask back over her
face. 'The vibes between you are as clear as—as this water… Oh, look, Craig's waving at us, shall we go back?'

Lucy took her time stroking toward the dinghy. Craig
and Heather were in love, that would explain the kind of
connection Heather had described. But she, Lucy, had
loved Phil—hadn't she? So why had she experienced sex
with Phil as a lack rather than a true joining? Whereas
when she was with Troy, no matter what they did—argue,
kiss or sail *Seawind*—she felt connected to him by a bond
she could neither describe nor break.

She mustn't fall in love with Troy.

That would be one impulse she would bitterly regret.

For lunch the next day Troy steered *Seawind* to a beach
on Copper's Island. Lucy arranged meats, cheeses and raw
vegetables on a platter and served them with chutneys and
wholegrain breads; she'd baked a banana loaf as well. After they'd eaten, Craig took the dinghy into shore. 'He
wants to buy me something at the boutique,' Heather said
fondly. 'He's such a sweetheart.' She took another sip of
her orange juice and added, 'I've got a favor to ask you,
Lucy.'

It was the Merritts' last full day, and if they'd made
love the night before Lucy hadn't heard them. 'Fire away,'
she said indolently.

'Troy told me you can do massage. Will you teach me
how to massage Craig's back and shoulders? He spends
so much time in front of his computer at work, I worry
about him.'

'Sure, I'd be glad to. Whenever he comes back.'

'Well, I'd really rather surprise him.' Heather smiled

with rather overdone innocence. 'You could demonstrate on Troy right now, couldn't you? You wouldn't mind, would you, Troy?'

Lucy dropped the celery stick she had been chewing. It was a set-up, she realized furiously, and could happily have pushed Heather overboard. 'I can't—' she began.

Troy almost knocked his can of Coke off the table. 'That's not such a—'

With another winning smile Heather overrode them both. 'Come on,' she coaxed, 'it won't hurt a bit.' She widened her eyes. 'And you'll get a fee massage out of it, Troy. If I were you, I'd be having Lucy give me one every day.'

Heather was one of nature's unstoppable forces, thought Lucy. Like the tides. Like the swell on the windward side of the islands. A man with a blond pony-tail, whom she'd dated when she was nineteen, had had the same kind of unquenchable charm that seemed to brush aside the wishes of others as if they didn't exist. Knowing when she was beaten, she struggled to don her most professional manner and said, 'I've got some cream in my cabin. I won't be a minute.'

It was only skin cream, but it would do. When she went back up, Troy and Heather had moved forward to the padded green mats that were tied to the deck under the headsail, a place where those who still believed in tanning themselves could do so. Lucy spread her blanket over the mat and said with impersonal pleasantness, 'You'll have to take your shirt off, Troy. Then lie face-down, would you?'

Without once meeting her eyes, he did as she asked. Lucy put a pillow under his ankles and eased the waistband of his shorts part way down over his hips, quelling the incipient riot in her nervous system as she did so. She then said to Heather, 'I'll put the cream on first. When you're doing a massage like this, without a table, you must be careful of your posture.' Moving up to Troy's head, she took a couple of deep breaths, telling herself that Troy was no different from any other client.

Client? Who was she kidding?

She warmed the cream in her palms, making a huge effort to transpose herself back to her studio in Ottawa, away from the soft wind and turquoise sea that surrounded her. Swallowing, she said, 'The other thing to remember is how you make and break your contacts—no rough movements, no shocks. Like this.'

Leaning forward, she brought her palms down until they rested with exquisite gentleness on Troy's bare skin. She felt the shiver in his flesh and her own pulse leaped to meet it. Fighting down a response that all her training told her was utterly inappropriate, she smoothed the cream on with long strokes that ran from Troy's shoulders to the base of his spine. Her hands separated, circling the rise of his buttocks, then traveling along his ribcage and over his deltoid muscles back to the nape of his neck. His muscles had the tone of a man in the peak of physical fitness; the smoothness of his skin, his body heat, flooded her with wave upon wave of primitive hunger.

She said in her best teaching voice, 'You can see when I lean forward how my body weight comes into play—I'm not just using my hands. You'll tire yourself out if you make all the strength come from your hands and wrists alone.' Leaving the fingertips of her left hand light on Troy's shoulder, she added, 'When I need more cream I keep contact with the client... You want him to relax, to trust you.'

Her words hung in the air, words meant more for Troy than for Heather.

Heather, to her credit, was paying close attention. Getting Lucy to massage Troy might have been a ploy; but her desire to learn was genuine enough.

Next Lucy kneaded the muscles in Troy's neck, one hand releasing its pressure as the other squeezed, working right up into his hairline where his blond hair, surprisingly soft, curled against his nape; she then smoothed the length of his spine again before deepening the pressure with long thumb-strokes all the way to his sacrum. 'Work on either side of the vertebrae,' she suggested, keeping to herself what she was learning about Troy's body as she worked on him. The tension in the deep layers of his musculature appalled her, and she could not flatter herself that it was sexual tension. Some of the more superficial tension might be. But most of it, she would have sworn, had been with him much longer than the week that he and she had known each other.

'Anger, she thought. Anger and pain, caught and held for too long. Unwittingly—and no doubt unwillingly—Troy was revealing the secrets of his body to her.

When she moved to Troy's left side, to do thumb presses along his scapula, she felt him wince at the pressure she'd applied. 'Sorry,' she murmured, 'is this better?' He grunted, his eyes closed. Forgetting Heather, and forgetting for a few moments that this was Troy, Lucy brought her whole focus on to what she was doing, working with all her skill to release the tightness in his rhomboid muscles.

'It looks like that hurts,' Heather remarked.

'It's counterproductive to cause pain... But you don't want to be so gentle that you don't soften the muscles, either. After you've done deep work like this, it's a good idea to smooth it out.' Suiting action to words, Lucy glided her palm from Troy's neck over the long curve of his shoulder. Her hand wanted to linger; oh, God, when could she end this travesty?

'Now we'll increase the pressure along the spine,' she said evenly, resting her outer hand over her inner as she stroked to his tailbone again, letting her body weight do the work for her. It was a good thing it was broad daylight and they were out on deck, she thought with a tinge of real desperation. Not once in all the years she'd been giving massages had her own sexuality been an issue with any of her male clients. She'd rather prided herself on her professional detachment.

Not any more.

Knowing she was being precipitate, and unable to prevent herself, Lucy said, 'We'll finish up now—a few more long strokes, each one with less and less pressure. No abrupt moves, no sudden stopping.'

As she completed the last slow sweep of Troy's back, she rested one palm at the base of his neck, the other in the hollow by his pelvis. Then she gradually lifted her hands until the contact was broken.

Her whole body screamed its protest. She could have stayed there all day, she thought, and prayed that her emotions didn't show in her face.

'That was wonderful,' Heather exclaimed. 'Thanks, Lucy—and thank you for being the guinea pig, Troy. I'm going down to my cabin to write down everything you showed me before I forget.' Shading her eyes, she said, 'There's Craig, heading for the dock—I'll have to hurry.'

She scrambled to her feet, leaving Lucy and Troy alone. Feeling as self-conscious as if she'd just given her first massage, Lucy said, 'Want me to get another pillow for your head? Maybe you could sleep for a while?'

Troy pushed himself up on his elbows. The breeze ruffled his hair; his eyes were at their most opaque. 'I'm certainly in no state to get to my feet,' he said.

It was a split second before she realized that he had been as affected as she by their recent intimacy. Gathering her scattered wits, she mumbled, 'Just don't tell Heather, that's all I ask.'

His eyes narrowed. 'Did the two of you cook this up when you were snorkeling?'

'No! She cooked it up all on her own.' Carefully Lucy capped the bottle of cream. 'Heather thinks you and I belong together.'

'She couldn't be more wrong, could she?' Troy said with brutal emphasis.

Lucy said quietly, 'I don't know, Troy. I don't know much of anything when I'm around you.'

'That's at least one thing we have in common,' he jeered. 'Go away, will you, Lucy? I've got to get my act together. I'm supposed to be running this show. As soon as Craig gets back I want to head to Great Camanoe— we'll moor there overnight if the swell's not too high.'

He was the skipper and she was the crew, that was the message she was getting. Lucy pulled the pillow from under his legs and stalked toward the cockpit. She couldn't put her nose in the air; she might trip over one of the hatches.

At five to twelve the next day Craig brought the last piece of luggage up the stairs. *Seawind* was anchored at the dock in Road Town. Heather asked Lucy to take a photo of her and Craig holding the wheel, then said, 'Now I want one of you and Troy together.' She jumped over to the dock, aiming the camera. 'Stand closer to Lucy, Troy, and put your arm around her, or else I can't get you both in… That's better.'

Lucy directed a strained smile at the lens. Troy's hip was bumping hers and his grip had nothing of gentleness in it. The minute the picture was snapped he let her go. There was a flurry of hugs and promises to write, in the middle of which Heather managed to whisper in Lucy's ear, 'Be sure and invite me to the wedding.' Then, waving, she and Craig walked away down the dock.

Lucy watched them go with mingled feelings. She didn't need to be told how thoroughly they had enjoyed *Seawind* and now they were happy to be by themselves again. Would she, Lucy, ever be the most important person in the world to a man whom she loved?

As she called one last goodbye she was aware of more than a touch of regret. For all Heather's machinations, Lucy had liked both her and her husband. Would she ever see them again?

Certainly not at a wedding—the idea was laughable.

She turned back to *Seawind* and to Troy. Stepping into the cockpit, she said, 'Now what?'

'At noon tomorrow the Dillons arrive. Victor and Leona and their two teenagers, Kim and Brad. We've got twenty-four hours to clean the boat from stem to stern and re-provision her with food and drink for six days.' Mockery twisted his mouth. 'Sure you don't want me to fire you, Lucy?'

'I can handle it—but can you, Troy?' she responded in deliberate challenge, and both of them knew she was not referring to the Dillons.

'We'll have to share the forward cabin this trip,' he said, his eyes trained on her face.

She paled. 'What do you mean?'

'There are three cabins off the saloon. One for Victor and Leona, one for Kim, who's a girl, and one for Brad, who's a boy. None for you, Lucy. So you'll have to join me up front.'

She would have nowhere to hide from him. For five nights she would have to lie in her bunk listening to him breathing, tormented by his closeness yet unable to escape.

'You don't look very happy about it. Just be glad there are two bunks.'

She gave a cracked laugh. 'Wouldn't Heather just love this?'

Troy said softly, 'When you take the Jeep to town to get groceries, are you going to head for the airport instead?'

Lucy—and this was nothing new—had no idea what he was thinking. Maybe he wanted her on the first flight out of here? He'd made no secret of the fact that he hated the way she aroused him sexually, resenting her for having that much power over him. Her nerves lacerated, her throat tight, she suddenly felt all her energy drain from her body, as if she were a broken glass whose contents had spilled on the floor. She couldn't fight him anymore. She was tired of fighting him. And to what end? He always took more than he gave. And day by day she was getting more deeply embroiled.

Her shoulders slumped, she said, 'If you want me to go, Troy—really want me out of your life because you can't stand the sight of me—why don't you just say so? In the long run it would be easier. On me, for sure, and on you too, I suppose.'

'No,' he said.

She jammed her hands in the pockets of her shorts, her voice rising. 'No, what? No, it wouldn't be easier? Or no, you don't want me out of your life?'

He paused, as though he was searching for the precise words he wanted. 'Years ago I used to sail on the west coast, out of Victoria. The tides would pull the boat one way, the wind blow it another, and then a rain squall would hit and the wind would shift between one moment and the next… That's how you make me feel, Lucy.'

Her nails were digging into her palms. 'Nothing like the trade winds?' she ventured.

His smile was mirthless. 'Steady from the east at fifteen knots? No, nothing like that.'

Knowing the question held her fate, she asked, 'Did you give up sailing on the west coast? Because it was frustrating and full of risks?' And then stood still, waiting for him to answer.

Her legs were braced against the bench, her shoulders rigid. But her chin was raised and there was unconscious pride in the blue-gray depths of her eyes. Troy said flatly, 'I've only just realized what your eyes remind me of… They're the color of the sea in the Strait of Juan de Fuca, where I used to sail. No, I didn't give up sailing there. Even though it was dangerous and unpredictable, and every year a fisherman or a yachtsman would drown, I still went out.'

She let out her breath in a tiny sigh. 'That takes courage,' she said.

'My mother had a different word. She thought I was crazy.'

Feeling as though she'd been granted a reprieve at the very base of the gallows, Lucy laughed. 'At the risk of disagreeing with your mother, I'll stick with courage.'

He hesitated. 'It took courage for you to ask me if I really wanted you to leave, didn't it?'

She nodded. 'You might have said yes.'

'And that matters to you?'

'Oh, yes,' she said, astonished that he even had to ask. 'But I would have gone.' It was her turn to hesitate. 'When

Phil was leaving with Sarah I begged him not to go, not to break our engagement. I guess what I learned then and what I've never forgotten is that it's useless to beg. I couldn't change Phil's mind—I couldn't change Phil. So I would have left Tortola, Troy. Left you. If you really hadn't wanted me here.'

'You're okay, Lucy,' Troy said slowly, 'you're okay.'

It was neither an effusive nor an articulate compliment. But Troy's eyes were smiling at her in a way that made her knees weak, and the sun was dancing on the water as though it didn't have a care in the world. Feeling as though she had traveled a very long way in the last five minutes, Lucy said, 'If we can get everything done that needs to be done before noon tomorrow, we'll both be okay.'

He laughed, his teeth white in his tanned face. 'You said it! I suppose, if I'm to be a skipper worthy of the name, I'd better pass out a few orders.'

'Yessir.'

'I'll take the laundry and the garbage into town, and pick up liquor and drinks. I'll leave you to clean the galley and make up the menus—feel free to repeat anything you served the Merritts.'

'You're not tired of my crab dip?'

'I can always invite Jack over.'

Lucy loved it when he teased her; the sun, if possible, shone even more brightly, and the seagull swooping over the mast was the most graceful bird she'd ever seen. 'I'll need fresh ice for the refrigerator,' she said. With an ingenuousness worthy of Heather she added, 'If you were a really god skipper, with the welfare of your customers truly at heart, you'd go to the spice shop and buy me the second volume of their cookbook series.'

'*Do* you ever cook when you're home, Lucy?'

'I give regular massages to the Italian woman who runs

the local pizza shop and to the old Chinese man who has a Szechuan take-out across the street from my apartment.' Her eyes twinkling, she added, 'It's called barter.'

'I suspected you were bluffing the day I hired you,' he said drily. 'You're to be congratulated—the Merritts thought you were a wonderful cook.'

'But then sex gives you an appetite…or so I've heard.'

He let his gaze wander the length of her body in its cotton shorts and brief tank top. 'Only for more sex, I'd suspect.'

Lucy blushed. 'Buy volume two, Troy—for the Dillons' sake.'

When he grinned at her, she suddenly saw another man, young and reckless, clinging to the mast of a Laser in the Strait of Juan de Fuca with the wind tugging at his blond hair. Feeling a lump gather in her throat, she heard him say, 'I promise… I'd better get moving. When I get back, I'll help clean the cabins.'

Five minutes later he was gone. Lucy decided to start by making up menus—a much more difficult task than polishing woodwork or scrubbing out the sinks. Troy had given her the Dillons' list of food preferences. With faint dismay she saw that Brad and Kim favored hamburgers, hot dogs and fried chicken, while their parents wanted poached seafood, salads with low fat dressings and fruit.

Great, she thought. I'll be spending the entire time in the galley. I'd better wait until I get my new cookbook, perhaps that'll inspire me.

When Troy came back, she'd cleaned the cabin that the Merritts had used for storage, and the stove shone like new. She quickly emptied the contents of the freezer so he could store the ice in it, saying, 'I'll do the refrigerator next—I'm going to miss the Merritts more than I thought.

The younger Dillons want to wallow in cholesterol and the older ones to eschew it.'

'Volume two,' Troy said, slapping the cookbook on the counter.

Wrinkling her nose at him, she said, 'I should have asked for the whole series.'

'I like your hair like that,' he said unexpectedly. 'You look—lighter somehow.'

I'm falling in love with you, Troy Donovan.

The words had come from nowhere. Her eyes wide with shock, her cheeks washed a delicate pink, Lucy heard them echo and re-echo in her mind. Troy muttered grimly, 'This is going to be one hell of a long five days—or should I say, nights? I'm going to wash out the coolers and put the beer on ice.'

It wasn't the beer he should be putting on ice, she thought numbly.

It was herself. Lucy.

CHAPTER SIX

TROY took the steps two at a time. Her fingers fumbling with the packages of frozen food, Lucy put them back in the freezer and latched the lid, and all the while her thoughts were whirling in crazy circles and her emotions were going up and down as rambunctiously as if *Seawind* were broadside to a swell.

Just because a man compliments you on your hairdo, you don't fall in love with him… But I adore it when his eyes soften and he looks at me as though I'm the only woman in the world… You don't know the first thing about him… I do! I know he's honest and he's hurting… Want to bet that he's still in love with someone else and that's why he's hurting…? He couldn't be so attracted to me if that was the case… That's a laugh. Sex is no basis for falling in love; you're old enough to know that… Oh, shut up!

Which seemed to bring an end to that particular inner dialogue.

Lucy polished the woodwork in the saloon, tidied the books, and went up on deck to shake out the cotton mats that lay on the floor. Then she sat down with the cookbook, scanning the recipes with a more knowledgeable eye than she would have had a week ago. She would have to prepare two meals each evening, that was obvious… Troy could help by barbecuing the hamburgers and chicken. Her pencil flew over the paper, and by the time he joined her she had piled the contents of the refrigerator on the counter and was making notes of what she had to buy.

He made a few entries in the logbook, then filled a pail with suds at the sink, standing so close to her she could have reached out and touched him. Touch…her area of expertise. She said impulsively, 'Troy, when I massaged you yesterday, your muscles were so tight that—'

He turned to face her, his expression far from friendly. 'I suffered through that massage—I already told you that.'

She bit her lip. 'I'm not talking about a superficial kind of tension—this was deep. It felt to me as though you've been carrying a huge weight on your shoulders for a very long time.'

'Stick to menus, Lucy—a much better use for your imagination.'

'I've been giving massages for years—touch is a language I know!'

'Lay off, will you?' he snarled, and swung the pail out of the sink.

How could she ever have thought she was in love with him? She hated his guts! She crammed the food back down into the refrigerator hatch, her mind anywhere but on what she was doing, and twisted to see if she'd left anything out on the counter. Troy was already halfway across the saloon, every inch of his body armored against her. Her eyes glazed with tears. The refrigerator door slipped through her fingers and slammed down on the back of her other hand.

She gave a startled cry of pain, gaping at the heavy wood and metal door that looked as though it had amputated her hand at the wrist. Before she could move, Troy had crossed the cabin, dumped the pail on the counter, and was lifting the door. She pulled her hand free, and as though it belonged to someone else watched it shaking like a leaf in the wind. Small drops of bright red blood appeared from nowhere.

He seized her arm, put her wrist under the cold tap and

turned the water on. The blood sheered off in pink sheets. 'Stay there,' Troy ordered. He pulled a first-aid kit out of a lower cupboard, extracted a gauze pad, turned off the tap and pressed the pad to the back of her hand. Then he steered Lucy over to the couch.

'I'm dripping on the floor,' she yelped.

'To hell with the floor!'

'You don't have to polish it,' Lucy said peevishly.

'These islands were the haunts of buccaneers... A bit of blood on the carpet'll add atmosphere to the place. Hold still, Lucy, this might hurt.'

She watched his fingers probe her bruised flesh, marveling at his gentleness. 'Nothing broken,' he said. 'And no need for stitches. But you'll be pretty sore for a couple of days. I'll put on an antibiotic cream and a bandage...and you're going to take it easy the rest of the day. I'll scrub out the bathrooms.'

'All right,' she said meekly. 'At least it's my left hand.'

He glanced up. She was very pale, her skin shadowed blue, her eyes bright with pain. He put down the cream, and with his thumbs slowly traced the curves of bone from her nose to her cheekbones, a gesture of such solicitude that she was touched to the heart. He said, 'We've got to stop this—fighting, I mean.'

'Yes,' she whispered. 'I shouldn't have said anything about the massage. I'm sorry.'

He said, choosing his words as meticulously as if each were a shell he was picking up from the beach, 'Everything you said was true... I'm just not ready to talk about it. Don't take that personally, will you, Lucy? I haven't talked to anyone.'

'I must stop pushing you.' She sighed. 'Although I do wish you'd tell me. Maybe I could help.'

His jaw tightened. 'Some things you can't change.'

It was a strange moment to remember her father, who between one day and the next had disappeared from her life forever. Resting her good hand on Troy's wrist, achingly aware of the jut of bone and the heat of his skin, Lucy said, 'When you're ready, you'll tell someone. And—who knows?—it might even be me.'

He pulled his hand away and said roughly, 'If it were to be anyone, it would be you. I don't have a clue how you do it, but you get past my defences every time.'

'Don't hate me for that,' she pleaded.

'I'll try not to.' His smile a mere movement of his mouth, Troy got up from the couch and brought the first-aid kit over to the table. Ripping open another gauze pad, he added, 'I knew when I hired you I was in for trouble. Knew it the first minute I saw you, when you said you were looking for *Seawind*. Now, hold still.'

The message was clear: he'd had enough of the personal.

Obediently Lucy held still, and equally obediently spent the next hour resting on the deck with a small bottle of juice in her good hand. 'Passionfruit', it was labeled. Not finding this very funny, she drained the bottle, finished her grocery list, and went below deck to polish the brass. If she took her time, her hand didn't hurt too much. Troy had finished the other cabins so she helped wipe the floor and then looked around with pleasure. 'Looks great. What would you like for supper?'

'I'm taking you out for dinner—Caribbean food. For the sake of my blood pressure, wear anything but that sundress. And if you want a shower, why don't you use my cabin? That way these'll stay clean.'

It was the sensible thing to do. But, when Lucy climbed down the ladder into the forward cabin, the shirt Troy had been wearing that morning was flung on his unmade bed, where she could see the indentation his head had made in the pillow. Panic warred with passion in her breast. She had no idea how she was going to get through the next five nights.

The shower was less than satisfactory because she didn't want to get her hand wet; it had been throbbing ever since she had hit it. She dried herself, dressed in her beige trousers with its matching crocheted top over a green silk camisole, and tried to hide the marks of pain with make-up. Her face looked back at her in the little mirror. Troy was right about her hair; the short clustered curls did become her. He's marking me, she thought, with a superstitious shiver of fear, and knew that one lesson she was struggling to learn from him was that of patience.

He had admitted she got through his defences. All she had to do was wait until they fell to the ground.

The restaurant was open to the ocean breeze and charmingly decorated with hibiscus and bougainvillaea; Lucy ate conch patties and flying fish and papaya ice-cream, and at any other time would have been totally happy, sitting across from Troy and watching the moon climb in the sky. But the throbbing in her hand had brought on a throbbing in her temples, and she felt very tired.

Troy called for the bill as soon as they'd finished eating. 'No bar hopping tonight,' he said. 'I'm taking you home.'

Home was *Seawind*. Home was where Troy was. 'I'm sorry—have I been bad company?'

The candle to one side of the table flickered over his features. 'You're the best company there is, and you look worn out.'

She was blushing again. 'I never know what you're going to say next, Troy Donovan.'

'Trade winds are dependable. But maybe a touch boring?'

Lucy chuckled. 'You have yet to bore me.'

He paid the bill, put a casual arm around her waist and steered her toward the Jeep. 'In the morning I'll go with you to do the groceries.'

He wasn't a man for flowery speeches, but he would be there when you needed him, Lucy thought. So in that sense he was like the trade winds. While dependability wasn't the most romantic of concepts, it could be very comforting.

She had never included words like dependability and comfort in her definitions of love before.

She had leaned into his arm, and when they reached the Jeep he put his other arm around her and without a word kissed her parted lips. The palm fronds rustled overhead, and in the bushes the crickets shrilled their monotonous nocturnal song. It was not a passionate embrace, it held none of the anger or desperation that so often had bound them together, but for Lucy it seemed as though another of Troy's defences had fallen—that he had allowed her one step closer to the man he really was.

When they drew apart neither had any need for words. He drove the Jeep to the marina, parked, and they walked arm in arm down the dock to *Seawind*, where the crickets' song was replaced by the metallic keening of the wind in the shrouds. Lucy had left her gear in the saloon, planning to sleep down there that night.

Troy said calmly, 'I'll put your bag in my cabin. When you're in bed, call me and I'll give you a painkiller; it'll help you sleep.'

'But—'

He stilled her protest with a finger on her lips. 'Lucy, I'm only going to say this once. You don't have to be afraid of sharing the cabin with me—I'll wait until you're asleep every night before I go to bed. If we ever make love, I want it to be in a proper bed with no one else on the other side of the wall, have you got that?'

If... The biggest word in the dictionary. Yet even while Lucy's heart was banging against her ribs at the thought of herself and Troy in a proper bed—with or without anyone on the other side of the wall—she also knew she could trust his word implicitly. He would never force himself on her. And, despite their cramped quarters, he would do his best to give her privacy.

'When you're angry with me,' she said unsteadily, 'I can handle you just fine. But when you're like this...I feel like crying—it's ridiculous. I go all mushy inside. Like melted papaya ice-cream—and don't you dare laugh at me. I'm serious.'

'The place for ice-cream that's melting is the freezer.'

'Or else,' she said recklessly, 'it should be eaten as soon as possible.'

Twin sparks flared in his eyes. 'Instead of "if" we make love, I should have said "when"...'

'That's one case where I certainly approve your use of the word "should",' Lucy said, with a lightness that didn't quite succeed.

Troy ran one finger along the soft curve of her lower lip, watching her eyes darken with desire. 'But "when" isn't tonight or the next five nights, Lucy. And, yes, I'm trying to convince myself as much as you.'

'I find that very encouraging,' she remarked.

He laughed, and deliberately stepped away from her. 'I'll put your bag in the cabin. Then you'd better get to bed.'

She watched him leave the saloon. 'When' was a very different word from 'if'. Was she a fool even to think of making love with Troy, a man who in so many ways was an enigma to her? Was this yet another impulsive action that afterwards she would bitterly regret? Troy knew she could only stay in Tortola for four weeks, that she had a job to get back to, an apartment, a circle of friends. So would they make love and then go their separate ways?

She couldn't bear that.

She trailed up the companionway steps, nursing her sore hand, her head pounding. Troy was getting himself a beer from the cooler that was lashed to the lifelines. She edged past him and climbed down into the cabin, where, after switching on the small brass lamp, she cleaned her teeth, undressed, pulled her nightgown over her head and got into bed.

Troy's bunk was perhaps two feet from hers. She gave a violent start as he called down the hatch, 'You ready?'

'Yes,' she croaked, and pulled the sheet up over her breasts as he came down the ladder, his bare feet automatically seeking out the rungs, his long legs moving with supple economy. He went into the bathroom and filled a glass with water. Stooping, he passed it to her and pulled a small vial of pills from the pocket of his shorts. 'One should do,' he said.

She took the white pill from his palm with the very tips of her fingers and swallowed it down. Only wanting him gone, she said, 'Thanks.'

'I'll raise the sails tomorrow—you can take the helm, that'll be easier for you. We'll only go to Norman and Peter Islands, the same as we did with the Merritts.' He smiled at her with impersonal kindness; in the soft light of the lamp his eyes looked almost blue. 'You should feel a lot better tomorrow.'

I love you, Lucy thought blankly. I don't have a choice anymore. I've fallen in love with you whether I want to or not.

'What's the matter?' Troy demanded.

'I—nothing. I'm just tired, that's all.'

She wasn't sure that he believed her. But he straightened, his big body throwing a bigger shadow on the wall. 'I'll see you in the morning,' he said, switched out the light and left the cabin.

Lucy lay down. She could see stars through the open hatch, and found herself remembering Phil. Technically Phil had been the more handsome of the two men. But the only time she'd been ill in the months she'd spent with Phil he'd kept his distance. 'I'll leave the doctoring to your mother,' he'd said with his most charming smile. He'd had lots of charm, she thought, gazing into the darkness. But he hadn't been kind.

In a flash of insight she realized that in his own way he'd been as distant as her mother and her two sisters. Certainly she'd never felt needed by him.

Troy needed her. On that she'd swear.

And she didn't just mean in bed.

When Lucy woke the next morning, rolling over to peer at the alarm clock she kept on her shelf, she bumped her elbow hard against a wooden ledge and sat up with a jerk. She wasn't in her cabin. She was in Troy's.

Her hand hurt.

The digital clock set in the wall said ten to six. Troy was still asleep. Scarcely breathing, Lucy let her eyes wander over him, and, with a deep inner certainty that took her a little further along the road called love, knew that she wanted to wake up beside him every morning for the rest of her life.

She had no experience on which to base this certainty, for her mother had never remarried and her two sisters were too devoted to their careers even to date very much, let alone marry. But she knew it to be true.

His face was turned to her, his thick hair tousled. The sheet had slid to his hips; he was bared to the waist. Even in sleep his fingers were tightly curled into a fist and there was a faint frown furrowing his brow.

Would he ever trust her enough to tell her what was wrong?

It would be so easy to leave her own bunk and crawl into his, to wrap her arms around him so he would wake to the warmth and softness of her body pressed into his. And then what would happen? Would he kiss her and caress her? Would he take off her gown so she was naked to him? Would he feast his eyes on her and let his hands wander to those secret places he had never touched?

He stirred, muttering something under his breath. In a flash Lucy lay down again, feeling the heat scorch her cheeks, a heat that reflected the insidious weakness of desire in her limbs. Troy's breathing slowed and deepened. She closed her eyes, trying to quieten the racing of her pulse, and knew that whatever this big blond man meant to her he was different from the rest.

Twelve hours later the Dillons were seated in the cockpit of *Seawind*, anchored off a quiet cove on Norman Island. Leona Dillon took another cracker spread with crab dip and said languidly, 'Delicious.'

Troy was barbecuing thick hamburgers; Lucy was baking fish with a lime sauce, to be served with wild rice and steamed vegetables. Nursing her left hand, she brought up more nachos and salsa for Brad, who was devouring them as if lunch was a meal that had never happened.

Brad was thirteen; despite his appetite he had yet to remove either his Walkman or his pose of world-weary sophistication. His sister, a year older, had made it clear within five minutes on the boat that she was not here by choice; but the sulky pout of her carmined lips hadn't prevented her from eating her fair share of the nachos, or from casting speculative glances, laced with emergent sexuality, at Troy.

Lucy served dinner in the saloon. She had taken considerable trouble with the meal and was rewarded when Leona asked for the recipe for the lime sauce and Victor cleaned his plate. Leona's simple linen shift would have paid for Lucy's return flight to Ottawa; her hair was a froth of copper curls and her fingernails wouldn't have survived a single turn of the anchor winch. In spite of her glamorous appearance, there was an earthiness to her that Lucy found rather appealing. But if her glamor was for Victor's benefit, Lucy soon realized, Leona was wasting her time.

Ever since he'd come on board, Victor, who was a cardiologist, had had his patrician nose buried in a medical journal. Lucy would have been willing to bet that at home he read while he ate. It had been Victor's decision to anchor in a quiet cove their first night; stubbornness rather than strength of character, Lucy had decided, had ensured he'd gotten his way over the objections of the three other members of his family.

She got up to fetch dessert, a fresh fruit salad along with puff pastries filled with cream and laced with a chocolate fudge frosting. The younger Dillons attacked the pastries, and Leona helped herself and Victor to the salad. Victor eyed the pastries wistfully and dug his spoon into his bowl of fruit.

Resting a predatory hand on Troy's bare arm, Leona said, 'Tomorrow we'll stay at a yacht club, didn't you say?'

'Right... There's a disco there and a steel drum band.

A little more action than Norman Island, whose only inhabitants are wild goats and pelicans.'

Leona gave a throaty chuckle. 'Not quite my cup of tea.'

'Troy, will you go with us to the disco?' Kim asked, tossing her hair back with a sultry smile.

Her father interposed, 'He's too old to be courting voluntary deafness, my dear.'

'I'll keep my eye on everyone,' Troy said. 'That's my job.'

'Excellent,' Victor remarked. 'I can catch up on some more reading while you're all ashore.'

Leona sent him a fulminating look and stroked Troy's arm with a provocative smile. 'I'm sure you're a wonderful dancer...a lot of big men are.'

Troy reached for the fruit salad, thereby dislodging her hand. 'You'll have to ask Lucy.'

Thanks a lot, Lucy thought in comical dismay. 'It's no trouble to find someone to dance with, and the band's great.'

'You'll like that, dear,' Victor said to his wife, pushing back his chair. 'If I stay here any longer, I'll succumb to one of those pastries—so I'll go and read for a while.' He gave Lucy a courtly bow. 'An excellent meal, thank you.'

Kim said sulkily, 'I wish there was a TV.'

'There's a bunch of games under the seat. We could play something after dinner,' Lucy suggested.

'Not my style,' Kim complained. 'I miss my boyfriend—he's a fullback on the school team... Although he's not as sexy as you, Troy.'

'Darling!' Leona protested half-heartedly.

'Well, he's not. I like older men.'

'You're so dumb,' her brother remarked, reaching for his Walkman and adjusting the headset.

'I am *not*.' Kim pulled a hideous face at him and

flounced up from the table. 'This is going to be the longest five days of my *entire* life,' she declaimed tragically, went to her cabin and slammed the door.

Leona's face settled into lines of discontent that were, Lucy was sure, habitual. 'She needs a man's hand. Victor's always so busy.'

'She needs an overdose,' Brad said, and turned up the volume on his tape.

'Bradley!' Her mouth drooping pathetically, Leona said, 'They're quite out of control—in effect, I'm a single parent. Victor said this was to be a family holiday—and where is he? Reading about lymphocytes and pernicious anemia.'

'Kim is a beautiful girl,' Lucy said diplomatically.

'I had her when I was much too young, of course,' Leona responded, pouting at Troy. 'Silly the things we do when we're teenagers, isn't it?'

Leona was at least forty.

Lucy embarked on a story about some of the more out-rageous of her sailing exploits and succeeded in making Leona laugh. After she'd washed the dishes, she suggested that she, Leona and Troy play three-handed bridge; Brad had long since retired to his cabin with his tape collection. When Victor wandered down to the saloon because it was too dark to read in the cockpit, Lucy cajoled him into joining them.

He played with erratic brilliance, as if only part of his mind was on the cards, and then sharp at ten, kissing his wife's cheek, said, 'I like to be up early in the morning. Goodnight, all.'

'And to think I married him because I thought he was fun,' Leona said with a total lack of discretion. 'Kindly don't wake *me* early in the morning.'

The cabin door shut smartly behind her. Troy said softly, for Lucy's ears only, 'The honeymoon's over.'

Lucy smothered a laugh. 'She's unhappy.'

'This is a chartered sloop—not the Love Boat.'

'You shouldn't be such a hunk.'

'Huh. If she'd dug her nails in any more deeply, I'd have bled to death.'

'I'm sure she's only trying to get Victor's attention.'

'Good luck,' said Troy, and put the cards away, yawning. 'We're going to earn our keep this trip, Lucy.'

Nor did the next few days prove him wrong. Troy, by a masterly combination of interest and indifference, got Brad to take the helm, a move that necessitated the removal of the Walkman. And despite his attempts to look bored, it was clear Brad enjoyed steering *Seawind*. Lucy took Kim to every boutique on every island that they passed, and as often as she thought she could get away with it endeavored to separate Victor from his cardiology journals. Leona spent a lot of time lying in the sun on the green mats, in a bikini that wasn't intended to go anywhere near the water.

On their third day they met up with Jack's charter, which included two teenage boys; Kim cheered up appreciably. On the morning of the fourth day they had a near collision with a bareboat captain who had never heard of the rules of the road. Troy's swift avoidance tactics and subsequent tirade at the unhappy skipper of the bareboat shifted Brad from world-weariness to hero-worship, as a result of which he then wanted to learn everything there was to know about sailing before he disembarked. Lucy was amused by his enthusiasm and touched by Troy's patience.

At their lunchtime anchorage Troy somehow managed to get Victor snorkeling, along with Kim and Brad; Lucy, now that her hand had healed, took the opportunity to offer Leona a massage. She worked in silence, bringing all her skill and concentration to play. When she finally sat back on her heels, she said gently, 'There...how does that feel?'

Leona fumbled with the strap of her bikini top and sat up. To Lucy's dismay she saw that Leona was crying, slow tears that leaked between the black fences of her lashes. 'Why doesn't Victor ever touch me like that?' Leona whimpered. 'As though he cares how I feel.' She grabbed for her cosmetic bag, which was never far from her, and took out a tissue. 'I still love him, you see—silly of me, isn't it? I could fight another woman. But medical journals and malfunctioning arteries... I've given up trying to compete with those. I used to flirt with every available man in sight—I even had an affair with a urologist once—and then I tried drinking too much, but all it did was make me sick.' She sighed, dabbing at her cheeks. 'I guess I'm stuck with it. And him.'

Remembering Heather and Craig, Lucy said impulsively, 'Maybe I could teach Victor how to give you a massage.'

'Maybe this boat will sprout wings.'

'I promise I'll try. We've still got all day tomorrow.'

'Honey, I've been married to him for sixteen years—you'll need more than twenty-four hours.'

Lucy was inclined to agree. 'I'd better go. I've got to start supper.'

This time Leona's long scarlet nails rested on Lucy's arm. 'Thanks, Lucy,' Leona said. 'You're a sweetie.'

That evening, as they were all eating Lucy's strawberry mousse, Victor said in his mild voice, 'Ever since we arrived, you've looked familiar to me, Troy. But I can't place you, no matter how hard I try. I've never taken a cruise before, so it's nothing to do with boats. For some reason I associate you with Tennessee—now, why would that be?' He closed his eyes, chewing a whole strawberry ru- minatively. 'It's your voice that I remember as much as your face.'

Troy glanced at the journal neatly aligned beside Victor's bowl and said casually, 'I gave a paper at a med- ical convention in Tennessee two years ago.'

Victor sat up straight, looking as energized as Lucy had seen him. 'Of course! You were the keynote speaker. The latest techniques on skin-grafting—fascinating material.'

As Lucy sat dumbstruck, Leona said speculatively, 'You're a doctor, Troy?'

Victor answered for him. 'An internationally known specialist in craniofacial repair—plastic surgery, my dear. Well, I'm delighted to meet you, Troy. What a pity I didn't speak sooner; we could have had many interesting discus- sions.'

Leona said bluntly, 'What are you doing this for, Troy?' Her gold bracelets jingling, she indicated the confines of the cabin.

'An old friend of mine runs this charter company. He developed appendicitis with complications and can't come back for another two weeks. I was down here on vacation anyway, so I took over for him.'

'How kind of you,' Leona murmured, running her tongue over her lips as she passed him her wine-glass for a refill; it wasn't an opportune time for Lucy to remember the urologist.

'Quite a change from surgery,' Victor said, looking very pleased with this turn of events.

Lucy got up to plug in the coffee. *She* wasn't pleased. She was, she realized, furious. Troy could tell a group of strangers about his real job but not her, whom he was contemplating taking to bed. From her he'd kept it a secret.

No wonder he'd been so deft at cutting her hair. And

how he must have laughed when she'd asked if he was a hairdresser!

With a sickening lurch of her heart she realized something else. His kindness the night she'd hurt her hand had been nothing but his bedside manner: he was being the perfect doctor. After all, a plastic surgeon would deal with women all the time—rich women, who didn't like the effects of aging or who wanted a prettier nose. Women like Leona. She'd been a fool to take it personally.

She wanted nothing more than to throw the remains of the strawberry mousse at the wall. Or at Troy. Instead Lucy arranged the coffee-cups and liqueur glasses on a tray and removed the dessert bowls from the table, smiling pleasantly the whole time. She smiled until her jaw ached, until she was sure an insincere smirk would be plastered to her face for the rest of the cruise. When everyone else went outside to watch the sunset, she stayed below, washing dishes with a ferocious energy that didn't soothe her spirits in the slightest.

She went to bed early, still fuming, and was wide awake when Troy came down the ladder. She should be sensible and lie still, and keep her eyes and her mouth shut. But she didn't feel sensible. She flicked the overhead light on and sat up. And instead of smiling, she glowered at Troy, as if he were a reincarnation of Raymond Blogden.

Not the man with whom she was secretly in love.

CHAPTER SEVEN

TROY was unbuttoning his shirt. 'What's wrong, Lucy?' he said in surprise. 'Can't you sleep?'

'You could write me a prescription for sleeping pills, Dr Donovan,' she said with heavy sarcasm. 'Why didn't you tell me you were a doctor?'

'You didn't ask.'

'Why would I? I assumed you ran the charter and that was your only job.'

'What's the big deal, Lucy? So I'm a doctor, so what?'

Her scowl, if anything, deepened. 'Are there any more little surprises lying in store for me?'

'You're acting as though I'm a drug pusher. Or a heroin addict.'

Lucy sat up straighter in the bunk, her skin gleaming through the lace on her nightgown. 'Let me tell you something. My mother's a forensic pathologist—that's how she met my father; he was one as well, he died when I was three. My elder sister's an immunologist, and my younger sister's an oncologist who's just been awarded a big research grant. I've had it up to here—' she drew her finger theatrically across her throat '—with doctors.'

He flung his shirt across the end of the bed. 'You're stereotyping me again.'

'No, I'm not!'

'Oh, yes, you are. First I'm a big blond hunk and now I'm a doctor. Which other of your prejudices am I going to activate, Lucy?'

'That's a horrible thing to say!'

'When are you ever going to see me as a real person?'

The angry retort on the tip of her tongue died away. His question was valid, she thought with painful truth. And she hated it when people misconstrued her own job. Swallowing her pride, she admitted, 'I—I've never felt at home in my family, and a big part of that's related to what they do... So I suppose I am prejudiced against doctors.'

Troy sat down across from her. 'Those specialties you mentioned—they involve very little contact with people.'

She should have realized he'd pick up on that. 'I don't think my family likes people very much.'

'You like people... Why didn't you specialize in family medicine?'

If she'd been smart, Lucy thought, she'd have rehearsed this conversation before embarking on it. 'Because when my parents were handing out the genes for mathematical skills, they skipped me. I can't do physics and chemistry to save my soul. So for three years in a row, to my mother's chagrin, I failed the medical admissions tests. I couldn't even get into physiotherapy, which was my second choice.'

'Does your mother like you?'

Lucy said fretfully, 'Your specialty's plastic surgery. Not psychiatry.'

'So she doesn't... Could it be that you missed out on mathematics but you inherited all the warmth and emotion in your family instead?'

Lucy's eyes filled with sudden tears. 'Is that what you think?' she said in a low voice.

Troy reached out a hand across the gap between their bunks, clasping her wrist. 'Is your family proud of what you do?'

She bent her head. 'Not really. It's not—respectable

enough, I guess. And I don't earn nearly as much money as they do.'

'But you like your job.'

'I love it! It's hands-on, it's so direct. I can make people relax and feel better about themselves even in one session. Touch is so important and so neglected nowadays, when either we don't have the time for it or else we sexualize it...' She stared down at his long fingers and added in a rush, 'I've never been turned on by any of my clients— not until you came along.'

He rubbed the little hollow in her wrist with his thumb. 'I'd be willing to bet you threaten the hell out of your mother and your sisters. You've got the courage to go your own way and you love people—I've watched you with Leona. And—you can trust my word on this—you've sure got lots of feelings.'

'*Me* threaten *them*?'

'Yep.'

It was not a point of view Lucy had ever considered before. Yet it made a crazy kind of sense when she thought about it. Feeling as though she'd just made a quantum leap along the steep path to maturity, she muttered, 'No wonder I always feel like a stranger in my own family.'

He was still rubbing her wrist with slow, hypnotic movements. Before she could lose her courage, she blurted, 'Is this just part of your bedside manner?'

He moved over to sit on the edge of her bunk, brought her palm to his lips and kissed it with lingering warmth. 'No,' he said, 'it's because it's your bedside.'

Lucy wasn't entirely convinced. Ever since Victor had spoken she had been aware of an ache of disappointment that Troy had feet of clay. 'You must see a lot of beautiful women, though.'

Troy glanced up, surprised. 'Hardly,' he said.

'But you're a plastic surgeon.'

He frowned at her. 'Did you think I went around doing face lifts and liposuction? Have a heart, Lucy. I deal almost entirely with children. Birth defects and trauma victims. Burns, car accidents—that sort of thing.'

'I'm sorry—I shouldn't have jumped to conclusions,' she said in quick contrition, adding naïvely, 'You must be famous to have been the keynote speaker at that conference.'

He moved his shoulders. 'Oh, well…over the years I've had a few successes.' Playing with her fingers, which were warm against his bare chest, he said huskily, 'The only way I've been able to keep my hands off you the past few nights is because you've been sleeping when I've come to bed.' He shifted restlessly. 'We'd better call it quits right now, or we'll be in trouble.'

'I suppose we should,' said Lucy.

'Your favorite word.' Taking her by the shoulders, he added with an intensity that made her tremble, 'When I came down here last night you were asleep with the moonlight on your face, and with every cell in my body I wanted to possess you… There's nothing I ever read in any medical text on human sexuality that could have prepared me for the way I felt.'

Lucy wanted so badly to tell him she loved him, and could only trust the inner voice that told her to wait, to have patience. 'It's new territory for me, too.'

His voice roughened. 'I own a villa on Virgin Gorda. I usually go there every February and again in April—I'd be there now if Gavin hadn't had his appendix out. We've got two days between the Dillons and the next guests…come to the villa with me, Lucy.'

A proper bed with no one else around. Wasn't that what he had said? 'All right,' she said faintly.

As if her reply had loosened a floodgate, Troy said, 'We'd only have twenty-four hours. But we'd be alone. The villa can't be reached other than by water, so it's completely private. It's the place I go when I've had too many patients I can't mend the way I want to, and too many parents whose fears I can't allay... Apart from a couple of days at the beginning of this month I haven't been there for nearly a year.'

So was it his job that had built up so much anger and tension in him? He was, after all, only human, and must constantly fall short of what he would wish to achieve for the children in his care. Lucy pushed the hair back from his forehead and smiled into his eyes. 'I'd love to go there.'

'It's my haven,' he said, his words muffled as he brought her fingers to his lips and kissed them one by one. 'In all the years I've owned it, I've never taken a woman there.'

Lucy believed him instantly, and in a rush of joy lifted his face in her hands and kissed him full on the mouth. It was the first time she had taken the initiative so boldly; mixed with joy was the new knowledge of her own power and the rapture of his response, flame leaping to meet flame in the most ancient of burnings.

They kissed for a long time, hungry kisses laced with a passionate tenderness that transported Lucy to a place she'd never been before. It was Troy who finally pulled back, his eyes the dark blue of the ocean depths. He said hoarsely, 'You're like *Seawind* when the wind catches her sails and she leaps to meet the waves... God, how I want you.'

'You shall have me,' Lucy whispered. 'All of me, nothing held back, nothing kept for myself.'

'I've never doubted your generosity.' His face con-

vulsed with longing, Troy kissed her one last time, a deep
kiss whose intimacy shivered along Lucy's nerves. 'Goodnight, dearest Lucy.'

I love you, Troy…I love you. While the words, unspoken, illumined her features, from some unacknowledged
source of wisdom she said, with just the right touch of
lightness, 'Do you think if the cook went on strike the
Dillons would go back to Tortola tomorrow instead of the
day after?'

His chuckle relieved some of the strain in his face. 'I
doubt it—Victor's still got four more journals to read.'

'And Brad wants to learn every nautical term in the
book.' She grimaced. 'Breakfast will be at the usual time—
provided I get any sleep. Judging by the way I feel right
now, that's not too likely.'

'For me, either,' said Troy. He reached up, turned off
the light, and moved over to his own bunk.

Lucy curled up, facing him in the darkness. Her body
ached to be held by him. But her heart was singing with
happiness. Dearest Lucy, she thought. Surely the two most
beautiful words in the language.

First thing the next morning Lucy enlisted Troy's help in
her campaign to teach Victor massage. 'If you told him
about the medical benefits of massage and suggested that
he could really help Leona by learning how to do it, he'd
pay a lot more attention than if I tried to persuade him.
He thinks you're the neatest thing since sliced bread.'

She was brushing her hair in front of the little mirror in
the bathroom; Troy was still in bed, propped against his
pillow. He said lazily, 'Could it be possible that I'm being
used?'

'Very probable, I'd say.'

'You're an unscrupulous woman.'

She grinned at him from the doorway. 'It's all in a good cause.'

'A better cause would be served were you to kiss me good morning.'

'Two kisses if you say yes.'

'Not just unscrupulous. Venal.'

'My true self is emerging,' Lucy said.

'I'll do it. Although I can't imagine that a couple of massage lessons will transform Victor into a model husband.'

It didn't seem very likely to Lucy, either. 'I have to try, though,' she said. 'For Leona's sake.'

Troy gave his rare smile. 'You're a nice person, Lucy Barnes.' His eyes darkening, he added, 'Come here. There's a small matter of two kisses. Whose duration you neglected to specify.'

'Clearly I need lessons in venality,' she said, and felt her heart begin to race as she approached his bunk.

Two kisses, she soon learned, could last quite a long time. She was pink-cheeked when she headed for the galley, and forgot to put nutmeg in the French toast. She served it with sausages, maple syrup and hot applesauce, and afterward was amused at how neatly Troy commandeered Victor for a talk up by the bow.

Troy then took Kim and Brad snorkeling, promising Brad a barracuda and Kim an angelfish. Victor, looking as though he was about to perform his first major operation, consented to be shown the techniques of a back and shoulder massage. Lucy did her best with the two of them, neither of whom was at all relaxed, and did at least leave them after the session sitting together on the green mat talking to one another.

Troy, Brad and Kim were chugging back in the dinghy.

The first moment they were alone, Troy asked, 'How did it go?'

'For a cardiologist,' Lucy answered drily, 'Victor knows almost nothing about matters of the heart.'

'One more doctor out of touch with his feelings,' Troy said.

He had spoken with an underlying bitterness that made it seem more and more likely to Lucy that his job was the source of his unhappiness. Tucking this thought away for future reference, she said, 'Lesson two is tomorrow morning, before we dock.'

'And then,' said Troy, 'we'll head for the villa.'

Heat scorched Lucy's cheeks. She was standing on the opposite side of the cockpit to Troy, but she felt bound to him as surely as if they were locked in each other's arms. 'I'll go and lift the anchor,' she mumbled, and turned away, then saw Leona stationed at the forepeak watching them.

'Privacy is beginning to seem a most desirable commodity,' she added between gritted teeth.

That day Brad took the helm every chance he got, Kim and Leona went shopping in Spanish Town, and Victor thereby was able to read two more journals in peace and quiet. Everyone was happy, thought Lucy, amazed that with all this activity the hours could creep by so slowly.

One moment she longed for it to be midday tomorrow, the next she was plunged into a cold sweat. Because she loved Troy, making love with him seemed both inevitable and right. But, because Troy had given no indication that he loved her, she was also afraid. She already knew that going to bed with him would make her vulnerable as she had never been before.

They would have, at the most, twenty-four hours at the villa. And then what?

*   *   *

Late that afternoon Lucy had the galley to herself. Jack's charter had joined them at the anchorage, so Brad and Kim were swimming with the teenagers in Jack's party; Victor had gone for a sleep in his cabin and Leona was sunbathing on the deck. Troy had taken the dinghy to Spanish Town on an unexplained errand. Humming to herself, she had put the last touches to a chocolate cheese-cake and was mixing herbs for wild rice when Leona descended the stairs.

After pouring herself a rum and Coke, Leona sat in the nearest swivel chair and said, 'I don't know how you persuaded Victor into that lesson—but thank you, Lucy.'

Lucy wasn't about to divulge the part Troy had played. 'Tomorrow—same time, same place,' she said, measuring water into a saucepan for the rice.

Leona leaned forward. 'You and Troy looked just like Kathleen Turner and Michael Douglas this morning... You know what I mean? Sort of sizzling.'

'Too much tropic sun,' Lucy said feebly.

'Who are you kidding?' said Leona. 'You looked like you belonged together. Like you were in love.'

'Then appearances are deceptive.'

'Hey, he's gorgeous. Most women, if a guy like Troy looked at them like that, would be out trying on wedding dresses. I know you're both single—I asked him that the first day we were on board—so what's the hold up?'

Leona was only a third through her rum, and Lucy was trapped in the galley. But after tomorrow, she'd never see the Dillon family again. Busily arranging sliced almonds on a tray to toast them, she confessed, 'Ever since I was in grade seven, the only kind of man I ever fell in love with was big, blond and handsome. Like Troy. But either I fall out of love or the man doesn't hang around long

enough for me to do so. I was engaged once—he upped
and left me. My track record, in other words, is lousy.'

'Troy doesn't look the type to take off.'

'Maybe it's my own feelings I'm scared to trust.'

'You've never been attracted to Burt Reynolds or Mel
Gibson or Tom Hanks?'

Lucy shook her head. 'But I'm a pushover for Robert
Redford and Nick Nolte.'

Leona's eyes narrowed. She took a long, thoughtful sip
of her rum. 'What colour's your father's hair?'

'My father?' Lucy repeated, puzzled. 'My father died
when I was three.'

'Oh, sorry—I didn't know that… But I dare say he still
had hair. In fact, if he died young, he probably had a full
head of it. What colour was it, Lucy?'

Lucy gripped the edge of the counter. The most vivid
memory of her early childhood, and almost her only memory of her father, was of herself being thrown high in the
air—so high that she was surrounded by apple blossoms,
pink and white against a blue sky—and then caught by a
giant of a man whose blond hair gleamed like gold in the
sunlight. He had been laughing, she remembered. Laughing and handsome and vibrantly alive.

'Blond,' she said numbly.

'I knew it!' Leona crowed. 'My analyst told me that
you're always attracted to men like your father. You often
marry them. Which might well account for the divorce
rates,' she finished cynically.

Stunned, Lucy stood still. Her father, her big, blond,
handsome father, had walked out of the house one day and
never come back. A heart attack, her mother had told her
years later. And she, Lucy, had been subconsciously
searching for him ever since. Falling in love over and over
again with men like him, men who often deserted her—

just as her father had left the little girl he had played with in the orchard.

She knew Leona was right; knew it in her bones. She also knew that she was going to cry. She said incoherently, 'I—I've got to— Excuse me, Leona,' and fumbled her way out of the galley and up the steps.

Troy was just climbing out of the dinghy. Averting her head, she clambered over the bench and scrambled forward, praying he wouldn't follow her. She almost fell down the ladder into their cabin. Flinging herself down on the bed, she stuffed her face into her pillow to muffle the sobs that were crowding their way from her throat.

Then she was being half lifted, and through a curtain of tears saw that it was Troy. Big, blond Troy. She could hear herself crying—thin, high sounds like an animal in pain. 'G-go away,' she wept, and felt him gather her into his arms and press her to his chest. He was warm and solid and very much alive; she sobbed all the harder, her fists clutching his shirtfront, her forehead hard against his breastbone.

He held her until she had cried herself out. Only then did he wipe her wet cheeks with a handful of tissues, waiting until she had blown her nose before he said, 'Lucy, dear, what's the matter?'

She scrubbed at her face with the back of her hand, her breath catching in her throat. For a moment she closed her eyes, wrapping her arms around him so tightly that he added, in mixed amusement and concern, 'I'm not going to go away. Just tell me what's wrong.'

'This is going to sound so silly,' she gulped. 'You see, I was crying for my father.'

'Your *father*? But he died years ago.'

'I know.' Lucy drew a couple of deep breaths and looked up at Troy, her nose splotchy, her eyes still swimming with tears; she desperately wanted him to understand. 'I don't think I've ever cried for him before. He vanished when I was three—I don't remember going to the funeral, and it was years afterward that my mother told me he'd had a massive coronary. When Leona and I were talking a few minutes ago...it suddenly hit me like a ton of bricks that I've been looking for him all my life. He was a big, blond, handsome man, you see.' She blew her nose again and stumbled on, 'It sounds corny, and I'm not trying to excuse myself...but I know that's why I kept falling in love with big blond men—I couldn't help it.'

Troy said warily, 'There's a certain logic to that.'

'I feel as though I've been in a cage all my life without even knowing it, and I've suddenly been given the key. Because I won't have to do that anymore. Troy, don't you understand? I can fall in love with whom I please.'

'I see,' he said, in a voice empty of emotion.

She hurried on before she could lose her courage, 'If I ever saw you as my father, I'm truly sorry. I know it won't happen again. You're you. Troy. Who happens to be big and blond and handsome.' Her smile was as dazzling as sun after rain. 'How could I have been so blind all these years? It seems so obvious now—about my father, I mean. Anyway, what I'm really saying is that I'm free to see you exactly as you are. For yourself.'

She seemed to have run out of words. Troy said, 'So you're not planning to fall in love with the first black-haired man you meet?'

'I'm planning to go to the villa with you tomorrow,' Lucy said steadily. 'If you still want me.'

'Oh, yes, I still want you.'

Aware of undercurrents, but having no idea of their nature, she added ruefully, 'Pretty silly to be crying for a man who's been dead for twenty-two years. I've heard of people delaying grief, but never to that extent, have you?'

'Not to that extent, no,' he said with careful precision.

'Is anything wrong, Troy?' She searched his face, finding nothing there but the guardedness that she had almost come to expect.

'Of course not,' he said shortly. 'Maybe you'd better go and find Leona. She looked rather as though she'd rubbed the magic lamp and an unexpectedly awesome genie had emerged.'

The words tripped from Lucy's tongue. 'Did you have a patient recently who died because of a heart attack?'

'No, Lucy. Off you go.'

His face was closed against her. Lucy got to her feet, washed her face in the bathroom and came back into the bedroom. She said evenly, 'Dinner's going to be late.'

'Doesn't matter. After dinner I thought we'd go ashore for a while. They're playing calypso music at the club, and Jack's lot will be there as well.'

Lucy felt more like going to sleep than going ashore. She climbed the ladder, went aft and found Leona in the cockpit, nursing what looked like the same glass of rum and Coke. Before the other woman could speak, Lucy said in a rush, 'I'm sorry I ran out on you like that—I've just cried my eyes out for a man who's been dead for over twenty years. Because you were right, Leona—I've been searching for him ever since he died, and thank goodness I didn't marry the big blond man I was engaged to a couple of years ago.' Impetuously she stepped closer and hugged Leona. 'Thanks,' she said. 'You changed my life by saying what you said.'

'I *did*?'

'Truly,' Lucy said with a watery grin.

'Wow,' said Leona. 'You know what? Victor and I had

the best—well, let's be honest—the *only* talk we've had in months after that massage.'

'So if dinner's a bit of a flop, it's been worth it?'

'You bet! Give me something to do and I'll help get dinner on the table.'

Lucy had no idea if it was against the rules for the guests to help the cook, but Leona looked more animated than Lucy had seen her, and Lucy wasn't about to quench that animation. 'Let's go,' she said.

The *pièce de résistance* of the meal was bananas *flambé*, the dark rum sending blue flames dancing over the fruit. They ate by candlelight—Lucy hoping to disguise the marks of her crying spell—and Troy plied the adults with wine; Lucy washed the dishes in a pleasant haze.

As she put away the last of the cutlery, she knew she'd told the truth to Leona: the insight about her father had indeed liberated her from a destructive pattern of many years. Paradoxically she felt much closer to the man who had fathered her. Troy had also shifted in her vision. She still loved the way the candle flames glimmered through his thick streaked hair, loved the breadth of his shoulders, the length of his legs. The play of muscles in his forearms kindled in her a fierce flame of desire, and the strong bones of his face, with its impenetrable slate-blue eyes and jutting cheekbones, drew her to him as the flowers of the hibiscus opened to the sun. He was blond, big and handsome; that hadn't changed. But she loved him because he was Troy. And every breath she drew told her that this time her love wouldn't alter. This was forever.

With a little jolt she saw that he had come back to the saloon and was standing watching her. He'd changed into a blue shirt and off-white cotton trousers, his untidy hair combed to a semblance of order. His eyes were indeed impenetrable, she thought with a tiny shudder of unease.

But all he said was, 'Can you be ready in five minutes, Lucy? The others are waiting.'

Twenty-four hours from now, what would she and Troy be doing?

Lucy said breathlessly, 'Sure,' and ran past him up the stairs. In the cabin she pulled on her sundress, hastily made up her face and daubed herself with perfume. Her eyes were very bright in the little mirror.

She was the last one to get in the dinghy. Kim was dressed to the hilt, because Jack's guests were going dancing as well; Brad sported a T-shirt with sailboats on front and back and a nautical cap. On shore the lanterns strung between the palm trees beckoned like multi-colored stars.

Troy and Jack pulled tables together so everyone could get to know each other, and even though her emotions felt about as stable as *Seawind* in a hurricane, Lucy coped valiantly with too many strangers and too much conviviality. She drank her fair share of rum punches, danced with every man at the table except Troy, and was somehow not at all surprised to find that he had disappeared when she came back to the table after five minutes of dodging Jack's leaden feet.

She switched to Coke, danced some more, and suddenly decided she too had had enough. Slipping between the tables, she headed toward the beach along a narrow dirt path that wound between the palms. To her overwrought imagination the fronds looked like unsheathed bayonets; sharp-edged, they clattered in the wind. When she reached the sand, she slipped off her sandals and walked barefoot, glad to be alone.

Mangroves had sculpted the beach into a series of curves, each hidden from the rest, some sandy, some piled with rocks and chunks of coral; imperceptibly Lucy began to relax. She was almost ready to head back to the dance-

floor when she caught a new sound over the soft ripple of
the waves and the susurration of the palms: a heavy rattle,
as though the rocks were being disturbed. It would take
something very large to make that much noise, she
thought, her nerves tightening. There it was again.

She was tempted to rejoin the crowds at the club, her
ears still able to catch the distant lilt of the music, but she
hadn't arrived in these enchanted islands by playing it safe.
She could creep closer in the shelter of the trees, just to
see what it was. Goats, probably. Or a wandering donkey.
They were loose everywhere.

Although it didn't seem too likely that a donkey would
be interested in rocks and coral.

As she edged nearer, until the next strip of beach came
in sight, she had enough caution to stay hidden behind the
thick leaves of a sea-grape shrub. The noise hadn't been
caused by donkeys or goats, she saw at once. And recognized immediately the man balanced on the rubble in his
light trousers and darker shirt. Even as she watched he
picked up a rock, and with concentrated fury threw it hard
against a huge boulder.

In a young boy this might have been seen as a game.
But for Troy it was in deathly earnest. Now that she was
closer Lucy could hear the harsh intake of his breathing,
almost like a sobbing in his throat. He bent, again hefting
a chunk of rock in his hand, then flung it at the boulder,
his feet braced in the jumble of coral. The explosion of
sound made Lucy shudder. She shrank back behind the
shrub.

His rage, so inarticulate, so ferocious, came as no surprise. She had lived with it for the last two weeks. She
had seen it erupt into violence in the stucco villa that belonged to Raymond Blogden. It had kept her at arms'
length from a man whom, foolishly or not, she had grown

to love. Even now, she knew she lacked the courage to confront him.

The job hadn't been invented that could have brought him to such a pitch of rage; she was sure of that. A woman. It had to be a woman. The first day she'd met him he'd warned her off. 'No male-female stuff,' he'd said. Why warn her if he hadn't been hurt, left so badly scarred that he was reduced to working off his anger on a lonely beach the only way he knew how? Any jealousy that Lucy had felt before was nothing compared to the ugly turmoil in her breast now; how intimate he must have been with this unknown woman; how much love he must have felt for her!

She jumped as the crack of rock on rock once more shattered the peace of the tropic night. He should have been dressed all in black, she thought wildly, for he was a man of darkness, a keeper of secrets. She was afraid of the force of his anger. Afraid of finding out about his past.

She might be frightened, but she was aware, too, that Troy had walked the length of several beaches in order to find privacy, that whatever demons he was trying to exorcise were his, and his alone, and that he wouldn't thank her for intruding.

She couldn't help him. She didn't know how.

Was this also love? This painful recognition that she was helpless? That all she could offer Troy was a silent prayer from the depths of her heart, and the solitude that he needed?

Like a gunshot, a hunk of dead coral struck the boulder. In the echoing silence she heard Troy's breath hiss between his teeth. Lucy turned around, torn by conflicting emotions, and hurried back along the beach. Maybe she was making the biggest mistake of her life to leave him… Did he really need solitude, or did he, unknown to himself, need the comfort of another human being? Was it respect for his struggle that had made her turn her back on him, or was it cowardice?

This was the man who was going to be her only companion in a lonely villa for twenty-four hours. Was she crazy? Or would he choose the villa, his haven, to tell her about the woman who had wounded him so grievously?

With no answers for any of her questions, Lucy ran along the dirt path toward the lights and music of the club. A huge part of her simply wanted to wrap her arms around the nearest palm tree and cry her eyes out. For the second time that day.

Was love inseparable from tears?

No one seemed to have noticed Lucy's absence; she slipped back into her seat and within moments was asked to dance by one of the more raucous of Jack's guests. Although she threw herself into the music, her skirt whirling about her knees, her hips gyrating, the ache in her heart didn't go away, and her eyes were constantly on the look out for Troy. When she went back to her seat, Victor rather ponderously asked her to dance. He was wearing a Hawaiian flowered shirt that Lucy was sure Leona had bought for him and he led her round the dance-floor with a flair she wouldn't have expected of him.

'Are you having a good time, Victor?' she asked.

'Well, yes,' he said, sounding rather surprised that this should be so.

Troy still hadn't come back, and perhaps it was this— along with two rum punches and a day that had been far from ordinary—that made Lucy say with conscious provocation, 'You know, Victor, you have a wife who really loves you—don't blow it, will you?'

He missed a step. 'I beg your pardon?'

'Troy would fire me if he knew I was speaking to you

like this,' she said, giving him the benefit of her most ravishing smile, 'but there's more to life than a stack of cardiology journals.'

'I enjoy reading them,' Victor said stiffly. 'It's only on holiday that I have the time.'

'Just as there's more to the heart than a bunch of valves.'

With a touch of humour that greatly encouraged her, Victor replied, 'Certainly that statement would be regarded as scientifically correct.'

'It's never a good idea to take a woman for granted,' Lucy persisted, exactly as if she knew what she was talking about. 'Leona's a sweetheart, and how long is it since you told her you loved her? Oh, lord, there's Troy. I'm going to shut up.'

'You are,' said Victor, 'a rather remarkable young woman.' And he steered her back to the table.

Remarkable could be interpreted any number of ways, not all of them flattering, Lucy thought, and sat down next to Troy. Victor or Leona would probably see nothing different about him; she, who knew him in ways she didn't fully understand, saw the bruised shadows under his eyes and a nasty scrape on his knuckles that hadn't been there earlier in the day. She said lightly, 'Dance with me, Troy?'

For a moment she thought he was going to refuse. Then he pushed back his chair and led her out on to the floor. Before he could reach out for her, she laced her hands around his neck, pressed her body to his and began to sway to the music. 'That's better,' she said softly. 'I needed this.'

She felt his hands slide past her waist to her hips, then one palm stroked its way up her spine to rest on the bare flesh of her back. His cheek was resting on her hair, and she knew she had been craving to be held by him ever since she had seen him on the beach. She had no need for words, letting her body do the talking for her in its surrender and its warmth.

She was no closer to knowing what Troy had been wrestling with on the beach but she did sense that the struggle had exhausted him, and that he, like her, simply wanted the intimacy of this silent embrace. She could have wished the music to last forever. When it eventually ended, Troy led her away from the other couples into a dark corner and murmured, keeping his arms around her, 'This is not what my mother intended me to learn when she sent me at the age of eleven to dance camp.'

'*I* like it,' said Lucy.

'I need so badly to have you to myself,' he muttered, and tightened his hold.

And what could she add to that? I love you, seemed the only answer. Yet they were three words she still wasn't ready to say.

Or he to hear.

CHAPTER EIGHT

PROMPTLY at noon the next day the Dillons stepped on to the dock in Road Town. Troy had taught Brad how to jibe that morning, and furnished him with a list of sailing schools; Victor had been given a second lesson in massage, and had finished reading his pile of journals, while Kim had presented Lucy with one of her favorite tapes. Leona, before disembarking, had hugged Lucy and said, a little too loudly for Lucy's taste, 'Don't forget what I said about wedding dresses.'

Lucy waved until they were out of sight. It seemed a lifetime ago that she had done the same thing with the Merritts. Heather had also made a remark about weddings.

She turned back to Troy. He said tersely, 'Let's get out of here before anything happens to delay us. We'll do all the housekeeping stuff when we get back tomorrow.'

They wouldn't even have a full day at the villa, Lucy thought as she went forward to hoist the anchor; they'd have to be here tomorrow afternoon to clean and re-provision the boat. She was beginning to develop a healthy respect for the skippers and crews of the chartered yachts that plied the harbor.

Once the sails were hoisted and trimmed, she went below and made sandwiches for lunch. As wind and waves worked their usual magic she began to relax, all the more so because *Seawind* was making a steady nine to ten knots and they were soon in sight of the shores of Virgin Gorda. It seemed a good omen when Troy pointed out a pair of tropic birds, their bills red as the blooms on the hibiscus, their slim, elegant bodies trailing long white plumes.

'They nest in the rocks along the coast every year,' he said, smiling at her in uncomplicated pleasure. He was slouched at the wheel, steering with one foot. He looked happy, she thought, and smiled back.

His villa was all she could have wished. They anchored off a narrow crescent of pure white sand, where the water was the clear turquoise of a gemstone. Once they'd put a few personal belongings in the dinghy they went ashore, lifting the dinghy well up on the beach. A path edged with rocks wound up a slope through a grove of coconut palms, widening into a garden that was a blaze of color.

Lucy stopped in her tracks. There were the usual tall bushes of scarlet hibiscus, but there were golden ones as well, and gorgeous white ones with vermilion centers. A frangipani tree, it's blooms a deep waxy pink, filled the air with scent. Yellow and red poinciana, purple wreath vine, white spider lilies, the gaudy fuchsia of bougainvillaea…'I feel as though I'm in a hothouse,' she marveled. 'Troy, it's beautiful! But who looks after it when you're not here?'

'Friends of mine live here ten months of the year, and do the upkeep in return. I have a thirty-foot ketch that they look after, too.'

A tiny hummingbird, its feathers flashing emerald fire, zipped past Lucy's nose, and from the woods she heard the soft cooing of doves. Troy led the way to the house, which was built of stone and stucco; the deck was shaded by latticework hung with vines, some with yellow trumpet-shaped flowers, others with plumes of mauve blossoms that quivered in the wind. A hammock was slung between two of the posts. Before she went inside, Lucy rested her hands on the railing, looking out over the water. 'I see why you love it here,' she said.

'Come and see the inside.'

Tile floors, pastel walls and wicker furniture gave a sense of coolness and space to the interior. There were a few exquisite watercolors of local scenes, while the plants that softened the corners of the rooms were glossy with health. Lucy had more than enough imagination to have filled in the gaps in Troy's job description; he would need a retreat, a place where beauty was effortless and no demands would be made on him. And here he had such a place, she thought, knowing that the last few minutes had furnished a few more pieces to the puzzle that was Troy. She said spontaneously, 'Thank you for inviting me here.'

'My pleasure. Want to go for a swim?'

She wasn't sure what she wanted. For a man who more than once had professed his desperate need of her, Troy seemed in no hurry to take advantage of the fact that they were finally alone together. He had put her bag in the white-painted bedroom, where a cool green spread decorated a bed that looked intimidatingly large, but he had made no effort to entice her into that bed. Didn't he want to make love to her anymore? Wishing she were not so conscious of how little time they had, she said, 'A swim would be lovely.'

And so it was. They shared the water with a pair of pelicans and a sleek brown booby, whose antics more than made up for any lack of conversation between Troy and Lucy. Then they wandered back up to the house, Lucy wondering why her bikini, which earlier had had such a satisfactory effect on him, now seemed to have none at all. 'There's a shower off the bedroom,' Troy said casually, 'why don't you use that one and I'll take the main bathroom? Then I'll pour you a drink.'

And after that it would be time to start dinner, she thought, and more of their precious time would have slipped past. Perhaps she had totally misinterpreted him. He hadn't wanted her as much as he'd wanted to be here in this enchanting retreat.

She closed the bedroom door behind her and looked around. The only photograph in the room rested on a set of bamboo bookshelves; its expensive gold frame surrounded a color print of an elderly couple standing against a background of fir trees. The man, who had an untidy of silver hair, had Troy's chin and strong cheekbones, while the woman, smaller, neater, had her son's gray eyes. This was the couple who considered strong feelings in bad taste, Lucy remembered, knowing she was looking at Troy's parents. He'd never mentioned any sisters or brothers; from the lack of any other photos she assumed he must have been an only child. A fig tree overhung a writing desk by one of the windows. The watercolor over the bed was of a crowded backstreet in Road Town, alive with people and cars and flowering trees, vines rampaging over the old buildings with their colorful wooden shutters. The bedroom, so cool and uncluttered as to be almost monastic, needed that painting.

As she went into the bathroom something else caught her eye. Pinned to the wall of the little hallway was a boldly printed scarf. Lucy had seen these in the boutiques she had visited with Kim, and had regretfully decided they were beyond her pocketbook. They were made to be worn as sarongs, draping the body in any number of ways. This one was emerald-green, turquoise and red, reminding her of the hummingbird, of the sea where she had swum with Troy and of the hibiscus blooms nodding outside the bedroom windows.

Her bag contained a clean pair of shorts and a matching

top, her sundress, and a nightgown that had not been bought with seduction in mind. Impulsively she loosened the pins, taking the scarf down and shaking it out. Going into the bathroom, she draped it over her bikini, where the bright hues brought out the blue in her eyes. Throwing it over the towel rail, she showered the salt from her hair and body.

Still wrapped in the towel, she went out on the deck leading from the bedroom and plucked a hibiscus flower, which she pinned into her hair in front of the bathroom mirror; this was a maneuver not as easy to accomplish as movie heroines might have had her believe. By the time she was finished her cheeks were flushed and her eyes wide with a mixture of emotions she was not about to categorize. The hibiscus, she had long ago decided, was a very erotic flower, and was she not doing her best to seduce Troy?

She spent several more minutes draping herself in the scarf. She didn't have the nerve to wear it around her hips with the rest of her body bare, and she didn't want to put her bikini top back on; it was too wet. So she compromised, by tucking the fabric low over her breasts. For reasons she couldn't fully have explained, this didn't seem the time or the place for make-up, perfume or jewellery. She wanted Troy to see her as she was. No more, no less.

The bedroom had a full-length mirror. The woman reflected in it was almost a stranger to her. Because the fabric was opaque, her skin glowed through it. It only covered her to mid-thigh; her legs looked impossibly long. In a panic she reached for her bag, to take out her sundress and pull it on, and heard Troy call, 'Lucy, are you all right?'

'I'll be out in a minute,' she quavered.

If Troy no longer wanted to be seduced, she was about to make a total fool of herself. She had to believe he hadn't changed, that he wasn't Phil or any of the other big, blond men who had briefly peopled her past. That his hunger for her was real and lasting, rooted in his integrity. He had never said he loved her, but he had never brought any other woman except herself to this place that was so close to his heart, either.

Calling on all her training, Lucy tried to relax. Then she opened the door and walked to the living-room, the tiles cold under her bare feet. Troy was standing with his back to her on the deck, looking out over the water. She pushed the screen to one side and stepped out into the open air.

As he turned to face her, he said, 'I was getting worried about— My God, Lucy.'

The breeze had flattened the sarong to her body, faithfully tracing the fullness of her breasts and her flat belly, the fabric revealing more than it concealed. The dappled sunlight patterned her bare shoulders and the slim length of her legs; her eyes, wide-held, were the gray blue of an ocean storm.

Lucy clutched the railing, her mouth dry, wishing she had opted for her sundress, wishing he would say something, but quite unable to think of anything to say herself. She should have been striking some kind of voluptuous pose, she thought frantically. She should be gazing at him through lowered lashes with her lips pouting. Instead of which she was frozen to the deck, paralyzed like a frightened rabbit. And about as alluring.

'I—I'll go and change,' she stammered, and backed up a step.

'Don't go!' He put his drink down on the weathered teak table and crossed the deck, stopping three or four feet away from her. 'You're very brave,' he said with a crooked smile.

'Or a lunatic.'

'You don't have to be afraid…'

'I'm scared witless,' Lucy said, and felt a little of her fear lift with the simple act of speaking the truth.

His hair was still damp from the shower; he was wearing a white T-shirt that molded his body like a second skin and a pair of denim shorts. Hoping he would take her in his arms, she watched him shove his hands in his pockets instead. He said roughly, 'I know I'm not handling this well—I'm sorry… You see, this house has always been an escape for me. From the realities of a job where I can so rarely do enough. Where all my skills of hand and brain aren't sufficient to heal the kids in my care the way I'd like to heal them. Then, on top of that, I've been stuck in a—a bad personal situation for a long time…too long. So I wanted this to be time out.' He hit his fist on the railing, making her jump. 'Dammit! It sounds like I'm talking about a hockey game instead of a romantic tryst—I wouldn't blame you if you told me to get lost.'

The same tumult of emotion that had held her paralyzed was twisting his mouth in an ugly grimace, and somehow this emboldened her to speak. 'I'm not going to do that. Not if you don't want me to.'

His short laugh had little humor in it. 'I want you here more than I can say.' Raking his fingers through his hair, he went on raggedly, 'I need peace and quiet. I need to lose myself in you, Lucy. Maybe that way I'll find myself again, I don't know.' He looked straight at her. 'I do realize I have no right to ask this of you.'

Lucy stood taller, her fear dropping from her as swiftly as if she had loosened the scarf to let it fall to the floor. Troy was a proud man, a man not used to speaking of his feelings; that he had revealed his needs to her was a nakedness at least as powerful, if not more so, than that of the body. She said, and it was the absolute truth, 'You may ask of me whatever you wish.'

'I don't know what I did to deserve you,' he muttered.

'I could say the same for myself.' Her smile faded. 'I was afraid I'd misread all the signals, that you didn't bring me here to make love to me after all. But you'd tell me if that was the case, wouldn't you? You see, Phil didn't tell me he'd fallen for Sarah for well over a month, and when I found out I was so humiliated. I loathe deception! Even if the truth hurts, I'd rather know what's going on than be kept in the dark.'

'Oh, Lucy,' Troy said, closing the distance between them and resting his hands on her bare shoulders. 'Beautiful Lucy…' His smile was rueful. 'The truth is that when I went to Spanish Town I went to the drugstore so I'd be prepared if we did make love. That's not very romantic, either, is it? But at work I so often see children that aren't wanted, and that suffer in consequence.' He paused, his face intent on hers. 'If you and I were ever to bring a child into the world, it would be because we both chose to do so.'

Was this Troy's way of saying he loved her? Lucy didn't know. She did know that the thought of bearing his child filled her with a bittersweet happiness. She and Troy had never talked of the future, of the time beyond the four weeks for which he had hired her; perhaps here, in this place, he would do so.

'Never think that I don't want you,' he added forcibly. 'If I'd followed my instincts, I'd have torn the clothes off you and ravished you on the sand before we'd even hauled the dinghy up on the beach. But—quite apart from the physical difficulties of making love on a beach—I didn't want to fall on you as though I was starving. I didn't want to rush you.'

Finally Lucy did what she'd wanted to do when she had first walked out on the deck. She reached forward, pulled Troy's T-shirt free of the waistband of his shorts, and slid her palms up his bare chest, tangling her fingers in his body hair. 'I don't feel the slightest bit rushed,' she said.

Her lips had curved in an enticing smile. With an inarticulate sound of gratification and passionate hunger, Troy pulled her closer and kissed her, teasing her lips apart, tasting all the sweetness of her mouth. Her sarong slipped a little.

Laughter warming her voice, Lucy said, 'Can they see us from the water? If you keep that up, I'm going to be stark naked.'

Troy glanced seaward, where two yachts were cruising the coastline. 'I'm not into sharing you...even long-distance,' he said. 'Let's go inside.' As she eased her hands free of his shirt, he added, letting his gaze wander down her body, 'Why is it that flesh showing through clothing is so erotic?'

Lucy blushed. Before she could move Troy had swung her up into his arms. Linking her fingers around his neck, she teased, 'You made that look awfully easy—I'm impressed.'

'Hey, I'm tough,' he rejoined. 'I knew there had to be a reason I lifted weights all last winter. Can you close the screen? Or the geckos will get in.'

'Lizards in my bed don't turn me on,' Lucy said primly.

He had reached the bedroom door. 'Are you going to tell me what turns you on in bed, Lucy Barnes? Or are you going to let me find out for myself?'

'That's easy,' she said breathlessly, as he put her down beside the bed and pulled back the covers. 'You turn me on, Troy Donovan. You don't have to do a darn thing.'

'You mean if I do this—' he stroked the rise of her

breast from her cleavage to her nipple, cupping it in his hand and watching her face '—it doesn't do anything for you?'

'Amend that last statement,' she said weakly. 'Everything you do turns me on.'

His answer was to kiss her again, a slow, tantalizing kiss that spread heat through her limbs like a tropic sun. She kissed him back, exulting in the flick of his tongue and the passionate single-mindedness with which he was besieging her.

She was clutching him round the waist. When he raised his head and started removing the hibiscus from her hair, she murmured 'You've got too many clothes on.'

'Complaining already, huh?'

'Suggestions for improvement are not the same as complaints.'

'In that case…' He stripped the T-shirt off, dropping it on the floor.

Lucy began to laugh, a delicious cascade of sound. 'I don't think I've ever been happier in my whole life than to be here with you, Troy,' she said. His face softened, and mixed with her laughter was a shaft of joy that, for now, she had made him forget the demons that drove him.

Taking her face in his hands, he said, 'You're a lovely woman, Lucy…beautiful in all ways.'

'Thank you,' she whispered.

His voice deepened. 'We could improve the situation still further, don't you think?' In a swift movement he pulled off his shorts and tossed them to the floor, so that for the first time she saw him naked.

If she'd had any doubts that he wanted her, she needed have none now. Her cheeks as red as the flower he had put on the bedside table, she said, 'You're beautiful, too,' and reached for the top of her sarong.

He stayed her hands. 'Let me.' He kissed her again. Then he was trailing kisses down her throat and along the arch of her collarbone, all the while loosening the sarong. When it slipped down to her waist his mouth followed it, exploring the silken valley between her breasts and the firm rise of her flesh. She ran her fingers through his hair, pressing him to her, and felt his tongue travel to the softness of her belly, his cheek against the jut of her pelvis. The sarong slithered to the floor, joining the small heap of his own clothes.

With the inevitability of the sun sinking to join the horizon, he sought out that secret place, where she was at once most vulnerable and most sensitive. Her response leaped like fire through her body. She threw back her head, crying out her pleasure, her body quivering like a bow strung too taut.

And then he was gone from there and she was being lifted to the bed to lie on her back, Troy's big body hovering over her. As she whimpered with need, he said huskily, 'There's time, Lucy. We have all day and all night and nothing but the two of us...'

Far beyond fear or shyness, she wrapped her legs around him and drew him down to lie on top of her, her hips moving under his. He took her breast in his mouth, his hands roaming all her softness and her curves until she thought she would die with the intensity of her desire. Then he was kissing her again, fierce, hard kisses whose demands she was more than ready to meet. She let her palms slide down his spine to circle his hips, and with a gentleness that yet had its own demand, she wrapped her fingers around the very center of his need.

A shudder ran through his body. He gasped her name, his face convulsing as she caressed him. Stilling her hand, he reached for the little envelope he had left by the bed;

only then did he thrust down to meet her. She was more than ready. Arching her hips, she took him in, watching the expression chase across his face one after the other: excitement and desire, tenderness and hunger, and the most elemental concentration as the storm gathered within him.

He rolled over on his side, slowing his strokes by an effort of willpower she could only guess at, touching her with a sureness and sensitivity that quickened her breathing until she was panting out loud, her nails digging into his arms. Then he was on top of her again and her body strained to meet his, unable to bear even the most temporary of separations. The tendons were corded in his neck, his breathing tortured in her ears.

Their bodies rocked and surged together, playing with surfaces, only to plunge deeper and deeper into the reefs of passion, where the water was the mysterious blue that blurred boundaries, where the never-ending dance of life and death was played out. The tides seized her, the currents whirled her about, the rhythms of her body inseparable from Troy's, until she lost all control, all sense of who she, Lucy, was. She became him, swam within him to depths that were shot with light, and in a crashing of foam in the black darkness of a cave lost herself and joined with him.

They clung together for what seemed like a very long time to Lucy, although it might have been only a few minutes. The din of her heartbeat gradually subsided; she grew aware of herself, of her body as a separate entity held in the arms of a man called Troy—and felt a pang of loss for a union that had been unlike any she had ever known. Troy's back was slick with sweat. Stroking it, she opened her eyes.

He was gazing at her face as if he had never seen it before, as though something new had been revealed to him that had knocked him off balance. He said hoarsely, 'What just happened... I've never felt like that in my life. I—I lost myself in you, Lucy.'

He suddenly dropped his head to her breast. She tightened her hold, whispering, 'I lost myself and found you.'

'It was like that for you, too?'

'Oh, yes...couldn't you tell?'

As he looked up emotions were chasing each other across his face, and none of them was less than intense. She said fiercely, with no idea where the words came from, 'You're safe with me, Troy. I swear you are.'

He let out a long, jagged breath. 'Deep waters,' he said. Too deep for me to know where I am... Too deep to see where I'm going. Lucy pushed his hair back from his forehead, feeling where it, too, was damp with sweat, and felt her heart clench with love for him.

He rested his cheek on her breast again. She curved her arms around him, knowing that, although she was sailing through unknown seas without a chart to guide her, she had never felt happier or more complete than she did now, in Troy's bed, with the heavy pounding of his heart against her belly.

The slow minutes passed. Lucy was almost asleep when Troy stirred, murmuring into her throat, 'I'll be back in a minute.'

He went to the bathroom. When he came back, he stood at the foot of the bed looking down at her. She was lying on her back, her mahogany hair a tangle on the pillow, her cheeks still flushed from the act of love. She raised one knee and gave him a lazy, provocative smile. 'Are you coming back to bed?'

He grinned at her. 'Is the sea blue?' Sitting down beside her, he let his eyes wander over the long lines of her body, so completely exposed to him.

In a low voice Lucy said, 'You don't even have to touch me, and I want you.'

He ran one hand from her ankle up the length of her leg, letting it rest where her thighs joined. 'So doing this has no effect?' he asked innocently.

'Well…I wouldn't go that far.'

His fingers moved with exquisite sensitivity. 'How far would you go, dearest Lucy?'

The tenderness in his face was almost more than she could bear. There was more than one way to tell him she loved him, she thought, and said quietly, 'To the land beyond the sea where the sun never sets…that far.'

'I believe you would.' Shifting to lie against her, he threw one leg over hers, its weight like an anchor holding her in a safe harbor. Then he kissed her parted lips.

They made love without haste, with a new sureness and a level of trust that both emboldened Lucy and let her expose her vulnerabilities more openly. This time the storm built slowly, although with the same inevitable momentum as before; Troy brought her to the very brink before releasing her along with his own shuddering surrender. Afterward he fell asleep in her arms, as suddenly as a child might, and she curled against the warmth and solidity of the body that was already so well known to her, and wondered, not altogether facetiously, if one could die of joy.

He didn't sleep for long, and when he woke Lucy had indisputable evidence that he was more than interested in her. She said, trailing little kisses across his shoulder, 'To think that when we went for a swim I was afraid you didn't want to make love to me.'

'You now have a choice—barbecued chicken or me.'

'Who's doing the cooking?'

'I am. Are you trying to tell me that chicken breasts

take preference over this?' He brushed her nipple suggestively with his palm.

He looked young and carefree and very happy. 'Are you serving salad with the chicken?' she asked, wide-eyed.

His hand moved lower. 'Indeed,' he said.

They came together in laughter; then they got up and shared the shower. Lucy wound the sarong low over her hips; Troy tucked another hibiscus behind her ear. They ate on the deck, watching the last vestige of orange fade from the sky, candles casting a small aura of light in the gathering darkness. Troy and she made easy conversation—he questioning her about her job, her apartment and her friends.

After he had fetched one of his shirts, which he put around her shoulders against the evening's chill, she smiled her thanks and said, 'You know, something's become very clear to me the last couple of weeks. I love my job—it's what I want to do—but I've been going about it all the wrong way, killing myself with busyness, working from eight in the morning often to eight at night. One massage after another with no rest in between. Totally counter to the whole spirit of massage… No wonder I got sick.'

He said bluntly, 'Why were you doing that?'

'I've always known my family didn't approve of what I do.' Lucy took another sip of wine, swirling the glass so the flames splintered against the crystal. 'So without ever thinking about it, I ran my job in a way they would approve. Worked from dawn to dusk, paid all my debts, built up a large clientele that's now running me instead of the other way round.' She grimaced. 'Stupid, huh?'

'Understandable, I'd say.'

'When I go back—' she looked down, feeling the full impact of her words '—I'll have to make some changes.'

Troy gripped her wrist with bruising strength. 'This has all happened so fast—too fast. We both have to go back, Lucy. Me to Vancouver, you to Ottawa.'

Where they would be separated by more than two thousand miles. 'I know we do,' she said, rather proud of the steadiness of her voice. And, partly because she was terrified of the abyss that yawned in front of her at the prospect of being separated from Troy, she said, 'I don't want to talk about it now. This is time out—isn't that what you said?'

'I'm not so sure that that particular phrase has any meaning where you and I are concerned.'

Only wanting to banish the grimness from his face, she went on, 'I've also figured out why sailing meant so much to me when I was a kid.'

'The best years of your life...'

She nodded, somehow not surprised that he had remembered. 'My mother and my sisters are all petite, elegant women. At thirteen I towered over them, and over everyone else in my class at school—including all the boys. I felt such a misfit, so out of place in a body that wouldn't stop growing. But when I went sailing, and discovered the magic of wind and water, everything suddenly made sense. Because I was tall, I could hoist sails and hike out with the best of them...so I forgot all about being self-conscious.' She said, with a touch of the old pain, 'It sure beat being a wallflower at school dances.'

With an underlying note of anger Troy asked, 'Did your mother know how you felt?'

'Oh, no, I couldn't have talked to her about it. She was so busy, always working or entertaining or going to concerts... You're the first person I've ever told.'

'You must have felt very lonely.'

'Yes…yes, I did.' Her voice had thinned, for to whom had she ever admitted that before?

'I'm glad you told me,' he said.

As she smiled into Troy's eyes, Lucy found herself wondering if this was yet another dimension of love: sitting up at midnight talking about things that mattered with someone who listened, understood and cared. Because Troy cared, she'd swear he did. With a start she realized something else. Her years of sailing had been the best years of her life because at the stern of a Laser she had become one—body and soul. The same thing had happened this afternoon. Every atom in her body, every fantasy and thought and wish and dream, had merged in her union with Troy, just as Heather Merritt had assured her it would. Body and soul, she was Troy's. And that, too, was what love meant.

She couldn't tell him that. Not yet.

'You've gone a long way away, Lucy.'

She glanced up. 'Sorry,' she muttered. 'This is all new to me—you and I together like this. I suppose I'm frightened.'

'Yeah,' he said, 'I know the feeling.' He looked down at his plate. 'Have you had enough? Do you want coffee?'

She stood up, his shirt falling open to reveal the pale gleam of her breasts. 'Take me to bed, Troy.'

He matched her urgency in the speed with which he pushed back his chair. Pausing only to blow out the candles, so the darkness was absolute, he led her into the house and down the hall to the bedroom. And there all Lucy's thoughts of past or future were lost in the immediacy of the present.

She woke sometime in the night. It was still dark. Through the window she could see the stars hanging low over the islands in the channel. Then Troy made a small, choked sound of pain, as though someone were strangling him, and she realized it must have been that that had wakened her. His fist was clenched on the pillow by her head; his shoulders, even in sleep, were hunched. Moving as carefully as she could, she knelt beside him and began stroking the length of his spine, her touch firm without being intrusive.

When his eyes flew open, she sensed the effort it took for him to adjust to where he was. He pushed himself up on his elbow, rubbing at his face. 'Lucy…was I dreaming?'

'I think you must have been.'

He reached out for her blindly. She sank down into his arms, feeling him pull her close with a desperation that in the last few hours had gone into abeyance. 'Hold on to me,' he rasped. 'Just don't let go… Oh, Lucy, you're so full of life and warmth, I need you so much.'

She clasped him with all her strength, and beneath the happiness that he should need her she was afraid again. 'Deep waters,' Troy had said earlier. Deep waters, indeed. And how was she to fathom them when she had been given less than twenty-four hours?

She stayed awake long after Troy had fallen asleep again, her eyes burning with tiredness, her brain going round and round the little she knew about him. Of facts she had painfully few. But she knew the essentials, she thought stoutly. She knew, because she had made love with him, that he was generous and passionate. She knew he could laugh. And now she knew that he needed her.

It had to be enough. Because it was all she had.

She did eventually go to sleep herself. When she woke in the morning, the bedside clock said nine-thirty and she was alone in the big bed; she could hear Troy showering, singing loudly and rather tunelessly to himself. She hadn't meant to sleep so late. They had so little time here—how could she have wasted it sleeping?

She cleaned her teeth and had a quick shower, then wrapped the sarong around her body and went out on the deck. In the far corner a lizard regarded her unwinkingly. A male lizard, she soon decided, as it performed the reptilian equivalent of a push-up and puffed a rather beautiful scarlet and yellow disc from its throat. It seemed content to keep on repeating this performance without any noticeable results. When Troy joined her on the deck, clean-shaven, with a white towel swathed around his hips, she said, 'If I were a lady lizard, I'd call him irresistible.'

Troy watched in amusement. 'Now, why can't I do that?' he said.

'I find what you do entirely adequate.'

'Only adequate, Lucy? I can see I'll have to expand my repertoire.'

He advanced on her, grinning. Sun and shadow patterned his deep chest, while the wind from the sea was playing with his thick blond hair. Lucy held her ground, wishing she could freeze time and keep him always with her, infected in spite of herself by the laughter in his face. 'I want breakfast,' she announced.

'You prefer papaya to me? Oh, Lucy...'

With a speed that took her by surprise he whipped his arms around her and lifted her off the ground, tossing her over his shoulder. As she shrieked in mock terror, he headed single-mindedly for the bedroom. Giggling helplessly, pounding with her fists on his back, Lucy gasped, 'Real pirates have beards. And eye patches.'

He flung her down on the bed and threw himself on top of her, pinioning her wrists to the mattress. 'Quit complaining—at least I own a boat.'

'An apprentice pirate.' Her eyes were laughing up at him and the sarong had slipped. The smile wiped from his face, Troy said with sudden harshness, 'You're so beautiful…so unbearably beautiful. Every time we make love, I end up wanting you more than the last time.' Still holding her captive, he began kissing her, impassioned kisses that spoke elementally of possessiveness.

Her arms might be immobile; her hips were not. Lucy thrust against him, and heard him groan her name deep in his throat. And not once, in the next half-hour, did she think about breakfast.

CHAPTER NINE

LUCY and Troy did eat breakfast eventually, croissants that Troy had taken out of *Seawind's* freezer, with fruit and iced coffee decorated with whipped cream. Lucy licked her lips. 'Decadent,' she said contentedly. She did feel content, far more than content; how could she not with Troy as her lover? She was also trying hard to ignore how rapidly the sun was climbing in the sky.

Echoing her thoughts, Troy said, 'Let's have a swim before we head back.'

Twenty-four hours had been just long enough to give her a taste of paradise—how could she leave here? 'All right,' she said.

'I don't want to go, either, Lucy. But we have to.'

'Another should,' she said wryly.

'The next family'll be with us for a week; we'll have lots to do back at the dock.'

'Who are they?'

'The name's deVries. Valerie, Charles and their nine-teen-year-old daughter Shannon. They're from Montreal, if I remember rightly.' He drained his coffee. 'I'll clean up the food—why don't you try out the hammock?'

He didn't want her company, was that what he was saying? Or was she being ridiculously over-sensitive? Lucy lay back in the hammock, feeling the soft cotton cord taut against her bare legs, letting the hammock rock back and forth so that the vines and the high clouds dipped and swayed in her vision. Nothing fixed, she thought, nothing firm, and wondered in cold terror if she would ever came back to this enchanted place.

She was being a fool. In the last twenty-four hours Troy and she had been intimate in ways she couldn't have imagined; he wasn't simply going to go away.

Back and forth her thoughts carried her, until she stopped the hammock by placing one foot on the floor. The lizard was watching her from the corner of the deck; her foot braced on the deck, one arm dangling, she craned her neck to keep it in sight, wondering if it would repeat its mating ritual. Staying absolutely still, she waited, feeling the pull of muscles across her belly.

'*Lucy*! My God, Lucy...'

Awkwardly, because she had a crick in her neck, she looked around. Troy was standing in the doorway staring at her. He was ashen-faced, half leaning against the frame as though he needed its support. 'What's wrong?' she cried, lurching to her feet. In a rustle of dead leaves the lizard slithered away through the undergrowth.

His voice scarcely recognizable, Troy said, 'For a moment I—I thought you were dead.'

'*Dead*?'

'The way you were lying, your head all twisted...'

She could have made some flip remark, but he was white about the mouth and she could see the tendons stand out in his wrist where he was gripping the wood. 'I'm fine,' she said prosaically, 'I was watching the lizard.'

He straightened, rubbing his palms down his shorts. 'I seem to have made a fool of myself,' he said levelly. 'Are you ready to swim?'

'I'm sorry I scared you.'

'It was nothing—a trick of the light. Let's go.'

For Troy the subject was closed; he pivoted and disappeared into the house. When Lucy went to put her bikini on he wasn't in the bedroom, and when she went outside on the deck she could see him running headlong into the sea, as if a pack of hounds were baying at his heels. He dove under the waves and surfaced doing a fast, efficient crawl. Alone, she walked down to the beach.

Although the water was deliciously warm and crystal-clear, Lucy knew she didn't want to be there. Troy was still stroking back and forth across the width of the bay without a wasted motion. In spirit as well as in body, she thought, watching him, he'd already left her behind. She lay on her back, floating idly, until he finally waded to shore. Shaking the water from his hair, he said, 'Why don't we shower on *Seawind*? It won't take me a minute to get our gear, and the couple who look after the house will be over later today.'

Lucy didn't want to think of anyone else in the rooms where she had known such happiness. She had meant to keep her feelings to herself but she blurted, 'I don't want to leave.'

As he reached for his towel, which he'd left lying on the sand, and rubbed at his chest, she felt a shaft of desire as piercing as if they'd never once made love in the big bed in his room. He said brusquely, 'You think I want to go? Get real, Lucy. No matter how many times I stay here, I never want to leave.'

She waded the last few feet into shore. 'So it's nothing to do with me—is that what you're saying? It's the place?'

'Are you trying to pick a fight?'

I want you to tell me you love me, she thought, and for a horrible moment was afraid she'd said the words out loud. 'I don't know what I'm doing,' she said, speaking the literal truth. 'We'd better go.'

'You knew before we got here that we only had a day.'

'Stop being so damned rational!'

'Oh, for Pete's sake,' he exclaimed, and marched up the beach toward the house.

Lucy watched him go, her nails digging into her palms. Sex, she thought. She'd been deceiving herself to think that the past few hours had had any significance for Troy other than the physical, that his need of her was anything more than a simple craving for her body. Her elder sister Marcia had always said—in her cool, well-bred voice— that men were like that. 'Trapped by testosterone,' had been Marcia's phrase. She, Lucy, should have paid more attention.

Because Troy hadn't said he loved her. Had never mentioned the word.

And they were back to fighting again.

Lucy discovered that she was shivering. She picked up her own towel and wrapped it around her, and as Troy reappeared went to help him with the dinghy. A few minutes later she was climbing on the transom of *Seawind*. Two weeks ago she couldn't possibly have imagined that she would ever be reluctant to do this.

The boat was exactly as they had left it. It was she who had changed.

She quickly went forward, found her loosest shorts and most unrevealing T-shirt, and got dressed. And as they motored out of the bay she didn't give the villa even one last glance.

Because Troy used the engine all the way back to Road Town, Lucy went below, where she worked out her menus and made a grocery list, cleaning out the refrigerator as she did so. She then stripped all the beds and bundled the laundry together. By the time Troy was ready to anchor *Seawind* at the dock, she had already started cleaning one of the cabins, concentrating grimly on what she was doing.

Jack caught the mooring lines as Troy flung them

ashore. 'Message for you,' he said affably, fishing in his back pocket. 'From your next lot of guests.' Maybe they'd cancelled, Lucy thought longingly. 'Think they want to come on board tonight,' Jack added.

Troy unfolded the sheet of paper. 'Their travel agent fouled up the hotel booking,' he grunted. 'As long as they come after dinner I suppose we could be ready—Lucy?'

She and Troy wouldn't even have tonight alone on *Seawind*. 'If that's what you want,' she said crisply.

He shot her an unfriendly glance. 'Gavin makes a point of giving extra service—that's how he's trying to increase his bookings. I don't think we have much choice.'

Jack raised his brows and wandered off, whistling to himself. Lucy said despairingly, 'Troy, I can't stand this.'

Her shoulders had drooped; she looked very unhappy. Troy said flatly, 'It was time to leave the villa, Lucy. You've got to accept that.'

'Don't you have any feelings for me at all?' she cried.

He gave an ugly laugh. 'I sure have... I think you've bewitched me.'

She wasn't at all sure she liked that word. 'You look less than ecstatic to be under my spell.'

'I don't know what the devil's happening to me!'

'Sex,' Lucy said, her chin raised defiantly.

He shot her a poisonous glance. 'Is that all it was for you? The twenty-four-hour equivalent of a dirty weekend?'

'That's what it was for you.'

'Don't you tell me what I'm feeling!' he roared.

'The entire dock's going to know what you're feeling!'

'I thought it was men who were always guilty of separating sex from emotion,' he grated. 'Not that we have the time to stand here arguing the subtleties of human sexual behavior. Give me the grocery list and the laundry and

I'll go and phone the deVrieses; they left me a contact number.'

'I have more than enough emotion for the two of us,' Lucy pronounced, and stamped down the companionway stairs.

He followed her, shoving the list in his pocket and picking up the bundled sheets and towels. 'Don't fall in love with me, Lucy. I'm warning you.'

'I wouldn't think of it,' said Lucy, and waited until he had gone before allowing herself the luxury of regaling the mahogany walls of the saloon with her entire stock of profanity. Then she started cleaning bathrooms, a task as far removed from romance as it could be.

Troy was in his cabin changing when the deVries family arrived. Lucy, now wearing her favorite purple shorts with a flowered shirt, heard them coming down the dock and went out on deck to meet them. She took to them instantly, for all three were blessed with the twin gifts of warmth and charm.

Charles, it transpired, played the cello in a chamber group that was establishing a solid reputation across the continent; tonsured like a monk, he sported a trim black beard. His wife, Valerie, had haunting dark eyes and a haircut as elegant as her bearing, and their daughter, Shannon, was stunning: dark blue eyes, sleek blonde hair that fell straight down her back, and an astonishing degree of self-assurance for someone her age. She was everything that Lucy wasn't: small and delicate, with a slender, almost boyish figure. Yet somehow this didn't bother Lucy; the stay at Troy's villa, however tempestuously it had ended, had removed any desire to look other than she did.

She welcomed them aboard, and called Troy's name. Then she led them down into the saloon, showing them the cabins. Shannon had just come out of the forward cabin she was going to occupy, and was laughing at something her father had said, when Troy came down the stairs. Lucy saw his eyes fly to the young woman with the sheaf of pale, silken hair. He stopped dead in his tracks, gripping the railing. He looked, Lucy thought blankly, as though someone had just punched him in the stomach. As though he couldn't breathe.

She made a tiny move toward him, for the agony in his eyes was beyond any she had ever seen, but then Charles stepped out of his cabin and said pleasantly, 'You must be our skipper... Charles deVries. My wife, Valerie, and our daughter, Shannon.'

Troy swallowed hard, and with a superhuman effort got himself under control. He let go of the railing and walked across the polished floor to shake hands, and only Lucy would have known that he moved with none of his usual lithe grace. He held Shannon's hand as briefly as politeness would allow, his smile a mere movement of his lips, and said, 'Lucy's planning hot chocolate and cookies on deck whenever you're settled. In the meantime I'll show you how the plumbing works and give you a tour of the boat.'

Lucy, who was so attuned to him, heard the strain under his commonplace words, and knew he hadn't yet recovered from the shock Shannon's appearance had caused him. He must have been in love with a woman who looked like Shannon, she thought sickly. Someone he had never told her about... The same woman who had fueled his rage that night on the beach. How else to explain his reaction?

The memory of Rosamund, to whom he had once been engaged and who had never stirred his emotions, couldn't possibly have dealt such an impact.

Obediently Lucy went to the galley to prepare the hot chocolate, which she served on deck along with fresh coconut cookies she had baked after supper. Valerie leaned back, gazing at the myriad stars. 'A perfectly lovely ending to a dreadful day,' she said. 'We were delayed in Boston, Lucy, and we only just made the flight in San Juan. Then to find there were no vacancies at the hotel... It was very good of you to take us on board this evening.'

'It means we can make an earlier start in the morning,' Lucy rejoined.

'Not too early...I'm on vacation.' At Lucy's look of inquiry Valerie added, 'I normally go to work at seven, I'm a hospital administrator.'

She looked too chic to do anything so mundane. Lucy glanced at Troy to see if he had heard this. But Troy was oblivious to Valerie and Lucy; he was watching Shannon, who was arguing amicably with her father over who should have the last cookie. 'Remember your tuxedo,' Shannon joked.

'I never do up the buttons when I'm playing,' Charles said loftily. 'Sugar's bad for your complexion, you know that.'

Valerie said mildly, 'You could break the cookie in half.'

'Or I could get more from the galley,' Lucy offered. 'And who'd like more hot chocolate?'

Charles, who was clearly a hedonist, pushed his mug across the table. 'Troy?' Lucy asked.

Troy was still staring at Shannon and didn't hear her. This is nothing to do with memory, Lucy thought in terror. This is about here and now. Troy's attracted to Shannon— moth to her flame. He can't take his eyes off her.

Clumsily she gathered the mugs and fled to the galley, but her thoughts pursued her like sharks after blood. Troy had fallen in love with Shannon. People did fall in love at first sight. They couldn't help it. It was a force of nature, ungovernable, impossible to resist. She herself had done it more than once.

It seemed the cruelest of ironies that Shannon should be blonde.

And how could he have fallen for Shannon only hours after making love with her, Lucy?

She dropped two cookies on the floor, had to sweep up the crumbs, and nearly let the milk boil over on the stove. But eventually she got herself together and went back up on deck. To a casual onlooker the scene could have been one from a tourist brochure: five vacationers relaxing on the deck of a yacht under a star-jeweled southern sky. But to Lucy, so acutely aware of the undercurrents, it was more like a scene from a surreal play. She talked and laughed, she discussed possible sailing routes and extolled the pleasures of snorkeling, and all the while she was watching her facile performance with a distant amazement.

Finally, to her infinite relief, Valerie got to her feet and stretched. 'I'm for bed,' she said.

Charles stood up too, slipping an arm around his wife's waist, and Shannon said with a gamine grin at Troy, 'I'd better get my beauty sleep if I'm going to learn to snorkel tomorrow.' She smiled at Lucy. 'Thanks for the wonderful cookies... See you tomorrow.'

The minute their backs were turned Troy pushed up from the table in an explosion of movement. Before Lucy could say a word, he'd leaped out of the cockpit and was striding forward. Lucy cleared off the table, put the food away in the galley, washed the dishes and set up the cof-fee-machine for the morning. Then she switched out the lights and went forward herself, stepping round the open hatches of the deVrieses' cabins.

Her blue duffel bag was sitting by the hatch to Troy's cabin. With another pang of terror she saw that Troy was standing waiting for her at the bow, holding on to the headstay. He said, so quietly that she had to strain to hear him, 'I've got to be alone tonight, Lucy—I'm sorry.'

The worst thing was that Lucy wasn't really surprised; unconsciously she had been expecting something like this. She stepped closer, aching to touch him yet afraid to do so. 'Please, Troy... Just tell me what's going on.'

As if the words choked him, he said, 'I can't.'

She made one more try. 'Were you in love with some-one who looked like Shannon...someone who died?'

'Leave it, Lucy. Just leave it, will you?'

'Don't shut me out!'

It was a cry of pain. He seized her by the arm and whispered furiously, 'We aren't going to have a fight within earshot of our guests—do you hear?'

She said bitterly, 'That's why you were waiting up here rather than in the cabin. So we couldn't quarrel.' She looked down, the sight of his long fingers on her flesh filling her with an agony of loss. He must have fallen in love with Shannon; it was the only way she could explain his behavior. Blindly she struck out at him.

He dropped her arm, and over the soft lapping of the water she heard his tormented breathing. Knowing she was going to weep, and far too proud to do so in front of him, she picked up her bag and steadily walked aft. She went down the stairs and into the stern cabin, closing the door.

Leaning against its smooth mahogany panels, she dis-covered with dull wonder that now she was alone she couldn't cry. Her throat was too tight, her misery too abject for tears. All her movements jerky and uncoordinated, she put her bag down, unzipped it and pulled out the night-gown that she had never worn in Troy's bed.

And not even that made her cry.

                    *   *   *

The next five days were the nearest Lucy could imagine to purgatory. It was the falsity of everything she did that was the most difficult to bear. On the surface everything was going smoothly. She cooked some excellent meals and kept the saloon and galley spotless. She crewed for Troy with an efficiency that perhaps only he would have seen as mechanical. She snorkeled with the deVries at the cluster of rocks called the Indians, guided them around the shops in Spanish Town, and led them through the huge tumbled boulders at the southern end of Virgin Gorda. The whole family was having a good time; Lucy had a dim sense of satisfaction that this should be so.

But underneath all this her heart felt as though it were congealing, turning slowly to ice in her breast. She had heard often enough that hearts broke. A clean event—sharp and painful in the moment, and then over and done with—that was how she had pictured it. But for her there was no clean break, only the protracted agony of being constantly in the presence of the man who had once been her lover. For Troy, whom she loved, had turned into a hard-eyed stranger.

There were times she thought she'd dreamed the twenty-four hours at his villa, that they were a figment of her imagination, an elaborate fantasy fed by the lush beauty of the islands and the heat of the sun. There were times she even wondered if she was going out of her mind. What she had believed to be real, more real than anything that had ever happened to her—Troy's arms around her, his body covering her, his kisses inflaming her—had vanished utterly. In place of that reality was another: a tall, blond man whom she couldn't reach. Who had turned his back to her with a profound finality.

It was a repeat of the old pattern, a pattern she had thought was gone forever.

Images stood out from those five days. The ugly spasm that had thinned Troy's mouth when Shannon rested a hand on his shoulder as she had jumped down into the dinghy. The tension in his big body when she had accidentally collided with him on the companionway stairs. The way her laughter always riveted him to the spot, his hands stopping whatever task he had been doing.

Once, only a few days ago, Lucy might have expected him to react to her this way. But not any longer.

Not that Troy was seeking Shannon out. If anything, he was avoiding her. He didn't flirt with her. He rarely spoke to her unless she spoke first. But Lucy could tell that he was always aware of her, tied to her by an invisible cord that was stronger than the lines on *Seawind*, and it was this that turned her heart to ice.

On the sixth morning Lucy took Charles, Valerie and Shannon to the boutiques at Soper's Hole, at the western tip of Tortola. Troy had anchored at the most distant mooring so she steered the dinghy between the yachts toward the wooden dock. Everyone got out. Lucy knew it was Valerie's birthday later in the week, and wasn't surprised when Shannon took her father's arm and said brightly, 'You go that way, Mum, we'll meet up with you in half an hour at the bar.'

Valerie smiled as the two of them marched away. 'Shannon has yet to learn the subtle approach… Lucy, why don't you go back to *Seawind*? We'll be at least an hour, it always takes Charles ages to make his mind up…and you look tired,' she finished delicately.

Lucy flushed, knowing Valerie was far too discreet to allude directly to the tension between Lucy and Troy, and far too intelligent to be unaware of it. 'Troy's expecting me to stay here,' she said lamely.

'It's never good to be too predictable,' Valerie remarked, watching the palm fronds curve in the wind.

Why shouldn't she go back to *Seawind*? thought Lucy.
She had nothing whatever to lose, and if all she gained
was a rip-roaring fight she might at least feel better afterward. 'Whenever you're ready to come back to the boat,
sit on one of the benches by the bar and I'll come and get
you,' she said, adding awkwardly, 'Thank you, Valerie.'

'I'm sure you're old enough to know that things aren't
always what they seem,' Valerie said with characteristic
obliqueness. 'Now, I'd better pick up some souvenirs for
my nephews.'

She wandered off, her silk skirt blowing against her
slender legs. Lucy got back in the dinghy and pulled the
starter cord quickly before she could lose her nerve. She
cut the engine before she reached *Seawind*, pleased to see
that two other dinghies were circling the area. She wasn't
sure why she wanted to catch Troy off-guard; perhaps because she had so few other weapons at her command.

But as she tied the dinghy's painter to the transom, she
heard music coming form the tape deck in the saloon. Troy
had never evinced any interest in the collection of tapes in
the drawer of the chart desk, she realized, frowning slightly
in puzzlement. The music was beautiful, a solo flute producing ripples and cascades of sound, joyous and unre-
strained: a performance entailing a formidable level of
technical ability.

She climbed out of the dinghy and stood still for a minute, letting the melody weave its spell, feeling something
akin to peace for the first time in many days. Maybe it
was a good sign that Troy was listening to such exquisite
music; she might finally be able to reach him.

She slipped off her canvas shoes and walked toward the
hatch, her bare feet soundless. But as she descended the

first of the steps into the saloon she came to a halt. Troy was sitting in one of the swivel chairs. His head was buried in his hands, his back a long curve of abject defeat.

She acted without thought. 'Troy...' she said, and took the rest of the stairs in a rush.

His head jerked up; his cheeks, Lucy saw, were streaked with tears. She stretched out her hand in compassion, but before she could say anything the bleakness in his slate-gray eyes was replaced by a fury that was instant and all-encompassing. He surged to his feet. 'Get out!'

'But—'

He advanced on her in two swift steps. 'Didn't you hear me? Get the hell out of here!'

Every instinct in her body was impelling her to run. But a vestige of courage—or perhaps mere stubbornness—kept Lucy glued to the floor. 'What's the *matter*?' she cried. 'I can't stand being left in the dark—if you've fallen in love with Shannon at least have the decency—and the guts— to tell me so.'

For a moment the torment in Troy's face was replaced by sheer incredulity. 'In love with Shannon? Of course I'm not.'

'Then what's going *on*?'

'I'll tell you what's going on,' he said viciously. 'You've intruded on the first five minutes of privacy I've had in weeks.'

Her nails digging into her palms, Lucy said, 'When you made love to me, you told me you needed me.'

'I sure don't need you poking and prying into my affairs!'

'What are you afraid of?' she flared. 'Showing an emotion—any emotion—that's not anger? Is that what you're afraid of?'

He took a single step toward her, his fists bunched at

his sides. 'Let me tell you something, Lucy. I'm entitled to my anger. I'm—'

'*Why*?' she demanded, and with a detached part of her brain heard the flute caress a series of notes as limpid as moonlight on water.

Deep lines scoring his cheeks, Troy said, 'I'll tell you why. And maybe that'll get you off my back. You hear that music? That's my kid sister playing. Lydia. She was studying music in New York, they predicted a brilliant future for her, and one evening last October she walked into her local corner store to buy a loaf of bread and was shot point-blank by the man who'd just robbed the till. They never caught him. She died instantly.'

The flute slipped effortlessly into a plaintive minor key and Lucy whispered, 'She looked like Shannon.'

'Clever girl,' Troy sneered. 'The man who fired that gun—I could kill him with my bare hands. How's that for an expression of emotion?'

Flawless and gloriously beautiful, the melody wove through his words. 'I'm so sorry,' Lucy said, and reached out one hand, her fingers lightly trembling.

'Don't touch me!' he grated. 'He killed her as easily as this—' In a gesture shocking in its violence he hit the stop button on the tape deck. With an ugly metallic click the music ceased as if it had never been.

Into the silence Lucy said, 'Have you ever cried for her, Troy? Sat down and wept your heart out because she's dead?'

Spacing each word as if it were a bullet, he said, 'Get out of here—now.'

Her cheeks as white as *Seawind's* sails, Lucy stayed where she was. 'You've got to grieve for her,' she said, the words tumbling one over the other. 'I was too young to grieve for my father so I carried him like an albatross

for years. The woman who played that music—she must
have been wondrously alive. She deserves your tears. Because otherwise you're choosing death, you're—'

'Are you quite finished?' Troy rasped. 'Because if you
are, you can go up those steps and out of my sight—I can't
stand being in the same room with you.'

He meant it. Meant every word. A hard lump clogging
her throat, Lucy groped behind her for the galley counter-
top and backed away from him. He'd said to her once that
he was unreachable and intended to remain so; he'd meant
that, too. Her ankle struck the lowest of the companionway
steps. Turning, Lucy bolted up them.

She tripped on the third step, barking her shins and grabbing at the hatch for support. At the top she whirled to
face Troy. 'I hate you,' she said in a choked voice. 'I wish
I'd never met you.' Then she ran for the dinghy, where
sunlight sparkled on water whose vibrant blues and greens
were the antithesis of violent death.

The dinghy started at the first tug on the cord. Lucy
hauled in the painter and headed for the opposite shore,
away from the boats and the marina. Turning off the motor, she let herself drift with the wind. Her hands gradually
stopped shaking; her heart-rate returned to normal. But her
ears echoed with the lambent strains of a flute played by
a young woman struck down in a senseless act of violence.
And in her brain, as inexorable as the ticking of a clock,
the same words sounded and resounded: it's over, it's over,
it's over...

She and Troy were finished. When they went back to
Road Town tomorrow with the deVrieses, she'd quit. Troy
could find someone else to cook and crew for him. She,
Lucy, was going home.

Because he was never going to change. And she
wouldn't beg. There was no point.

She looked around, suddenly loathing the picture post-card prettiness of the moored yachts and the quaint boutiques, not caring if she ever saw another palm tree in her life. She wanted the ordinary streets of home, the meandering Rideau Canal and the wide sweep of the St Lawrence River. She wanted her job and her friends and her family.

She'd never fall in love again. Never. It hurt too much.

Glancing at her watch, she saw that only forty minutes had passed since she'd left Valerie at the dock. She might as well head that way to pick her up.

Once there, Lucy sat down on one of the benches by the bar and ordered a lemonade. She felt blessedly numb inside; maybe her heart had finally frozen solid and was beyond feeling. With any luck at all it would stay that way.

Once she got away from Troy and didn't have to face him every minute of the day, she'd forget him. She'd forget the tragedy that had scarred him so deeply. She'd forget his corrosive rage, his dammed-up grief, his inability to let go of either one. She'd have to.

The lemonade had that reassuring blend of tartness and sweetness that Lucy remembered from childhood. As she was sipping it, Valerie sauntered over to her bench and sat down, showing her the gifts she had bought and describing a painting she was tempted to buy. Not by so much as a glance did she evince any curiosity about what had transpired on *Seawind*. Shannon and Charles arrived ten minutes later, laden with shopping bags and looking very pleased with themselves. 'All set?' Shannon said breezily.

A few minutes later, with immense reluctance, Lucy was following Shannon into the cockpit. But she needn't have worried. Troy didn't even look at her. Automatically she obeyed his soft-spoken commands as they sailed east into the wind, making good speed along the coast. They anchored off Peter Island for lunch.

Lucy was serving ice-cream and strawberries for dessert when Troy came up on deck. Until he spoke, she had had no premonition that the look of gravity on his face was anything to do with her. 'There's a phone call for you, Lucy,' he said in a neutral voice. 'It's your mother.'

The color drained from Lucy's face. Her mother would only call if something was wrong. The memory of Lydia's death flooding her mind, she looked down at the bowl of strawberries, wondering what to do with it, wondering if she was about to hear terrible news again, this time closer to home. As Valerie took the bowl out of her hands, Lucy managed to say, 'I'd better see what she wants,' and hurried below.

The connection was poor, their words booming as if trapped in a cave, but the gist of her mother's message was simple. Lucy's younger sister Catherine had been in a car accident. She was out of intensive care, but still in a serious condition.

'I'm sure she's going to be all right,' her mother said, 'but I—I'd really like to see you.' Even through the crackle of static Lucy could tell that her mother's voice, normally so perfectly controlled, was shaking. 'It's a lot to ask, I know, when you're on holiday, and if you'd rather not, I'd understand. You see, I need you, Lucy... It's funny, Marcia's been wonderful, naturally, but I don't dare cry in front of Marcia—you know how she feels about weepy women. *You* wouldn't mind if I cried, would you, Lucy?'

Catherine wasn't dead. Not like Lydia.

Somehow Lucy found her voice. 'No, Mum, I wouldn't mind. Of course I'll come. Just as soon as I can get a flight... Why don't I call you back in half an hour, once I know what's going on—will you be home?'

'Yes, I'll be here.' There was a pause. 'Thank you, Lucy.'

'I love you, Mum. Half an hour.'

Lucy hung up the phone, her thoughts in chaos. Competent, law-abiding Catherine had failed to slow at a yield sign. She drove a red sports car. Lucy had always liked that car, but today it had failed to protect her sister when another car had collided with it. Catherine could so easily have been killed... Her head spinning, Lucy groped for the nearest chair.

Someone was helping her, a hand guiding her to the chair. She looked down and saw a dusting of blond hair on the back of the hand and in a small, telling gesture thrust it from her. She couldn't bear Troy to touch her. She'd fall to pieces if he did.

Her mother, her cool, detached mother, needed her. Needed her because Lucy was the emotional one in the family, the one who wasn't afraid of tears.

From a long way away she became aware that Troy was speaking to her. 'What's wrong, Lucy? Tell me what's wrong.'

The concern in his face gave her a fleeting glimpse of the old Troy. Feeling her self-control slip another notch, she relayed her mother's message in a flat voice and saw him flinch. 'You'll have to go,' he said. 'I'll radio the airport. I know the people on the desk—we'll get you out on the first flight.'

No ifs or buts; Troy had understood immediately her need to be with her family. Lucy said faintly, 'Who'll cook for you?'

'I'll get in touch with Lise—the woman who used to cook for Gavin. I expect her son's back from San Juan by now.'

Within ten minutes Troy had her a seat on the afternoon flight out of Tortola and tentative bookings all the way to Ottawa, and Lucy had phoned home. When her mother heard she was coming she started to cry, the harsh sobs of someone not used to tears; Lucy's lip was trembling when she put the receiver back and she carefully avoided Troy's eyes.

'We'll head straight for Road Town, it's quicker for you to get to the airport by cab,' he said briefly. 'Let's go.'

Action was what Lucy needed. She hauled in the anchor, and as Troy put the diesel to full power she went to her cabin and packed. It felt strange to put on her skirt with its tidy little roses; it would be cold in Ottawa, she knew.

She was getting her wish. She was going home.

Biting her lip so hard that it bled, she pushed away the nightmare vision of a life without Troy and took one last look round the cabin to make sure she hadn't forgotten anything. Then she went into the galley and organized the evening meal as completely as she could. By then they were coming into Road Harbor. For the last time Lucy reeled out the anchor chain, obeying Troy's hand signals with a stony calm. She said goodbye to the deVrieses, suffering Valerie and Shannon to hug her and Charles to kiss her cheek, then Troy had picked up her bag and they were running along the dock.

'You'll only just make the flight,' he said. 'There's the cab I ordered—I'll tell him he'll have to hurry.' He scrabbled in the pocket of his shorts and pulled out a crumpled piece of paper and a stub of pencil. 'Write down your address and phone number.'

She took the paper, watching him run ahead to the window of the cab. Leaning on her wallet, she wrote in cramped letters, 'I can't bear your anger, Troy—it's better we don't stay in touch.' Then she folded the paper so her message was hidden. When she reached the taxi, she pushed the paper back in his pocket, inwardly shrinking from the contact, and watched him throw her bag in the back seat. She said, not looking at him, 'Thanks for arranging all this, Troy,' and tried to scramble in the cab.

He took her by one shoulder, pulling her round to face him, and said in a savage undertone, 'I know you haven't understood what's been going on. I was a fool not to have—'

'I'll be late,' she cried frantically. 'Let go!'

'I'll see you in Ottawa just as soon as I can get clear of *Seawind*.'

Lucy was doing her best to tug free, her face pale and pinched; it wasn't clear that she had heard him. He kissed her on the mouth with desperate urgency, branding himself on her flesh despite her struggles. 'You know how to reach the boat—let me know how your sister is... I'll see you soon, Lucy.'

No, you won't. You'll never see me again.

She dived into the back seat of the taxi and slammed the door. To her infinite relief the driver, who had a sense for melodrama, took off in a screech of tires. Clenching her hands in her lap, she did not once look back.

It's over, it's over, it's over...

CHAPTER TEN

AT TEN-FORTY-FIVE that night Lucy was ringing her mother's doorbell. She was dazed with tiredness, shivering in the raw night air. The brass knocker and mail slot, set neatly in a fashionably dark blue door, shone with cleanliness; as she remembered the lamps she had polished on *Seawind*, the gnawing pain that had accompanied her every mile of her journey surged up into her throat. Then the door swung open.

'Lucy,' Evelyn Barnes cried, threw her arms around her daughter and dissolved into tears. Lucy, taking the path of least resistance, started to cry too.

Evelyn was the first to pull back. 'Darling,' she quavered, 'you look terrible, and here I am keeping you out on the doorstep.' She pulled Lucy inside and closed the door, 'You'd better have a hot bath and then I'll make you some cocoa.'

'I'm the one who's supposed to be looking after you... Oh, Mum, it's so good to be home! How's Catherine?'

'Better. They've upgraded her condition from serious to stable. She has a broken pelvis and a cracked vertebra, so she'll be there a while. I told her you'd be in to see her in the morning. Now, upstairs with you, Lucy, and we'll talk in a few minutes.'

Lucy grinned. 'Yes, Doctor.'

Evelyn gave her a watery smile in return. 'I behaved so unprofessionally at the hospital this morning—I yelled at the surgeon because I didn't think he was paying enough attention to her symptoms.'

170

'Truly, Mum? I'd have loved to be there.'

'I'm very glad you weren't. Off you go.'

It was comforting to be told what to do. Lucy's old room at the top of the stairs still had her collection of blue teddy bears lined up on the shelf; the navy-flowered wallpaper and worn Persian rug welcomed her like old friends. She soaked in the hottest water she could bear and put on a fleecy nightgown with a woollen housecoat that she hadn't worn for years and went downstairs. Her mother had lit the fire in the den, where deep green curtains kept out the night. Sinking into her favorite wing chair, Lucy said, 'I feel human again. And you made cranberry muffins— you're an angel.'

Evelyn Barnes was wearing an elegant black caftan made of raw silk, her greying hair pulled back in its usual sleek chignon, her severe features, handsome rather than beautiful, unadorned by make-up. She tucked her tiny feet under her and said in a rush, 'I don't deserve this visit, Lucy—don't think I'm not aware of that.'

Lucy leaned forward, patting her mother on the knee. 'Sure you do.'

'No...' Her mother gazed into the flames. 'Catherine's accident was so sudden and so terrifying, an irrevocable change between one moment and the next. No going back. No re-establishing of the normal. Marcia was wonderful; she took charge of everything. But she was like a machine, and after I'd yelled at the surgeon she read me a little lecture about how medicine is a science and how mothers shouldn't be overly emotional. That's when it hit me— what a disservice I've done you. I know you've always been the odd one out in our family. What I realized today is that you're the only one who's in touch with her feelings. The only one of the four of us. And we made you an outcast because of it.'

With a depth of bitterness that shocked her, Lucy wondered what good it had done her in the past three weeks to be in touch with her feelings. Troy hadn't wanted them, and he had kept his own well-hidden from her. She said, 'Physically and mentally I didn't fit in either, though. Too tall and not clever enough.'

'You were clever in a different way,' Evelyn said drily, 'that we weren't clever enough to value.' She took a big gulp of the red wine she had poured herself and drew herself up a little taller in her chair. 'I even know how it happened. I've never talked to you very much about your father—I'm sorry about that, too. I loved him deeply. He was like you, full of feeling…I suppose that's why I married him. When he died, I buried that side of myself along with him and I never allowed it out again. Not even with my children.'

'Until tonight,' Lucy said gently. So her most vivid memory of her father was to be trusted: a big blond man, laughing, spontaneous, and very much alive.

'I was afraid if you didn't come until tomorrow—or next week—I'd lose the courage to tell you all this.' Evelyn looked right at her daughter. 'I knew how much I needed you today. You don't know how grateful I am that you came right away.'

A tear was coursing down her mother's cheek. Her mother, who never cried. Lucy fell on her knees by Evelyn's chair and hugged her. 'I'm so glad you did tell me.'

They sat up late that night, and as they talked the big blond man who had been Lucy's father became a real person rather than a shadowy figure from her past. When they finally turned out the lights and went upstairs, Lucy tumbled into bed and fell asleep instantly. But when she woke the next morning her first thought was of Troy.

Seawind would have left Road Town, was perhaps anchored in some quiet cove where many-hued fish swam among the coral. Another woman would have taken her place in the galley. And Shannon would still be on board, that beautiful young woman who reminded Troy of his dead sister.

Lucy burrowed under the covers, her body clamoring for Troy's touch, her soul aching for his presence, her mind despising herself for wanting someone who had so decisively turned his back on her. She would never see him again; the note she had written him would make sure of that. She had done the right thing, the only thing in the circumstances. She just wished it didn't hurt so much.

Lucy went to see Catherine as soon as visiting hours permitted. Although Catherine was well enough to be complaining about the public ward she was in, Lucy was shocked by her sister's pallor, by the complicated contraption that held her in traction and by the cuts and scrapes and bruises that marred the austere perfection of Catherine's features. She didn't stay long; Catherine also tired easily.

As she was going down the steps outside, buttoning her raincoat against a wind whose bite felt like winter, a woman's voice hailed her. Marcia, her elder sister, was tapping smartly across the parking lot. Marcia always looked as though whatever she was doing was essential to the smooth running of the world. Lucy offered her cheek to be brushed by her sister's lips. No hugs from Marcia. Marcia didn't like to be touched.

'How's Catherine?' Marcia asked.

As Lucy was describing how she had found her sister,

Marcia broke in, 'She's young enough that her bones will knit just fine... I don't understand why Mother's making such a fuss—she's really been impossible since the accident.'

Lucy had forgotten that Marcia rarely listened to the answers to the questions she asked. 'Mum was upset,' she said temperately.

'She's a doctor; she should know better. You look very tanned, Lucy—I hope you're aware of the dangers of UV. By the way, some man left a message for you with my secretary. I can't imagine why you gave him my number.'

Lucy's heart gave a great thump in her chest. 'Who?' she gasped.

With aggravating slowness Marcia searched through the papers in her neat leather purse, eventually extracting a bright pink slip. 'Troy Donovan,' she read. 'He left a number for you to call. I really would prefer that your personal life not overflow into my office.'

'I didn't give him your number. I didn't give him anybody's number,' Lucy said, crumpling the piece of pink paper into a tight ball. 'I'm through with him.'

'I'll have my secretary block his calls, then,' Marcia said briskly, glancing at her gold watch. 'I've only got five minutes to spare with Catherine before I have to be back at work. Nice seeing you, Lucy.'

Lucy clumped down the steps. She had recognized *Seawind's* code numbers right away. But she wasn't going to phone Troy. Not today. Not ever.

When she got home, there was a message from Evelyn's secretary that she was to call Troy Donovan. And when Lucy went to her own office, to pick up her mail and check her answering machine, the very last of a long string of messages made her heart plummet in her chest. To hear Troy's voice—deep, sure of itself, so well-remembered—

drained the strength from her knees, so that she sank down on the corner of her desk.

'Lucy,' he said over the hiss of static, 'I can't talk now—privacy and charters don't mix. Would you call me this afternoon and let me know you got home safely and how your sister is?' He then repeated *Seawind's* code and rang off.

She felt the first slow burn of anger and welcomed it with all her heart. Now that she was gone Troy suddenly wanted to talk to her. Too bad, she thought. You had your chance and you didn't take it. You're too late now. She then went back to the beginning of the tape, copied the other messages and erased them all. Thank goodness all four members of the family had unlisted numbers. At least he wouldn't be able to reach her at home.

Anger buoyed her up until bedtime, when more basic appetites vanquished it. Sex is the only issue here, she thought, pounding her pillow into a shape that would encourage sleep. It's nothing to do with love. I don't love Troy anymore, I don't—because if I do, I'm the worst kind of fool.

She was awake until three in the morning, then fell into a deep sleep from which she was awakened by the telephone that stood on the cherrywood desk in the hall. Staggering across the carpet, she picked the receiver up and croaked, 'Hello?'

'Did I wake you, darling?' Evelyn said. 'I'm so sorry, I thought you'd be up by now. Lucy, I've had the oddest phone call from a man called Troy Donovan... He wanted a number where he could reach you, but I thought I should check with you first. He sounded very persuasive, I must say. A gorgeous voice. He even got past Margaret.'

Margaret was Evelyn's secretary, a redoubtable woman.

'You're not to give it to him, Mum! I don't want to talk to him.'

'Is he the reason you look so unhappy?'

Lucy made a face into the telephone; she had thought she'd done a good job at disguising just how unhappy she was. 'That's irrelevant. You can tell him I never want to hear from him again.'

'I think you should be the one to tell him that.'

'Get Margaret to do it,' Lucy said irritably. 'That'll get his attention. I've got to go, Mum, I want to spend some time at the office and start letting my clients know I'm home. Bye.'

Damn him, she fumed, banging the receiver back in its cradle. Couldn't he take a hint? And quelled a traitorous urge to laugh that Troy had charmed his way past Margaret.

She didn't laugh at all when she pressed the message button on her answering machine at the studio. 'I'm coming up to Ottawa as soon as I can, and I'll find you if I have to ransack every goddamned massage outfit in the city,' Troy announced. 'I'll get down on my knees and apologize for being a total idiot, I'll smother you in roses, I'll throw you over my shoulder and haul you to the nearest bed—whatever it takes. But I'm going to see you, Lucy. I have to. Because I love you.'

As abruptly as he had begun, Troy broke the connection. The next message started—someone looking for an appointment. Lucy rewound the tape and listened again, and again Troy ended with the same three words. I love you.

He didn't mean it. How could he? It was lust he felt for Lucy, not love. Lust and rage and repudiation.

Emotions as highly colored as the flowers at Troy's villa tumbled and tossed within her. Lucy got to her feet, looking around as though she wasn't quite sure where she was, all her good intentions about getting to work evaporating. She craved action, anything to take her mind off a man whose next move she didn't even want to contemplate. Catherine. She'd go and see Catherine.

But when she got to the hospital Catherine was less than delighted to see her. A huge florist's box was lying beside her on the bed, the lid tossed to one side. The box was brimming with the most glorious red roses Lucy had ever seen; Catherine was frowning at the card.

As soon as she saw Lucy she demanded, 'Who's this man called Troy? I thought these roses were for me—I'm the one who's ill, after all—but they're for you. Really, Lucy, you might have a little more discretion than to conduct your affairs via my hospital bed.'

Marcia had said something to the same effect.

A rapt silence had fallen over the ward. Lucy blushed as red as the roses and snatched the card from her sister's fingers.

Dearest Lucy,
Red roses are a terrible cliché, I know. But I couldn't get hibiscus, and they do bring all my love.
Troy.

How dared he? How *dared* he? Lucy ripped the card in two and flung the pieces on the floor. 'As far as I'm concerned you can have every one of those roses,' she said, and burst into tears.

The old lady in the next bed, who had spent an enjoyable half-hour the evening before telling Lucy every detail of her hernia operation, sucked in her breath in a gratified sigh.

Catherine snapped, '*Lucy*! You and Mother between you are altogether too much.'

Lucy ripped a handful of tissues from the box by Catherine's bed and noisily blew her nose. 'I hate him,' she snuffled. 'I never want to see him again.'

'So why are you crying?' her sister asked with impeccable logic.

'Oh, Catherine, do shut up!'

'That's scarcely the way to speak to me when I'm so ill,' Catherine said haughtily.

She was right; it wasn't. Lucy scowled, her brain belatedly going into action. 'You know what these horrible roses mean? He's tracked you down. If he comes to Ottawa, this is the first place he'll look for me. He can't go to any of our homes because our phone numbers are unlisted. So he'll come here. What on earth am I going to do?'

'You're in love with him,' Catherine said distastefully, rather as if her sister were suffering from some unmentionable disease.

'Oh, Cat, I don't know.' The childish nickname slipped out before Lucy thought. 'I don't know anything anymore. I feel like I'm under siege, because every time I turn around he's phoning me, and I'm so unhappy I could die, and I'm so angry with him I could kill him, and of course I'm in love with him. Why else would I be making a fool of myself in front of a whole roomful of people?' With defiant panache she blew her nose again.

Catherine relented enough to smile. 'I'm glad I don't make a practice of falling in love if this is what it does to you.'

'He's the skipper of the boat I was on, he's handsome and sexy and he managed to sweet-talk his way past Margaret.'

Catherine's eyes widened with respect. 'He *did*?'

In sudden trepidation Lucy said, 'Cat, you've got to promise you won't tell him where my apartment is.'

In a ritual straight from their childhood, Catherine crossed her hands over her hospital johnny shirt and looked piously up at the ceiling. 'I swear.'

'You're a sweetheart. And now I'm going to take these roses and put them in the chapel downstairs,' Lucy said, jamming the lid on the box with scant respect for the contents, then tucking it under her arm. 'Somebody might as well enjoy them.' She kissed her sister on the cheek. 'Look after yourself... I'll scoot in to see you later today. And remember what you promised.'

The roses looked quite magnificent against the dark-stained woodwork in the chapel; with a pang of compunction Lucy turned her back on them and went outside. It was raining again and there wasn't a leaf to be seen on the trees. Forcing herself into action, she went back to her mother's—she couldn't quite bring herself to face her own apartment yet—and started on the long list of phone calls she had to make.

The next morning, after a night whose dreams would never have made it past the censor board, she went to her office, gave two massages and made a depressingly large hole in her bank account by paying all her bills. Since the delivery of the roses Troy had made no further attempts to get in touch with her. No more phone calls for Margaret, no more talk of love on Lucy's answering machine. Good, thought Lucy, he finally got the message; and tamped down the cold terror that was lurking in her belly as many-armed as an octopus in an underwater cave.

At five past twelve she decided to walk to her mother's for lunch. The house would be empty; she could relax for an hour before paying a quick visit to Catherine and then coming back to work. For the first time since she had arrived, the sun was shining. A pale sun with no noticeable warmth, she thought critically, and could almost feel beneath her sensible city shoes the burning sand on the beach at Troy's villa. The palms would be rustling in the wind, the hibiscus blooms drinking in the sunlight... She pushed open the wrought-iron gate to her mother's front garden and saw the man sitting on the front step.

Her hand froze on the latch. She was dreaming again, calling him up from a need too desperate to be acknowledged. Then Troy stood up and started walking down the path toward her.

He was far too solid-looking to be the figure in a dream. He was unshaven, his eyes dark-circled with tiredness; a leather jacket was slung round his shoulders, over a rumpled shirt and belted trousers. His hair, as usual, was untidy.

Lucy warded him off with a tiny gesture of panic. 'How did you find me here?'

'Catherine gave me the address.'

'She promised she wouldn't!'

'She promised not to give me the address of your apartment... She seems to think you're in love with me.'

'She'll be in more than traction by the time I'm finished with her,' Lucy said vengefully. 'Sure I'm in love with you—that's why I put those awful roses in the hospital chapel and why I haven't answered a single one of your phone calls. You'd better be careful—I'll charge you with harassment.'

He stepped closer. 'Lucy, I—'

'Don't touch me!' she cried. 'I don't know what the *hell* you're doing here but I don't want to talk to you. I don't want to see you ever again. You wouldn't even *talk* to me about your sister. I meant every word of that note I wrote to you in Road Town. I grew up in a family that never spoke of feelings and I don't want anything to do with a man who can't—or won't—share his.'

She seemed to have run out of words. Troy said evenly, 'I was a fool not to tell you about Lydia. But I was afraid if I did that I'd break down in front of Heather or Leona or Shannon—I couldn't handle that. Men aren't supposed to cry—my dad drummed that into me when I was only a kid.'

'Heather and Leona and Shannon weren't at your villa. Only us.'

'I wanted that twenty-four hours to be for you!' he said violently. 'You alone. I loved my sister dearly but I didn't want her intruding on those precious few hours you and I had together.'

A starling chittered from the telephone wire and a truck roared past in a haze of exhaust. 'Lydia comes along with you, Troy,' Lucy said. 'Part of the package.'

'I know that now. But I didn't then—for someone who can put a dozen letters after his name, I've been incredibly stupid.' He looked around unseeingly. 'Can we go inside?'

And Lucy, who had meant never to let him near her again, walked past him and up the steps, unlocked the dark blue door and ushered him indoors. After he had put his bag down on the polished oak floor, she led him into the den. The familiar surroundings steadied her, so that with new discernment she saw the deep lines of tension around his mouth, the exhaustion pulling at his shoulders. 'Would you like something to eat?' she asked.

He shook his head. Standing by her favorite wing chair, he said hoarsely, 'I've got to make you understand… Because if I don't, I've lost you. Don't think I don't know that.' He shrugged out of his jacket, letting it fall on the chair. 'Just tell me one thing, Lucy… Do you love me? Was Catherine right?'

Bracing her back against the other chair, knowing this was a time not for anger but for truth, Lucy said, 'Yes, I love you. But I won't be with you, Troy, unless you learn not to shut me out. It hurts too much when you do that…you've got to share your feelings.'

Insensibly the lines of his body relaxed. 'I love you, too,' he said. 'More than I can say.'

The dull, grinding ache that Lucy had carried with her ever since she had left his house by the beach began to loosen its hold. Feeling the shift in nerve and muscle, she was nevertheless deeply grateful that Troy made no move to touch her; intuitively he seemed to understand that there were things to be said before their bodies came together. 'Tell me why you were so unreachable,' she said.

He picked up a Venetian paperweight from the coffee-table and turned it over and over in his long fingers. 'Lydia's death nearly killed my mother and father. A murdered child—what parent can cope with that? So I've spent all my free time in the last few months, when I wasn't in the wards or the operating room, trying to hold Mum and Dad together… That's why I didn't get to the villa in February as I usually do. I wanted them to go with me, but they couldn't—it was one of Lydia's favorite places.'

Even in the midst of a compassion stronger than any she had ever felt, a great deal was coming clear to Lucy. 'The one person you didn't look after was yourself,' she said.

'Yeah…my parents came first, my patients second. Even there I wasn't managing very well. I didn't have the energy to care and to listen the way I had always used to, and then I'd feel guilty that I wasn't giving them the best that was in me.'

'You're only human, Troy!'

'When I met you, the timing couldn't have been worse. I'd been chained to Lydia's death for six months. I knew

I had to do something about it, but I didn't have a clue what…and then you applied for the job on *Seawind*.' He labored on, 'Right from the beginning I knew you were important. That you mattered in some way I couldn't define but that struck me to the heart. I had to take you to the villa, Lucy. I had to. I wanted to forget Lydia and savor you in all your beauty and your passion. But once we'd made love, I knew I was vulnerable again and it scared me blind. I loved you—that's what I realized when I woke with you in my arms in the big bed at the villa. I'd loved my sister and her death had devastated me. And now I was running the same risk again. With you.'

Lucy's eyes widened. 'That's why you couldn't get me out of there fast enough.'

'And then we picked up the deVries family and Shannon walked on board, looking so like Lydia that I could hardly bear it.' He rolled the smooth, heavy piece of glass in his hands, absently watching the colors swirl deep within it. 'I had to shut you out. If I hadn't, I'd have fallen apart.' In a voice so low she could hardly hear it, he added, 'Once they left *Seawind* I went to the villa, and for the first time since Lydia died I wept for her.'

His exhaustion was explained, as was so much else. Trusting her instincts, Lucy closed the distance between them and rested her hands on his taut shoulders. 'And then you came here.'

His muscles were rigid under her palms. 'I should have told you! I know that now and I even knew it at the time. But I'd smothered my grief for my parents' sake, and somehow it got caught. Trapped like a lump of granite in my chest.'

'I do understand, Troy.'

He looked at her, unsmiling. 'I'm sorry for what I put you through. I could see you hurting, but it was as if there

was a thick wall between you and me, and I couldn't climb
it or breach it. I tried... That was why I was playing one
of Lydia's tapes the day I was alone on *Seawind*. But you
came back on board before I was ready for you—and I
lost my cool and hurt you again.'

Lucy said softly, 'Come to bed with me, Troy. Right
now.'

His face stilled. 'If we go to bed, I'll make love to you.
Is that what you want?'

'Yes.'

'I don't want an affair with you, Lucy. I want to marry
you.'

Her heart skipped a beat. 'Is the wall gone? Or do you
think it'll come back?'

'I've learned how to climb it, Lucy. I'm only sorry it
took so long.'

She leaned against him, feeling his arms go around her.
His body was warm and hard and she hadn't forgotten the
smallest detail of their lovemaking. 'I do love you,' she
said.

'Marry me, Lucy.'

'Of course,' she said.

Visibly shaken, Troy muttered, 'I was afraid you'd turn
me down flat. It would have been no more than I deserve.'

'Troy, it goes without saying that I'll marry you.'

For the first time since she had seen him, waiting on her
mother's steps, Troy smiled at her, a smile wry with self-
knowledge. 'Nothing goes without saying. That's what
I've learned the last few days.' Smoothing a curl back from
her forehead, his voice made level with an obvious effort,
he said, 'We'll have to figure out how to manage our respective jobs. I'm sure I could get a position in Ottawa...I
know how hard you've worked to build up your clientele.'

Touched, Lucy shook her head. 'Thank you for offering.

But I think this would be a good time for me to start over, and this time run my business my way and not my family's way. Anyway, we could go sailing on the west coast. It beats the Rideau Canal.'

'I can't believe I'm actually standing here having this conversation,' Troy said huskily. 'Repeat after me—I love you, Troy, and I'll marry you as soon as possible.'

Her smile was dazzling. 'I love you, Troy, and I'll marry you as soon as Catherine gets out of traction. If it hadn't been for her, you wouldn't have known where to find me.'

'I'd have found you,' he said. 'If I'd had to go from door to door through the whole city.'

She believed every word of it. 'Now it's your turn,' she said.

But first he bent his head and kissed her, a kiss that in its intensity told her of his commitment and his hunger and his love. Letting his mouth slide down her throat, he said, 'I love you, Lucy, and we'll get married with Catherine on a stretcher in the aisle.'

'I could have red roses in my bouquet.'

'Only if I can't get hibiscus.'

She laughed. Head to one side, she said, 'Do we have to wait until then to make love?'

His smile had reached his eyes, sparking them with desire. 'We have to wait long enough for me to shower and shave.'

When he'd kissed her his beard had rasped her skin. 'That's a good idea…I could shower with you.'

'Your mother won't walk in? If she's anything like her secretary, I'm already terrified of her.'

'You? Who routed Raymond Blogden? Terrified of my mother?'

'We should invite him to the wedding, too. If it hadn't

been for his sexist views on massage, you and I might never have met.'

'I can manage without him,' Lucy said decisively. 'Him and his collection of jade. Although we should ask the Merritts and the Dillons. And you don't have to worry about Mum—she springs from the Puritan work ethic, and won't be home until six-thirty at the earliest.'

Troy looked over at the grandfather clock that was ticking ponderously by the fireplace. 'Five hours. Is that long enough for me to convince you you're the most beautiful woman in the world?'

'You'll never know until you try,' said Lucy.

They made love in her old bedroom, watched benignly by her collection of teddy bears. Passion, hunger and laughter were their bedfellows, and something else, something new to both of them. For this time, openly acknowledged, their love for each other lay between them and enfolded them. Lucy could see it naked in Troy's eyes, and feel it informing each of his caresses. To their mutual climax it gave depth and a fierce poignancy, for in that small death, thought Lucy, was also the first of many beginnings.

They lay for a long time in each other's arms, as Troy recounted some of his memories of his sister. Her veneration for Mozart; her addiction to Pepsi Cola, old Jimmie Stewart movies, and aerobic workouts to improve her wind; the oddly assorted clothing she wore, all second-hand; the single-minded focus she had brought to her music. Lucy wasn't even sure he was aware of the tears in his eyes as he spoke; to her they were beautiful, because they represented truth, and truth was what she needed from this complex and passionate man whom she loved, body and soul.

As if his words had freed him of some of the burden he had been carrying, he slowly started stroking her body, intimately relearning its geography and its responses. Without haste they made love again, a union that was an exploration of all the pleasures of the present as well as a gesture of trust in the future they would share.

It was the distant chiming of the grandfather clock downstairs that brought them back to reality. 'Was that six o'clock?' Lucy gasped.

Troy reached for his watch from the little stand by her bed. 'Yep.' He ran his hands the length of her body. 'You mean I have to get up?'

'I shall refrain from the obvious pun,' Lucy said demurely. 'I suspect my mother is fairly unshockable when it comes to matters of sex—she is a forensic pathologist, after all—but I still don't want her to find me in bed with someone she's never met.'

Troy kissed her firmly and at some length. 'I only hope I brought a clean shirt,' he said, nibbling at her lower lip in a way Lucy found very distracting. 'My mind wasn't on my packing.'

'I'll take you to my favorite Chinese restaurant for dinner,' she said. 'No dress code.'

'You mean your cooking days are over?'

She blinked. 'I forgot to ask you who's skippering *Seawind*!'

'I prevailed upon Gavin to come back with an extra man for crew. Answer the question, Lucy.'

'Not totally over. But I am in favor of take-out. Besides—' and she touched him very suggestively '—I'm not convinced the way to your heart is through your stomach.'

'Stop that! Or we *will* be testing your mother's level of shockability. It's just as well my mother was ahead of her time and taught me how to cook.'

Very reluctantly, Lucy stopped. So, when Evelyn Barnes

opened her front door fifteen minutes later, Lucy and Troy were sitting sedately in the den waiting for her.

'Ah,' said Evelyn, after Lucy had introduced him, 'you finally made it here. I rather thought you would.'

Troy kissed Evelyn on the cheek and said, 'I'm hoping you'll become my mother-in-law.'

'A pleasure,' Evelyn said. 'You made it past Margaret and you impressed Catherine, neither of which is a negligible recommendation.' She glanced at her daughter's radiant face. 'And Lucy, I must say, looks happier than I've ever seen her.'

'That,' said Troy, smiling at Lucy, 'is the best recommendation of all.'

The only one that really mattered, thought Lucy, and smiled back.

Sharon Kendrick started story-telling at the age of eleven and has never really stopped. She likes to write fast-paced, feel-good romances with heroes who are so sexy they'll make your toes curl!

Born in west London, she now lives in the beautiful city of Winchester – where she can see the cathedral from her window (but only if she stands on tip-toe). She is married to a medical professor – which may explain why her family get more colds than anyone else on the street – and they have two children, Celia and Patrick. Her passions include music, books, cooking and eating – and drifting off into wonderful daydreams while she works out new plots!

Sharon Kendrick's next book
FINN'S PREGNANT BRIDE
is available December 2002
in Modern Romance™.

SAVAGE SEDUCTION
by
Sharon Kendrick

For Tommy 'The Tiger' Crone – the amazing libel
lawyer. Thanks for your advice, Tom! And for Patti
'Pet' Crone, great wit and great lover of 'sparkling'!

CHAPTER ONE

'OH, HELL!'

Jade made the husky imprecation as she emerged from the gin-clear water, to see that the two would-be Romeos from her home city of London had none too subtly moved themselves even closer to her towel. She shook the droplets of water from her long hair, feeling decidedly disgruntled at the prospect of having to tell them politely to go away. Again.

The droplets of water had already begun to dry on her skin. The sea had been the temperature of warm milk and as soon as she'd left it the relentless heat of the sun had started beating down on her without mercy. But that was Greece for you.

The most exquisite place she'd ever visited—with sky which was bluer than a denim shirt and sand the colour of cream and the texture of caster sugar. Add to that the heady scents of lemon mingled with pine, the wine-dark sea and the drowse-inducing mass chorus of the cicadas, and you could understand why when people discovered Greece they felt they'd stumbled on Paradise.

If only it weren't so darned hot!

She picked her way over the burning sand, and one of the Romeos sprang to his feet, the sun glinting off his fair hair.

'Hi, there, beautiful,' he said, somewhat unoriginally. 'Can I get you a drink?'

'No, thanks,' answered Jade coolly, wondering what it was about some men which made them so dense in picking up the distinctly negative vibes she was sending out.

'How about—' He raised his eyebrows suggestively, as his glance strayed to her sopping bosom, and Jade felt a sudden stirring of apprehension as she picked up her sarong to cover the tiny yellow bikini she wore.

His leer increased. '—if I rub some sun-cream into your back—?'

'How about,' came a deep and softly menacing voice from behind Jade's back, 'if you left this beach and never returned?'

And Jade whirled round to see the man from the restaurant, her throat immediately drying with the powerful impact of his darkly rugged good looks.

The Londoner was foolishly attempting resistance. 'What's it to do with you?' he demanded belligerently.

'Move away from here,' came the flat and deliberate statement, 'before I am forced to remove you myself.'

There was something in his dark eyes which brooked no argument, and the two men blanched beneath their tans. Jade watched while they gathered their few possessions up into their arms and crept away like chastened dogs.

She stayed watching them go, unaccountably excited by the man's presence, yet oddly unsure of what to do next, and it was a moment or two before she could bring herself to look up at her rescuer, who stood silently surveying her, as though it was his every right to do so. He was a stranger, yes, and yet she recognised him instantly. A man once seen, never forgotten—with the kind of fiercely dominant presence which would imprint itself on any woman's psyche, as it had on Jade's. And yet they hadn't even exchanged a word when she had seen him at the taverna yesterday...

Jade had walked into the local village to buy her provisions, and as usual it had been baking hot, absolutely *baking*. She had scooped her hand back through her thick fair hair as she'd looked over longingly at the shady canopy of lemon trees in the taverna. Through the air she could scent the lamb smouldering on the barbeque with its big bunches of thyme strewn all over it. She saw the tentacles of the octopuses dangling over a line, awaiting their ritual dousing in lemon juice before cooking. She wasn't fond of eating alone in the restaurants where tourists abounded, but this one looked full of families, and, more interestingly, full of Greeks. It must be good, she'd thought as she made her way to a shaded table.

She had ordered Greek salad, a beer and a plate of olives and was sitting enjoying them until when a small child, all dark curls and heart-shaped face, waddled over to her table. The mother called the child back in Greek, but Jade turned and shook her head, smiling, and starting to play 'peep-bo' with the toddler, who eventually climbed on to her lap and began to pick up a strand of her blonde hair in wonder. Jade

pulled a funny face at the little girl who immediately
giggled back as she continued to play with the blonde
hair. The feeling of having the child in her arms was
a new and rather enjoyable experience, and Jade
couldn't help hugging her, delighted when the little
girl nestled back quite happily.

Jade had sensed, rather than seen, that someone
was watching her. Well, in fact, most of the restaurant
were. They were enjoying the little interplay between
the child and the young tourist.

But this sensation was different… Little hairs at the
back of her neck began to prickle with some nebulous
excitement.

She narrowed her eyes, looking into the dim air-
conditioned interior of the restaurant, and through the
gloom she saw a table, where a man sat surrounded
by three or four others. A man in a white shirt and
white jeans. A man to whom the others listened. A
man with eyes as black as olives and as hard as jet.
Eyes which gleamed and narrowed, frozen in a stare
as they captured her gaze over the head of the child.
For a stunned moment Jade stared back, unable to
look away—her mouth suddenly dry, her heart pounding erratically and an unfamiliar excitement stealing
over her as she gazed at the man, some unfamiliar
and primitive longing sweeping over her as their eyes
locked.

The man whose quietly menacing authority had
driven away the two tourists, and who now stood on
the beach in front of her.

The stranger was Greek; he could be nothing else.
He had the proud bearing and the superbly shaped

head of his ancestors. But he was tall for a Greek: a couple of inches over six feet, she hazarded. His skin was coloured a luminously soft olive, the kind of colour which made the sales of fake tan rocket, and it gleamed very slightly, the slight sheen emphasising the ripple of muscle. His hair was as black as tar, rich and thick—a mass of unruly waves worn just slightly too long. Today he was wearing nothing but a pair of sawn-off denims; very faded and very scruffy. Those and a pair of beaten-up sandals. She swallowed at the sight of so much naked flesh on show. She should have been frightened, and yet fear was the last thing on her mind as she returned his gaze. She stared into eyes as cold and forbidding and harsh as jet. Narrow eyes that glittered; eyes which studied her with a detached and yet strangely intense appraisal which was almost intoxicating in itself.

And all of a sudden, it happened again: a replay of the sensations she had experienced the last time she had seen him. She felt her senses clamour into life, felt her heart accelerate painfully, accepted the flood of colour to her cheeks and the almost debilitating dryness of her mouth as she battled to compose herself.

'Why are you here on your own?' came his terse interrogation.

The question floored her; she was so outraged at its implicit chauvinism. 'Because I like my own company,' she answered coolly.

He didn't respond to the inference. 'Well, do not do so again.'

Jade's eyes narrowed in disbelief. 'Don't do what?'

Jet eyes glittered dangerously. 'Do not put yourself at risk. This beach is too isolated; a woman is too vulnerable.'

He spoke, she thought suddenly, like a man used to giving orders, and having them obeyed.

'Who—are you?' she asked suddenly, in a voice which seemed to have deepened by at least an octave.

He stilled, his ebony eyes narrowed with suspicion. 'You don't know?'

'Oh, for heaven's sake! If I knew then I wouldn't be asking, surely?'

'No.' He was examining her face intently, like a man newly given sight, and that slow inspection stirred some answering response deep within her. He looked, she thought dizzily, like a king—there was something stately and proud in his bearing. And yet how could he when, to judge by his appearance, he was obviously a beach bum? She had been reading far too many romantic novels on this holiday—let that be a lesson to her!

'My name is Constantine Sioulas,' he replied, in a gloriously deep voice, with only the faintest trace of an accent, and again the black eyes pierced her with their intense scrutiny.

Constantine. She tested the name in her mind; found it the most beautiful name in the whole world, which was really rather appropriate, as the man in front of her was the most beautiful man she had ever laid eyes on.

'And you?' He lifted an enquiring eyebrow. 'What is your name?'

'It's Jade,' she said rather breathlessly, as though she'd just stopped running. 'Jade Meredith.'

'Jade.' He nodded his head, thoughtfully. 'Yes. It suits you,' he pronounced. 'Your eyes are the colour of jade.'

And her cheeks were now the colour of rubies, she thought ruefully as she blushed beneath the slow scrutiny of his gaze, revelling in the approbation on his face, and yet despising herself for the way she was behaving. Why not just fall down in reverence at his knees and kiss his feet, Jade!

'No, they're not,' she lifted her chin in a defiant little gesture. 'My eyes are pale green. Jade is darker.'

He shook his head. 'Sometimes,' he contradicted. 'The Chinese say that the colour deepens and intensifies as the wearer acquires wisdom. It would be an interesting experiment—to see whether that is true.' He gave a small almost reluctant smile, like the smile of a man not used to smiling. 'Shall I buy you jade, Jade Meredith?' he said softly. 'Jewels of jade for you to wear next to that pale, pale skin? Together we could watch it growing darker day by day.'

His words were so inappropriate considering that they'd only just met. And yet he spoke them with a coolly assured confidence which only renewed the throbbing of blood to her pulse points.

'My skin isn't pale,' she protested. After nearly three weeks in the sun, it had turned a pale golden colour—she was quite proud of it!

'Most certainly it is,' he contradicted, in the rich, glowing voice overlaid with its barely discernible yet totally seductive accent. 'Pale as milk—at least when you compare it with mine.'

And at his words she found her eyes drawn irresistibly to the dark olive of his bare chest and shoulders, the strong forearms, and the equally strong thighs. Her mind responded to his suggestion with frightening clarity as she pictured her lying on a bed with him, his dark limbs tangled with hers, strong brown thigh against a thigh as pale as milk... Jade had to close her eyes briefly to blot out the tantalising image, but it didn't work.

'Shall we?' he whispered silkily.

'Shall we what?' she echoed huskily, lost in some misty erotic world of her own.

He smiled, and it was a suddenly ruthless smile. The smile, she recognised with an unquestionable certainty, of a man who was used to getting whatever it was he wanted.

'I was referring to buying the jade,' he said softly. 'But we should have to go to the mainland to do that, and I don't want to waste precious hours doing that, not when there are so many more attractive alternatives.' He smiled. 'Come, I shall walk you back to your house.'

It was most definitely an order. Jade bristled. 'That won't be necessary.'

'On the contrary,' he answered smoothly, but there was a steely quality to his voice now. 'I insist.'

Most annoyingly, she found the arrogant protectiveness in his assertion extremely attractive, but a lifetime of paying lip-service to feminism couldn't be banished overnight! She met his gaze steadily. 'I said *no*, thank you.'

'I heard what you said, but it doesn't change a thing.'

Jade shook her head from side to side in a mixture of amusement and exasperation. 'Do you always insist on getting your own way?' she demanded.

He grinned then, the most heartbreakingly gorgeous grin imaginable, and *that* was her undoing. 'I always get my own way,' he murmured. 'Though not always by insisting. I don't usually have to,' he added arrogantly.

That she *could* imagine! Jade had to try very hard to suppress a smile as she watched while he bent down to retrieve her bag and her towel and tucked them under his arm with an old-fashioned courtesy— which she *certainly* wasn't used to. She knew she was fighting a losing battle here, and what was more, she was quickly discovering that it was a battle she didn't particularly want to fight anyway. 'Then I'll take you up on your offer of walking me home,' she said. '*Thank* you.' And she saw from the slight elevation of his eyebrows that he hadn't missed the sarcastic emphasis.

'My pleasure.' His eyes were mocking. Then. 'Those tourists—do not worry about them. They shall not bother you again.'

There was something about the grim, gravelly undertone to his voice which made it sound vaguely threatening. Jade swallowed; she hadn't thought that men like this existed outside films! 'Er—you wouldn't *hurt* them?' asked Jade anxiously. 'They weren't really doing anything.'

'Because I arrived.' His eyes glittered like coals from hell. 'I saw the way he was looking at you.' He made a terse exclamation in Greek.

Jade swallowed. Had she been blasé about the danger? She saw the hard, formidable lines in the handsome face, saw the ruthless glitter in the black eyes, and she knew a fleeting feeling of sympathy for the two hapless tourists. 'You won't—*hurt* them?' she whispered again, and was relieved to see a half-smile lift the corner of his mouth.

'What did you imagine I would do—beat them into pulp?' he queried softly, and then he gave an amused smile. 'Do not be concerned, little one. I shall merely speak to them—that will serve as sufficient deterrent.'

Feeling as though she'd been caught up in a sudden time warp, Jade stared curiously up at him. 'Do you always over-react like this?' she quizzed him, forcing her voice to be light.

He shook his head. 'It is not over-reacting at all.' Some feral light sparked at the depths of the coal-dark eyes. 'In Greece, you see,' he told her, 'we are protective of our women.'

He made her feel very small and very fragile, not a bit like her rather lanky five feet nine, and Jade couldn't repress a shiver of excitement. Put like that it sounded so darkly atavistic, so—well, so thrilling, the idea of someone like this black-eyed and powerfully built man actually protecting her. Because hadn't protection been in very short supply in her life up until now?

The sun beat down on their bare heads as they walked up from the beach to the narrow track which was masquerading as a road. Jade could see the heat shimmering hazily upwards into the endless blue of the sky.

'Put your hat on,' he said.

She obediently crammed the battered straw down on her head. 'Shouldn't you?'

He gave a little shake of his head. 'I am used to the sun.'

And hair that thick, that black, thought Jade, would surely protect him from its fierce rays?

Lizards ran swiftly along the sun-baked road, and he named them for her, pointing out tiny scrubby and fragrant plants that she'd never noticed before. His accent was entrancing; it lulled her into a dreamy sense of well-being, and when they arrived at last at the small house she was renting she stared up at him, aware of the disappointment thudding through her. I don't want this day to end, she thought suddenly.

'You want to know what we should do next?'

Could he guess so easily what she was thinking? she wondered dimly. Did her reluctance to see him go show on her face? 'I...' Her voice tailed off in hopeless confusion—*she* who everyone always said could talk her way into the record books!

'We have a number of choices,' he mused, as though this were the kind of bizarre conversation he was used to conducting every day. *Was* he? 'You could offer me some of your water and we could sit together and drink. Or we could walk down to the village and take some refreshment there. Alternatively, I could initiate what we both *most* want to do?'

And only the biggest fool in the world would have replied, 'Which is?'

'Why, to kiss, of course,' he replied, his voice a velvet caress which would have melted ice. 'That's what you want me to do, isn't it?'

Now she could feel her cheeks blanch—heaven only knew what harm this man was doing to her nervous system! He was virtually making love to her with his eyes. Jade Meredith the fearless reporter took stock of the potentially dicey situation she was in, and astonishingly *still* felt no fear. She used the gritty voice with which she'd fired questions at soap stars and the unsuspecting wives of footballers.

'Just who *are* you?' she demanded. She'd met confident men in her life before, yes, men who were arrogantly sure of their effect on women, yes—but never one who was *this* confident!

At the question, his eyes narrowed and he stilled, watching her intently from beneath dark, luxuriant brows. 'I told you.' His voice was a slumberous caress. 'My name is Constantine.'

'Yes—but…' Her voice trailed off helplessly. What could she say? Yes, you're right, you delectable man—I *do* want you to kiss me? More than I've ever wanted anything in my whole life? She was breaking every rule in the book by even standing here *listening* to him. What about all that assertiveness training she'd undergone? Did women allow men to change their minds for them? No, they most certainly did not! She gave him a conventional and dismissive nod. It was the hardest thing she'd ever had to do in her life. 'It was very kind of you to accompany me—but I think you'd better leave now.'

He smiled again. 'In time.'

He had moved closer now, and when he moved it was like poetry in motion. You could see the muscles moving in perfect symmetry beneath the olive perfection of his skin.

He really wasn't *that* tall, she reminded herself; plenty of men were taller than six feet, and she was only a few inches shorter herself. Yet there was something about the width of his shoulders and the magnificent breadth of a chest with its dark, dark whorls of hair. Something, too, about the powerful thrust of his thighs—as solidly carved as the trunk of an oak tree. All these things combined to make him seem the *biggest* man she had ever seen. She suppressed another little shiver of excitement.

He was smiling now as he let her give him the once over, again with that curiously cold smile—as though laughter was a stranger to his life. 'You aren't afraid of me.' It was a statement of fact; he sounded amused.

'No.' Perhaps that was the wrong thing to say. She knew that Greek men were notoriously old-fashioned. Would he have preferred it if she'd started backing away from him, white-faced and trembling? Oh, come *on*, Jade, she chided—why should you care what *he'd* prefer?

'Not even a little afraid?' he quizzed her softly. 'And yet you *terrify* me.'

Jade swallowed. Now he was talking in riddles. 'No, I'm not afraid of you,' she said firmly, and held her chin up stubbornly. 'But I happen to have a black belt in judo, just in case you're getting any ideas.'

This provoked a laugh, a low, rich chuckle, and Jade stupidly felt as though she'd just won the first prize in a raffle. 'Very commendable,' he remarked. 'But you know that your—black belt—in judo wouldn't do you any good at all?'

Such arrogance! Such *amazing* arrogance! 'Let me enlighten you,' she said quite calmly, which was astonishing considering how fast her heart was hammering away in her chest. 'Size has nothing to do with it.'

'Oh, really?' he teased softly, and her comment became something else completely. The black eyes glittered with mischief, and Jade coloured to the roots of her hair. *Now* what had she said?

'I mean comparative size,' she said firmly, refusing to back down or be intimidated. 'You are taller and obviously stronger than I am, but judo isn't about brute strength—it's all to do with control and balance, of observing your opponent and waiting for the right opportunity.'

'I know. And that isn't what I meant.'

'Oh? And just what did you mean? You implied that I'd be unable to defeat you.'

'Absolutely,' he said softly. 'And do you know why? Because I think that once we made contact…whoosh!' He lifted the palms of his hands in front of that magnificent bare chest in a flamboyant gesture that an Englishman could never have got away with.

Jade's heart had renewed its hammering. She

shouldn't be letting him talk to her like this; didn't Greek men notoriously think that Englishwomen were easy? Well, he was about to discover that Jade Meredith was not among that merry band of women who fell swooning into the arms of handsome islanders for two weeks of holiday bliss before being put firmly on the plane with a load of lies about writing. 'Is this your normal chat-up line?' she asked cuttingly. 'Because it if is I'd give you nought out of ten for subtlety!'

The dark brows knitted together. 'Chat-up line,' he mused. 'Considering that English is one of the most perfect and complex of languages, that phrase is rather—inelegant, wouldn't you say?'

It was rather shaming that someone to whom English was not a first language could express himself so eloquently, Jade thought with a touch of irritation. She had expected that to put him in his place, not to start some highbrow discussion about semantics!

The ebony brows remained knitted together. 'And if we're going to continue this—*fascinating* discussion—might I suggest that we do it in a little more comfort?' He looked pointedly at the table where the empty water jug sat. 'Shall we sit down?'

Excitement vyed with prudence. 'Why should we? I don't know you,' she said stubbornly.

'But you know enough to know that I won't hurt you?'

Jade stared at him. Enough, yes, to know that he would never physically hurt her, but...as she looked into those glittering black eyes, observed the slash of jaw and the high cheekbones, she suddenly felt some terrifying fear icing her skin. A knowledge that, yes, this magnificent creature with the cold smile and the eyes of jet *could* hurt her. That through him she could learn the real meaning of pain; indescribable, unbearable pain... She started to shake uncontrollably, a violent tremor which ran through her body like wildfire.

He saw her tremble. A warm hand was placed on her chilled forearm and she felt his strength like a warm embrace.

'Fear not—I will not hurt you,' he said quietly.

You will, she thought suddenly. Oh, this was *ridiculous*! Had three weeks in Greece had turned her into a clairvoyant? She shook him away inelegantly, but he captured her hand in his, raising it to his mouth where it stayed just centimetres away from the proud curve of his lips.

'Do you not know that in Greece it is customary to offer the traveller refreshment?'

Her breathing was inhibited, shallow, painful. She awaited the brush of his mouth on her hand.

In vain.

His eyes gleamed and he let her hand go, but somehow he had regained supremacy, and Jade was angry. Angry with herself for wanting him to press his lips on to her hand, and angry that he had not chosen to! And she wasn't sending him away with him thinking that she was some kind of desperado! She straightened her shoulders and gave her most English smile, spoke in her most chillingly polite tone.

'Then you must sit down and have a drink.'

'Thank you.' In response, he deepened his accent,

his eyes sparking with mischief, and Jade found herself wanting to giggle. So much for icy politeness!

'I'll fill the jug and fetch another glass,' she said hastily.

And she scrambled inside as he pulled out one of the wooden chairs, which now looked hopelessly insubstantial if expected to accommodate that large, muscular frame.

Jade filled the jug with water and ice and found the glass with fingers which were still trembling, her eyes lifting reluctantly to the small spotted mirror which hung on the whitewashed walls. A wild-eyed, fey stranger stared back at her. Her pale green eyes were almost unrecognisable as her own, the colour almost completely obscured by the deep ebony of two dilated and glittering pupils. Her mouth looked swollen and throbbing and redder than usual—had she been chewing it while talking to him? she wondered. Even her hair—baby-fine but masses of it—which she hadn't had a chance to brush since he'd disturbed her; it had dried into a thick, pale cloud—shimmered like an uncontrollable halo around her head. The sun had bleached it almost blonde. Did Constantine, she thought suddenly, like women with blonde hair?

She took the jug and glass back outside, half afraid that he might have disappeared, but he hadn't. He had spread those long olive legs beneath the table and was watching her return.

Walking suddenly seemed a skill she hadn't yet acquired, and she would have stumbled if a strong hand hadn't shot out and caught her. She managed to get the jug down on the table, but the tumbler slipped from her grasp; the sound of the glass shattering on the grey stone of the courtyard sounding piercingly loud to her ears.

'Oh, hell! Now look what you've made me do,' said Jade unreasonably, and, crouching down, she began gingerly to pick up the larger fragments.

He was beside her in an instant. 'Be careful,' he told her, but it was too late, a shard had pierced her forefinger, and crimson blood began to well and to drop in dark starry splashes on to the grey stone.

Her finger went up to her mouth, but he deliberately took it before it reached its destination, the black eyes fixed on hers as he put it into his mouth and sucked the blood away.

If there hadn't been glass all around them, Jade thought that she would have keeled over. She felt the blood drain from her face as she stared into the night-dark eyes.

'You—shouldn't have done that,' she said shakily.

He relieved the pressure, but her finger stayed firmly in the hot, moist cavern of his mouth. 'Why not?'

'It's dangerous,' she managed. 'Blood…'

He shook his head, as if he understood her meaning perfectly. 'I think not.'

'How can you know?' she demanded breathlessly. 'We've only just met.'

His eyes met hers. 'I know,' he said softly.

Another slow and deliberate suck; it was the most erotic thing that had ever happened to her in her life— and then he took the finger from his mouth, examined it and held it up for her inspection. 'The flow is stemmed,' he pronounced, and something in the formality of this statement, spoken with all the solemnity of a Victorian surgeon, instead of the more modern 'it's stopped bleeding', made Jade's lips twitch in amusement.

He saw the movement, and raised his eyebrows. 'What?'

'You have a very formal way of speaking,' she said honestly. 'But your English is absolutely superb.'

He inclined his head. 'And so it should be. I grew up with it as my second language.'

She shook her head, as if bemused by what was happening. 'Are you always like this—Constantine?' She said his name experimentally for the first time. Her tongue had to protrude a little in order to pronounce it properly, in the slightly lisping Greek manner. She liked saying it, liked the way his eyes flared as he watched her tongue snake out and then back in again.

'Like—what?'

Jade stared back into the glittering black eyes, realising that she actually felt as though she were high on something—if this feeling was ever marketed, the world would go into total chaos! 'So darned assertive!' she answered crisply.

He looked surprised. 'But naturally. Are not all men supposed to be assertive? The dominant ones?'

She smiled. 'That's not what the feminists would say.'

'Ah! The feminists! You are one of these?' He ran his eyes lazily over the bright and filmy covering of

her sarong, at the cloud of blonde hair. 'I don't think
so,' he observed.

Jade could not let that pass. 'You think that I
couldn't possibly be a feminist because I haven't got
cropped hair and am not wearing dungarees?'

A light flared in his eyes. 'But those are your
words, Jade,' he said softly. 'Not mine. No, I made
the comment because I could imagine you soft, and
pliant, loving and giving. *Very* feminine, but not a
feminist. There is a subtle difference, you know.'

Jade realised that she was letting him get away with
statements she would have emphatically disagreed
with if she'd been back at home in England. Persuasive kind of guy. She tried again. 'But men being so
dominant and assertive,' she said, 'it isn't really the
modern way.'

'But I,' he answered proudly, 'am not a modern
man. At heart all Greeks are ruled by the very same
passions which have existed since the beginning of
time.'

This was totally new, uncharted and terribly exciting territory, men talking quite openly of passion.
Jade shivered.

'But perhaps,' he said deliberately, 'you are not
used to assertive men?'

Oh, but she was—she most certainly was! But there
was a world of difference between the way all the
men at her office behaved, and the way that
Constantine was behaving. Her editor rode roughshod
over all the staff. However, perhaps that was less like
assertion, and more like bullying! Certainly there was

none of this man's cool assurance in her boss's behaviour.

'Well, are you?' he persisted.

She wasn't used to men at all, not in the sense that
he meant. Which was probably why she was respond-
ing in such a *pathetic* way towards this particular
man. Men had been deliberately put on ice until the
career which had meant so much to her had had a
chance to develop properly—the career which she
was now thinking of chucking in because she was so
disillusioned with it. A cynic already—and at the
tender age of twenty!

She stared into the black eyes, blinked, then looked
down at the thick fragments of glass which glittered
by their feet. Mostly from a desire to steer the conversation away from her shameful lack of experience
with the opposite sex, she began to turn away. 'I'd
better go and fetch a dustpan and brush—'

'No.'

There he went again, dishing out the orders! Jade
stared up at him, half in anger, half in admiration,
marvelling that it actually felt extraordinarily *good* to
be around such a masterful man. Shame on her!

'You put some covering on your finger. Go! I will
deal with the glass.'

She found herself obeying him without question. In
the tiny bedroom she found the box of Elastoplast she
had brought with her from England, and, after removing the wrapping, she shakily applied one to her
thumb. She could hear him moving around in the
kitchen, presumably looking for the dustpan and

brush. She didn't doubt for a moment that he'd find it!

She wondered fleetingly whether she had a touch of sunstroke. Surely *normal* women of her age didn't allow half-clothed perfect strangers the run of their house? And yet, given the outstanding attraction of the man, she didn't feel in the least bit threatened. She examined her finger carefully. Well, that wasn't entirely true. She felt a threat, all right, but it had absolutely nothing to do with thinking that he might be some mad axeman. It was more an interested kind of wondering just what *would* happen if she caught him in a judo stranglehold. That expressive little 'whoosh' sound he'd made…implying…mmmm…

She went outside to find him disposing of the last of the glass. It was strange to see such a self-proclaimed non-modern man doing it so competently, and yet to see Constantine brushing up the fragments of glass…it almost *emphasised* his masculinity, rather than detracting from it. Confusing, she thought fleetingly. He'd talked about the man assuming the dominant role, and had teased her about feminists, and yet he didn't seem to mind lending a hand. Interesting.

As she appeared, he straightened up.

'I will wrap it up tightly in newspaper,' he instructed. 'So no more cut fingers.'

Jade nodded, acknowledging the perverse sinking of her heart. There was something of the farewell in the way he spoke. Surely he wasn't going?

She ventured a smile. 'You didn't have your drink.'

'No matter. It is time I was going.'

She had been right. 'Yes.' Disappointment crept through her veins like a debilitating drug.

'I shall collect you at seven.'

'Collect me?' squeaked Jade, only keeping the excitement from her voice with the most monumental of efforts. 'What for?'

The mouth moved again in its curious smile. 'Why, for dinner, of course.'

'I'm having dinner with you?'

'Of course. Don't you want to?'

Which he asked with all the casual arrogance of a man who knew damned well that of course she wanted to have dinner with him! Who wouldn't? Jade had never experienced this overwhelming attraction before; it made you weak and it made you powerless. And she wasn't really sure whether she liked the feeling or not. Besides which—wouldn't it be totally foolhardy to go tripping off with him? Why should he *presume* that she'd just drop everything and have dinner with him? And what happened after dinner? What did he expect? Did he assume that because she was English she was going to fall into bed with him?

'What makes you think I'll say yes?'

He gave a slow smile, then raised that olive-skinned hand to her face. 'These,' he said softly, as he indicated her eyes. 'They give me one answer and one answer only. Then this—' And a finger brushed negligently over the bow of her mouth. 'It trembles with anticipation. And—' and here the eyes changed, the spark in their ebony depths becoming a feverish flame '—there are other outward signs of how much you want to see me again, but we will not go into those. Not now.'

She was innocent, but she knew exactly what he meant. She had been unsuccessfully trying to ignore the hot tingling as her tiny breasts thrust against the still damp material of her bikini top. The tips were as painfully hard as metal and yet the pain was bearable, pleasurable even, and her eyelids dropped to hide her confusion. She knew what she wanted, what she clamoured for. She clamoured for his touch. And, oh, heavens—wasn't it desperately shameful to want a complete stranger to touch her intimately? To run those strong brown fingers all over her pale breasts and to linger on the soft swell of her belly? Her cheeks burned.

He moved his hand beneath her chin, so that their eyes were locked on a collision course. In his eyes she could see reflected the febrile glitter in hers. 'I'll pick you up at seven,' he said huskily.

It wasn't fair, thought Jade. For a man to wield so much power over women—all women, she recognised with a violently jealous flare. I'll bet he never has to ask twice, she thought, with a sudden inexplicable anger, and was determined that in this, at least—she would be different. 'No, I can't,' she said stubbornly and immediately saw a momentary flare of irritation before it was replaced by a questioning look.

'You're busy?'

'That's right.'

'No, you're not,' he said quietly.

'Why, of all the—'

But he cut her off with an arrogant shake of his

black head. 'Listen to me, Jade,' he said quietly. 'You return to England shortly, yes?'

'In three days,' something compelled her to tell him.

'So.' The hand was still holding her face with gentle strength. 'We can either play foolish little games with each other. Or...'

'Or?'

His eyes narrowed; his expression was rueful—as though he was reluctant to complete the sentence.

'Or we can follow our hearts,' he said simply.

If anyone else had said it, she would have told them that they were being ridiculously corny, that no one said things like that and meant them, and yet it was the most romantic thing she'd ever encountered, and Jade felt a warm glow suffuse every pore of her body.

She stared up at him, a lost cause for assertive womanhood. 'OK,' she said, giving him a faltering smile as she looked into his eyes. 'I'll see you at seven.'

'Until seven,' he said, his hand falling from her face as he strode swiftly from the courtyard.

CHAPTER TWO

IN THE five hours until Constantine collected her, Jade experienced just about every mood-swing in the book. What the hell was she playing at? He could be *any-one*—anyone at all!

What did she know about him?

Absolutely nothing.

Well, that wasn't *quite* true. She knew his name and his nationality. Knew instinctively that he had a million times more experience than she had. And she also knew that he was the most devastating man she'd ever set eyes on.

But what was he thinking about her? Was he down in the village even now, boasting to his friends that the English girl had agreed with insulting speed to go out with a man she scarcely knew? Did men respect women who capitulated quite so easily?

Jade sighed. Suddenly, it became very important that he *did* respect her. I don't want him thinking I'm like this with everyone, she thought gloomily. But if she tried to tell him *that*—then wouldn't it bolster his already appallingly healthy ego?

She sighed again.

She didn't really have any option but to go. She didn't know where he lived, so there was no way she could duck out now. She supposed that she could always tell him that she'd changed her mind when he arrived at seven to collect her.

And yet...

Somehow she didn't see that as a realistic scenario at all. For a start, she *wanted* to see him, so her words would have the hollow ring of insincerity. And secondly, she couldn't really see him letting her get away with fobbing him off. She imagined him taking her ruthlessly into his arms, black eyes glimmering like a pirate, to kiss away every single objection she could think of.

Jade shivered as she walked into her bedroom. She would go, but her choice of garment would be crucial. Something demure, something which would definitely not give him the wrong idea...

The only trouble was that the clothes chosen for holidays in baking hot destinations tended to be all the things which *weren't* demure. Light, filmy fabrics. Lots of bare flesh on show. Oh, heck. Jade surveyed the six or so dresses she'd brought with her. She tried them all on, and each one in a different way made her achingly aware of her own body, unless...she stared at her naked reflection...unless Constantine had done that. Because never before had she been so conscious of the soft swell of her breasts above the slender line of her waist. Breasts which tightened just at the very thought of him. She remembered his comment about pale, pale skin when compared to his, and once again, with a lucidity which was shocking, given her inexperience, Jade closed her eyes and pictured her breasts laid bare. With a dark head bending to take each one in turn, to suckle with delectable sweetness as the dark waves of his hair teased and tickled her flesh…

Jade stared in the spotted mirror in horror, to see her nipples rucking into tight twin peaks, and she drew her hands over them to cover the shockingly sensual image with her palms, but even that didn't help, because she found herself wanting them to be *his* hands touching her, and she turned away from the mirror, sick with disgust.

But, after she had finally chosen an outfit, she managed to calm down. If she hadn't trusted him, then she'd never have accepted a date with him. And though he might *look* all strong and compelling charm, she also knew that the Greeks were courteous and charming to visitors. There would never need to be attentions forced… Frankly, she doubted whether he'd had to use an ounce of persuasion in his life. Which left it up to *her* to modify the pace.

He was bang on time.

Jade was sitting in the courtyard, reading, when his shadow fell over the pages of her book, and she looked up, unable to keep the smile off her face as she registered his narrow-eyed appreciation of her appearance.

'Hi,' she said softly.

'Hello,' he echoed. His voice was equally soft, and there was another brief flash of appraisal in his eyes as his gaze swept over her.

She wore a white sleeveless silk T-shirt, together with an ankle-length skirt in layers of white, swirling voile. The starkness of the colour emphasised the pale golden glow of her skin. At her waist was a soft leather belt of dark green, with an intricately scrolled silver clasp. On her feet were strappy leather sandals in the same green. She had left her hair loose, to fall down her back in a pale waterfall, and at her ears and throat and wrist she wore heavy and intricate silver jewellery.

'You look wonderful,' he said quietly.

She took in the snowy white of his shirt, tucked into dark, tapered trousers. His hair was still damp from the shower, falling into tendrils around his beautifully shaped head. 'So do you,' she said honestly.

He looked slightly bemused for a moment, and then he laughed, a deep and rich and glorious sound. 'Do you know,' he mused, 'that's the first time a woman's ever said that to me?'

Her cheeks hot, she stared down at her pink-painted toenails, wondering what in the world had made her come out with something like that. His women usually played it cool, obviously, she thought, and a spear of jealousy shot through her. 'I don't know what came into me—I don't usually say things like that either,' she said, her tone more defensive than she'd intended.

But his voice was warm, caressing, forcing her to meet his eyes. 'Don't apologise. That's the magic of the island,' he said softly. 'Working her spell on young lovers.'

Oh, lord. He *had* got the wrong idea. Well, it was about time she put him on the right track. Jade took a deep breath. 'I think you're assuming rather a lot, Constantine,' she said stiffly. 'I've agreed to have dinner with you—that's all, and I have absolutely no intention of becoming your lover. And if that's what you had in mind for the end of the evening, then perhaps you'd better leave right now.'

His eyes darkened, glistened like two fragments of hell's coal. She saw a muscle begin to work with ominous regularity in the side of the olive cheek, saw his mouth tighten into a hard slash, and then she *did* know the meaning of fear, saw suddenly the face of a ruthless man behind the shatteringly handsome mask. All power and strength.

'Is that what you think?' he gritted in a low, furious voice. 'That I am one of these men who expects sex as a form of payment for buying a woman dinner?'

He looked more than angry, she thought, he looked *furious*, as if she'd deeply offended his code of honour.

'Of course I don't!' she said hurriedly. 'It's just—'

'Just?'

She lifted her shoulders in bewilderment. 'I didn't mean to insult you. I don't know what I meant. When you made that remark about lovers…I didn't want you to think…'

'I didn't,' he said simply. 'And as for your confusion—do you think I don't feel it too? Do you think this happens to *me* every day of the week?'

'What?'

But he shook his head. 'Enough. All this talk on an empty stomach. Come. Let's go and eat.'

She fell into step beside him, giving him her hand when he held his out, walking down the dusty path towards the village, safe within the warmth of his grasp. Sinking into the distance, the giant dinner-plate of a sun flooded them with a rich, crimson light and it felt like being at the centre of some glowing and infernal jewel.

They walked into the village, past the restaurant where she'd seen him yesterday.

He saw the inquisitive rise of her eyebrows. 'There is little enough privacy in the village,' he explained. 'But even less there.'

'Oh? And why's that?'

He smiled down at her. 'My family owns it.'

So—he was in the restaurant business with his family. And he didn't want her to meet them! Some little English girl he was ashamed to be seen with. She began to pull her hand away, but he wouldn't let her, instead stopped still on the dusty track and turned her to face him.

'What's wrong?'

Peculiarly, it was too important to her to lie about. 'Of course, if you don't *want* me to meet your family—'

'*Agape mou*,' he laughed softly, 'there is a way that a man can behave with a woman which in Greece would have his family drawing up a wedding list.'

Her heart sounded very loud in her ears. 'And what way's that?'

'Never taking his eyes off her. Not wanting to eat. Not wanting to do anything other than kiss her and make love to her. I've seen it happen to other men before; but never to me. The way I intend to behave with you tonight, Jade,' he finished with quiet emphasis. 'And I would prefer not to have an audience.'

The darkness was falling and it camouflaged her

soft rise in colour, the sharp little intake of breath. It
had sounded as if… As if what? As if he was falling
in love with her? As she was with him? Oh, stop it,
stop it, she thought shakily. 'But surely,' she questioned, 'all the restaurants will be crowded tonight—
it's the height of the season.'

'Wait and see,' he promised.

In a dream she walked with him to the outside of
the village, to a white building which looked out over
the blue and green fragrant hills, the stars beginning
to glimmer in the indigo velvet of the sky.

A waiter led them to a terrace, where rose-coloured
candles burned incandescently on each table against
the ever-darkening night. This restaurant was obviously much more upmarket than the others in the village, thought Jade as Constantine held her chair out
for her, because crisp white tablecloths matched the
beautifully pleated damask napkins.

There was wine already chilling in the ice-bucket,
and Jade accepted a glass, together with the leather-
bound menu, her eyes wide with confusion.

'Where *is* everyone?' she whispered. 'Why are *we*
the only customers?'

He smiled, his teeth showing very white in the olive darkness of his face. 'Because, as I told you, I
wanted privacy.'

'But how—?'

His eyes narrowed. 'The proprietor owes me a favour,' he said implacably, and Jade once again got an
overwhelming feeling of a toughness emanating from
the man who sat opposite her.

She sipped at her drink nervously. 'You mean—

that we've got the whole restaurant to ourselves? As a favour to you?'

He gave a little nod. 'I do.'

'It must have been a very big favour.' In Jade's world, people just didn't *do* things like that. But this was, after all, Greece. Many parts of it a still very fundamental world, with values light-years away from the superficial mores of life in the highly developed west, or even from life in its capital, Athens. Without knowing why, goosebumps chilled her arms, even though the night air was warm and soft on her skin.

'Some day I'll tell you,' he smiled, and handed her one of the menus.

'Some day'…?

Did his words imply that they had some sort of future together?

Jade tried very hard to concentrate on the choice of food—grilled fish and meat mainly—and to stop reading things into what he was saying.

Constantine spoke in rapid Greek to the waiter, of which she understood not one word—bar his name, Kris, and moments later they were brought a dish containing the tiny hors-d'oeuvres known as *mezes*.

'So—' He popped a green olive into his mouth and chewed it. 'Tell me what such a beautiful woman is doing holidaying on her own?'

Jade looked at him suspiciously, scared that he was making fun of her. 'Very funny,' she said.

He raised his eyebrows. 'What?'

'I'm not beautiful,' she told him, her green eyes glittering with a challenge that dared him to lie to her.

He drew his brows together. 'On the contrary. I'm

being deadly serious. You are tall enough to model and you are extremely slender, almost too slender—I can see that I may need to feed you up. But truly, you are beautiful,' he stated. 'Quite astonishingly so.'

Beautiful? *Her*? Jade was sensible enough to know her good points and her bad points, but no one had ever called her beautiful before, and in common with others who had had a fragmented childhood her body image was poor. True, she was tall, but she'd always considered herself a bit of a beanpole, and yes, she found it almost impossible to put on weight—which was beneficial in a society so obsessed by thinness. But her mouth was much too wide for conventional beauty, and her narrow slanting eyes did not have the classic wide-eyed appeal which men were said to find attractive. Plus, in England—given the nature of the sexist men she worked with—she tended to sublimate her femininity with her hair scraped back into a sensible plait, and clothes which were designed to be functional but nothing more than that. She supposed that on *this* holiday she had allowed herself to relax the normal severity with which she dressed. But beautiful? Did he say that to all the girls? she wondered.

However, even this sobering thought couldn't abate her delight, and Jade found herself smiling at Constantine like an idiot. This was ridiculous—one compliment and she was like putty in his hands!

'So,' he continued. 'Tell me why you're here on your own?'

'I needed a break,' she said honestly.

'A break from what?'

Jade twirled the stem of her glass round and round

between her fingers, watching the condensation trickle slowly down the side.

Tricky. She wondered just how much to tell him.

True, Constantine was a Greek, whose family owned a tiny taverna on a small Greek island—he might not even have *heard* of the *Daily View*. But what if he had?

After she'd won the Young Journalist competition launched by the *Daily View*, they had offered her a job as reporter—a job she had accepted with eager gratitude, given the cut-throat world of journalism. *Then* she'd been proud to tell people that she worked on Britain's best-selling tabloid newspaper. But that was before she'd discovered what most people actually thought of the *Daily View*.

They despised it.

Time and time again, when she had explained who she worked for, she had seen an expression of scorn come into the faces of people who viewed tabloid writers as total drunks with no morals. So, in the end, she had stopped telling them. It made for an easier life.

She stared into Constantine's dark eyes and made her decision. This was one evening out of her lifetime, she reasoned; an evening scented with magic which would soon become nothing more than a distant memory. This was total fantasy, so why taint it with the bitter taste of reality?

She saw that he was waiting for her answer and gave a little shrug. 'I just wanted a break,' she said carefully.

'A break from something in particular?' he probed. 'A man perhaps?'

Now he really *had* got the wrong end of the stick! 'Heavens, no!' she exclaimed fervently, unaware of the small smile he gave to this. 'Nothing like that! I meant a break from city life.'

He sipped at his drink and surveyed her curiously. 'You're very young?'

'I'm twenty,' she answered, and then, more tentatively, because it suddenly seemed terribly important, 'And you?'

'Thirty.' There was a glimmer of a smile. Had he guessed what she'd been thinking? 'That is a good gap, yes? Ten years?' He stared across the table at her moonwashed hair, raising his glass to his lips. 'So tell me—what do you think of my island?'

'You don't actually happen to own it, do you?' she joked.

'You must forgive me yet another possessive Greek statement,' he said implacably.

'I love your island,' she said simply. 'I've never relaxed so much in my life. I've spent my whole time being thoroughly lazy, swimming every day—'

'I know.'

She looked into his eyes. 'How can you know?'

'Because I've watched you. Looking like a mermaid with that yellow hair, those mysterious green eyes, that secretive smile.'

'You were—*watching* me?' she asked, appalled at the way her heart galloped into action.

He nodded. 'I was your guardian angel. Like today. Didn't you know?'

Jade shook her head. 'No.' Thank heavens she *hadn't* gone topless!

'And do you mind?'

'I don't know really. Isn't it a loss of the privacy you were so keen to preserve this evening?'

He looked at her thoughtfully. 'Perhaps. But I couldn't stay away,' he said simply, as though this excused everything, then popped another olive into his mouth and smiled. 'Let's order.'

Jade was relieved to have something relatively ordinary to do to keep her attention from the lunatic thoughts which were buzzing around her head. For Constantine seemed to possess some powerful quality she'd never encountered in a man before. Something which touched and matched some deep, dark longing inside her, offering her a glimpse of a passionate side to her nature she hadn't dreamed existed.

And she already suspected—no, she *knew*, that this—relationship, if you could call it that, threatened to get out of control very quickly. And she knew what out of control meant. Shocking though it was, she wanted this arrogant and handsome man she'd only just met to make love to her. She wanted to taste the pleasures that she instinctively knew that only he could offer her. But no one in their right mind would allow such a wish to become reality. After all, what possible future could a London-based journalist have with a restaurant proprietor who lived on a distant Greek island?

None.

Jade forced herself to apply her attention towards the food, which was surprisingly good and simple.

They ate Greek salad, scarlet with tomatoes and white with feta cheese and black with olives, with strong olive oil drizzled all over it. 'And what do you do in England?' he pursued.

'Oh, it's just a boring old typing job,' she said vaguely. True, although she knew she was being economical with the truth—but what if *he* had the rest of the world's prejudices about tabloid journalists? The evening would be ruined before it had even got started. She dipped some bread into the olive oil, then ate it. 'And how about you? Are you a waiter at your family's restaurant?'

He paused with the fork halfway to his mouth, and the corners of his mouth twitched before he laid it down on his plate. 'Sometimes,' he said. 'And I help them—balance the books—as the English say.'

She looked around her and breathed in the scented air. 'It must be a heavenly place to live,' she told him.

'Oh, it is,' he agreed gravely. 'Indeed, it is.'

And after that the evening seemed to get better and better.

'You have brothers and sisters?' he asked.

Jade took a large swallow of wine. 'No. And you?'

Something indefinable came into his eyes as he shook his head. 'Just a brother. And a—' He hesitated, momentarily. 'Step-sister. But I like big families. And you?'

It was something she had never, ever considered until this moment. Children were somewhere off in a hazy, rosy future which she'd somehow never imagined happening, not to her. She had never given much thought to children, but tonight she *was*, and she had the strongest suspicion that he was, too. She remembered their eyes meeting over the head of the tousle-haired toddler, of that spark which had flown between the two of them; a spark born out of mutual need and understanding. But what on earth was she admitting to? That she wanted to stay here and have his children? To live on a Greek island with one of its inhabitants? She, who had always been so ambitious, so determined to succeed?

Yes, yes, *yes*!

'What's the matter?' He interrupted her silence. 'You don't approve of big families?'

As the truth dawned on her, it felt like coming home. 'Oh, no—I absolutely *love* them!'

He smiled, his eyes gently sweeping over her shining eyes, her dazzling smile. 'I'm glad,' he said softly.

Never had a meal seemed to take so long; Jade had no appetite for it. She remembered having odd dates where the meal had assumed the greatest importance because the man she was out with had seemed so dull. And yet tonight—delicious as the *barbouni* smelt, and however sweet and succulent its flesh, she couldn't wait to be away from here, to be some place alone with Constantine, to taste the delights of his lips, discover the safety of his arms.

At last they were away and walking back down the dusty road, until they reached her cottage. He hadn't tried to kiss her, not once, and when they stood outside her door Jade turned to him in confusion.

He nodded as he read her eyes. 'Not tonight, *agape mou*.' And then he said something in Greek softly beneath his breath.

'What did you just say?'

He gave a soft laugh. '*Epikindhinos*. It means dangerous. Just like you. There is danger in the witchy slant of your eyes, in the pale waterfall of your hair. And the dangers that lie within those dark red lips, and all the secret places of your body—ah! They are too manifold even to dare to imagine!'

Jade found herself laughing at his extravagance; somehow he had turned the tension into humour, and she found herself admiring him for it. The first man who hadn't tried to leap on her on a first date. Typical that it should be the only one she'd ever wanted to!

He picked up her hand and carried it to his lips, placed a fleeting kiss there. 'We shall spend the day together tomorrow.'

'Doing what?'

There was a fleetingly ruthless smile. 'Doing our best not to make love. Being—circumspect. That is what we must do. And now, my golden-haired angel—go and sleep. Dream of me until I arrive tomorrow morning.'

Not surprisingly, she *did* dream of him, and wonderful dreams they were, too—but the reality of the real man who arrived the following morning at eight o'clock far outshone the dream version.

He spent three days doing exactly what he had said he would do—being circumspect.

Jade was flattered; and frustrated.

She knew how much he wanted her, and how much she ached just to have him kiss her, but he didn't.

Instead, he took her snorkelling, took her round the island on the back of his motorcycle. They swam and they picnicked. He taught her elementary Greek and backgammon—he beat her—and she taught him some very corny jokes and Scrabble—she beat him. She never met a member of his family, and he seemed as reluctant to discuss his 'other' life as she was, and Jade found it very easy to simply put her London life into a compartment of her mind, and forget all about it.

For those three days they were together from early morning until midnight, and it was as though no world existed for them bar the island. There was no past; the future they did not dare to touch upon; instead there was just the glorious and golden present.

And then her last day arrived. They spent a morning snorkelling off a beach which was almost deserted, lunching again in the small restaurant which had become their regular haunt and where Kris, the owner, spent the whole time virtually bowing to Constantine.

He seemed terribly well respected, thought Jade, as she accepted the *metaliko nero*—mineral water—he handed her.

But as the day wore on, they both grew noticeably quieter and eventually he took her back to the cottage.

'Where shall we eat tonight?'

It was hard to be enthusiastic. Impossible, in fact. 'I don't mind.'

'It's your last night,' he said, and there was a strange, almost savage note to his voice.

'Yes.' She stared up, found herself mesmerised by the ebony glitter of his eyes. She saw that a pulse worked frantically in the side of his cheek. Her own pulse hammered; her mouth dried like dust and she found herself moistening her lips with the tip of her tongue, then blushed scarlet when his eyes narrowed as they watched the movement, afraid that he would interpret it as one of deliberate provocation. Embarrassed, she made to turn away, but he stopped her with one strong olive hand on the bare flesh of her upper arm.

'Where do you want to go tonight?' he repeated.

There was a pause. 'Nowhere,' she said quietly and honestly.

'We can't stay here,' he said, almost savagely.

'Why not?'

'You know why not.'

'OK, then, Constantine—you tell me where *you'd* like to go tonight?'

There was a long pause. 'Nowhere,' he said softly. His voice was unsteady as he spoke. 'I think that our days of being circumspect are numbered, don't you, *agape mou*?'

She was aware of the enormity of the question. Head bent, she nodded silently.

'Look at me,' he whispered. 'Jade. *Please*.'

Slowly, slowly, she raised her head. His eyes were dark.

'I'm almost afraid to kiss you,' he said huskily.

'I can't imagine you being afraid of anything, Constantine.'

'Not even of losing my sanity, my reason?'

'Then you'd better not kiss me,' she said firmly. 'I don't want to be responsible for—*oh*,' the gasp became an exultant little sigh as he locked her in his

arms, his heart thundering against her breast. Breathlessly, she waited with longing for his lips.

'Not kiss you?' It was a soft, mocking taunt. 'I
must. If only to tell myself that this is all some foolish
fantasy…'

His head came down and his mouth imprisoned her
in a sensual trap from which she never wanted to
escape. He tasted of wine, and of honey. He tasted of
man, primitive man; hot, hungry, and very, very
aroused.

His kiss was soft and sweet, cajoling her response,
so that her lips opened for him, and she heard him
make a murmured appraisal as he licked his way into
her mouth. She opened her mouth wider, felt their
tongues link together as the kiss deepened with an
intensity which was shattering.

Jade could feel her breasts tingling as she lifted her
arms up with a helpless sigh to lock them around his
neck, her fingers drifting upwards to entwine themselves in the black richness of his hair.

He lifted his mouth away from hers and stared
down into her upturned face, the feverish glitter in his
eyes as bright as moonlight. Very slowly and deliberately, he pulled her closer, so that she could feel
the shocking potency of his arousal.

Except that it did not shock her; it thrilled her immeasurably. She wanted that; him. Deep within her.
She wanted their bodies locked in the most basic
physical communion of all. She stared back at him,
rocked at the strength of her feelings, her eyes dark,
her lips trembling.

'Jade,' he said softly, and now the accent was more

pronounced than she'd ever heard it. 'Do you know how much I want to make love to you?'

'Yes,' she answered quietly. There was the evidence of that powerfully hard shaft which pushed against her lower belly through the filmy white voile of her dress—but she could have read his desire just as easily in the incandescent depths of his night-dark eyes. And his mouth, too, was trembling, as though what was happening to them had startled him, too.

'I want to touch your breasts,' he whispered against her mouth. 'To touch them until I know them better than you do,' and before she could say or do a thing he had pulled the silk T-shirt from beneath her belt, and was peeling it off and over her head, so that she stood before him, naked to the waist, her skin gilded golden and crimson by the dying light of the sun, her hair as bright and as glimmering as the stars which would later appear.

He just gazed down at her breasts, as if committing them to memory, nodding his head as he did so. 'I knew that you wore nothing beneath,' he murmured. 'Your breasts are small, yes, but all day long they have been aching, haven't they, Jade?'

She swallowed. This was madness. 'Yes,' she whispered.

'Waiting for my touch,' he murmured, and he cupped one small mound in the palm of his hand, his thumb reaching out to stroke with tantalising skill at the stiffened nub of her nipple.

'Oh!' breathed Jade, on a strangled note of disbelief, and her knees buckled beneath her, but he caught her, pulling her roughly into his arms, his mouth against hers.

'Let's go to bed,' he said, almost harshly.

Jade's eyelids fluttered open as she sought to reason with herself. She was alone in the middle of nowhere, with a man intent on making love to her. And she couldn't, she realised, on a shuddering sigh…she couldn't stop him; even if she wanted to.

And she didn't want to.

She was on fire with some strange magic, caught up in the throes of a spell so powerful that she felt she would die if he left her.

Was there, she wondered foggily as he picked her up and carried her into the cottage—was there such a thing as love at first sight?

Yes! she thought fiercely, and she reached up for him, and he dropped his mouth to hers again, kissing her as he walked until they were in her bedroom.

He laid her on the bed while he shrugged his way out of the white shirt he wore, and she saw the heaving of the powerful chest as he struggled to maintain his breathing, his eyes never leaving her.

Then he came to her, both of them half-naked, his eyes surprisingly soft as he looked down into her face. 'I have never desired a woman so badly,' he said, but his voice held an almost savage note to it, as though he was admitting to being fallible, and that infallibility came much more easily to him. 'Do you believe me when I tell you that?'

It didn't even occur to her to doubt it. 'Yes.'

He dipped his head to one breast, catching one hard and pointed little tip between his teeth, teasing and

tasting and tantalisingly grazing it, until her eyes
closed and her head fell back, and she felt herself
being sucked into an erotic vortex from which there
could be no escape. She opened her eyes, suddenly
frightened by behaviour which was so primitive, so
out of character for her.

He needed to know that, she decided. And *she*
needed him to know that.

'Constantine,' she said suddenly, and he looked up.

'What is it, *agape mou*?' From beneath hooded
eyes she could see the opaque glaze of desire.

Her gaze was drawn irresistibly down his body
where she could see the powerful thrust of his thighs;
see too the sheer male strength and power of his
arousal which was pushing insistently against the fine
linen of the trousers he wore. She imagined him in
the act of love, filling her with himself, found herself
wondering briefly whether it would hurt, yet knowing
that even if it did it would only be the prelude to
unimaginable pleasure. She trickled her fingertips
over the thick, dark whorls of chest hair, alighting at
last on one small male nipple, and she felt him shudder beneath her touch.

'What is it?' he asked harshly.

Jade took a deep breath. He needed to know. 'I've
never...' Her voice tailed off, embarrassed.

He stilled instantly, his fingers halting their rhythmic caress of her breasts, his eyes narrowing to char-
coal shards. '*What*?' he whispered, his voice dangerously soft.

'I've never—done—well, this...before.'

'You're saying—'

She nodded, swallowing, suddenly regretting that she'd opened her mouth. 'Yes. I'm a virgin, Constantine.'

He swore softly and profanely, and in more than one language, Jade thought, when to her horror and consternation he tore himself away from her and got up from the bed.

'Constantine.' She sat up, the white-blonde hair falling all over her bare breasts, and she heard him say something else, but this time she did not think that he swore; something soft and emphatic and very Greek, before turning his back to her.

'Put something on,' he commanded harshly.

'But—'

'Something to cover yourself. Do it *now*, Jade.'

Her silky T-shirt lay on the courtyard floor. In a confused daze, Jade climbed off the bed and foraged around in the old chest of drawers before extracting another T-shirt, not caring what colour it was or that it was inside out. Weary and sick at heart, she pulled it on and sat down on the bed.

Constantine had put his shirt back on and was buttoning it up with inelegant haste.

Jade watched him in bewilderment. Why on earth was he behaving this way, thrusting her away from him as if she were a hot potato?

He met her eyes again as he moved to sit beside her on the bed, putting one arm about her shoulder, as a doctor would to a patient to whom he was going to break bad news. He had decided that, for some reason, he no longer wanted her. OK. Fine. But Jade just wished he would *go*. Let her be humiliated in peace.

With one finger he lifted her chin up, so that she was imprisoned in the febrile glitter of his eyes. 'Why so sad, *agape mou*?' he queried.

She tried, fruitlessly, to shake the finger away. 'Just go away! Leave me!'

'You want me to?'

'Yes!'

'No. You want to know why I stopped?'

Jade swallowed. 'What makes you think that I wouldn't have stopped you myself?'

There was the trace of an arrogant smile. 'Because you were ready for me—'

It was the cool assurance that galled her most, even though she knew that he was being nothing but honest. 'Why—?' she raised her hand, but he caught it, pressed the palm to his lips and kissed it.

'You've been ready for me for days now. You wanted me to take you, to fill you, to make love to you until you cried out. Again and again and again. As you have wanted from the first moment we met. And I would have done that, Jade. Don't you think I don't want that, too? Quite desperately?'

All her insecurities came swimming to the surface. 'Then you don't respect me,' she stated.

'Why not?'

'Because I would have—have—'

'You would have let me?'

'Yes,' she admitted unhappily.

He caught both her hands in his. 'And that is exactly as it should be between a man and a woman.

Honesty and passion, no games or pretence—now *that* I respect. But you are leaving tomorrow, Jade. It is not a satisfactory way to begin a relationship and certainly not your first—a night of passion and then a parting. And then I did not imagine for a moment that you would be a virgin.'

That hurt. 'Why ever not?' she demanded.

He shrugged. 'Because English women do not guard their virtue so carefully. And most English women that I have met…' He gave a little movement of his shoulders, as if he was being diplomatic in not completing the sentence.

Jade felt absolutely *furious*. Not only had he shown that he no longer found her attractive, but now he was denigrating English women in general! 'I suppose you've had *hundreds* of English women?' she accused.

'Not at all,' he answered, unperturbed.

'What we don't do,' she said cuttingly, 'is use our virginity as some kind of bartering tool in the marriage market—'

'Enough!' he told her sternly, and caught both her hands in his. She angrily tried to shake her hands free, but he held them too securely.

'No, it is damned well *not* enough! I suppose I should be grateful that you didn't take advantage of me!' she lashed out at him. 'Do you like your women more experienced? Better used to casual sex? Less troublesome to the conscience, I suppose?'

Savagery returned to distort the handsome features into an impenetrable mask. 'Do you think I am that kind of man?' he demanded fiercely, and his accent became more Greek by the second; his presence more dominating. 'One who wants or even needs this one-night stand that you speak of? There is no joy in sex of that nature, and besides that there is something much more fundamental at stake here. You see, *I have fallen in love with you.*'

Jade stared at him wide-eyed, her heart starting to race in exultant beat. 'What did you say?' she said, very quietly.

The black eyes glittered. 'You heard me very well,' he said softly.

She wanted to believe him—oh, how she wanted to believe him. 'But you *can't* love me! You don't even know me!'

'Wrong!' he contradicted arrogantly. 'I knew you the moment I first set eyes on you. As you did me.'

'Oh, Constantine,' she said helplessly, feeling herself beginning to melt. 'I'm lost. Confused. What are you saying? What do you want?'

He moved the powerful shoulders in a tiny shrug. 'I want to spend every moment that I can with you. I want you in my arms when I fall asleep, and beside me when I wake up. I want to make love to you; I think you know how much. But first I intend to marry you.'

CHAPTER THREE

JADE sighed loudly as she settled back into one of the plush leather banquettes which adorned the foyer of the Granchester—undoubtedly one of London's finest hotels.

She had been sent here by Maggie Marchant, her editor—and was waiting to interview Russ Robson for the *Daily View*. Typical! It was just her luck to get stuck with the notoriously lecherous ageing rock-star, but that wasn't the real reason for the deep sigh.

It was because she missed Constantine.

She missed him like *hell*.

Sometimes she could hardly believe that it was only a week since he had stared down into her eyes and said those amazing words which had turned her world upside down: 'First I intend to marry you'.

And she had ecstatically agreed to let him do just that, and as soon as possible—in fact, as soon as he arrived in England, which Jade hoped would be very, *very* soon.

A buzz of excited chatter sounded over by the hotel reception, and she looked up to see Russ Robson approaching.

From a distance the rock-star looked quite good, slim and wearing the ubiquitous uniform of ripped jeans and a black leather jacket. But he was surprisingly small, and as he grew closer Jade could see quite clearly all the signs of a dissipated lifestyle: the bloodshot eyes and the ravaged and pock-marked skin. He swaggered over, and his eyes began a leisurely passage from the tip of Jade's head to her toes as she stood up to meet him.

'C'mon upstairs,' he leered at her as though she were some kind of groupie, 'and I'll give you the interview of a lifetime.' His hand went out to snake around her waist when there was the buzz of some other commotion and Jade looked up to see a group of men walking into the foyer, her mouth falling open in disbelief when she saw who it was, scarcely recognising the evidence of her own eyes.

Constantine.

Jade blinked.

It couldn't be. What on earth would Constantine be doing *here*, and dressed like *that*?

He hadn't seen her; he was deep in discussion with one of the group—another elegantly dressed businessman, who also looked Greek—and she was *sure* that he'd been one of the men seated with Constantine in the taverna, the very first time she'd seen him. She stared again at the impressive and unfamiliar sight he made. The thick and unruly curls had been trimmed and made sleeker, and the darkness of his chin was paler than the smoky growth of stubble which Jade was used to seeing, as though he'd shaved twice already that day.

But it was his outfit which completely knocked the stuffing out of her. He wore a beautifully cut linen suit, but it wasn't rumpled and crumpled like every linen suit *she'd* ever seen—it hung in elegant folds around the magnificently muscular frame. Beneath it he had on a shirt of the finest pure white silk, so fine that she could just make out the shadowy hint of the thick whorls of hair which grew in such riotous abandon across his broad chest. And, with the shirt, a tie of dark green silk. His shoes were of soft, black leather; hand-made, she'd bet. He looked... Jade swallowed. He looked so different.

He looked...rich.

Very, very rich.

It was all terribly confusing.

She shook her head a little. His family owned a restaurant on a small Greek island, for heaven's sake! He couldn't possibly be *staying* here!

'Hey, babe,' said Russ Robson impatiently, and Jade recoiled as his arm did actually make contact with her slender waist, sliding up so that his horrible heavily ringed hand brushed against her breast.

It was at that precise moment that Constantine looked over and saw her, before she had time to move, to shake off the revolting Robson's arm, and what happened next sickened her to the pit of her stomach.

She saw Constantine stiffen and still, frozen in beautiful, elegant pose. But there was no welcome or affection in that hard, bronzed mask of a face. She watched as his eyes narrowed to become so cold and so ruthless that Jade felt the icy fingers of pure fear chill her skin, saw the little tableau they must make— with Robson's hand resting intimately around her. She pushed the hand away angrily with a snort of disgust. Showbiz people were usually tactile, but Russ

Robson had really overstepped the mark and Jade tried to imagine what Constantine must be thinking. He must be appalled. He came from a land where values were much more robust, more fundamental…wasn't that one of the things that had made her fall in love with the land as well as the man?

Wordlessly, Jade stepped away from Robson, automatically moving towards Constantine, scarcely allowing herself to register that his mouth had thinned to a hard, cold line, that from his eyes blazed a stony kind of censure; a look which she defined all too quickly.

She started to walk towards him, aware of the murmured comment of one of the men he was with as she did so. She caught sight of herself in one of the glittering mirrors, at the blonde disarray of hair which had fallen out of her French plait to spill in profusion around her neck. At the two high spots of colour on her cheeks which seemed to compound a guilt she simply *shouldn't* be feeling. She'd done nothing wrong.

But you lied to him about your job, prompted an unnerving little voice inside her head.

'Constantine!' she called, just yards away.

The proud mouth curled. He made a small sound of disgust beneath his breath before speaking in rapid Greek to his companion. And then he walked right past her, as though she was invisible—no, worse than that, as though she was garbage. Walked right past her and straight into the lift without speaking.

CHAPTER FOUR

JADE stood in the centre of the foyer staring after Constantine, watching in disbelief as the lift doors closed behind him, feeling as though she'd just shot herself in the foot.

And then the questions began to crowd into her mind.

Like—just *what* was he doing in the Granchester dressed like that? And what right did he have to walk past her with that haughty look on his face as though she were something the dog had dragged in?

Every right, she admitted to herself gloomily. She had known instinctively that he would have a strongly possessive and jealous streak, and wasn't it part of his charm that he would use passion before logic? Perhaps to Constantine it might have appeared that the pose she struck with Russ Robson was intimate. And what else would she expect him to do while an ageing rock-star gave a display of the wandering hands syndrome? Rush up and ask to be introduced?

'Jade?' Brent, the *Daily View*'s staff photographer, who had been clicking away furiously, was now staring at her curiously. 'Do you know that guy?'

I thought I was going to marry him, thought Jade, which all goes to show that you can never be too old to believe in fairy-tales. 'You could say that,' she answered in a flat tone.

Brent's mouth had dropped open, but she scarcely took in the expression of disbelief on his face. 'How the hell can you—?'

She couldn't face his questions; not when she didn't have any answers which made sense; not even to her. She felt like opening her mouth and howling in disbelieving anger. What was Constantine doing *here*? she wondered in total confusion, feeling so dazed that she automatically sought solace in work. 'I have an interview to do,' she bit out crisply. 'And Mr Robson is waiting—'

'Call me Russ,' came a drawled voice by her side, and she looked up to find him surveying her with curiosity. 'Though perhaps I'm now making sense of those "keep off" vibes you keep sending out.' He jerked his head in the direction of the lift which Constantine had disappeared into, and grinned. 'Rich pickings, huh, baby? But it don't look like he's interested to me. So let's go up to *my* suite, huh?'

Jade's stomach turned over in revulsion. For two pins she felt like telling Mr Russ Robson what he could do with his interview; it was very tempting indeed. But she supposed that would be the height of unprofessionalism, and you didn't just throw in your job at the height of a recession without another to go to. She thought quickly, then gave him a briskly efficient smile.

'It just occurred to me, Mr Robson, that if we do the interview right here in the foyer,' and here Jade gestured to the exquisitely pillared seating area, 'then surely it would get you—er—noticed. And you know what they say about there being no such thing as bad publicity...'

Jade watched as the canny blue eyes considered what she'd said and wondered if he was remembering his last album, which had bombed so badly.

'OK.' He shrugged.

It took the most superhuman effort to put Constantine out of her mind, but an hour later Jade had her interview, in which she had somehow managed to discover that Russ Robson's main passion in life was breeding guppy fish!

'I can think of the headline already! ''From Yuppy to Guppy''!' laughed Brent as he pocketed a used roll of film in the top-pocket of his denim jacket.

But Jade felt sick at heart and couldn't even raise a smile. She found Brent staring at her unresponsive face as if sensing gossip. 'Let's share a cab back to the office,' he suggested, but Jade shook her head.

She couldn't face going back. Not yet. She wanted to be alone with the turmoil of her thoughts. She shook her head. 'Not just now, Brent—I'll catch you later—I've just had an idea for another feature.'

Brent shrugged, looking unconvinced. 'OK,' he said easily. 'See you later.'

At last he was gone and Jade stood hesitantly in the foyer. What should she do now? She needed to talk to Constantine more badly than she had ever needed anything before in her life. But would he agree to see her, and was he actually staying here? Presumably, as he had taken the lift. Should she enquire at Reception?

Unless…and here a cold, clammy sweat broke out on the back of her neck. Unless…

What could be the other perfectly legitimate reason for a man taking a lift to one of the hotel bedrooms? What if he was having an assignation with someone? Some beautiful woman lying naked and waiting for him? As willing a capitulation as hers in Greece had almost been…

But surely to believe that would be to believe that all Constantine's words to her had been lies. And yet perhaps the most logical explanation was that they *had* been lies. For what was the owner of a restaurant on a small Greek island doing walking around in costly clothes in one of London's best hotels?

But you lied to *him*, prompted the voice of her conscience. Letting him believe that you were some little goody-two-shoes office-worker instead of a tabloid journalist.

Well, she wasn't going to spend the rest of her life wondering what might have happened. I have to *know*, she decided, and, determinedly drawing her shoulders back, she walked over to the reception desk.

'My name is Jade Meredith,' she began.

'Yes, of course, Miss Meredith,' said the receptionist smoothly. 'Mr Sioulas is expecting you.'

Jade's heart hammered, though she couldn't decide whether it was with excitement or sheer fright. 'He is?'

'Certainly. He's in the Garden Suite. I'll get someone to show you the way.'

'Please don't worry,' said Jade hastily. 'I'll find it myself.'

The receptionist made no demur; he was obviously used to the capriciousness of guests. 'Certainly, Miss Meredith. You'll find the Garden Suite on the ninth floor.'

'Thank you.'

The smooth purring of the lift only increased her tension, and when it stopped at the appropriate floor Jade almost turned tail and ran, feeling more frightened than she'd ever done before in her life.

You pathetic little *coward*, she told herself, before stepping forward and rapping loudly on the door.

The door was opened by the man who had been talking to Constantine downstairs. The man she had been sure had been with Constantine in the taverna, thought Jade as she stared into impassive brown eyes.

She forced herself to stay calm. 'I'm Jade Meredith. I believe that Constantine is expecting me.'

A dark head made the faintest inclination, but he offered no introduction of his own. 'Mr Sioulas is inside.' He stepped aside to let Jade pass, and she got the strangest sensation of being summoned into the presence of some ancient potentate, an impression which was only partially dispelled by the sight of Constantine, his back to her, in the most rigid and forbidding of stances, an awesome stillness about him which completely unnerved her.

'Hello, Constantine,' she said, not surprised at the unusually high squeak in her voice.

He stayed unmoving. There was a rustle behind her, and the man who had shown her in rattled off what sounded like a question in Greek.

'*Ochi*!' Constantine's negation was savagely controlled, and the other man withdrew from the suite, one last curious look at Jade as he did so.

There was silence for a moment. This is ridiculous, thought Jade. Is he going to pretend I'm not here?

But he turned around then, and Jade wished that he hadn't, for it was as though the Constantine she had known had gone forever, and in his place was the face of a hard, cold and implacable stranger. She had seen a glimpse of it once, had suspected that it existed, that steely streak—but now she saw it revealed in all its true, formidable strength. And suddenly she knew that only a fool would have believed Constantine to be the owner of a restaurant on a tiny Greek island. This man was no small-time achiever, she realised with a sudden and penetrating flash of insight; here stood a ruthless tycoon.

'Hello, Jade.' But the greeting was denied any warmth by the cutting note of scorn which distorted it. 'To which, I would imagine,' he continued implacably, 'you reply, "Fancy meeting you here!"'

His mimicry, she thought bizarrely, was quite superb considering that it was not done in his native tongue. 'Wh-what are you doing here?' she blurted out, sounding nothing like a journalist and more like a schoolgirl confronting her head teacher with more than a little trepidation.

'What do you think I'm doing here, Jade?' he queried softly. 'Perhaps doing a little trading in the yoghurt or honey which our restaurant produces?'

'Dressed like that?' she blurted out.

He gave a little laugh; Jade had never heard anything more chilling in her entire life. 'Dressed like what, *agape mou*?'

But the term he had once used, she thought, with deep affection now sounded like nothing more then denigration when spoken in a tone which dripped scorn.

How dared he?

'Dressed in clothes which would probably cost a restaurateur's entire year's wages!' she returned. 'The man you allowed me to believe you were!'

He nodded. 'You're correct, you're absolutely correct, Jade. But I think that your accusation is a little misplaced. I did wonder,' he mused, almost as though she were not in the room with him, 'why you agreed marriage to a poor Greek so promptly. Why such a woman would be so willing, so eager to marry such a man—a man so many light-years away from the sophisticates she doubtless deals with in England.' He turned cold, black eyes on her. 'You are wasted in journalism, my dear—you should have turned your hand to acting. Such a fine performance! So convincing!'

It was like some awful dream. So much of what he said confused her, but one thing stood out in her mind: that he had somehow discovered her true identity. In a minute, surely—she would wake up? 'When did you find out that I was a journalist?' she asked quietly, her long fingers pleating at her skirt. 'Did you know on the island?'

He gave her a steady, stony stare. 'On the island?' His mouth twisted into a cruel parody of a smile. 'I think not. If I had known then...' He gave a deliberate pause while his gaze flicked to her breasts, and, hate-fully, humiliatingly, she felt them prickle with antic-ipation; his cold smile indicated that her reaction had not gone unnoticed. 'Then I should not have played the gentleman quite so assiduously.'

The implication was as clear as crystal. 'Then—when?'

He was shrugging out of the linen jacket now, throwing it negligently across the butter-coloured sofa. He walked across to the bar and poured himself a large shot of brandy. He didn't even offer her any, and Jade was suddenly more affronted by this simple lack of courtesy than by any of his earlier insulting remarks; because on Piros he had shown her more courtesy than she had ever received before.

'I'd like a drink, please.' Never in her life had she needed one more.

'Then get it yourself,' he ground out, in a voice of granite.

He watched while she walked over to the cabinet and picked up the heavy decanter with a hand which trembled uncontrollably, and she heard him make a muttered curse in Greek before taking the bottle from her and sloshing some brandy into a second glass.

'Here.' He pushed the glass into her hand, but even that brief contact of skin on skin was electrifying. Jade felt his touch like a whisper of fire to which her body screamed its instant response as if it were bone-dry timber, and she looked up to see his eyes darken, before an expression of disgust marred the autocratic features, and he stepped away from her, swallowing the rest of his brandy in an abrupt gesture of dismissal which spoke volumes.

He walked away from her and began talking softly. 'Let me see, where were we?'

Jade swallowed some of her brandy and the burning liquid to her stomach seemed to revive her. He will not intimidate me, she vowed, wondering why she chose to stay, to lay herself open to the inevitable hurt which would follow, rather than walk right out of that door. But she had to *know*. 'You were about to tell me when you found out that I was a journalist,' she said, amazed her voice should now sound so steady.

'Ah. Yes. When I began to make my plans to join you in England, I thought that as your prospective lover I should surprise you, as lovers often do—to meet you from work with the extravagant bunch of roses. Women appreciate these kind of gestures.'

I'll bet they do, she thought dully.

'But you, Jade, surprisingly, had neglected to give me your work number.' The voice had a steely ring. '*Not* surprisingly, as I now realise. So I rang you at home; late one night. You were not there. Night-clubbing, your flatmate told me. Then I asked her when you'd be back but she didn't know. Very late, most probably. The early hours.' The primitive censure in his voice was stark, the accusation plain, and Jade found herself automatically defending herself.

'There's no need to make me sound like Mata Hari! It's my job!'

His mouth tightened. 'So I believe. Then I asked for your work number—I would ring you first thing.

Imagine my astonishment to discover that you work for what can only be loosely described as a newspaper. The kind of newspaper which prints photographs of half-clothed women!'

Which Jade had always hated herself, but she couldn't really imagine convincing Constantine of that. 'How come Sandy didn't tell me any of this? She didn't mention that you'd rung!'

'Because I persuaded her not to,' he said with soft menace. 'I can be very persuasive, you know.'

Jade's mind was buzzing. 'Then today—you being here at the same time as me—you'd—you'd actually *followed* me?'

An expression of scorn mocked her. 'Followed you? After discovering *that*? No, I often stay at the Granchester when I'm in London.' He gave her a black look which could have come from the devil himself before continuing.

'No, Jade, my being here today was purely coincidence. Coincidence,' he reiterated savagely. 'The weapon of the gods. And that coincidence enabled me to see just how far you would go to get a story with that ridiculous singer downstairs whom you allowed to touch you so freely. But it did not surprise me. After all—you offered yourself to me without any of the normal persuasion a man has to use to bed a woman. Was that your brief? Is that what your editor instructed you to do? To get your interview with me—come—' and here his voice twisted with derision '—what may,' he finished softly.

She had never been so hurt and disgusted in her life, nor so angry. Too angry to question his absurd

suggestion that she had been sent to Greece to interview *him*, for heaven's sake. Why on earth should
she? A red flare of pure temper erupted and misted
in front of her eyes, and she slammed her tumbler
down on to one of the small tables and launched herself at him, wanting to punch him, kick him, scratch
him, wound him as he had wounded her, but he was
ready for her. His palms came up to deflect her flail-
ing hands, then with a swift movement he had captured both her hands in one strong hand, holding them
high above her head.

She tried to twist, to lock one leg behind his in
classic judo position, but he had countered with the
reverse movement and with his other hand he held
her waist in a vice-like grip, bringing her close into
his body, and she felt his hardness pushing against
her. She stared up in him in horrified disbelief to realise that even after all his vile insults he still wanted
her; wanted her very badly indeed, and then all
thought flew from a mind already punished by the
onslaught of emotion as he bent his head to take her
mouth in a savage kiss.

Jade opened her lips to protest as Constantine's
mouth brutally ground into hers but the movement
condemned her for he quickly used his tongue to
sweeten the assault.

Oh, no, she thought desperately, but the half-
hearted struggle she gave only reminded her all too
clearly just how aroused he was, and her body responded like a betraying stranger, so that she gave a
tiny cry, a mixture of anguish and desire as she felt
her breasts becoming heavy, their tips hard and pain-

ful and jutting against the thin silk of his shirt; and
they were so sensitive and aware that through them
she could feel the thick carpet of hair which roughened his chest.

The pressure on her mouth never ceased, and something was happening to her; something way beyond
her control. For his hungry, savage need was matched
by her own, overpowering her until she was nothing
but a slave to her own desire. Because she needed
him. Needed the man she knew lay beneath this pun-
ishing exterior. She wanted the real Constantine back,
the man she had grown to love in a few short idyllic
days. Surely he couldn't throw all that promise
away—that mutual passion which happened once in
a lifetime, and only then if you were very lucky? But
when his hand moved down to touch her breast she
stopped thinking altogether—about past or future,
right or wrong, because nothing that felt this good
could possibly be wrong.

It was as though he sensed her mental surrender,
for he gentled the kiss to one of such poignant sweetness that Jade felt a strange, lingering sense of triumph, knowing that all could not be lost if he could
kiss her like that. A proud man like Constantine, who
could call a halt on the brink of rapture as he had
done on the island—he would not be governed by the
needs of his body alone. Dared she hope that he still
cared for her? Still loved her?

She realised that he had freed her hands, that they
had fallen to rest on the broad spread of his shoulders,
and her fingers automatically began rhythmically to
massage at the solid wall of muscle, loving the warm

feel of his strength, longing to touch his naked skin instead.

He pulled his mouth away from hers. 'Come,' he commanded, his voice an unsteady, uneven rasp.

She had thought that he would take her into the bedroom, but he did not; instead he pushed aside the linen jacket which he had thrown down so casually, and moved her on to the sofa, which was scarcely wide enough for them both, forcing him to lie above her, his eyes staring down at her; hot, black coals which burned into her heart but told her nothing.

She stared back at him, her slanting eyes narrowing with confusion, wondering whether she was doing the most stupid thing imaginable, and yet rejoicing in the feel of his hard body pressed so intimately close to hers. Knowing that even if the hotel were falling down all around them she simply did not have the power to walk away from this.

He bent his head to hers, and with sweet savagery kissed away her final doubts. She locked her arms about his neck, her legs parting to receive his thrusting thigh. She did not know how long he kissed her for; she sensed his body's impatience, but none of that was evident in the honeyed seduction of his kiss. She felt an aching pull in the apex of her thighs, felt her breasts swell until it was almost too much to bear, and she began to move restlessly, her senses orchestrating these new movements as though she had been born to do only this.

And only then did he touch her breast again; little stroking movements, circling round and round the nipple through her shirt until she thought that she would die; and precisely as she thought it he captured the nipple between thumb and forefinger, rubbing it so that it stood even prouder, aching desperately to be freed of the confines of bra and shirt. 'Constantine!' she whispered. 'Oh, Constantine.'

His fingers never ceased, but he drew his mouth away from hers to look down at her as he touched her, his face starkly unfamiliar with passion, a rigid mask kept only under control by the restraint he was obviously exercising on his own needs.

'You like it?' He sounded almost casual.

'It's—heaven,' she breathed, but he shook his head.

'Not heaven. Not yet. Heaven comes later.' He moved his hand away from her nipple and she made a little moan of protest, but her mouth softened into a smile of anticipation as she realised that he was only doing so in order to unbutton her shirt, which he did slowly, degree by teasing degree until her small breasts, encased in a tiny sheer black lace and silk bra, thrust towards him for his delectation.

She didn't know what caused it, but his face darkened; his eyes like the blackest recesses of hell as he stared down at the flimsy, totally inadequate piece of underwear.

'What is it?' she asked him, her question husky, because her lips were swollen and tender from so much kissing.

For answer, he flicked at one nipple in a gesture which was almost casual, though the unsteadiness in his voice belied it. 'Do you always dress to tantalise, *agape mou*?' And then when she made no answer, began to speak again, as if to himself. 'I find myself wanting to rip this foolish little garment from your body. Shall I do that?'

But she didn't want her underwear torn off; not the first time. She wanted his gentleness; his understanding.

'Don't,' she said shakily.

His eyes narrowed as instead he unclipped it at the front, pushing the filmy fragments aside before lowering his head to take one swollen bud into his mouth with the gentleness she had dreamed of, and her head tipped back and she cried out as he made the slowest and most excruciatingly exciting journey from breast to breast, until she realised that she was pushing her hips into his, driven on by some urge she neither knew nor understood.

He moved away then, and she looked up to see that his face was grim as he pulled off his tie and tossed it away. 'Unbutton my shirt,' he ordered softly.

She hesitated, momentarily stricken by doubts, and he watched her from between narrowed eyes before briefly bending his head to suckle at her nipple, and Jade felt a sharp surge of pleasure, her doubts forgotten.

'Do it,' he urged huskily.

With faltering fingers, she started to undo his shirt, stumbling a little as she reached the last button because it was tucked beneath the belt of his trousers.

'Take it off,' he whispered, but she lowered her eyes as she did so. 'So shy, *agape mou*?' he queried mockingly.

For answer, she pulled the shirt off and let it flutter to the floor, and laid her head dreamily against his bare chest, running her cheek up and down it, her fingers losing themselves in the dark whorls of hair, just as they'd done so often in her dreams.

He found the side button of her skirt, and then unzipped it with ease, pulling it down past her knees until he could impatiently toss it aside, and she was left wearing nothing but a tiny pair of black silk panties which matched the flimsy bra.

He said something in Greek then, something very soft which she would have given her heart to understand, and his hand slid down to the soft skin of her inner thigh, teased her there until she moved so that his fingers would touch her where she most needed to be touched, and she heard him give a soft laugh as his fingers moved inside her panties, his hand at last on her moist, heated flesh, and he bent his head to her ear when he heard her helpless moan of pleasure.

'You want me, very much, *agape mou*?'

But Jade couldn't even nod; he was working some kind of magic with his hands, sending her out of her mind, so that she didn't feel like Jade Meredith at that moment, she was being reborn in Constantine's arms and she wondered whether the world would ever be the same place again.

He slid the panties down her legs and threw them off the sofa, while his other hand unbuckled the belt of his trousers, and she heard the zip being drawn down and her heart started beating even more frantically. He moved away to remove the last of his clothing and Jade lay there naked, but not in the least bit shy as she watched the formidable power of him springing free. She'd never seen a man naked before, and yet it felt so right. She allowed her eyes to feast themselves on his magnificent frame, on the massively muscular shaft of his thighs; on the narrow hips and the powerful evidence of his sex. And when he moved on top of her she revelled in the feel of his naked body on hers, of breast touching breast, belly on belly, thigh against thigh. She sighed on a broken little note of wonder.

He kissed her and touched her and she approached some unimaginably beautiful brink time after time, so that by the time he thrust powerfully into her, she was so ready for him, so at one—that there was none of the imagined pain. Indeed, she seemed to know instinctively what to do, entwining her thighs around his bare back so that each thrust went deeper and deeper, and she found herself thrusting back against each movement of his, until she reached the brink once again. But this time it was different; this time he didn't hold back, just kept on moving and moving inside her, harder and harder, until she tumbled over, crying out with wonder and relief as the first great wrenching spasm pulled ecstatically at her womb, and then he too uttered a word which sounded almost like a protest before he shuddered helplessly against her, and she locked her arms around him protectively until she felt him finally still inside her.

There was silence for a moment. His heartbeat sounded muffled and heavy as it gradually slowed down to something approaching normality.

Jade nestled her face luxuriously against his neck, lifting her mouth up to plant a lazy kiss there, when he forestalled her by withdrawing himself from her abruptly, his face averted, before getting up off the sofa.

Aware of the flush which had pinkened her neck and of her nakedness, so noticeable now that he had left her, Jade stared up at him in disbelief. 'Constantine?'

He didn't even look round. 'What?' he asked indifferently.

'Where are you going?'

The unbelievable was happening. He had started to pull on his trousers, and as he zipped them up he turned to look down at her, his face as forbidding as the devil's. 'I'm going to take a shower, then a nap. I don't know about you—' and he gave a lazy, insulting yawn '—but I feel I could sleep for a week.' His eyes glittered. 'But then good sex always makes me feel like that.'

Jade sat up, still not believing what she was hearing, and, seeing his eyes drawn to her still-naked breasts, she grabbed at her blouse in an attempt to cover herself.

His mouth twisted with a cruel kind of satisfaction. 'Oh, don't bother covering up, *agape mou*. I've seen it all, touched it all, *tasted* it all. Here,' and he bent to pick up her discarded clothes and threw them to land in her lap. 'Put your clothes on and get out of here.' And he began to turn away.

Filled with the most bitter, humiliating rage, Jade pulled on her panties and bra and haphazardly buttoned up her blouse, before leaping up to confront him. 'How *dare* you? You lousy—'

But he held one palm up with the calm authority

of a policeman stopping traffic. 'Please, no. We've
done all that once and once was enough,' he said, in
a bored sounding voice. 'Your pretended violence
served its purpose—it provoked me into taking you.'

Her anger became something concrete to focus on,
because the alternative to anger was tears, and she
would sooner die than give him the pleasure of letting
him see her cry. She swallowed, but her voice was
mercifully steady. 'Let me get this straight,
Constantine—you've just been to bed with me, and
now you're asking me to leave?'

He shook his head. 'But that's where you're wrong,
Jade. On both counts. I haven't taken you to my
bed—I've just had sex with you. And I'm not asking
you to leave—I'm telling you.' He gave a brief glance
at his watch. 'If you get a move on you might be able
to catch the man who was embracing you so fondly
in the foyer earlier.'

Jade stared at him. Was he referring to the creepy
Russ Robson putting his arm around her *waist*? 'You
can't honestly believe that I'd have...that I'd go anywhere near Russ Robson after what's just happened
between us?' she demanded hotly.

He gave her a cool, steady stare. 'Can't I?' he queried softly. 'Who knows what I should believe about
you, Jade? I was even lulled into believing that you
were virtuous—'

Her eyes widened. 'And n-now you're implying
that I'm not—?'

His eyes were cold and unblinking, and Jade was
reminded of the dangerous stillness of a snake.

'No implication. Statement of fact. Might I suggest

that next time you try and convince a man you're a virgin you try to feign a little innocence. Virgins don't usually make love with the kind of panache and fervour which you have just demonstrated.' And he began to turn away again.

Jade tasted salt at the back of her throat. 'You're sick,' she told him.

'Wrong. I am not sick, merely weary—of you. Now, are you going to go quietly, or do I have to ring down and ask Security to remove you?'

It was only by imagining a wax figure of him harpooned by pins, while pulling the rest of her clothes on, that Jade could stop herself from breaking down in front of him. She knew that he watched her, but she didn't dare look at him. Because if she looked at him she might just rake her fingernails all down that arrogant face of his.

It was only as she began to open the door that she looked at him, hatred burning from her eyes. 'Oh, Constantine,' she said softly.

The black eyes glittered as he raised his eyebrows in arrogant query. 'What is it?'

'I hope you rot in hell!' she shot, as, back erect, she walked out of his suite and slammed the door shut on his low, mocking laughter.

CHAPTER FIVE

JADE left Park Lane and walked and walked and walked, her body still aching and tingling, her mind in tatters—willing the tears not to come, because she suspected that if she started crying she might never stop. Eventually she found herself back at the offices of the *Daily View*, aware that the other members of staff were staring at her as though she'd just landed in an alien spaceship. And then she caught a sight of herself in one of the mirrors and immediately knew why; she was in shock. White-faced and distraught, she stared numbly while Maggie, the *Daily View*'s female boss, came bustling out of her office and propelled Jade inside.

I'm living my nightmare, thought Jade dully, as she stared in disbelief at the black and white photos which lay scattered all over Maggie's desk.

Photos of Constantine.

Reality became a distant memory. 'Where did you get these?' she asked dully.

'Brent took them surreptitiously. At the Granchester. Honey—do you actually *know* this guy?'

And Jade did the most unprofessional thing in the world and burst into tears.

Maggie dumped a box of tissues in front of her and hurried away to the coffee machine, bringing back a steaming polystyrene beaker and adding something to it, before giving it to Jade.

'Here. Drink this.'

Waiting until a shuddering sob had died away, Jade obeyed, immediately wincing. 'What have you put in it?'

'Brandy,' said Maggie, who drank a bucket of the stuff every day. 'Drink it. It'll do you good.'

What it *did* do was increase her sense of being removed from reality, which Jade wasn't sure was a good thing at all. Detached. As though what had just happened had happened to someone else. But then she felt the aching deep inside her, felt the tingling of her breasts where he'd bitten and suckled them, and she knew for sure that it *had* happened to her. Briefly, she closed her eyes.

She put the empty cup down on the desk and dabbed at her eyes. 'Just who is he?' she asked in a quiet voice.

Maggie's eyes widened. 'You mean you don't *know*?'

'Of course I don't know—if I knew I wouldn't be asking!'

'Who did you think he was?'

Jade felt muzzy. 'I met him on holiday. A gorgeous Greek guy I happened to fall for whose family run a restaurant.'

Maggie snorted. 'Restaurant! He probably owns every damned restaurant in the entire Aegean!'

Jade looked up from sniffing into her tissue. 'Who is he?' she repeated.

'He is Constantine Sioulas.'

'I know that.'

'He owns the biggest shipping line in the world. In the millionaire class, he's head and shoulders above the rest. For rich read *billionaire*.'

Jade blinked. 'Ha, ha,' she said, but Maggie's face didn't look as though she was joking. 'He can't do,' she protested. 'He wore jeans; drove the most beaten up old car I've ever seen in my life. He's just an ordinary—' But she bit the word back. No. Not ordinary. No way in the world was Constantine ordinary.

But Maggie had obviously caught her drift. 'He's Greek. They're all like that. No matter what they acquire—and believe me, Constantine Sioulas has acquired more than most—at heart they remain simple men with simple tastes. And simple appetites,' she added knowingly.

Jade was more confused than ever. 'Then why have I never heard of him; why didn't I recognise him?'

'Just because you work on a newspaper, it doesn't mean to say you've heard of every tycoon in the world, particularly one who keeps his head down and his nose clean. You're too young, for a start. Ten years ago when he was twenty, his father died and Constantine inherited—you'd have been about ten at the time, and in my experience ten-year-olds don't read newspapers. The Press went crazy—here you had this young Greek god of a man who was absolutely rolling in it. He stood about a year of it, and then he began to guard his privacy, and the privacy of his family, as if it were Fort Knox. He's always surrounded by at least one minder. He hasn't been interviewed in years.' Maggie chomped on her gum. 'What's he like, Jade?'

Jade's head was spinning. How to describe Constantine? 'He's…' What? Gentle? Ruthless? Both of these.

'Good lover?'

Jade nodded without thinking; the brandy was now making her feel as though she'd like to lie down on her bed and sleep for a year. Or a hundred years, until, like Sleeping Beauty, the kiss of Constantine would awaken her.

'And what would you say was the most impressive thing about Constantine?'

As the brandy seeped into her brain, Jade had the sudden overpowering compulsion to confide in her boss. 'His strength,' she said. 'Oh, Maggie—I can't tell you what he was like…'

'Try, dear.'

Perhaps if I had a mother who didn't spend her whole time criticising me, I could confide in her, instead of my hard-baked editor, she thought. Somewhere at the back of Jade's mind, a warning bell rang, but there must have been more brandy in the cup than she'd thought, because the warning bell very quickly became indistinct.

'He was so—charismatic. Sexy and strong and gentle and funny. We had a fantastic time. He even— asked me to marry him.'

The unshockable Maggie actually choked on her gum. 'You *are* joking?'

'Why would I joke about something like that?'

Although, as each minute passed, the idea did seem more and more bizarre.

'Jade,' Maggie's voice was breathless. 'Are you *quite* sure?'

'Of course I'm sure! How could I be mistaken about something like that?' Jade slammed her cup down on the desk. Her head was spinning and now she felt an unfamiliar lurching feeling in her stomach. 'Maggie,' she mumbled. 'I don't feel very well.'

'I'm ordering you a cab to take you home right this minute.'

'But I haven't filed my piece on Russ Robson.'

'Leave it,' said Maggie uncharacteristically. 'I'll find another piece to fill it.'

Just what that piece was, Jade was to discover the next morning when the demented buzzing of the doorbell bounced into her disturbed dreams about Constantine, and she glanced at the bedside clock to discover that it was almost eight o'clock. And with consciousness, the ghastly events of yesterday re-entered her memory with painful clarity.

The doorbell shrilled yet again.

Pulling her dressing-gown on, Jade stumbled out of bed, looked in the mirror and winced. Who on earth was that at the door? She wasn't expecting anyone, and Sandy, her television director flatmate, was away filming for a fortnight.

Hope, foolish hope, stirred to life within her. What if it *was* Constantine?

And what if it was? After the way he'd treated her? Now that her mind had cleared from the effects of

Maggie's brandy, common sense had prevailed. And if she saw the no-good brute just once more in her life, it would be once too often. If it *was* Constantine, she would tell him to go to the hell he deserved!

But it was not Constantine.

She opened the front door to mayhem. Flashbulbs exploded in her face as photographers and journalists, some of whom she recognised, jostled on the doorstep like a disturbed ants' nest.

'Miss Meredith—this way!'

'Over here, Jade!'

'Hey, Jade—would you like to comment on the item in this morning's *Daily View*?'

Another flashbulb temporarily blinded her with its lightning-blue flare.

'What's going on?' said Jade, bewildered, then wished she'd never asked, because an early edition of the *Daily View* was held up in front of her nose. She became aware of two things. Constantine's photo.

And hers.

Hers?

And then, she became aware of a third thing; of the headline—shockingly huge and clear and banner-like.

'My Steamy Nights of Love with Greek Tycoon!'

Under *her* byline!

Jade snatched the newspaper. 'Give me that!' She slammed the door in their faces, and, hands shaking like crazy, carried the newspaper into the sitting-room.

It was worse than she could have possibly imagined. It was a short piece, but to the point. And, apart from the headline, innocuous enough. But it would have repulsed even the strongest stomach with its opening sentence: 'Dewy-eyed cub reporter Jade Meredith described how stunningly handsome Greek billionaire Constantine Sioulas popped the question on an idyllic Greek island...'

Jade dialled the office with trembling fingers and asked to be put through to Maggie, who didn't even have the good grace to sound abashed.

'How could you do this to me, Maggie?'

'It's a good story!'

'But I *trusted* you!'

'The more fool you, Jade.' Maggie gave a shrill laugh. 'You should know by now, dear—once a journalist, always a journalist!'

'He'll sue. He'll sue you for every penny you've got.'

'He *can't* sue!' Maggie's voice was triumphant. 'I checked with our lawyer—and we've printed nothing that wasn't true!'

Jade didn't feel like enlightening Maggie that there had been no nights of love, merely a rather sordid episode in his hotel sitting-room. 'Then I'll sue. I didn't write that.'

'But all of it you said. And I have the tape to prove it.'

Jade listened in appalled silence. 'You *recorded* me?' she whispered.

'Sure. It's my job.' In the background, Jade could hear the sound of someone speaking very quickly. 'Listen, Jade—I have to hang up now.'

Jade sat on the sofa for the rest of the morning,

unable to eat or drink or move, feeling like a cornered fox while outside all the reporters bayed for her blood. She shut her eyes in horror. Yes, she'd been angry with Constantine's cold-blooded possession of her yesterday, but not enough to do this. Never to do something like this. She looked down to find that she was still clutching the *Daily View* like a lifeline, and immediately dropped the newspaper on to the carpet as though it were contaminated.

My God, she thought—if Constantine had disliked her before, then his loathing would now know no bounds.

Her reverie was interrupted by the telephone. It was Maggie again.

'Can you get in here right away, Jade?' she said urgently. 'I'm sending a couple of guys down to get you through the Press.'

And Jade did what she had been longing to do for almost a year, uncaring of the consequences. 'No, I can't, Maggie. In fact I'm tendering my resignation. As of now, I no longer work for you.'

There was an odd and somewhat strained quality to the normally robust editor's voice. 'Jade—I advise you to get down here right away. I advise you *very strongly indeed.*'

'Why?'

'I'm not at liberty to say any more on the phone.'

Not at *liberty*? 'Why?' asked Jade acidly. 'Has someone got a gun to your head.'

Maggie gave a strange, humourless laugh. 'Metaphorically speaking, yes. Can I expect you?'

Jade hesitated, her curiosity aroused by Maggie's

odd-sounding voice. Was it possible that Constantine *was* going to sue for libel, despite Maggie's bravado. Oh, how she hoped so. That would show them that they couldn't go around printing whatever they liked about people!

For the first time, Jade knew what it felt like to be on the receiving end of tabloid journalism. But she had never *tricked* anyone into giving her an interview—nor tape-recorded them without knowing.

'Jade?' came Maggie's strained voice. 'Are you still there?'

Jade looked around the room, realising that she couldn't sit in her flat for the rest of her life regretting what had happened, could she? What the hell! 'Yes, Maggie, I'm still here,' she answered coolly. Curiosity got the better of her. 'Send someone over then, and I'll come into the office. But I'm not confronting those vultures outside on my own.' I used to be one of those vultures, she thought. But no longer, thank heavens.

She felt like some minor celebrity when two burly men duly elbowed their way through the waiting Press and into a car, and when she walked through the office the atmosphere was more hushed than usual. At the sight of Jade, all conversation was killed stone-dead.

Head held high, determined that they shouldn't read any trace of emotion in her face, Jade walked towards Maggie Marchant's door, tapped it and opened it to see that it was not the editor who sat behind the cluttered desk.

It was Constantine.

CHAPTER SIX

JADE could only stare in disbelief at Constantine, incongruously seated in her boss's chair. He wore a suit; he looked impossibly elegant and unreachable. And about as friendly as a range of craggy mountains.

His dark eyes flicked over her, and she found herself wishing that she hadn't just thrown on the first items to hand, imagining his lips curling with disdain. But he surprised her. His face remained implacable; not a flicker of emotion whatsoever on the ruthlessly carved features as he took in her short, flared cotton skirt, worn with an old, closely fitting indigo shirt.

He switched his gaze to Maggie Marchant, who Jade now noticed was standing in one corner of the room, uncharacteristically silent and looking terribly out of place. She found herself blinking in surprise—what on earth was happening?

'Leave us,' ordered Constantine.

Jade expected Maggie to reply with a torrent of abusive rhetoric, because no matter how rich and how powerful Constantine might be, in the offices of the *Daily View* Maggie ran a tight ship, with the proprietor giving her an astonishing amount of freedom to run the paper as she saw fit. But no outburst followed; instead Jade was treated to the unbelievable spectacle of Maggie nodding her head and slipping silently out of the office like a messenger-girl.

Little hairs on the back of her neck bristled as she scented danger—the threat of it was emanating from every pore of that impressive frame. She wanted to run and hide from him, from the danger and the ever-present and still powerful attraction she felt towards him. And what a fool you are, Jade Meredith, she thought in abject disgust as she began to turn away.

'And where do you think you're going?' came a silky voice.

She injected steel into her voice. 'As far away from you as possible!'

'Perhaps to sell more details of our so-called affair?' And then the mouth *did* curl. 'I think not.'

A sense of fair play emerged as indignation righteously reared its head. It had been the same while she was at school—it was all very well being punished for something she had done, but not for something she *hadn't* done. But she wasn't going to crawl to him—she would give him the facts coolly and rationally. 'I want you to know I didn't write that story, Constantine!' But to her own ears it sounded blurted and made up. 'Honestly!'

He subjected her to a slow and contemptuous scrutiny. 'If I were you, I would think very carefully about using that particular word,' he suggested icily. 'It doesn't go at all well with your track record.'

'But I *didn't* write it! I wouldn't have had them print it in a million years—I'm just not the kind of person who goes around parading her private life in front of millions!'

He gave a soft, brutal laugh. 'Oh, really?' he mocked. 'Then how did the paper know that I'd been your lover? Or that I'd asked you—' and here he swore very softly and explicitly in Greek, and for the first time Jade was glad she didn't understand the language '—to marry me?' he finished on a note of harsh incredulity, as if questioning his sanity at the time of asking.

Oh, what was the use of trying to explain that she'd been trapped by a combination of her emotional state at being made love to and then dumped by him and the unexpected potency of brandy on an empty stomach? He'd never believe her in a million years, and even if he did, he'd never forgive her, not now. He was not, she recognised—a forgiving kind of man. 'Are you planning to sue?' she asked.

He ignored the question. 'Sit,' he ordered, indicating the chair in front of the desk with a cursory nod of the gleaming jet head.

And because the sheer emotion of seeing him sitting there after everything which had happened between them seemed to have reduced her legs to the consistency of jelly, Jade found herself sinking into the chair.

'Are you going to sue?' she repeated.

He gave an impatient nod of the dark head. 'No, I am not going to sue,' he gritted out tersely. 'There is little point in suing since what was published was the truth—or pretty close to it.' He leaned back in his chair, surveying her from hooded, hostile eyes. 'On a technical point, the article was, of course—inaccurate.' He closed his eyes and recited from memory. '"My Steamy Nights of Love with Greek Tycoon".'

Jade blushed with shame at the tasteless headline,

and he opened his eyes, which narrowed marginally as he took in the heated flares of colour which lay over her high cheekbones.

'As you know,' he ground out, 'there were no *nights* of love; and more fool me. For if I had not been so taken by your convincing little virginal act I would have taken you on the island when you offered yourself so willingly to me. *Over and over again*,' he said in a soft, cruel voice. 'Until I had satiated the aching in my loins, and rid myself of my obsession for you.'

And to Jade's astonishment and horror her body began to react to the brutal sexual boast, and she felt her breasts tingle into life, felt a hot frustrated aching begin at the pit of her belly, and the colour in her face deepened.

His eyes flicked to her breasts, to where she knew without having to look that the pointed outlines of her nipples were pushing against the thin material of her shirt, and his mouth gave another mocking twist.

'And as you know,' he continued relentlessly, 'the physical extent of our relationship lasted a little under an hour—'

Jade got quickly to her feet, her eyes flashing with humiliation and fury. 'I don't have to listen to a minute more of this, you swine!'

'Yes, you do,' he answered icily.

'I'm leaving right *now*!'

'I don't think so.'

Something in the cool and unswervable determination in his voice made her turn around, startled. 'Just try stopping me!' she challenged.

He gave a brief shake of the head. 'I intend to,' he said harshly. 'But not the way you want me to, at least not yet.'

Appalled, her mouth fell open. 'And what's that supposed to mean?'

He shrugged. 'Don't play innocent games, Jade—we've already established that your innocence is a sham. I'm talking about the usual scenario. You run for the door. I follow. You struggle. I kiss you and naturally, you kiss me back. And then I lock the office door, to take you right here. You would like it on the floor, perhaps—or do you prefer the desk?'

The blood thundered in her ears. How could she ever have believed that she cared for a man who could talk to her like this? 'You *arrogant*, unbelievable man—'

'But that's what happened last time.'

No, that's where you're wrong, she thought. Last time, I thought we were both motivated by love; now he had reduced it to the lowest possible common denominator. Lust. Now it was her turn to curve her lips with distaste. 'You disgust me.'

'I know. A pity you find it so exciting.'

She'd had enough. Shoulders back, she made an effort and walked to the door. '*Herete*,' she slung after her, using the Greek word for goodbye.

'I told you, you aren't going anywhere, not until you listen to what I have to say. You have angered me, Jade.'

'Good! You've angered me, too—so maybe we're quits!'

'Never before,' he mused, 'have I been made to look a fool by a woman—'

'Then maybe you should have done! And if you had, it might have made you more human!' she retorted, deliberately putting away the memory of him on the island. He had been human then—delectably human. Powerful yet persuasive, strong and yet gentle. She nudged the thought away. That Constantine did not exist; he had been playacting, too.

'All morning,' he ground out, his eyes dark and gleaming with anger, 'I have had family, colleagues and business acquaintances cabling me to offer their sincere congratulations.'

Jade stared at him in confusion. 'What for?'

Another abrasive laugh. 'On my forthcoming marriage.'

'I'm not with you.' Had he been hiding a fiancée up his sleeve all this time? In which case, he had no right to criticise *her* for supposedly flirting with Russ Robson!

'But yes, unfortunately, you are. You told the newspaper that I had asked you to marry me, and that you had accepted, and with those words I'm afraid that you have sealed your fate.'

Something in the way he spoke unnerved her, and Jade felt a shiver of apprehension trickle its way slowly down her spine. 'What in heaven's name are you talking about? Sealed my fate, indeed! How?'

The black eyes gleamed menacingly. 'I'm talking of marriage, naturally.'

Jade opened her mouth and the word squeaked out. 'Marriage?'

He made an impatient gesture with his hand. 'You will marry me, and as quickly as possible.'

There was a shocked, stunned silence as Jade stared at Constantine in disbelief. He'd flipped! Gone completely mad! She tossed her blonde hair contemptuously back over her shoulders and gave him a chilly smile. 'It may come as a surprise to you to learn that people who despise one another *don't* get married. That's a cute little custom we happen to have in this country!'

'So your answer is no?'

'Of course it's no!' And yet in those oh, so different earlier circumstances her answer had been an ecstatic yes. Unless… Her foolish little mind went into overdrive. What if he was genuinely sorry about the way he'd behaved on finding out that she'd lied about her job? Was he now regretting that savage seduction? What if the feelings that he'd had for her, or *claimed* to have had for her on the island, were real? What if he still wanted to marry her for…? Her mind dared not even admit the word to itself. But she had to know. 'Why do you want to marry me?'

'Wanting does not come into it. The world now knows that I proposed marriage, which you accepted—and I must honour that commitment.'

Jade's heart did a backward somersault. Of course he wasn't marrying her for love. Had he, since he'd arrived back in England, behaved like a man who was in love? The very opposite. 'I'm not sure that I'm hearing this right. You would marry me simply to honour a commitment?'

His eyes flared like sunlight bouncing off granite.

'Not simply for commitment,' he said harshly. 'For pride!'

'Pride?'

'Yes, pride, or, if you prefer it—honour.'

'I don't understand.'

'That I can believe—but it is a concept which shapes the whole life of a Greek,' he said proudly. 'If I back down now, having given my word that I would marry you—then I will be seen to be dishonourable, and for a man in my position that is something I simply will not countenance.'

Jade went cold at the unfeeling lack of affection behind his words. 'You must be mad,' she whispered, 'to think that I'd ever, *ever* marry you!'

'Don't make me force you, Jade.'

'*Force* me? This is London, you know, not the back of beyond—you can't throw me over the back of your horse and carry me off somewhere!' Even though just the thought of it sent a betraying little *frisson* of excitement through her body.

'More subtle force than that,' he answered, with smooth assurance.

'Oh, really?' She gave a disbelieving laugh, but there was something about the steely determination on his face which again stirred those misgivings into life. 'Like what?'

'Like the fact that two hours ago I bought your proprietor out and that I now own the major controlling interest in this newspaper.'

The room swayed. Jade swallowed. 'You can't have done!' she blustered. 'Not that quickly! This article was only published this morning. You can't possibly have bought the paper!'

'But that is where you are so wrong—with the right financial incentive anything is possible,' he answered, with a cynical smile. 'Surely you knew *that*, Jade?'

She eyed him with frosty disapproval. 'No, I didn't,' she answered witheringly. 'I'm not in the big money league. Besides, whether or not you've bought the paper is of absolutely no interest to me.'

'Oh, I think it is,' he said softly.

He obviously had no inkling of the fact that she was now no longer a member of staff! Jade gave him a superior smile as she savoured her moment of triumph. 'Wrong!' she retorted. 'I've already handed my notice in. So you see—whether or not you own the newspaper has nothing to do with me, because I no longer work here!'

'You wouldn't have done in any case—as my wife I would not have you working on such a scurrilous rag.'

Jade felt like shaking him, if his sheer size hadn't made him so immovable. 'I'm not going to *be* your wife, you ruthless tyrant! Don't you understand? The fact that you own the paper means nothing to me, absolutely *nothing*!'

'Then you care nothing about the fate of your former colleagues?' he enquired silkily.

Actually, no, certainly not Maggie, not after her betrayal, and most of the other journalists would find work on other newspapers.

She chewed anxiously on her bottom lip. Wouldn't they?

'Not particularly,' she said evasively, but her heart sank a little since she knew that several of them were mortgaged up to the hilt. 'Journalists are used to switching around—it's that kind of job.'

'But the others?' he persisted. 'The men in the print room, for example, who I am told by your editor you are rather fond of.' His mouth curled disdainfully. 'But then, they are men, are they not?' The insulting implication was made painfully clear. 'And some of these men,' he continued inexorably, 'look too old to start anew. *If they should lose their jobs*,' he said, with deliberate emphasis.

Jade stared back at him with fascinated loathing. 'You wouldn't,' she whispered. 'You wouldn't do that?'

'Wouldn't I?' he answered remorselessly. 'Believe me when I tell you that I would do whatever it takes.'

Jade often shared a snatched lunch break in the Lamb and Flag with the stalwarts of the print room. She thought of dear old Arthur, saving like mad for his retirement so that he and his wife could retire to a small complex in Spain. And Bill, whose married son was out of work, and whose wage meant that his grandchildren got toys at Christmas. And clothes for the rest of the year.

She stared into the cold, black eyes. 'Are you saying that I could save these people their jobs—'

'If you agree to marry me? Yes.'

This was preposterous—things like this just didn't happen in *her* world! 'You can't,' she protested. 'The unions will—'

'I can,' he said implacably. 'And I will.'

Jade ran her fingers wildly through her mussed hair, closing her eyes as she tried to piece her thoughts together. Could she bear to see people like Arthur and Bill thrown out of a job because of *her* foolishness, *her* indiscretion? And if the only way to put a stop to it was by marrying Constantine…

She looked up into the impenetrable black eyes, and perhaps he read the unwilling capitulation in hers, for the corners of his mouth lifted in an arrogant half-smile of triumph.

'So you'll marry me?' he asked.

'What choice do I have?' she answered bitterly. 'Only someone as heartless as yourself would dream of saying no.'

He made a soft laugh, and rose from behind the desk with all the stealth and grace of a jungle cat moving in for the kill, and Jade eyed him with a deep hatred which was nonetheless mixed with a deep longing which she couldn't seem to shake off. Cornered, she began to back away from him as he approached.

'I want to get a few things straight,' she said, and he immediately halted, eyeing her with a calculating interest. 'You're marrying me *just* to keep your word and maintain your honour?'

'Oh, no,' he negated mockingly. 'Not just for that.'

'It isn't?' Jade's eyes widened as she wondered just what other motivation there could be behind this preposterous marriage.

'No, indeed,' he repeated, on a deep, silky note, which made the little hairs on the back of her neck stand up like soldiers. 'An added incentive is that I desire you with a compulsion which I find profoundly disturbing; it disturbed me when I first met you, and making love to you just once seems to have only exacerbated it. By marrying you, it will enable me to have you whenever I like and how often I like, so that inevitably my desire for you will lessen, and—diminish,' he concluded callously.

Somehow, Jade managed to keep her face poker-straight. 'And then?'

He shrugged. 'Then, in a few months' time—we can divorce, if you wish it.' His mouth became an implacably hard line. 'I will probably have grown tired of you by then.'

'But surely that will heap even more dishonour on your head?' suggested Jade sarcastically.

He shook the black head emphatically. 'Not at all. My family and my Greek friends will doubtlessly expect the marriage to fail from the beginning—and they will blame its failure on the cultural differences between the two races. Besides, if we marry in England in a register office, it won't even be considered a proper marriage, no matter what the law says—because to all my family and friends only a church wedding in Greece will fulfil that function.'

He looked so cold, so hard, as if he were discussing some board-room take over. 'My God,' whispered Jade. 'You've got it all worked out, haven't you? Every single ghastly aspect.'

'But naturally,' he continued inexorably. 'It is the way I always operate. So,' the eyes glittered blackly. 'You agree to my proposal?'

Jade lifted her chin and glared at him. 'I will con-

sider it.' But his attention didn't seem to be on what
she was saying, for she saw that he was staring openly
at her breasts, and his eyes had darkened into glittering chips of black ice as he began to approach her
once more.

She watched as he moved, clasping her hands together to stop them trembling, knowing that she
should stray from his relentless path, but something
in his face stopped her. Oh, the fascinating planes and
shadows of that harsh and ruthless face! It was as
though everything which was dark and powerful and
savage and masculine—all the primitive qualities
which made some men so devastatingly attractive—
had been bestowed far too liberally on Constantine.
He made every other man she'd ever met seem like
insubstantial shadows by comparison.

'And now…' He was so close now: she could smell
that soapy fragrance mingled with the hot, salty and
aroused male tang of him. 'A kiss for your husband-
to-be…' His voice sounded like gravel scraping over
velvet.

He lowered his mouth with exacting precision over
hers, his tongue gently probing her half-protesting lips
apart, and she felt it move slowly into her mouth,
sliding erotically over her teeth…inexorably seductive…until there was no protest left in her, and she
kissed him back. And back…as the intimacy of the
kiss grew and grew. And, with each second that
passed, the kiss provoked a tense excitement which
built and built and built, so that her body and her heart
cried out for joy when he slowly and deliberately

swept his hand down over her breast, her belly, briefly alighting on one thigh before encircling her waist.

She felt the hot, fierce and wet release of desire and she gave a little moan, half-crazy with wanting. In the dimmest recesses of her mind some voice of reason spoke its protest, wondering how she could allow him to do this to her after all that had happened.

But the desires of her body seemed to have obliterated everything but its own intense need, and her mind and the voice of reason weren't getting a look in—not when his hand had moved down to unbutton her shirt and she felt the cool air on her skin, immediately closing her eyes with helpless pleasure as he slid his hand inside her bra, so that the exquisitely sensitive nub nudged insistently against his circling palm.

He hadn't stopped kissing her, and his other hand had begun to move her floaty skirt up, and was caressing its way oh, so slowly all the way up her bare and craving thigh, his fingers stroking feather-light touches over the soft skin there. With a muffled groan he pulled her body tightly into his and Jade's eyelids fluttered open as she felt the tantalisingly hard pressure of his arousal which pushed against her, and then, through dazed eyes, saw the familiar yet unexpected sight of her boss's office. Ex-boss, she corrected herself vaguely. Realised, with Constantine's hand almost on her panties, that if she didn't stop him soon, *now*, that he would take her right here, and with as little care or feeling as he had shown before in his hotel-room.

Her mind struggled for ascendancy over body, and

with a strength she hadn't known she possessed she
pushed him away from her, and stood hastily adjusting her clothing, her eyes dark with rage and passion,
her breathing heavy and laboured for exactly the same
reasons.

'Don't—don't *ever* do that again!' she declared,
once her breathing had steadied enough to allow her
to speak. 'Because here's the second of my terms,
Constantine. Yes, I'll damned well marry you—because I couldn't bear to see you put those poor men
out of work—but it'll be a marriage in name only!
And I'm afraid that you're in for a shock if you think
you're going to rid yourself of your desire for me by
making love to me—because I don't ever want you
to touch me like that again!'

His eyes glinted. 'Liar,' he taunted softly. 'Do you
really think you could stop me?'

She had the perfect counter-attack. 'You'd force
me, do you mean, Constantine? But surely your *pride*
wouldn't allow you to take a woman who didn't want
you?'

But to her fury, he merely laughed. 'You have an
astonishing and enchanting way of showing me how
much you don't want me,' he observed arrogantly.
'But don't worry, Jade—you won't have to fight me
off.'

Such an about-turn was mighty confusing. 'I
w-won't?'

He let out one notch of his belt, as though his trousers were unbearably tight, and Jade found herself
having to stare deliberately into empty space so as
not to be confronted with the visual evidence of ex-

actly *why* he was having to make the necessary ad-justment.

'No, indeed,' he concluded, still in that same, mocking voice. 'You see, living in such close confine-ment, I'm confident that, whatever your good inten-tions, you'll find it impossible to stay away from me.'

'Over my dead body!'

'And that if you'll be doing any fighting, Jade, it'll be with your own very healthy desires.'

CHAPTER SEVEN

JADE looked up into the hard black eyes. 'And when do you propose that this—wedding—take place?'

Constantine gave a chillingly ruthless smile. 'As soon as possible. I shall apply for the special licence today. We can be married by Wednesday.'

'And what happens until then—do I go home to my flat to prepare my trousseau?' she asked sarcastically.

'It is not necessary for you to return to your flat.'

'And if I insist?'

He raised his eyebrows mockingly. 'Have you not yet learnt that I will disregard your insistence? Besides, your flat is no longer suitable. Quite apart from its lack of space, you will have already seen how troublesome the Press can be.' His mouth twisted as if with the irony of his words. 'You will come straight with me to my suite at the Granchester.'

Jade shuddered. She couldn't face going back there…where… She lifted her chin up proudly. 'I'm not staying in that hotel room with you.'

'Why not?'

'Because I… Because there's nowhere to—' Oh, why not be honest about it? 'Where would you sleep?' she asked pointedly. 'On the sofa?' Oh, stupid, *stupid*, Jade! Why mention the wretched sofa?

He gave a complacent smile as he homed into her

thoughts immediately. 'I doubt it. That particular sofa
has far too many erotic memories to be conducive to
sleep, is still permeated with your scent...' He let his
voice tail off, heavy with suggestion, but then, surprisingly, as if noting her discomfiture at having been
reminded of an episode which she would have preferred to remain forgotten, he tried a different tack
altogether. 'Do not worry, *agape mou*,' he said, in a
gentler voice. 'It has two bedrooms. Propriety will be
observed.'

'But what will your family say,' she was unable to
resist asking, 'when they discover that you're sharing
a suite of rooms with a woman to whom you're not
married?'

'You think that this would be the first time it's
happened?' he queried softly, and the cruel taunt hit
her like a body blow.

Furiously Jade bit her lip and turned away, determined that he wouldn't be able to read such inappropriate jealousy in her eyes.

'Your exposé rather put paid to maintaining any
myth that we were prepared to wait until after the
wedding,' he drawled. 'But in any case, I am not in
the habit of living my life according to the dictates
of my family. I answer to no one.'

That, she could well believe. He wasn't a man she
could imagine many people standing up to.

Until now, she thought defiantly. And I meant what
I said. Yesterday, she had let her passion run away
with her, and she'd almost done the same today; but
not again. She had learnt her lesson painfully well.
He was prepared to take her in as brutal a way as

possible, without care and without feeling. She mustn't let him.

'And besides,' he added. 'After I have finished with my business in England, we will be returning to Piros. For our honeymoon,' he concluded softly.

Jade suppressed a shudder. 'Is that really necessary?'

'It is imperative. This wedding will be conducted with all due ceremony.' A strong hand was placed on her forearm, like a gaoler's grip. 'Come. Let us go,' he said. 'The car is waiting.'

Walking side by side, they made their way back out into the outer office, where Maggie was perched on the edge of the sports editor's desk, with the face of a woman who had just gambled away a fortune. Everywhere, fingers stilled on word processors and silence fell like a guillotine.

'One moment, Jade,' said Constantine, and paused, running one hand through his luxuriant hair and looking round at the hushed expectant workers. 'I know that there has been considerable speculation following my take-over. Therefore, I feel it only fair to inform you that there will be no redundancies at present,' he said, and there was an audible murmur of relief. 'And by the way, Maggie,' he remarked, looking around. 'We now operate a policy of no partially clothed women on *any* pages of this newspaper—is that understood?'

'Perfectly,' answered Maggie calmly, as though she had not just been asked to change the entire ethos of the *Daily View*! 'We'll think of something to replace them.'

'Something *suitable*,' murmured Constantine quietly. 'And in keeping with the new goals which I outlined earlier.' Piercing black eyes swivelled in Maggie's direction. 'Perhaps you would like to hold a meeting after we've gone—to outline the turnaround in our editorial policy. Any employee who feels that they would be unable to support such a turnaround will, of course, be free to leave.

'Oh, and by the way,' he remarked, almost casually. 'Miss Meredith is no longer employed by this paper—' He stilled the buzz of comment with the upraised palm of command. 'Because she and I are getting married. Good day, ladies and gentlemen. Come, Jade.'

As exits went, she would probably never better it, thought Jade, a flash of her customary humour returning as she observed the collective opening of mouths before following Constantine to the lift. How she wished she'd had a camera to capture the look on Maggie's face!

'What editorial turnaround?' asked Jade curiously, as they rode down in the lift together.

The back eyes glittered. 'It is quite simple,' he said. 'The *Daily View* is about to change and in future no one will be able to describe it as a "scandal sheet".'

'I see,' said Jade faintly. Well, it would certainly have to change a lot in order to qualify for that!

Outside, a blindingly shiny black Daimler stood parked by the front of the *Daily View* building. There was a chauffeur in the front seat, whom Constantine introduced as Tony. Beside him was the Greek man who had opened the door to her at the Granchester, and Jade found herself blushing as she wondered whether Constantine had told him of the outcome of that little meeting.

'This is Stavros,' said Constantine. 'My brother.'

His *brother*? Wait for the animosity, thought Jade, and then was surprised at the politely formal greeting.

'How do you do, Miss Meredith?' Stavros extended his hand. 'I saw you in Piros, but you will not remember me.'

Jade smiled; he had a kindly face. 'On the contrary,' she said. 'I remember seeing you in the taverna with your brother. Such a pity we did not meet.'

Stavros shrugged. 'Indeed. Constantine guarded you too well. But I am flattered that you noticed me,' he finished wryly. 'I thought that you and Tino had eyes only for each other.'

Jade's cheeks went pink. 'I'm pleased to meet you,' she said politely, if somewhat ironically.

She and Constantine sat in the back of the car, and he gave instructions in Greek to the driver, but Jade clearly made out the word 'Granchester'.

'Constantine—'

'What is it, *agape mou*?' he answered softly, and laid his hand on her forearm, only the lightest of gestures, but which had her senses on full alert immediately. It was…an almost…well, if not exactly a loving gesture, then certainly an affectionate one, and much too close to the way he'd behaved on Piros for her to derive anything but regret from it.

He's putting on an act in front of his brother, thought Jade, wriggling away from him. He must be. 'What about my things?'

'Things?'

'Yes, things. The kind of things which make such a difference to everyday living! You know—toothbrush, clothes. Little things like that.'

He laughed softly beneath his breath. 'I like it when you answer back, you know, Jade. I find your spitfire retorts *most* entertaining—'

'Well, they aren't supposed to be!'

'And as for your things—we can easily buy you another toothbrush.'

'And my clothes?'

'There is an answer to that which I do not think my brother and chauffeur should be privy to, but if you insist on wearing any then we can arrange to buy you anything you like.'

'But I don't want you to buy me clothes—I happen to have some perfectly decent ones in my own wardrobe.'

His face darkened, with the look of a man obviously not used to having his wishes thwarted. 'I'm talking about garments by the best designers the world has to offer,' he bit out impatiently. 'You can spend what you wish.'

'Keep them! I don't want your money, *or* your designer clothes' answered Jade emphatically. 'I want my own!' Through the glass partition, she was sure that she could see Stavros's shoulders silently shaking.

'As you wish,' he said tightly, and bit out some new instructions, then bent his mouth to her ear. 'So spirited,' he murmured. 'How I shall enjoy subduing that spirit.'

'I shan't let you!'

'We shall see. But I fully intend to.'

And there was no need to ask how he proposed doing that. Jade shivered, the sensual undertones of his murmured words creating vividly erotic pictures in her mind.

Although the car was big, it was none the less claustrophobic and she was intensely aware of his presence beside her. Such a strong and dominating presence. More to keep her mind off his undeniable physical attraction, she asked him a question which had been bugging her since they'd left the building. 'What made you change the policy on the *Daily View*'s pin-ups? Don't you approve of those kind of photographs?'

An expression of distaste masked his face and he crossed one long leg over the other. He stared out of the window at the slow-moving traffic. 'Of course I don't approve!'

Jade shrugged. 'But lots of men do.'

'Not this kind of man, Jade,' he said softly.

'And why do they offend you?' she persisted. 'Do all nudes offend your proprieties, or just some? Do Rubens or Renoir offend you? How about Botticelli's *Venus*, for example?'

He made an impatient sound. 'Nudity in art is different—that embraces and celebrates the female form; these others merely titillate, and of that I do not approve.'

'On purely moral grounds, then?'

He shook his head. 'I concern myself with welfare, too. Those women who pose—they all have mothers, fathers, brothers, sisters—maybe even young children of their own. How do you think that they must feel about it?'

She should have guessed! 'How very paternalistic of you!'

He shrugged. 'And what about you, Jade?' he queried coolly. 'Do you approve of such pictures?'

Jade sighed. 'No, of course I don't approve of them. I absolutely hate them! What woman wouldn't?'

He turned his head to face her, the black eyes piercing and direct. 'And yet you chose to work there?'

'Perhaps it was my only option. Lots of people do jobs they aren't particularly proud of.'

'Is that why you lied to me?' he asked, the timbre of his voice dangerously soft. 'Or do you just enjoy lying for the sake of it?'

Jade met his disapproving stare face on. 'You listen to *me* for a moment, Constantine! All your censure for my having lied about my job, and yet you were guilty of a similar lie. You allowed me to carry on thinking that you were no more than a humble restaurateur. Didn't you?'

'Yes, I'm guilty,' he grated. 'Of being foolish enough to fall for the innocent act you presented to me; foolish enough to believe that you had fallen for the man, and not all the trappings. For me, for the first time in my life, it was a delight to play at being two ordinary people, without all the pressures of wealth. If only—' his mouth twisted '—you hadn't happened to be a mercenary little bitch who knew *exactly* who I was—who would go to bed with me in order to get the story she wanted.'

Jade felt sick. 'But I *didn't* know who you were, I keep telling you! What do I have to do to make you believe me?'

'Hell will be frozen over before ever I do!' The black eyes narrowed to shards of jet. 'If you hated, as you claim, your job so much—then why do it in the first place?'

'It's a long story.'

'Really?' he queried with an almost polite disbelief. 'I'll bet it is! You must tell it to me some time.'

And she made up her mind to tell him right then because she simply couldn't bear anyone thinking so poorly of her, and it suddenly became tremendously important that he should know that things weren't quite as black and white as he seemed to see them, that she wasn't the hard-hearted villainess of the piece he thought she was. 'I'll tell it to you right now!' she announced, then, exasperated by his disparaging stare, 'But only if you stop glaring at me!'

Their eyes fused in a long gaze, the corner of his mouth tilted upwards by a mere millimetre. 'Very well.' And he leaned forward to close the glass partition between them and the two men in the front.

Jade laced her fingers together in her lap, remembering when she'd thought that the competition had been the answer to all her dreams. Some dreams! 'When I was seventeen and still at school, the *Daily View* ran a competition to find the country's most promising journalist. My teacher persuaded me to enter it, and, to my amazement—I won.'

'Congratulations,' he interjected mockingly.

Jade glowered at the implied criticism. 'Well, actually—I was *proud* of winning, *and* of the article I wrote. When they offered me a job on the staff—' She saw the expression on his face. 'Of *course* I accepted it! Who wouldn't have done?'

'I would have thought about it very carefully.'

'Well, you're a different kettle of fish, aren't you?' she retorted. 'You were rich and I was poor! You probably could have got your father to buy you a damned newspaper—the way you've just bought the *Daily View*! But this was like the answer to all my dreams—I'd imagined starting work on the local paper, so to be offered a job on one of the nationals—'

'But there are other newspapers, surely, more serious newspapers which carry more weight and are more prestigious—why not choose to work on one of those?'

Jade laughed sardonically. 'Oh, come *on*! I was eighteen, green as grass, politically naïve—serious papers don't go for people like that, they want university graduates.'

'And couldn't you have gone to university?'

'No,' Jade answered flatly.

He raised his eyebrows. 'Oh? I find that hard to believe. You certainly aren't stupid.'

'Thanks!'

'So why didn't you go?'

Jade could have shaken him by the shoulders for his total lack of comprehension as she remembered her father's strained face, regretfully informing her that going through college simply wasn't an option

open to her. 'For that very romantic reason of not
having enough money—except that the reality of it
isn't romantic at all! Besides, I thought that working
on the *Daily View* might get me a foot in the door.'

'But it didn't?'

She shook her head. 'No, it didn't. I didn't—learn
very much there.' She met a pair of frankly interested
black eyes. 'Actually,' she said, remembering some
of the *good* things about the *Daily View*, 'it wasn't
all bad there. They *do* do some very creditable in-
vestigative journalism. They raise a hell of a lot of
money for charity, and they certainly expose corrup-
tion in high places.'

'But that wasn't your particular line?' he queried.

'No,' said Jade bitterly. 'Because I'm a woman,
and a "cub"—I get stuck in features; showbiz. At
first it had novelty appeal, but now it's worn off. As
a matter of fact—'

'Yes?'

'Nothing.'

'Come on—I'm intrigued.'

She met his stare belligerently. 'If you must know,
I came to Piros with the idea of rethinking my future,
and to see whether I had a book in me.'

'And have you?' he asked quietly.

'I don't know yet. I didn't write much for the first
part of the holiday, and then I—'

'Met me?' he finished slowly.

'Yes.'

'I see.'

'And one other thing,' she blurted out. 'My editor
happened to *trick* me into talking about you. I was

upset and she gave me brandy and kindness and asked
me all about you, and all the time she had a tape-
recorder going! I certainly did not go to the Press
willingly about you!'

He muttered something violent beneath his breath,
the black eyes boring into her, before looking down
to study his hands, so that his expression was shielded
from her.

There was a moment's silence. He doesn't care, she
thought. Nothing you say will make any difference.
She bit her lip, staring sightlessly into the blur of
traffic, before returning her attention defiantly to his
dark gaze which was now fixed on her face once
more. 'Anyway, none of that matters. I don't work
there any more, do I?' Or anywhere, for that matter—
which didn't bode well for her future once that
Constantine had tired of her. She had tried to make
her voice deliberately bright but she knew that it
sounded put on, and he frowned at her, his lips parting
very slightly, and Jade's eyes were drawn to them,
and he watched her, his own gaze flickering down to
her lips. I want him, thought Jade unhappily. How
can I stop myself from wanting him? How is it possible to want a man who can treat you so appallingly?
Perhaps that's why I've never fallen for anyone before—perhaps I'm a masochist!

An uneasy silence descended and she had to concentrate very hard not to stare at his long legs; sitting
with her own knees held primly closed together, she
tried to force herself not to think about him, about
the way that he had brought her to that heart-stopping

climax yesterday afternoon on the sofa. But it was no good, the memories of it were too intense.

And he could feel it, too—she could sense that from the awkwardly tense way in which he held himself. A brittle stillness enveloped them both as the sexual tension grew. And Jade grew madder and madder with herself. How could she *possibly* still fancy him? The man was a brute!

She could have wept with relief when the car drew up outside her flat. 'Stop right here,' she said coldly. 'This is where I live.'

But, infuriatingly, he followed her inside, pushing his way through the couple of reporters who remained, ignoring all their called pleas for a photo, and slamming the door shut behind them. Once inside, he prowled around, those intelligent dark eyes taking in the simple surroundings—the white walls, the brightly coloured rugs, and, on the wall in pride of place, the water-colour she'd bought on Piros before she'd met him, showing the shaded, narrow streets with the tantalising azure flash of sky which glimmered through one of the arches.

He went to stand beneath it.

'A good choice,' he remarked sagely. 'I know the artist well.'

'I suppose you employ him?' she asked brittly.

'Her,' he corrected brutally. 'And no, I do not.'

Pain, fierce, sharp, unwilling and debilitating—punched at the pit of her stomach. Was the artist who had produced this as exquisite as her painting, with eyes as black as his and hair like the night? Tears threatened to sting the back of her eyes.

'I'll get my things,' she said, and scooted off to the bedroom before she made a fool of herself. Once there, she packed a suitcase full of clothes, hesitating as her gaze halted on the manila envelope on her dressing table. It contained the rough draft of her first chapter. She moved away, then hovered back again, torn with indecision.

If she really *was* going to go through with marrying Constantine, then what was she proposing to do while he went out to work? Surely this was an ideal time to complete the book?

She moved back and picked up the envelope, thrusting it to the bottom of her suitcase, when some sixth sense told her that the bedroom door had opened, and that Constantine had walked silently into the room. She didn't turn round, stayed looking at the suitcase, afraid to look at him, vulnerable in such an intimate setting as her bedroom. 'I'm almost ready.'

'Are you?' he said softly.

He was behind her; she could hear the soft rise and fall of his breathing.

'Please wait outside,' she said shakily, but now she could feel his warm breath on her neck, feel the strong hands at her waist, firmly turning her to face him, and the black ice-fire in his eyes almost blinded her. How could she stay immune to the stark, dark passion so evident in that cruelly handsome face? A passion that he had awakened in *her*; a passion of such strength and intensity that it terrified her.

And excited her beyond belief.

'I'm almost ready,' she said again, foolishly.

'Ready for what?' he queried softly. 'For this?' He

bent his head to plant a soft, soft kiss on her neck, and her body was drawn towards his with a trembling yearning.

'Please don't,' she whispered.

'But you want me to. You're ready for me.' One finger trickled with sensitive awareness to find the tip of her breast, and he pressed it with delicate precision, drawing attention to the fact that it was hard and hot and ready for him. Just as he'd said.

'Don't you?' And then he did take her in his arms, but he didn't kiss her, just held her very, very tightly with his arms wrapped around her shoulders, imprisoning her, and Jade had never felt so safe in her whole life. She shut her eyes against his shoulders, recognising one of the truths behind his attraction for her.

That was it; the secret of how he physically overwhelmed her with such ease. It was because the insecurity and chaos of her upbringing had left her feeling rootless, and because she had never met a man like him before. Someone so strong; so sure. Someone you could depend on; lean on.

But she couldn't lean on him, not really. He was motivated to marry her not by an urge to protect her, but through some outmoded concept of 'honour', and a physical ache for her.

That was all.

She should pull away, but the powerful warmth of his embrace held her to him more securely than any chains of metal could have done.

'Let me go,' she whispered weakly against his neck.

'Not yet. I have a much better idea. Let's go to

bed. Let me undress you again. God, how I want to do that. It is too long since I've seen you naked, Jade. Just twenty-four hours and yet not a second has gone by when I haven't thought about how it felt to have you naked and helpless beneath me, gasping with delight as I filled you—your body arching as you cried out your climax. Do you know, I didn't sleep at all last night for thinking about it, not at all. It was like a fever,' he whispered in a voice husky with hunger. 'I want to make love to you as with no other woman.'

Jade swallowed; unbearably and shamefully tempted. 'But your brother and chauffeur are outside waiting in the car.'

'Let them wait!' He pulled her closer. 'They can wait all night for all I care.'

She could feel the hard throb between his legs, and oh, she wanted to reach out and touch him there, she wanted to know and explore every gorgeous inch of him. 'But they'll know exactly what we're doing—' Her own voice sounded husky.

'I don't care!' he murmured against her hair. 'I care for nothing other than making love to you—'

She pulled away from him, her green eyes lighting with triumph as she saw the ache of frustration etching lines onto his handsome face. 'But we didn't make love yesterday! Did we, Constantine? We had, as you so charmingly put it, ''good sex'', and do you know, I regret every single minute of it! For two pins I'd like to have the gumption to call your bluff and tell you to get the hell out of here, because I honestly

can't imagine that *anyone* would threaten the liveli-
hood of a group of old men by sacking them—'

'Try me,' he taunted softly.

Jade shook her head, saw him watch the blonde
hair shimmering in angry tendrils over her shoulders.
'No, I shan't bother. You aren't just anyone—you're
ruthless enough to do anything. But let me tell you
one thing—we haven't made love and we aren't *going*
to make love, either—and if that makes you frustrated, then that's great!'

He gave her a cruel, mocking smile. 'Want to bet?'
he queried softly, as his eyes alighted on her strained,
pinched complexion. 'I'm not the only one feeling
frustrated around here, am I, Jade?'

Ignoring that, Jade drew her shoulders back and
continued to berate him. 'And let me tell you something else—that good sex might be enough for you,
Constantine, but it certainly isn't enough for me! And
now, if you'd like to pick up my suitcase, I really
don't want to keep Stavros and your driver waiting
any longer!'

And, so saying, her nose held as snootily aloft as
she could manage, Jade swept out of the flat.

CHAPTER EIGHT

JADE followed Constantine into the Garden Suite, keeping her eyes deliberately averted from the butter-coloured sofa. Talk about an ever-present reminder of her appalling surrender to his cold-blooded lovemaking; it made her cheeks flame just to think about it! And her heart race with humiliating irregularity.

She glanced down at her bright blue wristwatch. It was now almost five o'clock, and she was as weary as could be.

He loosened his tie and went to pour himself a glass of mineral water. 'Would you like one?'

Jade shook her head. 'No, thank you,' she answered stiffly.

He drank half the water and surveyed her slowly over the rim of his glass, from the tip of her head to her bare feet in their strappy sandals. 'I expect you'll want to freshen up. That's *your* room.' And the dark head was arrogantly nodded in the direction of a closed door. 'Over there.'

Let's hope there's a key to lock it, thought Jade. 'Thank you,' she replied automatically.

'I'll take you for dinner downstairs later. The food is excellent. Be ready at eight.'

It sounded far more tempting than it should have done, but she fought it. She remembered her assertiveness training. Start as you mean to go on. Maybe if she showed him her notoriously stubborn streak he might think twice about marrying her! 'That won't be necessary,' she said.

'I insist.'

'I'm not hungry.'

'So watch *me* eat.' The white teeth were bared and Jade shivered, reminded of a caged predator she'd once felt sorry for at Chessington Zoo. But *this* predator she didn't feel in the least bit sorry for!

'No, thank you.'

Slivers of ebony glittered with menace. 'So be it,' he said, in a voice so soft that she should have been reassured, and yet needles of ice were scraped with pinpoint accuracy up a spine which was suddenly cold and clammy. 'I'll allow you to play your little games with me, Jade—perhaps you look on it as some form of revenge at being forced into such an ill-conceived marriage to keep me at arm's length, when you know it causes us both nothing but frustration...'

Swine!

'But after the ceremony,' he vowed silkily. 'When you're legally *mine*...don't consider for a moment that I intend to let you play your shrinking virgin act with me—especially when we both know what a farce that particular act is.' He ended the sentence with a look of mocking contempt, but before Jade could even formulate an angry retort Constantine completely took the wind out of her sails by sauntering into his own room and shutting the door behind him, leaving her staring after him, her mouth hanging open like a stranded fish, feeling completely outmanoeuvred.

She went into her bedroom and quickly set about hanging her clothes up in the wardrobe, unable however to stop herself from admiring her surroundings. The room was just lovely, with an unmistakable air of quietly restrained luxury.

After she'd had the longest, most luxurious bath of her life, Jade deliberately stayed in her bedroom, determined to remain there all evening if necessary. She heard Constantine moving around next door, then the sound of the door closing at around eight. Then silence.

She should have been pleased that he'd taken her at her word, had left her alone and gone out to dine, but in reality she was absolutely *seething*! Which infuriated her.

Because why on earth was she wasting her time wondering just who he *was* dining with? What did she care?

Then she started to get very hungry indeed. It was all very well making a point, but Constantine wasn't even around to see her making it! And she hadn't eaten for what seemed like hours.

Jade resisted the temptation to chew on her fingernails. In books the heroines always seemed to go for days without food, so why couldn't *she* be like that? Any minute now, if she didn't get something in the way of sustenance, she might just be tempted to start gnawing at the hearth rug!

She picked up the telephone.

'Yes, madam?'

'Er—is it possible to order something to eat?'

'Certainly, madam.' Did the voice sound amused,

or was she just getting paranoid? 'Mr Sioulas said that you'd probably be feeling hungry.'

Swine!

But after a steak sandwich and the most expensive half-bottle of claret on the menu Jade felt a good deal better, good enough to find herself whistling a little tune as she hurled herself under the duvet, wearing her best pair of black cami-knickers, and the flimsy little top which accompanied it—just dying for the opportunity of fighting Constantine off when he came in from dinner.

Her next recollection was waking up at mid-morning and throwing on a matching black satin wrap to wander mid-yawn into the drawing-room, her hand raking back through the tousled blonde disarray of her hair to find Constantine, fully and immaculately dressed, as though he was going to an appointment in the city.

And Jade couldn't help the powerful pang which wrenched at her heart at the sudden and utterly devastating sight of him first thing in the morning.

The olive face was impassive, the black eyes secretive, but there was no mistaking the flash of hunger which lit them as they alighted on her semi-clothed state. 'Good morning. You slept well, I trust?'

Was that a twitch of amusement she saw at the corners of his mouth? She found herself wanting to demand what time he'd come in, why he hadn't come in to...oh, for heaven's sake, was she *mad*?

'Very well, thank you.'

'I've rung for some coffee.' He glanced at his

watch. 'I'm afraid that I shan't be able to join you, as I have a meeting to attend.'

Jade shrugged, feigning nonchalance, trying to convince herself that if he *had* joined her she'd be eager for him to be away. He was just using subtle psychology, that was all, probably following that old adage—what was it they said? 'Treat them mean, and keep them keen'. Well, he was in for a shock if he thought she was going to fall for that one!

He left minutes later, and Jade was left to fill up her day. In the event she had a wonderful day. All the time she'd lived in London and she'd never even been to St Paul's Cathedral, Westminster Abbey, the Tower...so she set off sightseeing with a vengeance.

But when she arrived back in the suite at just after four o'clock it was to find Constantine waiting for her, pacing the floor like an expectant father and resembling a caged panther even more strongly. As the door closed behind her, she saw the two big hands clench beside the muscular shafts of his thighs, the knuckles white, as though it were only through the most supreme effort that he didn't physically manhandle her.

'Where the hell have you *been*?' he demanded, before she'd barely closed the door behind her.

Jade knew enough about people to know when they had reached the end of their tether. 'Sightseeing,' she answered, frowning.

'*Sightseeing*?' He made it sound as though it warranted a gaol sentence. Black eyebrows knitted together in two formidable dark slashes. 'How?'

'Well, first you buy your ticket, and then you—'

'Silence!' he bellowed. 'I mean—how did you get there?'

Jade stared back in confusion. 'Well, by Tube, of course!'

He swore long and profoundly in his native tongue; incomprehensible to Jade, but it wasn't difficult to get his drift. 'You little fool!' he ground out in English, just in case she'd missed the message.

Jade looked up at him, her green eyes troubled. He sounded seriously worried. 'What have I done?' she asked in confusion—had she forgotten to pull the door shut? Had the suite been burgled while she'd been out?

He shook his head impatiently. 'Do you not realise that, as my fiancée, you are now the target for all kinds of lunatics?'

'What,' she ventured, 'exactly are you talking about?'

'I am talking about *kidnap*!' he emphasised harshly, then nodded grimly as he saw her wide-eyed look. 'Yes. It happens. Your clothes were here, and you were... I thought...' His face blackened with a terrifying rage again. 'In future you will use the car and the driver I have provided for you. Do you understand?'

She'd never seen a man so angry before; he was almost shaking with it. It was frightening to see someone who she had imagined to have an unbreakable control, to be that close to losing it completely. And he was intelligent enough for his fears to have some rational explanation to them, rather than just the nebulous fears of the over-cautious. Jade found a wave of sympathy washing over her as she registered the sharply defined lines which divided the very rich from the ordinary person. A life haunted by the threat of abduction. She might resent him for forcing her into marriage, yes, but not enough to send him over the edge.

'I should have left a note,' she said quietly. 'I won't do that again.' Then, to divert him, 'Shall we have some tea—I'm absolutely parched?'

He stared at her for a long, long moment, and then some spark fired at the depths of the coal-black eyes, something very like reluctant humour lifted one corner of his mouth.

'Tea?' he echoed faintly.

With equal reluctance, Jade smiled back. She could get quite used to seeing him look ever so slightly nonplussed, she thought. 'Yes, tea,' she reiterated. 'And if you spare me your "you English and your tea", speech, then I won't tell you that Greek coffee has the consistency of mud!'

He laughed then. 'But that's not true, is it, Jade? As I recall, you *loved* Greek coffee—'

She quickly turned away to pretend to look out of the window, afraid to speak, shaken with a strange, debilitating sadness and precariously close to tears at the intimate sound of that simple little memory. It was also, she realised, the first time she'd heard him laugh since the magical time they'd spent together on the island, when he hadn't seemed to stop laughing. In fact, he had marvelled about it at the time—that she had the ability to make him laugh, almost...as though that in itself were a rare commodity.

'I'll go and freshen up,' she said hastily, grateful that he said nothing, but aware of his watchful eyes on her retreating back.

When Jade went back out into the sitting-room, the tray of tea had arrived, and Constantine was stretched out in one of the armchairs, his eyes closed. His long legs were elegantly sprawled in front of him and there were lines of fatigue etched deep on the craggy features. Just for that one brief moment she was reminded of her own father; a million years away from Constantine in lifestyle perhaps, but looking similarly exhausted as he battled to earn the kind of money which would support the spending habits of his extravagant wife. A battle he had finally lost.

Silent though she was, the moment her foot went down on the soft carpet Constantine's eyes flickered open immediately, and Jade's senses prickled as she was caught up in the compelling blackness of his gaze.

'You look tired,' she said, without thinking.

His eyebrows were raised fractionally as if surprised by her solicitude. 'Yes. Your tea should revive me.'

'For what?'

His hand moved to rub wearily at the back of his neck. 'I have a business dinner.'

He said it with a quiet acceptance which caused her to look at him with new eyes. Suddenly she saw through to the loneliness and isolation of the tycoon, the omnipotent head of a vast organisation. Maybe there'd never been anyone in his life to tell him to slow down. She tried to dampen down another rush of definitely unwarranted sympathy. 'Do you *have* to go out on business tonight?'

'Why?' The voice was mocking, and the black eyes flickered over her watchfully. 'Are you offering me a more attractive alternative?'

Jade didn't react as she sat down in front of the tea-tray. 'I merely meant that you look as though you could do with a good night's sleep.'

'But I'm not going to get one, am I?' he queried silkily. 'Not when I know that you're right next door to me.'

'But you slept OK last night,' she pointed out.

'Did I?' he parried. 'Are you quite sure about that?'

'Tea?' asked Jade, a fixed smile upon her face as she picked up the heavy silver teapot, thinking rather hysterically that she sounded like one of the characters from a comic farce.

'Thanks.' He took the cup that she offered him, adding a wafer-thin slice of lemon, and for a while the scrumptious contents of the tray were enough to take her mind off their sleeping arrangements. Jade bent her golden head over the various plates as she busily examined and began selecting contents from the assortment of dishes on the tray.

'Mmm!' she murmured enthusiastically, slightly embarrassed when she looked up into a pair of bemused black eyes. 'I haven't had a cream tea for years!' she found herself explaining lamely.

'Haven't you?' He smiled. 'Me neither. Cholesterol be damned! Pass me one of those scones, please.'

In the end, it proved a surprisingly companionable meal as they both ladled thick home-made strawberry jam on to the fluffy scones, and compounded the damage by adding big spoonfuls of clotted cream.

Jade was absolutely starving and Constantine seemed amused by her delicate greed. 'Good?'

It was terribly easy to like him when he was in this kind of benign, indulgent mood, she thought. He'd been like that when she'd first met him and now, as then, she found it impossible not to return his rare smile. 'Mmm,' she murmured with satisfaction, as she leaned back in the armchair and stretched her arms above her head. 'That was delicious—I feel absolutely full.'

But with an abrupt movement he put his cup down on to the table. 'There are a number of things we must discuss.' His voice seemed to have assumed its habitually gritty quality, and their earlier mood of something resembling camaraderie was immediately broken.

Jade sat upright and took a sip of her tea. 'Such as?'

'Who you wish to come to our wedding.'

'You mean I have a choice?'

The black eyes flashed a silent warning. 'I mean that I have no intention of letting your ex-colleagues provide a ''scoop''—but that if you wish your parents to come, then obviously—'

'No,' cut in Jade quickly.

His eyes narrowed. 'You're quite sure?'

On the island they had not, she realised, done more than merely skate over their family life—he knew that she was an only child, and she knew that he had a brother and a stepsister. Her own reluctance to talk about it had been due to the highly unsatisfactory nature of her early years. Now, for the first time she began to wonder whether his own reluctance stemmed from a similar source.

'You don't wish for either of your parents to come?' he asked curiously.

'No.'

He frowned. 'I see.'

He didn't, not really. Jade realised that her bald answer must sound uncaring. Not that it could possibly matter if he thought her an unfeeling daughter. He couldn't possibly think any worse of her than he already did. But even so, she decided to elaborate, for her pride's sake more than any need to confide in him. 'My father is dead—'

'I'm sorry,' he said quietly, and a totally new expression came into his face.

She rushed on, not wanting to be affected by the sympathy which had softened the dark eyes. 'My mother is on her own—she lives in Devon. Her health is—frail. The journey would be too much for her.'

'Even if I arrange for a private jet?'

Jade swallowed. Even if he arranged for the reception to take place in the presence of the Queen, it would make no difference. 'Thank you, but no.' She saw the puzzlement darkening his eyes, and suddenly she wanted the score evened—why had he never talked about his own family? 'And your family?' she challenged. 'Will they be attending?'

'No,' he said determinedly. 'Just Stavros, as witness.'

'I see.' She put her cup and saucer down, understanding immediately his own reasons for not wanting a family celebration. Because why bother when the wedding was nothing but a farce? To have his family come dance at it would make further mockery of it. And yet, didn't it hurt more than a little bit to imagine a cold little signing of papers in some anonymous little register office somewhere, when she'd once imagined an enchanting union with them whispering their heartfelt vows to each other?

Jade rose to her feet, feeling drained, and knowing that her face was blanched of all colour. 'If that will be all,' she said, in the manner of a secretary speaking to her boss, rather than that of a prospective bride speaking to her husband-to-be. 'Then I'll go to my room.'

He inclined his dark head, but said nothing, and Jade, with the prospect of another long, empty evening ahead of her, found herself wishing that he had asked her to join him tonight, at his business dinner.

She would have said no, of course, but it would be nice to have been asked.

CHAPTER NINE

JADE, refusing to cower in her bedroom as though she'd done something wrong, was sitting in one of the armchairs watching the television—though she couldn't have described a single second of the programme she had been watching—when Constantine emerged from his room, ready for dinner. He had showered and changed and was wearing the most exquisitely cut suit in deepest blue, and a dark blue and white spotted tie of raw silk knotted around the strong sinews of his neck. The dark wavy hair was almost dry, but a tendril had fallen on to the wide and aristocratic forehead, and this one untidy deviation in an otherwise immaculate appearance somehow added even more to his physical appeal. As if he needed anything to do that, thought Jade ruefully.

He stood looking down at her for an instant, the lean face indifferent, but not as cold as before. 'Get some sleep,' he instructed. 'There are dark shadows beneath your eyes. Goodnight, Jade.'

She watched as the door closed quietly behind him and found herself again wishing that he *had* asked her to have dinner with him. But what would have been the point? Too many cosy get-togethers like the one they had shared this afternoon over tea would surely be detrimental? That way spelt danger, and the threat

133

of her succumbing to the subtle web of charm he could spin. And painted a false picture of him. Because the way he'd behaved while sharing scones with her was about as far removed as it was possible to be from the man who had ruthlessly seduced her, then taken over the newspaper and threatened to boot out half the staff if she didn't agree to his proposal of marriage.

Jade continued to try and concentrate on the documentary before giving up; and, going into her bedroom, she had a quick shower, then changed into an Edwardian nightgown of fine lawn, brushing her newly washed hair and leaving it hanging loose all the way down her back. She read a book, rang down for a salade Niçoise and a glass of milk, and after she'd eaten and brushed her teeth she took the book to bed with her to read.

It was a story which a few weeks ago she would have thoroughly lost herself in, but tonight the words on the pages bobbed around like midges, and eventually she gave up the struggle and turned out the light.

She thought she'd crash out as soon as her head hit the pillow, but sleep was surprisingly slow in coming. Behind closed eyes, she kept seeing Constantine's face in its many guises—stark with passion, dark with a fiercely controlled rage, exhausted and weary, and—this afternoon—like a rare jewel, the sight of his uninhibited laughter again. Pathetic really, to think how much that had warmed her in response.

Sleep came, but it was the deep yet restless sleep

which accompanied a troubled mind. Jade found herself far away from the comfort of her luxury hotel bed, poised instead in the doorway of an empty house, her panama school-hat on her head, the sunlight streaming in from the bright day behind her, even though the house was strangely dark. And cold.

'Mummy?' she called out tentatively into the silence. 'Mummy?' But the silence continued, growing more vast and more awesome by the second as she realised the implication of the sealed letter addressed to her father which lay on the hall table. '*No!*' she screamed. '*No!*'

'Jade!'

The deep voice penetrated her consciousness. Warm, strong hands were on her shoulders, shaking her awake.

'No!' she screamed again, and then fell into the blissful safety of an embrace, but a masculine embrace, not her mother's embrace. Her mother had never embraced her...

'Sssh.' His voice was strangely comforting, but it seemed to come from a long way away. 'Sssh. It's a dream, *agape mou*,' he murmured into her hair. 'Nothing but a dream.'

But if this was a dream, then she never wanted to wake up. Here, half awake in his arms, existed a kinder reality, an infinitely more attractive reality than the true circumstances of why they were together. In dreams, wishes could come true...

She didn't want to open her eyes; she wanted her dream to stay, never wanted to leave it. She allowed his arms to tighten around her, knowing that she had found what she wanted. She wanted this: Constantine's protection and Constantine's possession.

But he was breaking into the tender and blissful disorientation she felt at being within the strong circle of his arms. Breaking in with a question she didn't want to even acknowledge, for to do that would be to resurrect the unbearable pain of her childhood.

'Jade,' he whispered softly. 'What is it that troubles you? Is it the marriage?'

The marriage? Right at this moment, with her emotions swamping her senses, marriage to him seemed like a bedrock of heavenly security. If only the rock didn't happen to be built on sand...

'Is it the marriage?' he asked again, and she shook her head, her silky hair fanning over that warm, strong neck as she did so, and she heard him sigh.

'What, then?'

She shook her head.

'*Tell* me,' he urged her. 'I can help.'

Who could resist such a soft appeal from such a normally steely man? Certainly not Jade, half asleep, and half...half in love with the man... 'It was just a dream. I'm being silly—'

'Let me be the judge of that. Something made you dream badly. What was it?'

It came out in a rush then, like a bottle of champagne which had been shaken vigorously. 'When we talked earlier—'

'About the wedding?'

'Yes, but not that.'

'What then?' he urged, his voice deep and husky.

Jade submitted to its command. 'It was—when we were talking about my mother...' Her voice tailed off, ashamed, helpless.

'*Tell* me! I need to know.'

With her eyes still closed, she could picture it as though it were yesterday—the clarity of the un-welcome memory had not diminished over the years. 'I don't know what made me mention it. I was ten and my parents had taken me on holiday to Brighton. My mother went—' Jade's voice faltered. 'Out. It was pouring with rain, and the hotel was tiny. My father took me to a café for lunch. I think the waitress felt sorry for us, because she let us stay, and we sat there all afternoon, playing I-spy and watching the rain run down the windows.' Snake-like rivulets. Like tears. 'Then we went back,' she finished flatly.

'And your mother was waiting for you?' he asked curiously.

'That time, yes.' Her mother's voice had been slurred from too many cocktails at lunchtime, her cracked voice shrilling insults at her bewildered fa-ther. It had been their last family holiday; Jade had not known it at the time, but the cracks had been starting to widen irreparably even then.

'And the next time?' he prompted discerningly.

That soft, dark voice could coax blood from a stone, thought Jade as she found herself nestling fur-ther into the beating warmth of his chest. 'One day— oh, it must have been a year later—she didn't come back. She'd—she'd—met another man.' The passing of the years hadn't dulled the pain of memory. 'I came home from school one day to find that she'd—gone. I didn't see her for years, not until after my father died last year. I rarely see her now, and even now the relationship is…rocky…'

'I'm not surprised!' Constantine's eyes narrowed in disbelief. 'She *left* you? She left her child?'

'Is that so inconceivable to you?'

His voice sounded savage. 'Of course it is. The bond between mother and child is unbreakable.'

'Then you're very lucky, Constantine. That your mother wouldn't have dreamed of leaving you.'

He shook his head. 'Not in the way you speak of, no. She died when I was twelve.'

She opened her eyes immediately, struck to the very core by some indefinable note in his voice. It was the first time she had ever seen any trace of vulnerability in the severe lines of his face. No wonder he never talked of his family. 'I'm so sorry,' she whispered. 'I didn't mean to—'

He briefly laid a finger over his lips, shook his head. 'I know that.'

But his voice held no recrimination and the darkness gave her the courage to question him further. 'And your father?' she ventured.

In the shadowy half-light, she saw the faint outline of that hard mouth twist, though whether it was with pain or derision she couldn't guess. 'It broke him,' he said simply. 'It was a love match, you see. But he…' There was a pause.

'He?' she whispered.

Now there was definitely derision there. 'He married again a year later.'

Jade let out a sigh. 'Why?'

'Because he felt that Stavros and I needed a mother—especially Stavros, who was so young. As if *anyone* could have taken her place,' he said bitterly. 'Instead he found himself a wife and a stepdaughter whose sole purpose in life seemed to be the elimination of his fortune.'

She said nothing; nothing *to* say—but for answer she let her lips drift upwards to kiss his cheek, very very gently, and she heard him softly expel the air from his lungs.

'Now—' And he moved his hands purposefully to her shoulders, as if to distance her, but she couldn't bear to leave the safe haven of his embrace, here, where childhood scars were eased and soothed. And so she nestled closer into his chest, pushed her cheek against the strong column of his neck, his scent invading her nostrils and overwhelming her with its distinctive masculine aroma.

She felt his heart quicken beneath her breast, felt his arms imperceptibly tighten around her shoulders, and still he said nothing, just started to stroke her hair with a rhythmic caress which had her sighing with pleasure.

'Go back to sleep,' he urged her quietly.

She said nothing in response to this, but she felt her body answering for her—in the thrust of her nipples which had begun to nudge insistently against that hair-roughened chest, in the hot ache between her thighs and in her hungry lips which lay passively against his neck, but in whose centre beat an eager pulse which longed for his kiss above all else.

She heard him mutter something beneath his breath, felt him shift a little as if to move away from her. 'I must go,' he said with quiet emphasis.

But Jade did not want to be alone with her fears and her insecurities and her nightmares. More than that, she did not want him to go. Not tonight. Tonight she needed Constantine, as she needed no other. She laid her soul bare for him to see, and in doing so she felt completely empty. She needed Constantine to cover her, to fill her, to make her whole once more.

'Don't leave me,' she whispered.

'I must.'

She gave a tiny shake of her head. 'Stay.'

There was a sense of urgency in the deep voice. 'But if I stay, you know what will happen?'

'Yes.'

'Better another night.' She could hear his reluctance, but in her need, she chose to disregard it. 'When you aren't so…' He paused, as if searching for a gentle put-down.

He was giving her a way out, but she didn't want to take it. 'When I'm not so—what?' she whispered throatily. 'You told me you wanted my body; told me you wanted to slake your desire until it was no more.' Her eyes fluttered open to surprise a look of such naked, feral heat which burned in the depths of his eyes, but she began to tremble. 'Are you telling me now that you weren't speaking the truth?'

It was as though her own tremor had set up an answering response in his, for she felt a shudder rake through the length of his body.

'Were you?' she whispered. 'Speaking the truth?'

'You know I was,' he ground out. 'But then I spoke in anger. Tonight there is no anger between us; tonight...' His words tailed off.

'Tonight?' she prompted, in a husky whisper.

She caught the gleam of steel from behind the narrowed eyes. 'You are vulnerable tonight, *agape mou*. And your heart is aching—'

'Then take that aching away,' she said softly, astounded by her own daring, but urged on by needs which could not be constrained by the mere convention that the man should be the seducer, and not the woman.

There was a pause; she could almost hear him battling with his conscience—if a conscience he had.

But how could he have a conscience which was troubling him now, after he had taken her so cold-bloodedly and without compunction the other day?

Could it be because she knew and he knew that if he came to her tonight it would not just be 'good sex' as he had so ruthlessly said after that frantic coupling on the sofa just next door? Tonight, her emotions were too raw and exposed; she had laid herself open to him honestly, as he had to her, and she knew, with some kind of unerring instinct, that tonight he would have to respond to her in kind. With his heart.

If he came to her. She closed her eyes, prepared for him to take his leave of her.

'Open your eyes,' he commanded. 'And look at me.'

Weakly, she obeyed, fearful of what she would read in his, but she saw his own need shining through the dark waters of that ebony stare.

For a long moment, he stared down at her, and then, slowly, lingeringly, began to kiss her mouth as if he had all the time in the world.

It was a kiss so delectably sweet that she started to tremble again; she had never believed that a kiss could be so poignant and so tender. The last time she had lain in his arms like this, he had kissed her with all the masculine authority of the dominant sex, had branded her with fiery kisses which led straight into the blaze of sexual consummation. But this kiss—it was infinitely more subtle; and in its way far more distracting. She felt her eyelids flutter to a close again.

'No!' came the soft command, the accent very slightly emphasised. 'Watch me now, as I watch you. Drink in my body, Jade, as I do yours, and see the effect you're having on me. Keep your eyes open all the time, and watch me while I love you.'

Her gaze ran hungrily over him. He was still wearing the suit he'd had on earlier, and as if he'd captured her thoughts he gave a small, brief smile before momentarily releasing her to shrug out of the jacket where it fell to the floor with a whisper. He sat, motionless on the edge of the bed, his eyes fixed firmly on hers, compelling, waiting.

With trembling fingers she reached out to unknot the silk of his tie then to pull it off and discard it, so that it joined the jacket on the floor. Suddenly shy, she made as if to move her hand away, but he stopped her with a shake of his head.

'Continue,' he murmured. 'I like it.'

Jade swallowed as she slowly unbuttoned the shirt, until it revealed the olive-skinned torso, shadowed by the hair which grew there. He took the palm of her hand, laid it flatly over his heart, and she heard the dull thundering of his heart which hammered out his desire for her.

He took the shirt off, then pushed her gently back against the pillows before turning his attention to the fine white cotton of her nightgown. It was full of detail; she'd bought it for just that reason—tiny tucks and pleats, and a myriad minute pearl buttons, which he began to snap open, one by one.

'So English,' he murmured. 'So very, very English.' He peeled the nightgown over her head and threw it aside, staring down at her, his eyes blazing as he drank in her nakedness. She shut her eyes hurriedly; afraid to look into his eyes for fear of what she might read there.

'Open them,' he commanded again. 'There is no need for shyness.' His hand slipped to his belt, which he unbuckled with unhurried ease, so that he somehow managed to instil infinite grace into the act of stripping off the rest of his clothes, until he was as naked as she and he climbed into the bed and pulled the sheet over both of them.

For a moment he lay above her, his desire pressing hard and full against the softness of her belly, and she breathed a sigh of delectable anticipation, her mouth curving into a soft smile of pleasure. His eyes narrowed momentarily with some unknown question as he stared down at her, and Jade knew the briefest surge of uneasiness, but it was dispelled as his arms went about her, their bodies moulding even closer and their lips fusing in a heady union which threatened to stop her heart.

CHAPTER TEN

IT WAS the most perfect night of her life, and one which Jade would remember for the rest of her life, no matter what happened between them afterwards.

Her instincts had been right; it had not been 'good sex'—it had been much, much more than that. Constantine had made love to her over and over again, she had lost count of the times she cried out her pleasure into the silence of the night, but when she awoke in the morning he was gone.

As if he'd never been there; not one scrap of clothing remaining to show that he'd spent the night in her arms. Nothing to show, but plenty to feel. And not just the aching deep inside her, or the tiny bruises of teeth-marks on her swollen breasts—the discovery that he was no longer there beside her produced both anger and pain. She recognised bitterly that on the two occasions he'd made love to her he'd cast her off afterwards with a ruthlessness which left her feeling nothing short of cheap.

And why not? What did she expect? Nothing had changed. He still believed that she had deliberately deceived him, had tried to seduce him into getting a story. He still believed she had kissed and told by giving her story to the *Daily View*.

What she didn't understand was why he had been

so reluctant to make love to her last night, after boasting to her that he intended to talk his way into her bed.

And why she had been so reluctant to let him go back to his own room, after everything *she'd* said. Was it just that the man was capable of throwing all her senses into overdrive, or did it go deeper than that? Was she still, as she suspected—still in love with him?

Damn Constantine Sioulas, thought Jade, as she pulled on a bathrobe and padded through into the shower.

Half an hour later, she had just finished brushing her hair when there was a knock at the door. It was Stavros.

He gave her what appeared to be a genuine smile, which she returned, hoping against hope that she didn't resemble a woman who'd just spent the night being ravished by his brute of a brother. How many of those had Stavros seen over the years? she wondered. *I don't want to be just like all the others*, she thought, with a pang of regret for her *stupid*, impetuous behaviour—pleading with him to stay the night with her while knowing that there could only be one outcome if he did. And didn't men—particularly proud and possessive Greek men like Constantine— only respect women who fought them off? She sighed. What a mess everything was.

'Hello, Stavros.' She was *not* going to ask.

Was she?

'Er—do you happen to know where Constantine went?'

Shaking his head, Stavros gave a broad grin and a wink as if to say that her question as to his brother's whereabouts was entirely predictable. 'He didn't tell me—but he sure as hell looked *mad* when I saw him first thing.'

Her heart sank.

He narrowed his eyes—eyes like splinters of jet, so like Constantine's own, and yet lacking something of their enigmatic brilliance. 'Did you two have a fight or something?' he mused.

Not unless the dictionary version of fighting had undergone a radical change overnight. 'Um—not exactly.'

Stavros shook his head. 'What is it that you do to him, Jade? He's been like a crazy man since he met you, you know?'

'Yes,' answered Jade drily. Crazy was right. Sane men did not generally blackmail women they considered had wronged them into marrying them as some primitive form of revenge!

Stavros gave her a quick look. 'I know he's not always easy,' he began.

Jade almost laughed. 'You're certainly given to understatement!'

Stavros shook his head. 'He hasn't always had it easy himself, you know. People think that the money is an answer to everything, but it isn't.'

She knew that. She remembered his fear that she'd been kidnapped, his apparent isolation as he'd sat fatigued in his chair yesterday evening. But that wasn't really relevant to *their* situation.

But Stavros seemed to be possessed of a great need to present Constantine in a more favourable light. 'You know that our mother died?'

'Yes, he told me.' Her voice softened. 'You were very young?'

'She died giving birth to me,' said Stavros, and her heart went out to him as she heard the emptiness and confusion in his voice. 'I don't think my father ever got over it, really—even when he remarried—no, *especially* when he remarried. So Tino became like father and mother to me. He was only twelve.' He hesitated, the hero-worship there for her to hear as plain as day itself. 'Don't make the mistake, will you, Jade, of thinking that the harsh exterior you see is all there is?'

Jade said nothing, just stared at Stavros sadly. If only he knew. He was romantically, foolishly labouring under the misapprehension that she and Constantine were marrying for love. *She* might be in love, she realised with a sinking resignation but *he* certainly wasn't.

Stavros cut into her thoughts. 'What time do you want to leave?'

'Leave?' she echoed in confusion.

'Sure. He's left the car and the driver at your disposal.'

'What for?' Jade blinked, then remembered how he'd flipped because she'd trailed around London on her own yesterday, on the Tube. Perhaps he meant that she should play the tourist again.

And then another thought occurred to her, a thought which, surprisingly, she found infinitely more disturbing. What if Constantine had come to his senses after their night spent together—wouldn't that explain his hurried departure? Perhaps now that he'd had a night of passion with her he had slaked the lust he felt for her, and had decided to call the whole thing off. And perhaps the car was there to take her home to her flat, and out of his life forever.

Stavros cleared his throat. 'He said you should go and choose your wedding-gown. It's tomorrow, isn't it?'

Bang went her theory, and, infuriatingly, her heart accelerated! 'Oh, did he?'

'Mmm. You don't sound overjoyed.' Stavros eyed her speculatively. 'What's the matter? He's a good catch, my brother. Don't you know how many women have wanted to marry him?'

'I can imagine,' answered Jade acidly, then, seeing Stavros's almost hurt look of bemusement, she relented—it wasn't *his* fault that his brother was such a ruthless swine, after all!

Stavros frowned. 'You know that he hasn't invited our stepmother or her daughter?' He paused, and a fleeting narrow-eyed look crossed his face, making him look uncannily like his big brother.

Jade nodded. 'He told me.'

'Do you know why?'

Yes, she knew. Because they were just going

through the motions of a wedding, that's all—so why make it a farce by inviting all his relatives?

Stavros frowned. 'Marina—that's our stepmother—she won't particularly care one way or the other, but Eleni, that's her daughter—she's going to go absolutely *crazy*. She thinks the world of Tino.' He stared at Jade. 'Can't you make him invite her?'

'I don't think I can, Stavros.' She didn't imagine that it was possible to make Constantine do anything which he didn't want to.

Yet it seemed that he still wanted the wedding to go ahead, even if it was going to be a small and rather hushed-up affair, and if that was the case then she needed a dress to wear. A woman had her pride, after all!

So Jade spent the day being ferried round different shops in the low, sleek car—watching people peer into the interior whenever it stopped at traffic lights, obviously hoping to see someone famous. Sorry to disappoint you, she thought wryly, as she leant back against the soft, luxurious leather. She really could get used to this kind of life, she decided regretfully, remembering her own rainswept waits at bus-stops.

In the end she bought a cream linen dress with a matching hat, which looked stunning without breaking the bank, since she determinedly refused every one of Constantine's charge cards which Stavros tried to press into her hand.

'Take them,' he insisted.

'I don't want them.'

Stavros shook his head mournfully. 'He'll be mad.'

Good! 'That's not my problem,' she shrugged.

'Maybe that's what he likes about you—that you make him so mad!'

If only he knew, mused Jade as she walked back through the revolving doors of the Granchester, purchases in hand.

Constantine was in their suite, and to Jade's quickly stifled dismay she noted that his face was unwelcoming and tense as she appeared in the doorway. She didn't know what she had expected after she had given herself to him so passionately last night, but it was certainly not this cold and intimidating face he presented. He gave her a brief, terse nod, but that was it. No smile, no kiss, no embrace, nothing to let on how close she thought they'd been during the night. But perhaps that closeness had all been in her naïve and fevered imagination. She was relatively innocent; he was not. The kind of rapturous response which she'd demonstrated as he'd made such superb love to her was probably par for the course where he was concerned. How many women had sobbed out their pleasure in his arms and had their tears wiped away with his supposedly tender kisses? she wondered painfully.

'I have the licence,' he announced dispassionately. 'We marry tomorrow.'

Jade vowed to match his icy politeness. 'The sooner it's done, the sooner this farce of a marriage can be finished.'

A fleeting look of anger distorted his features, making his eyes as black as ink. 'The days, perhaps. But not the nights,' he taunted softly. 'Do you not want those to go on forever? Or did my ears deceive me last night when you begged me not to stop?'

Jade's cheeks flushed hotly. What a louse he was, to bring that up in broad daylight. She met his gaze full on. 'I was overwrought last night, not surprisingly. But it's a mistake which I shan't make again,' she vowed fervently. Even if it killed her.

'No?' A mocking smile twisted his mouth. 'Forgive me if I find that somehow hard to believe, Jade. You're hungry for me all the time. Even now, while you profess to hate me so much.' And his eyes dipped insultingly to her breasts, which tingled and throbbed under his blatantly sexual scrutiny, and she turned away from him, horrified by the betraying response of her body.

'So do I take it you won't be joining me for dinner tonight?' he asked silkily.

'Correct!' she rapped out.

'Beauty sleep before we take our vows? I guess you need it.'

The implication was brutally clear—she certainly hadn't got very much sleep last night. Oh, *what* had possessed her? Why did the night play such cruel, deceptive tricks? Last night he had seemed like security personified, solid as a rock in the dark loneliness of her nightmare, comforting her and loving her with his body. While now he was a cold-faced stranger who eyed her with nothing but lust, making mockery of the binding intimacy she had imagined they'd shared. 'I'm going to my room,' she said icily, and turned her back on him, but halted at the curt command of his next words.

'The wedding takes place at ten. We leave here at a quarter to the hour.'

Jade hesitated, wondering just what agenda he was proposing for their wedding-night. 'And afterwards?' she asked, as coolly as she could.

'Afterwards we travel to Piros.'

The blistering heat hit Jade like a sledgehammer, and she was so exhausted that she allowed Constantine's hand to support her back. His black eyes remained impenetrable and his mouth was a tense, thin line as he helped her out of the small rowing boat which had brought them from his luxury yacht, now moored just off the island of Piros. Seeing the island where they'd been so happy sent shock-waves of regret through her, but she determinedly kept her face poker-straight as she stared at the contrast of the deep lapis lazuli of the sea lapping against the white sand.

They had spent the last twelve hours travelling, flying from Heathrow to Athens after the wedding, then being driven to Piraeus Harbour to board the yacht.

'Tired?' he asked softly, his eyes narrowed as he watched her gaze flicker round to where people sat drinking and eating in the tiny quayside tavernas. Hard to believe that a few short weeks ago the two of them had roamed the island, hand-in-hand and carefree.

Jade nodded, swallowing to try to dispel the stupid lump in her throat. The journey *had* been long, and tiring, but it was the emotional strain of her whole wedding-day which had left her feeling as weak as a kitten.

However much of a farce the ceremony might have been, she had still found it unbearably painful to go through the motions of the simple wedding service. To have to say 'I will' to Constantine, and then to have him slip the ring on to her finger, and act like it meant nothing to her, when quite clearly it did. But the worse had been to come. After the registrar had pronounced them husband and wife he had pulled her into his arms and told her that she looked exquisite, before kissing her thoroughly in front of the registrar and a grinning Stavros and Tony so that she was left quite dizzy and breathless.

Because it had all been a front—that much was obvious since for the rest of the journey he had lapsed into a terse and moody silence, punctuated only by curt enquiries as to whether she wanted food, drink, another cushion, to sleep or to read. 'Just let me know if there is anything that you want,' he had said eventually, in the same hard, cold voice.

She knew exactly what she wanted. She wanted all this to be real. She wanted, not politeness, not even passion. She wanted love.

And now they were on Piros she knew neither for how long, nor for what purpose.

She held her head stiffly, unaccustomed to the heavy style of French plait, still dressed with the fragrant white flowers which Constantine had insisted on ordering for their wedding. 'And how long do you anticipate we'll be staying?'

He stared out at the dark blue band of the horizon. 'That depends,' he answered obscurely.

'On?'

'A number of factors, but I do not intend to discuss them here. You are tired, Jade. I will take you to my home.'

My home, she observed. Very territorial.

Before she knew it he was strapping her into the same beaten-up old jalopy as he'd driven her around in when she'd met him. In view of what she now knew of his lifestyle, his choice of car seemed decidedly incongruous. 'Why do you drive this, when in London you have a limousine?' she asked curiously.

He changed gear with a smoothness which was amazing, considering that the car seemed to be on its last legs. 'That's city life,' he shrugged. 'The world I move in expects symbols which demonstrate status and wealth. So I play the game. But I'm not turned on by cars.'

'As long as they get you from A to B?'

He shrugged. 'You have it in one.'

'This one might take longer getting from A to B than most!'

He laughed. 'Sure. But this car's very special to me.'

The dusty silver-green of the fragrant cypresses began to appear and Jade wound the window down to sniff their evocatively warm scent. 'Why?' she asked, as she looked at the doorknob which hung on only by a prayer.

He drummed long, olive fingers on the steering-wheel. 'I won it.'

'How?'

He gave a wry smile. 'In a fight, I am ashamed to admit.'

'Different!' murmured Jade, but her interest was alive. He didn't, she realised, give away much of his past. 'Who did you win it from?'

There was a pause. She thought that either he hadn't heard her, or that he wasn't going to reply.

But then he did.

'It's a long story.'

'I like stories. Car journeys are designed for story-telling.'

At this he grinned, which he didn't do very often. And when he grinned he was thoroughly irresistible.

'I grew up and was educated in Athens,' he began. 'But I used to come to this island every summer—even after my father died. He grew up on an island like this, you see, and he wanted me to know some-thing of the life he'd had. A simple life. But I was the city boy; the rich boy—always the outsider.' He swerved to avoid a rock, muttering something in Greek, and Jade was afraid that he would clam up just when she felt sure that she was about to get some insight into what really made him tick.

'Don't stop,' she said quickly.

He gave her a brief, sideways stare. 'There was one boy in particular—his name was Kris.'

Kris. Somewhere in the back of her mind, the name rang a bell.

'Kris always took particular exception to my being here. His dislike grew worse over the years. He fancied himself with the ladies and—' He made a little shrugging movement with his shoulders as his voice tailed away, and Jade didn't have to be told what one of the problems must have been. Even if the boy had been an Adonis, he wouldn't have got a look-in with the ladies with Constantine around.

'And he was the leader of the other boys,' he continued. 'He used to challenge me to fight him and, when that wouldn't work, to goad me into fighting him.'

'But you wouldn't?'

'I don't fight for fun.'

Jade shivered, in spite of the violent heat of the day. 'What happened?'

'One day, he went too far. He picked on a boy younger than himself.'

'And you—?' prompted Jade, with horrified fascination, thinking that this was the stuff that adventure films were made of.

'I taught him a lesson. He'd just bought a car. We fought for it.'

'And you won, right?'

He shrugged; smiled. 'Naturally.'

'But why d'you keep it?'

His face went suddenly tense. 'Because, for a long time it was the hardest thing I'd ever had to fight for…' His voice tailed off on a strange note as he glanced across at her, then back to the road.

Jade swallowed. 'But was he—all right?'

He actually laughed. 'Not for a week or so, but yes, he was all right—what did you think I'd do— kill him?'

'I wouldn't put anything past you, Constantine!' she said with feeling, then turned to study his strong profile. 'So that was the end of a beautiful friendship, was it?'

He grinned. 'For a while. Then, years later, he came to apologise to me, and to seek my help.'

'Your help?'

'He wanted to set up a restaurant.'

'And you helped him?' she asked incredulously.

'Sure. It was a good business proposition. And it's better in life to have a friend than an enemy. As a matter of fact,' he said coolly, 'you've eaten there. Often.'

'I have?'

'Sure. Remember that first night when I took you out for dinner—'

As if she wouldn't remember every second of it for the rest of her life. She saw the proud tilt of his jaw and recalled what he'd said at the time. 'The owner owes me a favour'. Kris! Of course! He'd waited on them. Good grief!

The car had been ascending the hilly interior, and Jade could see the bright glitter of a large white building which clung to one of the hills like a child to its mother's hips. She remembered the way their eyes had met over the head of the child in the taverna. Something preordained had happened at that moment. She had fallen hopelessly in love with him, however crazy that might seem. And suddenly she knew that, whatever else happened between them, her fate had been decided for her in that one long, shared look. She knew with a chilling certainty that her love for him would simply never go away, for it was part of her now, as much a part of her as her limbs.

Doomed, she thought gloomily. To love a man who is going to use our brief marriage to try to rid himself of his desire for me. 'Is that where we're going?' she asked, pointing up at the house.

'It is.' His voice was mocking. 'You wanted a honeymoon, didn't you?'

'Not particularly!'

'Liar!' he taunted softly.

She wore nothing but a short, sleeveless lemon dress, and she became quickly aware that the pinkening flush to her skin which accompanied just the *thought* of a honeymoon was easily visible all over her neck and shoulders, as well as on her face.

'I rest my case,' he added, with cruel observation.

Did *nothing* escape him? 'Well, if you're expecting to consummate this so-called farce of a marriage, you'll have a very long wait!' She turned to him, her voice quiet but determined.

'Bravo!' he applauded. 'Brave words, Jade! Fighting words! And empty words!'

'We'll see,' she challenged fiercely, although she knew that her argument was seriously flawed, because he was right, she *did* want him—incessantly. But she was not going to…not again. To have a wild and passionate night of bliss and the next day for him to behave in that cold and contemptuous way, as if the night had been nothing. And because he could not have even the most scant regard for her if he considered that sex was her motivating force. How amused her ruthless blackmailer would be if he discovered that it was love…

The car drove off the main road and on to a small track, then bumped up to the white building over which the rich velvet hue of a magenta bougainvillaea bloomed royally.

Despite her inner conflict, Jade couldn't stop herself from drinking in her surroundings with pleasure as she stepped out of the car, but Constantine's attention was elsewhere, and she heard a terse exclamation as she saw him stride to the side of the building, where another vehicle was parked beneath the shade of a lemon tree.

A car which couldn't be more different from the beaten-up one which Constantine had driven here.

It was a large and long, gleaming silver Mercedes. Jade shuddered to think of the cost of bringing such a car to such a small island.

'Who's here?' she asked him.

'We have guests,' he bit out, in a voice which could have sliced through metal quiet easily.

At that moment there was a flurry of sound, and the front door was flung open and a woman, who Jade judged to be in her late twenties, stood on the shadowed step. She possessed the proud patrician features and the strong dark colouring which immediately marked her out as Greek. There was a small silence before she stepped from out of the shadows into the full glory of the brilliant sunlight which bounced in a blue-black dazzle off her gleaming hair.

She was simply beautiful, thought Jade with a sudden sinking of her heart, and she was dressed in a spotless cream silk dress and coiffured to perfection. But then she looked into the woman's face and almost started with shock at the message revealed there. Her dark, almond-shaped eyes glittered with undisguised hostility as she stared directly into Jade's face.

'Surprise!' she called, with a husky Greek inflexion, and started to move towards them, her arms held out in greeting, pointed scarlet nails like talons outstretched. 'Welcome home, Constantine!'

CHAPTER ELEVEN

THERE was a moment's silence before Constantine stepped forward, a polite smile on his face as the beautiful brunette caught his hands and they exchanged a kiss on each cheek.

Constantine turned to Jade. 'Jade, darling,' he said smoothly, and Jade almost started at his use of the unfamiliar endearment in English. 'You must let me introduce you to Eleni—my sister.'

'Oh, Constantine,' chided Eleni, batting superb black lashes which didn't need one scrap of mascara to emphasise them. 'There isn't a drop of shared blood between us. I'm your *step*sister. Remember?' The coldness re-entered her brown eyes as they flickered from Constantine's face to Jade.

'So *this* is your bride,' she said haughtily, and there was a theatrical pause. 'Not at *all* what I would have expected. Hello, Jade,' she gushed insincerely.

And I can be just as insincere, thought Jade as she pinned a bright smile onto her lips. 'Hello, I'm very pleased to meet you,' she said, holding out her hand and receiving a limp imitation of a handshake in return.

Eleni's head was perched to one side, like a watchful bird. 'You're so very *young*,' she observed.

'Twenty,' Jade defended, her misgivings growing

by the second. There were all kinds of strange undercurrents going on here, she could sense them as easily as if they'd been visible to the naked eye. She could see an alertness and a rigidity about Constantine's stance, could sense the blatant sexual challenge which glittered at him from Eleni's eyes. *She wants him*, thought Jade, with a sudden sick feeling. What the hell had he brought her to?

He fired a question at Eleni in Greek, which only increased Jade's sense of being an outsider, and Eleni replied in the same language, giving Jade a smug stare as she did so, as though sensing her discomfiture.

Constantine turned to Jade, his voice softer. To sweeten the blow, she wondered fleetingly?

'My stepmother is inside. Come, we shall go and meet her.'

Eleni turned to Jade. 'We're *very* cross with Constantine for denying us the pleasure of attending his wedding. When I rang Stavros and he told me it was taking place yesterday—I couldn't believe it—'

'Damn Stavros!' swore Constantine succinctly. 'He was under strict instructions to tell no one.'

Eleni hooded her eyes with their heavy lids and slanted him a look. 'But for heaven's sake, why, Constantine?' she queried, mischief sparking her exquisite features. 'We've waited for so long for you to plight your troth, and then you rush away and do it in secret. Almost—' She gave a malicious smile. 'Almost as though you were ashamed of your beautiful young bride.'

Jade flushed, wishing that she could spirit herself

away from here by thought alone. What the hell was Constantine playing at?

'Unless, of course,' said Eleni maliciously, 'there's some *other* reason for the indecent haste?' And she looked pointedly at Jade's flat stomach.

Jade flushed. 'There's none,' she said smoothly, thinking that if Constantine didn't get her away from this woman in a moment, she wouldn't be responsible for her actions!

As if he'd homed in on her thoughts, he caught her elbow. 'Come,' he said softly.

The inside of the house was deliciously cool and dark. Jade got a brief impression of marble floors, of white walls and shuttered windows, before Constantine took her into what was obviously the formal drawing-room to meet Eleni's mother.

And if she'd been hoping for some dear little apple-cheeked old lady, she was in for a shock, because on first impression the pencil-thin beauty who sat on a high-backed chair looked little older than Eleni herself.

On first impression.

Closer to, Jade could see the ravages of time, made far more apparent by the older woman's determination not to give in to them. Thick foundation lay in the deep lines which tracked over her face, cruelly emphasising them, and the bright blue which glistened on the heavy eyelids—so like Eleni's—were like a throwback to the sixties, as were the thick black false eyelashes.

'Marina,' said Constantine. 'May I present to you my wife, Jade?'

Jade was subjected to another chilling scrutiny as she took the gnarled old hand in hers. Marina inclined her head briefly, then spoke in rapid Greek to Constantine, who shook his head.

'We will not, I think, speak in any language other than English since Jade is not yet familiar with Greek.'

'*Yet*?' mocked Eleni. 'And you plan to actually *learn* our language, do you, Jade?' she queried disbelievingly. 'Believe me, the English find it almost impossible.'

Some devil sparked insubordination in Jade's soul at the put-downs which the two women were loosely handing out. This marriage might be a farce as far as Constantine was concerned, but if he was playing the part of contented spouse, then she could go one better. And if it infuriated Eleni that she had married Constantine—then she would *really* give her something to get her teeth into! She gave a smile. 'I realise that, and I certainly don't underestimate how difficult it's going to be, but I'm quite determined, aren't I, Constantine? Especially if you teach me. He's the most *wonderful* teacher,' she confided glowingly. 'In just about everything!'

The black eyes glittered briefly at her in response before he turned back to his stepmother, a look of polite query on his face. 'This is most—unexpected,' he said carefully. 'To have company on our honeymoon.'

Eleni smiled without humour. 'You must allow us women our little foibles. We have brought Sophie with us to prepare a small wedding feast—but do not be troubled, Constantine—we are intent on leaving in the morning. And surely your bride will allow us one meal with you?'

Constantine gave a small nod of his head. 'You are, of course, most welcome to stay with us for as long as you like, and naturally Jade and I are honoured and delighted to share in a surprise meal with you. Have you—' and his black eyes looked as hard and as forbidding as metal '—planned to invite any others for this—er—feast?'

'Just the four of us,' said Eleni, a cool smile playing on her lips. 'Which will give us the chance to get to know each other better. Now please, Jade—sit. You stand like a stranger in your husband's house. Sit and Sophie will bring us refreshments—you must be parched after your long journey.'

'Thank you.' Jade sat down on the edge of one of the overstuffed chairs, her knees pressed tightly together, feeling a bit like a child invited to the party, who nobody had really wished to come.

Eleni picked up a small silver bell and rang it, and on cue a small, rather harassed-looking woman scurried in, her face lighting up with unconcealed joy as she sighted the tall form of Constantine who stood with his back to the window.

He strode over to embrace her, indulgently listening to her excited torrent of Greek, and then he turned and said Jade's name, and something else, very slowly in Greek, so that the woman beamed as she took Jade's hand.

'*Kalispera sas*,' said Jade, as her hand was grasped tightly. '*Pos issaste*?' And was rewarded for this extremely elemental greeting by a squeal of delight from Sophie, and a small, amused smile from Constantine, and it shook her how his approval could hearten her so.

There was stilted small talk until Sophie reappeared bearing a tray of coffee and four glasses of iced water. Eleni lifted up her stately blue-black head. 'It's Greek coffee, Jade,' she murmured. 'But I know that a lot of foreigners find it unpalatable. If you'd prefer it I can easily order some regular coffee for you?'

Jade swallowed as her smile remained in place. 'Thank you, but that won't be necessary—I happen to adore Greek coffee.' And she saw Constantine smile at her as she accepted one of the tiny cups with alacrity.

Constantine remained standing, and his immense height seemed to dominate the room. His eyes had flickered to Eleni's hand. 'You no longer wear your ring, Eleni? Your hand seems much smaller with the absence of such a magnificent diamond.'

Eleni shrugged narrow and elegant shoulders, her red-tipped fingernails fluttering as she spoke. 'I am no longer engaged,' she told him, her dark eyes slanting at him with some unspoken message as she did so.

Constantine's hand paused, the cup raised midway to his mouth. 'Oh?'

'She broke it off,' said Marina, a tight look of disapproval about her heavily red-glossed mouth.

Constantine's face hardened. 'Really?' he queried softly, his eyes gleaming with the crystalline brilliance of some dark, precious gem.

'I discovered that he wasn't what I wanted,' said Eleni quietly, her eyes never leaving Constantine's face. 'You see, I found that I'd been staring it in the face all along.'

'I see.'

'Do you?' asked Eleni huskily.

Jade felt as though she were in the midst of a nightmare, Eleni couldn't have made her feelings for Constantine more obvious if she'd had a great banner proclaiming her love erected and suspended from wall to wall. And surely the dark rage which simmered in the depths of Constantine's ebony eyes was due to the fact that Eleni was now free, but it had come too late for him. He had tied himself to a loveless marriage to Jade. What price honour now? For who in their right mind could possibly fail to love a woman as glitteringly sophisticated and beautiful as Eleni?

But wasn't she forgetting something? He *hadn't* tied himself to her, had he? Not really. The marriage was always intended to be brief. Would he now, as she suspected, abandon this so-called 'honeymoon' completely? With a hand that she willed not to shake, Jade put her half-full coffee-cup on the small table beside her.

Constantine's eyes searched her face, his ex-

pression obdurate as they registered the draining of
colour from her cheeks. He put his own cup down.

'Now,' he said smoothly, 'if you will excuse us,
we will go to our room and freshen up. Jade is, I
think, very tired.'

'But naturally,' murmured Eleni, her gaze taking in
Jade's simple little lemon cotton sundress. 'And you
will of course wish to change into something more
suitable for this evening.'

'Of course,' agreed Jade evenly.

'Dinner will be at eight.' Eleni's smile showed tiny
white teeth.

Like a ferret, thought Jade as she followed
Constantine out of the room in silence, summoning
up every bit of effort to smile politely at Eleni and
her mother, because the last thing in the world she
wanted was to let either of them know how much
Eleni's unsubtle and predatory attitude towards
Constantine had hurt her.

He led her along a cool, dim corridor and opened
a dark wooden door to reveal a simply decorated
room dominated by a vast double bed over which was
slung a blindingly white bedspread. Large patterned
cushions of white and blue added touches of colour,
as did the blue paintwork around the shuttered windows. Their two suitcases were standing side by side
on the floor, mocking her with their vision of unity.
She supposed that Sophie had brought them in from
the car while they had been sitting in the salon, drinking coffee.

Jade stared at the bed, her heart hammering as she

tried and failed to block the mental pictures which swam up to torment her. Had there been some form of relationship between Constantine and Eleni in the past? Was that why she had stared at him with that hungry, almost wild look of longing? After all, step-brother and sister were allowed to have a relationship by law, weren't they? Had his so-called *desire* for her now been deadened by the sight of his beautiful step-sister, freed from her engagement and obviously eager to find herself in Constantine's arms?

She fought the sick feeling in her stomach which threatened to swamp her, and stared up at Constantine, into the impenitent expression which had hardened the harsh features. It was over, she thought with immense sadness. It had never really begun.

He had moved towards her, and she knew that she had to put him straight before he touched her, because she couldn't trust herself to do the right thing if he touched her.

She backed away from him. 'I'm not sleeping with you here,' she told him quietly, and his eyes narrowed instantly into glittering black shards as she heard him draw in a deep breath.

'Oh, yes, you are,' he contradicted ruthlessly.

Her mouth dried. 'You can't *force* me...' she whispered.

'*Force* you?' He gave a cruel kind of smile. 'You little hypocrite! We both know that I wouldn't have to force you—erotic persuasion can be so much more effective, don't you think? But do not worry, Jade— I have no inclination to put it to the test. You can have the bed. I shall sleep in the chair—' His dark head indicated the roomy-looking but none the less unforgiving wicker chair which stood on the other side of the large room.

Her heart plummeted as she took in what he'd said. 'I have no inclination to put it to the test.' So he didn't even want her any more—the sight of Eleni had killed his desire stone-dead. But even knowing that, she was aware too that she wouldn't get a wink of sleep if he stayed in there with her. She would be longing for his possession, fighting every instinct she possessed to throw back the sheet and give him entry to her bed and body.

'Is that really necessary?' she demanded. 'There must be other bedrooms.' Including Eleni's, she thought with sick dismay.

His mouth tightened. 'Indeed there are. But I do not intend our marital spats to become public knowledge—not yet, in any case. There will be time enough for that. Marina and Eleni leave tomorrow morning. We can leave any decisions until then.'

So that was that, she thought, with a dull, empty ache in her heart. It was over. Eleni was his for the taking, and he wanted her now. And tomorrow he would release Jade from this farce of a marriage in order to pursue her.

Had that been the purpose behind his bizarre proposal in the first place? she wondered suddenly. Had she served her purpose by being brought here as his wife? Because perhaps Eleni was one of those women who were motivated by possessiveness—perhaps she hadn't realised how much she had wanted Constantine for herself, until she'd thought that some-one else had him.

He glanced at his watch. 'You have only two hours before we are due to dine. I am sure that you could fill them most productively.' His eyes mocked her startled expression. 'Oh, don't worry, *agape mou*— you won't have to fend off my advances. I'm going for a walk. Be ready by eight.'

'I'm not very hungry.'

'I don't care. Just be there.'

'You can't make me!' she challenged.

'No?' he said softly, and she quickly turned away, rage and desire filling her veins with a pounding fire.

The *bastard*! The cold-hearted, cynical bastard! Even knowing that it was over, he still couldn't resist any opportunity to demonstrate his power over her.

She turned her back on him. 'I'd like to use the shower now,' she said coldly.

His response was equally cold. 'But of course.' And he slammed his way out of the room.

The bathroom was adjoined to their room, and Jade was surprised to see the luxuriously appointed fittings, not expecting such mod-cons in a place which was, to all intents and purposes, in the middle of nowhere.

She showered and changed into a short vampy dress of black satin, against which the pale fall of her hair stood out in startling contrast. If she was going out, she had decided in the shower, she was going to do it in style! She was just applying some blood-coloured lipstick in front of the mirror when

Constantine returned. His face was set, and looked, she thought as she caught his reflection in the mirror, infinitely weary. She wondered whether he had in fact been out walking, or whether he had gone to Eleni, to seek solace in her arms, to make plans with her for their future.

He raised his eyebrows as he took in the amount of thigh she was showing, but gave her no greeting other than a short nod, then walked straight through to the bathroom.

She heard the sound of the shower running, and the hand which was applying mascara to her eyelashes began to tremble as her mind began reluctantly to conjure up images of Constantine naked; his statuesque and magnificent golden body standing under the streaming jets of water. An image which stubbornly refused to disappear, and just the thought of it played absolute havoc with her already tightly stretched nerves.

But that was nothing to the effect he had on her when he walked back in the room, gleaming droplets of water still clinging to the dark olive of his skin and the dark hair which shadowed it. He was wearing nothing but the skimpiest of white towels slung low on his narrow hips.

Sweat broke out in beads on Jade's forehead, but she doggedly continued to apply her mascara, splodging on far more than she'd intended, and wondering whether his mocking smile meant that he'd noticed.

Dinner was the longest meal she'd ever had to endure, and anything less like a celebration she couldn't have imagined. The food was excellent, and so were the wines, and the table set out on the scented terrace under the light of the moon and the candles was simply breathtaking. But Eleni was clearly in a sniping mood, and Constantine obviously on edge.

Marina retired early, immediately after the coffee had been served, but Eleni looked set for the night, and after two cups of coffee Jade rose wearily to her feet.

'I'm going to turn in now,' she said. 'Please excuse me.'

Eleni nodded, then turned to Constantine. 'Stay and have a brandy with me,' she urged him. 'It's been too long since I've seen you.'

Jade's whole world hung on his answer, then came crashing around her ears as he nodded his dark head.

'Very well,' he concurred. 'Just the one, but first I must take my wife to her room.'

Feeling sick at heart, Jade stared at him in horror, wondering what kind of a hypocrite *he* must be if he could actually use the word 'wife' so inappropriately. She shook her head, so that her long hair swayed in a pale cloud around her head, the long diamanté earrings she wore flashing starry light around her neck. 'It doesn't matter, Constantine. I know the way. Please don't bother.'

His mouth twisted. 'Very well.'

'Goodnight, Jade,' said Eleni, and Jade couldn't miss the brief note of triumph which hovered in her voice. 'It has been a delight to meet you.'

'Likewise,' said Jade evenly, then, before she gave

it all away, she turned quickly on her heel and away to her room.

She had thought that sleep would elude her, that she would stay awake all night in an agonised state, listening for the sounds of betrayal—the muffled giggles in the corridor, the deadened footsteps, even, she thought in horror—the creaking of the bed in another room. But perhaps she was wearier than she'd thought—perhaps in times like this nature could be almost kind and help her blot it all out until tomorrow, or perhaps she'd done so much thinking that her head simply couldn't take any more. Because, whatever the reason, she found herself drifting into the warm and numbing embrace of sleep, and when she opened her eyes again she blinked at the ceiling in bewilderment, at the patterns of sunlight which danced there, for a moment not remembering where she was.

And then it all came back, and she turned her head, expecting to find the room empty, but there sat Constantine in the wicker chair, his black eyes resting thoughtfully on her. He was, she registered dully, still in the suit he'd worn down to dinner last night. His face was etched with lines as though he hadn't slept, and that, together with the crumpled suit, seemed to bring her to her senses and she sat up in bed, her blonde hair tumbling in wild disarray all over the thin straps of her ice-pink camisole. She saw his eyes darken, and protectively reached out for the matching wrap and pulled it on.

'Jade—' he began, and she raised her hand to halt

him, because she knew that she could not bear to hear him say it. She wasn't going to break down in front of him. Let him have Eleni if he wanted, but let him not say it.

'I want to go home,' she told him, and saw the corners of his eyes crease in bewilderment.

'Home?' he echoed.

'Yes. Home. I'll get dressed, and then I'd like to leave as soon as possible. Please say goodbye to Eleni and her mother for me. And Sophie. I'd prefer not to see anyone, if you don't mind.'

'They've gone,' he said flatly.

Now it was her turn to echo. 'Gone?'

He shifted his position in the chair and loosened his tie. 'Yes, gone. Leaving us alone. At last. Because it's high time that you and I had a talk.'

'I don't think so.'

'You don't? Well, I do.'

And then she realised what had probably happened. Eleni had gone because it would be more diplomatic if Constantine terminated the marriage without his lover around. Perhaps there *was* that touch of kindness in him which Stavros claimed he had. Either that, or pity, or simply a dread of any scenes which might ensue. But Jade had her dignity; and she didn't want his kindness *or* his pity.

'It's all right, Constantine,' she said quietly, marvelling that her voice should hold no giveaway tremor. 'I know perfectly well what you want to say to me.'

His eyebrows rose to become lost in the blackness of his hair. 'You do?'

'Sure,' she said flippantly. 'You've made a mistake. You thought you wanted me and for a while you probably did. But now that Eleni is free—well, I want you to know that I understand. I'm releasing you from our marriage.'

A pulse began to beat insistently in the hollow beneath one cheekbone. 'Just what the hell are you talking about?' he demanded, from between gritted teeth.

'You know darned well what I'm talking about! You want *her*, not me—and she wants you. She wants you so badly, you can feel it in the air. You don't have to pretend any more. You spent the night with her, OK, I understand, but now I just want to get out of here, and as far away from you as possible.'

'I spent the *night*,' he repeated ominously. 'With *Eleni*?'

She'd had enough, flimsy nightdress or not, she jumped out of the bed and ran for the bathroom. 'You know you did!' she sobbed, and wrenched the door open, but he had waylaid her, pulling her violently into his arms, and she recoiled from the fury on his face, the contempt she read in his eyes.

'You think I'm that kind of man?' he thundered. 'That I could make love to a woman while my wife lay in the next room?'

'But I'm *not* your wife, am I?' she shouted back. Wives were loved, cherished. 'Not really! Not properly!'

'Then why don't you start being my wife?' he ground out, and he pushed her down on to the bed.

'No!' she screamed out, as she felt the sinewy weight of him on top of her, so hard against the softness of her body, and her hands reached out to grip convulsively at his shoulders, supposedly, she thought, to push him away, but suddenly she wasn't doing any pushing. 'No,' she pleaded on a broken whisper. 'Not like this.'

'How then?' And his lips brushed softly against hers. 'Like this?'

For answer she gave a great sob in his arms, and then he cradled her to his chest, murmuring words in Greek which she did not understand, but which soothed and calmed her. When she'd stopped, he opened each eyelid with a gentle finger.

'Do you really think I wanted Eleni here?' he quizzed.

'You asked her to stay for as long as she liked!'

'Because she is my stepsister, and because we Greeks show respect and hospitality to our family. I don't love Eleni,' he said.

'But she loves you.'

He sighed. 'Yes,' he admitted. 'Or rather she thinks she does. She is a spoilt child who wants to take everything she sees—she always has been. She imagines that no man can resist her if she puts her mind to it. And last night, after dinner, I was not, as you imagined, making love to Eleni—instead I was telling her that I intended settling down to a happy and, I hope, a very long life, with you, my wife—if you can bring yourself to forgive me.'

Tears shimmered in her eyes at his cruelty. 'Don't lie!' she husked. 'Don't tell me any of your lies!'

He shook his head. 'I'm not lying. I speak from the heart—and I love you, Jade.'

The time for pussyfooting, she decided, was long past. 'You don't love me! You don't even trust me! You think that I'm a heartless journalist who'd do anything for a scoop—even selling her own secrets. You think that I'm a seasoned seductress who pretended to be a virgin—'

'I think none of those things,' he said quietly. 'I think that I have been an arrogant and blind fool and nearly lost what is most dear in all the world to me.'

'No, you don't,' she sniffed.

'Listen to me,' he said. 'You knew that I fell in love with you when we first met?'

'So you said.'

'*Don't* you?'

Jade moved restlessly, refusing to make it easier for him, aware as she did so, that he still held her closely.

His eyes glittered with some satanic fire as he spoke the soft, husky words. 'For years women had told me I was cold, arrogant, unfeeling; and maybe I was. And in my heart of hearts I suspected that I was one of those men who never *can* fall in love. Perhaps the death of my mother made me equate love with loss. But even knowing that, logically, changed nothing. I did not seem able to feel emotion for a woman other than liking, and, occasionally—desire. But then I saw you, and it was like…' He shrugged, a rueful smile temporarily smoothing out the lines on his face. 'How can I explain what it was like? I don't think the words exist in either of our languages which could adequately describe it.

'An explosion, if you like. Or implosion. I was dizzy with it. Crazy. It was something to which no logic could be applied—overpowering—this need to be with you. I saw you and I fell in love with you. And then, when I met you—you were everything I dreamed you would be, only more. Intelligent, questioning, funny, sexy.' He gave a deep sigh. 'When you left the island I went half mad with wanting you. And that frightened me. For the first time in my life I felt no longer *in control*, and I found the experience disturbing. Profoundly disturbing. When I went back to work I found that I was restless, deferring decisions because I could not think straight and the only thing which occupied my thoughts, was you. Always you. I couldn't get you out of my mind.

'So I *forced* the rational side of my nature to try and analyse things—I told myself that I knew nothing about you. That it had all happened so quickly, on a magically beautiful island, that when faced with the stresses of everyday life the relationship would probably die a natural death. That I had kept my true identity secret, and that perhaps you would not care to be the wife of a very rich man—you who seemed content with the simple life we lived those few days.

'And then, when I found out who you were and

what you did for a living, after my initial rush of anger I was almost *glad* to learn what I'd discovered about you.'

'*Glad*?' Jade echoed, totally confused.

'Yes, glad. Believing you to have lied to me and betrayed me, meant that I now no longer had any reason to love you, and consequently I felt back in control.'

'So you seduced me ruthlessly,' she accused him bitterly, trying to wriggle out from beneath him, but his hips made her firmly their prey and she was made achingly aware of the fact that he was turned on.

'Yes, I seduced you,' he agreed grimly. 'Which is not something I should be proud of, and yet it proved to be my undoing. Even believing myself to be hating you, I fell completely under your spell again. I'd never experienced lovemaking like that in my life— it blew my head off. I tried to convince myself that it was just a physical ache, that I could exorcise my desire for you by making love to you over and over and over again.' The corners of his mouth turned down in self-deprecating mockery. 'But I was trapped, enmeshed by you. The more I was with you, the more I grew to like you. As well as love you. My little virgin,' he added gently.

Jade's head was spinning. She wanted to believe him, oh, how she wanted to believe him. 'You told me I was no virgin. You said—' Her cheeks became stained scarlet as she remembered his cruel gibes, but she forced herself to repeat them. 'You said that if I was pretending to be a virgin, then I shouldn't…' But she couldn't finish the sentence.

His face became grave, and his voice was filled with anger, that even she could tell was directed inwards. 'Because, my darling, my feelings were in complete turmoil; that's why I lashed out at you the way I did. I felt honoured, humbled to be the man to whom you should offer the great gift of your virginity. And yet I was sick with remorse at the manner in which I took that gift. I should have wooed you quite gently in our marital bed, not taken you like that—so swiftly and so savagely. And then—' He hesitated. 'I was wary, too.'

'Wary?'

He gave a self-deprecating smile. 'Indeed, since I recognised that my days as a single man were numbered. Because you see, I had discovered during that quite blissful interlude on the sofa that it was not going to be easy to give you up; indeed, I suspected that it was going to be damn nigh impossible.'

He reached his hand out to stroke one finger gently down her cheek.

She let him.

'So you bought up the newspaper?' she quizzed. 'A bit over the top, wouldn't you say, Constantine?'

He didn't look in the least bit abashed. 'The situation called for dramatic measures.'

'Like forcing me to marry you by bribery?'

He shrugged. 'What else could I do? When you walked into your boss's office and gave me such a look of withering contempt, I knew that you would never agree to see me willingly again. I had to have you, and I was prepared to go to any lengths to do so.' He stared down at her, the ebony eyes boring bright fire into her soul.

'But you were so distant towards me, the morning after you made love to me at the Granchester.'

He gave a small sound of disapproval. 'Because I was furious with myself. I had seduced you that first time, almost brutally—'

'Not really brutally,' she corrected, being perfectly honest, because even if the intentions had been brutal the act itself had been bliss.

'Single-mindedly, then. I used my experience quite ruthlessly to get you to capitulate. After that I wanted to show you how sweet seduction could be, but I wanted to do that *after* we were married, to make amends for my behaviour, if you like. That night, when you turned to me, I felt so close to you, and I wanted to show you that closeness didn't necessarily have to culminate in making love. But you persuaded me to stay. And once again, I demonstrated that around you, all my self-control amounted to nothing.'

Jade gave him a look of satisfaction.

'Yes,' he teased her. 'You can afford to look smug!'

'Why didn't you tell me all this in London?'

'Because our time in London had been tainted with nothing but bad experience and misunderstanding. I was afraid that you were going to call my bluff and leave me, in London. That is why I wanted to start again, on the island. Alone. I brought you back to the

island, where we had once been so happy—to redis-
cover our love for one another without the pressures
which surrounded us in London. It was to be a honeymoon of the most traditional kind. The last thing in
the world I imagined was to find my stepmother and
sister waiting here, with my stepsister attempting, and
managing, to drive a further wedge between us.' He
paused. 'I need to know, *agape mou*, whether you can
find it in your heart to forgive me, and whether there
is any of the love left which you once felt for me?'

She suspected that her beautiful, arrogant
Constantine already knew the answer to this question.
His mouth was now inches away, but, much as she
longed for him to kiss her, there were a few more
things which *she* needed to get off her chest. '*You*,
Constantine Sioulas,' she said firmly, 'are the most
arrogant man I've ever met in my life.'

'I agree,' he said gravely.

'You think you can just barge your way through
life, riding roughshod over people's feelings, doing
exactly what *you* want, in order to get your own way.
Don't you?'

'I do.' His lids hooded the spark in his eyes. 'And?'

'And I love you in spite of it, or because of it; I
have done since the moment I set eyes on you, and
it's never going to change, even though I probably
shouldn't be telling you that.' But the softness in her
eyes belied her words and she knew that, arrogant or
not—she would never hide her love from him. Because Constantine was strong, yes—but at a cost. The

cost of his lost years of childhood, unloved after his mother had died, a situation not unlike her own.

'Say it again,' he urged her softly, her powerful, beautiful man, and she needed no second bidding.

'I love you.'

He gave her a slow, slow smile. 'I don't think I could ever grow tired of hearing you say that.'

She vowed to tell him so every day of their lives, and the reality of their future suddenly hit Jade like a gloriously starry blow to the heart. 'Oh, Constantine,' she began, but the sentence was never completed because he started kissing her.

Some time later he raised his dark head and looked down at her.

'My main residence is in New York. Do you mind?'

'Mind?' She gave him a dazed, dreamy smile. 'I know that this is the most corny thing to say, but I'd live anywhere with you, Constantine.'

He wound a strand of bright gold hair round and round his finger. 'At the moment I travel all over the world, and I want you to travel with me, but when the babies come—well, then we won't be so no-madic.'

Babies! Jade wriggled her toes with anticipation, then kissed every inch of his face. 'Just so long as we can have our holidays here,' she murmured.

'I promise. But only if you promise me that you'll write that book you once told me you thought you had in you.'

She kissed the end of his nose, her eyes sparkling

with mischief. 'Funny you should say that—I happen to have the first twenty pages in my suitcase.'

'Then I am afraid I shall have to confiscate it,' he said gravely. 'This is, after all, our honeymoon—and I intend to spend the whole time making love to you.'

'Oh, Constantine,' she said breathily, helpless with a love for him which overwhelmed her, her feelings shining from her eyes, so that he grinned—that rare and bright and irresistible grin.

'Jade,' he whispered, and buried his head in her shoulder, and when he raised it again he looked like a man at peace with himself, but a man with something else on his mind too.

'And now,' he murmured, '*sweet* bride, what shall we do next? Any ideas?'

Her heart swelled with love, and her body tingled with the glorious anticipation of his touch. 'Oh, *yes*, my darling,' she whispered, and reached up to kiss him. 'More than you'd ever believe.'